THE PERRY MASON CASEBOOK

A Mystery Guild
Lost Classics
Omnibus

THE PERRY MASON CASEBOOK:

THE CASE OF THE SULKY GIRL
THE CASE OF THE CARELESS KITTEN
THE CASE OF THE FIERY FINGERS

by

Erle Stanley Gardner

with an exclusive
Introduction by Parnell Hall

Mystery Guild
Garden City, New York

THE CASE OF THE SULKY GIRL
Copyright © 1933 by Erle Stanley Gardner

THE CASE OF THE CARELESS KITTEN
Copyright © 1942 by Erle Stanley Gardner

THE CASE OF THE FIERY FINGERS
Copyright © 1951 by Erle Stanley Gardner

This edition published by arrangement with Hobson and Hughes, L.L.C.

ISBN 0-7394-2866-7

Manufactured in the United States of America.

CONTENTS

THE CASE OF THE SULKY GIRL   1

THE CASE OF THE CARELESS KITTEN   197

THE CASE OF THE FIERY FINGERS   393

HOOKED ON PERRY MASON

by Parnell Hall

I grew up on Erle Stanley Gardner. My parents were English lit teachers, and after a hard day of slogging through the classics, they would come home, put their feet up, and whip out a copy of the latest Perry Mason novel. As a young lad I was intrigued by this strange phenomenon, so I read one.

A whole new world opened up for me. I quickly worked my way through my parents' collection of books, and had to buy my own. As soon as I got my allowance I would rush to town to stock up on the adventures of Perry Mason, Paul Drake, and Della Street. The paperbacks were only a quarter. The covers tended to feature scantily dressed young women, and the salesladies looked at me askance. I didn't care. I was in heaven.

There are 82 books in the series. I have read all of them many times. In fact, the paperbacks in my bookshelf are so worn that many have no spines at all, and are merely unbound pages. I read them still.

Why are Perry Mason books so addictive?

To begin with, the books are built on intriguing premises, starting right with the titles. *The Case of the Fiery Fingers*. What's that all about? You're hooked before you turn the first page.

But the main thing is Mason himself.

Perry Mason is a gas!

Perry Mason was always doing such outrageous, outlandish, and downright illegal things, that a Perry Mason book was not so much a whodunit, as a how-will-he-get-away-with-it? Because Mason was never content to stay in his office and let the cases come to him, but was always out on the firing line, one jump ahead of the police, skating on thin ice, finding evidence, concealing evidence, juggling evidence, and planting evidence.

If you've only seen the TV show, you don't really know Perry Mason. The Perry Mason who appeared on television, particularly in the later made-for-TV movies, was a staunch, respected pillar of the community, and a far cry from the Perry Mason of old.

The Mason I loved would think nothing of showing up at a crime scene and firing a few extra bullets around, just to make the ballistic expert jump through hoops on cross-examination. Or hiding a piece of evidence, and retrieving it later right under the nose of the police guard. Or breaking into a house, and on getting caught red-handed by the police, calmly talking his way out of it. He was always racing around, interrogating witnesses, spiriting away witnesses, or, on occasion, hiring people to impersonate witnesses.

Mason's devil-may-care attitude was based on a fierce loyalty to his clients, and a willingness to go to any lengths to protect them. The clients, on the other hand, always lied to him, and left him in impossible positions. Watching him talk his way out of trouble was half the fun.

Of course, Perry Mason is most famous for his courtroom stunts. On TV, this translates largely into courtroom confessions. While this sometimes happens, in the books the tricks more often involve tiptoeing through legal land mines, and frustrating Hamilton Burger, the hapless district attorney. Mason was so exasperating, that Burger was usually more eager to pin something on him than to convict his client, and Mason was constantly dodging legal bullets. Erle Stanley Gardner was a lawyer himself, and the pitfalls he planned for Perry Mason were many and varied. Mason was always on the verge of contempt of court, but he might also be cited for abuse of process, suborning perjury, compounding a felony, and conspiring to conceal a crime. He would have his receptionist, for instance, stand up in court, point her finger at a witness she had never seen before in her life, and say, "That's him, all right," and then talk his way out of the resultant chaos. Or he would subpoena a witness too ill to appear in court, and when challenged to state what he expected her to testify to, stand up, say, "Nothing," and sit down again, leaving the judge apoplectic. (Needless to say, the fact the witness knew nothing would turn out to be the most important point in the case.)

The three novels in this volume offer a nice cross section of the Mason experience.

The Case of the Sulky Girl features Mason's debut in court. (The first Perry Mason novel, *The Case of the Velvet Claws*, had no trial.) As a result, the trial sequence is more fully described, as Gardner introduces the reader to courtroom procedure. If you've never read Perry Mason, it is an excellent place to start.

The Case of the Careless Kitten, a strong series entry from 1942, reminds us that the legal proceedings in Mason books take many forms. Though most frequently they are trials or preliminary hearings for murder, Mason also cross-examines witnesses at coroner's inquests, competency hearings, depositions, personal injury suits.

In *The Case of the Careless Kitten*, the charge is not murder, but merely concealing a witness. The stakes are no less high—in fact they are higher; as the defendant is Della Street!

The Case of the Fiery Fingers, as an extra treat, has not one but two trials. In the first, Mason defends a housekeeper from a charge of theft brought by her employer. Mason's cross-examination of her accuser is particularly delicious. The fact Mason gets another shot at him in the murder trial is almost too good to be true.

At any rate, welcome to the wonderful world of Perry Mason. If you're new to the series, I envy you. When you finish these three books, you'll have 79 to go.

Parnell Hall is the author of the Puzzle Lady, crossword puzzle mysteries, the Stanley Hastings private eye novels, and the Steve Winslow courtroom dramas. His courtroom books, written under the pseudonym J. P. Hailey, are a conscious attempt to emulate Erle Stanley Gardner's Perry Mason books. "The Anonymous Client" was actually intended as a Perry Mason novel, before being completed as a Steve Winslow book.

THE CASE OF THE SULKY GIRL

ONE

THE GIRL WALKED past the secretary who held the door open, and surveyed the law office with eyes that showed just a trace of panic.

The secretary gently closed the door and the girl selected an old fashioned, high-backed, black leather chair. She sat down in it, crossed her legs, pulled her skirt down over her knees, and sat facing the door. After a moment, she pulled the skirt up for an inch or two, taking some pains to get just the effect she wanted. Then she leaned back so that her spun-gold hair showed to advantage against the shiny black leather of the big chair.

She looked pathetic and helpless as she sat in the big office, dwarfed by the huge proportions of the leather chair. And yet there was something about her which gave the impression of having deliberately brought about that effect. There was a hint of feline efficiency in the care with which she had placed herself, in the very perfection of her helplessness.

Judged by any standard, she was beautiful. Her hair was silken, her eyes large and dark, the cheekbones high, lips full and well formed. She was small, yet perfectly proportioned, and well groomed. Yet there was a studied immobility of expression; an effect of complete detachment as though she had surrounded herself with a protective wall.

The door from an inner office opened and Perry Mason walked into the room. He paused when he had advanced two steps from the door, surveying the girl with patient eyes that seemed to take in every detail of her appearance. She bore the scrutiny without change of position or expression.

"You're Mr. Mason?" she asked.

Mason didn't answer until he had walked around behind the flat-top desk and dropped into the swivel chair.

Perry Mason gave the impression of bigness; not the bigness of fat, but the bigness of strength. He was broad-shouldered and rugged-faced, and his eyes were steady and patient. Frequently those eyes changed expression, but the face never changed its expression of rugged patience. Yet there was nothing meek about the man. He was a fighter; a fighter who could, perhaps, patiently bide his time for delivering a knock-out blow, but who would, when the time came, remorselessly deliver that blow with the force of a mental battering ram.

"Yes," he said, "I'm Perry Mason. What can I do for you?"

The dark eyes studied him warily.

"I," said the girl, "am Fran Celane."

"Fran?" he asked, raising his voice.

"Short for Frances," she said.

"All right," said Perry Mason, "what can I do for you, Miss Celane?"

The dark eyes remained fastened on his face, but the girl's forefinger went exploring around the arm of the chair, picking at irregularities in the leather. There was something in the probing gesture which seemed an unconscious reflection of her mental attitude.

"I wanted to find out about a will," she said.

There was no change of expression in Perry Mason's steady, patient eyes.

"I don't go in much for wills," he told her. "I'm a trial lawyer. I specialize in the trial of cases, preferably before juries. Twelve men in a box—that's my specialty. I'm afraid I can't help you much on wills."

"But," she told him, "this will probably be a trial."

He continued to watch her with the emotionless scrutiny of his calm eyes.

"A will contest?" he asked.

"No," she said, "not exactly a contest. I want to know something about a trust provision."

"Well," he said with gentle insistence, "suppose you tell me exactly what it is you want to know."

"A party dies," she said, "and leaves a will containing a clause by which a beneficiary under the will . . ."

"That'll do," said Perry Mason, "don't try that line. This is a matter that you're interested in?"

"Yes."

"Very well then," he said, "give me the facts, and quit beating about the bush."

"It's my father's will," she said. "His name was Carl Celane. I'm an only child."

"That's better," he told her.

"There's a lot of money coming to me under that will, something over a million dollars."

Perry Mason showed interest.

"And you think there'll be a trial over it?" he asked.

"I don't know," she said. "I hope not."

"Well, go ahead," said the lawyer.

"He didn't leave the money to me outright," she said. "He left it in a trust."

"Who's the trustee?" asked Mason.

"My uncle, Edward Norton."

"All right," he said, "go on."

"There's a provision in the will that if I should marry before I'm twenty-five, my uncle has the right, at his option, to give me five thousand dollars from the trust fund, and to turn the balance over to charitable institutions."

"How old are you now?" asked Mason.

"Twenty-three."

"When did your father die?"

"Two years ago."

"The will's been probated then, and the property distributed?"

"Yes," she said.

"All right," he told her, speaking rapidly now, "if the provision in regard to the trust was carried through in the decree of distribution, and there was no appeal from that decree, there can be no collateral attack, except under exceptional circumstances."

Her restless finger picked at the arm of the chair, and the nail made little noises as it dug into the leather.

"That's what I wanted to ask you about," she said.

"All right," said Mason, "go ahead and ask me."

"Under the will," she said, "my uncle controls the trust moneys. He can invest them any way he wants, and he can give me whatever money he thinks I should have. When I'm twenty-seven he's to give me the principal if he thinks that the possession of such a large sum of money won't spoil my life. Otherwise, he's to buy me an annuity of five hundred dollars a month for life, and give the balance to charity."

"Rather an unusual trust provision," said Perry Mason, tonelessly.

"My father," she said, "was rather an unusual man, and I was just a little bit wild."

"All right," said Mason. "What's the trouble?"

"I want to get married," she said, and, for the first time her eyes dropped from his.

"Have you spoken to your uncle about it?"

"No."

"Does he know that you want to get married?"

"I don't think so."

"Why not wait until you're twenty-five?"

"No," she said, raising her eyes again, "I want to get married now."

"As I understand your interpretation of the will," ventured Perry Mason cautiously, "there's complete discretion vested in your uncle?"

"That's right."

"Well, don't you think that the first thing to do would be to sound him out and see how he would feel about your marriage?"

"No," she said shortly, clipping the word out explosively.

"Bad blood between you and your uncle?" he asked.

"No," she said.

"You see him frequently?"

"Every day."

"Do you talk with him about the will?"

"Never."

"You go to see him on other business then?"

"No. I live in the house with him."

"I see," said Perry Mason, speaking in that calm expressionless voice. "Your uncle is intrusted with a whole lot of money, and given a discretion which is rather unusual. I take it that he's under bond?"

"Oh yes," she said, "he's under bond. As far as that's concerned, the trust fund is perfectly safe. My uncle is meticulously careful—too careful. That is, he's too methodical in *everything* he does."

"Does he have money of his own?" asked the lawyer.

"Lots of it," she said.

"Well," said Mason, with just a trace of impatience, "what do you want me to do?"

"I want you," she said, "to fix it so I can get married."

He stared at her for several seconds in silent, meditative appraisal.

"Have you got a copy of the will or of the decree of distribution?" he asked at length.

She shook her head.

"Do I need one?" she asked.

The lawyer nodded.

"I can't very well give you an interpretation of a legal document until I've seen the document."

"But I told you exactly what it said."

"You gave me your version of what it said. There may be a great deal of difference."

She spoke swiftly, impatiently. "I understand that conditions in a will which prevent a person from marrying can be set aside."

"That's not correct," he told her. "Generally speaking, a condition by which a party is prevented from marrying is considered against public policy and void. But that's subject to certain qualifications, particularly in the case of trusts of the type which are known as 'spendthrift' trusts. Apparently the trust which was created under your father's will was one of this nature.

"Moreover, you note that there is no restriction upon marriage after you have reached the age of twenty-five. As a matter of fact, your uncle seems to be given a wide discretion in the matter, and the provisions of the will as you have given them to me, merely indicate the circumstances under which he is to exercise his discretion."

She seemed suddenly to have lost her protective poise. Her voice rose, "Well, I've heard a lot about you," she said. "They say that some lawyers tell people what they can do and what they can't do, but that *you* always fix things so a person can do what he wants to."

Mason smiled, the smile of wisdom garnered from bitter experience, of knowledge amassed from the confidences of thousands of clients.

"Perhaps," he said, "that's partially true. A man can nearly always think his way out of any situation in which he finds himself. It's merely a paraphrase of the old saying that where there's a will there's a way."

"Well," she told him, "there's a will in this case. I want the way."

"Whom do you want to marry?" he asked abruptly.

The eyes did not waver, but stared steadily at him in dark appraisal.

"Rob Gleason," she said.

"Does your uncle know him?"

"Yes."

"Does he approve of him?"

"No."

"You love him?"

"Yes."

"He knows of this provision in the will?"

Her eyes lowered.

"I think perhaps he does now. But he didn't," she said.

"What do you mean he didn't?" asked the lawyer.

There could be no question now that the eyes were avoiding his.

"Just an expression," she said, "I didn't mean anything by it."

Perry Mason studied her intently for a few minutes.

"And I take it you want to marry him very much."

She looked at him then, and said in a voice that was vibrant with feeling: "Mr. Mason, don't make any mistake about it. I am *going* to marry Rob Gleason. You can take that as being final. You have got to find some way by which I can do it. That's all! I'm leaving that end of it up to you. I'm putting myself in your hands. I am going to get married."

He started to say something, then paused to study her carefully before he spoke.

"Well," he said, "you seem to know pretty much what you want."

"I do," she flared.

"Suppose then, you come back at this time to-morrow morning. In the meantime I will have looked up the court records."

She shook her head.

"To-morrow morning," she protested, "is too long. Can't you do it this afternoon?"

Perry Mason's patient eyes dwelt steadily on her face.

"Perhaps," he said. "Will four o'clock suit you?"

She nodded.

"Very well," he told her, getting to his feet. "Come back then. You can leave your name and address with my secretary in the outer office."

"I've already done that," she told him, arising from the chair and smoothing the line of her skirt. "I'll be back at four."

She didn't look back as she walked across the office, opened the door and swept out into the outer room.

Perry Mason sat at his desk, narrowing his eyes in thoughtful appraisal, as he watched the door through which the young woman had gone.

After a moment he extended a sturdy forefinger, and jabbed a button on the side of his desk.

A young man with unruly hair, and a face that seemed pathetically eager, popped his head through the doorway leading from a law library, then entered the room.

"Frank," said Perry Mason, "go up to the court house and find the papers in the Celane Estate. A Frances Celane was given property amounting to more than a million dollars in trust. The name of the trustee is Edward Norton. Check the decree of distribution, and also the will. Make copies of the trust provisions, then get back here as soon as you can."

The boy blinked his eyes swiftly, twice.

"Celane?" he asked.

"Yes," said Mason. "Carl Celane."

"And Norton?"

"Yes, Edward Norton," said Mason.

"Thank you," said the boy. He turned abruptly, crossed the office with nervous, self conscious haste, as though painfully aware of the gaze of Perry Mason, and plunged into the outer office.

Perry Mason rang for his secretary.

Della Street, his secretary, was about twenty-seven years old. Her manner radiated assurance and efficiency. She pushed open the door from the outer office.

"You rang?" she asked.

"Yes," he told her, "come in."

She stepped into the office and closed the door gently behind her.

"Let's check our impressions," he said, "about that girl."

"How do you mean?" she asked.

He stared at her moodily.

"I think," he said, "that I put the words in your mouth. You said she looked trapped or sulky. Now I am wondering which it was."

"Does it make a lot of difference?" asked Della Street.

"I think it does," he told her. "In your impressions you are usually right and you had a chance to see her when she wasn't posing. She started to pose as soon as she came into my office."

"Yes," said Della Street, "she's the type that would be good at posing."

"She sat down in the chair," he told her, "and figured just how to hold her head, just how to cross her knees and arrange her skirt, just what kind of an expression to put on her face."

"Did she tell you the truth?" asked Della Street.

"None of them tell the truth the first time," he told her, "at least the women don't. That's why I want to know just what kind of an impression she made on you. Did she look trapped, or did she look sulky?"

Della Street spoke thoughtfully, as though weighing her words carefully.

"She looked both trapped and sulky," she said, "as though she got caught in some kind of a trap and had turned sulky."

"Are you sure," he asked, "that it wasn't panic?"

"How do you mean?" she wanted to know.

"Lots of people," he said, "try to put on a poker face when they are in a panic and when they try to put on a poker face they look sulky."

"And you think she was in a panic?" asked Della Street.

"Yes," he said, slowly. "I think she was in a panic. I think she's a self-willed little devil who nearly always gets her own way and who has an ungovernable temper. I think she's caught in some sort of a trap and is trying to get out. When we know her better we'll find out more about her temper."

"A hell-cat?" asked Della Street.

He twisted his lips in a smile.

"Let's call her a hell-kitten," he said.

TWO

DELLA STREET PUSHED open the door of Perry Mason's private office. There was something almost surreptitious in her demeanor as she slipped through the door and carefully closed it behind her.

Perry Mason was seated at his desk. His eyes squinted carefully.

"Why the secrecy?" he asked.

She advanced a step or two into the room and looked at him, then turned to glance at the door and make certain that it was closed.

"There's a man in the outer office who gives his name as Robert Gleason."

"What does he want?" asked Perry Mason.

"He wants information about Miss Celane."

"The one who has just been here?"

"Yes."

"You didn't tell him she had just been here?"

"Certainly not."

"What did he say?"

"He said that he wanted to see you. I asked him what the nature of his business was and he said it was about a client of yours. I told him that he would have to give me the name of the client and tell me something of the nature of the business. He said that it was about Miss Celane and he was very anxious to see you about her."

"All right," Mason said, "what did you tell him?"

"I told him that I wasn't familiar with the names of your clients; that he would have to be more specific concerning his business. He's frightfully excited."

"What's he excited about?" asked Mason. "The girl, his business, or what?"

"I don't know. He's excited and nervous."

Mason squared his shoulders as though reaching a sudden decision. "Send him in," he said, "I want to talk with him."

She nodded and turned, holding the door open.

"You may come in," she said.

There was the rustle of motion. A man came into the room who radiated restlessness. He was a thin man with a very pointed nose and large ears. He walked with nervous jerky steps. He was in the late twenties or early thirties.

"You're Mason, the lawyer?" he asked, his voice quick with impatience.

Perry Mason surveyed him with patient eyes peering out from under heavy eyebrows.

"Sit down," he said.

His visitor hesitated, then sat down on the edge of one of the straight-backed chairs.

"Now, what did you want?" asked Perry Mason.

"I want to find out whether Frances Celane called on you to-day."

Perry Mason's face was patiently appraising.

"This is a law office and not an information bureau, Mr. Gleason," he said.

Gleason jumped nervously to his feet, made three swift strides to the window, stood against the light for a moment, then whirled to stare at the lawyer.

His eyes were dark and smouldering. He seemed to be fighting some overpowering emotion.

"Never mind the wisecracks," he said. "I've *got* to know whether or not Fran Celane was here talking with you."

Perry Mason's voice did not change its expression in the least. The other man's impatience dropped from his calm manner as easily as butter slips from a hot knife.

"Let's not have any misunderstanding about this," said Perry Mason. "You're talking about a Miss Frances Celane?"

"Yes."

"Do you know Miss Celane personally?"

"Of course I do."

Perry Mason made a frank, disarming gesture with his right hand as though the entire matter were dismissed as of no importance.

"That simplifies it," he said.

"What does?" asked Gleason, suspiciously.

"The fact that you know Miss Celane," said Perry Mason. "Under the circumstances, all you have to do is to ask her if she has consulted me. If she has not, there will be no necessity for you to return. If she has and doesn't want you to know it, she will doubtless find some way of concealing the fact. If she has consulted me and doesn't care if you know the fact, she will tell you."

He got to his feet and smiled at his visitor as though the interview were terminated.

Robert Gleason remained standing by the window. His face showed that he was laboring under a great strain.

"You can't talk that way to me," he said.

"But," explained Mason, patiently, "I have already talked that way to you."

"But you can't do it."

"Why not?"

"It would be all right to talk that way to a stranger," he said, "but I'm not a stranger. I'm close to Fran Celane. I've got a right to know. She's being blackmailed, and I want to know what you propose to do about it."

Perry Mason raised his eyebrows in polite interrogation.

"Who is being blackmailed?" he asked. "And by whom?"

Gleason made an impatient gesture.

"What's the use of all that hooey?" he asked. "I know she was here, and you know she was here. You know she's being blackmailed, and I want to know what you propose to do about it."

"I think," said Mason, "that under the circumstances I'm going to ask you to step out of the office. You see, when I asked you to come in, I thought that you had some matter of legal business to take up with me. As it happens, I am rather busy to-day, and I really haven't time to discuss with you the only matter which seems to interest you."

Gleason kept his position.

"At least," he said, "you can tell me *who* is doing the blackmailing. That's all I want to know. If you'll give me that information I'll arrange to take care of it myself."

The lawyer walked to the door, standing there very efficient and gravely dignified.

"Good-by, Mr. Gleason," he said. "I'm sorry that I can be of no assistance to you."

"That's final?" asked Gleason, his lips twisting with emotion, until he seemed to be snarling.

"That's all," said Perry Mason, in a tone of finality.

"Very well," said Gleason, and strode across the room and through the door without another word.

Perry Mason closed the door gently, hooked his thumbs in the armholes of his vest, dropped his head forward and started pacing the floor.

After a few moments, he went to his desk, and took out the typewritten paper containing the copy of the clause in the will of Carl Celane, setting forth the terms of the trust to Frances Celane.

He was still studying this typewritten document when Della Street opened the door once more.

"Miss Celane," she said.

Mason looked at her speculatively for a moment, then beckoned to her.

She interpreted the gesture, and stepped fully into the room, pulling the door closed behind her.

"Did Gleason go out of the office as soon as he left here?" he asked.

"Yes," she said, "in just about nothing flat. He acted as though he was trying to win a walking race."

"And Miss Celane just came in?"

"Yes."

"You don't think they met in the elevator?"

Della Street pursed her lips thoughtfully.

"They might have, Chief," she said, "but I don't think they did."

"How does Miss Celane seem?" he asked. "Excited?"

"No," she said, "cool as a cucumber, and she's trying to look her best when she comes in. She took out her compact and is making her face all pretty. She's got her hair arranged just so."

"All right," said Mason, "send her in."

The secretary opened the door. "Come in, Miss Celane," she said.

As Frances Celane walked into the room, the secretary slipped out through the door, and noiselessly closed it behind her.

"Sit down," said Perry Mason.

Frances Celane walked over to the same leather chair which she had occupied earlier in the day, sat down, crossed her knees and regarded the attorney from limpid black eyes in wordless interrogation.

"A Robert Gleason called on me a few minutes ago," said Mason, "and insisted on my telling him whether or not you had been here."

"Bob's so impulsive," she said.

"You know him then?"

"Yes, of course."

"Did you tell him you were going here?" he asked.

"I mentioned your name to him," she said. "Did you tell him that I had been here?"

"Certainly not. I told him to get in touch with you if he wanted to ask any questions about your affairs."

She smiled faintly.

"Bob Gleason wouldn't appreciate your talking to him like that," she said.

"He didn't," Mason told her.

"I'll see him," she said, "and tell him."

"Gleason," went on the attorney, "said that you were being blackmailed."

For just a fraction of a second there was a look of startled terror in the eyes of the young woman. Then she regarded the attorney with a placid and impassive face.

"Rob is *so* impulsive," she said, for the second time.

Mason waited for her to tell him more if she wished to take advantage of the opportunity, but she sat calmly placid, waiting.

Mason turned to the papers on his desk.

"I have copies of the trust provisions of the will, and the decree of distribution," he said. "I also find that there have been annual accounts submitted by the trustee. I'm afraid that I can't give you very much hope, Miss Celane, as far as the decree of distribution itself is concerned. The administration of the trust seems to be largely discretionary.

"You see, even if I should be able to get the provision in regard to marriage set aside, as being in violation of public policy, we would still be confronted with the fact that the distribution of the trust estate remains largely in the discretion of the trustee. I am afraid that your uncle would consider our attack upon the will in the light of an interference with the wishes of your father, and with his authority as trustee. Even if we should win our point in court, he would have it in his discretion to nullify our victory."

She took the blow without flinching, and said, after a moment: "That's what I was afraid of."

"There is another peculiar provision in the trust," said Mason, "to the effect that the discretion vested in the trustee is a personal discretion, due to the confidence which your father had in his judgment. The will and decree of distribution provide that in the event the trust should terminate because of the death, inability or refusal on the part of the trustee to continue to act, that then and in such event, the entire trust fund is to be vested in you unconditionally."

"Yes," she said, "I know that."

"There is therefore," said Mason, "some possibility that your uncle *might* be placed in a position where he could no longer act to advantage. In other words, we might make some legal attack upon his capacity to act as trustee—perhaps show a commingling of trust funds with his own accounts, or something of that sort. It's rather sketchy, and I'm mentioning it to you simply because it seems to be the only possible plan of campaign open to us."

She smiled at him and said: "You don't know my uncle."

"Just what do you mean by that?" asked Mason.

"I mean," she said, "that my uncle is meticulously careful, and is so obstinate that no power on earth can swerve him from anything he wants to do, or decides that he doesn't want to do. He is entirely self-sufficient."

For the first time during the interview, there was some feeling in her voice—a certain bitterness which colored her tone, though her eyes remained calm.

"Have you any suggestions?" asked Mason, watching her closely.

"Yes," she said, "I think that something might be done through Arthur Crinston."

"And who," asked Perry Mason, "is Arthur Crinston?"

"Arthur Crinston," she said, "is my uncle's partner. They are engaged in business together, buying, selling and mortgaging real estate, and buying and selling stocks and bonds. Arthur Crinston has more influence with uncle than any other living person."

"And how does he feel toward you?" asked Mason.

"Very kindly," she said, and smiled as she said it.

"Would there be any chance," asked Mason, slowly, "that Crinston could persuade your uncle to give up the administration of the trust and let you have the entire trust fund?"

"There's always a chance of anything," she said, abruptly, getting to her feet. "I'm going to have Mr. Crinston come in and see you."

"Sometime to-morrow?" asked Mason.

"Sometime this afternoon," she said.

He regarded his watch. "It's twenty minutes past four. I close the office at five. Of course I could wait a few minutes."

"He'll be here at quarter of five," she said.

"Do you want to telephone from here?" he asked.

"No, it won't be necessary."

"What," asked Perry Mason, snapping the question at her without warning, as she stood in the doorway of the office, "did Rob Gleason mean when he said that you were being blackmailed?"

She regarded him with wide, tranquil eyes.

"I'm sure," she said, "I haven't the faintest idea,"—and closed the door.

THREE

ARTHUR CRINSTON WAS forty-five, broad shouldered, and affable. He strode across Mason's private office, with his hand outstretched, and said in a booming voice of ready cordiality:

"Mighty glad to meet you, Mr. Mason. Fran told me that I must come in right away, so I dropped everything to run up."

Perry Mason shook hands and surveyed Crinston with his steady, appraising stare.

"Sit down," he said.

Arthur Crinston dropped into the same black leather chair which Frances Celane had occupied, fished a cigar from his pocket, scraped a match across the sole of his shoe, lit the cigar and grinned through the smoke at the lawyer.

"Wants to get married pretty badly, doesn't she?" he said.

"You know about that?" asked Perry Mason.

"Sure," said Crinston heartily, "I know everything about Fran. In fact, she's nearer being my niece than Edward's niece. That is, we get along together and understand each other."

"Do you think," asked Mason, "that anything could be done by a talk with Edward Norton?"

"Talk by whom?" asked Crinston.

"By you," Mason suggested.

Crinston shook his head.

"By Miss Celane then?" ventured Mason.

Again Crinston shook his head.

"No," he said, "there's only one person who could talk with Norton and do any good."

"And who is that?" asked Mason.

"You," said Crinston emphatically.

The lawyer's face did not change expression, only his eyes betrayed surprise. "From all I can hear of Mr. Norton's character," he said, "I would think my interference would be exactly the thing that he would resent."

"No it wouldn't," said Crinston. "Edward Norton is a peculiar chap. He doesn't want any sentiment to influence his business judgment. He's perfectly cold-blooded. He'd be far more apt to listen to you making him a purely business and legal proposition, than to either Fran or myself, who would have to talk with him on the ground of sentiment."

"You'll pardon me," said Perry Mason, "but that hardly seems logical."

"It doesn't make any difference how it seems," said Crinston, grinning, "and I don't know as it makes any difference whether it's logical or not. It's a fact. It's just the character of the man. You'd have to see Norton and talk with him in order to appreciate it."

Della Street opened the door from the outer office. "The young lady who was here this afternoon is on the telephone and would like to speak with you," she said.

Mason nodded and picked up the French telephone on his desk.

"Hello," he said.

He heard Miss Celane's voice speaking rapidly.

"Did Mr. Crinston come there?"

"Yes. He's here now."

"What does he say?"

"He suggests that I should interview your uncle."

"Well, will you please do so then?"

"You think I should?"

"If Arthur Crinston thinks so, yes."

"Very well. Sometime to-morrow?"

"No. Please do it to-night."

Mason frowned. "On a matter of this importance," he said, "I'd prefer to take some time to figure out the best method of approach."

"Oh that's all right," said the girl. "Arthur Crinston will tell you just what to say. I'll make an appointment with my uncle for eight thirty this evening. I'll pick you up at your office and drive you out there. I'll meet you at eight o'clock. Will that be all right?"

"Hold the line a moment please," Mason said, and turned to Arthur Crinston.

"Miss Celane is on the line and thinks I should see her uncle this evening. She says she'll make an appointment."

"That's fine," boomed Crinston, "a splendid idea. I don't know of anything that could be better."

Mason said into the receiver: "Very well, Miss Celane, I'll meet you at my office at eight o'clock, and you can drive me out."

He hung up the telephone and stared thoughtfully at Crinston.

"There's something strange about this affair," he commented. "There seems to be a frantic haste on the part of everyone concerned."

Arthur Crinston laughed.

"You don't know Fran Celane very well," he said.

"She seems to be a very calm and very poised young lady," Mason remarked tonelessly.

Crinston took the cigar out of his mouth to laugh explosively.

"You should be enough of a judge of human nature, Mason," he boomed, "to know that you can't tell a damned thing about these modern young ladies from the way they appear. Don't ever let her get her temper up. When she gets mad she's a hell-cat."

Mason regarded his visitor unsmilingly.

"Indeed," he said, in that same toneless voice.

"I didn't mean any offense," Crinston said, "but you certainly have missed it on Fran Celane. That girl is just plain dynamite.

"Now, I'll tell you what I'll do. If you're going to see Norton to-night, I'll run out a little bit in advance of your appointment, and try and soften him up a trifle. He's a peculiar chap. You'll understand when you see him. He's all cold-blooded business efficiency."

"Will Miss Celane have any difficulty making an appointment for this evening?" asked Mason, watching Crinston shrewdly.

"Oh no," said Crinston, "he's one of these fellows who likes to work nights. He has a regular office fixed up in the house, and he likes to do a lot of night work. He makes most of his appointments for afternoons and evenings."

He pulled himself to his feet, strode across to the attorney, and extended his hand.

"Mighty glad I met you," he said, "and I'll see if I can soften up Edward Norton a bit before you talk to him."

"Have you any suggestions," asked Mason, "as to the line of argument I should use with him?"

"None at all," said Crinston, "except that I would advise you not to make *any* particular plan of approach. You'll find that Edward Norton is very much of a law unto himself."

When Crinston had left, Mason paced back and forth for a few moments, then opened the door of his office, and stepped out into the outer room.

His private office was in the corner of a suite of offices which included two reception rooms, a law library, a stenographic room, and two private offices.

Perry Mason employed a typist, Della Street, combination stenographer and secretary, and Frank Everly, a young lawyer who was getting practical experience in Mason's office.

Perry Mason strode across the office to the law library, opened the door and nodded to Frank Everly.

"Frank," he said, "I want you to do something for me, and do it quickly."

Everly pushed back a calf-skin book which he had been reading, and got to his feet.

"Yes sir," he said.

"I think," said Perry Mason, "that a certain Robert Gleason has married a certain Frances Celane. I don't know just when the marriage took place, but probably it was several weeks ago. They've tried to cover it up. You've got to chase through the licenses to find what you want. Ring up some clerk in the license bureau, arrange to have him wait over after hours. They'll be closing in a few minutes, and you've got to work quickly."

"Yes, Chief," said Everly, "when I get the information where do I reach you?"

"When you get the information," said Mason, "write out whatever you find, seal it in an envelope, mark it personal and confidential, and put it under the blotter on the desk in my private office."

"Okay, Chief," said Everly, and started for the telephone.

Mason walked back to his private office, hooked his thumbs through the armholes of his vest, and started slowly and rhythmically pacing the floor.

FOUR

FRAN CELANE DROVE the big Packard roadster with a deft touch on the wheel, and skilled foot on the throttle.

When she had sat in the huge leather chair at the lawyer's office, she had seemed small, frail and helpless. Now that suggestion of helplessness had gone from her. The hint of the feline power in her nature was more pronounced. Her handling of the car was swiftly savage as she sent it hurtling through openings in traffic, coming to abrupt stops when the traffic lights were against her, leaping into almost instant speed as she got clear signals. Her face still held a pouting, sulky expression.

Seated at her side, Perry Mason studied her with eyes that were intent in watchful speculation.

The girl topped a hill, turned to a winding driveway in a scenic subdivision, and nodded her head in a gesture of indication.

"There's the place," she said, "down at the foot of the hill."

Mason looked down the winding road to the big house which showed as a blaze of light.

"Regular mansion," he said.

"Yes," she answered curtly.

"Many servants?" he asked.

"Quite a few; gardener, housekeeper, butler, chauffeur, and secretary."

"Would you call the secretary a servant?" asked Mason, watching her profile with mild amusement.

"*I* would," she snapped.

"Evidently you don't like him," Mason remarked.

She paid no attention to the comment, but swung the car around a curve at sufficient speed to bring a scream of protest from the tires.

"Incidentally," went on Perry Mason, "if you're feeling particularly savage about something, and want to take it out on the car, I'd prefer you let me get out. I have to move around in order to make my living. I couldn't gesture very emphatically to a jury with an arm in a sling."

She said: "That's all right. You might have both legs gone," and screamed the car into the next turn with an increased speed.

Mason reached over and shut off the ignition.

"We won't have any more of that," he said.

She slammed a foot on the brake, turned to him with eyes that were blazing with wrath.

"Don't you *dare* touch this car when I'm driving it!" she stormed. "Do you hear me, don't you *dare!*"

Perry Mason's tone was almost casual.

"Don't try to show off to me," he said, "by risking both of our lives. It isn't at all necessary."

"I'm not showing off to you," she blazed. "I don't give a damn what *you* think. I don't want to be late for our appointment. If we're as much as five minutes late, we're all through. He won't see us at all."

"*I* can do you a great deal more good," said Mason, "if I get there in one piece."

She had braked the car from high speed to a dead stop. Now she took her hands from the wheel as she turned to the lawyer with blazing eyes.

"I'm driving this car," she said, "and I don't want you to interfere with me!"

Suddenly she smiled. "Forgive me," she said impulsively, "I was wrong and I'm acting like a spoiled child. I guess I was in a hurry, that's all."

Mason remarked complacently: "That's all right, but you *have* got a temper, haven't you?"

"Of course I have," she said. "I thought you knew that."

"I didn't," he said, "until Crinston told me."

"Did he tell you?"

"Yes."

"He shouldn't have."

"And my secretary," he went on, calmly, "told me you were sulky. I thought at first she might have been right. But she wasn't. You're not sulky, you're just in a panic, that's all. You look sulky when you're frightened."

She whirled to face him with half parted lips and startled eyes. Then, wordlessly, she turned back to the road and started the car. Her lips were pressed into a thin line of determined silence.

Neither of them said anything more until she swept the car up the driveway and braked it to a swift stop.

"Well," she said, "let's go get it over with."

Mason got out.

"You don't intend to be present at the interview?" he asked.

She whipped the car door open and jumped to the driveway with a flash of legs, a flounce of skirt.

"Just long enough to introduce you," she said. "Come on. Let's go."

He followed her to the front door, which she opened with a latchkey.

"Right up the stairs," she said.

They walked up the stairs and turned to the left. A man was just coming out of a doorway, and he paused to stare at them. He held a stiff-backed stenographic notebook in his hand, and some papers under his arm.

"Mr. Graves," said Frances Celane, "my uncle's secretary. Don, this is Mr. Perry Mason, the lawyer."

Mason bowed and noticed as he did so, that Don Graves stared at him with a curiosity which he made no attempt to conceal.

The secretary was slender, well dressed, yellow haired and brown eyed. There was about him a certain alertness, as though he were just about to break into conversation, or just about to start running. Both his physical pose and his manner indicated physical and mental tension.

The secretary said, with a rapidity of utterance which made the words seem to tread each on the heel of the other:

"I'm very pleased to meet you. Mr. Norton is expecting you. If you'll go in, he'll receive you."

Perry Mason said nothing. His bow sufficed for an acknowledgment of the introduction.

The girl pushed on past the secretary. The lawyer followed her. Fran Celane led the way across an outer office which contained a stenographer's desk, a safe, a battery of filing cases, two telephone instruments, typewriters, an adding machine, a file of card indexes.

She pushed open the door of an inner office without knocking and Perry Mason found himself facing a tall man of fifty-five, who stared at them with a bland, expressionless countenance.

"You are late," he said.

"Not over a minute, Uncle Edward," said the girl.

"A minute," he said, "is sixty seconds."

She made no answer, but turned to the lawyer.

"This is my attorney, Perry Mason, Uncle Edward," she said.

The man said in those precise, expressionless tones: "I am very glad that you have consulted counsel. I think now it will be easier for me to explain certain things to you. You never would accept my word for them. Mr. Mason, I am very glad to meet you and very glad that you have called upon me."

He extended his hand.

Perry Mason nodded his head, shook hands, and sat down.

"Well," Fran Celane said, "I'll be running along and leave my future in your hands."

She smiled at them and left the room. As she closed the door of the private office, Mason heard her voice rattling in swift conversation with Don Graves, the secretary.

Edward Norton did not waste a single second in idle talk.

"Undoubtedly you have looked up the terms of the decree of distribution and the trust," he said.

"I have," Mason told him.

"You are familiar with them?"

"I am."

"Then, you understand, a great deal is left to my discretion."

"I would say a very great deal," said Mason cautiously.

"And I take it my niece has asked you to secure some specific modification of the provisions of the trust?"

"Not necessarily," said Mason, choosing his words cautiously. "She would like, I think to have a certain amount of latitude, and would like to know your possible reactions in the event she should do certain things."

"In the event she should marry, eh?" said Norton.

"Well, we might consider that as one of the possibilities," Mason admitted.

"Yes," said Norton drily, "we do so consider it. Her father considered it, and I consider it. You probably don't realize it yet, Mr. Mason, but my niece has one of the most ungovernable tempers in the world. She is a veritable tigress when she is aroused. She is also impulsive, headstrong, selfish, and yet thoroughly lovable.

"Her father realized that she had to be protected from herself. He also realized that leaving her any large sum of money might turn out to be the worst thing he could do for her. He knew that I shared his views, and that was the reason this trust was created.

"I want you to understand that in the event I exercise the discretion given to me under that trust, and disburse the money elsewhere than to my niece, I shall do it only because I consider it would be very much to her disadvantage to give her the money. Great riches, with a temperament such as hers, frequently lead to great suffering."

"Don't you think," said Mason diplomatically, "that it would be much better, however, all around, to accustom her to the handling of larger sums of money by gradually increasing the amount which she receives? And don't you think, perhaps, that marriage might exert a steadying influence?"

"I am familiar with all those arguments," said Norton. "I have heard them until I am tired of them. You will pardon me. I mean nothing personal. I say simply what I have in mind.

"I am the trustee of this estate. I have administered it wisely. In fact, despite the economic readjustment of values which has taken place in the last few years, I am glad to report that the trust funds have shown a steady increase, until now the amount of the trust is far in excess of what it was at the time it was created. Recently I have entirely cut off my niece's allowance. She is not receiving a penny."

Mason's face showed surprise.

"I see," said Norton, "that she has not confided to you the exact situation."

"I didn't know that you had cut off her income entirely," said Mason. "May I ask what is the reason for such a step?"

"Certainly," said Norton, "I have every reason to believe that my niece is being blackmailed. I have asked her about it, and she refuses to tell me who is blackmailing her, or what specific indiscretion she has committed which gives a blackmailer an opportunity to collect money from her.

"Therefore I have determined to place it out of her power to make *any* cash donations to *any* blackmailer. Under those circumstances, I am satisfied that another few days will force the situation to a head."

Norton stared at Mason with cold eyes which contained no trace of cordiality, yet no trace of hostility.

"You understand my position in the matter?" asked Mason.

"Certainly," said Norton. "I'm glad that my niece has consulted an attorney. I don't know if she has made arrangements for your compensation. In the event she has not, I propose to see that a sufficient amount is forthcoming from the trust fund to furnish you a reasonable fee. But I want you to impress upon her mind that she is legally powerless to do anything."

"No," said Perry Mason, "I'll take my fee from her and I'm not binding myself to give any particular advice. Let's talk about the *way* you're going to use your discretion, instead of whether you've got the right to use it."

"No," said Norton, "that is one matter which is not open to discussion."

"Well," Mason remarked, smiling affably and keeping his temper, "that is primarily what I came here to discuss."

"No," Edward Norton said coldly, "that phase of the discussion is entirely out of order. You will confine yourself to a discussion of the legal rights of your client under the trust."

Mason's eyes were cold and appraising.

"I've always found," he said, "that a legal matter has a lot of angles. If you'll just look at this thing from the human viewpoint and consider . . ."

"I will allow you to be heard," Norton interrupted, in cold, level tones, "upon no matter other than the question of the legality of the trust and the interpretation thereof."

Mason pushed back his chair, and got to his feet.

His voice was as cold as that of the other. "I'm not accustomed to having people tell me what I will talk about and what I won't talk about. I'm here representing the rights of Frances Celane, your niece, and my client. I'll say anything I damned please concerning those rights!"

Edward Norton reached out to a button and pressed it with his bony forefinger. The gesture was utterly devoid of emotion.

"I am ringing," he said, "for the butler, who will show you to the door. So far as I am concerned, the discussion is terminated."

Perry Mason planted his feet wide apart, standing spread-legged, he said: "You'd better ring for two butlers, and the secretary too. It'll take all of them to put me out of here before I say what I've got to say!"

"You're making a mistake, treating this niece of yours as though she were a chattel or a lump of clay. She's a high-spirited, high-strung girl. I don't know where you get the idea that she's being blackmailed, but if you have any such idea . . ."

The door of the private office opened, and a broad-shouldered, burly man, with a wooden face, bowed from the hips.

"You rang sir?" he asked.

"Yes," said Edward Norton, "show this gentleman out."

The butler put a firm hand on Perry Mason's arm. The lawyer shook him off, savagely, continued to face Norton.

"Nobody," he said, "is going to show me out, or is going to throw me out until I have had an opportunity to say what I want to say. If that girl is being blackmailed, you'd better act like a human being instead of a cash register, and give her a break . . ."

There was a rustle of motion, and Frances Celane rushed into the room.

She looked at Mason with black eyes, which gave the effect of being expressionless, with a face that seemed pouting.

"You've done all you can do, Mr. Mason," she said.

Mason continued to glower at the man behind the desk.

"You're more than a treasurer," he said, "or should be. She should be able to look to you for . . ."

The girl tugged at his arm.

"Please, Mr. Mason," she said, "please. I know you're trying to do me a favor, but it's going to have just the opposite effect. Please don't."

Mason took a deep breath, turned, and stalked rigidly from the room. The butler slammed the door shut behind him. Mason turned to Frances Celane and said: "Of all the obstinate, cold-blooded, unsympathetic icebergs I have ever met, that man is the worst!"

She looked up at him and laughed.

"I knew," she said, "that if I tried to explain to you how utterly obstinate my uncle was, you would never believe me. So I welcomed the opportunity to let you find out first-hand. Now you understand the necessity for taking legal steps."

"All right," said Mason, grimly, "we'll take them."

FIVE

PERRY MASON LET himself into the office with his key, walked to his desk and picked up the blotter. There was an envelope under it, marked "Confidential." He ripped it open and saw a notation in Frank Everly's handwriting:

"ROBERT GLEASON AND FRANCES CELANE TOOK OUT A MARRIAGE LICENSE ON THE FOURTH OF LAST MONTH. THEY WERE MARRIED IN CLOVERDALE ON THE EIGHTH."

The message was signed with the initials of the law clerk.

Perry Mason stared at it for several minutes, then hooked his thumbs in his vest and started pacing the floor of the office.

After a while he swung into the law library, took down a volume of *"Cyc."* dealing with wills, started reading.

He interrupted his reading to go to the book case and get a volume of the Pacific Reporter. He read the reported cases for some little time, then started taking other case books from the shelves.

He worked in cold, silent concentration, moving efficiently and tirelessly, his eyes hard and steady, his face without expression.

Somewhere a clock struck midnight, but Perry Mason kept on working. The pile of law books on the table grew larger and larger. He prowled around through the library, pulling down various books, turning to cases, studying intently. Once in a while he made a brief note. Frequently he book-marked cases, and placed them to one side.

About fifteen minutes past one o'clock in the morning the telephone rang.

Mason frowned and paid no attention to it.

The telephone continued to ring insistently, imperatively.

Mason uttered an exclamation, turned to the telephone and picked up the receiver.

"Hello," he said, "you've got the wrong number."

A voice said: "I beg your pardon, sir, but is this Mr. Mason, the lawyer?"

"Yes," said Perry Mason, irritably.

"Just a minute," said the voice.

Mason held the telephone, and heard a swift whisper, then the voice of Frances Celane: "Mr. Mason?"

"Yes."

"You must come at once," she said.

"Come where, and why?" he asked. "What's the trouble?"

"Come out to the house," she told him. "My uncle has just been murdered!"

"Has just what?"

"Has just been murdered!" she said.

"Do they know who did it?" he asked.

"They *think* they do," she said, in a low, almost surreptitious voice. "Come at once!" and the line went dead as the receiver slipped into place on the other end of the wire.

Perry Mason left the office without pausing to switch out the lights. The night watchman brought up the elevator and Mason pushed his way into it as soon as the door was open.

"Been working rather late, haven't you?" said the watchman.

Mason smiled mechanically.

"No rest for the wicked," he said.

He left the elevator, crossed the lobby of the office building, ran diagonally across the street to a hotel where there was a taxicab stand. He called the address of Norton's residence to the taxi driver. "Keep the throttle down to the floorboards," he said.

"Okay, buddy," said the driver, and slammed the door.

Mason was slammed back in the cushions, as the car lurched forward. His face was unchanging, though his eyes were squinted in thought. Never once did he glance at the scenery which whizzed past.

Only when the taxi swung off to the driveway which sloped down the hill, did Mason lose his air of abstraction, and begin to take an interest in the surroundings.

The big house was illuminated, every window was a blaze of light. The grounds in front were also illuminated, and more than a dozen automobiles were parked in front of the place.

Mason discharged the taxicab, walked to the house, and saw the bulky form of Arthur Crinston silhouetted against the lights on the porch.

Crinston ran down the three steps to the cement. "Mason," he said, "I'm glad you came. I want to see you before anybody else does."

He took the lawyer's arm and led him across the cement driveway, over a strip of lawn, and into the shadows of a hedge.

"Listen," he said, "this is a serious business. We don't know yet exactly how serious it is. I want you to promise me that you will stand by Fran. No matter what happens, see that she doesn't get mixed into this thing."

"Is she going to get mixed in it?" asked Mason.

"Not if you stand by her."

"Do you mean she's implicated in any way?" Mason demanded.

"No, no, not at all," Crinston hastened to assure him, "but she's a peculiar individual, and she's got the devil's own temper. She's mixed up in it somehow, and I don't know just how. Shortly before his death, Edward Norton telephoned the police station and wanted his niece arrested, or that's what the police claim."

"Arrested?" exclaimed Mason.

"Well, not exactly that," said Crinston, "but he wanted her disciplined in some way. I can't just get the straight of it. You see, she had his Buick sedan out driving it. According to the police, Norton telephoned in that the sedan had been stolen and wanted the police to pick up the car and put the driver in jail. He said it didn't make any difference *who* was driving it."

"Then that must have been after I left here, and before Norton's death," Mason said.

Crinston shrugged his shoulders.

"According to the police," he said, "it was at eleven fifteen. Personally I think it's all a lot of hooey. The police must have made a mistake. Norton had his faults, and there were plenty of them, but he loved his niece in his own peculiar fashion. I can't believe he wanted her arrested."

"Well," said Mason, "forget that. How about the murder? Do they know who did it?"

"Apparently," said Crinston, "that's all taken care of. Pete Devoe, the chauffeur, got drunk and killed him in order to get some money. He tried to make it appear that burglars had broken in from the outside, but he bungled the job."

"How was Norton killed?" asked Mason.

"Devoe beat his head in with a club. It was a messy job. He hit him a frightful lick."

"Did they find the club?" the lawyer asked.

"Yes," said Crinston, "that's where Devoe slipped up. He took the club and hid it in a closet in his room. He didn't think the police would search the place, because he tried to make it appear burglars had broken in from the outside. You see, the police discovered the crime a lot sooner than anyone thought they would. It's quite a story, and I'll have to tell it to you when we've got more time. Don Graves actually saw the crime being committed."

"Give me a quick outline," said Mason. "Spill it fast."

Crinston took a deep breath, then hurried into speech. "You know Norton is a night owl. He frequently keeps his office open until midnight. To-night he had an appointment with me, and I had an appointment with Municipal Judge Purley. I was late getting things cleaned up with Purley, so I persuaded Purley to drive me out here in his car, and wait for me. I only had to see Norton for a few minutes.

"I ran in and had my conference with Norton and then came out and started away with Judge Purley. Just as we started to drive away, Norton opened the window on the upper floor and called down to ask me if I would mind taking Don Graves with me. He was sending Graves after some important papers, and wanted him to go with us to save time. You see, they were papers that I had agreed to get for Graves—some documents relating to some of our partnership business.

"I asked Judge Purley if he had any objections, and Purley said it would be all right. So I called up to Norton to send Graves down, but Graves, anticipating it would be all right, by that time was at the door, and he ran right out and into the automobile.

"We started up the road toward the boulevard. You know how it curves and twists around. There's one place where you can look back and see into Norton's study. Graves happened to be looking back. He let out a yell. He said he had seen the figure of a man standing in Norton's study; that this man had a club, and had swung it down on Norton's head.

"Judge Purley ran the car to a place where he could turn around. He thought Graves might have been mistaken, but Graves insisted he couldn't have been mistaken. It was something he'd seen plainly. He insisted he was right. So Judge Purley drove back to the house, going pretty rapidly.

"When we got there, the three of us rushed into the house and up the stairs to the study.

"Norton was lying across his desk with the top of his head smashed in. His pockets were turned inside out. His wallet lay empty on the floor.

"We notified the police right away.

"There was a window in the dining room which had been jimmied open, and there were footprints outside in the loam. The prints were of very large feet, and the police think now that Devoe probably put a large pair of shoes on over his other shoes, in order to leave those prints and fool the police. You'll get the facts of the case when you go in."

Perry Mason stared thoughtfully into the half-darkness of the shadowed hedge.

"Why," he asked, "should Norton have accused his niece of stealing an automobile?"

"Probably a misunderstanding," said Crinston, "I don't think Norton had any idea his niece was the one who had the car. He just knew the car was missing, and telephoned the police. They were working on that when they were advised of the murder. So they're making inquiries, figuring the car business may have had something to do with it."

"Do they know that his niece had the car?" asked Mason.

"Yes. She's admitted having taken it out," said Crinston.

"It seems strange Norton would have wanted her arrested," persisted Mason.

"Well, he did," Crinston said, "unless the police got the wrong name, and that isn't likely, because they got the right car numbers. But Fran is a peculiar girl. You can't tell what she will do. For heaven's sake, talk with her, and don't let her get mixed up in this thing."

"You certainly don't think that she has anything to do with the murder?" asked Mason.

"I don't know," said Crinston, then hastily added: "No, no, of course not, she couldn't have. She's got a temper and they had quite a fight after you left. But she wouldn't have had the physical strength to strike such a blow anyway. And if she had had an accomplice ... Oh well, there's no use speculating about that anyway, because it's all foolishness. Devoe is the one that's guilty all right. But you know how a murder is. It's going to bring out a lot of complications. I want you to get in touch with Fran and keep her out of the complications."

"Very well," said Mason, starting once more for the house. "But either you think she's mixed up in it, or else you're keeping something from me."

Crinston grabbed Mason's arm.

"As far as compensation is concerned," he said, "there's going to be a big difference now that Norton is out of the way. The partnership that Norton and I had has some assets, and then there's quite a bit of money in the trust fund which will go to the girl without any question, as I understand it.

"I've got confidence in you and I want you to step right in the saddle as attorney for everything. Act as attorney for the estate, as well as for the girl, and stand between her and too much police questioning."

Mason stopped still and turned to face Crinston.

"You might just as well be frank with me," he said. "You seem to think that the girl can't stand too much questioning."

Crinston's jaw snapped forward and his eyes met those of the attorney in a gaze that was every bit as steady as the gaze of the steely eyes which stared into his.

"*Of course,* she won't stand too much questioning," he snapped. "Have I been talking to you all this time without giving you any idea at all of what I'm driving at?"

"Why," asked Mason insistently, "won't she stand too much questioning? Do you think she's mixed up in the murder?"

"I'm just telling you," said Crinston obstinately, "that she won't stand too much questioning. She hasn't got the temperament for it, in the first place, and she's a spitfire when she loses her temper. It isn't the murder, it's the incidental things that may come out in connection with the investigation. Now you get to her and keep the police from asking her questions."

Mason said: "All right, I just didn't want to misunderstand you, that's all. I wanted to know if you felt there was danger of her getting into trouble."

"Of course there is!" Crinston snapped.

"You mean about her private affairs?" asked Mason.

"I mean about everything," Crinston said. "Come on. Let's get in the house."

An officer stood at the front porch and questioned Mason.

"He's all right," said Crinston. "He's my attorney, the attorney for the estate, and also the personal attorney for Frances Celane."

"All right," said the officer, "you folks that live here can go in and out, but you understand that you're not to touch anything, or interfere with the evidence at all."

"Of course," said Crinston, and pushed on ahead of him into the house.

SIX

FRANCES CELANE WORE a short sport outfit, with a blue and gold sweater which set off to advantage the spun-gold effect of her silken hair.

She sat in her bedroom on an overstuffed chair, with her knees crossed, her dark eyes staring at the face of her lawyer. There was that about her which indicated she was warily watchful. She seemed to be listening, waiting for something to happen.

All about them the big house echoed with sounds; creaked with a suggestion of packed occupancy. Feet were constantly pounding the boards of floors, hallways and stairs in an endless procession. Doors made noise as they opened and shut. The drone of voices sounded as a distant rumble.

Perry Mason stared down at Fran Celane. "Go ahead," he said, "and tell me exactly what happened."

She spoke in a voice that was a low monotone, expressionless and thoughtful, as though she might be reciting a part that had been learned by rote.

"I don't know very much about it. I had a fight with Uncle Edward after you left. He was impossible. He was trying to make a chattel of me and break my spirit. I told him that that wasn't what father wanted, and that he was being false to his trust."

"What did you mean by being false to his trust?" asked Mason.

"I meant that father had created that trust only because he wanted to see that the money didn't go to my head too much, and make me too wild. He didn't intend that Uncle Edward should grind me down so I became just an automaton."

"All right," said Mason. "Did anyone know of the quarrel?"

"I guess so," she said dispiritedly. "Don Graves knew about it. And I think some of the other servants heard it. I got mad."

"What do you do when you get mad?" he asked.

"Everything," she said.

"Did you raise your voice?" he inquired.

"As high as I could."

"Did you do anything unladylike? That is, did you curse?"

She said, still in the same toneless voice: "Of course I cursed. I was angry, I tell you."

"All right," he said, "then what happened?"

"Then," she said, "I came downstairs and decided that I would run away and leave Edward Norton and his money and everything. I just wanted to get away."

"That was when you took the car?" asked Mason.

"No," she said, "I'm coming to that. I got things packed up as though I was going away, and then decided not to do it. I commenced to cool off a little bit. I've got a bad temper, but after I get over it, I can realize when I've made a mistake. So I knew that I'd make a mistake if I ran away. But I did want to get some air. I didn't want to go out and walk. I wanted to drive a car. I wanted to drive a car fast."

Perry Mason made a dry comment: "Yes, I can understand how you could keep your mind off your troubles by driving fast."

"Well," she said, "you have to do something to get your mind off your troubles."

"All right," he told her, "go on. What happened?"

"Well," she said, "I went to the garage. My Packard was in behind the Buick and I was going to have to move the Buick anyway, so I moved the Buick, and didn't see any reason why I should go back for my Packard."

"The Buick was your uncle's machine?" he asked.

"Yes," she said.

"He didn't allow you to use it?"

"He'd never forbidden me to use it," she said, "but I've never used it much. He babies it along a lot, keeps records of the mileage and the oil and gas, and all of that, and has it greased every so many miles, and the oil changed every so often. I don't bother with my Packard that way. I run it until something gets to sounding funny, and then I have it repaired."

"So you took the Buick without your uncle's consent?"

"Yes, if you want to put it that way."

"And where did you drive it?"

"I don't know. I just drove it around, taking curves as fast as I could take them."

"That was pretty fast?" he asked.

"Of course that was pretty fast," she told him.

"How long were you gone?"

"I don't know. I came back to the house a little while before the police arrived here. I must have returned ten or fifteen minutes after the murder."

"And while you were gone your uncle discovered the loss of the car—that is, he discovered that the car was missing. Is that right?"

"I think that Devoe must have told him," she said.

"How did Devoe know?"

"I don't know. Perhaps he heard me drive away, and went out to the garage to see what car I'd taken. I never did like Devoe. He's one of those big, cumbersome fellows who can't think a thought of his own, but goes through life making motions."

"Never mind that," he told her, "what makes you think that Devoe told your uncle?"

"I don't know," she said. "It was the time of uncle's telephone call, I guess, and then I always had him figured for a snitcher."

"What time was the telephone call?"

"Uncle called the police to report the car theft at about a quarter past eleven. I think the police records show that it was exactly eleven fourteen."

"When did you leave with the car?" he asked.

"About ten forty-five, I think it was," she said.

"Then you'd had the car for half an hour before your uncle reported the theft?"

"Yes, about that long I guess."

"And when did you return?"

"Somewhere around quarter past twelve. I was out about an hour and a half."

"What time did the police arrive here?"

"About an hour and a half ago."

"No, I mean how long before you returned the car."

"Ten or fifteen minutes," I guess.

"All right," he said, "what did your uncle tell the police?"

"All I know," she said, "is what they told me. One of the detectives talked with me and asked me if I knew any reason why my uncle should have reported the car as stolen."

"All right," he said, "what did your uncle tell them?"

"Well," she said, "according to what this detective told me, my uncle telephoned the police and said that it was Edward Norton talking, and that he had a criminal matter to report. Then there was a delay. I think he was cut off or something, and the police officer, I guess they call him a desk sergeant, held the telephone for a minute until Uncle Edward got another connection, and said that he wanted to report a crime—the theft of an automobile. And he described it, a Buick sedan, 6754093, with license number 12M1834."

"You seem to remember those figures pretty well," said Mason.

"Yes," she said, "they're likely to be important."

"Why?" he asked.

"I don't know," she said. "I just feel that they may be important."

"Did you tell the detective that you had the car?" he asked.

"Yes," she said, "I told him exactly what happened. That I took the car out about quarter to eleven, and brought it back about twelve fifteen, but that I hadn't asked my uncle's permission."

"The police seemed to take that explanation all right?" he asked.

"Oh yes," she said. "They have discontinued working on that end of the case. At first they thought that perhaps the burglars might have stolen the Buick for a get-away."

"They've about concluded now, I understand, that there weren't any burglars," said Mason.

"That's right," she said.

Mason paced up and down the floor.

Suddenly he whirled, and stared at the girl.

"You're not telling me the whole truth about this thing," he said.

She showed no resentment whatever in her manner, but stared at him with eyes that were coldly speculative.

"What is there in my story that doesn't hang together?" she asked, and her tone was impersonally thoughtful.

"It isn't that," he said, "it's something in your manner. You haven't told me the truth. You didn't tell me the truth when you first came to my office."

"What do you mean by that?" she wanted to know.

"About wanting to get married and all that," he said.

"Why what do you mean by that?"

"You know what I mean. You had been married already."

Every bit of color drained from her face, and she stared at him with eyes that were wide and round.

"Who told you that? Have you been talking with some of the servants?"

He countered her question with another.

"Do the servants know about it?" he asked.

"No," she said.

"Why then did you think that I had been talking with the servants?"

"I don't know," she said.

"You were married?" he asked her.

"That's none of your business," she said.

"Of course it's my business," he told her. "You came to me with a problem. You can't gain anything by lying to me, any more than you could by lying to a doctor. You've got to tell your lawyer and your doctor the whole truth. You can trust me. I don't betray communications made by my clients."

She pursed her lips and stared at him.

"What do you want me to tell you?" she asked.

"The truth."

"Well, you know it, so what's the use of my telling you?"

"You are married then?"

"Yes."

"Why didn't you tell me that before?"

"Because we were keeping it secret."

"All right," said Mason, "now somebody knows that secret. There is somebody blackmailing you."

"How do you know that?" she asked.

"Never mind that. Answer me."

She extended her right forefinger and started pushing it along the arm of the chair, squirming it around every irregularity in the cloth.

"Under the will," she said slowly, "now that my uncle is dead, does it make any difference if I am married?"

His eyes regarded her in cold, fixed appraisal.

"As I remember the provisions of the will," he said, "your uncle is given the option of turning the money over to charity in the event you marry before you are twenty-five."

"And on his death," she said, "the trust terminates?"

"On his death the trust terminates."

"Then if he can't exercise that option it doesn't make any difference whether I'm married or not?"

"Offhand," he said, "that would be my interpretation of the will."

She heaved a sigh of relief.

"Then," she said, "it doesn't make any difference whether anyone tries to blackmail me or not?"

Mason's eyes stared at the girl as though they would rip the mask from her face and probe the interior of her soul.

"I wouldn't," he said, "make very many comments about that, young lady."

"Why?" she asked.

"Because," he said in a low steady monotone, "if the police should stumble onto that theory of the case, it would show a most excellent motive for a murder."

"You mean that *I* murdered him?"

"It would mean," he said, stubbornly and steadily, "that you had an excellent motive for murdering him."

"Pete Devoe murdered him," she insisted.

"They might say that Pete Devoe was an accomplice," he told her.

"They *might*," she agreed, shrugging her shoulders, and regarding him with enigmatical black eyes.

"All right, all right," Mason said, his voice now showing a trace of impatience, "come down to earth. Suppose you try to be fair with me."

"Listen," she told him, speaking rapidly, "I'm going to come into a large sum of money. I'm going to need some one to protect my rights. I've heard about you, and I know you've got a wonderful mind. You're going to be well paid for everything you do for me—everything. You understand?"

"All right," he said, "what do you want me to do?"

"I want you to represent my interests and *my* interests alone. I am going to pay you a fee of forty thousand dollars, and if you have to do any work about getting the trust fund, that is, work like going to court or anything, I am going to pay you more."

He regarded her for a few moments in silent speculation, then said: "That's a lot of money to pay a person to protect your rights if there's nothing to be done."

"How do you mean?" she asked.

"If," he said, "you simply borrowed your uncle's car without his permission and went out for a ride, returned the car and found him murdered, there is no necessity for paying an attorney forty thousand dollars to protect your rights."

She twisted her fingers together and asked: "Are you going to argue with me about that?"

"No," he said, "I simply made that comment. I wanted you to understand the facts."

"You understand what I mean when I say that I will pay you forty thousand dollars if you protect *my* rights?" she inquired.

"Yes," he said.

She got up and crossed the room with quick, nervous stride, dropped into a wicker chair in front of a writing desk, pulled a piece of paper to her and scribbled out a document in pen and ink, which she signed with a flourish.

"Here you are," she said, "my promissory note to pay to you the sum of forty thousand dollars as soon as I have received that amount from the inheritance left me by my father. And I also mention that if there is any litigation about the inheritance, I will pay you more."

Mason folded the note and dropped it into his pocket.

"Have the police questioned you in detail?" he asked.

"No," she said, "they aren't annoying me at all. You see, the fact that I had the car out when the murder was committed gives me an alibi. That is, they know I wouldn't know what took place in the house at the time of the murder."

"What time was the murder?" he asked.

"They can fix that very exactly," she said. "It was about eleven thirty-three or eleven thirty-four. You see, Mr. Crinston had Judge Purley with him in the car, and Judge Purley wanted to get home. He started away from the house promptly at eleven thirty. He remembers because he looked at his wristwatch and I believe some comment was made about the fact that he had been here less than half an hour. I think Mr. Crinston promised Judge Purley that if the judge would drive Mr. Crinston out here, he would be detained less than half an hour in all. Mr. Crinston had an appointment with my uncle for eleven o'clock, and he was seven minutes late.

"I guess you saw enough of my uncle to know how he would feel about that seven minutes. Mr. Crinston kept urging Judge Purley to 'step on it,' all the way out here."

"I still don't see," said Mason, "how that fixes the exact time of the murder."

"Well, you see," she explained, "Don Graves saw the murder committed. Now, if the car started from the house at eleven thirty, it would have taken about three minutes to get to the point in the driveway where Graves could look back and see the persons clubbing my uncle."

"Persons?" he asked.

"Person," she amended quickly.

"I see," said the lawyer dryly.

SEVEN

PERRY MASON ENCOUNTERED Don Graves just after that individual had been released from police questioning.

Graves mopped his forehead and smiled at the attorney.

"Never had such an ordeal in my life," he said. "I certainly am glad that *I* wasn't here."

"What do you mean by that?" asked Mason.

"They might have tried to pin it on me," he said. "They tear you to pieces and doubt everything you say."

"I wonder," said Mason, "if you'd mind giving me an outline of just what you told them?"

Graves sighed wearily.

"I've told the facts so often now," he said, "that I'm hoarse."

Mason took the young man's arm and piloted him unsmilingly through the dining room to a solarium, where there were some chairs grouped around a wicker table.

"Smoke?" he asked, extending a package of cigarettes.

Graves nodded eagerly.

Perry Mason held a match to the cigarette. "Get started," he said.

"Well," said Graves, "there isn't very much that I can tell. That's the trouble with it. The police want me to tell too much. At first, when I saw the murder being committed, Judge Purley thought that I was crazy because he claimed I couldn't have seen all that I said I saw through the window, and now the police are jumping on me because I don't tell them more, and seem to think I'm holding something back."

"You saw the murder?" asked Mason.

"I guess so," said Graves wearily. "I've been hammered around so much now that I don't know what I saw."

Perry Mason made no comment.

"Well," said Graves, exhaling twin streams of smoke from his nostrils, "Mr. Crinston had an appointment for eleven o'clock, and was seven minutes late. Mr. Norton was very much exasperated over several things that had happened—one of which was your visit, and then he had some trouble with his niece afterwards. But Mr. Crinston says that I'm not to mention that trouble with Fran Celane unless somebody specifically questions me about it.

"Well, Crinston was late for his appointment, and you know how that would affect Norton. He was in one of those cold rages. He showed it by being cold-blooded, efficient, and exceedingly disagreeable.

"I don't know what Crinston talked about with him. They were having some violent difference of opinion. Frankly, I think Crinston was pretty much exasperated when he decided to leave. He had promised Judge Purley that he would leave not later than eleven thirty, and at just about eleven thirty Crinston came out of the inner office.

"Mr. Norton wanted him to stay. Crinston refused. He said he'd promised Judge Purley to leave at eleven thirty. Then Mr. Norton made some sarcastic remark that Crinston would keep him waiting seven minutes, and think nothing of it, but wouldn't think of detaining a municipal judge for as much as ten seconds. He was mad, all right—good and mad.

"Crinston had only been gone a minute or two when Mr. Norton came out and told me that he wanted me to rush out to Crinston's house and get some papers. They were some agreements that he and Crinston had been discussing, and Crinston had promised to send them to Norton. Norton suddenly decided that he didn't want to wait, but wanted them right away. He told me to wake up Devoe, that's the chauffeur, and get him to drive me out to Crinston's house and pick up the agreements.

"At that time, Crinston and Purley were just about to drive away. They had, I believe, started their car.

"Then Mr. Norton suddenly got the idea that if I should drive out with Mr. Crinston, I could save a little time. He intended to have Devoe, the chauffeur, come in and pick me up. But it was going to take Mr. Crinston a few minutes to get the documents, after I got there, and the chauffeur would take a little time dressing and getting the car out; so Norton thought he could save time by having me go in with Mr. Crinston. There wasn't any sense to it. Devoe could have driven me there just as well, but I mention it to show how excited Norton was. He was simply furious.

"So Mr. Norton raised up the window in his office and called down to Mr. Crinston to wait a minute. I'm not certain, but I think Mr. Crinston got out of the machine and walked back so that he stood under the window to hear what Mr. Norton said. I heard Norton ask if it would be all right for me to ride in with them, and I heard Crinston say that he'd go over and ask Judge Purley if there were any objections.

"I knew right away there wouldn't be any objections, so I started hot-footing down the stairs. The way Norton felt, I didn't want to waste a second.

"Crinston had asked Judge Purley, and was standing beneath the window, talking with Mr. Norton, when I got down. Mr. Crinston said to me: 'Hurry up, Graves, I've promised Judge Purley that he would leave here promptly at eleven thirty, and he's in a rush to get home.' So I ran right across and jumped into the machine. I think that I got into the machine before Mr Crinston did, or maybe we got in together, at any rate, Mr. Crinston got into the machine at just about the same time.

"Judge Purley had the engine running, and just as soon as the door slammed, he started the car. I was in the back seat, and Mr. Crinston was sitting up in front with Judge Purley.

"You know the way the road winds around up the side of the hill. Well, I don't know what prompted me to look back through the window at the house. Maybe it was just curiosity, maybe it was some sense of what was happening.

"Anyway, I was looking back through the rear window of the car, and just as it rounded the curve where I could see into the study, I saw people in the study, and a man swinging a club."

"How many people?" asked Perry Mason.

Don Graves did not answer for a moment. Then he took a deep breath and said slowly: "Only one that I was sure of. That is, I saw one person raise his arm and strike another person."

"That you were *sure* of?" said Mason.

"Yes sir," said Graves, "that I was sure of."

"There *might* have been another person present?" asked Perry Mason.

Don Graves said in a very low voice: "I don't think, if I were you, sir, that I'd go into that."

"Why not?" asked Perry Mason explosively.

"I'd rather not state," said Graves, squirming uncomfortably. "But you might find, if you pressed that line of inquiry too far, that it wasn't of any particular advantage, either to you or your client."

"I think I see," said Perry Mason softly.

Graves sighed his relief.

"You were, of course, some distance away?" asked Mason.

"Yes," said Graves, "I was some distance away."

Mason looked at the young man searchingly, but Don Graves kept his eyes averted.

"How clearly could you see?" Mason pressed.

Graves took a deep breath. "I could see quite clearly that somebody was standing over somebody else, and striking a blow," he blurted.

"And did you see that other person fall?"

"I don't think so. You know, it was quite a distance away, and I only had a flash as the car was swinging around the curve in the road."

"Could you say that there were *only* two people in the room?" asked Mason.

"No, of course not, because I couldn't see the entire room."

"Could you say that you only *saw* two people in the room?" Mason inquired.

"I *did* say that," said Graves, and added after a moment, "to the police."

Perry Mason's voice was low. "Let's not misunderstand each other, Graves. In the event that you saw anything which indicated that there was another person in the room, did you see anything that would identify that person?"

Graves spoke very softly and with obvious reluctance. "Confidentially, Mr. Mason, one can't trust one's impressions in a momentary glimpse like that. It isn't as though you had a photograph of it. And yet there's something that's etched on my brain that I haven't mentioned— to the police. I might tell *you*, in strict confidence, that, if there was another person in that room, and if I saw such a person, *that person was a woman*."

Perry Mason stared steadily at Graves, then asked:

"Could you identify that woman?"

"I have not mentioned to anyone that I saw that woman," said Graves slowly, "and I would not care to make any identification."

"But," said Mason, "have you been absolutely positive and emphatic in saying that you did *not* see such a person?"

Graves met his eyes. "I have tried to tell the truth, Mr. Mason. So far, whenever the question has been asked me, I have answered in such a way that the inquiry has taken another turn. You understand that I am going to answer questions truthfully when I get on the witness stand, if I get on the witness stand. But you will also understand that everyone of us is exceedingly loyal to your client."

"Meaning?" asked Mason.

"Meaning Miss Celane."

"Do I understand," said Mason very softly and almost ominously, "that such a loyalty would lead you to protect her against a murder charge?"

"No," said Graves frankly, "it would not. But it certainly would be sufficient to lead us to keep her name out of an investigation which could only be abortive at any rate."

"And what do you mean by that?" pressed the attorney.

"I mean by that, that inasmuch as Miss Celane was not in the house at the time, it would naturally have been impossible for her to have been in that room."

"Then you did not see a woman in the room?" Mason asked.

"I didn't say that either," said Graves. "I said that *if* there had been another person in the room that I had seen, that person would probably have been a woman."

"Why," asked the lawyer, "do you say that?"

"Well," said Graves, "there is in my mind a more or less confused impression of a woman's head and shoulders showing momentarily in one corner of the window. But of course I couldn't be sure of it, because my glance was riveted on the man with his arm upraised."

"One more question," said Mason. "Did the police take down, in shorthand, the answers which you gave to the questions they asked you, when they inquired about what you had seen?"

"Yes," said Graves.

"And you didn't mention anything about a woman at that time?"

"No."

Mason said slowly: "You understand, Graves, that there is something very peculiar about this. Both you and Crinston have intimated to me that my client might be in some danger. Yet, apparently, she was not anywhere near the house at the time."

"That's right," said Graves eagerly, "she wasn't here."

"Then how could she be in any danger?" asked Mason.

"She isn't," said Graves. "That's the point I'm trying to make. And I'm trying to protect her against any insinuations which might be made, because, you understand, there's a motive which might be attached to her."

"Very commendable," said Mason dryly. "I wouldn't want you to commit any perjury, Graves, but you will, of course, understand that if you tell your story a few times without mentioning the woman, and that story is recorded in shorthand, or reported in the press, and *then* you should subsequently be placed upon the stand and asked specifically if you saw a woman or had the impression that a woman was there, an answer which tended to change your previous story wouldn't do my client such a great amount of harm. One the other hand, it wouldn't do you such a great amount of good."

Graves said with dignity: "I am prepared to make some sacrifices in order to protect the good name of Miss Celane."

"And," went on Perry Mason, ominously, "when you did amplify your story to include a woman, as being present in that room, I'd rip you wide open."

"Sure," said Graves, readily.

"And," Mason told him grimly, "when I say wide open, I mean wide open."

At that moment, a door opened and a detective looked into the room, stared at Mason, then shifted his eyes to Graves, and beckoned.

"Graves," he said, "we want you back upstairs. There are one or two questions we want to ask you. When you gave your statement, you seemed to have evaded answering one of the questions. That is, the chief thinks that you did, now that your statement is being read over."

Graves looked at Mason with eyes that were suddenly apprehensive.

"You won't mind answering these questions?" asked the detective.

"Not at all," said Graves, and walked from the solarium.

When the door closed behind Graves and the detective, Perry Mason pulled a paper from his pocket, unfolded it and examined it with thoughtful appraisal. The paper was Frances Celane's promissory note for forty thousand dollars.

EIGHT

THE WOMAN SLIPPED in through the door of the solarium and stared at Perry Mason, watched him pacing back and forth, following him with her eyes, studying every motion.

There was a keen concentration in the intentness of her gaze; she might have been a motion picture director, studying a new star for the strong, as well as the weak, points. She was short and broad, but not particularly fat. She seemed heavily muscled and big-boned; a woman of immense strength, capable and self reliant, and in her eyes was a glitter of greedy vitality.

Her features were rugged; the chin rounded and heavy, the nose distended at the nostrils. The lips were not thin, but uncurving. The mouth was a straight line, stretching under the nose and calipered at the ends by wrinkles which came from the nostrils. The forehead was rather high, and the eyes black and snapping—highly polished eyes that glittered as though they had been huge, black glass beads.

Perry Mason continued his pacing for several seconds before he sensed her presence. Then, as he turned, the woman's form struck his vision, and he came to an abrupt pause.

Mason looked at her with eyes that were steady in their scrutiny, yet seemed to take in every detail of the woman's appearance from head to foot.

She said: "You're the lawyer."

"Yes," he said, "I'm Perry Mason."

"I want to talk with you," she told him.

"Who are you?"

"I'm Mrs. Mayfield."

"I don't know that that conveys anything to me, Mrs. Mayfield," he said. "Could you be more explicit?"

"I live here," she told him.

"Indeed," he said tonelessly.

"Yes, sir," she said, "my husband and myself."

Mason stared at the broad shoulders, the thick arms, the black dress which covered the rugged lines of her body.

"You're the housekeeper?" he asked.

"Yes."

"And your husband?"

"He acts as gardener and general man about the place."

"I see," said Mason, unsmilingly, "and what was it you wanted to talk with me about?"

She took three steps toward him, lowered her voice, and said: "Money."

Something in her tone caused the lawyer to glance over her shoulder to the door of the room. Then he took her arm and led her to the far corner of the room.

"Exactly what," he asked, "was it about money that you wanted to discuss with me?"

The woman said in a low, intense voice: "You're an attorney. You're not in business for your health. You're representing Miss Celane. She's going to get a lot of money, and when she gets it, you're going to get a big slice of it. I want some money. I want some from you, and I want some from her."

"Just why," asked Mason, "should you want money from her and from me?"

"Because," said the woman, slowly, "if I don't get it, you don't get it."

"Exactly what do you mean by that?"

"Just what I say. If you think you can deal me out on this, you've got another think coming."

Mason laughed, a laugh that was utterly mechanical.

"Really, Mrs. Mayfield," he said, "you have got to explain. Things have been happening rather rapidly to-night, and I was called in at the request of Miss Celane. I don't know exactly what my duties will consist of, but I presume it is possible that I may have charge of handling the estate. I don't know whether or not there was a will."

"Never mind that," said the woman, "it isn't Norton's estate that I'm talking about. I'm talking about the trust money."

Mason simulated surprise, but his eyes were patiently watchful and very hard.

"Why," he said, "that matter is all taken care of by a decree of distribution made months ago. Miss Celane doesn't have to employ an attorney to collect that money for her. It will be distributed to her by an order of the court under the provisions of the trust."

"You're not fooling me any with all that line of talk," said the woman.

"Exactly what," asked Mason, "do you have reference to?"

"I have reference that if she ain't careful she don't get any of that money at all," said the woman.

"And you are intimating, I take it," said Mason, cautiously, "that you can assist her in being careful?"

"I don't know what you're driving at now," she said, "but I think you've got my idea."

She smirked and put her hands on her broad hips, tilted her chin upward, and stared with unwinking intensity into the attorney's face.

"Suppose," he said, "you should be more explicit."

"The girl's married," she said.

"Indeed," said Mason.

"Yes," she said, "does that mean anything?"

"Not now it doesn't," said Mason. "In the event what you say is true, I understand that Mr. Norton had the right to terminate the trust by delivering a small amount of the principal to Miss Celane, and giving the balance to charitable institutions. But that was something entirely in his discretion. He died without the discretion having been exercised. Therefore, the trust has terminated."

"Don't be too sure he didn't do anything about that trust," said the housekeeper.

"Did he?" asked Perry Mason.

"Suppose," said the woman, without directly answering his question, "Fran Celane and her uncle had a big fight after you left last night? And suppose that he then and there told her he would give her five thousand dollars of the money, and give all the rest to charity?"

"Did he?" asked the lawyer.

"I'm asking you what would happen if he had."

"Well," said Mason, "there certainly isn't any evidence that he did, is there?"

"There ain't now," she said.

"Exactly what do you mean?" he asked.

"Suppose there should be some evidence like that?"

"We'll cross that bridge when we come to it," said Mason.

"Well," she snapped, "if you don't do business with me, you'll come to it."

"That's hardly possible," said the lawyer. "Come, come, Mrs. Mayfield, if you want to make any insinuations against Miss Celane, you will have to make them in a manner which will be substantiated by the circumstances of the case.

"The evidence in this case shows that Miss Celane left the house before eleven o'clock and didn't return until after the police had arrived."

"Yes," said the woman, "that's what the evidence shows, and you'd better see that it ain't changed."

"I still don't get what you mean," said Perry Mason.

"You will," said the woman, "when you've made Fran Celane come clean and quit pulling the wool over your eyes. I'm not going to stand here and have you high hat me with your lawyer talk. I've told you what I want, and I'm too smart to make any threats."

"In other words," said Mason, "you want money."

"Yes."

"Very good," said Mason. "I take it that everyone wants money."

"You know what I mean," she said, "and if you want to get some more evidence, you might look up what Bob Gleason was doing at the time this murder was committed."

"Gleason?" said Mason, arching his eyebrows. "Why Gleason wasn't even here in the house."

"Oh wasn't he?" said the woman.

"Was he?" asked Mason.

"Ask your Frances," she said.

Mason suddenly turned, planted his feet wide apart, and stared at her.

"Look here, my woman," he said, in his best courtroom manner, "I don't know whether it's ever occurred to you, but you may be guilty of a very serious crime. If you are seeking to frighten me or to frighten Miss Celane into paying you money by making insinuations, you are guilty of a crime known as extortion, and in a case of this kind it might be a very serious crime."

The beady black eyes stared at him snappingly with hostility reflected from their burnished surfaces.

"You're not frightening me a bit," she said.

"And," said Perry Mason, "may I advise you that *you* are not frightening *me* in the least?"

"I ain't trying to frighten you—yet," she said. "I just told you certain things."

"What things?" he asked.

"That I'm going to get some money out of it. Otherwise, nobody gets any money."

"Nobody?" he asked.

"Neither you nor the girl," she agreed.

"That would be unfortunate," said Mason tonelessly.

"Wouldn't it?" she said. "And then again I might find somebody that would pay me, if you didn't see which side of the bread had the butter. Some of these charities for instance."

"Really," said Mason, "I don't get you. You've got to give me more particulars of what you're driving at."

She said: "I'm too smart for you, Mister Lawyer. You go ahead and make your own investigation. Don't think that you're dealing with an ignorant woman, because you ain't. You talk with Frances Celane, and then you can talk some more with me."

"I have talked with Miss Celane," said Mason.

The woman's laugh was harsh and bitter.

"Oh no, you haven't," she said, "you've listened to her. Frances Celane is the best little liar in the world. Don't listen to her. *Talk* to her. Make her mad and *then* see what she says."

And the woman turned and walked from the room with quick, vigorous strides, a veritable bundle of energy.

Perry Mason stared at her broad back until she had left his field of vision. His eyes were clouded with speculation.

He was standing so, when a man with keen gray eyes and bushy white hair came walking through the room beyond, to the door of the solarium. His manner was grave and dignified, his walk unhurried, his face placidly serene.

Perry Mason bowed to him.

"Judge Purley," he said, "I have practiced before you, Judge."

The judge fastened his keen eyes upon the attorney, and nodded.

"Perry Mason, I believe. Good evening, Mr. Mason."

"We can call it morning, I think," said Mason. "It will be daylight pretty soon."

Judge Purley frowned.

"I was in a hurry to get home too," he said. "I was very, very tired."

"The police about finished with their investigation?" asked Mason.

"I think so," said Purley. "They've got the man who did it, beyond any doubt."

"This chap, Devoe?" asked Mason.

"That's the chap. He made rather a bungling job of it, too, if you ask me."

"I didn't get the details," said Mason invitingly.

Judge Purley selected one of the reclining chairs, stretched himself in it, gave a sigh of weariness, and took a cigar from his waistcoat pocket.

He carefully clipped off the end of the cigar, smelled the wrapper and muttered: "Pardon me, Mr. Mason, but this is my last, and I need it."

"Go right ahead," said Mason, "I only smoke cigarettes anyway."

"Yes," said the judge, speaking gravely and judiciously, in measured tones, "the thing that confused the murderer, of course, was the fact that our machine turned around and came directly back to the house. He had counted on an interval of half an hour or so during which he could have masked his crime.

"However, when he heard us returning to the house, he knew that the only thing for him to do was to get into bed and pretend he was dead drunk. He managed to get the odor of whisky pretty well on his breath, and put up rather a credible imitation of intoxication.

"In fact, it is possible he imbibed enough so that he was genuinely intoxicated. A man can drink a lot of whisky in a short time."

Perry Mason smiled.

"That is, judge," he said, "if he has it to drink."

The judge saw no humor in the remark. He looked at Perry Mason with judicial appraisal.

"Well," he said, "this man had plenty to drink."

"He's the chauffeur, I believe?" asked Mason.

"Yes, the chauffeur."

"Wasn't he going out some place?" asked Mason. "Didn't Norton telephone for him to take one of the cars and run an errand?"

"If my understanding is correct," said Judge Purley, "that is what happened. Norton wanted his secretary to get some papers at Mr. Crinston's house, and the chauffeur was to go and pick him up."

Perry Mason eyed the judge in shrewd appraisal.

"Well," he said, "let's see if we can figure out what happened. Norton asked you to permit Graves to ride in your car, is that right?"

"That is correct. That is, Norton addressed his comment, I believe, to Mr. Crinston, but I, of course, heard it. He called out the window."

"Okay, then," said Mason. "Let's start from there. Graves went downstairs to join you two. It's reasonable to suppose that Norton then sent for the chauffeur. He probably simply told him to come to his office. Now, it would have taken the chauffeur a minute or two to get there."

"That's right," said Judge Purley wearily. "But if you'll pardon me, counsellor, I don't see as there's anything to be gained by going over the ground."

"No," said Perry Mason, almost dreamily, "I was just wondering how much time the two men had to quarrel."

"What do you mean?" asked Judge Purley with sudden interest.

"If," said Perry Mason, "the murder was committed by the time your car had arrived at the top of the hill, and if during that time Norton had summoned the chauffeur, and there had been a quarrel, the quarrel would, of necessity, have been of long standing."

"That doesn't follow at all," Judge Purley said. "The quarrel could have started right then. In fact, it isn't reasonable to suppose that Norton would have retained Devoe in his service if there had been a previous quarrel between them."

Perry Mason's eyes glinted.

"Then," he said, "you must agree that there wasn't opportunity for a great deal of premeditation."

Judge Purley regarded him quizzically.

"Just what are you leading up to?" he asked.

"Nothing," said Perry Mason noncommittally.

"In the eyes of the law," said Judge Purley, as though he were pronouncing some judgment, "there is no particular time required for premeditation. An instant's premeditation is all that is necessary to make a crime first degree murder."

"All right," said Perry Mason. "Now, let's look at the case from another angle. As I understand it, one of the windows had been jimmied open, and there were the marks of footprints under the window. These things tended to indicate that a burglar had entered the place."

"All a frame-up," said Judge Purley. "The police have demonstrated that."

"Precisely," said Perry Mason. "But it took some time to plant these clews. Now, the point I am getting at is that there is nothing in the evidence to show whether they were done before the murder, or afterwards. The police have been inclined to the theory that they were done afterwards. But it is barely possible they were done before."

Judge Purley looked at him through the blue haze of his cigar smoke, with a forehead that was wash-boarded in thought.

"In that case," he said, "the fact that Norton sent for the chauffeur would have had nothing to do with it. The chauffeur would have been waiting our departure, in order to enter Norton's study."

"Now," said Perry Mason, nodding his head, "you're commencing to get to the meat of the situation."

Judge Purley studied the tip of his cigar.

Perry Mason said, in a low tone of voice: "You were in the room where the crime was committed, Judge?"

"Yes. The police allowed me to look through the place. Because of my position, they gave me every liberty."

"Then," said Perry Mason, "if it's a fair question, did you notice anything unusual?"

Judge Purley acted as though the question had given him a great deal of satisfaction. He settled back in his chair, and spoke in slow, deliberate tones, gesturing once in a while with the tip of his cigar.

"The man had been struck from behind," he said, "apparently while he was seated at his desk. He had fallen forward across the desk, and had never moved after the blow crushed in his head. The telephone instrument was at his left hand. There were some papers on the desk, an envelope, I think, and a blank sheet of paper, and an insurance policy for the stolen automobile."

"Ah," said Perry Mason, in a voice that was purring. "The stolen car was insured then?"

"Of course it was insured," said Judge Purley. "Naturally, it would be."

"Are you certain the policy was for the stolen car?" asked Mason.

"Yes," said Judge Purley. "I checked it, and the police checked it. The policy covered a Buick sedan numbered 6754093. It was a policy of full coverage."

"Did you," asked Perry Mason, "know Edward Norton in his lifetime, Judge?"

"No, I had never met him. I am quite well acquainted with Mr. Crinston, Mr. Norton's business partner, and Mr. Crinston has spoken to me so often about Mr. Norton and his peculiarities that I feel as though I had known him personally. But I had never met him. Mr. Norton was a bit difficult to approach, and I had never had any business dealings which would have caused me to make his acquaintance."

Perry Mason suddenly turned to face Judge Purley.

"Judge Purley," he said, "Edward Norton wasn't killed as the result of a quarrel."

Judge Purley shifted his eyes.

"You're referring again to the time element?" he said. "The fact that there wasn't time for a quarrel?"

"Partially," said Perry Mason. "Devoe wouldn't have had time to get to the room, have a quarrel with the man, and work himself up into the frenzy of rage necessary to result in murder. Furthermore, the clews which were planted, and were for the purpose of directing suspicion toward a couple of burglars, indicate the murderer knew the logical motive for the killing was that of robbery."

Judge Purley fidgeted uncomfortably. He seemed struggling with the desire to make a statement, and a reluctance to do so. Perry Mason watched him as a sailing hawk might study a sloping hillside.

"Well," said Judge Purley, at length, "I must say, counsellor, that you have done a very nice bit of reasoning. I wasn't supposed to mention it, but inasmuch as you seem to know, there can be no harm in my confirming your suspicions, or perhaps I should say, your deductions."

"The motive, then," asked Perry Mason, "was robbery?"

"The motive was robbery," said Judge Purley.

"Money?" asked Mason.

"A very large sum of money. Mr. Norton had on his person at the time of his death, something over forty thousand dollars in currency. That money was in a wallet in his inside pocket. When the body was found, the pockets had been rifled and the wallet was gone. That is, it had been lifted from the inside pocket and lay near the body, empty."

"Were any of the other pockets disturbed?" asked Perry Mason.

"Yes. They had all been turned wrong side out," Judge Purley said.

"Have the police found any of the money?" asked the lawyer.

"That is something which probably won't come out until later, counsellor," said Judge Purley. "But I don't mind telling you in confidence that they have. They found two one thousand dollar bills in Devoe's trouser pocket. Those bills can be identified by their numbers as being part of the currency which Norton had in his possession, and Devoe has made the mistake of stating, in his maudlin way, that he doesn't have any idea how the bills got there."

"Has it been brought out why Norton had such a large sum of cash in his possession?" Mason wanted to know.

Judge Purley started to speak, then checked himself.

"I think, counsellor," he said, "that I have given you all of the information which I should give you. After all, your interest in this matter, while it is parallel with that of the police, is not, of course, identical. Much of the information which was given to me was given to me in confidence because of my judicial position, and I do not think that I should disseminate it carelessly."

There was a faint twinkle of amusement in the eyes of the attorney as he surveyed the ponderous form of the magistrate. Judge Purley radiated a sense of exaggerated self-importance.

"Of course, judge," said Perry Mason, "one must understand and respect your position. I didn't want you to think I was merely curious. I was trying to get a mental picture of what had happened. I am advised by the interested parties that I will be in charge of the estate, and, under those circumstances, I wanted to have complete information."

"That's true, of course," said Judge Purley, nodding his head, "and that's the reason that I gave you as much of the inside information as I did. You will, however, counsellor, regard it as strictly confidential."

"Oh yes, of course," said Perry Mason, and there was just a trace of mockery in his voice, which caused the judge to look up quickly. But the face of the lawyer was bland and innocent.

NINE

SUN STREAMED IN through the window of the room, and shone upon Edward Norton's massive desk.

A police representative sprawled in one of the chairs, a cigarette drooping from his lips, a pencil poised over a notebook. Don Graves, the efficient secretary of the dead man, checked off the documents.

The furniture in the room was in exactly the same position it had occupied the night of the murder. According to police orders, things were to be disturbed as little as possible.

Perry Mason, as the attorney representing the interested parties, was engaged in making a survey of the business affairs of the murdered man.

Don Graves, standing in front of the safe, turned to Perry Mason.

"This compartment of the safe, sir, contains all of the documents relating to the partnership business of Crinston & Norton."

"Very well," said Mason. "You're familiar with the details of those documents, I take it?"

"Oh, yes, sir."

"Generally, what is the financial state of the partnership?"

"The partnership had a few rather unfortunate investments, sir. There were some commitments which ran into rather a large deficit, amounting to something around a million dollars. But, aside from that, the affairs were in good shape. There was, I believe, something like eight hundred thousand dollars on deposit in various banks. Would you like the exact figures?"

"You might give them to me," said Mason. "I want to get just a general idea of the financial set-up."

Graves took a book from the safe, opened it, and read off a column of figures.

"The account was in a little better shape than I thought, sir. There's a balance of eight hundred and seventy-six thousand, five hundred and forty-two dollars and thirty cents at the Seaboard Second National Trust Company, and two hundred and ninety-three thousand, nine hundred and four dollars and fifty cents in the Farmers and Merchants National.

"There are notes, representing the partnership loss, which are held at the Wheeler's Trust and Savings Bank in an amount of nine hundred thousand dollars, with some interest due on them, I believe, and there's a deposit in that bank of seventy-five thousand dollars."

"How about the trust funds?" asked Mason. "The funds representing the trust in favor of Frances Celane?"

"Those are in excellent shape," said Graves. "There is over a million dollars in stocks, bonds, and securities. There's a list of them in this ledger. Mr. Norton was particularly careful about his trust obligations, and kept the account right up to date."

"Are there any liabilities in the trust account?" asked Mason.

"No, sir. There's not a dollar of indebtedness. The assets are all net."

"Then how about Mr. Norton's individual account; that is, outside the partnership of Crinston & Norton?"

"That's something that I can't tell you very much about," said the secretary. "Mr. Norton kept his private business in such shape that it required but little bookkeeping, and carried most of it in his head. Virtually all of the commercial transactions were in the partnership of Crinston & Norton. Mr. Norton's private affairs were confined to the purchase of gilt-edged stocks and bonds, which he kept in a safety deposit box."

"How about a will?" asked the lawyer.

"Yes, sir, there's a will. I don't know where it is. I think it's somewhere in the safe here. I understand generally it leaves everything to Miss Celane. Mr. Norton had no close relatives, you understand."

The police representative said casually, the words coming through an aura of cigarette smoke which seeped out from his mouth as he talked: "Pretty good thing for this Celane woman all around. She gets her trust account free and clear, and also gets a gob of money from the old man, himself."

Perry Mason made no reply to the comment, but continued to address Don Graves.

"Just where is the will?" he asked. "Can you find it?"

"Most of his personal papers were kept in this pigeon-hole in the safe," said Graves, indicating a pigeon-hole.

Perry Mason walked over to the safe, reached in the pigeon-hole, and pulled out a bundle of papers.

"Life insurance policy with the Prudential," he said. "Amount, five hundred thousand dollars. The beneficiary is the estate."

"Yes, sir," said the secretary. "You'll find several life insurance policies in cash to the estate. Those were taken out in order to have sufficient ready cash in the estate to pay inheritance taxes without necessitating a sale of securities at a loss."

"Good idea," said the lawyer. "Here are some more policies. You can list those."

He pulled out a small pasteboard-backed notebook from underneath the policies.

"What's that?" asked the police representative.

Perry Mason turned it over slowly.

"Looks like a car register," he said, "of mileage."

Don Graves laughed.

"Yes," he said, "that's one of the things about Mr. Norton. He always wanted appointments kept to the minute; always carried watches that were adjusted to the second; always kept an account of every mile that was traveled by one of his automobiles. He wanted to know exactly how much mileage he was getting to every gallon of gas and oil. I presume you can tell to within a fraction of a cent how much it cost him to operate every automobile."

"How many cars did he have?" asked Mason, fingering the notebook carelessly.

"He had three: The Buick sedan, a Ford coupe, and a Packard roadster."

"The Packard roadster was the one that Miss Celane usually drove?" asked the lawyer.

"It was," said Graves, "and you won't find any figures on that. That was the despair of his life. Miss Celane simply wouldn't turn in mileage figures."

"I see," said Mason. "But the others are accurately accounted for?"

"Yes."

"Miss Celane wasn't in the habit of operating the others?"

Don Graves flashed the lawyer a meaning glance.

"No," he said, shortly.

Perry Mason carelessly opened the notebook to the division which had to do with the Buick sedan, and noticed the different mileage reports which were in there. Apparently for every mile the Buick had traveled, there was a note as to the kind of road it had gone over, the place to which it had been driven, the general average speed, and much other data which represented a mass of detail that would have been considered useless to any save a mind that gloried in figuring costs to a fraction of a cent.

Perry Mason maintained a pose of casual interest as he fingered the pages until he came to the last entry covering the Buick sedan, which was as follows: "15,294.3 miles. Left house and drove to bank. Arrived bank at 15,299.5 miles. Left bank and returned to house at 15,304.7 miles. Instructed Devoe to fill tank."

Perry Mason glanced at the date, and saw that it was the date on which Norton had met his death.

"I see," he remarked casually, "that he went to the bank the day of his death."

"Did he?" said Don Graves.

"I wonder," said Perry Mason, "if that was when he got his money . . . that is, the cash that he carried."

"I'm sure I couldn't tell you, sir."

"Does anyone know why he had such a large sum of cash in his possession?" asked the lawyer.

"No," said Graves, emphatically.

"Almost looks as though he might have been blackmailed or something," said Mason, his patient eyes peering out from under his level brows at the face of the secretary.

Don Graves met his glance without changing expression by so much as the flicker of an eyelash.

"I hardly think so, sir," he said.

Mason nodded and slipped the book into his pocket. "Just a minute," said the police officer. "Shouldn't that book be kept here with the rest of the papers?"

Mason smiled.

"That's right," he said. "It looks so much like a notebook that I sometimes carry, I mechanically dropped it into my pocket."

He handed the book to the secretary, got up, and yawned.

"Well," he said, "I guess I've covered about everything I need to, as a first preliminary survey. Of course, we'll have to take a detailed inventory later on."

"We can take the detailed inventory now if you want," said Graves.

"Oh, I don't think so," said Mason, yawning again. "There's going to be a lot of detailed stuff to check over here, and I'll probably want my own stenographer here to take notes when I go into it in detail. I hate detail work."

"How about the will? Should we make any further search for the will?" asked Graves.

"Oh, let's close things up now, and I'll have my secretary come out and we'll tackle it to-morrow," said the attorney.

"Very well, sir, just as you say," said Don Graves.

The police representative flipped away his cigarette and remarked, "Any time suits me. I'll be around here all the time."

"Fine," said Mason, without enthusiasm. He lit a cigarette, and walked casually from the office.

He went down the broad flight of stairs, opened the front door, and stood in the sunshine, inhaling the fresh morning air. When he was certain he was not observed, he stepped off the porch, walked to the driveway, and went up the driveway to the garage. He slid back the door of the garage, slipped inside, and walked over to the Buick sedan which stood, obviously well cared for and polished by the chauffeur who was now in jail, charged with murder.

Perry Mason opened the door of the sedan, slid in behind the steering wheel, switched on the dashlight and looked at the speedometer. The figures showed 15,304.7 miles.

The lawyer stared at them for a moment, then switched off the dashlight, slid out from behind the wheel, and carefully closed the door. He walked out of the garage, looked to see if anyone had been observing him, then retraced his steps to the front door.

As he stepped inside, he encountered the form of the housekeeper.

Her glittering black eyes surveyed him uncompromisingly.

"Good morning," she said.

"Good morning," said Perry Mason.

She lowered her voice slightly.

"I'm going to be wanting an answer, sir," she said, "very soon."

"You shall have it," said the attorney, "and, by the way, where is Miss Celane? Is she up yet?"

"Yes, sir, she's up. She's having breakfast in her room."

"Give her my compliments," said the lawyer, "and ask her if I can see her at once."

The glittering black eyes of the housekeeper surveyed his face searchingly, and Perry Mason met her stare with a look of weary patience.

"I'll see," said the housekeeper. She turned and walked with swift, aggressive steps toward the girl's bedroom.

Perry Mason lit a cigarette with a steady hand, took only a single appreciative inhalation, then stood studying the smoke as it eddied from the tip of the cigarette.

He heard the steps of the housekeeper as she pounded toward him.

"Miss Celane says you can talk to her while she's eating breakfast," said the housekeeper. "Right this way, please."

The lawyer followed the housekeeper down the corridor and to the door of the girl's room.

The housekeeper held it open.

"There you are, sir," she said. "Step right in," and added in a lower tone, "and remember, I want an answer."

Perry Mason walked in and heard the door slam viciously behind him.

Frances Celane, in a silken negligee, sat curled in an over-stuffed chair. A small stand at the side of the chair held a tray containing empty dishes. A huge coffee pot had been pushed to the side of the tray, and a steaming cup of coffee was at the fingertips of her right hand. Her left held a cigarette.

Her dark eyes, seeming purposely expressionless, surveyed the attorney. Her face showed a hint of rouge, but there was no lipstick on her mouth. The negligee seemed to have been chosen for appearance rather than warmth.

"Good morning," he said, barely sweeping his eyes over the negligee. "Did you sleep any?"

"After I finally got to bed, I did," she said, staring at him steadily. She took the cigarette from her mouth and tapped the ashes into the edge of the saucer under the coffee cup.

Perry Mason moved over and dropped ashes from his own cigarette into the saucer.

"I presume," she said, "that you want money."

"What makes you ask that?" he inquired.

"I understand attorneys always want money."

He made a gesture of impatience with his hand, and said: "That isn't what I meant. Why did you choose this particular time for bringing up the subject?"

"Because," she said, "I have some money for you."

His eyes were coldly cautious. "A check?" he asked.

"No," she said, "cash. Would you mind handing me my purse? It's over there on the dresser."

Mason reached for the purse and handed it to her. She held it at such an angle that he could not see the contents. She opened it and fumbled with her fingers for a few moments, then produced a sheaf of currency.

"Here," she said, "is something by way of retainer."

He took the money, crisp new one-thousand-dollar bills. There were ten of them. He looked at her for a few moments, then folded and pocketed the money.

"All right," he said, "where did you get it?"

Her eyes suddenly contained expression. "That's none of your business," she snapped. "You're an attorney paid to represent me; not to inquire into my personal affairs."

He stood with his feet apart, smiling down at her rage.

"Your temper," he told her, "is going to get you into trouble some day."

"Oh, you think so, do you?" she flared.

"I know it," he said. "You're getting on thin ice. You've got to learn to keep your temper and use your head."

"Just what do you mean by that crack about thin ice?"

"I was referring," he said, in cold tones, "to the reason that you were spared more detailed questioning last night, or, rather, early this morning."

"What was that?"

"The fact that you had taken your uncle's Buick sedan without his permission, and were, as I remember your story, speeding around the country trying to settle your nerves."

"I always do that," she said, her voice suddenly cautious, "after I've been in a rage. It calms me down."

He continued to smile frostily at her.

"Do you know how far you drove the automobile?"

"No. I drove it an hour or so. I had my foot pretty well down on the throttle. I drive like that most of the time."

"How unfortunate," he said, "that the speedometer was disconnected."

She stared at him, with her eyes suddenly wide and very dark.

"What are you talking about?" she asked, slowly.

"About the fact that your uncle's notebook shows every mile that the Buick was driven."

"Does it?" she asked, warily.

"Yes," said Mason dryly. "He made a note of driving the car from the bank to the house, showing that he started with the speedometer registering 15,299.5 miles, and arrived at the house registering 15,304.7 miles."

"Well," she asked, "what if he did?"

"When I inspected the speedometer on the Buick sedan this morning," he said slowly, "it showed 15,304.7 miles."

She stared at him with her eyes dark with panic. Her face had suddenly gone white. She tried to set down the coffee cup, but missed the saucer. The cup balanced for a moment on the edge of the tray, then crashed to the floor, spilling its contents over the rug.

"You hadn't thought of that, had you?" asked Perry Mason.

She continued to stare at him mutely, her face white to the lips.

"Now," said Perry Mason suavely, "you will perhaps pardon a repetition of my question. Where did you get this money that you gave to me just now?"

"I got it," she said slowly, "from my uncle."

"Just before his death?" asked Mason.

"Just before his death," she said.

"Oh," said the lawyer meaningly, *"before* his death."

The significance of the accented word suddenly dawned upon her.

"You don't think," she began. . . .

There was a knock at the door of the room, and the housekeeper walked in. She stared at them.

"Did I hear you drop something?" she asked.

The girl indicated the coffee cup on the floor.

"You have," said Perry Mason meaningly, "rather remarkable ears."

She met his stare with her eyes snapping and defiant.

"I was given a good pair of ears," she said, "and *I use them.*"

"Even to the extent of listening at doors?" said the lawyer.

Frances Celane spoke steadily.

"That will do, Mr. Mason," she said. "I think that I am perfectly capable of disciplining the servants when they need it."

The housekeeper stooped, picked up the coffee cup, set it back on the tray, turned her back to the attorney, and said to Frances Celane: "Shall I bring you another cup and saucer?"

"Yes," she said, "and a hot pot of coffee."

The housekeeper picked up the tray, and swept from the room.

Perry Mason's tone was rasping. "If I'm going to handle this case," he said, "I don't want you interfering. That woman was spying on us. She tried to blackmail me early this morning."

Frances Celane seemed hardly interested.

"Indeed?" she said, absently.

Perry Mason stood, staring down at her.

"Yes, indeed," he said, "and I'm still waiting for an explanation of why your trip made in the Buick sedan at such a high speed, didn't show on the speedometer."

Frances Celane jumped from the chair, and, totally ignoring the presence of the lawyer, started pulling garments from her slender body.

"What are you doing?" he asked.

"Going to get dressed and put some mileage on that Buick, you fool!" she blazed at him.

"And are you going to tell me anything about where you were last night at the time of the murder?"

She whipped off the last of her lounging garments and started dressing.

"Don't be a fool," she said.

"I can help you a lot more," said Mason, "if you let me know the facts."

She shook her head. "Get out," she said.

Perry Mason turned to the door with dignity.

"Very well," he said, and jerked the door open.

The housekeeper was on the other side of the door, regarding him with malevolent, glittering eyes, and a smile which held a trace of sardonic triumph. In one hand she held a coffee cup and saucer, and in the other hand a pot of coffee.

"Thank you, sir," she said, "for opening the door," and slipped into the room.

TEN

GEORGE BLACKMAN TRIED to present an impressive appearance. He combed his hair well back from his high forehead, cultivated a deep, booming voice, and wore nose glasses from which dangled a wide, black ribbon. He might have been a congressman or a banker, but was, in fact, a criminal lawyer.

Only a slight uneasiness of the eyes belied the picture of stolid, intellectual respectability which he tried to present to the public.

He stared across the desk at Perry Mason. "I understand that you're the attorney for the family," he said.

Perry Mason's eyes were hard, and patient.

"I'm representing Miss Celane in the termination of her trust matter," he said, "and I'm representing Arthur Crinston, who is the surviving partner of the partnership. There's some talk about having me represent the executor under the will, but I can't very well represent both the surviving partner and the executor."

Blackman grinned, and there was a trace of envy in his grin.

"Pretty soft for you," he said, "with all of those fees coming in."

"Was that what you came to talk about?" asked Mason, coldly.

Blackman's expression changed.

"I came to tell you," he said, "that I'm representing Peter Devoe, the chauffeur, who is charged with the murder."

"Got a good case?" asked Mason casually.

The other man winced.

"*You* know all about the case," he said.

"To tell you the truth," said Mason, speaking with elaborate carelessness, "I don't. I've been so busy with other angles of the matter that I haven't had time to look into the murder case at all."

Blackman said, "Baloney!" explosively.

Mason looked dignified and resentful.

Blackman leaned forward and tapped the desk impressively.

"Look here, Mason," he said. "You're playing things pretty foxy. But I just want you to know that you're up against somebody who's going to play just as foxy."

"Meaning?" asked Perry Mason.

"I mean that you can't sit back and rake in all the money, and keep all *your* people out of it, while you railroad Devoe to the gallows."

"I'm not railroading anybody to the gallows."

Blackman squirmed under the cold glare of the man across the desk.

"Look here," he said, "I'm talking facts now. There's nobody here to hear us. It's just a conference between us two. You know the game as well as I do. You defend persons accused of crime whenever there's a good fee in it, and so do I. When you defend a person, you're representing him and nobody else on earth. You'd fight the whole world to protect the rights of your clients."

"Sure," said Mason, patiently, tonelessly, "that's the duty of an attorney."

"All right," Blackman said. "I just want you to know that *I'm* going to be faithful to *my* duties."

"Go on," said Mason. "You've said too much or not enough. I can't tell which yet."

"All right," Blackman told him. "I mean just this. You're keeping this Celane woman pretty much in the background. You've managed to do it rather adroitly. After all, the only case against Pete Devoe is one of circumstantial evidence, and it's pretty weak circumstantial evidence, at that. He was lying there in bed, drunk, and *anybody* could have planted that club in his room and the two thousand dollars in his clothes."

"You overlook," said Mason, "the testimony of Don Graves, who actually saw the murder being committed. You overlook the fact that, according to Crinston's testimony, Edward Norton was sending for his chauffeur as Crinston left the place."

"I overlook nothing," said Blackman impressively, his eyes boring belligerently into Mason's face. "And I don't overlook the fact that there was a woman mixed up in the thing somewhere."

"Yes?" asked Mason in a tone of polite but surprised interest.

"Yes," said Blackman, "and don't be so damned surprised at it. You know it, as well as I do."

"Know what?" asked Mason.

"Know that Don Graves saw a woman in that room at the time the murder was being committed."

"Don Graves doesn't say so in the statement that he made to the police, as I understand it," Mason remarked.

"The statement he made to the police hasn't got anything to do with it," said Blackman. "It's the statement he is going to make on the witness stand that counts."

Mason looked at the ceiling and said, impersonally: "In the event, however, that the statement he makes on the witness stand doesn't coincide with the first statement he made to the police, it might have a tendency to weaken his testimony, particularly as far as the woman was concerned."

"Yes, it *might*," said Blackman.

There was silence for a moment, then Blackman lowered his voice and said emphatically, "All right. You know where I stand now. You're controlling all the money in this case, and I'm representing the man who has been picked for the fall guy. I want the family to coöperate in this thing, and I want some money. Otherwise, I'm going to tear the lid off."

"What do you mean by coöperation?" asked Mason.

"I mean that I want the family to convey the impression to the police that they're not at all vindictive; that if Devoe did anything, he was drunk when he did it, and that if the District Attorney will take a plea of manslaughter they'll be just as well satisfied. And then I'm going to want some of the gravy."

"You mean," said Mason, "that you want Frances Celane to see that you get paid to plead Pete Devoe guilty of manslaughter so as to hush up any scandal? Is that what you're trying to convey to me?"

Blackman got to his feet with ponderous dignity.

"I think, counsellor," he said, "that you understand my errand perfectly. I think that I have stated my position fairly and frankly, and I do not care to commit myself by replying to the rather crude summary which you have attempted to make."

Perry Mason pushed back the chair from his desk, stood with his feet planted well apart, his eyes staring at Blackman.

"Don't think you can pull anything like that, Blackman," he said. "We're here alone. You're going to tell me what you want, and tell it in so many words."

"Don't be silly," Blackman told him. "You know what I want."

"What do you want?"

"I want money."

"What are you going to give in return for it?"

"I'll coöperate with you in keeping Miss Celane in the background."

"To the extent that you'll have Pete Devoe plead guilty to manslaughter?"

"Yes. If I can get a plea."

"Is he guilty of manslaughter?" asked Perry Mason.

"Why the hell bother about that?" said Blackman irritably. "I told you that he'd plead guilty to manslaughter."

"How much money do you want?"

"I want fifty thousand dollars."

"That's too much money for a fee," Mason remarked, in a voice that was almost casual.

"Not for the work I'm going to do it isn't."

"The work for Devoe?" asked Mason.

"The work for Frances Celane, if you want to put it that way," Blackman told him.

"All right," Mason went on, "as you, yourself, expressed it, we're here alone. There's no reason why we can't talk frankly. Did Pete Devoe kill Edward Norton?"

"You ought to know," said Blackman.

"Why should I know?"

"Because you should."

"I don't know. I'm asking you if he did."

"Why worry about that? I'll get him to plead guilty to manslaughter."

"For fifty thousand dollars?"

"For fifty thousand dollars."

"You're crazy. The District Attorney wouldn't accept any such plea. This is a murder case. Second degree murder would be the best you could get."

"I could get manslaughter," Blackman said, "if the family would coöperate, and if Graves would change his story a little bit."

"Why should Graves change his story?" Mason inquired.

"Why should anybody do anything?" Blackman asked in a sarcastic tone of voice. "Why should I do anything? Why should you do anything? We're not mixed in it. We're doing things for money. Don Graves would do things for money too."

Slowly, almost ponderously, Perry Mason walked around the big desk toward Blackman. Blackman watched him with greedy eyes.

"Just say it's all right," said Blackman, "and you won't hear anything more about it."

Perry Mason came to a stop in front of Blackman. He looked at him with eyes that were cold and sneering.

"You dirty scum," he said, his voice vibrant with feeling.

Blackman recoiled slightly. "What the hell are you talking about?"

"You," said Mason.

"You've got no right to talk to me like that."

Perry Mason took a swift step forward.

"A dirty shyster," he said, "who would sell out his client for a fifty thousand dollar fee. Get out of this office, and do it right now!"

Blackman's face twisted in surprise.

"Why," he said, "I thought you were going to listen to my proposition."

"I listened to it," Mason told him, "and heard all I wanted to."

Blackman suddenly bolstered up his courage, and brandished a rigid forefinger in front of Mason's face.

"You're mixed in this thing pretty deep yourself," he said. "You're either going to accept this proposition, or you're going to hear a lot more about it."

Perry Mason reached up and grasped the extended forefinger in his left hand. He twisted the other's hand down and around, until the lawyer exclaimed with pain. Mason abruptly released the forefinger, spun the other lawyer halfway around, grasped the back of the lawyer's coat with his big, capable hand, and propelled the lawyer to the door. He jerked open the door of the private office, gave Blackman a shove that sent him sprawling off balance, into the outer office.

"Get out, and stay out!" he said.

Blackman almost ran for half the distance across the outer office, then turned, with his face livid with rage, his glasses dangling at the end of the black ribbon.

"You're going to regret that," he said, "more than anything you ever did in your life!"

"Get out!" said Perry Mason, in a slow, even tone of voice, "or I'm going to do some more."

Blackman groped for the knob of the outer door, pulled it open, and stepped into the corridor.

Perry Mason stood in the doorway of his private office, shoulders squared, feet planted widely apart, staring belligerently at the slowly closing door.

"What happened?" asked Della Street, in sudden concern.

"I told the cheap heel where to get off," Mason remarked, without looking at her, his cold eyes still fastened on the door from the outer office.

He turned and walked back to his private office, leaving Della Street staring at him with wide, apprehensive eyes.

The telephone was ringing as he reached his desk. He scooped the receiver to his ear, and heard the voice of Frances Celane.

"I've got to see you at once," she said.

"All right," he told her, "I'm in my office. Can you come in?"

"Yes, unless you can come out here."

"Where are you?"

"Out at the house."

"All right," he told her, "you'd better get in that Buick and come in here."

"I can't come in the Buick," she said.

"Why not?" he asked.

"The police have sealed it up. They've locked the transmission and padlocked the wheels."

Perry Mason gave a low whistle over the telephone.

"In that event," he said, "you'd better get in the Packard and come here just as fast as you can. You'd better grab a suitcase and put some clothes in it, but do it without attracting too much attention."

"I'll be in in twenty minutes," she said, and hung up.

Perry Mason put on his hat, and paused for a moment to talk with Della Street as he went out.

"I'm expecting Miss Celane in here," he said, "in about twenty or twenty-five minutes, and I think I'll be back by the time she arrives. But if I'm not, I want you to put her in my private office and lock the door. Don't let anyone in. Do you understand?"

She looked up at him, swiftly apprehensive, and nodded her head in a gesture of affirmation. "Has anything gone wrong?" she asked.

He nodded curtly, then smiled and patted her shoulder.

He walked out of the door, took the elevator down, and walked a block and a half to the Seaboard Second National Trust Company.

B. W. Rayburn, vice president of the bank, regarded Perry Mason with hard, watchful eyes, and said: "Yes, Mr. Mason?"

"I'm representing Miss Frances Celane, the beneficiary under a trust fund which was administered by Edward Norton," said Mason. "Also, I'm representing Mr. Arthur Crinston, who is the surviving partner of Crinston & Norton."

"Yes," said Mr. Rayburn. "So I understand from a conversation I had this morning with Mr. Crinston."

"On the day of his death," said Mason, "Mr. Norton made a trip from his home to a bank and back again. I am wondering if the trip was to this bank, or to the Farmers and Merchants National, where I understand he also had an account."

"No," said Rayburn slowly, "he came here. Why do you ask?"

"I understand," said Mason, "he came here to secure a large sum of money in one thousand dollar bills. I am anxious to know if there was anything peculiar about his request for that money, or anything peculiar about the bills."

"Perhaps," said Rayburn significantly, "if you could be a little more explicit, I could give you the information you wanted."

"Did Mr. Norton," asked the lawyer, "say specifically for what purpose he wanted those bills?"

"Not specifically," said Rayburn, with the secretive manner of one who is determined only to answer direct questions.

Mason took a deep breath.

"Did he ask you in advance," he said, "to get for him a certain number of thousand dollar bills bearing consecutive serial numbers?"

"He did," said the vice president of the bank.

"And did he further state to you that, through your banking affiliations, he would like very much to have you make note of the numbers of those bills and ascertain when the bills were presented for deposit at any bank in the city?"

"Not exactly in those words," said Rayburn cautiously.

"Did he state that he intended to use that money to make a payment to a blackmailer, and would like to find out the identity of the person who deposited the currency?"

"Not in exactly *those* words," said the banker again.

"I think," said Perry Mason, smiling, "that I have all of the information I can ask you to give me, and sufficient for my purpose. Thank you, Mr. Rayburn."

He turned and walked from the bank, leaving behind him a cold-eyed individual who surveyed his back in a gaze of shrewd speculation.

Mason returned to his office and beckoned Della Street to his inner office.

"Get Drake's Detective Bureau for me," he said, "and say that I want Paul Drake, himself, to handle a matter of the utmost importance. Say that I want Drake to come to my office posing as a client, and that I want him to wait in the reception room until I give him a line on what he's to do. During the time he's waiting, he is to appear merely as a client."

She looked at him with eyes that showed grave apprehension.

"Is that all?" she asked.

"That's all," he told her.

"And you don't want that Celane woman to know anything about who Paul Drake is?"

"Get this straight," Perry Mason told her. "I don't want *anyone* to know who Drake is. As far as anyone who comes into the office is concerned, Drake is a client who is waiting to see me."

"Okay," she said.

She paused for a few moments, watching him with eyes that made no effort to conceal their concern.

He grinned reassuringly.

"Don't worry," he said, "it's okay."

"You're not getting in trouble?" she asked.

"I don't think so."

"Is Miss Celane?"

"She's in already—up to her neck."

"Does she know it?"

"I think so."

"You won't let her drag you into it?"

He shook his head slowly.

"No," he said, "I don't think so. I can't tell just yet."

"When can you tell?" she asked.

"Not until Miss Celane tells me the truth."

"When will that be?"

"Not until she gets worse frightened than she is now."

Della Street frowned, then said, quickly: "Suppose we frighten her?"

Perry Mason shook his head and smiled.

"No," he said, slowly, "I don't think we'll have to."

ELEVEN

PERRY MASON, THUMBS hooked in the armholes of his vest, paced back and forth across the floor of his private office.

Frances Celane, perched in the big black leather chair which she had occupied on her first visit to the office, regarded him with eyes that moved steadily back and forth, following the pacing of the lawyer.

"Well," she said at length, "you haven't asked me anything about why I wanted to see you."

"I don't have to," he said, "I know what's happening better than you do. What I'm trying to do is to think far enough ahead so I can find the proper place to head them off."

"I'm in an awful mess," she said.

"Of course you are," he snapped, and resumed his steady pacing of the floor.

There was a period of silence, then he paused in his walk to plant his feet far apart and stare down at her.

"Where did you get that money you gave me?" he asked.

"Just as I told you before, I got the money from my uncle," she said, in a thin, weak voice.

"Before he was murdered or afterwards?" pressed Perry Mason.

"Before."

"How much before?"

"Not very much before. That is, just before Mr. Crinston came to the house."

"What happened?"

"There was forty-eight thousand dollars," she said. "He gave it to me, and told me he was sorry he'd been holding out my regular allowance. He said he'd decided to change his mind."

"Had he accused you of being blackmailed before that?"

"No."

"And he gave you this money in cash?"

"Yes."

"You came to him and told him that you needed cash?"

"I told him that I simply had to have some money and have it right away."

"And he didn't say anything about you being blackmailed?"

"No."

"*Were* you being blackmailed?"

She bit her lip and looked down at the floor.

"Is that any of your business?" she asked.

"Yes," he said.

"Yes," she said, "I was being blackmailed."

"All right," he said. "Was it by the housekeeper?"

She started, and raised her eyes to his with a look of alarm.

"How did you know?"

"I suspected," he said. "How much did you give her?"

"I gave her all of it," she said. "All except the ten thousand dollars that I gave you."

"Does that mean," he said, "that *you* haven't any of those thousand dollar bills in your possession?"

"That's right."

"Now listen. Let's not have any misunderstanding about this, and let's get it straight. You're in a jam, and I'm going to get you out, but it's important I know *exactly* what happened with that money. You haven't *any* of it in your possession?"

"Not a bit," she said.

Perry Mason took the ten thousand dollars which she had given him from his wallet and fingered the bills.

"You knew," he asked, "that all of these bills were numbered consecutively, and that various banking institutions in this city had been given a list of those numbers?"

"No," she said in a wan, frightened voice.

"Well," he told her, "that's a fact. Thousand dollar bills aren't so numerous but what they attract attention when they're deposited, and it's almost necessary to take them to a bank to change them. Merchants don't ordinarily carry change for a thousand dollars in their tills."

Perry Mason went to the desk, picked up a long envelope of heavy manila paper, sealed the ten thousand dollars in currency in the envelope, unscrewed the cap from a fountain pen, and addressed the envelope to Carl S. Belknap, 3298 15th Street, Denver, Colorado, and jabbed his forefinger on the button on the side of his desk, which summoned his secretary.

When Della Street opened the door, Perry Mason tossed her the envelope with a careless gesture.

"Stamp and mail this," he said. "First Class."

She looked at the address.

"I didn't know we had any correspondence with a Mr. Belknap," she said.

"We have now," he told her. "Send it registered mail."

She nodded, flashed one swiftly appraising glance at Frances Celane, then slipped back through the door to the outer office.

Perry Mason turned to Frances Celane.

"All right," he said. "That envelope will be in the mail for the next few days. Eventually it will come back to me. In the meantime, nobody is going to find that money on me. Now why didn't you tell the police about that in the first place?"

Her eyes suddenly snapped black fire.

"That's my business!" she said. "I hired you as an attorney to represent my interests. Don't think that you can stand there and tell me what I'm going to do, and what I'm not going to do. . . ."

He took a stride toward her and said: "You're either going to control that temper, or you're going to march up the gallows and have a black bag put around your neck. Did you ever think of how you would like to be hung?"

She got to her feet and drew back her hand as though she intended to slap him.

"You've been a spoiled spitfire all your life," Perry Mason told her. "Now you're facing a situation you can't handle by yourself. Just as sure as you're standing there, you're going to be arrested within the next forty-eight hours, and the case that's going to be built up against you is going to be so black that I don't know whether I can get you out of it or not."

Sheer surprise pushed her rage to one side, and showed in her dark eyes.

"Arrested? Me, arrested?"

"Arrested," he told her, "for murder."

"Devoe was arrested for murder," she said. "He's the one that did it."

"Devoe didn't do it," said Perry Mason, "any more than I did. That is, if he did do it, no one is ever going to prove it. He's got an attorney that knows the ropes, and he's going to drag you into this."

"How do you know?" she asked.

"Because he was here in this office less than an hour ago and told me so."

She sank back in the chair and stared at him, all of the temper gone from her eyes, which were now dark and pathetic.

"What did he want?" she asked.

"Money," he said.

Her face showed a trace of relief.

"All right," she said. "We'll give it to him."

"We will *not*," he said.

"Why?"

"Because," he said, "he'd blackmail you to death. He doesn't know for sure that you are in a bad jam, but he suspects it. He wanted to make sure. If I'd talked terms with him, he'd have been sure. He's heard whispers somewhere. He wanted to verify them. If I'd given in to him on the money end of it, he'd have been sure."

"But," she asked, "what did you do?"

His voice was grim.

"I threw him out of the office," he said.

"How much does he know?" she asked.

"Not much, but he suspects a lot."

"I'm afraid of him," she said, in a voice that was almost a wail.

"You've got a right to be," he said. "Now I want to get at the bottom of this thing. Tell me *exactly* what happened when your uncle was murdered."

She took a deep breath and said in a low monotone, "I was in the house. I had had a quarrel with him. He had been very bitter, and I lost my temper and said things that hurt."

"You would," said the lawyer drily.

"I did," she said, without expression.

There was a moment of silence.

"Go on," said the lawyer.

"He took some money from his wallet," she said. "It wasn't all of the money that was in there. There were some bills left. I don't know exactly how many, but he pushed the currency toward me and told me to take it. He said that he had intended to cut down on my allowance to bring me to my senses, but that he'd come to the conclusion I would never come to my senses. He said it was really my money and if I wanted to throw it away, that was my business."

"So you took the money," he told her.

"Yes, of course."

"Then what?"

"Then," she said, "I gave all of it except ten thousand dollars to Mrs. Mayfield."

"Why did you do that?" he asked.

"Because she knew I had been married, and was threatening to tell my uncle about it."

"Was that before Crinston came to the house, or afterwards?"

"You mean when I gave her the money?"

"Yes."

"Afterwards."

"Who saw you give the money to her . . . anyone?"

"Rob Gleason."

Perry Mason whistled.

"So Gleason was there, eh?" he asked.

"Yes," she said slowly, "Gleason was there. That's why I said I wasn't there."

"All right," he said grimly, "tell me about *that*."

"You know that we are married," she said. "Rob drove up in his car, a Chevrolet. There's a porch which opens out from my room, and he came to that porch and I let him in. He was worried about Mrs. Mayfield and about what my uncle was going to do. I told him that I'd seen my uncle and I thought things were all right.

"While we were talking, Mrs. Mayfield came in and demanded money. She had been listening, and knew that my uncle had given me some money. She didn't know how much.

"I told her I'd give her all I had. I opened my purse and let her take it out. But, before I did that, I had ditched ten of the one thousand dollar bills, because I knew you were going to need some money, and I was saving it for you. That was all I needed money for—just you and her. I thought then that things would be all right, with you representing me, and Mrs. Mayfield keeping quiet. I thought we could work the thing out some way."

"And Crinston had arrived by that time?" asked Mason.

"Yes," she said, "he had come before that. I heard him drive up. In fact, I was leaving my uncle's office when Crinston came up."

"And Graves, the secretary, was in the outer office all the time?" asked the lawyer.

"Yes, he was there all the time, and knows pretty much what happened. He knows a lot more than he lets on. He knows a lot about my uncle's affairs, and I have an idea he knows something about what Mrs. Mayfield is doing."

"All right," said Mason, "then what happened?"

"Well," she said, "Mrs. Mayfield went out, and I went out and sat on the porch with Rob. Then there was a commotion, and I heard running steps from the front of the house, and shouts, and heard something about my uncle having been murdered. I knew that it would never do for Rob to be there, so I told Rob to get in his car and drive away."

"And you went with him?"

"Yes, I went with him."

"Why did you do that?"

"Because I didn't want to be there."

"Why?"

"I thought that I could fix up an alibi for Rob."

"How did you get out of the grounds?"

"There's a way out through an alley in the back, to the driveway. We went out there, and nobody heard us, I guess."

"All right, then what happened?"

"Then I came back home; that is, I had Rob drive me to a place about two blocks from the house, and got out there. I sneaked into my bedroom and talked with Don Graves. I found out from him that my uncle had reported the Buick as having been stolen, and they thought that I was driving it. I figured that was a good alibi for me, and would let Rob out of it, so I said that I had been driving the Buick, and nobody questioned my word."

"All right. Then what happened?"

"You know the rest. Everybody took it for granted that I had been driving the Buick, and I thought everything was all right until you came and told me about the speedometer records not checking up. I went out to put some mileage on the Buick, and found an officer there, who grinned at me and told me that the Buick was going to be held for evidence."

"They'd sealed it up?" asked Perry Mason.

"Yes. They put a padlocked chain around the front axle and through the spokes of the wheel, and they'd also locked up the transmission."

"That," said Mason drily, "makes it nice."

She said nothing.

After a moment Mason resumed his regular pacing of the floor, and the girl watched him with dark, anxious eyes, her head never moving, but the eyes following him back and forth as he paced rhythmically.

"You," he said, at length, "are going to have a nervous breakdown. I know a doctor I can count on. He's going to examine you and order you to a sanitarium."

"What good will that do?" she asked.

"It's going to give me a little time," he said.

"But won't that make them more suspicious when I run away?"

"They can't get any more suspicious," he told her. "The minute they sealed up that Buick, it showed they were working on this other angle of the case. I tried to slip that notebook containing the mileages into my pocket, and make it appear I was doing it casually; but the officer wasn't so dumb. He called me on it, and I had to put the notebook back."

"Did you know about the mileage then?" she asked.

"I suspected it."

"How did it happen you suspected it?"

"Because I knew you'd been lying to me."

Her eyes blazed.

"Don't talk to me like that!" she said.

He simply grinned at her. After a moment the angry light left her eyes.

"You've got to figure you're trapped on that car business," he told her. "You've got to switch around on that."

"But," she said, "that's going to bring Rob into it. If they know Rob was there, that's going to make an awful mess, because there was bad blood between Rob and my uncle."

"Did Rob see your uncle the night he was murdered?" asked Mason.

She shook her head, hesitated a moment, then nodded it.

"Yes," she said, "he did."

"And the reason you changed your story just now and admitted it," he said, "is that you suddenly remembered there is someone who knows Rob saw your uncle. Who is that someone—Don Graves?"

She nodded her head again.

Perry Mason stepped to the door of the outer office.

"Dell," he said, "get me Doctor Prayton on the telephone right away. Tell his nurse that it's vitally important—a matter of life and death. Get him on the telephone personally, and do it now."

"Yes," she said. "There's a Mr. Paul Drake in the office who wants to see you about a personal matter. He won't tell me what it is."

"All right," snapped Perry Mason. "Tell him to wait," and he stepped back into the office, slamming the door.

"Now," he told the girl, "you're going to have a nervous breakdown. You'll be sent to a sanitarium under another name. The police will find you sooner or later. But I want it to be later. Don't let anyone know who you are, don't show any undue interest in the newspaper reports of the case, and, no matter what happens, don't get stampeded."

She stared at him searchingly.

"How do I know I can trust you?" she asked.

He met her gaze with a steady stare.

"That's one of the things you can use your own judgment about," he said, "and it's going to make a hell of a lot of difference what you do."

"All right," she told him, "I'm going to trust you."

He nodded.

"Under those circumstances," he said, "I'll order the ambulance right now before Doc Prayton gets here."

TWELVE

PAUL DRAKE, THE detective, bore no resemblance whatever to the popular conception of a private detective, which was, perhaps, why he was so successful.

He was a tall man, with a long neck that was thrust forward inquiringly. His eyes were protruding, and glassy, and held a perpetual expression of droll humor. Nothing ever fazed him. In his life, murders were everyday occurrences; love nests as common as automobiles, and hysterical clients merely part of an everyday routine.

He sat in the big high-backed leather chair in Perry Mason's office, and turned sideways, so that his long legs were crossed over the right hand arm of the chair. A cigarette was in his mouth, hanging pendulously at an angle from his lower lip.

Perry Mason, seated back of the big desk, stared at the detective with patient eyes that were calmly watchful. His manner was that of a veteran fighter relaxed in his corner, waiting for the sounding of the gong. He looked like a man who would presently lose his relaxed watchfulness, spring from the chair, and engage in swift conflict, with the ferocity of a tiger.

"Well," said Drake, "what's eating you?"

"Awhile back," said Perry Mason, "you were telling me something about a rough shadow."

Paul Drake inhaled placidly on his cigarette. His glassy, protruding eyes watched Perry Mason with an expression of quizzical humor.

"You must have a good memory," he said. "That was a long time ago."

"Never mind when it was," Mason told him. "I want to get the lowdown on it."

"Somebody trying it on you?" asked the detective.

"No," said Mason. "But I have an idea I can use it. Give me the sketch."

Paul Drake removed the cigarette from his mouth, pinched it out, and dropped it into an ashtray.

"It's a stunt in detective work," he said. "We don't ordinarily talk about it—not to outsiders, anyway. It's a psychological third degree. It's predicated on the idea that a man who has something on his mind that he's trying to conceal, is likely to be nervous."

"How does it work?" Mason asked tonelessly.

"Well, let's figure that you're working on a case, and you figure somebody has got some knowledge—not just ordinary knowledge, but a sort of guilty knowledge that he's trying to conceal. You've got two or three ways of approaching him in order to get him to spill the beans. One of them is to use the routine stunt of getting an attractive woman to get acquainted with him, and start him boasting. Another one is to plant some man who becomes friendly with him, and gets his confidence.

"Usually one of those ways works out. But sometimes they don't work. Sometimes a man won't fall for a woman, or, if he does, won't start boasting, and he'll get suspicious if one of your operatives starts getting friendly with him. That's when we use the rough shadow. It takes two men to work a rough shadow job. First, you have your contact man who makes a contact with the suspect, but can't seem to get under his hide, can't get him to talk.

"Well, you pick the time and a suitable place, and have your rough shadow trailing along behind. The contact man starts the fireworks by giving a signal.

"Of course, you understand, shadowing is a job in itself. The public gets goofy ideas about the work of a shadow, and how he operates. The public gets the idea that a shadow puts on disguises and ducks into doorways or hides behind telephone poles, and all that sort of stuff. They get that way from looking at the movies and reading a lot of detective stories written by guys that don't know anything about the detective business.

"As a matter of fact, your real shadow is a smooth guy who almost never uses a disguise. He's just a casual, innocent-looking bystander. No matter what happens, he never gets rattled and never does any of this business of ducking in a doorway. He looks so matter-of-fact that the suspect always takes him as part of the general scenery, and never thinks of him as an individual."

"I know all that, in a general way," Perry Mason told him. "What I want to get straight is just how this rough shadow game is worked."

"Well, that's simple," said the detective. "It's like all of the good things—they're simple when you come right down to analyze them. The rough shadow simply acts the way the suspect figures a shadow should act. In other words, he quits being a regular shadow, and becomes crude. He does all the things that the suspect naturally expects a detective would do. He hides behind telephone poles and ducks in doorways, and all of that stuff."

"So that the suspect knows he's being shadowed?" asked Perry Mason.

"That's the idea," said Drake, taking another cigarette from a case in his pocket, and tapping it gently on his thumb nail.

"You see, the contact man has established a certain amount of friendly relations with the suspect. The suspect, however, is a guy who won't talk about the thing that the contact man wants him to talk about, so the contact man gets a shadow to tail along behind. The suspect never knows that he's being tailed, because the shadow is a smooth worker. But, when the circumstances are right, the contact man gives a signal, and then the shadow gets crude about his methods. He starts ducking around behind telephone poles, putting on disguises, and doing the hundred and one amateurish things which defeat the very purpose of a skilled shadow. Naturally, the suspect takes a tumble that he's being tailed.

"Now, it's a funny thing about a man finding out that he's being shadowed, particularly a man who ain't used to it. As soon as he finds that somebody's tailing him around, he starts getting nervous. Usually the first thing he does is to start walking faster, and looking back over his shoulder. Naturally, the contact man has the rough shadow game sprung when he's walking with the suspect, and the contact man always slows down and saunters along.

"So the suspect wants to hurry things up a little bit, and he's nervous and jumpy all over. After a while, ninety-nine chances out of a hundred, he'll turn to the contact man and say that there's a detective following him and he wants to ditch the shadow. The contact man helps him to do it, and that makes the suspect loosen up and take the contact man into his confidence."

"Suppose the suspect doesn't say anything to the contact man?" asked the lawyer.

"Then," said Drake, "the contact man says something to the suspect. He taps him on the shoulder, and says: 'Listen, old man, I don't want to get personal, but do you know there's somebody shadowing you?'

Or else, he may say: 'Say, look at that fellow behind us. I believe he's shadowing me.' If it's a crime he's working on, the contact man usually pretends that the rough shadow is tailing him, and opens up and confesses to the suspect that he's been guilty of a crime somewhere, and that he's afraid the dicks are on his trail. He asks the suspect to help him ditch the rough shadow. They rush into buildings, go up and down elevators, mingle with crowds, and all that sort of stuff, and when the contact man gives a signal, the rough shadow steps out of the picture, and the suspect thinks he's been ditched.

"It's just an angle of the game that sometimes brings results. You can nearly always get a man talking when you pull a rough shadow on him."

"All right," said Perry Mason, "I want to work a rough shadow game."

"Maybe you won't need a rough shadow," Drake pointed out. "It's something we use only as a last resort. Usually we can build up a friendship and get people to talk. A slick operative has a knack of making people spill facts."

"No," said Mason, "this is an unusual case, and I want a contact operative who is of a certain type."

"What's the type?" asked the detective.

"A middle-aged woman who can pretend she has had to work hard all her life. Get somebody who hasn't any particular beauty or figure; who has wrinkled hands and a heavy figure."

"Okay," said Drake. "I've got just the woman. She's clever, and she's hard-boiled. Who do you want to have her contact?"

"Mrs. Edna Mayfield, the housekeeper for Edward Norton."

"The man who was murdered?"

"The man who was murdered."

Drake whistled.

"Think she's mixed up in the murder?" he asked.

"I don't know just what she's mixed up in," Perry Mason said slowly, "but she's got information. I want that information."

"They've got the fellow that did the murder, haven't they?" asked the detective, his glassy eyes suddenly losing their expression of droll humor, and containing a glint of quick appraisal. "Wasn't it the chauffeur or somebody that pulled the job?"

"So I understand," said Mason noncommittally.

"You're representing Frances Celane, the young woman who's the beneficiary under the trust fund and the will?"

"Yes."

"Okay, now just what do you want me to get out of her?"

"Anything that she knows," said Perry Mason slowly.

"You mean about the murder?"

"About anything."

Paul Drake let his glassy eyes study the tip of the cigarette and the smoke which eddied upward from it.

"Look here," he said, "let's be frank with each other. I know you well enough to know that if you're getting me to start work on this murder case, that there's an angle to it that the police haven't got."

"I didn't say I wanted you to work on the murder case," Perry Mason said slowly.

"No," said Drake significantly, "you didn't *say* that."

There was a moment or two of silence, then Perry Mason said, slowly and impressively: "I want you to find out everything that that housekeeper knows. I don't care what it's about."

Paul Drake made a gesture with his shoulders.

"Don't get me wrong," he said. "I'm not curious, and I don't want you to misunderstand me. But just suppose that some of the information this woman spills wouldn't look so well for your client?"

"I want to get the information," said Perry Mason.

"Sure, I know," said Drake. "But suppose that we get it through a couple of operatives that I'll put on the case. And suppose the information should be something you would want to keep under cover? I try to get dependable people to work for me, but things have a habit of leaking out in time."

"Yes," said Perry Mason slowly, "in time."

Once more there was an interval of silence.

"Well?" asked the detective.

"I think," said Mason, "that this is another case where I'm going to be working against time. I don't think there's any information that your operatives will get that the police won't get sooner or later. I want to have it sooner, and want the police to get it later."

Drake nodded.

"All right," he said, "I get the sketch. I just wanted to be certain there wasn't any misunderstanding between us. Misunderstandings in my business make for dissatisfied clients, and I want to keep my clients satisfied."

"All right," Mason told him. "We understand each other on that.

"Now, there's one other thing. A fellow by the name of Don Graves, secretary to Edward Norton, was a witness to the murder, itself. He's told the police one story, and me another. He may be dangerous. I want to find out confidentially whether he really did see a woman in the room at the time the murder blow was struck, or whether he's going to say he did, which amounts to the same thing.

"Now, do you suppose that you could get someone to contact him without creating too much suspicion, and find out just what he's really going to testify to? If there's any way of doing it, I'd like to get a written statement out of him."

"Any money for expenses?" asked the detective.

"Plenty of it," said the lawyer.

"Well, suppose I get somebody to go to him and tell him he's representing a tabloid newspaper, or a true detective story magazine, and wants the account of an eye-witness, get him to submit the manuscript signed and sworn to, and offer to pay him by the word?"

"Okay," said Mason, "provided there aren't too many words."

The detective grinned.

"You mean, provided the words are of the right kind."

"Well," said the lawyer, "I guess that amounts to about the same thing."

Drake got up and flipped his cigarette into a brass cuspidor.

"Okay," he said, "I'll get started."

"You'll let me know progress?"

"I'll let you know progress."

"Concentrate heavy on that housekeeper. She's a tartar and you'll have to watch her."

"Mail reports?" asked the detective.

"No. Make them orally or not at all."

There was a knock at the door, and Della Street glanced significantly at Perry Mason.

"That's okay," he said, "tell me what it is, Della."

"Mr. Crinston is out here. He says his business is important and he can't wait."

"Very well," said Mason, "I'll see him."

He flashed a meaning glance to Drake and said to the detective in a tone of voice sufficiently loud to carry into the outer office, "That's quite all right, Mr. Drake. I'm busy on an important matter right now, and I can't give it my immediate attention, but you've got ten days within which to make an appearance, and I'll draw up a demurrer and file it in court. That'll carry the thing along and keep you from being in default until we can go into greater details."

He shook hands with Drake in the doorway, and beckoned to Mr. Crinston.

"Come in," he said.

Crinston pushed his way into the inner office with that aggressive suggestion of booming authority which characterized him. He gave the impression of sweeping away all obstacles from his path by the very blast of his forceful personality.

"Hello, Mason," he said, shaking hands. "Glad to see you. Guess you've been pretty busy, haven't you?"

Mason watched him with speculative eyes.

"Yes," he said. "I've been busy."

Crinston sat down in the big chair, and filled it completely. He took a cigar from his pocket, clipped off the end, scraped a match on the sole of his shoe.

"Well," he said, "it's been a mess all around."

"Yes," the lawyer told him, "it's still a mess."

"Oh, I think it's going to come out all right," said Crinston, "but why didn't you follow my instructions?"

"What instructions?"

"About keeping Frances out of it."

"I have kept her out of it the best I could. The poor girl is hysterical. She came to the office and had a complete breakdown. I called a physician, and he prescribed complete rest. He's taken her to a sanitarium somewhere, and won't tell even me where it is, for fear that I might call her."

Crinston puffed out the first whiffs of blue smoke from the cigar, and stared at the lawyer thoughtfully.

"Not bad, that," he said.

"Her nerves were really on the ragged edge," said Mason with dignity.

"Yes, yes, I know," Crinston said impatiently. "No need to waste your time and my time with that stuff. I understand. What I dropped in to find out was whether you know a man by the name of George Blackman, an attorney here?"

"Yes, I know him," said Mason.

"He got in touch with me on the telephone and told me I should see you right away on a matter of great importance."

Mason kept his voice flat and expressionless in an even monotone.

"Blackman came to see me earlier in the day," he said, "and suggested that it might make matters better for the family all around if Devoe should plead guilty, to manslaughter."

"Why, damn it!" stormed Crinston. "He's a murderer! That was a dastardly cold-blooded murder!"

"That attitude on the part of the family was the thing that Blackman wanted to speak to me about," said Mason, still speaking in the same even cautious monotone. "He said that if the family were going to adopt a vindictive attitude toward his client, it would be necessary for him to adopt a vindictive attitude toward the family and try to show that the case was a frame-up against his client."

"How could he do that?" asked Crinston.

"Oh, there are various ways," said Mason, in his steady monotone. "It's an axiom of criminal law that a man should try everyone except the defendant. You know, sometimes you can try the prosecuting attorney. Very frequently you can try the prosecuting witness. You can start digging around, cross-examining on extraneous matters, trying to show some sort of a motive for murder. Then, if you can get a motive before the jury, you start showing opportunity, and if you can get motive and opportunity, you suddenly switch the accusation and claim there's just as much ground to suspect the prosecuting witness as there is the defendant."

"You mean to switch the guilt to Fran Celane?" asked Crinston.

"I didn't mention any names," said Mason. "I simply told you how criminal lawyers play the game."

"Look here," said Crinston. "Did you find out *exactly* what he wanted?"

"He *said* that he wanted a fee," said Mason, "and the assurance that a request would go to the District Attorney to look at the matter as leniently as possible and accept a plea of manslaughter."

Crinston studied the lawyer thoughtfully.

"You say that's what he *said* he wanted?" he commented.

"Yes."

"You act as though you didn't think it was what he really wanted."

"I don't."

"Why?"

"Because I don't think the District Attorney would consider a plea of manslaughter. I think he'd prosecute either for first degree murder, or not at all."

"Then what *did* Blackman want?" Crinston demanded.

"I think he wanted to find out what our reactions would be to a proposition of that kind. If we'd been willing to go ahead, he'd have taken as much money as he could get, and then blackmailed us for as much more as possible, and then double-crossed us at the time of trial."

Crinston studied his cigar thoughtfully.

"He didn't impress me as being that kind of a man," he said slowly. "Not from the impression he made over the telephone, anyway."

"If you'd seen him, he'd have made a better impression," Mason told him.

Crinston put the cigar back in his mouth and chewed on it thought-fully.

"Look here," he said suddenly, placing his parted fingers to his mouth, and jerking out the chewed cigar, "I don't like the way you're handling this case."

"No?" asked Perry Mason coldly.

"No!" said Crinston explosively.

"And what don't you like about it?" asked the lawyer.

"I think you're letting a golden opportunity slip through your fingers. I think there's a good chance to get this thing all cleaned up by playing ball with Blackman."

Mason's answer was curt and without explanation.

"I don't," he said.

"Well I do, and I'm giving you orders right now to get in touch with Blackman and give him what he wants. Anything within reason."

"He doesn't want things within reason," Mason said. "His type never does. He'd find out what we consider reasonable, and then raise his sights."

"All right. Let him raise them. There's a hell of a lot of money involved in this thing, and we can't afford to bungle it."

"Are you afraid," asked Perry Mason, "that Frances Celane can't stand too much pressure?"

"That's a great question to ask me!" Crinston almost shouted. "When you've had to let her have a nervous breakdown in order to keep her out of the hands of the police."

"I didn't say that I did it to keep her from the police," Mason reminded him.

"Well, *I* said it," said Crinston.

"Yes," Mason told him, "I heard you, and furthermore, you don't need to shout."

Crinston got to his feet, flung the half smoked cigar into the cuspidor, and glowered at Mason.

"All right," he said, "you're finished."

"What do you mean I'm finished?"

"Just what I say. You're not representing me anymore, and you're not going to represent Frances Celane anymore."

"I think," Mason told him slowly, "that Miss Celane will be the best judge of that. I'll wait until she tells me that I'm not to represent her anymore."

"She'll tell you fast enough, as soon as I get in touch with her."

"Where," asked Mason, smiling thoughtfully, "are you going to get in touch with her?"

"Don't worry," Crinston told him, "I'll get in touch with her all right, and then you're going to be finished. You're a bungler. You've been smart enough on some things, but you've let the case get into a hell of a mess. I'm going to get some attorney, and . . ."

Abruptly, Perry Mason got to his feet. He strode purposefully around the desk. Crinston watched him come with eyes that remained steady, but seemed to hold just a trace of panic. Mason planted himself firmly in front of the other man, his eyes cold, hard, and ominous.

"All right," he said, "let's not have any misunderstanding about this. From now on I'm not representing you, is that right?"

"You bet that's right!"

"And don't think," said Mason, "that your business is so damned important. Miss Celane would have let me handle the estate if it hadn't been for the fact that I couldn't place myself in the position of acting as attorney both for the estate, and for the surviving partner."

"Well," Crinston told him, "you don't need to worry about that anymore. On the other hand, don't think you're going to represent the estate. You aren't going to represent anything or anybody. I'm going to get another attorney to represent me, and he's going to represent Frances Celane, as well."

Perry Mason said, slowly, ominously: "Just to show you what a fool you are, and how you've walked into a trap, the man that you're going to get to represent you is one that was suggested to you by Blackman."

"What if he is?" Crinston demanded.

Mason's smile was frosty.

"Nothing," he said. "Go right ahead. Walk into the trap just as deeply as you want to."

Crinston's eyes softened somewhat.

"Look here, Mason," he said, "I've got nothing against you personally, but this is a business matter. I think you're bungling things, and I think you're too damned ethical. I don't want you to misunderstand me. Frances Celane means a lot to me. I'm just like an uncle to her. She's a kid that I've taken a lot of interest in, and I'm going to see that she gets a square deal. I think that this case requires someone who can deal with Blackman. He says he wouldn't deal with you anymore if you were the last man left on earth."

Perry Mason laughed a bitter, mirthless laugh.

Crinston went on doggedly. "No matter what happens, I'm for Frances Celane. I don't know what the evidence may disclose before it gets done, but I'm going to stick by the kid no matter what happens. Get that, and get it straight. I'm a business man, and she doesn't know a thing about business. I'm going to see that she gets a square deal, beginning immediately."

He turned and walked with ponderous dignity toward the door.

Perry Mason watched him with thoughtful concentration.

"What a sucker you are," as Crinston jerked the door open.

Crinston whirled on him. "I hate that word!" he said. "I don't let anybody call me a sucker."

"You'll hate it a lot worse before you're done," said Mason, and, turning on his heel, walked back to his desk.

Crinston hesitated a moment, then turned and walked back into the room.

"All right, wise guy," he said, "now I'm going to tell you something.

"You've bungled this case from the time you started in on it. I know that *I* can't fire you as Miss Celane's lawyer. That's something that's entirely up to her. *I'm* going to advise her to let you go. In the event she doesn't, however, I'm going to give you one tip, and that's watch Purkett, the butler."

"Now," said Perry Mason, "you interest me. Go ahead and tell me what you're driving at."

"Oh," said Crinston sarcastically, "you *do* want to take a little advice, eh?"

"I want you to tell me why you made that remark about Purkett," said Perry Mason, his eyes cold.

Crinston's eyes surveyed the lawyer in thoughtful appraisal.

"If I told you," he asked, "would you have sense enough to use the information?"

Perry Mason said nothing, but held his head slightly on one side, after the manner of a person anxious to hear that which is about to be said.

"The evidence in this case," said Crinston, "pointed unmistakably to Devoe. A *good* lawyer would have seen that the police never had a chance to consider the possibility that such evidence wasn't conclusive. However, you sat back and did nothing while the police began to doubt that evidence and make other investigations.

"Then, when that investigation was under way, you did nothing to keep them from involving your client. Now, if Devoe is guilty, that's the end of it. If he isn't guilty, someone else is. There's a stronger probability that that someone else is Purkett than anyone else. Yet you're letting him keep entirely in the background."

Crinston stopped speaking and stood in an attitude of glowering belligerency.

"Is that all you have to say?" asked Perry Mason.

"That's all."

Perry Mason smiled.

"Blackman's address," he said, "is in the Mutual Building. I thought I would save you looking it up in the telephone book."

Crinston's face showed a slight flicker of surprise, then set in grim lines.

"Very well," he said, jerked the office door open, and slammed it behind him.

Perry Mason sat for a few minutes, then clamped his hat down firmly on his head. He walked through the outer office, saying to his secretary as he went past, "I don't know just when I'll be back, Della. Close up the office at five o'clock."

THIRTEEN

PERRY MASON WALKED into the garage where he stored his automobile and asked for the mechanic.

"How much of a job would it be," he said, "to turn a speedometer back a few miles? That is, suppose you had a speedometer that registered around 15,350 miles, and you wanted to turn it back to 15,304.7 miles. How much of a job would it be?"

"Not much of a job," said the mechanic grinning, "only, if you were going to turn it back that far, you should make a good job of it and turn it back to 3000 miles and sell the car as a demonstrator."

"No," said the lawyer, "I didn't mean to slip one over on the car dealer or on a customer. I was trying to find out about evidence. How long would it take to set the speedometer back?"

"Not so very long," said the mechanic. "It's a simple job."

Perry Mason gave him half a dollar and walked from the garage, his head bowed in thought.

He stepped into a drug store and telephoned the number of Edward Norton's residence.

The voice that answered the telephone, apparently that of the butler, was filled with that type of formality which comes when one has answered a telephone innumerable times in connection with some tragedy which has attracted much public interest.

"I want to talk with Mr. John Mayfield, the gardener," said Mason.

"I beg your pardon, sir," said the voice, "but it's rather unusual for calls to come through for Mr. Mayfield. I don't know whether he's supposed to take calls on this telephone or not, sir."

"That's all right," said Mason, without disclosing his identity. "This is in connection with some police business. Get him on the phone, and don't waste time."

There was a moment of hesitant silence at the other end of the line, and then the butler's voice said: "Very good, sir. Just a moment, sir."

After a delay of several minutes a heavy, stolid voice said: "Hello," and Perry Mason spoke rapidly.

"Don't tell anybody who this is," he said, "but this is Mason, the lawyer, who represents Frances Celane. Your wife spoke to me about getting some money for her, and I can't locate her. Do you know where she is?"

"I think," said the man, "she went to the District Attorney's office. They called for her in a car and took her there."

"All right," said Mason. "It's important that I get in touch with you and talk with you about this business matter which your wife took up with me. Now, the question is, can you take one of the cars and come in to meet me?"

"Maybe I could, sir, but I'm not certain. I'd much rather walk up and meet you at the corner of the boulevard if you could drive out here, sir."

"All right," said Mason, "I'll do that. You meet me at the boulevard, and don't tell anybody that you're meeting me there."

Mason returned to the garage, got his car, and made time out to the place where the curving roadway which led to the Norton residence intersected the boulevard.

A man who was stooped of shoulder, heavily framed and big-boned, stepped out from the gathering dusk as Mason parked the car.

"You're Mr. Mason?" he asked.

"Yes," said the lawyer.

"I'm John Mayfield. What was it you wanted?"

Mason got partially out of the car and stood with one foot on the running board, and surveyed the man with keen scrutiny.

He saw a stolid, unemotional face, with sullen eyes and heavy, unsmiling lips.

"Did you know what your wife spoke to me about?" he asked.

"My wife told me she had had a talk with you," said the man, cautiously.

"Did she tell you what she talked about?"

"She told me that maybe we were going to get some money."

"All right," said Mason. "Now, in order to know where I stand on this thing, you've got to tell me about that speedometer."

"About what speedometer?" said the man.

"About the speedometer on that Buick car. You set it back, didn't you?"

"No, sir," said the gardener.

"Would you say that you set it back if I completed the business arrangements with your wife?" asked Mason.

"What do you mean?"

"Never mind what I mean," said the lawyer. "You simply tell your wife that if business arrangements are going to be completed between us, I would want to know first whether there would be testimony that the speedometer of that Buick automobile had been set back."

"What's that got to do with it?" asked the gardener.

"Just this," said Mason, making little jabbing motions with his forefinger to emphasize his statements. "We know that Edward Norton telephoned in to the police that his Buick had been stolen.

"Now that means that the Buick most certainly wasn't in his garage at the time he telephoned. *Somebody* had that Buick out. It doesn't make any difference whether Miss Celane was home or not. Somebody had the Buick out. That Buick was missing at the time Norton telephoned. Now, when the police got there, the Buick was in the garage, and the speedometer on the Buick was set back to the same mileage that it showed when it was taken out. So somebody set that speedometer back. Now, the question is, *who did it?*"

"I didn't, sir," said the gardener.

"How about Devoe, the chauffeur?"

"I don't know about him, sir."

"How about the butler?"

"I don't know about him."

"All right," said Mason. "You don't know very much about anything, but your wife has a pretty good idea about what's going on. I want you to tell her that *if* we are going to do business *she has got to find out who set the speedometer back* on that car."

"You mean the person that had it out, sir?"

"No," said Mason, "I don't care a damn about the person who had it out. I'd just as soon the police figured it was Miss Celane who had the car out. What I want to do is to prove that the speedometer was set back, and I want to find out who set it back. Do you understand?"

"Yes, I think I do now. Yes, sir."

"When is your wife coming back?"

"I don't know. Some men from the District Attorney's office came and talked with her. Then they told her they wanted her to go to the office and make a statement."

"All right," said Mason. "Do you think you can give her my message?"

"Yes, sir, I know I can."

"All right. See that you do," Mason told him. "Now there's one other thing that I want to find out about, and that's where you were at the time the murder was committed."

"Me?" said the man. "I was asleep."

"You're certain about that?"

"Of course I'm certain. I woke up with all of the commotion going on."

"Your wife wasn't asleep," said Mason.

"Who says she wasn't?" demanded Mayfield, his sullen eyes showing some trace of emotion.

"I do," said Mason. "Your wife was around the house. She hadn't gone to bed when the murder was committed. You know that."

"Well, what of it?" said Mayfield.

"Just this," Mason remarked, lowering his voice impressively, "there was a woman in the room with the man who struck that blow. Now your wife had intimated that woman was Miss Celane, or may have been Miss Celane. I want you to tell your wife that I now have evidence which leads me to believe that *she* was the woman who was in the room at the time."

"You mean," said the man, bristling, "that you're accusing my wife of murder?"

"I mean," said Mason, standing his ground and staring at the belligerent gardener, "that I'm telling you I have evidence that indicates your wife was the woman who was in the room at the time the blow was struck. That doesn't mean that she struck the blow. It doesn't mean she knows anything at all about the fact that a blow was going to be struck. But it does mean that she was in the room at the time."

"You want me to tell her that?" asked Mayfield.

"I want you to tell her that," said Mason.

"All right," said Mayfield, "I'll tell her that, but she won't like it."

"I don't care whether she likes it or not," said Mason. "I told you to tell her that."

"All right," said Mayfield. "Is there anything else?"

"No," Mason told him, "except that you want to be sure and tell her about this interview when no one is listening. In other words, I don't want the representatives of the District Attorney's office to know about it."

"Oh, sure," said Mayfield, "I know enough for that."

"All right," said Mason, and got in his car and drove down the boulevard.

He drove in to a cafe, where he dined leisurely and thoughtfully.

By the time he had finished dinner, the newsboys were crying papers on the street, and Perry Mason bought one, took it to his automobile, lounged back against the cushions, turned on the domelight and read the headlines which spread across the top of the page.

"NEW MYSTERY IN MILLIONAIRE MURDER. . . . WOMAN IN ROOM AT TIME OF CRIME IS CLAIMED. . . . POLICE TRACING MARKED MONEY TAKEN FROM BODY OF MILLIONAIRE. . . . HEIRESS SECRETLY MARRIED AND HUSBAND SOUGHT AS MATERIAL WITNESS. . . . BEAUTIFUL NIECE MYSTERIOUSLY DISAPPEARS FOLLOWING VISIT TO PROMINENT LAWYER."

Perry Mason read through each word of the sensational story which followed; a story in which the reporters told as much as they dared in between the lines; a story which stopped short of actual accusation, yet which left the public to infer that the police were far from satisfied with the case against Pete Devoe, the chauffeur, and were considering a sudden change of front which would involve persons of wealth and prominence.

Perry Mason carefully folded the paper, thrust it into the door pocket of the car, and drove, not to his bachelor apartment, but to a downtown hotel where he registered under an assumed name and spent the night.

FOURTEEN

PERRY MASON WALKED into his office, said good morning to Della Street, then went into his private office where the morning newspapers were spread on his desk.

Della Street opened the door and followed him into the private office.

"Somebody broke in and searched . . ."

He whirled on her, placing his finger to his lips. Then, while she ceased talking, started making a round of the office. He moved pictures, peering behind them, swung out the revolving bookcase and inspected the wall space, then crawled under the desk. He straightened, smiled, and said: "Looking for a dictograph. There's just a chance that they'd have one planted."

She nodded.

"Somebody broke into the office last night," she said, "and went through everything. The safe was opened."

"Did they smash it?"

"No, he must have been some clever crook who knew how to work the combination. The safe was opened, all right. I could tell, because the papers were disturbed."

"That's all right," he told her. "What else is new?"

"Nothing," she said, "except three police detectives watching the office, and I have an idea they're waiting for someone to come in."

He smiled wisely and said: "Let them wait. It will teach them patience."

"Did you read the papers?" she asked.

"Not the morning papers," he told her.

"The late editions say that they've identified the club that killed Norton," she told him.

"Yes?"

"Yes. It was a heavy walking stick, and they've found out that it belonged to Rob Gleason, the husband of our client."

"That'll mean," said Perry Mason, "that they'll charge him with first degree murder, and let the charge against Devoe go."

"They're also going to charge the woman," she said, "unless they have already."

"So?" he asked.

"Yes. This secretary, Don Graves, has given some additional information which has changed the entire complexion of the case, according to the *STAR*. Graves was shielding some one. The police broke him down and he gave additional evidence."

"Well," he said, "that makes it interesting. If anybody comes in, give them a stall."

She nodded her head, staring at him apprehensively.

"You're not going to get mixed into this thing, are you?" she asked.

"Why should I get mixed into it?" he inquired.

"You know what I mean," she said. "You do too much for your clients."

"What do you mean by that?"

"You know what I mean. You had Miss Celane have a nervous breakdown, and leave here in an ambulance."

He smiled at her. "Well?" he asked.

"Isn't it a crime," she said, "to conceal someone who is wanted by the police?"

"Was she wanted by the police then?" he inquired.

"No," she said, dubiously, "not then, I guess."

"Furthermore," said Mason, "I am not a physician. I might make an incorrect diagnosis. I thought she was having a nervous breakdown, but I called a physician to verify my impression."

She frowned at him and shook her head.

"I don't like it," she said.

"Don't like what?"

"Don't like the way you mix into these cases. Why can't you sit back and just do your stuff in a court room?"

"I don't know, I'm sure," he told her, smiling. "Maybe it's a disease."

"Don't be silly," she told him. "Other lawyers walk into court and examine the witnesses and then put the case up before a jury. You go out and mix yourself into the cases."

"Other lawyers," he told her, "have clients who get hung."

"Sometimes they deserve it," she pointed out.

"Perhaps. I haven't had one hung so far, and I haven't had one who deserved it."

She stood staring at him for a moment, then smiled, and there was something almost maternal in her smile.

"Are *all* your clients innocent?" she asked.

"That's what the juries say," he told her. "And after all, they're the ones to judge."

She sighed and shrugged her shoulders.

"You win," she said, and went back into the outer office.

As the catch clicked, Perry Mason sat down at his desk and spread out the newspapers. He read for fifteen minutes without interruption, and then the door opened.

"There's a Mrs. Mayfield out here," Della Street told him, "and I have an idea you'd better see her while the seeing is good."

Perry Mason nodded.

"Send her in," he said, "and make it snappy. There'll probably be a police detective following on her trail. Stall him off just as long as you can."

The girl nodded, opened the door, and beckoned to the woman who sat in the outer office.

As the broad form of Mrs. Mayfield hulked in the doorway, Perry Mason saw his secretary blocking as much of the passage as possible. Then, as the door was closing behind the housekeeper, he heard Della Street's voice saying: "I'm very sorry, but Mr. Mason is in an important conference right now and can't be disturbed."

Perry Mason nodded to Mrs. Mayfield, got up, crossed the office and turned the lock on the door.

"Good morning, Mrs. Mayfield," he said.

She stared at him in black-eyed belligerency.

"Good morning!" she snapped.

Perry Mason indicated the black leather chair, and Mrs. Mayfield sat down in it, her back very stiff and her chin thrust forward.

"What's this about the speedometer being set back on the Buick automobile?" she asked.

There was the sound of scuffling motion from the outer office, then the noise of bodies pushing against the door, and the knob of the door twisted. The lock held it shut, and Perry Mason kept his eyes fastened on Mrs. Mayfield, holding her attention away from the noise at the door.

"Mr. Norton," said the lawyer, "reported the Buick automobile as having been stolen. At the time, we thought that Miss Celane was driving it. Now it appears that she was not. Therefore, the Buick must have been gone at the time Norton reported its theft to the police. However, we have the mileage record of the car, and it shows that he returned it to his house at 15,304.7 miles.

"That means the person who was using it the night of the murder must have either set the speedometer back or disconnected the speedometer when he took it out."

Mrs. Mayfield shook her head.

"The car wasn't out," she said.

"Are you certain?" he asked.

"Purkett, the butler," she said, "sleeps right over the garage. He was lying awake in bed, reading, and he'd have heard anyone take a car out. He says that the garage doors were closed, and that no car went out."

"Could he have been mistaken?" pressed Mason.

"No," she snapped. "The doors make a noise when they're opened. It sounds very loud up in the room over the garage. Purkett would have heard it, and I want an explanation of this crack that you made to my husband about me being in the room when the murder . . ."

"Forget that for a minute," Mason interrupted. "We're talking about the car, and our time's short. I can't do any business with you unless I can prove that speedometer was set back."

She shook her head emphatically.

"You can't do any business with me anyway," she said. "You've got things in a fine mess."

"How do you mean?"

"You've handled things in such a way that the police have dragged Frances Celane into it."

The black eyes snapped at him in beady indignation, and then suddenly filmed with moisture.

"You mean *you're* the one that got Frances Celane into it," said Mason, getting to his feet and facing her accusingly. "You started it by blackmailing her about her marriage, and then you wanted more blackmail to keep her out of this murder business."

The glittering black eyes now showed globules of moisture.

"I wanted money," said Mrs. Mayfield, losing her air of belligerency. "I knew it was an easy way to get it. I knew that Frances Celane was going to have plenty. I didn't see any reason why I shouldn't have some of it. When she hired you, I knew you were going to get plenty of money, and I didn't see any reason why I shouldn't have some.

"All my life I've been a working woman. I've married a husband who is a clod, and hasn't ambition or sense enough to come in out of the rain. All my life I've had to take responsibilities. When I was a girl

I had to support my family. After I was married, I had to furnish all the ambition to keep the family going. For years I've waited on Frances Celane. I've seen her live the life of a spoiled lady of leisure. I've had to slave my fingers to the bone doing housework and seeing that she had her breakfast in bed, and I'm tired of it. I didn't see any reason why I shouldn't have some money too. I wanted lots of money. I wanted people to wait on me. I was willing to do anything to get the money, except to get Frances into real trouble.

"Now I can't do anything about it. The police cornered me and made me talk, and they're going to arrest Frances Celane for murder. For murder! Do you understand?"

Her voice rose almost to a shriek.

There was an imperative pounding on the door of the office.

"Open up in there!" gruffed a voice from the outside.

Perry Mason paid no attention to the commotion at the door, but kept his eyes fixed upon Mrs. Mayfield.

"If it would help clear up this mystery," he said, "do you think you could find someone who would testify that the car was taken out and that the speedometer was either disconnected or set back?"

"No," she said, "that car didn't go out."

Mason started pacing the floor.

The knocking at the outer door was redoubled in intensity. Someone shouted: "This is a police detective. Open up that door!"

Suddenly Mason laughed aloud.

"What a fool I've been!" he said.

The housekeeper blinked back the tears and stared at him with wide eyes.

"Of course," said Mason, "that car didn't leave the garage. No car left the garage." And he smacked his fist down upon his palm.

He whirled to the housekeeper.

"If you want to do something for Frances Celane," he said, "talk with Purkett again, and in detail. Go over the case with him and strengthen his recollection so that, no matter what happens, he can't be shaken in his testimony."

"You want him to say that the car didn't leave the garage?" asked the housekeeper.

"I want him to tell the truth," said Perry Mason. "But I want him to tell it with sufficient firmness so that he won't be rattled on the witness stand by a lot of lawyers. That's all I want him to testify to— just the fact that the car did *not* leave the garage at any time on that night; that the garage doors were closed, and that they remained closed, and that no person could have taken a car from the garage without his hearing it."

"Well," she said, "that's the truth. That's what he says."

"All right," he told her, "if you want to do Frances Celane a favor, you get to him and see that no pressure on earth can change that testimony of his."

"I'll do it," she said.

He asked hastily: "What did you tell the police about getting money from Frances Celane?"

"Nothing," she said. "I told them that she gave you money but I didn't know how much, or whether it was in large bills or small bills."

The door creaked under the weight of a body which had been thrown against it.

Perry Mason walked to it, snapped back the lock, and opened the door.

"What the hell do you mean," he demanded, "by trying to bust into my private office?"

A burly man with square shoulders, thick neck and scowling forehead, pushed his way into the room.

"I told you who I was," he said. "I'm a police detective."

"I don't care if you're Mussolini," said Perry Mason. "You can't break into my office."

"The hell I can't," said the detective. "I'm taking this woman into custody."

Mrs. Mayfield gave a little scream.

"On what charge?" asked Perry Mason.

"As a material witness in a murder case," said the detective.

Mason remarked: "Well, you didn't get the urge to take her into custody as a material witness until after she came to this office."

"What do you mean?" asked the detective.

"Exactly what I say," said Mason. "You sat outside and watched this office until you saw Mrs. Mayfield come in. Then you telephoned your superior for instructions, and he told you to pick her up as a material witness before she had a chance to talk with me."

"Pretty smooth, ain't you?" sneered the detective.

Mrs. Mayfield stared from one to the other and said: "But I haven't done anything."

"That ain't the question, ma'am," said the detective. "It's a question of keeping you as a material witness where you won't be annoyed or inconvenienced."

"And," sneered Perry Mason, "where you won't have a chance to talk with anybody except representatives of the District Attorney's office."

The detective glowered at Perry Mason.

"And we understand," he said, "that you received ten one thousand dollar bills that were stolen from the body of Edward Norton."

"Is that so?" said Mason.

"That's so," snapped the detective.

"Just where do you think those bills are?" asked the lawyer.

"We don't know, but we intend to find out," the detective told him.

"Well," said Mason, "it is a free country, or it used to be once. Go ahead and find out."

"When we do," said the detective, "you're likely to find yourself facing a charge of receiving stolen property."

"Well, you've only got three things to do," said Mason.

"What three things?" asked the detective.

"Prove that the money was stolen, prove that I received it, and prove that I knew it was stolen when I received it."

"You know it's stolen now."

"How do I know it's stolen?"

"Because I've told you it was. You're on notice."

"In the first place," said Mason, "I'm not admitting that I have any ten thousand dollars. In the second place, I wouldn't take your word for anything."

The detective turned to Mrs. Mayfield.

"Come along, ma'am," he said, "we'll handle this lawyer later."

"But I don't want to go," she said.

"It's orders, ma'am," he told her. "You won't be annoyed. We're simply going to keep you where you'll be safe until after we can get your testimony."

Perry Mason watched the pair depart from his private office. His rugged face was expressionless, but there was a glint of smouldering hostility in his patient eyes.

When the door of the outer office had closed, Perry Mason walked to his secretary's desk and said: "Della, I want you to ring up the STAR. Tell them who you are. They've got a reporter there named Harry Nevers. He knows who I am. Tell the city editor to have Nevers come and see me. I'll see that he gets some sensational news."

She reached for the telephone.

"You want me to tell that to the city editor?" she asked.

"Yes," he told her. "I want Nevers sent here right away."

"You don't want to talk with the editor?"

"No, he'd plug a rewrite man in on the line, listen to what I had to say, call it an interview, and let it go at that. I want you to tell them who you are, tell them to send Nevers over here for a hot yarn. They'll try to pump you about what it is. Tell them you don't know, and that I'm not available."

She nodded and lifted the receiver from the hook. Perry Mason walked back to his private office and closed the door.

FIFTEEN

HARRY NEVERS WAS tall and thin, with eyes that looked at the world with a bored expression. His hair was in need of trimming, and his face had that oily appearance which comes to one who has gone long without sleep. He looked as though he had been up all night, and had, as a matter of fact, been up for two.

He walked into Perry Mason's office and perched himself on the arm of the big black leather chair.

"I'm going to give you a break," said Perry Mason, "and I want a favor."

Nevers spoke in a dull monotone of low-voiced comment.

"Sure," he said. "I had that all figured out a long time ago. Where is she?"

"Where's who?" asked Mason.

"Frances Celane."

"Who wants to know?"

"I do."

"What's the big idea?"

Nevers yawned and slid back over the arm of the chair, so that he was seated cross-wise in the chair.

"Hell," he said, "don't try to surprise me. That's been tried by experts. I doped out the play as soon as I got the call. There was nothing to it. Frances Celane had a nervous breakdown and was rushed to a sanitarium. Last night the District Attorney uncovered evidence which made him decide to put a first degree murder rap on her. She was secretly married to a chap named Gleason. They've picked up Gleason, and they're getting ready to go after Frances Celane.

"You're Frances Celane's attorney. You've got her under cover somewhere. It's a cover that's deep enough to keep her from walking into a trap until you're ready to have her surrender. But you can't keep her under cover when the newspapers broadcast that she's wanted for murder. You've got a doctor mixed up in it, and a hospital. They wouldn't stand for it, even if you wanted them to. So it's a cinch you've got to turn her up, and you just picked on me to get the news, because you wanted something. Now tell me what you want, and I'll tell you whether we'll make a trade."

Perry Mason frowned thoughtfully, and made little drumming noises with his fingertips on the edge of the desk.

"I don't know what I want, Harry," he said.

Harry Nevers shook his head lugubriously.

"With the hardboiled bunch I'm working for, brother, if you don't know what you want, you're never going to get it. If you're going to make a trade you've got to make a trade right now."

"Well," said Perry Mason slowly, "I can tell you generally what I want. Somewhere along the line I'm going to try to get two or three people back at the Norton residence, under conditions that were similar to those which existed at the time of the murder. I don't know just how I'm going to do it. Somewhere along the line I'm going to make a point about the fact that the Buick automobile, which was reported stolen, wasn't taken out of the garage. All I want you to do is to see that I get a reasonable amount of publicity on those two points."

"Wait a minute," said Nevers, speaking in that same dull monotone, "you said you were going to make a point that the Buick car hadn't been taken out of the garage. You mean that you're going to claim that it was taken out, but the speedometer was either disconnected or set back, ain't that right?"

"No," Mason told him. "I'm going to make a point that it wasn't taken out of the garage."

For the first time since he had entered the office, the voice of Harry Nevers showed a trace of interest; a touch of tone.

"That's going to be a funny angle for *you* to play," he said.

"All right," said Mason, "we'll talk about that when the time comes. I'm just telling you now what I want. The question is, do we make a trade?"

"I think so," said Nevers.

"Have you got a photographer lined up?"

"Sure. He's down in the car waiting, and I've got a space held on the front page for a picture."

Perry Mason reached for the telephone on his desk, took down the receiver, and said to Della Street, in a low voice:

"Get Doctor Prayton on the line. Find out what sanitarium he put Frances Celane in. Get him to make out a discharge from the sanitarium, and telephone it over. Tell him that Frances Celane is going to be charged with murder, and I don't want him to get mixed up in it. Get the telephone number of the sanitarium, and after he's telephoned in the discharge, get Frances Celane on the line for me."

He hung up the telephone.

"Now listen," said Nevers earnestly, "would you do me a favor?"

"What is it?" asked Mason cautiously. "I thought I was doing you one. You're getting exclusive photographs and all that."

"Don't be so cagy," Nevers told him. "I was just asking an ordinary favor."

"What is it?"

Nevers straightened up slightly in the chair, and said in his low monotone: "Get that jane to show a little leg. This is a picture that's going to make the front page, and I want to have a lot of snap about it. Maybe we'll take a close-up of her face for the front page, with a leg picture on the inside page. But I want to take back some photographs that have got a little leg in them."

"Well," said Perry Mason, "why not tell her so? You can be frank with her."

"I'm going to be frank with her all right," said Nevers, "but you're her lawyer, and she'll have confidence in you. Sometimes we have a little trouble getting these janes to pose right when they're excited. I want you to see that I get a break."

"Okay," Mason told him, "I'll do the best I can."

Harry Nevers took a cigarette from his pocket, lit it, and looked appraisingly at the attorney.

"If we could get her to come down to the *STAR* office and surrender herself to our custody," he said, "we'd see that she got a better break."

Mason's tone was firm.

"No," he said, "you're going to get the exclusive story and photographs. That's the best I can give you. She's going to surrender to the District Attorney, and I want to be sure there isn't any misunderstanding about that. In other words, I want the newspaper account to tell the public the truth."

Nevers yawned and looked at the telephone.

"Okay," he said. "I wonder if your secretary's got the calls through yet. . . ."

The telephone rang, and Mason took down the receiver. He heard Frances Celane's voice, eager and excited, at the other end of the line.

"What is it?" she asked. "They won't let me have newspapers here."

"All right," said Mason. "The show's starting."

"What do you mean?" she asked.

"They've arrested Rob Gleason for murder." He heard her gasp, and went on, "They've identified the club that killed Edward Norton. It was a walking stick that belonged to Rob Gleason."

"Rob Gleason never did it," she replied swiftly. "He called on my uncle, and they had quite an argument. He left that walking stick in Uncle's study, and . . ."

"Never mind that," interrupted Perry Mason. "There's a chance this line is tapped. They may have detectives listening in on us. You can tell me when you get here. I want you to get in a taxicab and come to the office right away, prepared to surrender yourself for murder."

"You mean they're going to arrest me too?"

"Yes," he said. "I'm going to surrender you into custody."

"But they haven't charged me with murder yet, have they?"

"They're going to," he said. "I'm going to force their hand."

"*Must* I do it?" she asked.

"You said you were going to have confidence in me," he told her. "I say you must do it."

"I'll be in there," she said, "in just about half an hour."

"Okay," said Mason, and hung up the telephone.

After a moment he jiggled the receiver and said to his secretary: "Get me the office of the District Attorney. I want to talk with Claude Drumm if he's in."

He hung up the telephone and faced the reporter.

"Listen," Nevers told him, "you're going to step on your tonsil there. If you tell the D.A. you're going to surrender the broad, they'll cover your office and pick her up when she comes in. They'd rather have her picked up than have her surrender."

Mason nodded.

"That's why you're going to listen to my talk with the D.A.'s office," he said. "It'll avoid misunderstandings."

The telephone rang, and he picked up the receiver.

"Hello," he said. "Hello, Drumm? This is Mason talking. Yes, Perry Mason. I understand that Rob Gleason has been charged with the murder of Edward Norton."

Drumm's voice came cold and cautious over the telephone.

"He is charged as *one* of the principals."

"There's another one then?" asked Mason.

"Yes, probably."

"Have charges been filed?"

"Not yet."

"A little birdie," said Mason, "tells me that you want to charge Frances Celane as being the other principal."

"Well?" asked Drumm, his voice still cold and cautious. "What did you call me up for?"

"I called you up to tell you that Frances Celane is on her way to surrender herself into custody at your office."

There was a moment of silence, then Drumm said: "Where is she now?"

"Somewhere between where she is and your office. That is, she's on the road."

Drumm asked cautiously: "Is she going to make any stops in between times?"

"I'm sure I couldn't tell you," said Mason.

"All right," said Drumm. "When she comes in, we'll be glad to see her."

"Will there be bail?" asked Mason.

"We'll have to talk that matter over after she makes a statement to us."

Mason smiled into the telephone.

"Don't misunderstand me, Drumm," he said. "I told you that she was going to surrender into custody. There won't be any statement."

"We want to ask her some questions," said Drumm.

"That's fine," said Mason. "You can ask her all the questions you want. She'll be only too glad to have you do so."

"Will she answer them?" asked Drumm.

"She will *not*," said Mason. "If there's any talking to be done, I'll do it."

He heard Drumm's exclamation of exasperation, and hung up the receiver.

Nevers looked over at him with bored eyes.

"They'll double-cross you," he said. "They'll figure that she's going to come to the office, and they'll send men to arrest her here. They'll make it appear she was arrested, rather than giving herself up."

"No," Mason said, "they think she's going directly from the sanitarium to the D.A.'s office. And, anyway, you've heard the conversation. That'll eliminate misunderstandings."

Mason opened a desk drawer, took out a flask of rye, and set out a glass. The reporter slid the glass back to him along the desk and tilted the bottle to his lips.

When he lowered the bottle, he grinned at the lawyer. "My first wife hated to wash dishes," he said, "so I got out of the habit of dirtying them. You know, Mason, this may be a hard morning, and I haven't had any sleep for a couple of nights. If I put this bottle in my pocket, it might keep me awake."

Mason reached out and took the bottle.

"If I keep it in the desk," he said, "I'll know that you don't get an over-dose."

"Well," Nevers told him, "under those circumstances, there's nothing to keep me from going down and getting the photographer," and he slid down from the arm of the chair and walked through the door which led to the outer office.

He was back in five minutes with a photographer who carried a camera in a canvas case in one hand, and tripod in the other.

The photographer wasted no time in greetings, but scrutinized the office with an eye that soaked in the lighting arrangements.

"What sort of complexion has she got?" he asked.

"Spun silk hair," said Mason. "Dark eyes, high cheeks, and a good figure. You won't have any trouble with her when it comes to posing. She's expert at placing herself where she looks well."

"I want her in that leather chair," said the photographer.

"That's where she'll go," Mason told him.

The photographer raised the shades on the windows, set up the tripod, adjusted and focused the big camera, poured some flashlight powder into a flashgun.

"Why don't you use electric bulbs?" asked Perry Mason, eyeing the photographer with interest. "I understand they do better work, and they don't get a room all filled with smoke."

"Try telling that to the eagle-eyed bird that audits the expense account," said the photographer, "and it's *your* office. *I* don't care about the smoke."

Nevers grinned at Mason.

"That's the sweet spirit of coöperation that we have over at the *STAR*," he said.

Mason looked at the ceiling of the room and muttered: "I presume I can move out of here for a half an hour just because you fellows want to save the cost of a flashlight globe."

"Give him a shot out of that bottle," said Nevers, "and maybe he won't load the flash quite so heavy."

Mason slid the bottle over to the photographer.

"Listen," Nevers said, almost moodily, "something seems to tell me you've got a trick up your sleeve, Mason."

"I have," Mason told him.

Nevers nodded to the photographer.

"All right, Bill," he said, "better get a photograph of the lawyer at his desk. Drag out some law books. Get that bottle out of the way, and get a couple of shots."

"Don't waste your film," Mason told him. "They won't publish my picture unless it's in connection with a courtroom scene, or walking down the street with Frances Celane, or something like that."

Harry Nevers looked at him moodily, and said, in that bored monotone: "I'm not so certain. It depends on what you've got up your sleeve. You've pulled a couple of fast ones lately, and I'll have these pictures for the morgue in case we need 'em. You can't ever tell what's going to happen."

Perry Mason looked at him shrewdly.

"In other words," he said, "you've heard that there's some talk of arresting me as an accessory after the fact."

Nevers chuckled, a dry, rasping chuckle.

"You've got a good mind, Mason," he said. "But you've got funny ways of trying lawsuits and representing clients. Now that you mention it, it seems to me I *did* hear something about some stolen money that you'd received on a fee and hadn't surrendered."

Mason's laugh was scornful.

"If I *had* received any money, what a sweet spot it would put my client in if I walked into the D.A.'s office, and laid the money down on the table and said, virtuously: 'Here it is.' "

"Did you receive any one thousand dollar bills from your client?" asked Harry Nevers, in the tone of one who asks a question without expecting an answer.

Perry Mason made a gesture with his hand.

"If I did," he said, "I'd either have the bills on me, or some place in the office. The office has been searched from top to bottom."

"This morning?" asked Nevers.

"Some time last night," Mason told him.

Nevers jerked his head toward the photographer.

"Better take three pictures, Bill," he said. "Get him at the desk, get him standing up, and get a close-up."

SIXTEEN

FRAN CELANE SAT in the big, black leather chair, stared at the camera on the tripod, looked at the face of Perry Mason, and smiled, a wan, pathetic smile.

"Hold that smile," said the photographer.

"Wait a minute," said Nevers, "there's going to be a sex angle to this, and I want a little more leg."

Fran Celane continued to smile wanly. She reached down with her left hand and moved her skirt up an inch or two.

"Face the camera," said the photographer.

Harry Nevers said: "Wait a minute. It still ain't right. I want a little more leg."

The smile left her face, her black eyes blazed furiously. She reached down and pulled the skirt far up over the knee with an angry gesture.

"That's too much, Miss Celane," the photographer said.

"All right," she blazed at Nevers, "damn you, you wanted leg! There it is!"

Mason explained patiently.

"You understand, Miss Celane, that these men are friendly to our side of the case. They're going to see that you get some favorable publicity, but, in order to do that, they've got to have a picture that will attract the interest of the public. Now, it's going to help your case a lot if you can get just the right kind of a smile on your face, and at the same time, show just enough of a sex angle to appeal to the masculine eye."

Slowly the glitter faded from her eyes. She adjusted her skirt down over her knee, and once more the wan, pathetic smile came on her face.

"That's oke," said Nevers.

"Hold it," said the photographer, and, "don't blink your eyes."

A puff of white light mushroomed up from the flashgun and a little cloud of smoke twisted and turned as it writhed toward the ceiling.

"All right," said the photographer, "let's try one with a slightly different pose. Handkerchief in the left hand as though you'd been weeping, face mournful. Let the mouth droop a little bit. Not quite so much leg."

Frances Celane flared: "What do you think I am, an actress or a mannequin?"

"That's all right," soothed Perry Mason. "You'll have a lot of this to go through with, Miss Celane. And I want to caution you to keep your temper. If you flare up and show temper, and the newspaper reporters start playing you up as a tiger-woman, it's going to be a bad thing for your case. What I'm trying to do is to get the case brought on for trial, and get a quick acquittal. You've got to coöperate or you may have some unpleasant surprises."

She stared at Perry Mason, sighed, and took the pose they had suggested.

"Chin a little lower and to the left," said the photographer. "Eyes downcast, but not so far that they give the impression of being closed. Get the point of that shoulder a little bit away from the camera, so I can get the sweep of your throat. All right, that's fine. Hold it!"

Once more the shutter clicked, and once more the flashlight gave forth a puff of white smoke.

"Okay," said the photographer. "That's fine for those two."

Perry Mason crossed to the telephone.

"Get me Claude Drumm at the District Attorney's office," he said.

When he had Drumm on the line, he said: "I'm awfully sorry, Drumm, but Miss Celane is very much indisposed. She's had a nervous breakdown and was ordered to a sanitarium by her physician. She left the sanitarium to come in and surrender herself into custody when she knew that the police were looking for her. She's at my office now, and she's suffering from nervousness. I think you'd better arrange to pick her up here."

"I thought you said she had left your office when you telephoned before," said Drumm, with a trace of annoyance in his voice.

"No," said Mason, "you misunderstood me. I said that she had started for your office. I told you I didn't know what stops she intended to make on the way. She was nervous, and stopped in here because she wanted me to go with her."

Drumm said: "All right, the police will be there," and slammed up the telephone.

Mason turned and grinned at Nevers.

"If I'd let them know she was coming here to surrender herself, they'd have had men parked around to grab her before she got here," he said.

"Oh, well," said Nevers. "It's all in the game. I could stand another drink of that whisky if you've got it handy."

"I could stand a drink myself," said Fran Celane.

Mason shook his head at her.

"No, we're going to be in the middle of action pretty quick, and I don't want you to have liquor on your breath, Miss Celane. You've got to remember that every little thing you do, and everything you say, will be snapped up and dished out to the public.

"Now remember that under no circumstances are you to talk about the case or to lose your temper. Those are two things *you've got* to remember. Talk about anything else, give the reporters plenty of material. Tell them about the romance of your secret marriage with Rob Gleason. Tell them how you admire him and what a wonderful man he is. Tell them all about the childhood you had, the fact that your parents died and that your uncle was the same as a father and a mother to you. Try to get the note of the poor little rich girl who has neither father nor mother, but is rolling in coin.

"Give them all the material that they want to write sob sister articles and character sketches, and that stuff. But the minute they start talking about the case, or what happened on that night, simply dry up like a clam. Tell them that you're awfully sorry, that *you'd* like to talk about it, and you don't see any reason why you couldn't, but that your lawyer has given you specific instructions that he's to do all the talking. Tell them you think it's silly, and that you can't understand why your lawyer feels that way, because you've got nothing to conceal, and you'd like to come right out and tell the whole circumstances as you remember them, but you've promised your lawyer, and you're not going to break your promise to anybody.

"They'll try all sorts of tricks on you, and probably tell you Rob Gleason has made a full confession, or that he has told the officers he has reason to believe that you committed the murder, or that you made certain incriminating statements to him, or they'll tell you that he has come to the conclusion that you are guilty and has made a confession in order to take the jolt so that you'll be spared. They'll try all sorts of stuff. Simply look at them with a dumb expression on your face, and say nothing. And for God's sake, don't lose your temper. They'll probably do things that will make you want to kill them, but if you lose your temper and fly into one of your rages, they'll spread it all over the front pages of the newspaper, that you've got an ungovernable temper, and are one of these tiger women."

"I understand," she said.

There was the sound of a siren drifting up through the windows of the office.

Frances Celane shuddered.

"Well," said Nevers to the photographer, "get your camera all loaded up, boy, because some of these cops will want to get their picture in the paper, taking the suspect into custody. Probably Carl Seaward will show up from the Homicide Squad. He's one of those birds that likes to stick his stomach in front of a camera and put his hand on the shoulder of the prisoner, with a photograph for the front page labeled: *'Carl Seaward, intrepid investigator of the Homicide Squad, taking the suspect into custody, marking the termination of a case which has baffled the entire police force for the past forty-eight hours.'*

"Maybe I'd better get in this picture too. I wonder if my hair is on straight. I can pose as the *STAR* reporter who assisted the police in locating the suspect."

And Nevers struck a pose in front of the camera, grinning.

Frances Celane surveyed him in scornful appraisal.

"Show a little leg," she said.

SEVENTEEN

PAUL DRAKE PERCHED on the edge of Perry Mason's desk and shook tobacco from a cloth sack into a brown paper which he held expertly between cigarette-stained fingers.

"Well," he said, "we've got our contact with Mrs. Mayfield. But it isn't getting us anything. We had one devil of a time. The police had her in custody as a material witness for a while."

"Have you worked the rough shadow business on her yet?" inquired Mason.

"Not yet. We're building up to it. We've got a woman operative who's posing as a woman who's been abroad as a governess, and is now out of work. We've checked back on Mrs. Mayfield and found all about her early associates. We managed to run one of them down and got all the dope from her about the names of the people she knew, and all that sort of stuff."

"This woman is getting across all right?" asked Mason.

"I'll say she's getting across. She's got Mrs. Mayfield confiding in her, all of her troubles with her husband, and all that sort of stuff."

"But she hasn't said anything about the murder?" asked Mason.

"Not a peep so far. That is, of course, she mentions that she was taken to the District Attorney's office and held for awhile as a material witness until they got a signed statement out of her, and a lot of that stuff. But she isn't going into details. All that she's telling is simply a rehash of what she's told the newspapers."

"How about Don Graves?" inquired the attorney. "How are you getting along with him?"

Paul Drake put the finishing touches on the cigarette.

"We're making some *real* progress there," he said, "We've got a young lady operative who has contacted him, and Graves is falling for her like a ton of brick. He's telling her everything he knows."

"About the case" asked Mason.

"About the case, about everything. He's turning himself inside out."

"This woman must be good," said Mason.

"I'll say she's good," explained Drake enthusiastically. "She'd knock your eye out. She's got one of those confiding techniques that snuggles up and looks at you with big eyes, and seems to listen all over. You just naturally ache to tell her things. My God, every time I go out with that broad, I sit down and start telling her all of *my* troubles; about the girl that jilted me in my childhood, so that I never got married, and all that stuff.

"You've seen a guy when he's about nine-tenths drunk, going around and weeping on the necks of total strangers and telling all of his private affairs? Well, that's just the way this jane works. She affects the fellows just about like nine-tenths of a drunk. They fall all over her and spill everything."

"That's fine," said Mason. "What have you found out?"

"So far, just stuff you don't want to hear," said the detective. "It don't help your client a damn bit."

"All right," said Mason, "give me the lowdown, and don't try to put a sugar coating on it. Give me the facts."

"The facts are," said Drake, "that this Celane girl had on a pink negligee the night the murder was committed. Graves was sent by Edward Norton to ride up with Judge Purley and Arthur Crinston to get some documents. He kept looking back toward the house as they went around the curves in the road and when they got to the point in the road where he could look up at the window in Edward Norton's study, he saw somebody standing back of Norton, who was seated at his desk.

"More than that, he says that he saw the man swing a club down on Edward Norton's head, and Norton collapsed across the desk. He says that he saw the arm, shoulder and head of a woman, and that he thinks he is positive of the identity of both the man and the woman. The woman had on a pink negligee."

"He made that statement to the District Attorney's office?" asked Mason.

"Yes, he's made it, and subscribed and sworn to it."

"That isn't the statement he made the first time," Mason pointed out. "When they were making their first investigation, Graves said that he saw the man in the room, who struck the blow, and didn't see anyone else except Norton."

"That won't help you any," said Drake casually. "You can't prove that."

"They took the statement down in shorthand," said Mason.

Drake laughed.

"Those notes have been lost. I'm just telling you in the event you don't know it," he said. "I made it a point to ask one of the newspaper reporters to inquire of the shorthand stenographer who took down the statements there that night. Strange as it may seem, something happened, and the notebook had been misplaced. It's disappeared."

He grinned at the lawyer.

Perry Mason stared down at the surface of his desk, his brows in straight lines of frowning concentration.

"The dirty crooks," he said. "The D.A. always howls to high heaven about the crooked criminal lawyers who manipulate the facts. But whenever the D.A. uncovers any evidence that gives the defendant a break, you can bet something happens to it."

The detective shrugged his shoulders.

"The D.A.'s want convictions," he said.

"Can your operative get into Mrs. Mayfield's room in Norton's residence, Paul?" Mason asked.

"Sure. That's a cinch."

"All right, I want her to make a report on every dress that's in there. In other words, I want to see if there's a pink dress or a pink negligee in there."

Paul Drake squinted at the lawyer significantly.

"It wouldn't be such a hard job to *put* one in there," he said.

"No," said Mason, "I'm going to play fair."

"What's the use of playing fair?" asked Drake. "They didn't play fair with you."

"I can't help that," said Mason. "I think I've got an out in this case, and I'm going to play it fair and square. I think I can beat the rap if I can get a decent break."

"Listen," said Paul Drake, drawing his feet up to the desk, and sitting cross-legged on the corner of it, "you haven't got an out in this case. They've got your client as good as convicted right now. Look what they've got on her. She's the one that would have benefited by the old man's death. In fact, with that marriage hanging over her head, she either had to kill him, or lose an estate that's worth a big bunch of money.

"This fellow, Gleason, may have married the woman because he loved her, or he may have married her because he wanted her money. Nobody knows which, but he gets all the credit for marrying her for money. The theory of the prosecution is that when he found out about the trust provision, he and the girl tried to reason with Norton. When Norton wouldn't listen to reason, Gleason made up his mind he'd bump him off. They had a big squabble. He'd have killed Norton right then if it hadn't been for Crinston coming to keep an appointment. So Gleason waited around until Crinston left, then jimmied a window to make it look as though burglars had broken in from the outside. Then he cracked down on Norton's head.

"He probably hadn't figured on any robbery at the time. He just wanted to make it look like robbery, so he turned the pockets inside-out. He found so much money in the wallet, he decided to keep it. Then he heard Crinston coming back, and had to do something quick. He knew the chauffeur was drunk, so he dashed down and planted as much of the evidence on him as he could, and then beat it.

"Frances Celane was with Gleason when the murder was committed. She's got the devil of a temper when she gets aroused. Probably she was in a rage, but Gleason married her for her dough. It was a deliberate crime on his part. He'd probably worked out the burglar plant while Crinston was talking with Norton. When he heard the car coming back, he realized he must have been seen, or that something had gone wrong, so then he framed the chauffeur, just as a second string to his bow."

Perry Mason stared at the detective with his eyes cold and hard.

"Paul," he said, "if they go into court on that theory, I'm going to bust it wide open."

"You're not going to bust anything wide open," Drake told him. "They've got all kinds of circumstantial evidence. They've caught the girl in half a dozen lies. Why did she say that she was out in the Buick sedan when she wasn't? They can prove that the car never left the garage. Mrs. Mayfield has worked up that end of the case for them, and the butler will swear positively that the car was there all the time. They can prove the ownership of the club that killed Norton, and they can prove that the girl had some of the money that came from Norton. . . ."

Perry Mason jerked to rigid attention.

"They can prove the girl had the money?" he asked.

"Yes," said Drake.

"How?" asked the lawyer.

"I don't know exactly how, but I do know that it's part of their case. They've got it all worked up. I think it's through the Mayfield woman."

"Well," said Mason wearily, "we're going to have a chance to find out. I'm going to force them to bring that case to an immediate trial."

"Force them to an immediate trial?" exclaimed Drake. "Why I thought you were stalling for delay. The newspapers say that you are."

Perry Mason grinned at him.

"That," he said, "is the way I'm forcing them to a trial. I'm yelling for continuances, and asking for additional time, as though my clients would be stuck if I didn't get them. Naturally, they're opposing my continuances. After I've got the D.A.'s office to make that opposition sufficiently vigorous, I'm going to admit that I'm licked, and let them bring the case on for trial."

Drake shook his head.

"They won't fall for that one," he said, "it's too old."

"It won't be old the way I dress it up," said Mason. "What I want you to do is to play this rough shadow business on Mrs. Mayfield, and also on Don Graves. I want to see if we can't frighten some facts out of them. Neither one of them is telling the truth—not yet. And I want to find out more about that money, whether the District Attorney had proof or just suspicions."

"You going to try and saddle the murder off on Mrs. Mayfield and her husband?" asked Drake.

"I'm going to represent my client to the best of my ability," Mason insisted.

"Yeah, I know that line," the detective told him, "but what does it mean?"

Mason tapped a cigarette end on the polished surface of the desk.

"The way to get to the bottom of a murder," he said, "is to pick out any pertinent fact which hasn't been explained, and find the real explanation of that fact."

"Sure," said Drake, "that's another generality. Get down to earth. What are you talking about?"

"I'm talking about the reason Norton had for claiming the Buick sedan was stolen," said the lawyer.

"What's that got to do with it?" Drake wanted to know.

"Everything," insisted Perry Mason. "That's an unexplained fact in that case, and until we get the explanation of that fact, we haven't got a solution of the murder."

"That's a good line of hooey for the jury," commented the detective, "but it doesn't really mean anything. You can't explain everything in any case. You know that."

"Until you can explain it," doggedly insisted Mason, "you haven't got a complete case. Now remember that the prosecution is going to rest its case on circumstantial evidence. In order to get a conviction on circumstantial evidence, you've got to exclude every reasonable hypothesis other than that of guilt."

The detective snapped his fingers.

"A lot of lawyer talk," he said. "That doesn't mean anything to the newspapers, and the newspapers are going to be the ones who will determine whether or not your client gets convicted."

"Well, before I get done with this case," Mason remarked, "the newspapers are going to figure that Buick car is the most important fact in the entire case."

"But the automobile wasn't stolen. It didn't leave the garage."

"That's what the butler says."

Drake's face suddenly became hard with concentrated attention.

"You mean that the butler is lying?" he asked.

"I'm not making any statements right now," said Mason.

Drake spoke in a monotone, as though thinking out loud.

"Of course if the butler had taken the car and disconnected the speedometer, and maybe gone for a little drive, and Norton had telephoned the police that the car was stolen, and he wanted the driver picked up, no matter who it might be, and then the butler had come back and found out about that telephone call . . ."

His voice trailed off into silence. He sat motionless for a few minutes, then shook his head sadly.

"No, Perry," he said, "that won't work."

"All right," said Mason, smiling, "I'm not asking you what'll work and what won't work. I want facts out of you. Get the hell off of my desk, and let me go to work. Put your rough shadows to work just as soon as you can. I'm anxious to find out what they uncover."

"You're representing both Gleason and the woman, eh?" asked Drake.

"Yes, I am now. Frances Celane is going to stand by her husband. She's told me to represent him."

"All right, I'm going to ask you something that's been asked me by a dozen different people, I hope you won't take any offense, but it's for your own good, because everybody in town is talking about it. They're saying that if the lawyer for the defense has any sense why doesn't he try to get separate trials and try the man and the woman separately? In that way they'd have to try the man first, and you'd have a chance to find out all their evidence and cross-examine all their witnesses before they got down to a trial of the woman."

"I couldn't get separate trials for them," said Mason. "The court wouldn't allow it."

"Well, you could at least make the attempt," said the detective.

"No," said Mason with a smile, "I rather think I'm satisfied the way things are now. I think we'll try them together."

"Okay," said Drake, "you're the doctor. I'll get the rough shadows at work just as soon as I can."

EIGHTEEN

PERRY MASON APPEARED at the entrance to the visitors' room in the huge jail building.

"Robert Gleason," he told the officer in charge.

"You're Gleason's attorney?" asked the officer.

"Yes."

"You didn't appear for him as his attorney when he first came in."

Perry Mason frowned. "I'm his attorney now," he said. "Do you want to bring him out, or do you want me to go into court and show that the officers have refused to permit me to talk with my client?"

The officer stared at Mason, shrugged his shoulders, turned on his heel without a word, and vanished. Five minutes later he opened a door and escorted Mason into the long room.

A table ran the length of this room. Along the middle of the table, stretching to a height of some five feet above it, was a long screen of heavy iron mesh. The prisoners sat on one side of this screen. The attorneys sat on the other. Robert Gleason was seated about half way down the table. He got to his feet, and smiled eagerly as he saw Perry Mason approaching. Perry Mason waited until the officer had moved out of earshot, then dropped into the chair, and looked searchingly across at the man accused of murder.

"Keep your voice low when you answer questions, Gleason," said Mason, "and tell me the truth. No matter what it is, don't be afraid to tell me the exact truth."

"Yes sir," said Gleason.

Mason frowned at him.

"Did you make a statement to the District Attorney?" he asked.

Gleason nodded his head.

"A written statement?"

"It was taken down in shorthand by a court reporter, and then written up and given to me to sign."

"Did you sign it?"

"I haven't yet."

"Where is it?"

"It's in my cell. They gave it to me to read. That is, they gave me a copy."

"That's funny," said Mason. "Usually they try to rush you into signing it. They don't let you have a copy."

"I know," said Gleason, "but I didn't fall for that. They tried to rush me into signing it, and I told them I was going to think it over."

"It won't do you much good," the lawyer told him, wearily, "if you talked in front of a court reporter, he took down everything you said, and he can testify to the conversation from his notes."

"That's what the District Attorney's office told me," said Gleason. "But I'm not signing, just the same."

"Why not?"

"Because," said Gleason, in a low voice, "I think that I'll repudiate what I said."

"You can't do it," the lawyer told him. "Why the devil did you have to shoot off your mouth?"

"I can do it the way I intend to," Gleason told him.

"Can do what?"

"Repudiate the confession."

"All right, show me," said the lawyer.

"I intend to take the entire responsibility for the murder," Gleason told him.

Perry Mason stared at the man through the coarse screen of the partition.

"Did you commit the murder?" he asked.

Gleason bit his lips, turned his head so that his eyes were averted from those of the attorney.

"Come on," said Perry Mason. "Come through, and come clean. Look up at me and answer that question. Did you commit the murder?"

Rob Gleason shifted uncomfortably in the chair.

"I'd rather not answer that question just yet," he said.

"You've got to answer it," Perry Mason told him.

Gleason wet his lips with the tip of a nervous tongue, then leaned forward so that his face was almost against the coarse iron screen.

"Can I ask you some questions before I answer that?" he inquired.

"Yes," Mason said, "you can ask me all the questions you want, but you've got to come clean on that before I leave here. If I'm going to act as your attorney, I've got to know what happened."

"The District Attorney's office told me that Frances had been caught with some of the money that Mr. Norton had in his possession when he was killed."

"Don't believe everything the District Attorney's office tells you," Mason answered.

"Yes I know. But the point is, *did* she have that money?"

"I'll answer that question by asking you another," said Perry Mason. "Did Mrs. Mayfield make any statement to the District Attorney about having money in her possession, that she had received from Frances Celane?"

"I don't know," said Gleason.

Perry Mason chose his words carefully. *"If,"* he said, "the District Attorney's office has any *proof* of Frances Celane having any of that money, it came through Mrs. Mayfield. In other words, they found Mrs. Mayfield with the money, and she passed the buck to Frances Celane. Now, if that happened, there's just as much reason to believe that Mrs. Mayfield was in the room at the time of the murder, and took the money from the body of the dead man, as to believe that Frances Celane gave it to her."

"Are they *sure* that there was a woman in the room at the time of the murder?" Gleason inquired.

"Don Graves says there was."

"He didn't say that the first night."

"We can't prove what he said the first night because the police have torn up the notes of the statement he made."

"He says now that there was a woman there?"

"Yes, he says there was a woman. I think he's going to say it was a woman who wore a pink negligee."

"Did he see her plainly enough to identify her?"

"He saw her shoulder and arm, and part of her head—probably the back of her head."

"Then Mrs. Mayfield is trying to pin this crime on Fran?" asked Rob Gleason.

"I'm not saying that," said Mason. "I'm simply giving you the facts as I know them. If the District Attorney's office has proof of any money, that's where they got it."

"How much chance do you stand of getting Fran off?" asked Gleason.

"One never knows what a jury is going to do. She's young and attractive. If she keeps her temper and doesn't make any damaging admissions, I stand a pretty good chance."

Gleason stared through the screen at the lawyer for a few moments, and then said: "All right, I'm not attractive. I haven't got any of the things in my favor that Frances has. How much chance do you stand of getting me off?"

"It depends on the kind of a break I can get, and on what you've told the District Attorney," said Mason. "Now, I'm going to tell you what I want you to do. You go back to your cell and get some paper. Say that you want to write out what happened, in your own handwriting. Take that paper and scribble a lot of meaningless stuff on a few pages of it, and then tear it up. Let them believe that you used up all the paper, but take the rest of the paper and write out a copy of the statement that the District Attorney has given you to sign. In that way, I'll know exactly what you said, and what you didn't say."

Rob Gleason swallowed twice painfully.

"If," he said, "you don't get the breaks, they may convict Fran?"

"Of course, she's charged with first degree murder, and there's some circumstances in the case that don't look so good."

"Would they hang her?"

"Probably not. She'd probably get life. They don't hang women, as a rule."

"Do you know what it would mean to a girl of her fire and temperament to be shut up in a penitentiary for the rest of her life?" asked Gleason.

Perry Mason shook his head impatiently.

"Of course I know," he said. "Let's not start worrying about that now. Let's get down to facts. Tell me, did you, or did you not, murder Edward Norton?"

Gleason took a deep breath.

"If," he said, "the case commences to look hopeless for Fran, I'm going to confess."

"Confess to what?" asked Mason.

"Confess to the murder of Edward Norton; confess that I married Frances Celane for her money; that I didn't care very much about her. I liked her well enough, but I wasn't crazy about her. She had a great big bunch of money, and was a good catch. I wanted the money bad enough to marry her, and I married her. Then I found out that because she had married, her uncle had the right to cut her off with almost nothing. Her uncle didn't know about the marriage until the night he was killed. He found it out then. He was going to exercise the discretion given to him under the trust, and turn everything over to the charitable institutions, leaving Fran with just a lousy thousand or two. I went in and argued with him. He wouldn't listen to reason. Fran went in and argued with him, and that didn't do any good. Then Crinston came, and he had an appointment with Crinston, so we had to let our matter go. Fran and I went back down to her room. We sat and talked things over. Mrs. Mayfield came in, and was furious. She'd been blackmailing Fran, threatening to tell Mr. Norton about the marriage, unless she got a bunch of jack. Edward Norton had found out about the marriage, and that had killed the goose that laid Mrs. Mayfield's golden eggs.

"I heard Crinston drive away. He took Don Graves with him. I went out to have a last word with Mr. Norton. I went up to his study, and on the stairs I ran into Mrs. Mayfield. She wore a pink negligee, and she was still weeping about the money that she'd lost. I told her if she'd keep her head, we could have lots of money. She wanted to know what I meant, and I told her I was going to give Norton one more chance to come through. If he didn't take it, I was going to smash his head for him before he had a chance to give Frances Celane's money to charity. She went with me up the stairs and into his study. I gave Edward Norton his ultimatum. I told him that if he didn't give Frances her money, he was going to be sorry. He told me that he was not going to give her a cent; that he was going to turn it all over to charity, and then I cracked him on the head. I went through his pockets, and he had a big bunch of dough in his pockets. I took some, and Mrs. Mayfield took some. We were talking about how we were going to make the murder look as though burglars had done it. Mrs. Mayfield said we could pry up a window and leave some footprints outside in the soft loam. I wanted to plant it on the chauffeur because I knew he was drunk. While we were talking it over, we saw the lights of an automobile coming down the hill, and I figured it must be Crinston coming back. Mrs. Mayfield ran down and fixed the window so it looked as though burglars had come in, and I ran down and planted a stick and a couple of the thousand dollar bills in Devoe's room. Then I jumped in my car and beat it."

Perry Mason looked at the young man thoughtfully. "What did you do with the money that you had?" he asked.

"I buried it," said Rob Gleason, "where it will never be found."

Perry Mason drummed with the tips of his fingers on the table. "So help you God," he asked, "is that what happened?"

Gleason nodded his head.

"That's in confidence," he said. "I'm going to beat the rap if I can. If I can't, I'm going to come clean so that Frances Celane won't have to take the jolt."

"Did you," asked Perry Mason, "take out the Buick automobile on the night of the murder? Did you use it at all?"

"No."

Perry Mason pushed back the chair.

"All right," he said. "Now I'm going to tell you something. If you ever spill that story, you're going to get Frances Celane sent up for life, if you don't get her hung. Probably you'll get her hung."

Rob Gleason's eyes grew wide.

"What ever in the world do you mean?" he asked.

"Simply," said Perry Mason, "that nobody will believe the story the way you tell it. They'll believe just half of it. They'll believe that you committed the murder all right, but they'll figure that it wasn't Mrs. Mayfield that was with you. They'll figure that it was Fran Celane, and that you're trying to protect her by dragging Mrs. Mayfield into it."

Gleason was on his feet, his face white, his eyes wide.

"Good God!" he said. "Can't I save Frances by telling the truth?"

"Not that kind of truth," said Perry Mason. "Now go back to your cell and get me a copy of that statement the District Attorney wants you to sign. In the meantime, keep your head and don't tell anybody anything."

"Not even the truth, the way I told it to you?" asked Gleason.

"The truth is the last thing in the world you want to tell," said Perry Mason, "the way you're situated. Because nobody's going to believe you if you do tell the truth, and you're a rotten liar."

He turned on his heel and walked away from the screen meshed table, without a single backward glance. The officer opened the locked door, and let him out of the visiting room.

NINETEEN

IT WAS THE first time Frank Everly had ever been in court with Perry Mason; the first time he had ever been behind the scenes in a big murder case.

He sat at the side of Perry Mason and stared surreptitiously at the crowded courtroom, at the nine men and three women who were in the jury box, being examined as to their qualifications as jurors. He strove to give the impression of being thoroughly at home, but his manner betrayed his nervousness.

Perry Mason sat at the counsel table, leaning back in the swivel chair, his left thumb hooked in the armhole of his vest, his right hand toying with a watch chain. His face was a cold mask of rugged patience. Nothing about the man gave any indication of the terrific strain under which he labored.

Behind him sat the two defendants: Frances Celane in a close fitting costume of black, with a dash of white and a touch of red, her head held very erect, her eyes calm and a trifle defiant.

Robert Gleason was nervous, with the nervousness of an athletic man who finds himself fighting for his life under circumstances that necessitate physical passivity. His eyes smouldered with the sullen fires of suppressed emotions. His head jerked from time to time as he turned to face the various speakers in the drama which so intimately concerned him.

The courtroom was filled with that peculiar atmosphere which permeates a crowded room where spectators are in a state of emotional unrest.

Claude Drumm was acting as the trial deputy for the state, but there was a rumor that the District Attorney himself would come into the case as soon as the jury had been selected, and the routine evidence disposed of.

Drumm had been on his feet much of the time in his examination of the jurors. He was tall, well-tailored and self-contained, yet forcefully aggressive, without displaying too much force. His manner held the easy assurance of a professional who is fully at home and who is driving steadily toward a predetermined goal which he is assured of reaching.

Judge Markham, beneath the cloak of his austere judicial dignity, held himself with wary watchfulness. Perry Mason had the reputation of being able to "stampede," every case he tried, and Judge Markham was determined, that while the trial would be conducted with impartiality, it would be conducted with a proper regard for the dignity of law and order; that there would be no errors in the record, no opportunities for the dramatic manipulation of emotions which so frequently turned trials in which Perry Mason participated into spectacular debacles for the prosecution, crashing across the front pages of newspapers in glaring headlines.

"The peremptory," said Judge Markham sternly, "is with the people."

Claude Drumm dropped back to his chair and engaged in a whispered consultation with his assistant. He interrupted, to glance up at the court.

"If I may have a moment's indulgence, Your Honor."

"Very well," said the judge.

Everly looked at Perry Mason inquiringly, and caught a glint in the lawyer's eyes.

Mason leaned forward and whispered:

"Drumm wants to get number three off of the jury, but he thinks we have got to get off jurors nine and eleven. We've got twice as many peremptory challenges as he has, so he's wondering if he dares to pass his peremptory and hold it in reserve until he sees what the jury looks like later on."

"Does he dare to do it?" asked Everly.

"That," said Perry Mason, "remains to be seen."

There was a moment of tense silence, then Drumm got to his feet and bowed to the court.

"The people," he said, "pass their peremptory."

Judge Markham looked down at Perry Mason, and his lips moved to form the words: "The peremptory is with the defendants."

But the words were never uttered, for Perry Mason, turning toward the jury with a casual glance of appraisal, as though the entire matter had just claimed his attention, said, in a clear voice: "Your Honor, this jury seems *entirely* satisfactory to the defendants. We waive our peremptory challenge."

Claude Drumm was caught by surprise. Eyes of those who were wise in courtroom technique, saw the quick intake of his breath as he started unconsciously to register a protest which his consciousness knew would be futile.

Judge Markham's voice rang out through the crowded courtroom: "Let the jurors stand and be sworn to try the case."

Claude Drumm made an opening statement to the jury which was remarkable for its brevity.

"Gentlemen," he said, "we expect to show that, at the exact minute of eleven thirty-two on the twenty-third day of October of this year, Edward Norton met his death; that he was murdered by a blow on the head, struck with a club held in the hand of the defendant, Robert Gleason; that at the time of the murder, there was present as an active accomplice, the defendant, Frances Celane; that at the time of the murder, Edward Norton had a large sum of money on his person in the form of one thousand dollar bills.

"We expect to show that at the hour of eleven fourteen on that date, Edward Norton telephoned to the police station, reporting the theft of one of his automobiles, a Buick sedan; that Frances Celane was, in fact, present in the study of Edward Norton at the hour of eleven thirty-two P.M., on the date of the murder, but that, for the purpose of trying to establish an alibi, and knowing that Edward Norton had reported this Buick sedan as having been stolen at the hour of eleven fourteen, the said defendant, Frances Celane, then and there stated falsely and wilfully that she had been distant from the scene of the crime, in the said Buick automobile, from the hour of approximately ten forty-five until approximately twelve fifteen.

"We expect to show that immediately following the commission of the crime, the defendants left the bloody club with which the crime had been committed, and two of the one thousand dollar bills which had been stolen from the body of the deceased, in the bedroom of one Pete Devoe, who was then and there asleep and in an intoxicated condition; that this was done for the purpose of directing suspicion to the said Pete Devoe.

"We will also show that the defendants forced open a window and made footprints in the soil beneath the window, in an attempt to lead the police to believe burglars had entered the house.

"We also expect to show that immediately thereafter the defendant Robert Gleason fled from the scene of the crime; that both defendants gave false and contradictory accounts as to their whereabouts; that the club with which Edward Norton was struck down was a walking stick belonging to the defendant, Robert Gleason.

"We expect to show that an eye-witness actually saw the murder committed, and will identify Robert Gleason as the man who struck the blow, and will identify Frances Celane as the young woman who, attired in a pink dress or negligee, aided and abetted the commission of the crime."

Claude Drumm stood staring at the jurors for a moment, then sat down. Judge Markham looked inquiringly at Perry Mason.

"If the court please," said Perry Mason, "we will withold our opening statement until the time we start to present our case."

"Very well," said Judge Markham. "You may proceed, Mr. Drumm."

Claude Drumm started building up the case with that calm, deadly efficiency for which he was noted. No detail was too small to claim his attention; no link in the chain of evidence was to be overlooked.

The first witness was a surveyor who had mapped and photographed the premises. He introduced diagrams drawn to scale, showing the room in which the body had been found, the furniture in the room, the location of the windows. Then he produced a photograph of the room, other photographs of various corners of the room. Each of these photographs was identified by locating it on the diagram of the room. Then followed photographs of the house, and finally, a map showing the house with reference to the winding road which climbed up to the boulevard. Following that came a contour map showing the various elevations of the windows in the house, with reference to the road along which the automobile had traveled.

"So that," said Drumm, suavely, indicating a place on the diagram where a curve in the road was shown, "it would be perfectly possible for a person traveling along this section of the road which I am indicating, in an automobile, to glance back and see into the room marked number one on the map, People's Exhibit A?"

Before the surveyor could answer the question, Perry Mason got to his feet and raised his voice in protest:

"Just a moment, Your Honor," he said. "That question is leading. It also calls for a conclusion of the witness. It calls for a conclusion which the jury is to draw in this case. It is one of the points upon which we intend to convince this jury of the improbability of the People's case. Whether or not . . ."

The gavel of the judge banged down upon his desk.

"The objection," he said, "is sustained. The argument, Mr. Mason, is unnecessary."

Mason dropped back to his chair.

With the manner of one who has scored a victory even in defeat, Drumm bowed smilingly to Mason.

"Counsellor," he said, "you may inquire on cross-examination."

With the eyes of everyone in the courtroom riveted upon him, Perry Mason, fully aware of the dramatic advantage of the moment, and the interest which would attend upon his first question, strode to the map which had been fastened to the blackboard with thumb tacks, placed the index finger of his right hand upon the curve in the line which indicated the roadway from the house to the boulevard, placed the index finger of his left hand upon the location of the study in the house, and said, in a voice which rang with challenge: "Exactly how far is it from the point which I am indicating with my right forefinger, and which is the curve in this roadway, to the point which I am indicating with my left finger, and which is the point where the body was found?"

"If," said the witness in level tones, "your right forefinger is exactly at the point where the curve swings farthest south, and your left fore-finger is at a point representing the exact point where the body was found, the distance is exactly two hundred and seventy-two feet, three and one-half inches."

Perry Mason turned, his face showing surprise.

"Two hundred and seventy-two feet, three and one-half inches?" he exclaimed incredulously.

"Yes," said the witness.

Mason dropped his hands to his sides with a gesture of finality.

"That," he said, "is all. I have no further questions to ask of this witness."

Judge Markham looked at the clock, and an anticipatory rustle of motion stirred the courtroom, as dead leaves on a tree are stirred by the first current of an advancing breeze.

"It has," said the judge, "approached the hour of adjournment. The court will adjourn until ten o'clock to-morrow morning, and during that time, the jury will remember the admonition of the court not to converse amongst themselves about this case, nor permit others to converse with them or in their presence about it."

The gavel banged on the desk.

Perry Mason smiled craftily, and remarked to his assistant: "Drumm should have carried on the examination until the hour for adjournment.

Giving me the opportunity to ask that one question, will make the newspapers feature it to-morrow morning."

Everly had his eyes puckered in concentration.

"Two hundred and seventy-two feet is a long distance," he said.

"It won't," Mason assured him grimly, "get any shorter as the case goes on."

TWENTY

THE NEWSPAPERS PREDICTED that the first major witness for the prosecution would be either Arthur Crinston, the business partner of the murdered man, or Don Graves, who had been the only eye-witness of the murder.

In this, the newspapers showed that they underestimated the dramatic trial tactics of the chief trial deputy. Drumm would no more have plunged into the drama of that murder without preparing the minds of the jurors for the gruesome tidbit, than would a playwright have opened his presentation with a crisis lifted from the third act.

He called to the stand, instead, Judge B. C. Purley.

Necks craned as the Municipal Judge, coming in from the back of the courtroom, strode down the aisle with the stately bearing of one who realizes to the full the dignity of his appearance, and the importance of his position.

White-haired, ponderous, deep-chested and heavy-waisted, he held up his right hand while the oath was administered to him, and then took the witness chair, his manner indicating a respect for the tribunal and what it stood for, a dignified tolerance of the attorneys and jurors, a calm disregard of the restless spectators.

"Your name is B. C. Purley?" asked Claude Drumm.

"Yes sir."

"You are now a duly elected, qualified and acting Judge of the Municipal Court of this city?"

"I am."

"And, on the night of October twenty-third of this year you had occasion to be in the vicinity of the residence of Edward Norton?"

"I did."

"At what time did you arrive at the residence of Edward Norton, Judge Purley?"

"At precisely six minutes after eleven."

"And what time did you leave that vicinity?"

"At precisely thirty minutes past eleven."

"Will you explain to the jury, Judge Purley, why it is that you are able to testify with such exactness as to the time of arrival and departure?"

Perry Mason recognized the trap, yet had no alternative but to walk into it.

"Objected to, Your Honor," he said. "The witness has given his testimony. The mental processes which led up to it are incompetent, irrelevant, immaterial, and, at best, matter only for cross-examination."

"Sustained," said Judge Markham.

Claude Drumm's smile was ironically sarcastic.

"I will withdraw the question, Your Honor," he said. "It was an error upon my part. After all, if Counsellor Mason desires to go into the matter, he is at liberty to do so upon cross-examination."

"Proceed," said Judge Markham, pounding his desk with the gavel.

"Who was with you on the occasion of your visit?" asked the deputy district attorney.

"Mr. Arthur Crinston was with me when I went to the vicinity of the house, and both Mr. Arthur Crinston, and Mr. Don Graves were with me at the time I departed."

"What happened while you were there, Judge Purley?"

"I arrived at the grounds in the vicinity of the house, stopped my car to allow Mr. Crinston to get out, turned my car, shut off the motor, and waited."

"During the time that you were waiting what did you do?"

"Sat and smoked for the first ten or fifteen minutes, and looked at my watch rather impatiently several times during the last part of the period I was waiting," said Judge Purley.

And he glanced, with just a trace of subdued triumph, at Perry Mason, his manner indicating that, being fully familiar with court procedure, he was going to get the damaging parts of his testimony in, whether the defense wanted them in or not. The inference to be drawn from the fact that he had glanced several times at his watch was that he was aware of the exact minute of his departure, and he was sufficiently adroit to get that inference across to the jury without violating the ruling of the court.

Perry Mason eyed the witness with placid indifference.

"Then what happened?" asked Claude Drumm.

"Then Mr. Crinston came out of the house to join me. I started the motor of my car, and at that moment the window of the house in the southeast corner of the building was opened, and Mr. Norton thrust his head out of the study window."

"Just a moment," said Claude Drumm. "Do you know of your own knowledge that that was Mr. Norton's study?"

"No sir," said Judge Purley. "I only know it from the fact that it was the room in the southeast corner on the second story of the house, and is the room marked on the map and diagram as room number one, Mr. Norton's study."

"Oh," said Drumm, "then the room is that which is indicated on Plaintiff's Exhibit. A by the figure one marked in a circle?"

"Yes sir."

"Very well," said Drumm, "what did Mr. Norton say?"

"Mr. Norton called down to Mr. Crinston, and said, as nearly as I can remember: 'Arthur, would it be all right for you to take Don Graves in to your house in your car and let him get the documents? Then I will send the chauffeur to pick him up.' "

"And," said Drumm, "what happened next?"

"Mr. Crinston said, as nearly as I can remember: 'I am not in my own car, but with a friend. I will have to ask my friend if it will be all right.' "

"Then what happened?"

"Mr. Norton said: 'Very well, do so, and let me know,' and withdrew his head from the window."

"Then what happened?"

"Then Mr. Crinston came to me and said that Mr. Graves was to get some documents . . .."

"Objected to," said Perry Mason in a casual tone of voice. "Anything which took place without the hearing of this defendant is admissible only as a part of the *res gestae*. By no stretch of the imagination can this be considered as a part of the *res gestae*."

"The objection is sustained," said Judge Markham.

"Very well. Then what happened?" asked Drumm suavely, smiling over at the jury as much as to say: "You see how technical the defense is in this case, ladies and gentlemen?"

"Then," said Judge Purley, "Mr. Crinston went back to a position under the study window, and called up, as nearly as I can remember his words: 'It's all right, Edward. He can go with us.' And at about that moment, the front door opened and the figure of Mr. Graves ran down the steps, Mr. Graves saying 'I am ready,' or words to that effect."

"And then what happened?"

"Then the three of us got in my automobile, Mr. Crinston sitting in the front seat with me, Mr. Graves sitting in the rear seat. I started the machine and started to drive up along the road, lettered on the map 'People's Exhibit B' as *'Winding Roadway.'* We traveled up that road until we were in a position on the curve . . ."

"Just a moment," said Claude Drumm. "Can you take a pencil and indicate the exact point on the curve which you had approached when the event took place, concerning which you were about to testify?"

Judge Purley nodded, got to his feet, and walked with ponderous dignity to the blackboard, turned up the map and marked a small oblong on the curve in the roadway.

"This represents the approximate position of the car."

"And what happened when the car was in that position?" asked Claude Drumm.

"Mr. Graves looked back through the back window and exclaimed . . ."

"Objected to," snapped Perry Mason. "Hearsay, incompetent, irrelevant, and immaterial, not part of the *res gestae*, not binding upon the defendant."

"Sustained," said Judge Markham.

Claude Drumm made a helpless gesture.

"But surely, Your Honor, in view of what is to take place . . ."

"The objection," said Judge Markham coldly, "is sustained. You may call Mr. Don Graves at the proper moment, counsellor, and let him testify as to anything he saw. As to anything which was said or done outside of the presence of this defendant, and which is not a part of the *res gestae*, the objection is well taken."

"Very well," said Drumm, turning to the jury, and all but bowing, "at the proper time I will call Mr. Don Graves, and Mr. Don Graves will testify as to exactly what he saw at that place.

"Go on, Judge Purley, and tell the jury exactly what was done at that time and place, with reference to what you, yourself, did in relation to the operation of the automobile."

"I did nothing at exactly that place, but proceeded along the winding road, as indicated there on the map, for a distance of several rods, until I came to a place in the road which was wide enough to turn. There I turned the car by backing and twisting, and went back down the winding roadway, stopping once more in front of the house of Edward Norton."

"And then what did you do?"

"Then Mr. Graves and Mr. Crinston entered the house, and at their request I accompanied them. The three of us went up the stairs and into the room marked by the numeral 'one' in a circle on People's Exhibit

A, and saw there a body, which was subsequently identified to me as that of Edward Norton, lying sprawled across the desk, with its head badly crushed. The body was lifeless at the time of my arrival. There was a telephone near one hand, and several papers, including a policy of automobile insurance, on the desk."

"Did you notice, Judge Purley, what automobile was covered in that policy of insurance?"

"Objected to as incompetent, irrelevant and immaterial," said Perry Mason.

"Your Honor," said Drumm, "this is vital, and I propose to connect it up. It is a part of the theory of the prosecution that the defendant, Frances Celane, made a statement to the effect that she was out driving this Buick automobile; that these statements were made after she had been advised that police had been notified that the Buick automobile had been stolen. In other words, she knew that Edward Norton had telephoned that the Buick automobile had been stolen. Frances Celane, knowing that . . ."

"Very well," said Judge Markham, "there is no necessity for further argument, counsellor, as to the relevancy of the testimony. Upon the assurance of the prosecution that the matter will be connected, I will overrule the objections as to its relevancy, and permit the question to be answered, subject to a motion on the part of the defense to strike out if the evidence is not subsequently connected.

"This ruling, however, goes only to the relevancy of the testimony. It is, of course, apparent that the evidence called for by the question is not the best evidence. The automobile insurance policy, itself, is the best evidence of its contents, but there seems to be no objection made upon that ground."

Judge Markham looked down at Perry Mason with a puzzled expression on his face.

Perry Mason seemed to smile, the faintest trace of a quiver at the corners of his lips.

"No, Your Honor," he said, "there is no objection upon *that* ground."

"Very well," snapped Judge Markham, "the objection, as made, is overruled. Answer the question."

"The policy," said Judge Purley, "as I noticed at the time, or a few minutes later, covered a Buick sedan number 6754093, with a license number 12M1834."

Claude Drumm made a gesture with his hand.

"You may cross-examine the witness, Mr. Mason," he announced.

Perry Mason regarded Judge Purley with a placid smile.

"Judge Purley," he said, "did I understand you to say that when you went into the study you saw the body of Edward Norton lying across the desk?"

"You did *not*," snapped Judge Purley. "I stated that I saw the body of a man who was subsequently identified to me as being that of Edward Norton."

Perry Mason looked crestfallen.

"My mistake," he said.

There was a moment of silence, during which Judge Purley gazed at the courtroom with an air of complacent self-satisfaction, the air of one who has given testimony in a very credible manner, and the manner of one who has confidence in his ability to avoid any trap which can be set for him by cross-examining counsel.

"You see," explained Judge Purley, "I had never personally met Mr. Norton, despite the fact that I was quite friendly with Mr. Crinston and had, upon at least one prior occasion, driven Mr. Crinston to Mr. Norton's house."

Perry Mason seemed to be smiling.

"On how many occasions had you discussed any business matters with Mr. Norton on the telephone?" he asked.

Judge Purley showed his surprise.

"Why, I never talked with the man on the telephone in my life," he said.

"Then you'd never discussed the trust fund of his niece, Frances Celane, with him?"

Judge Purley's eyes bulged with surprise.

"Good heavens, no! Of course not!"

"Had you," asked Perry Mason, "ever discussed this trust fund with anyone else?"

Drumm was on his feet.

"Your Honor, that is objected to, not proper cross-examination, hearsay, incompetent, irrelevant, immaterial. Counsel has simply started upon a round-about way of calling for conversations which could not possibly . . ."

"Sustained!" snapped Judge Markham.

Drumm sat down.

There was silence in the courtroom. Perry Mason's face was expressionless.

"Any further questions?" asked Judge Markham.

"No, Your Honor," announced Perry Mason, to the surprise of the courtroom. "There is no further cross-examination."

TWENTY-ONE

"CALL SERGEANT MAHONEY," said Claude Drumm.

Sergeant Mahoney, attired in a uniform, stepped to the front of the clerk's desk, held up his right hand to be sworn, then took the witness stand.

"Your name is Sergeant E. L. Mahoney, and you were, on the evening of October twenty-third of the present year, acting as desk sergeant at the Central Police Station in this city?" asked Claude Drumm.

"Yes, sir."

"You received a telephone call at about the hour of 11:14?" asked Drumm.

"Yes, sir."

"Just describe that call, Sergeant."

"Mr. Edward Norton called, sir, and . . ."

Perry Mason started to his feet, but Claude Drumm was the one who interrupted the witness.

"Just a moment, Sergeant," he said. "Let me caution you that you are under oath, and are to testify only to the things which you know of your own knowledge. You didn't know that that call came from Edward Norton. You only know that someone called."

"He *said* he was Edward Norton," blurted the sergeant.

There was a ripple of laughter, which ran through the courtroom, and was promptly silenced by a banging of the judge's gavel.

"Just tell what was said to you over the telephone," said Drumm, and glanced sidelong at Perry Mason, waiting for the attorney to object.

But Perry Mason remained placidly indifferent.

Judge Markham said: "Is it claimed that this is part of the *res gestae,* counsellor?"

Drumm looked uncomfortable.

"There is no objection to it, in any event, Your Honor," said Perry Mason.

"Very well," said Judge Markham. "Proceed, Sergeant."

"This call came in, and I noticed the time of it," said Sergeant Mahoney. "It was fourteen minutes past eleven. The man said that he was Edward Norton, and that he wanted to report a stolen automobile, that a Buick sedan, belonging to him, No. 6754093, with a license number of 12M1834 had been stolen, and that he wanted the car picked up and the driver arrested, no matter who the driver might be. I believe that he stated that even if the driver should be related to him, he wanted him or her arrested."

"You may inquire, counsellor," said Claude Drumm, with the smiling gesture of one who had landed a telling blow.

"Did that call come in all at once?" asked Perry Mason, casually.

"How do you mean, sir?"

"I am just testing your recollection," said Perry Mason.

"Of course it came in all at once," said the sergeant.

Perry Mason reached in his brief case and took out a newspaper.

"You made a statement to the newspaper reporters when this matter was more fresh in your mind, Sergeant?"

"Well, I believe I said something to them the next morning, yes."

"And didn't you state at that time that the call was interrupted?"

"Just a moment," said the Deputy District Attorney. "That is not the proper way to lay a foundation for an impeaching question."

"I am just refreshing the recollection of the witness, if the Court please," said Perry Mason.

Sergeant Mahoney made frantic gestures.

Judge Markham smiled and said: "I think from the demeanor of the witness that his recollection has been refreshed. Proceed, Sergeant."

"That's right," said Sergeant Mahoney, "I remember now. The call came in, and he was cut off right in the middle of the conversation— right at the first part of it, I think it was. He gave his name and address and wanted to know if he was talking with the police department, and said he had a crime to report. Then the line went dead. I looked up his telephone number in the book, to call him back, when the call came in again, and he went right along talking. He said he'd been cut off."

"That," said Perry Mason, with emphasis, "is all."

Claude Drumm looked puzzled.

"What's that got to do with it?" he asked sharply.

Judge Markham banged his gavel on the desk.

"Order!" he snapped. "Is there any redirect examination, counsellor?"

"None," said Claude Drumm, but his eyes were thoughtful as he stared at Perry Mason.

"The next witness," said Judge Markham.

"Arthur Crinston," snapped Claude Drumm.

Arthur Crinston arose from a seat within the bar, walked to the clerk, was sworn, and took the witness stand.

"Your name is Arthur Crinston, and you are the surviving partner of the firm of Crinston & Norton, the said firm being composed of yourself and Edward Norton?"

"That is correct, sir."

"Edward Norton is dead?"

"He is, sir."

"Did you see the body of Edward Norton, Mr. Crinston?"

"Yes sir. On the twenty-third day of October of this year."

"At about what time?"

"I saw his body at approximately eleven thirty-five or eleven thirty-six."

"Where was his body?"

"Lying across his desk in the study, with the top of the head crushed in."

"What did you do then?"

"I notified the police."

"Did you see the defendant, Frances Celane, on that night?"

"I did."

"At about what time?"

"At approximately midnight or a little before."

"Did you tell her anything about the death of her uncle?"

"I did."

"Did you mention anything about the reported theft of a Buick automobile?"

"I did."

"Did she make any statement to you at that time as to the said Buick automobile?"

"That can be answered yes or no," said Judge Markham, in a cautioning tone of voice. "It is preliminary merely."

"Yes, she did," said Arthur Crinston.

"At what time was this?"

"At about midnight."

"Who was present?"

"Miss Celane, Mr. Don Graves, and myself."

"There was no one else present?"

"No sir."

"What did she say?"

"She said that she had taken the Buick automobile at about ten forty-five o'clock and gone for a ride, returning at approximately fifteen minutes past twelve, midnight."

"What was Mr. Norton doing the last time you saw him alive, Mr. Crinston?"

"Standing in the window of his study calling down to me."

"What did he say?"

"He asked me if Don Graves could accompany me to the city; that is, to my residence."

"And what did you tell him?"

"I told him that I would have to ask Judge Purley, in whose car I was riding."

"Then what happened?"

"I stepped across to ask Judge Purley, and received an affirmative answer from him to my request. Then I returned to notify Mr. Norton. He was standing in his study—a few feet back from the window at that time. I called up to him that it was all right, and Mr. Graves, who had anticipated Judge Purley's consent, was then coming down the steps from the front doorway to join me."

"Then what happened?"

"Then I got in the front seat of the automobile with Judge Purley, Mr. Don Graves got in the rear seat, we started up the winding road shown on the map, until we came to a certain point, where we turned around and went back to the house. I take it that I cannot state any conversation that took place in the automobile?"

"That is the ruling of the court, Mr. Crinston."

"Very well. I returned in the automobile, re-entered the house, and found Mr. Norton's body as described, whereupon I notified the police."

"Cross-examine," snapped Claude Drumm unexpectedly, turning to Perry Mason.

Perry Mason surveyed Arthur Crinston with an expressionless face for a few seconds, then said abruptly: "You had been in conversation with Mr. Norton during the evening?"

"Yes. I had an appointment and was a few minutes late for that appointment. I arrived there at six minutes past eleven, I think."

"What," asked Perry Mason, "did you talk with Mr. Norton about?"

Arthur Crinston made a swift grimace and shook his head at Perry Mason. The gesture seemed to be one of warning.

Claude Drumm, who had jumped to his feet to object, caught that gesture of warning, and suddenly smiled. He sat down.

Arthur Crinston looked at Judge Markham.

"Answer the question," said Perry Mason.

Arthur Crinston blurted: "*You* don't want to have me answer that question."

Judge Markham banged with his gavel on the desk.

"Is there any objection, Mr. Drumm?" he asked.

The Deputy District Attorney shook his head smilingly. "None whatever," he said. "Let the witness answer the question."

"Answer the question," said Judge Markham.

Crinston fidgeted.

"Your Honor," he blurted, "it isn't to the advantage of the defendant, Frances Celane, that I should testify to what was said, and Perry Mason has reason to know that. I don't know what his idea is in asking any such question . . ."

The gavel of Judge Markham banged upon the desk.

"The witness," he said, in tones of icy frigidity, "will confine his comments to the answers of such questions as may be asked of him. The witness certainly should know that any such statement coming in court, particularly in a trial of this nature, is a contempt of court. The jury are admonished to disregard that statement, and are admonished to disregard any statements of the witnesses except those which are elicited as a part of the testimony. Mr. Crinston, you will answer that question or be held in contempt of court."

"We talked," said Crinston in a low voice, "about an attempt that had been made to blackmail Miss Celane."

A grin of triumph suffused Claude Drumm's face.

"An attempt at blackmail, made by the housekeeper, Mrs. Mayfield?" asked Perry Mason.

The grin faded from Claude Drumm's face. He jumped to his feet. "Your Honor," he said, "that is objected to as incompetent, irrelevant, and immaterial, leading and suggestive. Counsel well knows that Mrs. Mayfield is an important witness for the prosecution in this case, and this is an attempt to discredit her . . ."

"Leading questions are permitted upon cross-examination," said Judge Markham. "You did not object when Counsel asked the witness as to what the conversation consisted of, and since this is cross-examination, I am going to permit the question."

Claude Drumm slowly sat down.

Crinston squirmed uncomfortably in the chair.

"Mrs. Mayfield's name was not mentioned," he said at length, in a low voice.

"You're certain of that?" asked Perry Mason.

"Well," said Crinston, "it *might* have been mentioned as a possibility."

"Oh," said Perry Mason, "so it was mentioned as a possibility? Is that right?"

"It might have been," said Crinston.

Perry Mason abruptly shifted his attack.

"Edward Norton had secured rather a large sum of money during the day of October twenty-third in one thousand dollar bills, had he not, Mr. Crinston?"

"So I understand," said Crinston, surlily.

"You didn't secure that money for him?"

"No, sir."

"Did you go to any of the banks during that day in which the firm of Crinston & Norton had an account?"

Arthur Crinston scowled thoughtfully.

"Yes," he said, "I did."

"Which bank?"

"The Wheeler's Trust and Savings Bank."

"Whom did you talk with there?"

Suddenly Crinston's face changed color.

"I would prefer," he said, "not to answer that question."

Claude Drumm jumped to his feet.

"The question is objected to," he said, "as incompetent, irrelevant and immaterial, and not proper cross-examination."

Perry Mason smiled, a slow, drawling smile.

"Your Honor," he drawled, "if I may present a brief argument?"

"Very well," said Judge Markham.

"This witness has testified on direct examination that he was a surviving partner of Crinston & Norton. I let that question go in, although it probably calls for a conclusion of the witness. But I have the right to cross-examine him as to his activities as a co-partner, and the reasons upon which that conclusion was founded."

"Not at a remote time," said Judge Markham.

"No, sir," said Perry Mason. "That is why I am confining the question to the date of October twenty-third—the day of the death."

Judge Markham stared at Perry Mason with eyes that were suddenly hard and wary.

Mason returned the gaze, his eyes wide with candor.

Claude Drumm was on his feet.

"The partnership affairs have nothing whatever to do with it," he said.

"But," said Judge Markham, "you, yourself, qualified him as a member of a partnership."

"But only for the purpose of showing the intimacy of his acquaintance, Your Honor."

Judge Markham shook his head.

"I am not convinced," he said, "that the question is proper cross-examination, but in a case of this nature I am going to err, if at all, on the side of the defendants. The witness will answer the question."

"Answer the question, Mr. Crinston," said Perry Mason. "Whom did you talk with?"

"With Mr. Sherman, the president."

"And what did you talk with him about?"

"About the partnership business."

"You talked with him about meeting the indebtedness of approximately nine hundred thousand dollars which the partnership had with that bank, did you not; an indebtedness which, as I understand the facts, was evidenced by notes which had been signed by you as an individual alone, isn't that right?"

"No sir, that is not right. Those notes were partnership notes, signed by Crinston & Norton."

"That is, signed by the partnership name of Crinston & Norton, per Arthur Crinston. Isn't that right?"

"I think that is right," said Arthur Crinston. "The main business of the partnership as far as banking activities were concerned, was transacted by me; that is, I signed the partnership name to notes, although in a majority of instances the checks were signed by both of us. No, I'll amend that statement. I guess that the Wheeler's Trust and Savings Bank notes were signed with the partnership name per myself, and that checks were drawn out in the same way."

"You went out to Mr. Norton's house to see him about the maturity of those notes, did you not?"

"That is correct."

"Then," said Perry Mason, "how did it happen that you talked about the blackmailing of Frances Celane by the housekeeper?"

"I didn't say it was by the housekeeper," snapped Arthur Crinston. "I said that her name was mentioned as a possibility."

"I see," said Perry Mason. "My mistake. Go ahead and answer the question."

"Because," said Crinston, "the business matter relating to those notes occupied but a few minutes of our discussion. The question of his niece's being blackmailed weighed very heavily on Mr. Norton's mind, and he insisted upon postponing all further business discussion in order to ask my advice about that."

"And why did he say she was being blackmailed?" asked Perry Mason.

"He thought that she was being blackmailed over something she had done."

"Naturally," said Perry Mason. "Did he mention *what* it was?"

"No, I don't think he did."

"Did he mention what it might have been?"

"He mentioned that she had an ungovernable temper," said Crinston suddenly, and then bit his lip and said: "Wait a minute, I'll withdraw that. I don't think he said that. That was my mistake."

"Your mistake," asked Mason, "or are you trying to protect the defendant, Frances Celane?"

Crinston's face purpled.

"I'm trying to protect her a lot better than you are!" he roared.

Judge Markham's gavel banged upon his desk.

"Mr. Crinston," he said, "the court cautioned you once before. The court now pronounces you in contempt of court, and assesses a fine of one hundred dollars for contempt of court."

Crinston, his face purple, bowed his head.

"Proceed with the case," said Judge Markham.

"Was anything else discussed by you and Mr. Norton, save the matter of indebtedness to the bank, the partnership affairs, and the possibility that his niece was being blackmailed?"

"No, sir," said Arthur Crinston, evidently with relief that the question was no more searching as to the possibilities of the blackmail.

Perry Mason smiled urbanely.

"I may desire to recall Mr. Crinston for further cross-examination later on, Your Honor," he said, "but I have no more questions at the present time."

Judge Markham nodded.

"Any redirect?" he asked.

"Not at this time," said Claude Drumm, "but if counsel reserves the right to recall the witness for further cross-examination, I would like to reserve the right to recall the witness for further redirect examination."

"Granted," snapped Judge Markham. "Proceed."

Claude Drumm raised his voice dramatically.

"Call Mr. Don Graves," he said.

Don Graves arose and pushed his way forward, while the spectators turned to exchange swiftly whispered comments. The murder trial was proceeding with a dispatch which was unusual, and the attorney for the defense seemed to be overlooking many opportunities in his cross-examination. Yet those who knew Perry Mason knew him as one whose trial technique was a by-word among attorneys.

And it was equally apparent that Judge Markham was mystified, as well as the spectators. From time to time, his eyes dwelt upon the placid face of Perry Mason with thoughtful speculation.

Don Graves cleared his throat and looked expectantly at Claude Drumm.

"Your name is Don Graves, and you were employed on the twenty-third of October of this year, and had been employed for some time prior thereto, as the confidential secretary of Mr. Edward Norton?"

"Yes, sir."

"You were with Mr. Norton on the evening of October twenty-third?"

"Yes, sir."

"When did you last see him on that evening?"

"At approximately eleven thirty in the evening."

"You had seen him before that?"

"Oh, yes. Mr. Crinston left about eleven twenty-seven or eleven twenty-eight, and Mr. Norton came out of his private office when Mr. Crinston left. They talked for a minute or two and Mr. Norton asked me to get some papers which Mr. Crinston had at his house."

"Then what happened?" asked Claude Drumm.

"Then Mr. Crinston went downstairs, and Mr. Norton told me to call Mr. Peter Devoe, the chauffeur, and get him to drive me to Crinston's residence. Then, just as I was starting for the stairs, he said: 'Wait a minute. I have another idea,' or words to that effect, and went to the window and called down to Mr. Crinston to ask if I could accompany him.

"Mr. Crinston said that he was with Judge Purley and would have to get Judge Purley's permission, and I, knowing that Judge Purley would give his permission and that time was valuable, ran down the stairs and was just coming out of the front door when Mr. Crinston called up that Judge Purley said he would be glad to accommodate me.

"I ran across and got in Judge Purley's automobile, getting in the rear seat, and then Judge Purley started the automobile and we drove up the winding road until we came to a spot, the approximate location of which Judge Purley has marked on the map."

"And then what happened?"

"At that point," said Don Graves dramatically, "I turned and looked back, and saw through the rear window of the automobile into the study window of Edward Norton."

"And what did you see?" purred Claude Drumm.

"I saw a figure raise a club and strike Mr. Norton on the head."

"Could you recognize who that person was?"

"I thought I could," he said.

"Who did you think it was?" asked Drumm.

"Just a minute," said Perry Mason, "that is objected to as calling for a conclusion of the witness, and as leading and suggestive. The witness has stated that he *thought* he could make the identification."

Judge Markham looked at Perry Mason as though expecting to hear an extended argument upon this crucial point. There was no argument.

He looked at Claude Drumm.

Claude Drumm shrugged his shoulders.

"He has stated that in his opinion he could make an identification," he said. "The word 'thought' is merely a colloquial expression."

"You'd better clear the matter up," said Judge Markham.

"Very well," said Claude Drumm.

"Mr. Graves," he said, "you say that you thought you could identify the witness. Just what do you mean by that?"

"I believe," said Don Graves, "that I know who that man was. I think that I recognized him. I did not see his face clearly, but I think that I could recognize him by the manner in which he held his head, from his shoulders and the general outline of his body."

"That is sufficient, if the court please," said Claude Drumm. "A man doesn't need to see the facial characteristics of another in order to make an identification. The objection goes to the weight, rather than the admissibility of the evidence."

Judge Markham looked expectantly at Perry Mason.

Perry Mason said nothing.

"I will overrule the objection," said Judge Markham. "Answer the question, young man."

"That man was Robert Gleason," said Don Graves in a low voice.

"Was there anyone else in the room?" asked Claude Drumm.

"Yes, sir."

"Who was that other person?"

"A woman, sir, who was attired in a pink garment of some sort."

"Could you see that woman?"

"I saw part of her shoulder, just a bit of her hair, and her arm."

"Could you recognize that woman from what you saw of her?"

Judge Markham interrupted.

"I think, counsellor," he said, "that while I permitted the first identification upon the ground that the objection went to the weight rather than the admissibility of the evidence, that where a witness can see only a relatively small portion of a woman's figure at the distance which was shown upon this map, the objection really should go to the weight as well as the admissibility of the evidence, and I will sustain the objection as to the identity of the woman."

"Your Honor," said Perry Mason softly, "there was no objection made as to the identity of the woman."

"No objection?" said Judge Markham.

"None, Your Honor," said Perry Mason.

"Very well," said Judge Markham, "I shall sustain an objection if one is made."

"There will be none made," said Perry Mason.

A rustle sounded throughout the courtroom.

"Very well," snapped Judge Markham, his face purpling, "answer the question."

"Yes, sir," said Don Graves. "I think that that woman was Frances Celane. I am not as certain in her case as I was in the case of the man, but I think it was Frances Celane. She was dressed like Frances Celane, and the color of her hair, and the contour of her shoulder made me think it was Frances Celane."

"How long have you known Frances Celane?" asked Claude Drumm.

"For more than three years."

"You have lived in the same house with her?"

"Yes, sir."

"Did she, at that time, to your knowledge, have a dress or some garment of the color which you saw upon the woman who was standing in that room?"

"Yes, sir."

"Very well," said Claude Drumm. "What did you do, if anything?"

"I told the other gentlemen what I had seen, and asked them to turn the car around."

"I will strike that out on my own motion," said Judge Markham. "It is incompetent, irrelevant, and immaterial. The question is what the witness did next, with reference to what had taken place in this room. Conversations between parties outside of the presence of the defendant which are not part of the *res gestae* will not be permitted."

"Very well," said Claude Drumm. "Then what happened? What did you do with reference to Mr. Edward Norton?"

"I returned to the house, climbed the stairs to his study, and found his body slumped across the desk, with the top of his head beaten in," said Don Graves.

"Cross-examine," snapped Claude Drumm.

Perry Mason got to his feet and stared slowly and fixedly at Don Graves. An electric tension ran around the courtroom. The spectators sensed that this was to be the crucial part of the trial.

"Your eyes are in good condition?" asked Perry Mason.

"Yes."

"You think that you were able to sit in a speeding automobile at this point on the road, and, in the momentary glance which you had through the rear of the automobile, recognize the occupants of the room in that study?"

"Yes, sir. I know I could."

"How do you know it?"

"Because I saw them at that time, and because in order to test my own ability, I have made subsequent tests."

"The last part of that answer may go out," snapped Judge Markham.

"There was no motion to strike it out," said Perry Mason. "If the court please, I would like to follow that point up."

"Very well," said Judge Markham.

"You say you have made subsequent tests?"

"Yes, sir."

"In an automobile?"

"Yes, sir."

"With occupants in the room?"

"Yes, sir."

"Who were the occupants in the room?"

"Mr. Drumm, the Deputy District Attorney, and two people from his office."

"You were able to recognize those people?"

"Yes, sir. You see, sir, the windows are very wide, and the lighting in that study or office is very good."

"The automobile in which those tests were made wasn't driven very rapidly, was it?" asked Perry Mason.

"Just about the same rate as the automobile in which I was riding on the night of the murder."

"That was Judge Purley's automobile?"

"Yes, sir."

"But you haven't made a test in Judge Purley's automobile, have you?"

"No, sir, in other automobiles."

"Then the tests weren't made under the same conditions; that is, the machine wasn't the same, the window in the rear wasn't the same."

"They were similar," said Don Graves.

Perry Mason stared accusingly at the witness.

"But the tests weren't made under *exactly* the same conditions."

"No, sir."

"Would you," thundered Perry Mason, "*dare* to make a test under the *same* conditions?"

"Objected to as argumentative," snapped Claude Drumm.

"I think," said Judge Markham, "that it may be argumentative, but it has a tendency to show the interest or bias of the witness. The question was, whether or not he would be *willing* to make a test under certain conditions."

"But such a test wouldn't prove anything more than has already been proven," said Drumm.

"The question," said Judge Markham, "is, whether or not he would be willing to make such a test. I think I will permit the witness to answer."

"Answer the question," said Perry Mason.

"Yes, I would be willing to make such a test."

"If Judge Purley will furnish his automobile, *will* you make a test while you are riding in such automobile?"

Claude Drumm was on his feet.

"The question is now different, Your Honor. It is not question now of whether he is willing to make such a test, but if he *will* make such a test."

"Yes," said Judge Markham, "if you desire to object to that question, I think that I shall sustain an objection to it."

Perry Mason turned to face the jury.

"In that event," he said, "there is no further cross-examination."

"No further cross-examination?" asked Claude Drumm.

"No. The fact speaks for itself," snapped Perry Mason. "You are afraid to have a test made under identical conditions."

The gavel of Judge Markham banged sharply on the desk.

"Counsellor," he said, "you will please refrain from personalities and address your remarks to the court, rather than to opposing counsel."

"Your pardon, Your Honor," said Perry Mason, but his voice held no trace of humility, and his eyes twinkled with amusement.

Claude Drumm stared at Perry Mason, and his forehead creased in thought.

"Your Honor," he said, "might I ask at this time for an adjournment until to-morrow morning at ten o'clock? I have been rather surprised at the unexpected progress which this case has made."

"You are no more surprised than the court," said Judge Markham. "Agreeably surprised, I may say. It is customary for murder cases to be drawn out to such prolonged length that it comes as rather a startling innovation to have a case move with such rapidity as this. Your request is granted, Counsellor, and court will adjourn until ten o'clock to-morrow morning, during which time the jury will remember the usual admonition of the court against discussing the case or allowing it to be discussed in their presence."

The gavel banged.

Perry Mason swung about in his chair and turned to face the dark eyes of Frances Celane.

He smiled at her reassuringly.

Rob Gleason, sitting at her side, was haggard and drawn, showing the effects of the ordeal; his posture tense and strained, his eyes filled with a lurking fear.

The girl was calm and collected, her eyes gave no hint of her feelings. Her chin was up, and her head back.

Perry Mason leaned toward her.

"Have confidence in me, please," he said.

Only when she smiled at him was there evident the changes which had taken place in her during the ordeal preliminary to the trial. There was a touch of sadness in the smile; a hint of patience that had not been in her face before. She said nothing, but her smile spoke volumes.

Rob Gleason whispered: "A word with you, sir? And in private, please."

A deputy sheriff moved forward, touched Frances Celane on the shoulder. Perry Mason said to him: "Just a moment, please," and led Rob Gleason to one side.

Gleason spoke in hoarse whispers.

"Looks pretty black, doesn't it?"

Perry Mason shrugged his shoulders.

"If," whispered Gleason, "it's going against us, I want to take it all."

"Meaning?" asked the lawyer.

"Meaning," husked Gleason, "that I want to confess and take the sole blame. I want to free Fran of any responsibility."

Steadily, purposefully, remorselessly, Mason's eyes studied Gleason's features.

"It hasn't come to that yet, Gleason," he said. "And it won't. Keep your mouth shut."

He turned and signaled the waiting deputy that the conference was over.

TWENTY-TWO

PERRY MASON SAT at his desk in the office, looking across at Harry Nevers.

Nevers, with his hair trimmed, his face clean-shaven, wearing a newly pressed suit, twisted his legs up over the arm of the leather chair, and let his eyes study Perry Mason in bored appraisal.

"Sure I'll do you a favor," he said, "if it's anything I can do. The office is friendly toward you. You gave us a nice break on Frances Celane's surrender."

"All right," said Perry Mason, his eyes hard and watchful. "I want you to bear down heavy on the fact that the District Attorney has conducted secret tests to determine whether Don Graves could be telling the truth."

Nevers nodded and yawned.

"I suppose you mean that you want to have an intimation between the lines, that the D. A. wouldn't have had those tests made unless he'd had a little doubt in his own mind about the testimony."

Perry Mason nodded.

"Well," said Harry Nevers, in that expressionless monotone which was so characteristic of him, "that's already been done. I gave you that much of a break in advance."

"All right," said Mason. "Now here's something else. I want you to emphasize the events that happened just before court adjourned; the fact that the District Attorney refused to make a test under identical circumstances."

Nevers inclined his head in a gesture of assent.

"All right," he said, "what's back of it?"

"Back of what?" asked the attorney.

"Back of this test business."

"You can see for yourself," said Mason. "The District Attorney conducted tests. That shows he had some doubt of the ability of the witness to see the occupants of that room, as he claims he did. Furthermore, he has now refused to conduct a test, or permit a test to be conducted under exactly identical circumstances."

"Baloney," said the reporter. "That's a good line to hand to the jury, but I'm asking you for the lowdown."

"There isn't any lowdown," Mason told him.

"The hell there ain't," said Nevers. "Don't think I'm going to pull chestnuts out of the fire for you. You've given me a break in this case, and I'm willing to give you a break. But don't think I'm going to run around playing cat's paw for you, and get my fingers burnt unless I know whether the chestnut is worthwhile reaching for."

Mason shook his head.

"You've got me wrong, Harry," he said. "I simply want to have a test arranged under exactly identical circumstances."

"Well," said Nevers, "we'll talk that over for a while. What do you mean by exactly identical circumstances?"

"Well," said Perry Mason, "here's the way I want the test arranged. I want it so that I'm riding in the front seat of the automobile with Judge Purley. I'll be in the position that Arthur Crinston occupied. I'm perfectly willing to allow Drumm, the Deputy District Attorney, to sit in the back seat with Don Graves."

Harry Nevers stared at him with eyes that showed a glint of surprise.

"Have you gone crazy?" he asked.

"No," said Perry Mason shortly.

"Why you poor damned innocent babe in the woods!" said Nevers. "Don't let Claude Drumm fool you with any of that bushwa about being fair. He's one of the crookedest campaigners in the game. He's the one that ditched the notes that contained the first statement Don Graves made to the police—the one in which he said he recognized Devoe as the murderer, and didn't say anything about there being some other person in the room."

"That's all right," said Mason. "What if he did?"

"Why, simply this: He'll have things arranged so that Don Graves could be blindfolded and still make a one hundred percent identification. If you let him sit within nudging distance of Don Graves or where he can whisper or signal to him, you're just a plain fool."

Perry Mason shook his head and smiled.

"All right, then," said Nevers, "tell me what's up or you don't get a bit of coöperation out of us."

"There are times," said Perry Mason, "when a person has to use a little strategy—for instance when one is stalking a flock of geese it's always advisable to get behind a horse to walk up on the geese."

"What does that mean?" Nevers inquired.

"It means that geese are wild things, and they take flight whenever they see something they can't understand, or something that looks like a hunter," said Perry Mason. "But they're accustomed to the sight of a horse and when they see a horse walking around them, they don't pay any attention to it."

"So you're walking behind a horse?" asked Harry Nevers.

Perry Mason nodded his head.

Nevers slid his feet off the arm of the chair, stood up, and looked steadily at Perry Mason.

"Look here," he said, "you've got a reputation among lawyers of being a fast worker, and a two-fisted campaigner. You've got the reputation of jockeying a case around so that you get in a position to give one knock-out punch and then concentrate on that one punch. You don't go around wasting your energy in a lot of little taps that don't mean anything. Now I want to know what the knock-out punch is in this case."

"I'm not certain yet," Perry Mason told him. "There may not be any."

"The hell there ain't," said Nevers. "Look at the way you've tried this case. You have sat back and let the prosecution put in every damned bit of evidence they wanted. You haven't cross-examined the witnesses so as to bring out anything that's to the advantage of either of the defendants."

"What do you mean by that?" inquired Perry Mason in low, ominous tones.

"Keep your shirt on," Nevers drawled tonelessly. "You aren't fooling me any with that stuff. You know as well as I do that Don Graves made a statement to the police the night of the murder, in which he either said, or at least intimated, that the person who struck the blow was Devoe, the chauffeur. He said there wasn't a woman in the room at the time the blow was struck, or at least he failed to say he saw a woman in the room. You've gone ahead and let him testify in this case, and haven't brought that out, or even intimated that he ever made a contradictory statement."

"It wouldn't do any good if I did," Perry Mason said. "The notes of that statement have been destroyed, and Graves would swear, either that he never made such a statement, or that Frances Celane asked him to give her a break, and he tried to leave her out of it."

"Baloney," said Nevers.

Perry Mason slid open a drawer in his desk and took out a flask of whiskey.

"I'll tell you this much, Harry," he said. "If you'll play ball with me, you won't be sorry."

"Meaning by that?" asked Nevers.

"Meaning by that you can stick around on this test that's made and save a big slice of the front page for a blow-off."

Harry Nevers pushed back the glass which Mason had handed him with the bottle, and tilted the bottle to his lips. He took half a dozen swallows, then handed the bottle back to the attorney.

"When's this blow-off going to come?" he asked. "Right after the test?"

"I don't think so," said Perry Mason. "I think I'll have to do a little manipulation."

The reporter spoke as though he might have been thinking out loud.

"We can force the D. A. into making that test," he said. "It's a test that is bound to come out all right. But you've got something up your sleeve. You're trying this murder case with no more apparent fight about you than as though you were covering a coroner's inquest. You're going through it with a hop, skip and jump, and letting the prosecution get in all the damaging evidence they want. Everybody in town is talking about what a poor defense you're putting up."

"Yes?" asked Mason, raising his eyebrows.

"Oh forget it!" said Nevers, with a trace of feeling in his voice. "You know damned well they are. A kid out of law school would have tried this case better than you're trying it. Everybody is commenting on it. The town is divided into two camps—those that think you're shrewd as the devil, and have something up your sleeve, and those that think you've just been lucky on your other cases, and haven't got anything on the ball. Naturally, it's an important case. A woman who's got as many millions as Frances Celane at stake; a secret marriage; a sex angle, and all that sort of stuff makes front page news. It's the opportunity of your life to drag this case along, fighting every inch of the way, keeping your name on the front page of the newspaper for two or three weeks. In place of that you're acting like a dub. For a murder case, this thing is streaking through the court like a greased pig going between a farmer's legs."

Perry Mason corked the whiskey bottle, and slid it back in the drawer of his desk.

Nevers looked at him searchingly.

"Going to say anything?" he asked.

"No," said Perry Mason.

Nevers grinned and wiped the back of his hand across his lips.

"Okay," said Nevers. "I've done my duty. I'll tell the city editor I tried my damnedest to get something out of you. Maybe I'll fake some piece of inside information that the readers can pick out between the lines."

Perry Mason took the reporter's arm and escorted him to the door of the outer office.

"Listen, Harry," he said, "if you fake anything, be sure you fake it right."

Perry Mason paused in the doorway, suddenly turned and faced the reporter.

"All right," he said, "I'll give you a bit of inside information. Rob Gleason is intending to make a complete confession and take the blame for the crime, exonerating Frances Celane."

Nevers stared at him.

"You can't give me that for publication," he said.

"Why not?" asked Perry Mason.

"It would be violating every professional confidence."

"That's all right," said Mason easily, "you're not using my name, that's all. Simply put it down as coming from a source that is close to the inside."

"My God!" said Nevers. "That would be the worst kind of libel if we couldn't back it up!"

"You can back it up," said Mason. "If anybody calls you on it, you can disclose the source of your information."

"Meaning that it came from you?"

"Meaning that it came from me," Mason told him.

Nevers took a deep breath.

"Listen, Perry," he said, "I've seen 'em come, and I've seen 'em go. I've been in on all kinds of cases, interviewed all kinds of people. I've seen those that were foxy, and those that just thought they were foxy. I've seen those that were dumb, and didn't know it, and those that were dumb, and thought they were smart, but you've got the whole world cheated. This is the damnedest interview with a lawyer I ever had!"

Mason placed his right hand between the reporter's shoulder blade and gently pushed him into the outer office.

"All right," he said, "I've given you a break. Give me one."

Frank Everly was standing in the outer office, his manner filled with impatience.

"Did you want to see me?" asked Perry Mason.

Everly nodded.

"Come in," Mason told him.

Everly walked into the inner office. Perry Mason stood in the door until Harry Nevers had gone out through the outer door, then Mason closed the door of the inner office, and turned to face Everly.

Everly coughed and averted his eyes.

"Didn't the case move rather expeditiously, Mr. Mason?" he asked.

Mason smiled at him with patient, tired eyes.

"In other words," he said, "you've been hearing some comments that I've stubbed my toe on the defense, and the prosecution is walking all over me, is that it?"

Everly turned red and said in a choked voice: "I didn't say anything like that, Mr. Mason."

"Did you ever hear the story," asked Perry Mason, in a kindly tone of voice, "of the man who brought suit against his neighbor, claiming to have been bitten by the neighbor's dog? The neighbor filed an answer in which he denied that his dog was vicious, denied that the dog had bitten the man, and denied that he ever had a dog."

"Yes," said Frank Everly, "I've heard that yarn. It's a classic around law school."

"All right," said Perry Mason. "The defense in that case became humorous because it took in too much territory. Now, when you've got a doubtful case, it's all right to try and have two strings to your bow. But remember that when you have two strings on a bow, while increasing the factor of safety, you lose the efficiency of the weapon. A bow that has two strings won't break a string, but it won't shoot an arrow one quarter of the distance that it would if it only had one string to it."

"You mean you're sacrificing everything in this case to concentrate on some one point?" asked the law clerk.

"Yes," said Perry Mason, "the innocence of Frances Celane and Rob Gleason is virtually shown by the evidence as it exists at the present time. The guilt of the defendants simply cannot be proved beyond a reasonable doubt. But I want to do more than raise a reasonable doubt in the minds of the jurors. I want to make a complete solution of the case."

Frank Everly stared at Perry Mason with wide, incredulous eyes.

"My heavens!" he said. "I thought that everything that went in to-day clinched the guilt of Frances Celane and Rob Gleason. I thought that unless we could break down the stories of some of those witnesses, we could just as well figure on a verdict of first degree murder."

Mason shook his head wearily.

"No," he said, "the big point I wanted in the case has already gone in. What I'm trying to do now is to crash that point home to the jury in such a dramatic manner they'll never forget it. And remember this—I've got Claude Drumm so badly rattled the way that case is going that he's on the verge of panic right now. He figures I must have an ace up my sleeve somewhere, or I wouldn't be giving him all the breaks."

"The jury," suggested Frank Everly, "looked rather unsympathetic."

"Of course they looked unsympathetic," said Perry Mason. "And they'll probably look more unsympathetic. You notice what Claude Drumm is doing. He's putting in the *corpus delicti* with just a smattering of testimony. Just before he gets ready to rest his case, he'll start introducing photographs of the dead body slumped over the desk, of the bloody blotter, of the insurance policy, spattered with the life blood of the dead man, and all of that stuff. Then, he'll throw the case into our laps, and leave us to face a jury that's hardened its heart to bring in a death penalty verdict."

"What I don't see," said Everly, "is how you're going to stop him."

"I'm not going to try to stop him," smiled Perry Mason, "I'm going to head him off."

Della Street walked into the room.

"Mr. Drake is out there," she said, "and says it's important."

Perry Mason smiled at her.

"He'll have to wait just a minute," he said, "I'm explaining something to Frank Everly."

Della Street looked at Perry Mason with eyes that were warm with tenderness.

"I can remember," she said softly, "when I made you explain something to me. After that, I've had enough faith in you so I don't need any explanations."

Perry Mason watched her with speculative eyes.

"You've read the papers?" he asked.

"The afternoon papers, yes."

"And you know how the trial is *going?*"

"Yes."

"You gathered that I was putting up a pretty weak defense?"

She stiffened slightly, and looked accusingly at Frank Everly.

"Who said that?" she asked.

"It's intimated in the newspapers," said Perry Mason.

"Well," said Della Street, "I just made a bet of half of my month's salary, with Paul Drake, that you were going to get both defendants acquitted. That shows how much faith I've got in you."

"Then," said Perry Mason, "Drake must have some bad news. You two get out of here and let me talk with him. You know he's doing some work for me on this case. He's probably got some inside information. It wasn't very sporting of him to bet on his inside information."

"That's all right," Della Street said. "He was square about it. He told me he had some inside information."

"Did he tell you what it was?"

"No, he just said he had it, and I told him I had some too."

"What did you have?" asked Perry Mason, staring speculatively at her.

"Faith in you," she said.

Mason waved his hand.

"All right," he said, "you folks get out and let me talk with Drake. We'll see what he's got to say."

Drake came into the inner office, sat down, grinned, and rolled a cigarette.

"Well," he said, "I've got the lowdown for you."

"All right," Perry Mason said, "what is it?"

"The rough shadow did it," said Drake.

"Never mind the methods," said Mason. "I want the facts."

"Well," said Drake, "the story goes like this. This Mrs. Mayfield is a hard-boiled baby."

"I knew she was," said Mason. "She tried to hold me up a couple of times."

"Yes, I got all the lowdown on that, too," said Drake. "The only trouble is, Perry, that it looks like hell for your clients."

"How do you mean?"

"Well, in the first place, Mrs. Mayfield doesn't know quite as much as she tried to pretend she did. She made the mistake of going to bed at the wrong time. She went to bed just about fifteen or twenty minutes before the murder was committed. But she'd spent the evening snooping around.

"It all starts in with the fact that she found out Gleason and Frances Celane were married. She started in trying to capitalize on that knowledge. She took quite a bit of money from Frances Celane; I don't know how much, around ten thousand dollars, I think. And then, in some way, Edward Norton got wise that Frances Celane was paying blackmail. He got her in and tried to make her tell him whom she was paying money to and why. Naturally, she didn't dare to let him know. But Norton was a pretty obstinate individual, and, in order to find out, he shut off the girl's allowance. That put her in the position of having no money with which to pay any blackmail.

"On the other hand, Mrs. Mayfield said that she could capitalize on the information elsewhere, and if Frances Celane wouldn't give her money, she was going to sell the information to some of the charitable institutions who would benefit by the knowledge.

"Of course, this was all bluff, but Frances Celane didn't know it. The whole situation came to a head on the night of the murder. Frances Celane had a stormy interview with Norton, and they quarreled bitterly. Norton said that before he went to bed that night he was going to execute a written document terminating the trust and giving to Frances Celane the annuity provided by the terms of the trust, and letting the balance go to charity.

"Whether that was a bluff on his part or not I don't know. Anyhow, that's what he said. Then Mrs. Mayfield went to bed. Next morning Frances Celane had money, lots of it. She gave Mrs. Mayfield twenty-eight thousand dollars to keep quiet. Mrs. Mayfield promised she would.

"Rob Gleason was there in the house that night, and participated in at least a part of the interview with Norton. Norton was furious, and accused the girl of all sorts of things. She got mad and used language that must have raised a blister on his ears.

"Afterwards, Gleason went down to the girl's room. That was after Crinston came, and before the murder. Along about that time Mrs. Mayfield went to bed. She doesn't know exactly what happened, except that she's certain Frances Celane didn't go out in the Buick automobile. Therefore, she knows that the alibi Frances Celane was trying to make was false.

"She went to you and tried to shake you down for money to keep Frances Celane out of it. You turned her down hard, so she started concentrating on the girl, and actually collected from her. Then she found out that the money she'd taken from Frances Celane was in thousand dollar bills that were numbered consecutively, and knew that these bills would be traced in the event that she tried to change them for smaller bills. So she has these bills hidden, and has tried to create the impression that Frances Celane gave you twenty-eight thousand dollars to apply on a fee. She has told the District Attorney's office that that is what happened, and the District Attorney's office has been trying to locate the twenty-eight thousand dollars. They've made examinations at your banks, and have even gone so far as to search the office. They have now come to the conclusion that you must be carrying the twenty-eight thousand dollars on your person.

"The District Attorney is intending to use her as a surprise witness. She's going to testify as to the falsity of the girl's claim that she was out in the Buick automobile, and also to the quarrel that took place.

"It's the theory of the prosecution that a bitter quarrel was interrupted by Arthur Crinston; that the two people hatched out this murder plot and waited until Crinston had left to carry it into execution; that, as soon as Crinston drove away, they dashed up to the office and killed Mr. Norton, then planted the evidence in Pete Devoe's room in order to make it appear Devoe was the guilty party, in the event the officers didn't fall for the jimmied window and the footprints in the soft soil."

"How about Graves?" asked Perry Mason. "Have you done anything with him?"

"I've done lots with him. That girl has turned him inside out. He's going to be a bad man for you to handle, but he tells the girl that he's trying to protect Frances Celane, or that he *was* trying to protect her until the District Attorney brought pressure to bear on him."

"Look here," Mason said, "my theory of this case is that Norton *gave* Fran Celane that money before Crinston called. Now, Graves must have some information that'll support that theory."

"That," said Drake, "is the worst part of his testimony. He says he could hear every word of the conversation; that Norton took out his wallet and showed the girl forty thousand dollars, telling her he had originally gotten the money to give her, but that he wasn't going to give her anything except a small amount for current expenses. Then he took out two one thousand dollar bills and handed them to her.

"Don Graves has the idea the girl took the one thousand dollar bills, and that she and Gleason planted *those* one thousand dollar bills in the pocket of Devoe, the chauffeur, while Crinston was talking with Norton; that the girl and Gleason came back afterwards and killed Norton, taking the balance of the money from his wallet to use for the purpose of bribing the housekeeper to silence and paying you a sufficient cash retainer so you would interest yourself in the case. That's the theory Graves has.

"The District Attorney had things planned so that most of this would come out on cross-examination. He was going to slap you in the face with it. The fact that you've restricted your cross-examination so much has got Drumm worried. He's going to try and bring out all of this stuff on redirect examination now, asking permission to recall the witnesses."

Perry Mason stretched his long arms, stared at the detective, and laughed.

"Paul," he said, "there are times when caution is a vice."

"What do you mean by that?" Paul Drake asked.

"I mean," said Perry Mason, "that at times it is wise to stake everything on one dramatic blow, one crashing knock-out punch. I've only got one string to my bow in this case. If it breaks, I'm finished. But if it doesn't break, I'm going to shoot an arrow right through the bull's-eye of the whole case."

Drake said: "Well, Perry, if you can figure this thing out, you can do a lot more than I can. The more I see of it, the more mixed up and confused it looks."

Perry Mason started pacing the floor back and forth.

"The thing that I'm afraid of," he said, "is that I'm not keeping my real objective sufficiently concealed."

"How do you mean?" the detective inquired.

"I'm stalking a bunch of geese behind a horse," said Perry Mason, "and I'm afraid the horse may not be big enough to give me the concealment I want."

Paul Drake started for the door.

"Listen," he said, as he paused, with a hand on the knob of the door, "don't worry about that. I've seen a lot of murder cases in my time, and I've talked with a lot of lawyers who thought they had a point when they didn't have. If you think you're going to be able to save either one of your clients in this case, you've got more optimism than I have. I just bet half of Della Street's salary for this month, that your clients were going to be convicted, and, after talking with you, I'm going out and try and get a bet for the other half. That shows how much confidence I've got."

As he closed the door, Perry Mason was standing in the center of the office, with his feet spread wide apart, his jaw thrust forward, heavy shoulders squared, staring in steady concentration at the closing door.

TWENTY-THREE

HEADLINES STREAMED ACROSS the front page of the *STAR*.

"WITNESS TO MILLIONAIRE'S MURDER REFUSES TO MAKE TEST."

Perry Mason, with the paper propped up in front of him on the table, cracked his three-minute eggs and smiled with satisfaction. Down below the large headlines were smaller headlines:

"DISPUTE OVER VISION OF STATE'S STAR WITNESS. DE-FENSE CHALLENGES TO MAKE TEST AND PROSECUTION RE-FUSES."

Perry Mason salted and peppered his eggs, dropped in a square of butter, reached for a slice of crisp toast, and chuckled.

He read the verbatim account of the trial, noticed that the challenge which he had hurled at the prosecution was printed in black-faced type, finished his breakfast, folded the newspaper, and went to his office.

"Any news?" he asked Della Street.

She regarded him with a wistful, half-maternal smile on her lips.

"You've got it in your pocket," she said.

He grinned at her.

"If the District Attorney refuses to accept the challenge now, I've got the case won in front of the jury," he said.

"What will you do if he *accepts* the challenge?" she wanted to know.

Perry Mason walked to the window and stared thoughtfully out at the morning sunshine.

"Now that," he remarked, "calls for another question. Did you double your bet with Paul Drake?"

"Yes."

"Good girl!" he said.

"You think the D. A.'ll consent to the test?" she asked.

"Yes."

"How are you going to determine that it's a fair test?"

"I can't," he told her, "but there's no harm in trying."

"Well," she told him, "you've got some good advertisement in this case, anyway. Every morning newspaper is speculating what it is you've got up your sleeve. You're referred to a dozen times as 'The Old Fox of the Courtroom,' and most of the reporters state that the chief trial deputy was plainly worried at the manner in which the case was expedited."

"You mean," he told her, "the newspapers figure I couldn't possibly be as dumb as I seem."

She laughed. "I'm betting on you," she said.

"The D. A.'s got a couple of surprise witnesses," Perry Mason said.

"Surprise to whom?" she inquired.

"That's the question," grinned Perry Mason, and walked to his inside office.

He had no sooner closed the door than the telephone rang.

"This is Drumm on the line now," said the voice of Della Street.

"Hello," said Perry Mason.

"Good morning, counsellor. This is Drumm speaking. I have been thinking over your demand for a test of the vision of Don Graves, and have decided to consent to making a test under exactly identical circumstances. I shall ask the court for an adjournment over the week end to enable the test to be completed and thought I would let you know."

"Nice of you," said Mason.

"Not at all," snapped Drumm.

Mason chuckled.

"I meant letting me know," he said.

"Oh," said Drumm.

"Have you any plans worked out for making the test?"

"I will announce that in court," said Drumm. "Good-by."

Perry Mason was still chuckling as he slipped the receiver back on its hook.

Perry Mason pressed the button which called Frank Everly to his office.

"Everly," he said, "there's going to be a continuance granted in that trial this morning, so that arrangements can be completed for a test which is to be made. I'm not going up to court, but am going to send you up, to be there and arrange for the continuance. There will be nothing except the formality of getting the case continued over the week end. Drumm will undoubtedly have some scheme worked out under which he'll want the test made and he'll try to rush you into a consent to that scheme, while you are there in court in front of the jury.

"Simply tell him that you were sent up to represent me for the purpose of consenting to the continuance, and that you have no authority to conclude the terms under which the test is to be made. That will necessitate his getting in touch with me when we are *not* in front of a jury."

Frank Everly nodded his approval, and there was a look of admiration in his eyes.

"You forced him into it, eh?"

"I don't know. He's consenting to the test. That's all I want. I don't care *why* he's doing it."

"And by this means," said Everly, "you keep from having to quibble over the details in front of the jury?"

"Exactly," smiled Perry Mason. "Tell him that I'll be in my office this afternoon to arrange the details of the test with him, or that I'll meet him at any mutually satisfactory place. Be sure when you make the statement that you do it with an air of the utmost candor and frankness. The jury will be watching you closely and there's been a little too much talk in the newspapers about my being an old fox."

"Okay, Chief," said Everly, and swung out of the office, his face flushed with enthusiasm.

Perry Mason got Harry Nevers on the telephone.

"Just wanted to let you know," said Mason, "that the Deputy District Attorney just called up and told me he was going to consent to a continuance over the week end this morning, so that a test could be made."

The voice of Harry Nevers sounded in a husky, bored monotone over the telephone.

"I can go you one better on that," he said. "I was just going to call you and give you a tip. The D. A.'s office has a scheme framed up for that test. They're going to put it up to you in front of the jury. You won't like it, but you won't dare to argue with it in front of the jury."

"All right," Perry Mason said, "I can raise you one on that. I'm not even going to be in in court. I've sent my assistant up to consent to a continuance. He hasn't any authority to stipulate in regard to the conditions of the test."

Harry Nevers laughed. "That sounds a little more like it," he said. "Will the court order the test?"

"No," Mason said. "I don't think the court will want to have anything to do with it. It's something that will have to be handled by stipulation. We'll make the test and then let the witnesses testify Monday morning."

"When are you going to figure on the details of the test?" asked the reporter.

"Probably right after the court adjourns," Mason told him. "Drumm will get in touch with me. I thought I'd give you a ring and let you know that I can't control the publicity that comes out of the D. A's office, but as far as I'm concerned you're going to have an exclusive on the details just as soon as I reach an agreement with the District Attorney's office."

Harry Nevers gave a dry chuckle.

"I guess," he said, "it's a good thing that I had the photographer get a couple of pictures of you when he was over in the office. Something seems to tell me we will be running them about Tuesday morning, or in the evening editions Monday night."

"There's one other thing I want you to do for me," Mason said.

"Gee, you're full of those suggestions," the reporter told him.

"That's all right. This is a simple thing."

"All right, shoot."

"When that test is arranged, I'm going to have things fixed so that Drumm and I will be downstairs in the automobile, and Graves will be upstairs. We'll summon him by some kind of a signal. When we give that signal, I want you to detain Graves up there in that room."

"For how long?" asked Nevers.

"As long as you can."

"What's the idea of that?"

"I want to get him rattled."

"You can't rattle that bird. He's a foxy guy, if I ever saw one."

"He may think he's foxy, but he can be rattled just the same. I want you to put up some proposition to him that will hold him behind until he has to appeal to the District Attorney."

"Now," said the reporter, "you're asking something that's making me suspicious."

"It doesn't need to," Mason told him. "If you'll do that, I'll give you a break afterwards so that you can claim you participated in the final result."

"Maybe I don't want to participate in the final result," said Nevers. "Those final results sometimes ain't so hot."

"You won't have to unless you want to," Mason pointed out. "I'll take *all* the responsibility. You can share in the credit."

"I think," Nevers told him, "I'd better come over and talk this thing over with you a little bit."

Mason chuckled.

"I knew you wouldn't forget it," he said.

"Forget what?" asked the reporter suspiciously.

"That bottle of whiskey in my desk," said the attorney, and slipped the receiver back on the hook.

TWENTY-FOUR

THE NORTON MANSION blazed with light, every window in the place was illuminated. More than a dozen automobiles were parked along the curb, or crowded into the driveway. Men came and went through the open door, and four or five police officers strutted importantly about the premises.

Up in the study where Edward Norton had been murdered, Claude Drumm stared speculatively at Perry Mason.

"I don't know what you could ask for that is more fair than this," he said.

"Well," Perry Mason told him, "it doesn't seem particularly complete to me as a test. Don Graves has only a fifty percent chance of guessing wrong even if he were blindfolded."

"I don't see what you're getting at," said Claude Drumm with purposeful stupidity.

"You've got two women here," said Perry Mason, "one in a black dress and one in a pink dress. You've got three men, all of whom are known to Graves. Now the idea is, as I understand it, that Judge Purley will drive his car up the roadway at exactly the same rate of speed, as nearly as he can remember, that he drove it on the night of the murder. When the car reaches a certain position in the roadway, Judge Purley is to shout: 'Look!' And at that time Graves is to turn and look.

"After we have started up the roadway, the figures will arrange a pantomime. One of the three will stand with a club in his hand, and one of the women will stand so that her head, shoulder and arm are visible to a person going up the roadway."

"That is correct," said Drumm.

"Very well," said Perry Mason. "Now the point that I am making is this: As far as the men are concerned, if Graves simply guessed, he would stand one chance in three of being right. As far as the women are concerned, if he simply guessed, he would stand an even chance of being right."

"Well," said Drumm, "you can't ask to have conditions any more favorable to your side of the case than they were at the time of the murder. Now there were only two women in the house at that time. There was Mrs. Mayfield, the housekeeper, and Frances Celane, your client. Now, it's conceded that there was a woman in the room at the time of the murder . . ."

"No it isn't," snapped Perry Mason.

"Well, according to my theory of the case, and according to the testimony of Don Graves, a disinterested witness, there was," said Drumm, "and, if the test is going through, that has got to stand. Now that woman who was in the room either had to be Mrs. Mayfield or Miss Celane. Similarly, there were three men who might have committed the murder. There was Pete Devoe, the chauffeur, who was drunk when we found him, but who, nevertheless, was under suspicion; there was Rob Gleason, the defendant in the action, and Purkett, the butler. One of those three men must have been the one to swing the club."

"That," said Mason, "is taking for granted that the evidence of the footprints under the window, and the window that had been jimmied open, is evidence that was planted."

"Of course it is," said Drumm. "You wouldn't want us to have the whole city standing here in the room because there might have been someone in the city who had broken into the house. You can't have this thing all *your* way."

"I should have it enough my way so that we can tell whether Graves uses his eyes, or whether it's just a lucky guess."

Claude Drumm showed a glint of triumph in his eyes.

"I have arranged this test," he said, "under circumstances which are identical to those which surrounded the commission of the crime. This test is made as the result of a challenge by you. Now, if you are afraid to have Graves go ahead with it, all you have got to do is to say so, and we'll call the test off, because you didn't dare to let the witness go through with it."

Mason shrugged his shoulders.

"Very well," he said, "if you're going to put it on that ground, go ahead."

The glint of triumph which had been in Drumm's eyes became a light of victory, and he grinned with blatant assurance.

"All right," he said to the compact group that had gathered about the two men, "I think you two gentlemen understand the situation perfectly. We are to go up the hill in the car. I will be seated in the back seat with Mr. Graves. Mr. Mason, the attorney for the defendants, will be seated in the front seat beside Judge Purley.

"After the car has started up the hill, you gentlemen of the press will select one of these women, who will stand so that her head, neck, shoulder and arm will be visible through the window, to anyone standing on the curve in the road at the point where Graves looks back. You will also select one of the three men, each of whom is attired in a distinctly different suit of clothes, to stand with a club in his hand, leaning over the chair in which Edward Norton was sitting when he was killed.

"I think that covers the situation. The reputation and integrity of Judge Purley will be sufficient to guarantee that whatever may happen in the automobile will not subsequently be distorted by either party."

Perry Mason said: "Just a minute. Before Don Graves leaves this room I want to have a confidential word with Judge Purley."

Drumm looked at him suspiciously.

"Not unless I am along," he said. "This is a test, and if you are going to have any confidential words with anyone, I'm going to hear what they are."

"I have no objection to your listening," said Perry Mason, "but naturally, inasmuch as this is a test, I *don't* want Don Graves to hear it."

"Very well," said Drumm. "You can wait here, Graves, until we call you."

"We'll blow the horn on the automobile," said Perry Mason, "when we are ready."

In frigidly dignified silence, the two opposing attorneys walked down the broad stairs, through the front door, and to the automobile where Judge Purley sat in ponderous dignity, surrounded by flashlight photographers, his face wearing an expression of satisfaction which he endeavored to conceal beneath the cloak of a judicial and ponderous dignity.

"Are you ready, gentlemen?" he asked.

"It is understood," said Perry Mason, "that I am to sit in the front seat with Judge Purley; that you, Mr. Drumm, are to sit in the rear seat with Don Graves?"

"That is so understood," said Drumm.

"Under those circumstances," said Perry Mason, "I am going to ask that you remove your glasses."

"That I what?" snapped the Deputy District Attorney.

"That you remove your glasses," Perry Mason said. "You will readily understand that if you are wearing your glasses so that your vision is fully corrected, and you should turn at the same time that Don Graves turns, it *might* be that by some involuntary exclamation or motion, you would signal Don Graves which one of the three men you thought was holding the club. In which case I should be having a test made with two pairs of eyes instead of one."

"That sir," said Claude Drumm, "is an insult to my veracity."

"No," said Perry Mason, "it is no such thing. It is merely a matter of precaution against an involuntary betrayal."

"I refuse to consent to it," said Drumm.

"Very well," said Perry Mason, "I shall not insist. I have merely mentioned the matter. One other thing is that I am going to ask Judge Purley to keep his eyes straight ahead on the road."

"No," said Drumm, "I am not going to consent to that condition, because when Judge Purley was driving the car on the night the murder was committed, and Don Graves gave his exclamation, it was only natural that Judge Purley should have looked back to see what it was that had caused the exclamation, and in doing this, he naturally slowed down the car, which gave Graves opportunity for a much longer and steadier look."

Perry Mason sighed wearily, after the manner of one who has been out-generated.

"Very well," he said, "summon Graves."

Judge Purley pressed the button of the horn on the automobile.

They waited a few minutes, and Perry Mason reached over and again pressed the button of the horn.

There was still no Graves, and Judge Purley pushed his left palm imperatively against the button on the steering post of the car, looking expectantly up at the window.

There was a commotion for a moment, and then Don Graves stood in the window and shouted: "One of these newspaper reporters wants to change the conditions of the test."

Claude Drumm gave an exclamation, slammed open the door of the car, strode across the street, and stood under the window. "The conditions of that test were fully arranged when we left the room," he said. "Don't discuss the matter with any of the newspaper reporters. If they can't coöperate in this thing they'll be excluded. Come down here at once!"

"Very well, sir," Don Graves said, and left the window.

Almost at once Harry Nevers thrust out his head and called: "This test isn't fair. We should have the right to have one of the men stand where Graves claims the woman was standing, if we want to. That would determine whether Graves could actually see that the other occupant of the room was a woman. It might have been a man."

"In a pink negligee, eh?" sneered Drumm. "Now listen, the only function that you gentlemen have is to pick which one of the three men, and which one of the two women, will stand in that position. That was definitely understood, and that is the condition of the test. If an attempt is to be made to change it, I will call off the test."

"Oh, very well," said Nevers, "have it your own way. But it doesn't seem fair to me."

Don Graves came down the stairs, left the front door, and said in a low voice to Claude Drumm: "The man is drunk. He made a nuisance of himself up there, but I didn't want to offend him because I didn't want his newspaper to roast me."

"All right," snapped Drumm, "leave him to me. Are we ready?"

"All ready," said Perry Mason.

They took their positions in the automobile for the last time. Flashlights boomed up in puffs of dazzling flame as newspaper photographers took action pictures of the car pulling away from the curb.

Judge Purley snapped it through the gears and drove up the winding roadway at a fair rate of speed.

"It is understood," said Perry Mason, "that Don Graves will not look back until Judge Purley indicates the place on the road where Graves first gave his exclamation."

"So understood," snapped Drumm.

The car purred up the roadway, swinging around the curves.

"Now!" said Judge Purley.

Don Graves pushed his face up against the rear window of the automobile and cupped his hands around his eyes.

Perry Mason flashed a glance at the study window of the house.

The figures could be seen for a single brief glimpse, standing in position.

The car swept around the curve in the roadway, and the house vanished from view.

"I got it, sir," said Don Graves.

"Who was it?" asked Judge Purley, braking the car to a stop.

"The man in the blue serge suit with the dark hair, and the woman in the pink dress," said Don Graves.

Claude Drumm heaved a sigh.

"There, counsellor," he said to Perry Mason, "goes your defense in this case—blown to smithereens!"

Perry Mason said nothing.

Judge Purley sighed ponderously.

"I will now turn around and go back," he said. "I presume the newspaper people will want to make some more photographs."

"Very well," Drumm told him.

Perry Mason said nothing. His rugged face was expressionless. The patient, thoughtful eyes stared meditatively at the face of Judge Purley.

TWENTY-FIVE

THE COURTROOM WAS jammed with spectators as Judge Markham marched in from the chambers in the rear of the bench.

"Stand up," shouted the bailiff.

The spectators arose and remained standing while Judge Markham strode to the judicial chair and the bailiff intoned the formula which convened the session of court.

Judge Markham sat down, and banged the gavel, and spectators, attorneys, jurors and defendants dropped into their seats.

The atmosphere of the courtroom was electric, but sympathies were all with the prosecution.

In man there is implanted a sporting instinct to side with the underdog, but this is in man, the individual. Mob psychology is different from individual psychology, and the psychology of the pack is to tear down the weaker and devour the wounded. Man may sympathize with the underdog, but he wants to side with the winner.

And the results of the test had been spread to the public through the pages of every newspaper in the city. It had been dramatic and spectacular. There had been about it something of the element of a gambling proposition. The defense had staked much on the happening of a certain event, on the turn of a single card, and it is human nature to crowd breathlessly forward as spectators when men are risking high stakes on a single card.

Therefore the reading public eagerly devoured the newspaper accounts of that which had happened. The outcome of the case was now a foregone conclusion. Don Graves had vindicated his ability to identify the occupants of the room from the exact point where he had seen the murder committed, and under exactly similar circumstances.

The gaze of the spectators in the courtroom had shifted now from the witnesses, and was fastened upon the defendants, particularly upon the shapely and slender figure of Frances Celane.

Old campaigners who have participated in hard fought legal battles will agree that this is the most ominous sign which a courtroom can give. When a case first starts, the attention of the spectators is fastened upon the defendants. They strain their necks with curiosity, watch the faces of the defendants for some flicker of expression which will convey a hint of their feelings. The average spectator likes to look at a defendant, try to visualize the defendant in the midst of the circumstances surrounding the crime, and reach an opinion as to the guilt or innocence of the prisoner, to the extent that he or she seems visually to fit into that picture.

Then, after the trial is under way, the auditors become interested in the unfolding of the story of the crime itself, in the battle over testimony. Their attention is centered upon the witnesses, upon the judge, upon the dramatic personalities of the attorneys as they match wits in legal arguments.

So long as the issue is in doubt, so long as the interest remains centered upon the outcome of the case, so long will the spectators continue to fasten their eyes upon the witnesses; upon the actors in the drama that is being unfurled. But let some event crash the testimony to a climax, remove the element of uncertainty, convince the spectators of the guilt of the defendant, and the eyes of the spectators will automatically shift to the defendant; not trying now to visualize how the defendant looked in the commission of the crime, but staring at the prisoner with that morbid curiosity which comes to men who look at one who is about to die. They like to terrify themselves by thinking of the morning when the inevitable hands will drag the protesting prisoner from the cell and march the lagging footsteps along that last grim walk.

It is the sign which lawyers dread, the verdict of these masses, the thumbs-down signal which shows the turning point has been passed, and that the prisoner is condemned.

Never a veteran trial lawyer who has fought his way through the intricate web of many cases, but has learned to appreciate the dread portent of that shifting attention. Defendants do not know its fatal significance, often they smirk with satisfaction as they see themselves the sudden cynosure of the eyes of the spectators; but not so the attorney who sits at the counsellors' table, his law books piled in front of him, his face calm and serene, but his soul shrinking from the portent of that silent verdict.

In this case the silent verdict had been rendered. It was guilty of murder in the first degree for both defendants, and there was no recommendation of mercy.

Judge Markham's level tones cut the tense silence of the courtroom.

"Mr. Don Graves was on the witness stand," he said, "and was being cross-examined. The case was continued from last week, pursuant to a stipulation by counsel that a test was to be made with this witness—a test that had been suggested by the defense, and stipulated to by the prosecution.

"Gentlemen, do I understand that the results of that test were to be received in evidence?"

Claude Drumm rose to his feet and said sneeringly: "It was a test which was conducted with every possible degree of fairness to the defense, at the challenge of the defense, and pursuant to stipulation. It was participated in by this witness under conditions identical to those which surrounded the commission of the crime, and I asked that it be received in evidence."

Judge Markham looked at Perry Mason.

Perry Mason rose to his feet.

"If the court please," he said, "there is no objection to that. It is, however, not a part of my cross-examination. That is, it must come in as a part of the redirect examination of this witness, and the question is therefore not properly before the court at the present time. But, when the question does come before the court, if the District Attorney desires to examine this witness as to the test, *I shall make no objection*, subject, however, to the fact that I shall have the right to cross-examine the various witnesses to that test, as to the actual circumstances surrounding it."

It had been said of Judge Markham that the lawyer did not live who had ever brought an expression of surprise to the face of the magistrate when he was sitting in a court of law. Now Judge Markham stared at Perry Mason as though he would try to read what might be in the mind of the counsel for the defense, and his eyes were wide and thoughtful.

Perry Mason met his gaze calmly and placidly.

"Shall I proceed with the cross-examination of the witness?" he asked.

"Proceed," snapped Judge Markham.

"You are familiar with the business affairs of Edward Norton?" asked Perry Mason in an even monotone of passionless inquiry.

"I am fully familiar with all of those affairs," said Don Graves.

"You are then familiar with the expiration date of the insurance policy which lay upon the desk of Edward Norton?" asked Perry Mason.

"I am."

"What was the expiration date of that insurance policy?"

"The twenty-sixth of October of the present year."

"Ah! Then the insurance policy expired but three days after the murder of Edward Norton?"

"That is correct."

"Is it a fact, Mr. Graves, that you have some animus, some prejudice against the defendant, Frances Celane, in this case, due to the fact that she is married to Robert Gleason?"

The question came as a surprise, and there was that suppressed rustle of motion from the courtroom which indicates a sudden snapping to attention on the part of the spectators, a craning of necks, a pushing forward to the extreme edges of the seats.

"That is not true!" protested Don Graves, with a show of feeling. "I did everything I could to keep the name of Frances Celane out of this. I am testifying in this matter only because I was forced to court under a subpoena."

"And you have no bias against Frances Celane for any other reason?"

"None."

"Or against Robert Gleason?"

"No. I hold no feeling of friendship for Robert Gleason because I know him but slightly; but for Miss Celane, my feelings are entirely different. I would not say a word in this courtroom which would connect her in any way with the murder of Edward Norton unless I knew absolutely and beyond all reasonable doubt that what I said was true and correct."

"No further questions," said Perry Mason, with the air of a man who has been defeated.

Claude Drumm got to his feet, and said with just a trace of a sneer in his air of triumph: "I have a few questions to ask upon redirect examination. You were asked upon cross-examination, Mr. Graves, whether you had ever made a test, under circumstances identical with the circumstances surrounding the murder of Edward Norton, to determine if you could recognize persons in the room where Edward Norton was murdered."

"Yes," said Don Graves, "I was asked that question."

"Since that question was asked you," persisted Claude Drumm, "have you made such a test under exactly identical circumstances?"

"I have," said Don Graves.

"Describe the circumstances under which that test was conducted, and the result of it," said Claude Drumm.

"The test was made at night," said Don Graves slowly, and in a low tone of voice, while spectators held their breath. "There were three men in Edward Norton's study and two women. One of the women was dressed in black, and one in pink. One of the men had on a blue serge suit, one had on a tweed suit, and one had on a plaid suit. I knew each one of the men, but had never seen the women before. There were present representatives of the press, and there were present Mr. Drumm, the Deputy District Attorney, also Perry Mason, the attorney for the defense."

"Then what happened?" asked Claude Drumm.

"Then," said Graves, still speaking in that low, strained voice, "we got in the automobile and went up the winding road which goes over the hills toward the main boulevard. When Judge Purley had the car at the place where it had been the night of the murder, when I gave the exclamation, he told me to look back. I looked back, and continued to look until the car had swung around the curve, and out of sight."

"What did you see?" asked Claude Drumm.

"I saw a woman, the one who had the pink dress on, standing in about the same position that Frances Celane was standing when Mr. Norton was killed, and I saw the man who wore the blue serge suit holding a club over the chair where Mr. Norton had sat on the night of the murder."

"Cross-examine the witness," said Claude Drumm triumphantly.

Perry Mason's voice was almost drawling.

"You haven't told *all* that happened there during the test, have you, Mr. Graves?"

"Yes sir, all of the important points."

"Wasn't there a newspaper reporter there who annoyed you and delayed you somewhat?" asked Perry Mason.

"Yes sir. There was a chap named Nevers, I believe, who kept insisting upon certain changes in the way the test was being made. I had no authority to make any change in the conditions of the test. Those were agreed upon between Mr. Drumm and yourself, and I told this reporter so. But he kept hanging on to me, even hooking his finger in the buttonhole of my coat, and holding me."

"Where were we at that time?" asked Perry Mason.

"You were down in the automobile."

"How did you finally get free from him?" Mason inquired.

"I called down to Mr. Drumm, and he told me definitely that there were to be no changes in the conditions under which the test was to be conducted. When this reporter heard Mr. Drumm make that statement, he seemed to realize that he was out of order, and let me go."

Spectators who had been straining their necks to listen, now glanced curiously at one another.

"That is all," said Perry Mason.

"Call your next witness, Mr. Drumm," said Judge Markham.

"Just a moment, Your Honor," interrupted Perry Mason. "Before the prosecution goes on, I would like to recall Arthur Crinston for further cross-examination."

"Very well," said Judge Markham. "The proceeding has been slightly irregular, but, under the circumstances, the matter being entirely in the discretion and control of the court, I will permit you to cross-examine any of the other witnesses that you may care to call. The court is not unmindful of the fact that various new conditions have entered into the case since your *very brief* cross-examination of the other witnesses."

Judge Markham could not resist a slight emphasis upon the words describing the brevity of the cross-examination; an emphasis which was in the nature of a very faint judicial rebuke to counsel who would so lightly dispose of the cross-examination of important witnesses in a murder case.

Arthur Crinston came forward, his face grave, his eyes solemn.

"You have already been sworn," said Perry Mason. "Just take your position in the witness chair, if you please, Mr. Crinston."

Mr. Crinston sat down, crossed his legs and turned to look at the jury.

"Mr. Crinston," said Perry Mason, "you were in conference with Mr. Norton on the night of the murder?"

"Yes sir, I have already testified to that effect."

"Yes. You arrived there, I believe, at seven minutes past eleven, and left at about eleven thirty?"

"Yes," said Mr. Crinston, and went on to volunteer a statement: "I can fix the time of my arrival with certainty because Mr. Norton was a stickler for keeping appointments on time. I was seven minutes late for my appointment, and he pointed that matter out to me rather sarcastically."

"Yes," said Perry Mason. "And from seven minutes past eleven until eleven thirty you were in conference with Mr. Norton?"

"That is correct, yes sir."

"As a matter of fact, Mr. Crinston, wasn't that conference in the nature of a quarrel?"

"No sir, I don't think I can add anything to the statement that I made before, as to what was said at that time."

"Mr. Crinston, the partnership has an indebtedness at the Wheeler's Trust & Savings Bank of some nine hundred thousand dollars?"

"Yes sir."

"With deposits in that bank of only seventy-five thousand dollars."

"Yes sir, approximately that amount."

"Yet it has deposits of eight hundred and seventy-six odd thousand dollars at the Seaboard Second National Trust Company, and deposits of approximately two hundred and ninety-three thousand dollars at the Farmers & Merchants National Bank?"

"Yes sir."

"Now, Mr. Crinston, isn't it a fact that the indebtedness of nine hundred thousand dollars which was incurred at the Wheeler's Trust & Savings Bank on a promissory note which bears only your signature, was money that was borrowed without the knowledge of Mr. Norton, and was money that was not used for partnership purposes, but was used solely for your own individual speculations in the stock market?"

"No sir!" snapped Arthur Crinston. "That is not the case."

"Why was it necessary for the partnership to borrow nine hundred thousand dollars from one bank, when it had over a million in liquid assets in other banks?"

"That was because of certain business policies. We had some large purchases we were intending to make, and we desired to keep cash assets to that amount on deposit in those banks. We didn't wish to borrow from that particular bank or those particular banks, because we wanted to keep our cash there readily available. If we had made a large note at those banks and checked out all of our cash, there would have been some explanation required. Therefore, inasmuch as the Wheeler's Trust & Savings Bank had been very anxious to get our account, and had intimated that we could have an unlimited amount of short term credit, we executed the notes there."

"It is a fact, Mr. Crinston, is it not, that those notes at the Wheeler's Trust & Savings Bank came due some two days prior to Mr. Norton's death?"

"I believe so, yes sir."

"And the bank sent out notices through the mail, did it not?"

"I believe so, yes sir."

"And isn't it a fact that Mr. Norton received one of those notices on the day that he was killed?"

"I'm sure I can't tell you, sir."

"Isn't it a fact that on that day Mr. Norton knew for the first time of the indebtedness at this bank?"

"No sir."

"Isn't it a fact that Mr. Norton called you into conference that evening in order to tell you that he had given you a certain limited time to make restitution to the partnership, and, you having failed to make such restitution, Mr. Norton was going to notify the police?"

The spectators could see that Mr. Crinston was visibly worried. His face had turned a few shades whiter, and his knuckles showed white as his hand clenched tightly, but his voice remained even and steady.

"Absolutely not," he snapped.

"And," persisted Perry Mason in the same even, imperturbable tone, "isn't it a fact that when you advised Mr. Norton that you had been unable to make restitution, and could not do so, he took down the telephone receiver, called police headquarters and said: 'This is Edward Norton speaking. I have a criminal matter to report to you,' or words to that effect?"

"No sir," snapped Arthur Crinston, and his voice now, for the first time, showed the strain under which he was laboring.

"And," said Perry Mason, slowly rising to his feet, "isn't it a fact that when he had made that statement, you crashed a club down on his head and caved in his skull?"

"I object!" shouted Claude Drumm, getting to his feet. "This examination has gone too far afield. There is absolutely no ground for . . ."

"The objection is overruled," snapped Judge Markham. "Answer the question, Mr. Crinston."

"No, I did nothing of the kind!" shouted Arthur Crinston.

Perry Mason stood on his feet, staring at Arthur Crinston until the courtroom had grasped the full significance of the question, and all that it implied, until the spectators, leaning breathlessly forward, had made of the courtroom a vault of silence.

"And," said Perry Mason, "isn't it a fact that you then placed the receiver back on the hook, stared tremblingly about you, and suddenly realized that Edward Norton had given his name to police headquarters when he made his call and stated that he had a criminal matter to report—didn't you know then that when the body of Edward Norton was discovered, the police would check back and find a record of that call, knowing then the exact time that Mr. Norton had been killed, and being able to surmise something of the motive for his murder?"

"No sir," gulped Arthur Crinston, but his forehead was glistening in the light which came from the high windows of the courtroom, as the beads of perspiration oozed through his skin.

"And isn't it a fact that with the consciousness of guilt upon you, you knew that it was necessary to explain that call to the police in some way; that you saw the insurance policy lying on his desk; that you knew this insurance policy lay there because Mr. Norton, who was very methodical, had intended to make certain that the insurance had been renewed before the expiration date. Isn't it a fact that this insurance policy gave you an inspiration, and that you immediately called back the Police Headquarters and stated to the desk sergeant that you were Mr. Norton, who had just called; that you had been cut off, and that you desired to report the theft of an automobile, and that you then and there read the description of the Buick automobile from the insurance policy which lay upon Mr. Norton's desk?"

"No sir," said Arthur Crinston in a tone of mechanical defiance.

"And isn't it a fact that then the door opened, and Don Graves came into the room; that Don Graves had been your accomplice and assistant in connection with the embezzlement of the nine hundred thousand odd dollars which you had lost in speculations upon the stock market, using partnership funds to cover your individual losses? And isn't it a fact that you and Don Graves then and there fixed up a plan by which the murder of Mr. Norton would be blamed upon others?"

"No sir," came the same mechanical denial.

"Isn't it a fact that you knew that Judge Purley did not know Edward Norton personally, and therefore would not recognize his voice from the voice of any other man? Isn't it a fact that you and your accomplice, Don Graves, sneaked down to the room of Pete Devoe, the chauffeur, and planted evidence in that room which would have a tendency to connect Devoe with the murder? Isn't it a fact that you jimmied a window and left footprints in the loam on the soil outside of the window so that it would appear that Mr. Devoe had made a clumsy attempt to divert suspicion from himself?

"Isn't it a fact that you then went back to the study where the dead man was slumped across his desk, and that you arranged with Mr. Graves so that you were to go down the stairs and start for Judge Purley's automobile; that Mr. Graves was to raise the window in Mr. Norton's study, keeping the desk light well to his back, so that Judge Purley would see nothing but the blurred outline of a human form, and that Mr. Graves, pretending to be Edward Norton, would call down and ask you to take Don Graves in the automobile to your home, and that you then and there arranged that you would go to ask Judge Purley for his permission, and that Don Graves would then move away from the window, rush downstairs, and be standing by your side, while you pretended to call up to Mr. Norton, whom you pretended that you could see in the window, saying that it was all right, and Judge Purley had given his permission?"

"No sir," said Arthur Crinston.

"That," said Perry Mason, in tones that rang through the courtroom until they seemed to make the rafters in the ceiling vibrate, "is all the cross-examination I have of this witness."

Judge Markham glanced at Claude Drumm.

"Is there any redirect examination, counsellor?" he asked.

Claude Drumm made a sweeping gesture. "None, Your Honor. A very pretty theory has been advanced, but there has been no evidence to support it. The witness has denied . . ."

Judge Markham banged his gavel on the desk.

"Counsellor," he said, "you will make your argument to the jury at the proper time. The question of the court was whether there was any additional redirect examination. Your answer was in the negative, and the witness will stand aside."

"Recall Judge Purley for further cross-examination," said Perry Mason.

Judge Purley came to the witness stand. Gone was the judicial assurance which had clothed his manner earlier in the trial. His face was drawn and strained, and there was a haunting doubt in his eyes.

"You also have been sworn in this case, so there is no necessity for you to be sworn again," said Perry Mason. "Take your place on the witness stand."

Judge Purley heaved his big bulk into the witness chair.

"When this test was being made over the week end," said Perry Mason, in the tone of voice of one who is pronouncing a final and solemn judgment, "you sat in your automobile under the window of Edward Norton's study, in exactly the same place and position as that you occupied on the night of the murder, did you not?"

"I did, sir, yes, sir."

"And from that position, by craning your neck, you could see the study windows in Edward Norton's house?"

"Yes, sir."

"But because the top of the automobile was so low as to interfere with your vision, you could only see those windows by craning your neck, is that right?"

"Yes, sir."

"And isn't it a fact, Judge Purley, that while you were seated there in that automobile, in exactly the same position that it occupied on the night of the murder, Don Graves came to the window of the study and called down to you, or to Claude Drumm, who was with you in the car?"

"Yes, sir," said Judge Purley, taking a deep breath.

"And isn't it a fact," thundered Perry Mason, extending his rigid forefinger, so that it pointed directly at Judge Purley, "that now the matter has been called to your attention, and your recollection has had an opportunity to check over the circumstances of what happened upon that fateful night of the murder, that you *now* realize that the voice which called down to you from that second story window on the night of the test, was the same voice which had called down from that window on the night of the murder?"

Tense, dramatic silence gripped the courtroom.

Judge Purley's hands tugged at the arm of the witness chair, and his face writhed in agony.

"My God!" he said. "I don't know! I have been asking myself that question for the last ten minutes, and I cannot answer it satisfactorily to my conscience. All I know is that *it may have been!*"

Perry Mason turned half around and faced the jury. His steady, unwavering eyes surveyed the faces of the nine men and the three women.

"That," he said, in a tone of finality, "is all."

For a long moment the courtroom remained silent, then there were rustlings, whispering, half-gasps. Somewhere in the background a woman tittered hysterically.

Judge Markham banged his gavel down on the desk.

"Order!" he said.

Claude Drumm bit his lip in an agony of indecision. Dare he go into the matter on redirect examination, or dare he wait until he could talk privately with the Municipal Judge?

And, in that moment of indecision, in that moment when the attention of every human being in the courtroom was fastened upon him, Claude Drumm hesitated for one second too long.

The attention of the crowd shifted.

Perry Mason, leaning back in his chair, his eyes placidly surveying the sea of faces, saw it shift. Judge Markham, sitting on the bench, wise in the ways of the courtroom, veteran of a hundred murder trials, saw it shift.

As with one motion, as though actuated by some subtle, psychic command, the eyes of the jurors, the eyes of the spectators, turned away from Claude Drumm, and fastened themselves upon the agonized face of Arthur Crinston.

It was the silent verdict of the courtroom, and that verdict exonerated the two defendants, and fixed the guilt of Edward Norton's murder squarely upon Arthur Crinston and his accomplice.

TWENTY-SIX

PERRY MASON SAT in his office. The light from the window streaming in upon his rugged, virile features made him seem somehow older, brought out the strong lines of his face.

Frances Celane sat in the big black leather chair, her forefinger poking and twisting as she slid it along the smooth arm of the chair. Her eyes were dark and filled with emotion.

Robert Gleason stood leaning against the book case, his heavy, dark face twisted into that agony of silence which comes to those inarticulate men who have much to say, yet cannot find a means of expression.

Through the open windows, from the street below, came the cries of the newsboys, shouting their extra edition of the *STAR*.

Perry Mason tapped the newspaper on his desk; a paper which was still damp from the presses.

"That," he said, "is clever journalism. Nevers had that paper on the street before you had gone from the courthouse to my office. He had the thing all figured out and blocked out. All he needed to do was to add a brief summary of the testimony of Judge Purley, and the headlines."

He slid his forefinger along the headlines which streamed blackly across the top of the newspaper: "MURDER CASE DISMISSED."

Frances Celane said softly: "It wasn't the journalism in this case that was so remarkable, Mr. Mason; it was your wonderful analysis of what must have happened, and the steps you took to reconstruct the scene so that Judge Purley would be convinced. I watched him when he was on the witness stand the first time, and I could see the problem that you had with him."

Perry Mason smiled.

"Judge Purley," he said, "is rather opinionated, and he would very much have disliked having to confess himself in error. In fact, if I had asked him that question the first time he was on the witness stand, he would have indignantly denied that such could have been the case, and the denial would have so impressed itself upon his own mind, that no amount of subsequent testimony could ever have caused him even to entertain the faintest notion that he might have been mistaken.

"But the fact that I managed to duplicate the conditions in such a manner that his mind was totally unprepared for what was taking place, gave me the opportunity to approach him on a blind side, so to speak.

"Of course," went on Perry Mason, "I had all of the facts in hand at the moment that Arthur Crinston, in telling me about the murder, discussed the telephone call to the police as though he had no knowledge of it, except what he had learned through the police.

"That was the slip that Crinston made, and the fatal slip; that, and failing to report that telephone conversation in his testimony to the jury.

"You see, he was so obsessed with the idea that he must keep the authorities from knowing what had transpired in that room when Norton was murdered, that he made up a story out of whole cloth, and stuck to it.

"That is not skillful lying. It is not the proper way to commit perjury. The skillful perjurer is he who sticks to so much of the truth as is possible, and only departs from it when it becomes absolutely necessary. These men who make up stories out of whole cloth usually leave a few loose threads somewhere.

"Yet it is a strange thing about the human mind: It has many facts constantly thrust upon it, and it doesn't properly correlate those facts. I had the facts at my command for some time before I knew what must have happened.

"You see, Crinston had borrowed heavily on the partnership credit. The partnership was, of course, solvent, but Crinston's credit as an individual was all shot to pieces. He had made Graves an accomplice, and, together, they were deceiving your uncle; but when the bank sent the notice to your uncle, then Edward Norton learned for the first time what had happened.

"We can imagine what happened next. He gave Mr. Crinston a definite deadline, at which time Crinston was to have returned the money, or else be reported to the police. When Crinston failed to make the payment, your uncle, acting with that cold-blooded efficiency which is so absolutely merciless, picked up the telephone and called Police Headquarters.

"Crinston sat there behind him, watching dumbly, knowing that the words which Norton was to say next would lead to his confinement in a penal institution. He heard Norton say: 'Police Headquarters, I have a criminal matter to report,' and then Crinston acted upon a blind, murderous impulse. He struck Norton down without warning and probably without any great amount of premeditation.

"When he had done that and hung up the receiver, he suddenly realized that the police must have a record of that call which Norton had sent in, and that this would lead to his detection. So he did a very clever thing. He called Police Headquarters right back and pretended that he was Norton. He had to have something to report in the nature of a criminal matter, because your uncle had already said that he had such a report to make.

"The policy of automobile insurance was lying on the desk, and Arthur Crinston plunged blindly into that lead. Then, when you heard of your uncle's murder, and knowing that Rob Gleason had been in the house with you, and that there might be some possibility you would either be implicated, or have to explain what Gleason was doing there, you seized at what seemed to be the best opportunity to establish an alibi for yourself, by stating that you had been driving the Buick automobile at the time that your uncle reported it lost.

"On the face of it, it was almost mathematical. In other words, a man with a trained mind, sitting down and concentrating upon the evidence, should have been able to point his finger to the murderer at once. Yet I confess that the circumstances were so dramatic and so unusual that I was confused for some little time, and failed to realize what must have happened.

"When I did realize it, I knew that I was up against a most serious problem. I felt certain that I could explain my theory well enough to raise a reasonable doubt in the minds of the jury, and get either an acquittal or a hung jury, but I realized also that unless I could trap the murderers into betraying themselves, I could never entirely remove the stigma of doubt from your names.

"I recognized at once that Judge Purley was the key witness, and knew that the man's conceit and love of posture, would render any ordinary cross-examination futile. Therefore, I had to devise some means by which a doubt would be raised in his own mind before he knew that the doubt was there, and then crash it home to him with dramatic force."

Fran Celane got to her feet with tears showing in her eyes.

"I can't begin to tell you," she said, "what it has meant to me. It's been an experience that will always leave its imprint."

Perry Mason's eyes narrowed. "You're lucky," he said, in a tone of tolerant patience, "to have escaped with nothing but an unpleasant experience."

Frances Celane smiled and blinked tears back as she smiled. "I didn't mean it that way, Mr. Mason. I meant that it has been an experience I wouldn't have missed for anything!"

He stared at her.

"I mean it," she said. "Not the murder trial, but the being in jail, getting a glimpse of the sufferings of other people. It gave me a chance to see things in a different light. I think it's helped cure my fiendish temper.

"And then it brought out the loyalty in Rob. He knew that I couldn't be guilty, but he knew that the evidence was against me, and that I stood a chance of being convicted. In those dark hours when you didn't take us into your confidence and things seemed to be stacking up so much against us, he came forward and was willing to give his life to save mine."

"Yes," said Perry Mason, looking thoughtfully at Rob Gleason, "it was a noble and magnanimous thing to do, but if I hadn't been sure of my theory of the case, he would have thrown me entirely off my stride. His confession was most convincing, save for the fact that he claimed he had taken the thousand dollar bills from the body. I knew that he couldn't have done that, because you had given me ten of those bills the next morning. And then you, Miss Celane, weren't frank with me. You kept certain things back, trying to protect yourself."

"I know it," she told him. "It was all on account of that first lie about the Buick automobile. I couldn't tell the truth after that. I grabbed at the story about being out in the automobile as the best way to prove an alibi, and then I found I was trapped. I couldn't even tell you about getting the money from my uncle, because I was supposed to have been out in the automobile at that time."

There was a knock at the door, and Della Street entered the room.

She looked at Perry Mason with eyes that were starry with pride. When she spoke, her voice had something of caressing tenderness in it.

"There is a telegram for you," she said.

Frances Celane walked quickly across to Perry Mason and extended her hand.

"Rob and I will be going," she said, "and there's no use trying to tell you how much we appreciate what you've done. We can compensate you financially, but in addition to that we want you to know . . ."

Her voice shook, and there were tears in her eyes.

Perry Mason gripped her hand, then nodded. "I know," he said.

When the door leading from his private office to the corridor had closed on them, he turned to Della Street.

"Here," she said, "is the telegram. If you can make sense from it, you can do more than I can."

He took the telegram and read:

"SENDING YOU SPECIAL DELIVERY AIR MAIL PHOTOGRAPH OF UTMOST IM-PORTANCE IN CASE I AM ABOUT TO PRESENT. KEEP PHOTOGRAPH AND AWAIT ME IN YOUR OFFICE WITHOUT FAIL.

(Signed) EVA LAMONT."

Perry Mason stared at the telegram curiously.

"Did the photograph come?" he asked.

"Yes," she said, "a few minutes ago." She opened a drawer in her desk and took out a photograph. It was the photograph of a young woman, generously displaying a beautiful pair of legs. Below the photograph was a typewritten caption which had been pasted to it. The caption said, simply: "THE GIRL WITH THE LUCKY LEGS."

The photograph did not show the woman's face, merely her shoulders, hips, arms, hands, which held the skirts very, very high, and the legs. They were slim, straight legs, perfectly formed, stockinged and gartered.

"Now," said Perry Mason, his curiosity aroused, "what the devil does *that* mean?"

"I don't know," said Della Street, "but I'm going to make a file—*The Case of the Girl With the Lucky Legs.*"

Perry Mason looked at his watch. The weariness had dropped from his face, and his eyes were sparkling.

"I wonder," he said, "just what time Eva Lamont is due here."

THE CASE OF THE
CARELESS KITTEN

ONE

THE KITTEN'S EYES, weaving back and forth, followed the ball of crumpled paper that Helen Kendal was waving high above the arm of the chair. The kitten was named Amber Eyes because of those yellow eyes. Helen liked to watch them. Their black pupils were always changing, narrowing to ominous slits, widening to opaque pools of onyx. Those black and amber eyes had an almost hypnotic effect on Helen. After she had watched them a little while her thoughts seemed to slip. She would forget the near things, like to-day, and this room, and the kitten; she could even forget about Jerry Templar and Aunt Matilda's eccentric domineerings, and find herself suddenly thinking about things that were far away or long ago.

It was one of the long-ago things this time. Years and years ago. When Helen Kendal was ten, and there was another kitten, a grey-and-white one, up on the roof. So high up that it was afraid to come down. And a tall man with kind grey eyes had fetched a long ladder and was standing up at the wobbly tip of it, patiently coaxing the kitten toward his outstretched hand.

Uncle Franklin. Helen was thinking about him now as she had thought about him then. Not as she had learned to think about him afterward, from other people. Not as Aunt Matilda's runaway husband, not as Franklin Shore, the Missing Banker, in the big headlines, not as the man who had inexplicably thrown away success and wealth and power and family and lifelong friends, to lose himself, moneyless, among strangers. Helen was thinking of him, now, only as the Uncle Franklin who had risked his life to rescue a scared kitten for a sorrowful little girl, as the only father whom that little girl had ever known, a gentle, understanding, friendly father, remembered, after all these years, with a love that knew and would keep on knowing, against all seeming proofs to the contrary, that it had been returned.

That knowledge, suddenly rediscovered, made Helen Kendal absolutely sure that Franklin Shore was dead. He must be. He must have died long ago, soon after he had run away. He'd loved her. He must have loved her, or he wouldn't have risked sending her that picture post card from Florida soon after he disappeared, just when Aunt Matilda was trying so hard to find him and he trying even harder to keep her from doing it. He couldn't have lived very long after that or there'd have been another message for Helen. He'd have known how she'd be hoping for one. He wouldn't have disappointed her. He was dead. He'd been dead for almost ten years.

He was dead, and Helen had a right to the twenty thousand dollars he had left her in his will. And that much money now, with Jerry Templar home on a week's leave——

Helen's thoughts slipped again. The Army had made a difference in Jerry. His blue eyes were steadier, his mouth grimmer. But the change in him only made her surer that she loved him, and surer than ever, for all his tight-lipped silence on the subject, that he'd kept on loving her. He wasn't going to marry her, though. Not when it might mean that Aunt Matilda would turn her out of the house, to live on his Army pay. But if she had money, money of her own, money enough to let Jerry feel perfectly sure that no matter what happened to him, she'd never be homeless or hungry——

There was no use in thinking about it. Aunt Matilda wasn't going to change her mind. It wasn't that kind of a mind. Once it was made up, even Aunt Matilda herself couldn't change it. And it was made up permanently to believe that Franklin Shore was alive, and just as permanently and immovably made up not to take the steps at law that would declare him legally dead and allow his will to be proved. Aunt Matilda didn't need her share of the estate. As Franklin Shore's wife, she controlled the property he had left behind him almost as completely as she could hope to control it as his widow and executrix. She controlled Helen, penniless and dependent, far more completely than she would control her after that twenty-thousand-dollar legacy was paid.

And Aunt Matilda enjoyed controlling people. She'd never willingly give up her purse-string power over Helen, especially not while Jerry Templar was here. Aunt Matilda had never liked him nor approved of Helen's liking him, and the change the Army had made in him only seemed to make her dislike more explicit than ever. There wasn't a chance on earth of her letting go of that legacy before Jerry's leave was up. Unless Uncle Gerald——

Helen's thoughts shifted again. Uncle Gerald, three days ago, telling her he was going to force Aunt Matilda's hand. His brother's will left him the same sum it bequeathed to Helen. Sixty-two and looking older, still practising law for his living, he could use his money and already felt he'd waited for it long enough.

"I can make Matilda act, and I'm going to do it," he'd said. "We all know Franklin's dead. He's been legally dead for three years. I want my legacy and I want you to have yours."

His eyes had softened and warmed as they studied her, Helen remembered, and his voice had been warmer, too, and gentler.

"You're more like your mother every time I see you, Helen. Even when you were little you had her eyes, with the violets in them, and her hair, with the red just showing under the gold. And you've grown up to have her tall, slim, lovely body and her long, lovely hands, and even her quiet, lovely voice. I liked your father, but I never quite forgave him for taking her away from us."

He had stopped. And there had been something different about his voice when he went on. "You're going to need your twenty thousand dollars before long, Helen."

"I need it now," she had said.

"Jerry Templar?" Her face must have been answer enough, because he hadn't waited for her to speak. He'd nodded slowly. "All right. I'll try to get you that money." He'd sounded as if he meant to do more than just try. And it had been three days ago. Maybe——

Amber Eyes had stood it as long as he could. He flashed up in a leap toward that maddening ball of paper, clutching with teeth and claws; then, starting to fall, struck instinctively for Helen's wrist, clinging with needle-sharp claws trying to save himself from a fall to the carpeted floor.

Violently startled, she screamed.

Aunt Matilda called sharply from her room, "What's the matter, Helen?"

"Nothing," Helen said, laughing nervously as she grasped the kitten's paw with her free hand, disengaging the clutching claws. "Amber Eyes scratched me, that's all."

"What's the matter with Amber Eyes?"

"Nothing. We were just playing."

"Stop playing with that kitten. You're spoiling it."

"Yes, Aunt Matilda," she said dutifully, stroking the kitten and regarding the scratches on the back of her hand.

"I suppose," she said to Amber Eyes, "you don't know that your little claws are sharp. Now I've got to go and put something on my hand."

She was in the bathroom, at the medicine cabinet, when she heard the sound of Matilda's cane; then the door of the bedroom opened, and Matilda stood frowning at her.

Matilda Shore, at sixty-four, had a full ten years of deterred vengeance behind her. Sciatica had not improved her disposition. She was a big-boned woman. In her youth, she must have had a certain Amazon type of beauty, but now she had lost all regard for personal appearance. Flesh had wrapped itself around her frame. Her shoulders were stooped. She habitually carried her head pushed forward and down. There were deep, sagging pouches under her eyes. Her mouth had taken on a sharp, downward curve. But none of the encroachments of time had been able to eradicate from her features the grim determination of a woman of indomitable will who lived with a single, definite purpose in mind.

"Let me see where the cat scratched you," she demanded.

"It wasn't the kitten's fault, Aunt Matilda. I was playing with it, and holding out a piece of paper for it to jump at. I didn't realize that I was holding it so far from the floor. Amber Eyes just tried to hang on, that's all."

Aunt Matilda glared at the scratched hand. "I heard somebody talking a while ago. Who was it?"

"Jerry." Helen tried her best not to say it defensively, but Aunt Matilda's eyes were too much for her. "He only stayed a few minutes."

"So I noticed." It was clear that Aunt Matilda took a grim pleasure in the brevity of the visit. "You might as well make up your mind to it, Helen. It's quite plain that he's made up his. He has sense enough to see he can't possibly marry you. And it's a good thing for you that he can't. You're just fool enough to do it if he asked you to."

"Just exactly fool enough," Helen said.

"Meaning you aren't a fool at all." Aunt Matilda sniffed. "That's what fools always think. It's lucky for you that what you think doesn't matter. He's the worst possible type for a girl like you. He's a man's man. He'll never be any good to a woman. That padlocked, shut-mouthed repression of his would drive you mad. You've got enough of it for two, yourself. I've been married twice and I know what I'm talking about. The only sort of man you'll ever be happy with is somebody like George Alber, who——"

"Who leaves me absolutely cold," Helen said.

"He wouldn't if you saw more of him. If you'd get rid of this ridiculous idea that you're in love with Jerry Templar and mustn't be even civil to any other man. When even you can't possibly be fool enough not to see that he can't marry you on his private's pay. When——"

"Jerry won't be a private much longer," Helen said. "They're sending him to an officers' training camp."

"What of it? When he gets his commission—if he gets it—he'll only be shipped off to the ends of the earth and——"

"He'll be at the camp first." Helen spoke quickly, before Aunt Matilda could say anything about what would happen afterward. Helen wasn't letting herself think about that. "He'll be there for months, and I could be there, too, or somewhere near by. Near enough for us to see each other sometimes."

"I see." Aunt Matilda's voice was heavily ironic. "You've thought it all out, haven't you? Except, of course, for the trivial matter of what you'll live on while all this is happening. Or——" She stopped. "I see. Gerald's been talking to you. He's made you think he can make me give you the money Franklin left you. Well, you can put that idea out of your head. That money isn't due to you till Franklin's dead. And he's no more dead than I am. He's alive. One of these days he'll come crawling back, begging me to forgive him."

She laughed, as if the word were comic. Helen suddenly understood, for the first time, why Aunt Matilda clung so fiercely to her belief that Franklin Shore was alive. She hated him too bitterly to bear the thought of his having gone beyond hatred's power to follow. She had one dream left and she lived on it, and in it—the dream of his coming back. Coming back for the only reasons that could drive him back. Old, alone, beaten, in want. For her to take payment from him in kind and in full for what he had done to her.

Komo, the houseboy, appearing silently from nowhere, stood in the doorway. "Excuse pleassse," he said.

Matilda said. "What is it now, Komo? The door's open. Come in. And don't be so damned pussyfooting when you walk."

The houseboy's dark glittering eyes surveyed Matilda Shore. "Party on telephone, pleassse," he said. "Statement made that call is most important."

"All right. I'll be there in a minute."

"Receiver is left down on extension in your bedroom," Komo announced, and turned to walk back down the corridor with quick, light steps.

Helen said, "Aunt Matilda, *why* don't you get rid of that houseboy? I don't trust him."

"Perhaps *you* don't. *I* do."

"He's Japanese."

"Nonsense. He's Korean. He hates the Japanese."

"He may *say* he's Korean, but that's just . . ."

"He's been saying so for twelve years."

"Well, he doesn't look like a Korean to me. He looks like a Japanese, he acts like a Japanese, and . . ."

"Ever know any Koreans?" Aunt Matilda interrupted.

"Well, no—not exactly, but . . ."

"Komo is a Korean," Matilda said positively, and turning, walked back to her bedroom, pulling the door closed behind her.

Helen returned to the living-room. Her hand smarted from the scratches and the sting of the disinfectant. The kitten was nowhere in evidence. She sat down and tried to read, but her mind refused to concentrate on the printed page.

After some fifteen minutes, she tossed the magazine to one side, sat back and closed her eyes. The kitten, appearing from nowhere, seemed properly apologetic as it rubbed, purring, against her ankles. At length it jumped up on the arm of her chair. Its rough tongue scraped against the skin of her arm.

Helen heard the telephone ringing, heard Komo's light steps as he went to answer it, then he was standing beside her chair as though he had silently materialized from thin air.

"Excussse, please. This time, call for Missy."

Helen walked out to the hall where the telephone was placed. She picked up the receiver, wondering if this might not be Jerry calling to . . . "Hello," she said, her voice eager.

The voice which came over the telephone wire was quavering with some emotion. "Is this Helen Kendal?"

"Yes, of course."

"You don't know who this is?"

"No," Helen almost snapped. People who rang up and asked her to guess who was speaking irritated her.

The voice seemed a little stronger now, more steady. "Be very careful what you say that might be overheard. You remember your Uncle Franklin?"

Helen's mouth was suddenly very dry. "Yes, yes, but . . ."

"This is your Uncle Franklin."

"I don't believe it. He's . . ."

"No, Helen, I'm not dead." The voice broke with emotion. "I'm very much alive."

"But . . ."

"I don't blame you for not believing it. You'd know me if you saw me again, wouldn't you?"

"Why, I . . . why, yes—of course."

The man's voice went on more firmly now. "You remember the time the dog chased the kitten up on the roof of the house? You begged me to get him down, and I took a ladder and climbed up. Remember the New Year's party when you wanted to try the punch and your Aunt Matilda told you you couldn't, and you sneaked some in the pantry, anyway? Remember how I followed you up to your room and talked to you until you developed a laughing jag—and how I never told anyone—not even your Aunt Matilda—about it?"

Helen felt a peculiar tingling sensation round the hair at the back of her neck. "Yes," she said in a voice which was hardly more than a whisper.

"Now do you believe me, Helen?"

"Uncle Frank . . ."

"Careful! Don't mention my name. Is your aunt at home?"

"Yes."

"She mustn't know that I've rung up. No one must know. Do you understand?"

"Why, I . . . why . . . No, I don't understand."

"There is only one way to straighten things out. You'll have to help me."

"What can I do?"

"You can do something that no one else can do. Have you ever heard of a lawyer named Perry Mason?"

"I've heard of him."

"I want you to see him this afternoon, tell him the entire story so that he'll know the facts. To-night at nine o'clock I want you to bring him to the Castle Gate Hotel. You know where that is?"

"No."

"You can look it up. It's a cheap hotel. Don't be frightened. Bring Mason to that hotel, ask for Henry Leech. He'll take you to me. Don't let anyone else know about this conversation or what's happening. Be sure you aren't followed. Tell Mason everything, but swear him to secrecy. I'll . . ."

She heard a quick, gasping intake of breath. Abruptly, the receiver clicked at the other end of the line, and there was only that peculiar singing of an open telephone line. She jiggled the receiver hook several times. "Operator," she called. *"Operator!"*

Through the partially-opened door, Helen heard the unmistakable sounds of her aunt's approach, the slow, laboured steps, the steady *thump . . . thump . . . thump* of the cane, the dragging shuffle of the right foot.

Hastily, she hung up the receiver.

"Who is it?" Aunt Matilda asked, entering the hall as Helen turned away from the telephone.

"I think it's a date," Helen said, trying to sound casual.

Aunt Matilda lowered her eyes to Helen's right hand. "How did that cat happen to scratch you?" she asked. "You're lying to protect it. I'm not going to keep it if it's becoming vicious."

"Don't be silly," Helen said. "I tell you, I was teasing it with a piece of paper."

"Well, it had no business to scratch you. Was that your soldier boy on the telephone?"

Helen laughed evasively.

"What are you so excited about? You're all flushed." She shrugged her heavy shoulders contemptuously. "It would be just like that fool, Jerry Templar, to propose to a girl over the telephone. It wouldn't surprise me at that. . . . Helen, what in heaven's name is the matter with that kitten?"

Helen sighed wearily. "I told you it was my fault. I . . ."

"No, no! Look at him!"

Helen moved over, impelled by her aunt's fixed stare. "He's just playing," she said. "Kittens play that way."

"It doesn't look like he's playing to me."

"Kittens do that when they're stretching. They have to flex their little muscles. They . . ."

Helen felt the words fading from her tongue as she lost assurance. The kitten was acting most peculiarly, its motions very different from the stretches by which kittens coax their immature muscles into growth. The little spine arched backwards. The paws were stretched out to the fullest extent. Little spasms sent tremors through the body. But what arrested her attention and filled her with apprehension was the expression in the amber eyes, the manner in which the kitten's jaws were clamped together, bits of froth oozing from beneath curled, pale lips.

"Oh, dear, something's wrong! Amber Eyes is sick!" she exclaimed.

Matilda Shore said, "Don't go near it. The cat's gone mad. Cats do that just the same as dogs. You'd better go and see a doctor at once about that hand."

"Nonsense!" Helen said. "The kitten's sick. . . . Poor little Amber Eyes. What's the matter? Did you hurt yourself some way?"

Helen reached down to the rigid little body. As soon as her fingers touched the fur, the cat went into a very definite convulsion.

"I'm going to take that cat to a vet, right away," Helen said.

"You watch out. You'll get hurt," Aunt Matilda warned.

"I'll take care of that," Helen promised, dashing to the closet and struggling into her coat.

"You get something to wrap that cat in," Aunt Matilda said, "so it can't scratch you. . . . Komo. . . . Oh, Komo."

The swarthy little man materialized almost at once in the doorway. "Yes, ma'am."

Helen said, "Get an old blanket or a quilt out of the closet. Something to wrap the cat in."

Komo regarded the kitten with a peculiar expression in his lacquered eyes. "Kitten sick?" he asked.

"Don't stand there asking foolish questions," Matilda said impatiently. "Of course the kitten's sick. Do what Miss Helen told you. Get that blanket."

"Yes, ma'am."

Helen hastily adjusted her hat in front of the mirror, then stooped to bend over the kitten.

"Keep away from him," Matilda warned. "I don't like the way he's acting."

"What is it, Amber Eyes?" Helen asked, her voice soothing.

The cat's eyes were staring fixedly, but at the sound of Helen's voice, he made a slight motion as though to turn his head. That little motion brought on another of those swift spasms, this time more violent.

Just as Komo brought the blanket, Helen heard steps on the outer porch. The door opened. Her uncle, Gerald Shore, crossed the hall to the living-room, taking off his hat and light coat as he moved. "Hello, everybody," he said cheerfully. "What seems to be the trouble?"

There was reassurance in his deeply resonant voice. It never seemed necessary for him to raise that voice, yet he could be plainly heard, no matter how large the room.

"It's Amber Eyes," Helen said. "He's sick."

"What's wrong with him?"

"We don't know. He's having spasms. I'm taking him to a veterinary," Helen said. "I'm . . . Here, Komo, help me get the blanket round the cat. Watch out he doesn't bite now."

They wrapped the blanket round the kitten. Helen clasped the tense little body to her and could feel another spasm tighten the muscles as she started for the door.

"Come on," Gerald Shore said. "I'll drive the car. You can hold the cat."

"The cat's already scratched Helen," Matilda said.

"I washed it with alcohol," Helen explained.

"Cats can go mad just the same as dogs do," Matilda insisted.

Komo, smiling and nodding, said, "Fits. Excussse, please. All cats have fits. This very typical cat fit."

Helen turned to her Uncle Gerald. "Come on. *Please* let's get started."

Matilda Shore said to the houseboy, "Komo, you've let me run out of stout again. Now you go all the way up-town to the market and get me six bottles. Don't disturb me when you come back. I'll lie down until dinner. Helen, don't take on so over that kitten. Find a better outlet for your affections. Now get started, all of you."

She entered her bedroom, slamming the door shut behind her.

"Come on, Helen," Uncle Gerald said sympathetically.

Suddenly Helen remembered the telephone call. Curiously, she had forgotten it completely in the excitement over Amber Eyes. In a way it seemed unreal, like something that had never happened. Uncle Franklin! As soon as she took care of Amber Eyes, she would try to reach this Perry Mason.

TWO

GERALD SHORE HAD never had his brother's flair for making money, or rather, for keeping money. Where Franklin had watched his ever-growing fortune with the tight-lipped determination of a man who knows how to say no, Gerald had spent money recklessly on the "easy come, easy go" theory. Prior to 1929, he had considered himself a wealthy man. Within a few short weeks, he not only had been completely stripped of his property, but had found himself dependent upon his law practice to give him even a living.

This period of transition had been most embarrassing. Having adjusted his practice on the theory that he would not waste his time with small cases, that he would see clients by appointment only, and would take only such cases as interested him, Gerald suddenly found himself eager to accept any honourable employment where there was even a fair possibility of a fee.

Holding the kitten close, feeling the convulsive waves that racked its little body, Helen thought gratefully that Uncle Gerald was more sympathetic, more understanding, than any man she knew. She wondered if he had always been like this. Certainly his difficulties and his trouble had not hardened him. It seemed even that since the crash he had been more gentle, more tolerant, than before. Whereas Aunt Matilda's idea was for Komo to put the kitten out of the way, Uncle Gerald obviously recognized a major emergency that relegated traffic laws to the background. It was but a matter of minutes before they had Amber Eyes in the hands of a competent veterinary.

Dr. Blakely, making a quick diagnosis, reached for a hypodermic needle.

"It isn't—isn't rabies, is it?" Helen asked.

"Probably poison," he said. "Here, hold the cat's head. Hold him tightly by the neck and shoulders. Hold firmly now. Don't let go if he starts fighting."

He inserted the hypodermic needle, carefully regulated the amount of fluid which he injected, withdrew the needle, and said, "Temporarily, we'll put him in this cage. The kitten's going to eject the contents of its stomach. In that way, we'll get rid of any poison which remains. How long ago was it when you first observed any symptoms?"

"I don't think it could possibly have been over five or ten minutes," Helen said. "It didn't take us over three minutes to get here, and ... well, perhaps ten minutes ago."

"We stand a good chance," Dr. Blakely said. "Nice little kitten. Hope we can save it."

"You think it's poison?"

"I think so. The treatment isn't going to be particularly pleasant. You'll think the animal is suffering even more than it is. You two had better wait out in the office. If I need any more help, I'll call you."

He drew on a pair of thick leather gloves.

"You're sure there's nothing we can do?" Helen asked.

He shook his head. "I can let you know more in a few minutes. It had been playing out in the yard, hadn't it?"

"No, I don't think so. I don't remember distinctly, but I *think* the kitten had been in the living-room all the time."

"Well, we'll find out more about it after a while. Go sit down and wait."

Out in the waiting-room, Gerald Shore settled himself in a chair, fished a cigar from his waistcoat pocket, bit off the end and struck a match. The flame, which was held in his cupped hands, illuminated the sensitive outlines of his features, the sweep of a high, contemplative forehead, kindly, tolerant eyes, about which were little crow's-feet of humour, a mouth which was uncompromising and determined without being too stern.

"Nothing we can do now, Helen. May as well sit down and take it easy. We've done everything we can."

They sat silently for several minutes, Helen's mind tumbling around between that strange telephone call and Amber Eyes and poison, and what she should do about her Uncle Franklin. In spite of what he had said, she wanted to confide in Uncle Gerald, but she hesitated. He was quite evidently lost in thought, his mind occupied with a problem that plainly required concentration.

Abruptly he said, "Helen, as I told you a few days ago, we're going to do something about Franklin's will immediately. Matilda has been hanging on to what belongs to us long enough."

"Perhaps we ought to wait—just a little," Helen murmured uncertainly.

"We've waited long enough."

He saw that Helen was hesitating, trying to make up her mind to speak or to keep silent.

"Well," he asked, "what is it?"

Helen suddenly made up her mind with a rush. "I . . . I had a queer experience to-day," she blurted out.

"What?"

"A man telephoned."

Gerald chuckled. "I'd say it was queerer if any man who knew your number *hadn't* telephoned you. If I weren't your uncle and . . ."

"Don't be ridiculous! This man said—— Oh, it just doesn't sound plausible. It *can't* be true!"

"If you'd be just a *little* more explicit," Gerald murmured encouragingly.

Her voice dropped almost to a whisper. "He said he was Franklin Shore. He seemed to recognize my voice, wanted to know if I recognized his."

Gerald Shore's face showed baffled, incredulous surprise. "Nonsense!" he exclaimed.

"It's true."

"Helen, you're excited. You . . ."

"Uncle Gerald, I swear it."

There was a long pause.

"When did the call come in?" he asked finally.

"Just a few minutes before you came to the house."

"Some impostor, of course, trying to . . ."

"No. It was Uncle Franklin."

"Look here, Helen, did you—that is, was there anything familiar about his voice?"

"I don't know. I couldn't be sure of the voice—but it was Uncle Franklin all right."

He frowned at the tip of his cigar. "It's impossible! What did he say?"

"He wants me to meet him to-night at the Castle Gate Hotel—that is, I'm to see a man named Henry Leech there, and Henry Leech will take me to Uncle Franklin."

Gerald Shore relaxed. "That settles it. Obviously an impostor after money. We'll go to the police and set a trap for your friend."

Helen shook her head. "Uncle Franklin told me to see that well-known lawyer, Perry Mason, tell him the whole story and bring him to the meeting to-night."

Her uncle stared at her blankly. "It's the damnedest thing I ever heard. What does he want with Perry Mason?"

"I don't know."

"Look here," Gerald said somewhat sternly, "you don't *know* that was Franklin talking, do you, Helen?"

"Well——"

"Then stop referring to that person as Franklin. That might affect the legal situation. All you know is, you heard a man's voice over the telephone. That man *told* you he was Franklin Shore."

"He said things that proved it."

"What?"

"A lot of things out of my childhood that only Uncle Franklin would know about: the time the kitten got up on the roof of the house and couldn't get down, and he rescued it; all about the New Year's party when I was thirteen and sneaked the punch and got tipsy. No one ever knew about that except Uncle Franklin. He followed me up to my room, and was so perfect about it. He just sat down and started talking. Even when I developed a laughing jag, he pretended not to notice. He told me that he didn't agree with Matilda's idea of bringing me up, that I was getting to be a big girl, and would have to experiment about life myself, but that it would be better if I learned how dangerous drink was—and learned to gauge just how much I could take. And maybe for a few years it would be better if I didn't drink at all. And then he got up and walked out."

The other's brows were level with thought. "And this person told you all about that when he rang up?"

She nodded.

Gerald Shore got up from the chair, walked over toward the window, stood with his hands in his pockets. Outwardly he seemed calm and thoughtful. Only the rapid little puffs of cigar smoke which emerged from his mouth showed nervousness.

"What happened after that?" he asked.

"Then Uncle Franklin—this man, whoever he was—asked me to get Perry Mason and be at the Castle Gate Hotel at nine o'clock and to ask for Henry Leech."

"But, good heavens, Helen, if it was Franklin who was talking over the telephone, why in the world didn't he come home and . . ."

"That's what I kept wondering about, and then I thought perhaps—well, you know, if he's gone away with some other woman . . . I guess he wants to pave the way for coming back and probably wants someone to sound out Aunt Matilda on how she'll feel."

"But why didn't he call *me*? I'm his brother. I'm a lawyer. Why did he call *you*?"

"I don't know. He said I was the only one who could help him. Perhaps he tried to reach you and couldn't."

"And what happened after that? How did the conversation terminate?"

"He acted as though something had surprised him, as though someone had come in the room or something. He gave a quick little exclamation and hung up the telephone very abruptly."

"He asked you not to tell anyone?"

"Yes. But I—well, I thought I should tell you—under the circumstances."

"You didn't tell Matilda?"

"No."

"Sure she hasn't any suspicion?"

"No. I'm sure she thought I was talking to Jerry. And right after that she noticed the kitten was having spasms. Poor Amber Eyes! How could he possibly have got poison?"

"I don't know," Gerald said somewhat shortly. "Let's quit thinking about the kitten for a moment and think about Franklin. This doesn't make sense. Ten years' silence, and then this fantastic stage play of a return! Personally I always thought he'd run away with that woman. I felt sure he'd left Matilda some note that she'd suppressed. I thought, as time passed without any word except that card from Miami, that things probably hadn't gone so well. I always considered the possibility that he might have committed suicide. He'd have preferred that way out rather than face the humiliation of an ignominious return."

Gerald pushed his hands down more deeply into his pockets, stared out of the window. After a time he turned round and said to Helen, "When Franklin left, Matilda had a lot of the property in her name. If Franklin should show up he's not going to have much left for himself. You and I will have nothing. Franklin's my brother. He's your uncle. We both hope he's alive, but he is going to have to prove it."

Dr. Blakely came out from the operating room. "Your kitten was poisoned," he said to Helen.

"You're certain?"

"Absolutely."

Gerald turned again from the window to regard the doctor gravely. "What did you find?"

"Some poisoned meat had been administered but a very short time before the kitten was brought here. There were tablets of poison in the meat—perhaps more than one. I recovered a part of one tablet which hadn't as yet fully dissolved. It had probably been embedded in a piece of meat, and the kitten's digestive juices hadn't thoroughly dissolved it."

"Will—will he live?" Helen asked.

"Yes. He's going to be all right now. You can come back and get him in an hour or two, but you'd better let him either stay here for a few days, or let some friend keep him. Someone very deliberately tried to poison your kitten. You probably have some neighbour who doesn't like animals, or has some particular reason for disliking you."

"Why, I can't believe such a thing's possible," Helen said.

Dr. Blakely shrugged his shoulders. "Poisoned tablets packed in small wads of meat such as was given this kitten indicate the work of a deliberate poisoner. We have trouble with poisoners in various parts of the city: usually they're after dogs. They prepare little balls of meat and toss them into a yard. The dog grabs them eagerly. It's rather unusual that a kitten as young as this one gets such a big dose of poison."

Gerald said abruptly, "You want the kitten to stay away from the house for a few days, Doctor?"

"Yes."

"Is he out of danger now?"

"Yes. But I want to give him some further treatment—an hour or so."

Helen said, "Let's come back right after dinner and get him, Uncle Gerald. Then we can take him down to Tom Lunk—the gardener. He has a little bachelor shack that's out of the neighbourhood. Amber Eyes loves him and will be happy there."

"That sounds like an excellent plan," Dr. Blakely said.

Gerald Shore nodded. "All right. Come on, Helen, you've got a lot to do."

Four or five blocks from the veterinary's Gerald Shore pulled into the kerb in front of a drug-store.

"That appointment with Perry Mason," he explained. "I know him slightly, so I'll telephone for you. It will be a miracle if we can catch him now. He's a law unto himself as far as office hours go—and a lot of other things."

A few minutes later he emerged. "In an hour at his office. That all right?"

Helen nodded. "Hadn't you better come with me?"

"No. You'll tell him the story better if you do it in your own way without having me there. I'm particularly anxious to see how he reacts to it—if he gets the same impression I do. I told him I'd meet you somewhere in front of the Castle Gate Hotel at nine."

"What's your impression, Uncle Gerald?"

He smiled affectionately, but shook his head. He concentrated on his driving for a moment, then turned to Helen. "You really don't know whether that kitten was outdoors late this afternoon?"

"I've been trying to think, Uncle Gerald. I remember he was out in the back yard about three o'clock, but I can't remember that he was out after that."

"Who was at the house this afternoon?"

"Komo and Aunt Matilda and the cook."

"Who else?"

Under the direct impact of his eyes, she felt herself colouring. "Jerry Templar."

"How long before the kitten developed those spasms?"

"Not very long."

"Was George Alber there?"

"Yes, only for a few minutes. He came to see Aunt Matilda and then kept hanging around—until Jerry came—then I got rid of him in a hurry. Why?"

A muscle flickered in Gerald's cheek, as if his jaws had tightened. "How much do you know about this—this devotion of Matilda's to George Alber?"

"I know she likes him," Helen said. "She's always——"

"You don't know what's behind it, then? You don't know that she almost married his father?"

"I never knew that. It—it's hard to imagine Aunt Matilda as ever having been——"

"She was, though. In 1920, when she was forty or so, she was an attractive widow. And Stephen Alber was a good-looking widower. George is a lot like him. It wasn't any wonder to us that they fell for each other. It was a good deal more of a wonder when they had a quarrel and Matilda married Franklin. I always thought she did that mainly to hurt Stephen. It did hurt him, too, but he got over it. Married, two or three years afterwards. You probably remember when he was divorced, about 1930."

Helen shook her head. "It's hard to believe anybody could ever have been in love with Aunt Matilda. And it's even harder to imagine her being in love."

"But she was. So much in love that I don't think she ever got over it. I think she's still in love with Stephen Alber. I think the biggest of her reasons for hating Franklin isn't that he walked out on her. She knew he'd always hated Steve Alber, and I'm pretty sure that the thing she can't forgive him for is what he did to Steve."

"What did he do?" Helen said.

"Nothing, really. The bank did it after Franklin disappeared. But I shouldn't wonder if he'd been getting ready to do it before he left. The big smash in '29 hit Alber pretty hard, along with everybody else, but he managed to save some of the pieces. He hung on to them till '32, just after Franklin left. Then the bank put on the screws. I shouldn't wonder if Franklin had been intending to do it himself. He certainly didn't like Alber. Anyway, Alber went under and never came up. Perhaps that wasn't what killed him, but I guess it helped. And Matilda——" He stopped. They were almost home. "I'm going with you to-night. I'll be outside the Castle Gate at nine."

Helen hesitated. "Uncle Franklin said I mustn't bring anybody except Mr. Mason. He sounded terribly in earnest about it."

"No matter," Gerald said. "I'm going with you." His voice dropped a tone as he stopped in front of the house. "Be careful what you say. There's George Alber."

THREE

GEORGE ALBER WAS coming down the steps. If he looked as much like his father as Uncle Gerald said he did, Helen thought, it was easy enough to believe that twenty-odd years ago Aunt Matilda—and plenty of other women, probably—had fallen rather hard for Stephen Alber.

They would have had to be the kind of women, though, who lose their hearts to photographs of cinema actors. Retouched photographs, Helen told herself. There was something of that artificial quality about George Alber's handsomeness, as if some careful pencil had drawn the Greek straightness of the nose, given the eyebrows that precisely perfect line, sketched a little extra wave into the thick, brightly dark hair.

But the retoucher hadn't taken quite enough pains on the mouth. It was too full-lipped, and the jaw was too prominent. They marred the picture a little, that chin and mouth; they let coarseness into it, and vanity, and a kind of ruthlessness that might easily be cruel.

"What's this about the kitten's going mad?" His voice was something like his face, Helen told herself. Retouched so that instead of being just right, it was just a little too right to be real. "The cook says it scratched you. Let's see that hand."

He reached for it. His fingers were long and strong and beautifully kept, but Helen didn't like their touch. She jerked her hand away.

"My hand's all right. And Amber Eyes wasn't mad. He——"

"You can't afford to take that for granted." He wagged his head. "From what the cook says——"

"The cook got her information second-hand from Aunt Matilda," Helen interrupted. "The kitten was poisoned."

"Poisoned!" Alber exclaimed.

"That's right."

"You're certain?"

"Absolutely."

"But I can't understand that."

Gerald Shore, opening the left-hand car door and sliding out from behind the steering-wheel, said dryly, "There's no particular reason why you shouldn't be able to understand it. Pellets of poison were embedded in several particles of meat and fed to the animal by someone who wanted to make a very thorough job of killing the kitten. I don't know how I can explain it to you any more plainly."

George Alber apparently failed to notice the sarcasm. He said, smiling, "I didn't mean that I couldn't understand *what* had happened. I can't understand *why*."

Gerald said, "The answer is obvious. Someone wanted the kitten out of the way."

"But why?"

It was that question which suddenly impressed Helen. She turned to her uncle, her forehead puckered into a frown. "Yes, Uncle Gerald, *why* should anyone want to poison Amber Eyes?"

He dismissed the subject, rather brusquely, she thought. "You can't account for the psychology of an animal-poisoner. People go along and drop poisoned bits of meat into yards. The veterinary says they're rather prevalent in certain sections of the city."

Helen watched George Alber's eyes lock with those of her uncle. There was, she realized, a certain innate combativeness about the younger man which made him advance under fire rather than retreat. "I doubt very much if the kitten could have been poisoned in that way," he said. "One scrap of meat, perhaps, yes. But several scraps—well, I doubt it."

Gerald Shore, on the defensive and somewhat nettled by finding himself in that position, said, "Several scraps of meat might have been tossed into the yard within a space of a few feet. I see no reason why a kitten couldn't pick them up."

George Alber turned back to Helen. "When was the kitten out last, Helen?"

She said, "I don't know, George. I can't *remember* that it went out after three o'clock."

"Could it have picked up the poison then?"

"The veterinary says that it must have been administered within a few minutes of the time of the first spasm, not very long before we got it to the hospital. That's all that saved the kitten's life."

He nodded slowly as though that merely confirmed some idea which he had had in mind all along, then said suddenly, "Well, I'll be on my way. I only dropped in. Be seeing you later. Sorry about Amber Eyes. Take good care of him."

"We will," Helen said. "We're going to let Tom Lunk keep him for a few days."

George Alber walked across to the kerb where his car was parked, jumped in, and drove away.

Gerald Shore said with an intensity of feeling which came as somewhat of a surprise to his niece, "I definitely and distinctly dislike that man."

"Why, Uncle Gerald?"

"I don't know. He's too—too damned assured. You can take it in an older man, but what the devil has he ever done to warrant his assuming such a cocksure air? How does it happen he isn't in the Army?"

"Defective hearing in his left ear," Helen explained. "Haven't you ever noticed he always turns so his right side is toward you?"

Gerald snorted. "It's his profile. Notice the way he holds his head. Trying to ape the pose of some matinée idol in the pictures."

"No, he isn't, Uncle Gerald. That's unfair. It's on account of his hearing. I know that for a fact. He tried to enlist."

Gerald Shore asked abruptly, "When does Jerry Templar go back to camp?"

"Monday." She tried not to think how near Monday was.

"Does he know where they're sending him?"

"If he does, he isn't telling."

They were at the door of the house. Gerald pushed it open for her, but he didn't follow her in.

"I've got some things to see to uptown. You'll have to get down to Mason's office on your own." He glanced at his watch. "You'll have to start pretty soon, too, and you won't be back in time for dinner, so you'd better say you're having it with me. That'll satisfy Matilda and let you give Mason all the time he wants. He'll want plenty, unless I miss my guess. I'll be waiting for you outside the Castle Gate at nine."

He shut the door before she could remind him again that Uncle Franklin had very positively told her that nobody except Perry Mason was even to know about that appointment at the Castle Gate.

FOUR

PERRY MASON HAD that peculiar, confidence-inspiring magnetism which is so frequently found in tall men. In repose, his features and his manner had the weathered patience of hard granite. It was only in times of stress that his irrepressible personality flooded through. Before a jury, for instance, he could summon the skill and grace of a finished actor. His voice was a responsive instrument that accompanied and emphasized his words. His questions held a razor-edged sharpness which cut through the clumsy falsehoods of sullen, stubborn perjurers. In critical courtroom crises he was a fast-moving, quick-thinking force, moulding men's minds, playing on their emotions, out-thinking his antagonists; dramatic, persuasive, agile, yet never forsaking the fortress of deadly logic which buttressed every contention.

Della Street, his secretary, unlocked the door of the lawyer's private office, and entered to find him seated in the swivel chair behind his desk, his long legs elevated, the ankles crossed on a corner of the big desk.

"Well, here I am," she announced, taking off her gloves and slipping out of her coat.

Mason said nothing until she emerged from the cloak closet, having deposited her hat and coat. Then he said, "Della, virtue has been rewarded. I told you this morning that we shouldn't clutter up our minds with that equity case, even if there was money in it. Eight hours later we get *this*."

"There was a ten-thousand-dollar fee in that equity case," Della said frostily. "What's in this?"

Mason grinned. "It's an adventure that will make you feel ten years younger."

"Most of your cases make me feel ten years older!"

Mason ignored her. "This has none of the dull, routine angles that drive me to drink. It sparkles with mystery, adventure, romance. To put it another way, it's cock-eyed crazy and doesn't make any sense at all— one hell of a swell case."

"So I gathered when you telephoned," she observed, crossing over to seat herself on the opposite corner of his desk, conscious of that peculiar gleam in his eyes which came only in moments of inner excitement.

Perry Mason had the rare ability so seldom found in professional men, to derive enjoyment from his work. After a certain period, the doctor who has run the gamut of experiences with human illnesses acquires a certain impersonal efficiency. He regards the patients not so much as persons as depositories of various symptoms or anatomical structures which are to be coaxed or carved back to health. The lawyer, having acquired a sufficient background of experience, is apt to become imbued with the mechanics of procedure. But Perry Mason had a mind which was only content when it was detouring the technicalities of legal red tape. He not only regarded each case as a venture studded with excitement, but became impatient with the delays of routine procedure. More and more, as his practice developed, he became interested in personalities. More and more, his methods became dazzlingly brilliant, increasingly dangerous, and highly unorthodox. And Della Street knew that this peculiar light in his eye meant that in this new case he had found a tantalizing puzzle.

Perry was staring at her, and automatically she looked at herself through his eyes. Her brown suède pumps were good. Her legs were perfect. If the beige tailored suit didn't fit it was not because she hadn't been to a good tailor. Her face was all right, and she had a new shade of lipstick. Her hat was outrageous. She hoped he was satisfied.

"Della," Mason sighed, "sometimes I think you are getting blasé."

"Yes?" she drawled ominously. "Do tell me about it."

"You're getting conservative, mercenary, cautious. You're more interested in periods than you are in question marks."

Della relaxed. "Someone about this office has to be practical," she said. "But if it's not too much to ask, what's all the excitement about? I don't mind leaving half a good dinner uneaten and rushing over here, but I would like to know which missionary ate the cannibal."

"It was after you'd left the office," he said. "I was getting ready to leave—doing some work on that brief in the Johnson case. A lawyer whom I know slightly telephoned and wanted an appointment for his niece, and a little later she came in and talked to me."

Della Street slipped from the desk to pick up a note-book from her desk. She drew up a chair, and her informal manner gave place to secretarial efficiency. "What were the names?" she asked.

"Gerald Shore's the lawyer, has an office in the Debenture Investment Building. As I remember it, he handles rather a specialized branch of practice—does a good deal with mining corporations. Think he's something of a gambler himself, does work largely for promoters, and takes fees partly in cash and partly in stocks in the companies he organizes."

"Any money in it?" Della Street asked.

"Don't be so damned mercenary," Mason said, grinning. "I think he makes more out of it than money."

"How do you mean?"

"He's always chasing mirages. Our realistic philosophers hold that as being poor economy. Simply because a mirage has no definite substance, they overlook the fact that it's such a lovely object to chase. They also lose sight of the fact that the mirage-chaser is getting great joy out of life. He's always interested in what he's chasing, which is more than you can say of many men who struggle toward more practical goals. Interest in life is the very best form of wealth."

"Any retainer?"

"Not yet," Mason admitted.

"I see. The niece's name?"

"Helen Kendal."

"Age?"

"About twenty-four. Very exciting violet eyes. On the blonde side. Nice chassis, nice assembly, nice accessories—definitely nice."

"*And* no retainer," Della Street muttered. "You say she's a niece of Gerald Shore?"

"Yes. I'll give you a brief sketch of the family history." He reached for some scrawled notes and began to dictate. Swiftly and compactly, the salient facts in the case went into Della Street's note-book.

On a January evening in 1932, Franklin Shore, then fifty-seven and in vigorous health, went into his study after dining with his wife. There he received a caller whom he must have admitted himself, since no servant had answered the door. A maid had seen somebody coming up the drive, and thought she recognized him as Gerald Shore, and Matilda Shore also thought that the voice she heard in the study was Gerald's, but she had not heard it clearly enough to be sure, and Gerald himself denied having been there.

Whoever the visitor was, he wanted money. Matilda Shore distinctly heard her husband's voice, lifted in anger, refusing to lend it, saying something about the world's being crowded with jackasses who only needed a few thousands to get back on Easy Street, when even a jackass ought to know that there was never going to be any such street again.

That was all the talk she overheard. She went upstairs to read in bed and didn't hear the visitor leave. She did not find out until next morning that Franklin Shore had also left.

Those were the days when a whisper could break a bank, so that Shore's wife and business associates did not take the police into their confidence until he had been missing for some days. Every effort, official and private, was thereafter made to locate him, but no trace of him could be found. The bank's affairs proved to be in perfect order, so that, in spite of the headlines, the institution suffered no damage from its president's disappearance. His own affairs were also in order, so instead of explaining his action, that made it more mysterious, because, except for a few hundred dollars he habitually carried with him, he had apparently left without funds. His cheque-book was found on his desk, with the date on a blank cheque filled in, and a broken line indicating that he had begun to write the name of a payee and then evidently had either changed his mind or been interrupted. The book showed a balance of $58,941.13 in his joint account with his wife, and this balance was proved correct except for one cheque for $10,000, drawn on a blank taken from another cheque-book, about which Shore had telephoned his secretary before the disappearance.

There were the usual whispers. Several times during the few months before he vanished, he had been seen with a woman unknown to any of those who reported having seen the pair, but good-looking, noticeably well dressed and somewhere in the thirties. But there was nothing to suggest that she had left in Shore's company, except for a picture post card, from Miami, Florida, postmarked June 5, 1932, which his niece had received six months after the disappearance. The message, in handwriting identified by experts as unmistakably that of Franklin Shore, read:

> No idea how much longer we shall be here, but we're enjoying the mild climate and, believe it or not, swimming. With lots of love,
> YOUR UNCLE FRANKLIN.

The plural pronouns, of course, seemed to justify the whispers about the blonde unknown, but the investigators who were hurried to Miami found no trace of Franklin Shore. He had a number of acquaintances there, and the fact that none of them had seen him argued that he could not have made any long stay.

His will was found. It left the bulk of his estate to his wife, with twenty-thousand-dollar legacies to his niece and brother.

"How about them?" Della Street looked up hopefully from her book.

"They haven't been paid. The niece has been living with her aunt for years. Gerald Shore has, I think, had some indirect benefits. But the legacies are still payable—that is, they will be if Franklin Shore is dead."

"But nothing has been heard from him for . . ."

"That's just the point," Mason said. "Something has. He telephoned his niece to-day. She's to meet him to-night. He insisted that I should be present at the interview. I'm going to take you along."

"Do I take a note-book?" she asked.

"By all means a note-book," Mason said. "We're going to have notes, so we'll know everything that's said, and be able to discuss the significance of the things that aren't said."

"But why doesn't he get in touch with his wife and come back home?"

"That's just the point. There was something mysterious about his disappearance, some talk at the time of his having run away with a younger woman. Apparently he isn't too certain of the reception his wife will give him."

"She knows nothing about his being here now?"

"No. Franklin specifically instructed his niece to say nothing to any-one. She did confide in her Uncle Gerald, the one who telephoned me."

"Is Matilda Shore the forgiving kind?" Della Street asked.

Mason grinned. "Definitely not, and reading between the lines of Helen Kendal's story, I'd say she's a most objectionable, peculiar char-acter. What's more, there's an old love affair involved, too. The man is dead, but his son, George Alber, is the spitting image of his father, and Matilda is very much attached to him. I gather that Gerald Shore views that relationship with alarm."

"Why?"

"In young Alber," Mason said, "she sees the image of the man whom she once loved. Her only living relatives being Gerald Shore and Helen Kendal, ordinarily, they'd be the beneficiaries under her will. Some time ago, before young Alber read 'Welcome' on the mat, she intimated that they were not only her heirs but would inherit the entire fortune."

"It is a fortune?"

"Yes."

"Enter Alber!"

Mason grinned. "Enter Alber. Gerald Shore thinks he's turning loose all his charm, and there's no question about the fact that he has become a frequent visitor at the house."

"Good heavens, you don't mean that this woman of sixty-four is going to marry this . . ."

"Probably not," Mason said. "But she wants her niece to marry him. And Alber seems to like that idea. Matilda has become quite a despot, and she controls the purse-strings. However, you haven't heard all the ramifications of the case yet. Not only was there this mysterious telephone call, but a kitten was poisoned this afternoon."

Della raised her eyebrows. "What has the poisoned kitten to do with the return of Franklin Shore?"

"Perhaps nothing, perhaps a lot."

"In what way?"

"It was probably an inside job."

"Why inside?"

"Because, checking up as best they can, the cat doesn't seem to have been out of the house after three o'clock in the afternoon. The symptoms of poisoning developed round about five o'clock. The veterinary says the poison was administered not over fifteen or twenty minutes before the cat was brought to him for treatment. That was about a quarter past five."

"What kind of poison?" Della Street asked. "A kind that could have been administered to a human being?"

"That's the rub," Mason admitted. "Apparently it was a strychnine poisoning. Strychnia has a bitter taste. An animal would swallow it if the poison were skilfully embedded in small balls of meat, because animals seldom chew. But a human being would have detected the bitter taste; particularly if the meat had been cooked."

"And you want me to go with you to-night?"

"Yes. A man by the name of Leech is going to escort us to the place where Franklin is hiding."

"Why's he hiding?"

Mason laughed. "Why did he disappear in the first place? I've often wondered about that, Della. Why a man who was enough of a realist to keep selling stocks short during the years which followed the crash of twenty-nine, who was making money hand over fist, who had everything that he wanted in life, should suddenly disappear *and take none of the money with him.*"

"Perhaps he'd been salting some away," Della Street said.

"Not in these days of income-tax," Mason pointed out.

"He might have falsified his books."

"An individual with a smaller income might have done that, but

Franklin Shore's affairs were too complex. No, Della, we're in the way of solving an ancient mystery. The solution is going to be interesting and may be highly exciting. You want to get the picture of Matilda Shore as Helen Kendal painted it. A morose, strong-minded woman with over a million dollars locked in her grasping hands, approaching the end of life, something of a Tartar, addicted to chirping lovebirds, a servant who has always posed as a Korean, but who acts, looks, and talks like a Japanese. She's kept alive by one thing—the desire to be there waiting when her husband finally returns. Come on, Della, we're on the trail of another adventure in crime!"

Della grimaced. "There's no crime yet," she pointed out.

"Well," Mason said, walking over to the hat closet and whipping on his coat, "at least we have one attempted crime."

"What's that?"

"The kitten."

"The case of the poisoned kitten?" she asked.

She slipped a note-book and half a dozen pencils into her purse, and then stood by the desk as though worried about something.

"Coming?" demanded Perry impatiently.

"Chief, have you ever seen a kitten eat?"

"Does a duck swim? Why?"

"A cat usually picks at its food. That kitten must have been terribly hungry to gulp down those balls of meat."

"This kitten was just careless, I guess. Hurry up."

"Very careless," nodded Della. "I think when I open the file for this case I'll call it 'The Case of the Careless Kitten.' "

FIVE

IN MASON'S CAR, driving toward the Castle Gate Hotel, Della Street asked, "Did Franklin Shore put *all* his property in his wife's name?"

"Just about all, as I understand it. There were joint accounts in the bank."

"How long before the disappearance?"

"It had been going on for three or four years."

"Then if she wants to keep him from coming back, she could . . ."

"Couldn't keep him from coming back physically," Mason interrupted, "but she certainly could embarrass his come-back financially. Suppose, the moment he showed up, she filed suit for divorce, asked for a property award, and all that out of what little property remains in his name? Get the sketch? She'd claim that the other property was all hers."

"You think that's what she's planning?"

Mason said, "He certainly has *some* reason for wanting me there at the conference. I don't think he wants me to play tiddlywinks."

They were silent for several blocks, then Della asked, "Where do we meet the others?"

"A block from the Castle Gate Hotel."

"What kind of a place is it?"

"Second-rate, down-at-the-heel hotel, an outward front of respectability, but it's a thin veneer."

"And Henry Leech wanted Helen Kendal and you to come along?"

"Yes."

"Think he'll object to the four of us?"

"I don't know. There are some peculiar angles, and I want notes taken so I'll know what is said, and what isn't said. . . . Up on the next corner is where we meet the others. Here's a good parking place."

Mason eased the car into the kerb, switched off the lights and ignition, helped Della Street out, and locked the door. Two figures detached themselves from the shadows of a doorway. Gerald Shore came forward to shake hands. Introductions were performed in a low voice.

"Coast all clear?" Mason asked.

"I think so, yes."

"You haven't been followed?"

"Not as far as we can tell."

Helen Kendal said, "I'm quite certain no one has followed us."

Mason nodded toward the building in the middle of the next block where a section of blank wall rising above the top of the nearest house had been lettered "CASTLE GATE HOTEL. *Rooms One Dollar and Up.* MONTHLY RATES. TRANSIENTS. *Restaurant.*" The sign had been faded and sooted by the grime of a big city.

Mason took Helen Kendal's arm. "You and I will go first," he said. "Shore, you and Miss Street can follow, after an interval of twenty or thirty seconds. Don't appear to be with us until we start up in the elevator."

Gerald Shore hesitated. "After all," he said, "the person *I* want to see is my brother Franklin. I don't care about seeing this man Leech. If my presence may frighten him, I'd prefer to sit and wait in the automobile."

Mason said, "Miss Street is going with me. That'll make three of us. You may as well make four."

Shore reached a sudden decision. "No, I'll wait here in the automobile, but the minute you meet my brother, I want you to tell him I'm here and that I simply *must* see him before he talks with anyone. Do you understand? Before he talks with *anyone.*"

Mason regarded the man quizzically. "Before he talks with me?"

"With anyone."

Mason shook his head. "If you want any such message delivered, deliver it yourself. The man has sent for me. He probably wants to consult me professionally."

Shore's bow was courtly. "My mistake. I'm sorry. But I'll wait here just the same. I doubt that my brother is in that hotel. When you come out with Leech, I'll join you."

He walked back to a place near the corner where he had parked his automobile, unlocked the door, got in, and sat down.

Mason smiled reassuringly at Helen Kendal. "We may as well go."

They walked along the echoing, all but deserted sidewalk to the drab entrance of the out-dated hotel. Mason held the door open for the two young women, followed them in.

The lobby was some twenty feet wide, running back to terminate in a U-shaped desk and counter behind which was a switchboard. A somewhat bored clerk sat, reading one of the more lurid "true" detective magazines. Across from the clerk were two automatic elevators. There were some fifteen or twenty chairs in the lobby, for the most part arranged in a row along one wall. Half a dozen individuals sprawling disspiritedly in these chairs raised their eyes to look, at first casually, then with sharpened interest, at the two trim, slim-waisted young women followed by the tall figure of the lawyer.

The clerk at the desk glanced up from his magazine, and did them the honour of letting his attention remain on them.

"You have a Henry Leech registered here?" Mason asked, as he reached the desk.

"Yes."

"Been here long?"

"About a year."

"Indeed! What's his room?"

"Three-eighteen."

"Will you ring him, please?"

The clerk, who apparently was also the telephone operator, moved over to the switchboard and plugged in a line. He pressed a button several times while holding an earpiece against his left ear. His eyes studied Della Street and Helen Kendal with an interest which he made no effort to conceal.

"I'm sorry. He isn't in."

Mason looked at his watch. "He was to meet me here at this time."

The clerk said, "I didn't think he was in. A man came to see him two or three hours ago. He was out. I haven't seen him come back. I . . ." He broke off as a special delivery messenger came up to the desk.

"Got a special delivery for the clerk at the Castle Gate," the boy said.

The clerk signed for the special delivery, opened the letter, read it, then looked up at Mason. "Are you Mr. Perry Mason?" he asked.

"That's right."

"Well, I guess Leech was to meet you all right. It's really for you— but he addressed it to me."

He handed Mason a sheet of paper on which a message had been neatly typewritten:

To clerk at Castle Gate Hotel:
    A gentleman will call for me to-night. He is Perry Mason, lawyer.

Please tell him I cannot keep appointment, but he is to come at once to place indicated. Circumstances have necessitated a change in plans. This is unfortunate. Tell him to drive, please, to reservoir near top of road behind Hollywood according to course traced on map enclosed herewith. Once more excuse, please, change in plans. It is unavoidable.

HENRY LEECH.

The signature as well as the message was typewritten. The map which was enclosed with the letter was an Auto Club map of Hollywood and vicinity. An ink line had been traced along Hollywood Boulevard, turning to the right on Ivar Street, then following a winding course to a spot on the map marked STORAGE RESERVOIR.

The clerk said, "I *thought* he went out—a couple of hours ago. I haven't seen him return."

Mason studied the special delivery letter, abruptly folded both letter and map, and shoved them down into the side pocket of his coat.

"Let's go," he said.

SIX

THE HEADLIGHTS OF the two automobiles twisted and turned, alternately showing dazzling circles against a cut bank, then swinging out to send parallel cones of light across dark canyons. The road snaked its way up the mountains, climbing steadily. Mason and Della Street drove the car in the lead, Gerald Shore and his niece following in their car.

"Did it strike you that there was anything strange about that letter of instructions?" Mason asked Della, deftly spinning the wheel to follow the curves in the road.

Her eyes shifting alternately from the map to the road ahead, she said, "It has a vaguely familiar sound as though I knew the person who had written it—sort of a style of expression, I guess you might call it."

Mason laughed. "If you heard it read aloud in the proper tone of voice, you'd recognize at once what it was."

"I don't get you."

Mason said, "Try bowing and smiling as you read the lines out loud. Read them without expression, in a monotone, and see what you get."

Della Street unfolded the letter from the envelope, started reading. At the end of the fourth line she said, "Good heavens, it's the way a Japanese would write."

Mason said, "You couldn't have made a letter sound more Japanese if you'd deliberately set out to do it. And notice that the signature is typewritten—also that the letter is addressed simply to the clerk at the Castle Gate Hotel. Leech has been staying there for a year. He'd almost certainly have known the clerk by name, and would have addressed the letter accordingly."

"Then you don't think we'll find Leech up here? You think this is a wild-goose chase?"

"I don't know. I noticed that peculiar style of expression and wondered if you'd noticed it, too."

"I hadn't at the time. I suppose I would have if I'd heard it read aloud. Now that you've pointed it out, it's perfectly plain."

Mason shifted the car into second, pushed the throttle well down, sent the big machine screaming round the curves. For the space of several minutes his hands and arms were busy with the steering-wheel; then the road straightened somewhat and levelled off. All around them was a black rim of quiet mountains. Above this rim were the steady stars. Below and behind, a carpet of twinkling lights extended in a huge crescent for mile upon mile, marking the location of Los Angeles, Hollywood, and the suburban towns, an apparently unbroken cluster of myriad pin-pointed lights, interspersed here and there with blobs of colour from neon signs. Against this vast sea of illumination, the outlines of the mountains up which they had climbed were dark, patient silhouettes.

Mason slipped the car back into high gear, eased the pressure on the throttle, and the powerful silent motor in the big car became a mere whisper of synchronized power. Through the open windows the silence of the mountains seeped in, a silence that was broken only by the sound of tyres gliding over the road, and the ominous *whooo whooo whooo* of an owl.

A moment later, the lights of Gerald Shore's car were reflected back from windscreen and rear-view mirror in Mason's car, partially blinding him by their glare, so that it was not until Mason was almost on top of the parked unlighted automobile that he saw it and swerved sharply to the right. A few yards ahead, the road curved abruptly, and a circular fringe of eucalyptus marked the location of a reservoir.

"This is it," Della said.

Mason pulled his car to the side of the road and parked. Gerald Shore swung in behind the lawyer. Both drivers switched off headlights and motors.

Almost instantly, the silence of the mountain spaces engulfed them. From under the hood of Mason's car, the cooling motor block gave forth little cracks of sound which were magnified by the surrounding silence until they became as distinct explosions. The sound of Gerald Shore's feet coming up from behind seemed unusually loud.

Adjusting his voice to the quiet which surrounded them, Gerald Shore said, "That must be the car back there, but I didn't see anyone in it."

There was an uncertain note in Della Street's laugh. "It doesn't look

like much of a party to me," she announced with nervous flippancy.
"Are you sure they said Tuesday night?"

Helen Kendal's voice from behind Gerald Shore was sharp with
apprehension. "There's someone in the automobile, sitting behind the
steering-wheel. He hasn't moved, just keeps sitting there, waiting."

"Got a torch?" Shore asked. "Somehow I feel uneasy about this
whole business. There's no reason why my brother should have decoyed
us up here simply to meet him."

Mason said, "I'll get a torch." He opened the glove compartment
of the car, pulled out a three-cell electric torch, and said, "Come on,
let's go."

They formed a compact little group as they marched back along the
road, the torch spraying a circular spot of white light on the ground.

The parked automobile remained dark, silent, and motionless. There
was no sign of life from within it.

Abruptly, Mason raised the spotlight so that the rays shone through
the windscreen. Helen Kendal only half checked the exclamation of
startled horror which came to her lips.

The body was slumped awkwardly against the steering-wheel. The
right arm was half circled around the wheel. The head was tilted to one
side and rested against the shoulder. A sinister red stream had flowed
down from the left temple, had divided at the line of the cheekbone,
contrasting in colour with the hue of the dead flesh.

Mason stood still, holding the spotlight focused on the inert body.
He said over his shoulder to Gerald Shore, "I don't suppose you could
identify this man Leech."

"No. I've never met him."

"This isn't your brother?" Mason asked, moving a little to one side
so that the spotlight would illuminate the features to better advantage.

"No."

"You're certain?"

"Yes."

Mason deliberated a moment, then said, "Lieutenant Tragg of Homicide is always claiming that I violate the law by moving bodies and
destroying clues before the police get on the job. This time I'm going
to be above suspicion. If Miss Kendal isn't afraid to stay here, I'm going
to leave you two to watch the body while Miss Street and I rush down to
the nearest telephone and notify the Homicide Squad."

Shore hesitated for a moment, said at length, "It will only take one
to do the telephoning. I'd like more than one witness here."

"Willing to stay?" Mason asked Della.

She met his eyes. "Of course."

"Okay. . . . Miss Kendal, what's your aunt's telephone number?"

"Roxwood 3-3987. Why? Are you going to notify her?"

"No," he said, "but I thought I might ring up the house. I may want to ask the houseboy a question."

Mason jumped in his car, hurriedly slammed the door shut, stepped on the throttle, and went snarling in second gear down the winding hill. He stopped at the first house where he saw a light, ran up the steps, and rang the doorbell.

It was a somewhat pretentious mansion, typical of California sidehill construction, one floor on the street side; then descending in a series of floors and balconies on the downhill side away from the road.

Mason saw the figure of a man moving leisurely across a corridor. A porch light clicked, etching him into sharp brilliance. A small window in the door slid back. A pair of keen, grey eyes surveyed the lawyer. "What is it?" a man's voice asked.

Mason said, "My name is Perry Mason. I want to use your telephone to notify the Homicide Squad that a man's body has been found in an automobile up by the reservoir at the top of the hill."

"Perry Mason, the lawyer?" the man asked.

"Yes."

"I've heard of you. Come in."

The door opened. The man, wearing a smoking-jacket and slippers, peered curiously at Mason, and said, "I've read a lot about you in the newspapers. Never thought I'd meet you this way. The phone's there on that little stand."

Mason thanked him, picked up the phone, dialled Homicide, and asked for Lieutenant Tragg. A few moments later, he heard Lieutenant Tragg's crisp, incisive voice on the line.

"Perry Mason," the lawyer said. "I have something to report."

Tragg said, "You aren't going to tell me you've found another body?"

"Certainly not," Mason replied promptly.

"Well, that's better. What's the trouble?"

Mason said, "*I've* quit discovering bodies, but one of the persons who was with me discovered a body in an automobile up near a reservoir above Hollywood. If you want to start now, I'll meet you at the corner of Hollywood and Ivar and show you the way up."

"Oh," Lieutenant Tragg said with elaborate politeness, "someone who was *with* you discovered the body."

"That's right."

"Since you've used up your quota," Tragg said sarcastically, "I presume you've let your very estimable secretary claim the credit for this one?"

Mason said, "It's all right with me if you want to sit at the phone making wisecracks instead of investigating a murder, but it'll sound like hell in the newspapers."

"Okay, you win. I'll be right out."

Mason hung up the telephone and dialled Roxwood 3-3987.

After several seconds during which he could hear the sound of the ringing bell at the other end of the line, a woman's voice answered the telephone. "Yes. What is it?" she asked in sharp, high-pitched accents.

"You have a Japanese houseboy," Mason said. "I'd like to talk . . ."

"He isn't Japanese. He's Korean!"

"All right, whatever nationality he is, I want to talk with him."

"He isn't here."

"Oh, he isn't?"

"No."

"When did he leave?" Mason asked.

"About an hour or so ago."

"Who are you?"

"I'm the cook and housekeeper. It's supposed to be my night off, but I came in just as they left and they told me to stay here and answer the telephone in case anyone rang."

"Could you tell me if this *Korean* servant had been in the house all the evening?"

"Well—I couldn't exactly—I think he was out for a while."

"Where is he now?"

"Out."

"Can't you give me any more information than that?"

"No."

"I'm Mr. Mason. I'm calling on behalf of Gerald Shore and I want to know where this houseboy is now."

"You're calling for Mr. Shore?"

"That's right."

"If I tell you where Komo is now, you'll see that—there won't be any trouble?"

"No. I'll take care of that."

"He's taken Mrs. Shore to the Exeter Hospital."

"To the Exeter Hospital?" Mason repeated in surprise.

"Yes. She was taken very sick, all of a sudden like, looked as though she'd been . . ."

"As though she'd been what?" Mason asked.

"Nothing."

"When did this happen?"

"About a quarter to nine, I think."

"Looked as though she'd been what?" Mason insisted.

The woman at the other end of the line hesitated a moment, then said sharply, "Poisoned. But don't tell anyone I said so," and hung up the telephone.

SEVEN

THE HOMICIDE SQUAD car, screaming along Hollywood Boulevard, swerved and swayed through frozen traffic. Pedestrians stood staring at the speeding car, watching it swerve and twist until the red tail-light disappeared and the normal traffic once more came to life and motion.

Mason stepped out from in front of his parked car to stand in the beam of the headlights of the oncoming police machine. As the big car slid to a stop, a door swung open, and Lieutenant Tragg said tersely, "Get in."

Mason climbed in, noticing that the rear seat beside Tragg had apparently been reserved for him.

"Where to?" Tragg asked.

Mason took the folded map from his pocket. "There's the map which gave me my directions."

"Where'd you get it?"

"It came in a letter."

"Where's the letter?"

Mason passed it over. Tragg took it, but held it, making no attempt as yet to read it.

The officer who was driving the car looked back for instructions.

Tragg said, "Take it easy a minute, Floyd. The man up there in the automobile is dead. *He* isn't going to make any moves that will confuse us. Mr. Mason is very much alive."

"Meaning that *I'm* apt to make confusing moves?" Mason asked with a smile.

Tragg said, "Well, I always like to interview you as soon as possible after one of your nocturnal adventures makes my presence necessary. I find it sometimes simplifies matters."

"I didn't discover this body."

"No? Who did?"

"A lawyer named Gerald Shore."

"Never heard of him."

"He doesn't do much court work and no criminal work. I think you'll find he's a very respectable member of the profession."

There was a certain grudging admiration in Lieutenant Tragg's eyes as he looked Mason over. Tragg was utterly unlike the popular conception of a police detective. Not quite as tall as Mason, he was slender, suave, sophisticated, and thoroughly imbued with a knowledge of his profession. When he started following a trail, he was not easily detoured. He had imagination and daring.

"Now this letter," he said, balancing it in his hand as though trying physically to weigh the evidentiary importance of the document. "Where did you get this?"

"From the clerk of the Castle Gate Hotel."

"Oh, yes. The Castle Gate Hotel, rather a second-rate, shoddy affair; and in case you're interested, Mason, it's down on our list as being somewhat friendly to persons who don't have exactly the best reputations—or perhaps you hadn't heard about that."

"I hadn't heard about it."

"In any event, it's hardly an hotel which *you'd* have picked as a stopping place."

"That's right," Mason admitted. "I wasn't registered there."

"Therefore, it's logical to ask you what you *were* doing there? . . . Drive ahead slowly, Floyd. We're getting too much of an audience round here."

One of the officers in the front seat said, "I can start 'em moving and keep 'em moving."

"No, no," Tragg ordered impatiently without taking his eyes from Mason. "Drive on. Dispersing crowds takes time. Mr. Mason wants to tell us his story while it's still fresh in his mind, don't you, Mason?"

The lawyer laughed.

Tragg pushed the map across to the front seat. "Here, Floyd. Take this map. Follow the road. Don't give her the gun until I tell you to. Now, Mason, you were about to tell me why you went to the Castle Gate Hotel."

"I went there to see a man. If you'd read that letter, you'd understand."

"The man's name?" Tragg asked, still holding the letter in his hand, but keeping his eyes on the lawyer.

"Henry Leech."

"And what did you want to see him about?"

Mason made a little gesture with his hands as though tossing something away. "Now there, Lieutenant," he said, "you have me. I went to see Mr. Leech at the suggestion of Mr. Leech. He wanted to tell me something."

"The invitation came directly from Leech?"

"Indirectly."

"Through a client?"

"Yes."

"The client's name?"

"Helen Kendal, and I presume she came to me through this attorney, Gerald Shore."

"They knew what Leech wanted to see you about?"

"Mr. Leech was to take me to see someone else, as I understood it."

"Oh, a case of a mysterious witness taking you to a mysterious witness?"

"Not exactly. The person I was to see was a man who had disappeared some time ago and . . ."

Tragg held up his hand, half closed his eyes, snapped his fingers twice, said, "Wait a minute—wait a minute! I'm getting it now. What was his name?"

"Franklin Shore."

"That's right. The most baffling disappearance of 1932. I've placed your lawyer, Gerald Shore, now. Leech knew something about this disappearance?"

"Of course," Mason said, "I'm only giving you hearsay. You can perhaps do better by communicating with the parties who really know the background."

"Rather subtle that," Tragg conceded. "But I think I'd prefer to have *your* story first, Mason."

Mason said, "Leech was, I understand, going to take Miss Kendal to see Franklin Shore. Really, Lieutenant, I think you'd be wise to try and get up there as soon as possible. What happened there may well be a clue to something more important."

"Yes, yes, I know," Tragg said. "You always have some very acceptable red herring which gets dragged tantalizingly across the trail just when I'm getting somewhere; but there's a little more I want to find out first, Mason. . . . Just keep driving slowly, Floyd. . . . Now, how did it happen that Leech promised to take you to see Franklin Shore?"

Mason's voice rasped with sudden impatience. "I don't know, and

I think you're wasting valuable time. The message came to me through Miss Kendal."

"But he did promise to take you?"

"Who?"

"Leech, of course," Tragg said. "Quit sparring for time."

"No," Mason replied. "So far as I know, Leech didn't talk with Miss Kendal. It was a telephone communication with another party that sent her to Leech."

"Oh, I see," Tragg said. "Someone else did the talking, and I take it you're going to say you don't know who this party was?"

"No," Mason said. "I don't *know* who he was."

"I see. One of those anonymous conversations?"

"Not at all, Lieutenant. The man gave his name, and furthermore gave some rather interesting information to establish his identity."

"And the name?" Tragg asked.

It was Mason's turn to smile. "Franklin B. Shore."

For as long as a second, Tragg's face was changing expression as his mind digested the import of that information; then he snapped a command to the driver. "Step on it, Floyd. Give it everything it's got. Get up there—fast!"

Mason settled back in the seat, took a cigarette-case from his pocket, and offered one to Tragg. "I thought you'd like to get up there. Lieutenant. Have a smoke."

Tragg said, "Put that damn thing back in your pocket and hang on. You don't know Floyd."

Mason reached for a cigarette, was all but thrown from his seat as the car lurched round a turn and dodged another automobile coming through an intersection.

"Get that siren going," Tragg ordered. "And get some speed."

The siren started its eerie screaming. The big, powerful car kept picking up momentum as it climbed. Mason, bracing himself, managed to get a cigarette from his case and up to his lips. He returned the case to his pocket, then was forced to hang on with both hands, having no opportunity to strike a match.

The car climbed rapidly, the screaming siren alternately roaring back in echoes from precipitous banks, then being swallowed up in the vastness of deep mountain canyons to return in muffled echoes from distant hillsides. The driver skilfully set the two red-beamed spotlights at such angles that no matter which way the winding road twisted up the mountain, a spot of illumination was thrown on the road.

At length the headlights on the police car illuminated the two parked automobiles, showed Della Street, Helen Kendal, and Gerald Shore standing closely together, their faces white ovals as they watched the approaching car.

Mason said, "Swing your headlights so they illuminate that first car, Lieutenant."

"That the one that has Leech's body?" Tragg asked.

"I don't know," Mason said. "I don't know Leech when I see him." Tragg looked at him sharply. "You mean this body isn't that of Leech?"

"I don't know."

"Who does?"

"I'm sure I couldn't tell you. I don't know whether anyone in my party can make an identification."

The police car lurched to a full stop.

Tragg said, "All right, let's look around, boys Mason, go over and see if anyone in your party can identify the body."

If Lieutenant Tragg's request had been intended to keep Mason from observing the police inspection of the car, it failed, for Mason merely raised his voice and called, "Come on over here—the three of you."

"I didn't say that," Tragg said irritably.

Mason said, "I thought you wanted to know whether they could identify the body."

"I do, but they don't need to come over here and get in the way."

"They won't get in the way. How are they going to identify a body if they don't see it?"

"They've taken a good look at him by this time," Tragg said. "Trust you for that."

"On the contrary," Mason assured him, "two of these people haven't been near the car."

"How do you know they haven't?"

"Because I left instructions for them not to do so."

"How do you know they followed instructions?"

"Because Della Street was here."

Tragg frowned at him and said, "The elaborate precautions you're taking in this case make it look as though you had already stuck your toe in the water and found it mighty hot."

Mason looked hurt. "You've got a nasty, suspicious mind, Tragg." Then he grinned. "I'll admit, though, that I try to remember the story of the guy who wanted to go swimming at night and dived into the pool without finding out whether it was filled."

By that time, spotlights were blazing on the interior of the car. A photographer had set up his camera on a tripod and was inserting a bulb in the synchronized flash gun.

"Move over to this side," Tragg said. "You can see his face from there. Any of you know him?"

Solemnly they moved round to the side of the car to examine the features.

"I have never seen this man before," Shore said solemnly.

"Nor I," Helen Kendal supplemented.

"You?" Tragg asked Della Street. She shook her head.

Tragg said, "None of you know Leech?"

There were two "No's" and a shake of the head.

The photographer said, "Okay, Lieutenant, get 'em out of the way."

An officer pushed the group back, and the instantaneous brilliance of the torch bulb cut the night apart with a quick stab of light.

"Hold it," the photographer said. "I'll get another shot from this angle, then one from the other side. Then you can have him."

As the little group moved away from the car, Mason managed to get Della Street and Helen Kendal off to one side. "When Lieutenant Tragg questions you," he said, "answer his questions frankly; but it might be a good plan not to *volunteer* any information . . . particularly unimportant information."

"Such as what?" Della asked.

"Oh," Mason said, with an elaborately casual manner, "any of the family gossip or anything of that sort. Tragg will ask you what he wants to know. Don't take up his time with a lot of unimportant incidentals, such as the fact that Gerald Shore didn't come into the hotel when we went in to call on Leech—things like that. Of course, if he asks you specifically, that's different, but there's no necessity to waste time telling him things in which he isn't interested. He'll ask you about everything he wants to know."

Helen Kendal nodded innocently enough, but Della Street manœuvred Mason off toward the rear of the car. "Why the secrecy about Gerald Shore not going into the hotel?" she asked. "And what's significant about it?"

Mason's manner was deeply thoughtful. "Hanged if I know, Della. For some reason, I don't think he wanted to go into the hotel."

"You think he really knows Henry Leech?"

"He may—or he *might* have been in there earlier to-night and didn't want the clerk to recognize him."

She puckered her lips to give a low whistle.

"Mind you, that's just a guess," Mason warned. "There's probably nothing to it, but I . . ."

"What are *you* two talking about?" Tragg demanded, coming round from the other side of the car.

Mason said, "Wondering whether he was shot from the left side by someone hidden by the side of the road or from the right side by someone sitting in the car."

Tragg snorted, "Pardon me! From the secret huddle you're in, I thought you might be discussing something confidential—like who won the last World's Series. Just to satisfy your curiosity, he was shot from the left side by someone who was outside the car. The bullet entered the left side of the head, and the murderer stood far enough away so that the weapon left no powder burns. Probably it was a .38 revolver, and it *may* have been an automatic. We're going to look for the empty cartridge-case. Is there anything else you want to know?"

"Quite a lot," Mason said. "In fact, virtually all the details."

"Got a nickel?" Tragg asked casually.

Mason pushed his hand down in his pocket. "Yes. Why? Did you want to telephone?"

"No," Tragg said, grinning. "Keep your nickel. You can buy a newspaper with it to-morrow and get *all* the details. Right now, I'm only going to tell you what I want you to know."

Tragg walked past them to the side of the car. By this time, the deputy coroner had completed his examination, so the men began searching the body.

A few moments later, Tragg walked over to the police car and said, "I'd like to have you four come over here. Mason, I'm going to ask you to let me do the talking for a moment, and not say anything unless I ask you some specific question."

Mason nodded.

"Now then," Tragg said, turning to the others, "what was it Mason told you *not* to tell me about?"

Mason said, "What makes you think . . ."

Tragg silenced him by holding up his hand. He kept his eyes on Helen Kendal. "All right, Miss Kendal, I'll ask you. What was it?"

In a loud, droning voice Della Street started in reciting: " '*Will you come into my Parlour,' said the Spider to the Fly*——"

"Stop that!" Tragg looked angry. "I'm asking Miss Kendal. Come on, Miss Kendal. What was it?"

Helen Kendal seemed embarrassed for a moment, then, looking straight at Lieutenant Tragg, said, "He told us to answer all your questions fairly and frankly."

"That all?"

"He said not to waste your time by interpolating a lot of trivial little things."

"Such as what?" Tragg asked, pouncing upon her answer with the alacrity of a cross-examiner who has found a weak point in the story of a witness.

Helen Kendal's big, violet eyes were wide. "Such as the things you didn't want to ask us about," she said. "Mr. Mason said that you were very skilful and that you'd ask questions which would cover every single angle of the case about which you wanted information from us."

Tragg's face showed angry determination. "And don't think I won't," he promised grimly.

EIGHT

IT WAS A good half-hour before Lieutenant Tragg completed his searching questions. By that time, the men had finished their examination of the body and the car.

He said wearily. "All right, you four stay right here in this automobile. I want to go back to that other car and check up on some things."

Gerald Shore said, as Tragg moved away, "Rather a searching interrogation, it seemed to me. There was an element of cross-examination in it. He would almost seem to suspect our motives."

Mason was soberly thoughtful as he said, "Tragg senses that there's something else behind this. Naturally, he wants to know what that something else is."

Shore said, very casually, "You didn't suggest to *me* that I should withhold any information which might seem trivial from Lieutenant Tragg."

"That's right," Mason conceded.

"What specifically did you have in mind?"

"Oh, minor matters—things which enter into the general background, but don't seem particularly pertinent to the case."

"Did you have some *particular* thing in mind?"

"Lots of little things," Mason replied. "The poisoned cat, for instance."

Helen Kendal's quick inhalation betrayed her surprise. "Surely, Mr. Mason, you don't think the poisoning of the cat has anything to do with *this*?" and she motioned toward the parked sedan in which the body had been discovered.

Mason said suavely, "I was merely mentioning it to illustrate the trivia in which I felt Lieutenant Tragg *wouldn't* be interested."

"But I thought you said the thing you didn't want us to tell him was . . ." She caught herself abruptly.

"Was what?" Gerald Shore asked.

"Oh, nothing."

Shore looked at Mason suspiciously.

"I think the only thing I specifically mentioned," Mason went on suavely, "was something that I suggested by way of illustration—just as I mentioned the poisoned cat just now."

"What was the illustration that you used?" Shore asked.

Helen Kendal blurted out, "About you not going into the Castle Gate Hotel when we drove up there to-night."

Gerald Shore's body seemed wrapped in that rigid immobility which is the result of a conscious effort not to betray emotion. "What in the world would *that* have to do with it?"

Mason said, "That is just it, sir. I mentioned it as one of those trivial details which might clutter up the case and unnecessarily prolong the examination of the witnesses. It's in exactly the same category as the poisoning of the kitten."

Shore cleared his throat, started to say something, then thought better of it, and lapsed into silence.

Lieutenant Tragg returned to the automobile, carrying a white bundle.

"Open the car door," he said to Mason. "Move over so I'll have a place to put these things. Now, I don't want anyone to touch any article here. I do want you to look at them carefully—but just look at them."

He spread out the bundle, which proved to be a handkerchief upon which rested a gold watch, a penknife, a leather pocket-book and a card-case, a gold pencil, and a fountain-pen encrusted with gold, on which initials had been engraved.

"I have some theories about these things," Tragg said. "But I'm not going to tell you what they are. I want you to tell me if you've ever seen any of these before; if any of them look at all familiar."

They leaned forward to stare down at the articles, Shore peering over Mason's shoulder from the front seat of the automobile, Della Street and Helen Kendal leaning over the back of the front seat.

"They mean nothing to me," Mason announced promptly.

"How about you, Shore?" Lieutenant Tragg asked.

Shore craned his neck, frowning thoughtfully.

Mason said, "He can't see very well from that position, Lieutenant. Suppose I get out, so he can look at them more closely."

"All right," Tragg said, "but don't touch any of the articles."

"Is it in order to ask where you got them?" Mason inquired.

"They were done up in this handkerchief in a little bundle such as you see here, and were on the seat of the automobile beside the body."

"Indeed," Mason said, squirming round so that he could get out of the front door without brushing against any of the articles. "It's all right to touch the handkerchief, isn't it, Lieutenant?"

"Yes. We won't get any fingerprints from the cloth."

Mason fingered the handkerchief. "Good grade of linen," he said. "A man's handkerchief. Touch of rather a peculiar colour, isn't there, Lieutenant?"

"There may be."

As Mason slid out of the door, Gerald Shore, leaning over, exclaimed, "Why, that's my brother's watch!"

"You mean Franklin Shore?" Lieutenant Tragg's manner was tense.

"Yes," Gerald said, his voice showing his excitement. "That's his watch all right, and I believe . . . yes, that's his fountain-pen!"

"The initials 'F.B.S.' are engraved on it," Tragg said dryly. "It made me think perhaps it *might* have been your brother's."

"It is. It's his."

"How about the pencil?"

"I'm not certain about the pencil."

"Or the pocket-book and card-case?"

"I can't help you there."

"The knife?"

Gerald shook his head. "But that's his watch all right."

"Is the watch going?" Mason asked.

"Yes."

Mason said, "Perhaps we could manipulate the handkerchief so we could look at the face of the watch."

"It's a plain, open-faced watch," Tragg said. "But you'll notice there's a scroll on the back of the watch, a scroll made by the initials 'F.B.S.' "

"Highly interesting," Mason said. "We might look at the face of the watch to see whether it has any added significance."

The lawyer picked up the handkerchief, moved it round so that the watch slowly turned over.

Mason glanced significantly at Della Street, closed one eye in a quick wink. She promptly lowered her hands to the catch of her purse.

Mason said. "That's interesting. A Waltham watch. There's something written on the dial. What is it? . . . ." He bent over the handkerchief. "Hold that spotlight there just a moment if you will, Lieutenant."

"It's a trade name and description of the watch," Tragg said.

Mason bent over it. "That's right. The printing is rather fine. The word *'Waltham'* is printed in a straight line, and down below it in a curve is *'Vanguard 23 Jewels.'* Notice this, Lieutenant. There's a winding indicator on the top, right by the figure twelve. It indicates when the watch has been wound up and when it's run down. There are twenty-four hours on the dial and you can tell roughly from the position of the hand how long since it's been wound—about six hours in this case. Rather interesting—don't you think?"

Tragg said, "Yes. It indicates that the watch was fully wound up about six hours ago—although I can't see that the point has any particular significance."

Mason consulted his own watch. "It's about ten-thirty," he remarked, thoughtfully. "That would indicate that the watch was wound up about four-thirty or five o'clock this afternoon."

"Exactly," Tragg said. "But you'll pardon me, Mason, if I don't get very excited over it. Somehow or other, I've always noticed that when you start pointing out clues, it isn't because you're so anxious to have me become interested in the things you're mentioning as to keep me from becoming interested about some other thing which you carefully avoid mentioning."

Helen Kendal grimaced over her shoulder at Della Street and in a loud stage whisper observed, "I'm glad *I'm* not Lieutenant Tragg's wife!"

Mason looked at Helen appreciatively. She was coming on fast. "The lieutenant isn't married," he told her.

"Mr. Mason, I'm not at all surprised. Are you?"

"No, Miss Kendal, I'm not," he replied gravely. "They tell me that once . . . All right, Tragg, all right. Carry on."

"That's his fountain-pen all right," Gerald Shore said. "I remember now that he was very fond of it."

"Carried it in his pocket all the time?" Tragg asked.

"Yes."

Mason slid out of the car, peered over the back of the seat to make certain that Della Street had interpreted his signal correctly.

She had her shorthand note-book on her knees and was taking down the conversation.

He took a pencil and note-book from his pocket and scribbled a series of figures.

Lieutenant Tragg said, "Quite obviously, that is the body of Henry Leech. There's a driving-licence in his pocket. It shows that it was issued to Henry Leech who resides at the Castle Gate Hotel. Evidently, he must have been a permanent tenant there. There are also some other cards in the wallet. It's Leech all right."

Gerald Shore said excitedly, "Look here, Lieutenant, this man was going to take us to my brother. I think you can appreciate the extreme importance of clearing up that old mystery."

Lieutenant Tragg nodded.

"If my brother is alive and well, that is a matter of the greatest importance. It might even overshadow the murder of this man. I feel that you should lose no time in running down every available clue."

Tragg's eyes narrowed. "Now, why should that overshadow a murder?"

"I'm speaking as a lawyer."

"Exactly. And I'm speaking as a detective."

Shore glanced at Mason; then turned hastily away. "My brother was a man of some importance. I take it this man Leech who lived at a questionable, second-rate hotel was not."

"Keep talking," Tragg said. "You haven't said anything—yet."

"Well, there might be a lot of difference in the legal situation. You see—well, I think you'll understand what I mean."

Tragg thought for a moment, then snapped a question. "A will?"

"I wasn't referring to that."

"You had it in mind?"

"Not particularly."

"But it's an angle?"

"Yes," Shore admitted reluctantly. "It's an angle."

Mason intervened with a suggestion. "Look here, Lieutenant, don't you think, under the circumstances, we're entitled to see everything that was in the pockets of the dead man?"

Tragg shook his head emphatically. "I'm handling *this* investigation on my own, Mason. You're entitled to see nothing."

"At least," Mason said, "we should be permitted to go with you to Henry Leech's room in the Castle Gate Hotel and see what you uncover there in a search. After all, this is Gerald Shore's brother we're looking for, and Shore should have some rights in the matter."

Shore said hastily, "As far as I'm concerned, I have unlimited confidence in Lieutenant Tragg's ability. I don't want to do anything which would interfere. However, if there's anything I can do to help, I want to place myself and every bit of my time and ability at the lieutenant's disposal."

Tragg nodded absently. "I'll call on you when I need anything."

Mason said, "Tragg, I want to go to the Castle Gate Hotel with you. I want to see what's in this man's room."

Lieutenant Tragg shook his head in a gesture of finality. "No, Mason, I'm going to run this investigation in my own way without any suggestions or interference."

"But you're going there now," Mason insisted. "At least, we can follow along and . . ."

"Nope," Tragg said. "You're all done. Your car's parked down by Hollywood Boulevard, Mason. Go on down and get in it and go about your business. I'll let you know in case I want anything. I'll leave a man here with this body. I want a fingerprint man to go over every inch of the car. Okay, Floyd, let's get started. And remember, Mason, I don't want you to try following me. You stay away from the Castle Gate Hotel until I've completed my investigation. Good night."

He gathered up the handkerchief and once more tied the corners together, making a compact bundle of it.

Mason slid back into the front seat. "Well," he remarked to Shore, "I guess Tragg doesn't want any of our assistance. You might drive me back to where I've left my car parked. And," he added in a lower voice, "get started before the lieutenant changes his mind."

"Why, what do you mean?" Shore asked, stepping on the starter.

Mason said, in a low voice, "If I hadn't apparently been so eager to have him let us accompany him to the Castle Gate Hotel, he might have insisted on it."

Shore turned to Mason defiantly. "Well," he asked, "what's wrong with that?"

"Something else has happened that I thought we might want to investigate before the police stepped in. Matilda Shore is in the Exeter Hospital. She's been poisoned."

"Good God!" Shore exclaimed, swinging the car into a quick turn. "Helen, did you hear that?"

"I heard it," she said calmly.

"Easy, easy," Mason warned him. "Don't make it seem that you're too anxious to get away. Drive along rather slowly until after the police car passes you. And that won't be long. That fellow Floyd drives like the devil."

They had gone about three hundred yards when they saw the red spotlights on the police car blossom into ruddy brilliance, heard the sound of gears meshing, and then the big car came roaring up behind them.

"Pull over," Mason said, "and let's hope he doesn't think things over and change his mind."

The police car didn't even hesitate, but went screaming by, swaying into the first down turn of the long, winding grade.

Mason settled back in the seat. "All right," he said to Gerald Shore, "put her in second gear and turn her loose."

NINE

MATILDA SHORE, PROPPED up in the hospital bed, surveyed her visitors, her eyes showing her anger.

"What is the meaning of this?" she demanded.

"Why," Gerald Shore explained, "we heard you were ill, and naturally wanted to see if there was anything we could do."

"Who told you?"

"Mr. Mason learned about it."

She turned to Mason. "How?" she demanded.

Mason bowed. "Just casually."

Gerald put in hastily, "We *had* to see you, Matilda. Some things have happened which you should know about."

"I've been sick. I don't want visitors. How did you know where I was? Why did you bring these people?"

"Perry Mason, the lawyer, and Della Street, his secretary, are interested in certain matters which are important to you."

She swung her big head on its thick neck, surveyed Perry Mason, and said, "Humph!"

"How did you know where I was?" she asked after a moment.

Helen Kendal said, "Komo was very much alarmed about you. He said you'd been poisoned, that you acted just like the kitten. You told him to drive you to a hospital."

"Why, the little slant-eyed hypocrite," Matilda Shore said. "I told him to keep his mouth shut."

"He did," Mason said, "until after he learned that we knew all about it. *I* am the one who found out about what had happened. I didn't talk with Komo. Your niece talked with him *after* I had told her where you were."

"How did *you* find out?"

Mason merely smiled. "I must protect my sources of information."

Heaving herself up to a more erect sitting position, Matilda Shore said, "And will you kindly tell me why my whereabouts and my physical condition should be any of your business?"

"But, Matilda," Gerald interrupted to explain, "there's something about which you have to know. We simply had to reach you."

"Well, what is it? Stop beating about the bush."

"Franklin is alive."

"That's no news to me, Gerald Shore. Of course he's alive! I've always known he was alive. Ran off with a trollop and left me to twiddle my thumbs. I suppose this means you've heard from him."

"You shouldn't condemn him too hastily. Aunt Matilda," Helen Kendal said in a voice which failed to carry the least conviction.

"No fool like an old fool," Matilda grumbled. "Man who was almost sixty running off with a woman half his age."

Mason turned to Gerald Shore. "Perhaps you'd better tell her how it happens you know he's alive."

"He telephoned us this afternoon—rather, he telephoned Helen."

The bed-springs heaved as Matilda twisted her big body round. She opened a drawer in the table near the bed, took out a pair of steel-rimmed spectacles, adjusted them to her nose, and looked at her niece as though she were examining a microbe through a microscope.

"So—he telephoned—*you*. Afraid of me, I suppose."

The door opened. A nurse glided into the room, her starched uniform giving forth a businesslike rustle. "You mustn't excite the patient," she warned. "She really isn't supposed to have visitors. You can only stay a few minutes."

Matilda glared at her. "I'm all right. Please leave us alone."

"But the doctor . . ."

Matilda Shore motioned imperiously toward the door.

The nurse hesitated a moment. "I'll have to notify the doctor," she murmured, then withdrew.

Matilda swung back to Helen Kendal. "So he telephoned you, and you didn't say a word about it. *That's* gratitude. For ten years I devote myself to your——"

Gerald Shore spoke hastily. "You see, Matilda, she thought she might be dealing with an impostor, and she didn't want to disturb you with the news until she had made certain."

"Why did he telephone *her*?" Matilda demanded.

"That's just it," Gerald said placatingly. "Everything indicated that we were dealing, not with Franklin, but with some impostor who wanted to impose upon the family. We thought it would be better to establish a preliminary contact before telling you anything about it."

"I'm not a child."

"I understand, Matilda, but we thought it was better this way."

"Humph!"

Helen Kendal said, "He told me particularly that I couldn't see him unless I followed his instructions to the letter."

"Did you see him?" Matilda asked, peering through her spectacles at her niece.

"No, we didn't. A man by the name of Leech was to lead us to him—and something happened so that Leech couldn't do it."

Matilda Shore said, "It was Franklin all right. Sounds just like him—trying to sneak in the back way—wants to get hold of Helen, play up to her, get her sympathies aroused, and get her to intercede with me. Tell him to stop hiding behind a woman's skirts and come out in the open and meet me. I'll tell him a thing or two. I'll file suit for divorce the minute he shows his face. I've been waiting ten years for this."

Mason said, "I trust your poisoning wasn't serious, Mrs. Shore."

She rolled her eyes toward him, said, "Poisoning is always serious."

"How did it happen?" Gerald asked.

"Got hold of the wrong bottle, that's all. Had some heart medicine and some sleeping tablets in the medicine cupboard. Had a bottle of stout before I went to bed. Then went to get some sleeping tablets. Got the wrong bottle."

"When did you suspect it was the wrong bottle?" Mason asked.

"Had a little spasm," she replied. "Rang for Komo, told him to get out the car, to notify my doctor, and get me up to the hospital. Had enough presence of mind to drink a lot of mustard water and to get rid of as much of the stuff as I could. Told the doctor about how I'd gone to the medicine cabinet in the dark to take some sleeping medicine after I'd had my stout, told him I'd got the wrong bottle by mistake. Not certain he believes me. Anyhow, he got busy and fixed me up. I'm all right now. Want you to keep your mouth shut about that poisoning. I don't want to have the police interfering in my business. Now then, I want to find Franklin. Let's get him out into the open."

Mason said, "Has it ever occurred to you, Mrs. Shore, that there might be some connection between the return of your husband and the two instances of poisoning which have occurred in your household?"

"Two?" she asked.

"The kitten and you."

Matilda Shore studied him for the space of several seconds, then said, "Fiddlesticks! I got the wrong bottle, that's all."

"I'm asking you if the idea has occurred to you that the drink was poisoned."

"Bosh! I tell you I got the wrong bottle."

"Don't you think you owe it to yourself to do something about it?"

"What should I do?"

Mason said, "At least, you should take steps to prevent a recurrence. If someone has made an attempt on your life, you certainly should do something about it."

"You mean the police?"

"Why not?"

"The police!" she exclaimed scornfully. "I'm not going to have them messing in my life and giving out a lot more stuff to the newspapers. That's what always happens. You call in the police to protect you, and some idiot who wants to see his picture in the paper rushes out to the reporters and tells them the whole story. I won't have it. Besides, I just made a mistake."

Mason said, "Unfortunately, Mrs. Shore, after what's happened to-night, there is going to be a lot of publicity."

"What do you mean, after what happened to-night?"

"This man Leech who was to lead us to your husband failed to do so."

"Why?"

Mason said, "Because someone stopped him."

"How?"

"By a .38 calibre bullet in the left side of his head, fired while he was sitting in an automobile waiting to keep an appointment with us."

"You mean he's dead?"

"Yes."

"Murdered?"

"Apparently."

"When did it happen?"

"We don't know exactly."

"Where?"

"By a reservoir up behind Hollywood in the mountains."

"Who was Leech? I mean how does he fit in?"

"Apparently, he was a friend of your husband."

"What makes you think so? I never heard of him."

Gerald Shore said, "When Franklin telephoned Helen, he told her to get in touch with Mr. Leech, that Leech would take her to Franklin."

Matilda motioned to Helen. "Get these men out of here. Get my clothes out of that closet. I'm going to dress and go home. If Franklin's around, he'll be pussyfooting out to the house, trying to wheedle me.

I've been waiting ten years for this, and I'm not going to be shut up in any hospital when it happens. I'll show him he can't walk out on *me*!"

Mason made no move to leave. "I'm afraid you'll have to get your doctor's permission. I think the nurse has gone to telephone him."

"I don't need anybody's permission to get up and go out," Matilda said. "Thanks to that emetic I took, I got off with a very light dose of poison. I have the constitution of an ox. I shook it off. I'm all right now. I'm going out under my own power."

Mason said, "I wouldn't advise you to get up and put any strain on your heart. We wanted to let you know about your husband, and we wanted to find out what had happened, and what you intended to do about this poisoning."

"I tell you it was an accident, and I don't want the police . . ."

A knock sounded on the door.

Gerald Shore said, "That's probably the doctor or a couple of husky attendants called on by the hospital to eject us forcibly."

Matilda Shore called out, "Well, come on in. Let's get it over with. Let them eject me."

The door pushed open. Lieutenant Tragg and a detective entered the room.

Mason greeted them with a bow. "Mrs. Shore, may I have the honour of presenting Lieutenant Tragg of the Homicide Squad. I think he wants to ask you a few questions."

Tragg bowed to Mrs. Shore, turned, and bowed again to Mason. "Rather cleverly done, Mason. The more I see of you, the more I am forced to respect your very deft touch."

"Referring to what this time?"

"Tne manner in which you threw me off the trail, temporarily, by insisting that you and your friends should be permitted to accompany me to the Castle Gate Hotel. It wasn't until after I'd left you that it began to occur to me you'd tossed me a bait and that I'd very credulously grabbed at it."

"Putting it that way makes it sound very much like a conspiracy."

"Draw your own conclusions. I started checking all angles of the case just as soon as I realized that your insistence on accompanying me had led me to let you go. Now, Mrs. Shore, if you don't mind, I'll hear about the poisoning."

"Well, I *do* mind," Mrs. Shore snapped. "I mind very much."

"That is unfortunate," Tragg announced.

"I ate something that disagreed with me, that's all."

"The hospital records indicate that you took some medicine by mistake," Tragg pointed out.

"All right, I went to the medicine cabinet and took some medicine by mistake."

Tragg was suavely solicitous. "That's unfortunate. May I ask what time this was, Mrs. Shore?"

"Oh, about nine o'clock, I guess. I didn't notice the exact time."

"And, as I understand it, you had prepared for bed, had your regular nightly glass of stout, turned out the light, and went to the medicine cabinet in the dark?"

"Yes. I thought I was taking sleeping tablets. I got the wrong bottle."

Tragg seemed particularly sympathetic. "You didn't notice any difference in the taste?"

"No."

"Your sleeping medicine is in the form of tablets?"

"Yes."

"Kept in the medicine cabinet?"

"Yes."

"And you didn't notice any difference in the taste of the tablets you took?"

"No. I washed them down with water. Had a glass of water in one hand, tossed the tablets into my mouth with the other, and washed them right down."

"I see. Then you were holding the glass of water in your right hand as you tossed the tablets into your mouth with your left hand?"

"That's right."

"And you put the cap back on the bottle and returned it to the medicine cabinet?"

"Yes."

"That took both hands?"

"What difference does it make?"

"I'm simply trying to find out. That's all. If it was an accident, there's nothing to investigate."

"Well, it was an accident."

"Of course," Tragg said soothingly. "I'm simply trying to get the facts so I can make a report that it was an accident."

Mollified, Mrs. Shore explained, "Well, that's what happened. I screwed the top back on this bottle."

"And put it back in the medicine cabinet?" Tragg asked.

"Yes."

"And then picked up your glass of water, holding the tablets in your left hand?"

"Yes."

"Tossed them into your mouth and drank the water immediately?"

"Yes."

"You didn't notice a bitter taste?"

"No."

"I believe it was strychnine poisoning, wasn't it, Mrs. Shore?"

"I don't know."

Tragg's voice showed his sympathy. "Most unfortunate," he said, and then asked casually, "And what were the strychnine tablets doing in your medicine cabinet, Mrs. Shore? You were using them for some particular purpose, I suppose?"

Her eyes studied the detective's countenance. "They're a heart stimulant. I kept them there in case I needed them."

"On a doctor's prescription?" Tragg asked.

"Yes, of course."

"What doctor prescribed them?"

She said, "I don't think that has anything to do with you, young man."

"How many tablets did you take?"

"Oh, I don't know. Two or three."

"And you put the bottle back in the medicine cabinet?"

"Yes. I've told you that before."

"Right next to the bottle of sleeping tablets?"

"I guess so. I tell you it was in the dark. I reached up in that general vicinity and got down the bottle which I thought contained the sleeping tablets."

Tragg said, "It's most unfortunate."

"What is?"

"The fact that a search of your medicine cabinet reveals that there are neither sleeping tablets nor strychnine tablets in it."

Mrs. Shore straightened up still further. "You mean that you've been to my house and searched my medicine cabinet?"

"Yes."

"What authority did you have to do that?" she demanded.

Tragg said, without raising his voice, "Perhaps, Mrs. Shore, I'd better ask you a question instead. What do you mean by lying to the police about an attempt which was made to poison you?"

"There wasn't any attempt to poison me."

"I believe that a kitten was poisoned at your house this afternoon and taken to Dr. Blakely's small animal hospital?"

"I don't know anything about a kitten."

Tragg smiled. "Come, Mrs. Shore, you'll have to do better than that. Falsifying evidence, you know, constitutes a crime. There are two attorneys in the room who will bear me out in that. If there was poison in that bottle of stout, the police want to know about it, and it would be exceedingly unwise for you to hamper their investigation."

The door of the hospital pushed open. A man, entering hastily, said, "What's going on here? I'm the doctor in charge of this case. This patient isn't to be disturbed. She's had a severe shock. I'm going to ask you all to leave—immediately."

Matilda Shore looked at him and said, "I guess you mean well, Doctor, but you got here just five minutes too late."

TEN

GERALD SHORE, STRANGELY thoughtful and silent, drove his car up to the big, old-fashioned house which had remained virtually unchanged since the night the president of the Shore National Bank had vanished into thin air.

"Better get out here, Helen," he said, "and keep an eye on the house. I'll run Mr. Mason and his secretary out to Hollywood where he left his car."

"I can go and keep you company on the way back," Helen Kendal offered.

"I think you'd better be at the house. Someone should be here to take charge of things."

"When will Aunt Matilda be home?" she asked.

Gerald Shore turned to Mason, silently passing the question on to him.

Mason grinned. "Not until she's answered every question Lieutenant Tragg wants to ask."

"But the doctor insisted that the questioning was to be limited to five minutes. He said that Aunt Matilda's condition wouldn't stand for more than that."

"Exactly," Mason said. "And the doctor is in charge while she's in the hospital. But Tragg will put a couple of men on guard. He'll see that she doesn't leave the hospital until the doctor says she's entirely cured. When the doctor says she's completely recovered, Tragg will get the answer to his questions—either there at the hospital or down at headquarters."

"Lieutenant Tragg seems to be a very clever and a very determined young man," Gerald Shore said.

"He is," Mason agreed, "and don't ever underestimate him. He's a dangerous antagonist."

Gerald Shore was looking searchingly at Mason, but there was nothing in his face which indicated that his remark about Tragg had held any hidden significance.

Helen slipped out of the automobile and said, "Well, I'll stay here, then, and hold the fort."

"We won't be long," her uncle promised.

She shuddered a little. "I wonder what's going to happen next. I wish I knew where I could get hold of Jerry Templar."

"Wouldn't you like me to stay with you?" Della said impulsively.

"I'd love it," Helen confessed.

"Sorry," Mason said flatly. "I need Della."

Helen's face fell. "Never mind. I'll be all right—I guess."

Driving out toward Hollywood, Gerald Shore returned to something that seemed to be worrying him. "You've mentioned two or three times, Mason, that Lieutenant Tragg was a dangerous antagonist."

"Yes."

"Am I to assume that perhaps there was some particular significance which was attached to your remarks?"

"That all depends."

"Upon what does it depend?" Gerald Shore asked, his manner that of a courteous but insistent cross-examiner.

"Upon what you have to conceal."

"But suppose I have nothing to conceal?"

"In that case, Lieutenant Tragg would not be a dangerous *antagonist* because he would not be an *antagonist*. But Lieutenant Tragg would always be *dangerous*."

Shore studied Mason's profile for a minute, then turned back to keep his eyes on the road.

Mason went on smoothly, "There are several things about this case which are rather significant. In the first place, if you and your brother had parted on the best of terms, there is no good reason why he wouldn't have rung you up, rather than have subjected his niece to the shock of hearing his voice and learning that he was alive.

"That, however, is a minor matter. The point is, he particularly and specifically suggested that Helen should consult me and take me with her to call on Mr. Leech, that no other member of the family should be present."

Gerald Shore said, "You've either said too much, Mason—or too little."

"Yet," Mason went on calmly, "*you* insisted upon coming along."

"I don't see what you're getting at, Mr. Mason. It was only natural that I should want to see my brother."

"Quite right. But it seemed that you deemed it necessary to see him *before* anyone else talked with him."

"Can you explain just what you mean by that?"

Mason smiled. "Of course I can. I'm looking at it now from the angle a person of Lieutenant Tragg's mentality and temperament would take in approaching the problem."

"Go right ahead."

"Tragg will eventually find out that while you left the house with us, that while you were with us when we drove up to that reservoir to keep that appointment with Leech, you *weren't* with us when we went into Leech's hotel."

"My interest was in my brother, not in Leech," Shore said.

"Exactly. Even Lieutenant Tragg would be willing to concede that, although inasmuch as Leech was the only link with your brother, it would seem that your interest should have been transferred to him. However, he would be quite willing to accept that—*if* there were no other complicating factors."

"Such as?"

"Oh," Mason said, "let's suppose that, just to be on the safe side, Tragg would get one of your photographs and take it to the clerk on duty in the Castle Gate Hotel, ask him if you'd been making inquiries about Henry Leech, ask if perhaps you'd ever called to see him—or if they remembered having seen you around the hotel at any time."

Gerald Shore was silent for a matter of seconds; then he inquired, "What would be the object in that?"

"I am hardly in a position to know all the facts, but—still looking at it from Tragg's viewpoint—there are things which are most significant. Your brother disappeared abruptly. His disappearance must have been brought about by some rather unusual factors. Immediately prior to his disappearance, he had had an interview with someone who had been either asking for or demanding money. There was some evidence indicating that this person was you. There seems to have been some conflict in this evidence. I presume, however, that you were questioned about it, and I presume that the records will show that you denied that you had seen your brother the night in question. Now Tragg might reason that it would be rather embarrassing to you if your brother should now appear on the scene and not only tell a story in direct conflict to that, but indicate that what you had been talking about had had something to do with his disappearance.

"Having reasoned that far, Lieutenant Tragg would then doubtless say to himself, Franklin Shore is in existence. For some reason, he doesn't want to make himself known. He doesn't care to go directly to his house. He wants to communicate with some of his relatives. He avoids his own brother and communicates instead with his niece, a very attractive young woman to be certain, but a young woman who must have been only thirteen or fourteen years of age when he disappeared. Gerald Shore, whom the brother has ignored upon his return, immediately steps into the picture and insists that he is going to go along with the niece. Henry Leech is the connecting link between Franklin, who is either unable or unwilling to come directly to the house and his relatives. Henry Leech goes to a lonely spot and is killed. There is a typewritten letter indicating that Leech has gone to this place of his own volition, but there is nothing to indicate that Leech himself wrote that letter. In fact, there is every reason to believe that he didn't write it. Of course, a great deal will depend upon what Lieutenant Tragg finds as to the time of death from a post-mortem examination. However, from certain bits of evidence which I saw when I was at the scene of the crime, I'm inclined to believe the time of death will be fixed perhaps about four hours prior to the time we arrived on the scene.

"Having reasoned that far, if Lieutenant Tragg finds any evidence indicating that you tried to get in touch with Leech earlier in the evening or actually *did* get in touch with him, it would be only natural for him to consider you as a very logical suspect."

Mason ceased talking, took a cigarette from his case, lit it, and settled back in the seat.

Gerald Shore drove silently for some ten blocks, then said, "I guess it's about time I retained you to act as my attorney."

Mason took the cigarette from his mouth long enough to observe, quite casually, "Perhaps it is."

"How about your secretary?" Gerald Shore asked, indicating Della Street who was sitting silently in the back seat.

"The soul of discretion," Mason assured him. "You may speak freely—and it may be the last opportunity you'll have to speak freely."

"You'll represent me?"

"That will depend," Mason said.

"Upon what?"

"Upon the circumstances, and upon whether I think you're innocent."

"I am innocent," Shore said with feeling, "entirely innocent. I'm either the victim of the damnedest set of circumstances fortune could conjure up, or of a deliberate conspiracy."

Mason continued smoking in silence.

Shore slowed the car, so driving that it would not require quite so much attention on his part, and said, "I was the one who called on my brother the night he disappeared."

"You denied it afterwards?" Mason inquired.

"Yes."

"Why?"

"For various reasons. One of them was that too much of my conversation had been overheard, and made public. You'll remember that the person who was with Franklin immediately prior to his disappearance had been heard to ask for money and had intimated that his own financial affairs were in desperate straits."

Mason nodded.

"I was engaged in carrying out some promotional transactions at the time. These would have shown a very considerable profit if I could have carried them through to completion, and would have shown a staggering, ruinous loss if I failed. The only thing which was enabling me to keep my head above water was the fact that the other parties in the transaction never for a moment suspected the possibility that I didn't have ample capital behind me."

"Your brother?" Mason asked.

"Well, my brother's connections perhaps had something to do with it. They didn't think he was directly interested. They *did* think that I had plenty of capital, and that if anything happened and I found myself in need of more than I had available, my brother was always ready to stand behind me."

"So," Mason said, "you didn't dare to admit that you had been the one who had been with your brother because so much of that conversation had been published in the newspapers."

"That's exactly it."

"Didn't your brother's disappearance have a bad effect upon the transaction?"

"I'll say it did," Shore said with feeling, "but I was able to find and interest a man who furnished me the necessary capital—taking, as it happened, the lion's share of the profits. The fact that the affairs of the Shore National were so promptly investigated, the fact that my brother left so large a cash balance—those all helped."

"You didn't confide to Mrs. Shore, perhaps, that you were the one who had been with Franklin?"

"I didn't confide in anyone. I didn't dare to at the time."

"And after the necessity for the secrecy was removed?" Mason prompted.

"I stuck to my story. Put yourself in my position, and you'll realize I had to."

"Go ahead."

"To-night, when Helen told me that Franklin had telephoned her, I was sick with apprehension. I felt that I *had* to see Franklin before anyone else did."

"So while Helen returned to the hospital to see how Amber Eyes was getting along, you were out trying to get in touch with your brother. Is that right?"

"Yes. Helen went to the hospital directly after dinner to pick up the kitten. She then took the kitten down to the place where our gardener maintains a little bachelor shack, and then went up to keep her appointment with you."

"And during that interval of time, you went to the Castle Gate Hotel?"

"Yes. That was why I didn't come up with Helen to see you."

"You were trying to see Leech?"

"Yes."

"Any success?"

"No. I inquired first over the telephone, and was told that he had gone out with a man, but would be back soon. That left me in something of a spot. I thought the man might well have been my brother, Franklin. So I went to the hotel and waited. I didn't know Leech, but I felt certain he was with Franklin and that he'd be back within an hour."

"You waited?" Mason asked.

"Yes. I sat there waiting until it came time to go and meet you."

"He didn't come in?"

"No. At any rate, I don't think so. I do know Franklin didn't come in."

"And the clerk noticed you?"

"Yes. He spotted me as not being one of the regulars. I sat there by the door, and he kept looking at me. He may have thought I was a detective. As I gather from what Lieutenant Tragg said, the hotel apparently caters for men who have somewhat shady backgrounds, and that must make them suspicious of strangers. At first I intended to park my car near the door and wait in the car; but I couldn't find a parking place within half a block, so I decided I'd go inside and wait."

"And the fact that you were afraid the clerk might identify you as being the man who had been waiting earlier in the evening made it absolutely essential that you shouldn't be seen in the hotel."

"Yes—that, of course, is in the strictest professional confidence."

Mason said, "I think you can rest assured Tragg will reason all this out for himself."

There was a vacant space at the kerb. Shore swung his car to the side of the road, parked it, and shut off the motor. "I can't keep on driving," he said. "Give me a cigarette, will you?"

Mason handed him a cigarette. Shore's hands were shaking so that he could hardly hold the flame from the match to the end of the cigarette.

"Go on," Mason said.

"That's all there is to tell you."

Mason glanced back at Della Street, then said to Gerald Shore, "It's all right, except the motive."

"What is wrong with the motive?" Shore asked.

"You wouldn't have done what you did and as you did unless the necessity for seeing your brother before anyone else did had been much greater than would have been the case if you were merely trying to protect yourself against an original discrepancy in your statements."

"I see that I've got to be frank with you."

"It's always an advantage," Mason observed dryly. "As a practising attorney, you should realize that."

Shore said, "I think you'll realize that no one ever knows exactly how honest he is. He goes through life *thinking* he's honest, because he's never been confronted with a sufficient temptation; then suddenly he's confronted with some crucial situation where he finds himself facing ruination on the one hand and with a chance to turn defeat into victory by doing something which seems very simple but which is— well, not dishonest, but not strictly legal."

"Never mind the excuses," Mason said somewhat sharply. "Don't underestimate Tragg. When he works on a case, he works fast. I want facts. You can fill in reasons and excuses later. And get this straight. All that you've told me before this is what I had already deduced. All you've done so far has been to cross the t's and dot the i's. The thing you're coming to now—if you tell me the truth—is going to be the determining factor in whether I represent you."

Shore nervously took the cigarette from his mouth, dashed it out of the window to the sidewalk. He took off his hat and ran his hands through the wavy splendour of his grey hair. "This is something which must never, never come out," he said.

"Go ahead," Mason said.

"I begged and pleaded with my brother. I had to have ten thousand dollars. He read me a lecture on my general business methods—a lecture which I wasn't in a position to appreciate because, if I didn't get that ten thousand dollars, I was completely ruined. If I did, I felt I'd clean up enough money on that one deal so I could quit taking long chances and become more conservative. My brother finally promised that he would help me. He said that he had some other matters to attend to that night, but that before he went to bed, he would write a cheque for ten thousand dollars and put it in the mail."

"A cheque payable to you?" Mason asked.

"No. A cheque payable directly to the party to whom the money was due. Time was too short to have a cheque go through my account."

"Your brother did that?" Mason asked.

"My brother didn't. He disappeared without doing that."

"Then we can take it for granted that after your visit, he was confronted with a certain urgency which made his disappearance so imperative that he forgot his promise to you."

"I suppose so."

"When did you learn of the disappearance?"

"Not until the next morning."

"And that day was the last day you had in which to take some action?"

Shore nodded.

"You had, perhaps, already assured your associates that the matter had been taken care of?" Mason inquired.

"At nine-thirty that morning," Shore said with feeling, "I rang up the party to whom the payment was due and told him that he would have his cheque before the banks closed that afternoon, that the cheque would be made payable to him and would be signed by Franklin B. Shore. About ten minutes after I'd hung up the telephone, Matilda got in touch with me and asked me to come over at once. She told me about what had happened."

"Now, as I remember it," Mason said, "the fact of the disappearance was kept from the public for a day or two."

Shore nodded.

Mason looked at him shrewdly. "During that time, several large cheques were cashed," he said.

Again he nodded.

"Well?" Mason prompted.

"Among them," Shore said, "was a cheque to Rodney French for ten thousand dollars."

"Rodney French was the man to whom you owed the money?"

"Yes."

"And to whom you had promised the payment?"

"Yes."

"And that cheque?" Mason asked.

Gerald Shore said, "That cheque was made out and signed by me. I forged my brother's signature. My brother had promised me that I could count on that cheque. I felt that—that I was entitled to do what I did in all honesty."

"And Matilda Shore never knew that the cheque was forged?"

"No one ever knew it was forged. I—I made a good job of it. As it happened, my brother had called up his bookkeeper late that night in connection with some other matters, and had mentioned that he was making out this cheque to Rodney French for ten thousand dollars.

"I don't suppose, Mr. Mason," Shore went on, emotion choking his voice, "I could ever explain to you what all this meant to me. It was the turning-point in my career. Prior to that time, I'd been mixed up in a lot of get-rich-quick schemes—legitimate all right, but, nevertheless, promotional gambles. I'd been intent on making money. I guess my brother's influence furnished the spur which goaded me on. I wanted to be like him. I wanted to show that I, too, had the ability to make money. I wanted the things which went with financial security.

"After the devastating experience which I had that time, I took stock of myself. I wasn't particularly impressed by what I found. That's been ten years ago, Mr. Mason. I think I can truthfully say that I've changed since then—changed in a great many respects."

"Go on," Mason said. "I'm interested."

"For one thing, I've realized that there's something more to life than making money."

"You mean acquiring wisdom, or a philosophy of life?" Mason asked.

"No, I don't," Gerald Shore said. "I mean in the duties and responsibilities a man has toward others."

"In what way?"

"I used to think a man's life was his own to live as he wanted to live it. I realize now that isn't true. A man isn't entirely a free agent. He's constantly influencing others by his character, by what he says, by the way he lives, by . . ." His voice choked, and he became silent.

Mason waited, smoking quietly.

Shore went on after a few seconds. "Take Helen, for instance. She was a girl of fourteen, standing, to use a trite expression, on the threshold of life. She had always looked up to me and respected me. She was approaching a time in life when moral values were about to become more significant to her. If something happened, if she had discovered that—well, Mr. Mason, from that time on, I changed my entire goal in life. I got a completely different set of objectives. I began to try and pattern my life so that those who looked up to me wouldn't—— Oh, what's the use?"

"There's a great deal of use," Mason said, his voice kindly.

"That's all there is to it," Shore said shortly. "I quit trying to make money. I began to take more of an interest in people, not for what they could do for me, but for what I could do for them. I realized that, to younger persons at least, I was a trustee for certain standards. And I," he continued bitterly, "a confessed forger, am ranting all this stuff, *I* who have committed a crime and who thought that crime would go undiscovered, had the temerity to think that I could avoid paying for what I had done."

Mason waited until his emotion had subsided, then inquired, "How about Rodney French? Did he ask any questions?"

"No. He *did* go as far as to telephone Franklin's bookkeeper and ask him if Franklin had said anything about making out that cheque. That was when it wasn't in the morning mail. Upon being assured that Franklin had so advised his bookkeeping department, French took the money and kept quiet."

"Otherwise, he might have resorted to a little blackmail after he learned of Franklin's disappearance?" Mason asked.

"I don't know. I suppose that after he heard of the disappearance and heard my denial that I had been with my brother, he became rather suspicious."

"And just why," Mason asked, "did that make you feel that your brother would have become estranged from you?"

"Don't you see?" Shore said, unmistakable anguish in his voice. "The newspapers dug up a lot of stuff. A lot of the details about my brother's financial transactions were given to the public, the amount of his bank balance, the cheques which had been drawn in the last few days—and there was, of course, mention made of the fact that the last cheque which he had drawn had been one in favour of Rodney French to an amount of ten thousand dollars."

Mason gave the matter thoughtful consideration. "You don't think your brother forgave you—under the circumstances?"

"I had hoped that he would understand and forgive," Gerald said, "but when he saw fit to make himself known by calling up Helen instead of me, I—— Well, you can draw your own conclusions."

Mason pinched out the end of his cigarette. "If Lieutenant Tragg ever gets hold of *all* these facts," he said, "he'll convict you of murder."

"Don't I know it!" Gerald Shore exclaimed. "And there's nothing I can do. I feel like a swimmer who's being carried along by a current against which he can't struggle, headed toward a deadly whirlpool."

Mason said, "There's one thing you *can* do."

"What?"

"Keep your mouth shut. Let me do the talking—and that means let me do *all* of it."

ELEVEN

HELEN KENDAL HAD taken off her coat, hat, and gloves and was reading a book when she heard a car in the drive.

She glanced at her wrist-watch. Surely no one could be coming at this hour, but unmistakably, the car was turning into the private drive. Then, as the driver kicked out the clutch and she heard the succession of knocks and bangs which came from under the hood, her heart caught, skipped a beat, then started pounding. She felt certain there was only one motor in the world which was in quite such a state of disrepair, yet still running.

She went quickly to the door.

Jerry Templar was getting out of the car, moving with that slow efficiency which seemed almost to border on awkwardness, yet which somehow managed to accomplish so much. He looked slim and straight in his uniform, and she realized the Army training had given him a certain determination, an assurance of his ability to accomplish things which had not been there a few months earlier. This man was in some ways a stranger to her, a familiar friend who had become invested with a new, breath-taking power to affect her life, to make her heart skip beats, then pound wildly.

On no account would she mention the murder or anything of the family complications, she decided. He had come to-night, unannounced, to see her. With Jerry, there were more important things to talk about. Perhaps to-night——

"Oh, Jerry!" she exclaimed. "I'm so glad to see you!"

"Hello, darling. I saw lights and thought perhaps you hadn't gone to bed. Can I come in for a few minutes?"

She took his hand, drew him into the hall, and closed the door. "Yes," she said, rather unnecessarily.

Helen led the way into the big living-room and dropped down on the davenport. She watched Jerry curiously to see where he would sit. Was he going to the chair on the other side of the fireplace, or was he coming over to her on the davenport? Shamelessly she willed him to come over beside her, but he just stood there in the middle of the room.

"You look tired, Jerry."

He seemed surprised. "Tired? I'm not."

"Oh! My mistake! Cigarette?" She held a box toward him.

That did it. He crossed the room slowly, took a cigarette and settled down beside her.

"Where have you been all the evening?" he demanded.

Her eyes dropped. "Out," she said.

"I know that. I've rung up four times."

"Twenty cents! You shouldn't throw money around like that, Jerry."

"Where were you?" It was almost an accusation.

"Oh, here and there," she replied evasively. "No place special."

"Alone?"

Helen looked up at him, and her eyes were mocking. "You're mighty curious, soldier," she drawled. "Do all your women sit at home every night on the chance you may call?"

"I haven't got any—women," he said roughly. "You know I——"

"Go on."

Instead of going on, however, Jerry jumped up and began pacing the floor.

"Where's your aunt?" he demanded suddenly. "In bed?"

"She was, the last time I saw her." Then, very casually, "So are Komo and the housekeeper."

"Your aunt doesn't like me!"

"Such perception, Jerry! I'm amazed."

"What's she got against me?"

There was a silence. "I guess I won't answer that one," Helen finally decided.

There was another silence. "Were you out with George Alber to-night?"

"It's none of your business, of course, but as it happened I was with Uncle Gerald all evening."

"Oh!"

He looked relieved and settled down on the davenport again.

"When are you going to your officers' training camp, Jerry?"

"As soon as I get back to the outfit next week, I guess."

"Monday—six days more," Helen murmured. "You're not thinking about anything much or anybody these days except the war, are you?"

"Well, there *is* a job to be done."

"Yes, but we've still got to live," she said softly. If she could only get him to break through that self-imposed wall of silence. If he would only stop being so ridiculously noble, so self-disciplined, and let himself go for once. She turned toward him, chin up, lips half parted. They were all alone in the big house. The ticking of the grandfather's clock in the hall was loud.

Jerry seemed to steel himself against her. He started speaking, and there was no verbal fumbling. His words were swift, close-clipped. His grey eyes looked into hers with tenderness, but with that determination she had seen so much of the last few days. "I don't know what's ahead of me," he said. "You don't know what's ahead of me. There's a nasty job of mopping up. After that, there's got to be some face-lifting in the world. Don't you see that at a time like this a man has to abandon and try to forget some things that mean more to him, personally, selfishly, than anything else in the world? If a man's in love with a woman, for instance——"

His voice trailed off as, suddenly, from Matilda Shore's bedroom, they heard the sound of some article of furniture crashing to the floor. Then, a moment later, came the unmistakable *thump . . . thump . . . thump* of a cane, and the shuffle of heavy steps crossing the floor. The caged lovebirds started throaty, shrill chirpings as they chattered excitedly.

"Your Aunt Matilda," said Jerry in a hollow voice.

Helen tried to speak, but for a moment her throat was constricted so that the words wouldn't come.

He looked at her curiously. "What's the matter, darling, you look scared?"

"That's—that's not Aunt Matilda."

"Nonsense. You can't mistake those steps. The shuffle-and-thump; and shuffle-and-thump. You can even hear the peculiar dragging sound of her foot when she . . ."

Her fingers clutched his arm. "Jerry, it isn't she! She isn't at home. She's in hospital."

There was a moment while her words and her fear penetrated into Jerry's consciousness; then he was on his feet, brushing her to one side despite her efforts to cling to his arm.

"All right, let's see who it is."

"No, no, Jerry! Don't go alone. There's danger! Something horrible happened to-night. I didn't want to tell you, but . . ."

He might or might not have heard her. She only knew her words had no effect. With his jaw set, he moved swiftly toward the closed door into the corridor leading to Matilda's bedroom.

"Where's the light switch?" he asked.

She raced to his side, suddenly aware that Jerry, a stranger to the house, was groping his way through half darkness.

She clicked on the light switch. "Jerry, be careful. Oh, my dear, please . . ."

From behind Aunt Matilda's bedroom door, there was a silence as though the intruder might be standing still—or might be moving with catlike stealth to surprise him when he opened the door. Only the high-pitched chatter of the lovebirds grew to an hysterical crescendo of bird talk.

"Please, Jerry," Helen whispered. "Don't open it. If someone should be in there and . . ."

He said, "Let go of my arm."

She still clung to him.

"Let go of my arm," he repeated, shaking her off. "I may need that arm. Let's see what this is all about."

He turned the knob of the door, raised his foot, and kicked it open.

A gust of cold air billowing in from an open window came sweeping through the doorway into the corridor. The room was dark save for the illumination which flowed in from the lighted hall, an illumination which threw a grotesque, distorted shadow of Jerry Templar along the floor of the bedroom. The birds became suddenly silent.

"The lights," Helen said, and darted past Jerry's side to reach for the light switch.

He grabbed her shoulder. "Don't be a fool. Keep out of this. Tell me . . ."

A stabbing spurt of flame came from the dark corner near the head of Matilda's bed. A bluish red spurt of flame that was ringed with orange. The report of the gun boomed through the confines of the room. She heard the bullet smack against the door jamb, even as a swift whisper of air brushed her face. She saw the drab darkness of the wood burst into lighter coloured splinters as the wood beneath the aged exterior was ripped into view by the bullet. She felt the blast of fine particles of wood and plaster stinging her skin.

Jerry had her shoulder then, was jerking her back, shielding her body with his own.

The gun roared again.

That second bullet hit with a meaty *"smok"* against something at her side. She felt Jerry's body, close to hers, spin round in a quick half circle. His hand was reaching out, clutching. Then she was frantically trying to support a dead weight. His legs buckled and he went crashing to the floor, taking her with him.

TWELVE

MASON, GETTING INTO his own car, waved good night to Gerald Shore, watched the tail-light on his client's car disappear, then started his own motor.

"Whew!" Della Street exclaimed. "You certainly pick cases! If Lieutenant Tragg ever uncovers those facts . . . Good night!"

Mason grinned. "There's only one way to keep him from uncovering those facts."

"What's that?"

"Give him so many other facts to uncover he won't have time to bother with these."

"That will only hold him back for a while," she pointed out.

"It's the best we can do—now."

He swung his car into Hollywood Boulevard, drove half-way to Los Angeles. "I guess the time has come to call in Paul Drake," he decided.

Della sighed. "More overheads! What do you need a private detective for? Couldn't I do it?"

"No, you could not."

"Well, Paul's out anyway. He's taking this week off and he swore that he wouldn't go to the office or take on any job for love or money."

"The devil! I'd forgotten."

"You'll have to get one of his operatives. That sweet little guy who looks like a Bedlington terrier is good. What's his name?"

"He won't do," Mason said decidedly. "I need Paul."

"He'll just hang up on you if you call him. You know Paul."

"Yeah, I know Paul. I guess you're right. He'd just dust me off."

They cruised on down the Boulevard.

"Is it really important, Perry?"

"What?"

"Getting Drake."

"Yes."

Della sighed resignedly. "All right, pull up by that all night lunch counter ahead, and if they've got a telephone booth, I'll see what I can do for you."

"You? What makes you think you can get Paul out of bed in the middle of the night if I can't?"

Della's eyes dropped demurely. "You just don't know how to appeal to Paul's higher instincts," she murmured. "I don't say I can make him *work*, but if I can get him down to the office you ought to be able to handle him from then on."

He stopped in front of the lunch counter, and followed Della in. She looked round, frowning.

"Go ahead and do your stuff," Mason said. "I'll order something to eat."

Della shook her head. "This joint won't do."

"What's the matter? It looks clean enough."

"There's no telephone booth."

"There's a phone on the wall over there, stupid."

"What I've got to say to Paul calls for a *booth*," she drawled. "A wall telephone won't do. Come on, we'll have to try somewhere else."

A few blocks farther on he stopped the car again in front of a brilliantly lighted dining-room. He looked in through plate windows at the interior, shining with chromium and glass, and locked the car.

"We're eating here whether there's a telephone booth or not. I'm hungry."

Inside the door, he pointed to the telephone booth and headed for the counter.

"Ham and eggs and coffee for me," she called after him.

Mason said to the man behind the counter, "Two orders of ham and eggs. Keep the eggs straight up and fry them easy. Plenty of French-fried potatoes. Lots of hot coffee, and you might make up two cheese-burger sandwiches on the side."

Five minutes later Della joined him at the counter.

"Get him?" Perry demanded.

"Yes, I got him."

"Is he coming down to the office?"

"He's coming down to the office—in thirty minutes."

"Swell. Say, what's the matter with your face? You haven't got a fever, have you?"

"I'm blushing, you lug! I'll never do that again, even for you. I want my coffee now."

"Well, I'll be damned," Perry Mason said softly.

The man drew two steaming cups of fragrant, golden-brown coffee, and slid them across the counter. "You'll like that," he said. "Best I can buy. I make it in small quantities and keep it fresh."

They perched themselves on stools, placed elbows on the counter, sipped coffee, and watched the food cooking on the gas plate, the appetizing smell of frying ham swirling past their nostrils.

"Now tell me why you need Paul Drake," Della said.

"I need a lot of facts dug out before Tragg closes the case with a lot of half-truths."

"Do you think Shore was telling you only half-truths?"

He thoughtfully regarded the steaming surface of the coffee in his cup. "He was telling us the truth as he sees it. But he was seeing only a part of the picture. There's nothing so deadly as a case built on circumstantial evidence composed of half-truths."

The cook slid hot, thick platters across the counter. Generous slices of ham, the golden yellow of fried eggs, and the rich brown of French-fried potatoes furnished a tempting visual background for the smells which came drifting up. "We eat," Mason said, "and do our thinking afterwards."

"Your cheeseburgers are coming right along," the man promised, picking up the toasted buns, putting the fillings in them, spreading them thickly with white, chopped onions. "Do you want mustard?"

"Lots of it," Mason said.

They ate silently, concentrating on their food.

Della Street pushed her coffee-cup across the counter for a refill.

"Why did Matilda Shore try to keep Lieutenant Tragg from knowing someone had poisoned her?"

"Quite evidently because there's some connection between that and the poisoned kitten."

"Was it an attempt on her life?"

"Looks that way."

"Any ideas?" Della asked.

"It depends on the time element. Apparently the stout was kept in an ice-box."

"What makes you think it was?"

"Wouldn't go flat so quickly after it was opened and poisoned. Probably she keeps several bottles in an ice-box."

"How did the poisoner make certain she was going to take the poisoned drink if she keeps several bottles on hand?"

"Probably by poisoning the nearest one—or perhaps by poisoning several."

He shoved a five-dollar bill across the counter and looked at his wrist-watch.

The attendant at the lunch counter handed him his change. "More coffee, yes?"

"About half a cup," Mason said. "That's all I have time for." He pushed back twenty-five cents out of the change, scooped the rest into his pocket, said, "Mighty good grub. We'll be back again sometime."

"In a hurry?" the attendant asked.

"Uh huh."

He peered at them shrewdly through the upper part of his spectacles. "If anybody'd ask me," he said, "looks as though you two was headed for Yuma on a marryin' party."

"Nobody asked you!" Della Street said, smiling.

Mason took another twenty-five-cent piece from his pocket, slipped it under his plate.

"What's that for?" the man asked.

"The idea," Mason said, grinning. "Come on, Della. Let's go."

They raced through the streets to the building where Mason had his office. Paul Drake's detective agency was on the same floor as the lawyer's office but nearer the elevator. Mason opened the lighted door, looked in on the man who ran the office at night. "The boss in yet?"

"Hello, Mr. Mason—no, he is taking this week off. I thought you knew."

"If he should drop in, don't mention me," Mason grinned. "Just forget you saw me."

They walked down the long, vacant corridor, their steps echoing hollowly against the walls. Dark doors on each side lettered with the names of business firms seemed like silent sentinels of dead business. The air in the passage was musty and stale. Mason opened the door of his private office, switched on the lights. Della Street paused as he held the door open. "That's the elevator coming up again," she said. "I'll bet this is Paul Drake."

Mason disappeared into the law library and closed the door. He could hear the steady rhythm of the approaching steps.

"It's Paul, all right," she whispered from the other side of the door. "Nothing ever seems to change the tempo of that walk. He's not stopping at his office."

There was a soft knock on the door into the corridor. Della opened it a crack. Drake pushed it open the rest of the way, stalked in, slammed the door behind him. He looked at her with slightly protruding eyes which held no hint of expression. Then he smiled sardonically. Tall, somewhat stooped, he had the manner of a professional undertaker making a midnight round of the mortuary.

"Hello, kid," he said.

"Hello, Paul." Della's voice was uncertain.

"That was a good act. I didn't know you had it in you." He crossed swiftly to the door concealing Perry Mason and flung it open. "Come out of there, you cheap shyster! I'll teach you to try the badger game on me."

Mason came out, grinning. "I had a hunch you didn't fall for it, but I didn't say anything."

There was a wail from Della Street. "You played up and led me on and pretended you thought I was serious, and all the time you were laughing at me!"

"Shucks, Della, I was admiring you. I wasn't laughing at you." His slow drawl was expressive, pungent. "I just know you too well."

"Why did you come, then?" she demanded, pointing at him.

Paul Drake's head drew in like a turtle's, then lunged forward and snapped at the tinted red finger-nail a few inches away from his face. "I figured Perry needed me, and I guess I've had enough vacation. I was bored stiff," he confessed, with his peculiar husky chuckle.

"Get this woman off my neck, Perry, and let's get to work." He squirmed his way into his favourite, crossways position in the big, overstuffed leather chair. "What's the excitement?"

For ten minutes Mason talked rapidly. Drake listened with his eyes closed.

"That's the picture," Mason wound up.

"Okay. What do I do?"

"Find out everything you can about Leech. Find out anything you can about all the members of the family, particularly what they've done since the hue and cry over Franklin's disappearance died down."

"Anything else?"

"Yes. This man who telephoned Helen Kendal seems to have identified himself unmistakably as Franklin Shore, but in a case of this sort, you can't overlook the possibility of an impostor. Now, this man Leech has either been in contact with Franklin Shore or else trying to slip over a fast one. Here's a number," Mason went on, opening up his note-book and tearing out a sheet of paper.

"Car licence?" Drake asked.

"No. Laundry mark. Laundry mark on a handkerchief that was tied round some personal stuff that seems to have belonged to Shore. It was on the seat of the car beside Leech. Leech evidently brought them along to show that he actually was acting as intermediary for Shore."

"Why the intermediary?"

"You've got me. Maybe Shore didn't want to come back until he'd tossed his hat in the door first."

"Would it have been kicked out?"

"Hard."

Drake gave a low whistle. "Like that, eh?"

Mason nodded.

"Tragg know you've got this laundry mark?" Drake asked.

"I don't think so. I fumbled around and pretended to be interested in the watch. That laundry mark struck me as being peculiar, Paul. I haven't seen laundry marks inked on the hems of handkerchiefs for some time. Most laundries don't do it any more. We should be able to trace Franklin Shore from that laundry mark."

"Anything else?"

"That Castle Gate Hotel seems to be . . ."

"I know the dump," Drake interrupted. "Bunch of promoters hang out there. Slick stock men. Phoney mining-company stuff. Get-rich-quick oil businesses and that sort of thing. They don't promote their rackets from the hotel, but use the Castle Gate as a place to hibernate when things go sour. If they start hitting the jack-pot, they move into swanky hotels and apartments and put on the dog. If the police don't get anything on them and the racket pays off, they move into the big-time. If the police do get something on them, they go to San Quentin. But when a racket doesn't pay off, and the police haven't anything on them, they sneak back to the Castle Gate to make contacts with each other and lie low until the beef has passed."

"Okay," Mason said. "Now, here's another angle. Look back in the newspapers in 1932 and you'll find they published a list of cheques which had cleared through Franklin Shore's account within a few days of his disappearance. You can be sure the police have dug up everything they could find out about those cheques as of 1932. I want you to make a fresh investigation as of 1942."

"Anything else?" Drake asked, jotting down notes in a leather-backed, loose-leaf note-book.

"As an incidental development," Mason said, "a kitten was poisoned out at Matilda Shore's house. I think Tragg will be covering all the drug-stores looking for poison purchases, and it won't do any good for us to trail along behind the police. They have the organization and the authority. They'd be bound to get the facts before we could. But you might bear in mind the poison angle."

"What's the kitten got to do with it?" Drake asked.

"I don't know, but Matilda Shore was fed poison from some source—apparently the same sort of poison that was used on the kitten. There's a chap by the name of Komo who works as houseboy. There's some question whether he's Japanese or Korean. Tragg has a letter and map which was mailed, special delivery, about six-thirty from a Hollywood branch post office. It sounds very Japanesy—almost too Japanesy. However, you can't tell a thing by that. Komo might have written it, or it may have been someone who thought Komo, because of his nationality, would make a good bait for the police to snap at. You can probably get a photostatic copy of that letter. Tragg will be searching for typewriters which could have written it, and will have had an expert check it over. You can probably find out from one of the newspaper boys what has been reported by this expert—the make and model of typewriter it was written on. It looked to me like a portable owned by someone who didn't do any serious typewriting, quite probably a man who's owned the machine for some time."

"What gave you that impression?" Drake asked.

"Letters badly out of line, a faint ribbon which looked as though it had dried out from lack of use, dirt in the loops of the e's and the a's, a few strike-overs and cross-outs, poor spacing of the letter on the sheet of paper, and irregularities in the letters which indicated a ragged touch. However, Tragg will have seen all that almost at a glance, so don't waste too much time on the letter. There's no use duplicating the police effort, and we can't expect to engage in competition with them on the things they'll be covering."

"Okay," Drake said, "I'll . . ."

Della Street said, "The phone keeps ringing in the outer office. Hear that peculiar buzzing sound? That's the way the switchboard sounds when the lines are out and someone's ringing on the main line. It's been doing that at intervals for the past five minutes."

Mason glanced at his watch, said, "On a hunch, Della, see who it is."

She got up and went through to the outer office, and in a few minutes came running back.

"What is it?" Mason asked.

"Helen Kendal. Someone broke into the house and shot her boyfriend—the one who's on leave from the Army. She notified the police and called for a taxicab. She's at the hospital now. They're operating, on a desperate chance. They don't expect him to live through the operation. She's been ringing for the last five minutes."

Mason nodded to Paul Drake. "Let's go, Paul."

Drake shook his head. "*You* go. By the time you get there, Lieutenant Tragg will have things sewed up so tight you'll have to pay admission to get within a block of the place. I'll put in the time working these other angles while Tragg's busy out there."

Mason said, "There may be something to that."

"This new development will keep him occupied," Drake said, "and leave my hands free."

Mason was struggling into his overcoat. "Want to come, Della?"

"Try holding me back."

Drake looked at Mason, with his peculiar, lop-sided smile twisting his features. "Where was *your* client when this last bit of shooting took place?" he asked.

Mason looked at his wrist watch, narrowed his eyes thoughtfully as he made a rapid mental calculation, and said, "That's one of the first things Lieutenant Tragg is going to ask. For all I know, he's asking it right now—and getting an answer. And, as I figure out the time clement, my client could have made it back to the house in time to do the shooting."

THIRTEEN

THE BIG, OLD-FASHIONED house in which Franklin B. Shore had reigned as a financial power was lighted from cellar to garret. Two police cars were parked in the drive. Under the contagion of excitement, adjoining houses showed lighted windows, mostly in the upper stories, and these oblongs of light, in a neighbourhood which was otherwise wrapped in slumber and darkness, held in themselves a certain portent of tragedy.

Mason drove past the house twice, then parked his car on the opposite side of the street and said to Della Street, "I'll make a preliminary survey. Do you want to sit here in the car?"

"Okay."

"Keep your eyes open. If you see anything suspicious, strike a match and light a cigarette. Otherwise, don't smoke. When you strike the match, hold it for a second close to the windscreen, then cup your hands and bring it up to the cigarette. It won't do any harm to let the first match go out and strike a second, just in case I'm where I don't get your first signal."

"Are you going up to the house?"

"Eventually. I want to snoop around the yard first."

"Want me to go with you when you do make the house?"

"I'll let you know. I want to check up here first. Notice that window over on the north side of the house, the one on the ground floor? It's wide open and the curtains aren't drawn. I saw the light from a flash bulb on the inside of that room just now. It looks as though they were photographing the window. That's significant."

Della Street settled down in the car. "I suppose Tragg's already on the job in person."

"Oh, sure."

"And your client, Gerald Shore?"

"May have walked right into the middle of things," Mason said. "I hope he has sense enough not to give them his alibi."

"What *is* his alibi?" Della Street asked.

"He was with us—I hope, I hope."

She said, "I don't think we've ever furnished an alibi for a client, have we?"

"No. That's why I hope he keeps his mouth shut."

"Wouldn't Tragg accept your word?"

"Tragg might, but put yourself in the position of someone in a jury-box. A lawyer comes into court defending a man charged with one murder. Another murder gets linked up with him. He says, 'At that time I was with my lawyer,' and the lawyer who is defending him, and his secretary, get on the stand and glibly try to prove the alibi. Doesn't look very well, does it?"

She shook her head. "Not to a jury it wouldn't."

"That is why the better lawyers withdraw from a case when they have to be witnesses," Mason said.

"You mean you'd withdraw if you had to make an alibi for Shore?"

"I wouldn't want to be both a witness and an attorney in a case."

"*I* could be a witness."

"We'll talk it over later," Mason said, and buttoning his overcoat against the chill of the night wind which was sweeping down from the north-east, walked diagonally across the street toward the lighted house.

She watched him through the windscreen of the car, her eyes darting about, searching the shadows. As he neared the yard and started to cut across the strip of lawn, Della saw the motion of a shadow near the hedge.

Mason had turned so that he was facing the window on the north. The shadow was moving toward him.

She hurriedly lit a match. Mason, with his back to her, didn't notice the signal. Della reached to the dashboard and switched the headlights on and off, twice.

Mason turned, then—too late.

Della, rolling down the window of the car, could hear the conversation.

"Mr. Mason?"

Only one who had been intimately associated with Perry Mason for years would have noticed anything unusual in his voice as he said, "Yes. This is Mr. Mason. Why?"

The man moved forward. "Lieutenant Tragg wants to see you. He said you'd probably be along and for me to keep an eye out for you."

Mason's laugh was hearty. "My compliments to Lieutenant Tragg. When do we see him?"

"Now."

"Where?"

"Inside."

Mason linked his arm through that of the officer. "It's a little chilly outside, anyway. Care for a cigar?"

"Don't mind if I do."

They marched up the steps and into the house. Della Street settled back against the cushions of the automobile.

Lights in the hall beat into the lawyer's eyes, so that he squinted against the sudden glare. A plain-clothes officer, seated by the door, got to his feet.

"Tell Tragg Mr. Mason's here."

The guard looked curiously at Mason and said, "Okay," and vanished.

Mason's escort held a match to the cigar, tilted his hat back on his head. "We stay here," he said. "I don't think the lieutenant would like to have you rubbering around the house until he's ready to talk with you."

They heard the sound of quick steps. Tragg came through the door which opened from the living-room. "Well, well, Mason," he said, "nice of you to call! I wanted to talk with you. Rang up your office but you weren't there."

"I endeavour to anticipate your every wish," said Mason with mock formality.

"That's very thoughtful of you."

Lieutenant Tragg turned, pushed his head through the door, called out to someone, "Close that bedroom door."

He waited until the sound of a door slamming shut indicated that his order had been obeyed.

"Come on in, Mason."

He led the way into the living-room. Mason's eyes, by this time thoroughly adjusted to the light, took in the significant details with photographic clarity.

Gerald Shore, apparently perfectly calm and composed, was sitting in an easy chair, his knees crossed, puffing placidly at his pipe. A plain-clothes officer stood unobtrusively in the shadows, his hat brim pulled down so that his face was completely in the shadow. The ruddy tip of a lighted cigarette glowed and paled alternately as he smoked. A man whom Mason took to be Komo, with a distinctly Oriental cast of countenance, was seated within a few feet of the officer.

That end of the long room was thrown into shadows by a relatively dim illumination, but the end over toward the hall leading to Matilda's bedroom and the hall itself blazed with the brilliant light thrown by powerful floodlights in reflectors which were supported on metal stands. These lamps quite evidently had been used to give illumination for photographic purposes. The wires which led to them from outlets in various parts of the living-room and hall criss-crossed over the floor.

The closed door and the end of the hall concealed the interior of the room beyond. The blazing floodlights standing just outside the door, showed quite plainly that Lieutenant Tragg had wanted photographs of the bedroom, and the sinister red stain on the hardwood floor by the door showed why.

"Sit down, Mason," Tragg said. "I don't want to take any unfair advantage of you. I have asked you for co-operation in times past. I'm not doing that now, because I'm in a definitely hostile position."

"How so?" Mason asked.

"Mr. Shore says you're his attorney. He isn't doing any talking. I don't like that."

"I don't blame you," Mason said.

"And," Tragg went on, "I don't propose to stand for it. When a man tries to conceal something from me in a murder case, I consider it an admission of guilt."

Mason's nod was sympathetic.

"I'm hoping," Tragg went on, "that *you'll* talk. It's going to be unfortunate for your client if you don't."

Mason nodded to Gerald Shore, sat down in a chair by the table, and said, "Of course I'll talk, Tragg. I'm always willing to talk."

Tragg drew up a chair.

Shore removed the pipe from his mouth. "Lieutenant Tragg has been asking me questions. I told him you were my lawyer."

Tragg said, "That doesn't prevent you from answering questions about an entirely different matter."

"How do you know it's an entirely different matter?" Mason asked.

"Because it must have occurred *after* he'd employed you."

"I see."

Shore tamped the tobacco down into the bowl of the pipe with his finger and said, "It's an axiom of the profession, Lieutenant, that a lawyer who seeks to advise himself has a fool for a client."

"The point is," said Tragg, "Shore refuses to tell me where he was when this crime occurred."

Mason said, "Suppose you tell me what crime we're talking about, Tragg."

Tragg said, "All right—I'll tell you that. Helen Kendal was sitting on that davenport talking with Jerry Templar, her—well, if she's not engaged to him, she ought to be. They heard a noise in Mrs. Shore's bedroom."

"What sort of a noise?" Mason asked, his eyes showing keen interest.

"As though a bedside stand or something of the kind had been knocked over."

"By an intruder climbing in through that window on the north side?" Mason asked.

Tragg hesitated for a moment, then said, "Well, yes."

"Go on."

"Naturally, Helen Kendal was startled," Tragg said, "as she knew that her aunt was not in her bedroom. After that they both heard sounds that *should* have been Matilda Shore walking across the room, the thump-thump of a cane and the slightly dragging steps. It's significant that if Miss Kendal hadn't known that Mrs. Shore was in the hospital, she would not have paid any attention to the sounds, thinking that her aunt had accidentally overturned some object in getting out of bed to go to the bathroom. But since she knew Mrs. Shore was not in the house, they started to investigate."

"Mrs. Shore *was* in the hospital?" Mason asked.

"She was. I can vouch for that. Templar opened the door. While he was fumbling for the light switch, someone who was in the room shot him with a revolver. Two shots were fired. The first missed. The second struck him in the left side."

"Killed?" demanded Mason quickly.

"No. I understand his chances of recovery are about fifty-fifty. The doctors are performing an emergency operation."

"This seems to be one of your more lurid nights, Tragg," Mason broke in dryly.

The other ignored him. "They ought to have that bullet shortly, if they have not already recovered it. I've got here, though, the bullet which missed him and hit the woodwork just to the side of the door. It missed Helen Kendal's head by a scant inch or two. It's a .38 calibre slug, apparently fired from a conventional double-action, self-cocking revolver. I haven't as yet matched it up with the bullet which killed Henry Leech, but I won't be at all surprised if all three shots were fired from the same gun. That means, of course, they were fired by the same person."

Mason drummed softly with the tips of his fingers on the arm of the chair. "Interesting," he observed.

"Isn't it?"

Mason nodded. "If we concede in advance that all three shots were fired from the same gun and that, therefore, they must have been fired by the same person, we can exclude Leech because he is dead, Matilda Shore because she was in a hospital at the time the last crime was committed. Gerald Shore because he has a perfect alibi for that same period, also Helen Kendal and Jerry Templar. Moreover . . ."

"I'm quite capable of working out the theory of elimination," Tragg interrupted. "What I am interested in is your statement that Gerald Shore has an alibi."

"He has."

"Well, what is it?"

Mason smiled. "You haven't told me the time the crime was committed."

"Then how do you know he has an alibi?" Tragg countered quickly.

"That's right," Mason said, smiling. "I don't, do I? Now let's see. The person who entered that room knew that Mrs. Shore wasn't in the room, but *didn't know that Helen Kendal knew it.*"

"How do you make that deduction?" Tragg asked, interested.

Mason said, "Because he tried to deceive Helen by impersonating Mrs. Shore, and walking across the room just as Mrs. Shore would have done. That proves Gerald Shore couldn't have done it. Gerald knew that Helen knew her aunt wasn't in the house."

Tragg frowned. It was plain that Mason's reasoning impressed him, and also upset some theory he had formed.

Suddenly the guard at the other end of the room said, "This Jap's doing a lot of listening. Lieutenant. His ears are sticking out a foot."

Tragg turned, his face showing annoyance. "Get him out of here."

Komo bowed. "Excussse please," he said with dignity. "I am not Japanese. I am Korean. My sentiments for Japanese are not friendly."

"Get him out!" Tragg repeated.

The guard clapped a hand on Komo's shoulder. "Come on, Skibby," he said. "Out!"

Tragg waited until Komo had been escorted from the room to the kitchen. Then he turned to Mason. "Mason," he said, "I don't like your attitude, nor that of your client."

Mason grinned. "If we're going to play a game of Truth, Lieutenant, it's my turn. I don't like the way you dragged me in here as though I were a second-story man."

Tragg said, "And perhaps you won't like what I'm going to do now any better. When my men checked on the Castle Gate Hotel, the clerk said there were *three* of you in there when the letter was received. Four of you went up to the mountain. Now, why didn't one of your party want to go in the hotel? Just hold everything a moment."

He got up, walked out to the telephone in the hall, leaving the door open behind him. He dialled a number, and after a moment said, "The Castle Gate Hotel? The night clerk? . . . This is Lieutenant Tragg, Homicide. . . . That's right. . . . What time did you come on duty last night? . . . Six o'clock. All right, do you know a man named Gerald Shore? . . . Let me describe him. About sixty-two years, rather distinguished looking, a high forehead, clean-cut profile, five-feet-eight or eight and a half, weight a hundred and sixty-five pounds, flowing grey hair which sweeps back from a high forehead, wearing a grey checked suit, a light blue shirt, and a blue-and-red necktie with a black pearl scarf pin. . . . He was! When? . . . I see. . . . For how long? . . . I'll be up to see you within the next half-hour. In the meantime, don't talk with anyone about this."

He slammed up the telephone receiver and came back to stand where he could look from Gerald Shore to Perry Mason. "I think I begin to see a very great light," he said. "Perhaps, Mr. Shore, you will tell me why you went to the Castle Gate Hotel early this evening and waited—and waited—and waited."

Gerald Shore calmly removed the pipe from his mouth and pointed the stem toward Perry Mason. "He's my lawyer."

Tragg nodded. His smile was triumphant. "Okay, Jerry," he called to the guard in the hall, "Mr. Mason has got to go. If you see him hanging around remind him that he has an engagement elsewhere—until we meet again, Mason!" Then he held up his hand for attention. "And I'm telling everyone here that as soon as Franklin Shore is found I want him as a witness to testify before the grand jury—and you'll all kindly remember that."

Mason turned without a word and started for the front door and opened it. Tragg said to Gerald Shore, "This is going to be about your last chance to say something."

Mason hesitated, listening for the reply. "Have you got a match, Lieutenant?" Shore asked calmly.

The guard bustled Mason out to the front porch. The door slammed shut.

Another officer, evidently waiting to see that he left the grounds promptly, stepped up beside him. "I'll walk with you to your car."

"No need to."

"Oh, I'd better. No telling what might happen around here to-night. Wouldn't want anything to happen to *you*, Mr. Mason."

Perry walked down the drive, the officer marching at his side. Peering across the street, he saw only the vacant kerb. There was no sign of his automobile nor of Della Street. For a moment only, he was puzzled. He hesitated just enough to throw the officer out of step with him.

"What is it?" the latter asked.

"Little kink in my leg," Mason said, walking toward the corner.

"Say, Mr. Mason! Your car's on the other side. You'd better... Where the hell *is* your car?"

Mason said, "My chauffeur took it back to the office. I had an errand I wanted done."

The officer looked at him suspiciously. "Where you goin' now?"

"I'm going to take a walk—a long walk—to get some air. Would you like to come along?"

Said the officer, with feeling, "Hell, no!"

FOURTEEN

MASON'S UNLISTED TELEPHONE was ringing as he opened the door of his apartment. He switched on the lights, crossed over, picked up the receiver and said, "Let's have it."

It was Della Street. As soon as she started talking he realized that she was in a nervous funk and trying to cover up. "Gosh, Chief, is that you?" She was off at the tempo of a pneumatic riveter exploding into action. "I think I may be violating the form, force and effect of the statutes in such cases made and provided, and my actions are probably against the peace and dignity of the People of the State of California. I guess I've graduated into a full-fledged criminal."

"They tell me prison is a great experience," Mason assured her. "You'll learn a lot."

Her laugh was high-pitched, and there was a catch in the middle of it. "Paul Drake warned me that I'd wind up in jail if I went on working for you, but I was too stubborn to listen to him."

"Well, you haven't been sentenced yet. What have you done?"

"I've k-k-k-kidnapped a witness," she wailed.

"Done what?"

"Snaked him right out from under Lieutenant Tragg's nose, and am holding him incommunicado."

"Where?"

"In my automobile—or rather, your automobile."

"Where are you?"

"At a service station about four blocks from your apartment."

"Who's the witness?"

"He's sitting out in the car now. His name's Lunk, and he . . ."

"Wait a minute," Mason interrupted, "what was the name?"

"Lunk. He's the gardener out at the Shore place. And he's the temporary custodian of the poisoned kitten."

"How does he spell his name?"

"L-u-n-k. Thomas B. Lunk. That part's all right. I've already managed to get a look at his driver's licence."

"What does he know?"

"I don't know exactly, but I think it's awfully important."

"Why?"

"He got off a street-car about two blocks from the house. It was just after that guard collared you and took you inside. I saw the street-car come to a stop and this man get off. He's an old, weather-beaten, outdoor type of man. He came hurrying toward the house. Occasionally he'd break into a run for a few steps. You could see he was in a great rush."

"What did you do?"

"Followed a hunch," she said, "started the car, and drove down a block to meet him, got out of the car and asked him if he was looking for the Shore residence."

"Then what?" Mason asked, as she hesitated.

"I'd rather not tell you all this over the phone."

"You've got to. At least the part that you don't want him to hear."

"Well, he was so excited he was stammering. He just kept nodding his head and couldn't talk at first. Then he said he had to see Mrs. Shore right away. I turned on my best manner and asked him if he knew Mrs. Shore when he saw her—just sort of sparring for time and trying to find out what it was all about. He said then that he'd worked for her. That he's the gardener who's been with the place for twelve or thirteen years."

"But he doesn't live there?" Mason asked.

"No. The address on his driving licence is 642½ South Belvedere. He says he lives in a little bachelor shack at the back of a house. He used to live in a room over the garage up at the Shore place. Then he went down to live in this little shack."

"What's he know?"

"I don't know. He was so excited he could hardly talk. He said he had to see her at once, that something had happened, and I told him that Mrs. Shore wasn't at home, that I happened to know where she was and I could take him to see her. I got him in the car, drove away from the place, and then started stalling, pretending that I needed oil and gas, and then let the attendant at the service station here talk me into changing sparking plugs. I told him that Mrs. Shore was where she couldn't be disturbed right away, but that we could see her in fifteen or twenty minutes and I'd take him to her. All the time, of course, I kept calling up, hoping that you'd get a taxi and come in. When I didn't hear anything from you, I bribed the service station attendant to let the air out of one of my tyres and tell me that I had a puncture that had better be fixed right away. He got the tyre off and kept fooling around with it. Now my boy-friend's getting nervous and a little suspicious. I've got to let the attendant here put that tyre back on, and you'll have to get here in a rush."

"What's the address of the service station?"

"On the corner, four blocks down the boulevard from your apartment."

"I'm coming right down. Wait there," Mason said.

"What'll I do when you get here?"

"Just follow my lead," Mason said. "I'll size him up. Tell me about him."

"He has steady, blue eyes, with a far-away squint, a weather-beaten face with high cheekbones, a drooping moustache, about fifty-five or maybe sixty, gnarled hands, stoop shoulders, long arms, slow-moving, and has a single-track mind. Sort of simple, but obstinate and sullen when he gets suspicious. I think he'll believe anything you tell him, if you can make it sound plausible. But I was so excited and—well, he's getting terribly suspicious. You'll have to get down here right away or he'll walk out on me."

"On my way," Mason promised, and hung up.

He switched out the lights, went down in the elevator, crossed the street and waited in the shadows to make certain he wasn't being followed. Having convinced himself on that point, he walked rapidly for three blocks, and paused long enough to be certain once more that no one was on his trail. Then he walked to the all-night service station where an attendant in white uniform was just finishing tightening the bolts on the left hind wheel of his car.

Mason walked up to Della, apparently without noticing the man in his late fifties at her side, raised his hat, said, "Good evening, Miss Street. I hope I didn't keep you waiting."

She searched his eyes for a signal, hesitated a moment, then said, with some show of feeling, "Well, you certainly *were* late! If it hadn't been for finding a nail in this tyre I couldn't have waited."

"Too bad," Mason said. "I was unavoidably detained. You know, I told you I could get you an audience with Mrs. Shore. But, you see, she's . . ."

He broke off, apparently seeing, for the first time, the man.

Della said, "It's all right, this is Mr. Lunk. He's working out at the Shore place as a gardener. He wants to see Mrs. Shore, too."

Mason said, "Mrs. Shore is at a hospital. She was poisoned. She *says* she took poison by mistake, but that isn't what the police think, and they're making it a matter for police investigation."

"Poison!" Lunk ejaculated.

Della Street registered dismay. "Can't we see her? Mr. Lunk says his business is terribly important."

"We can try at least," said Mason. "I thought everything was arranged, but the way things have turned out . . ." He shifted his position so he could watch Lunk from the corner of his eye. "You see," he went on, "with a police guard on the premises, the minute wc tried to see her, they'd begin asking *us* questions."

"I don't want no police," Lunk burst out. "I've got to see Mrs. Shore personally and private."

Mason raised his eyebrows. "You say you work there?"

"I'm the gardener."

"Live there?"

"Nope. I come to work on the street-car and go home on the street-car. I lived there for a while. That was years ago. She wanted me to stay on, but I can't stand having a darned Oriental snooping around. I want to be by myself and be private-like."

"Oriental?" Mason asked.

"Yeah. That houseboy she's got. I don't know why she hasn't fired him long ago. To tell you the truth, I've been looking for the F.B.I. to come around and . . . Well, I guess I ain't goin' to say nothin' more."

Mason didn't press him, but nodded sympathetically. "Well, as I understand it, if we can fix things so we can see Mrs. Shore without the police grabbing us, you want to see her. Otherwise, it can wait. Is that it?"

Lunk said, "It *can't* wait."

"That important?"

"Yes."

Mason gave the matter thoughtful consideration. "Well, let's go down and see if the coast is clear."

"Where is she?"

"She's in a hospital."

"Yeah, I know. But what hospital?"

"I'll drive you there."

He eased the car past the street intersections. "At this hour of the night, you don't ordinarily meet anyone on these intersections, but if you do meet someone, he's driving like the devil. You can get smacked at an intersection as easy as not."

"Uh huh."

"So you've been working for Mrs. Shore for some twelve years?"

"Yes, goin' on for thirteen."

"You knew her husband then?"

Lunk glanced at him sharply, saw nothing except an expressionless profile as Mason's eyes held steady on the road ahead.

"Yes. One of the finest men that ever set foot in a garden."

"So I've heard. Peculiar about his disappearance, wasn't it?"

"Uh huh."

"What do *you* think about it?"

"Who? Me?"

"Yes."

"Why should I think anything about it?"

Mason laughed. "You do think, don't you?"

"I'm paid for gardening."

"It's an interesting family."

"You know 'em?" Lunk asked. "All of 'em?"

"I've met some of them. I'm doing some work for Gerald Shore. How do you like him?"

"He's all right, I reckon. He ain't like his brother Franklin, though, about the lawn and flowers. He don't seem to care much about 'em, so I don't see much of *him*. Mrs. Shore gives the orders—except when that damned Jap tries to horn in. Know what that heathen devil was trying to do just a little while ago?"

"No."

"Get her to take a trip for her health. Wanted the whole family to get out and let him give the house a thorough cleaning inside and out. Guess he wanted to take three or four months doing it. Wanted her to go to Florida and take the niece with her. And I happen to know he'd been talking with George Alber about it. May have been Alber's idea. You know him?"

"No."

"He's the fair-haired boy child right now. Seems like the old lady liked his daddy—or he liked her—ain't sure which. I do my work and want to be left alone. That's *all* I ask."

"How is Komo? A pretty good worker?"

"Oh, he *works* all right, but you always have the feeling that his eyes are staring through your back."

"You said you lived at the Shore place for a while. Have any trouble with Komo while you were living there?"

"No fights—nothing open. My brother was the one that had the trouble with him."

"Your brother?" Mason asked, taking his eyes from the road long enough to flash a quick glance at Della Street. "You had a brother living there with you?"

"Uh huh. For about six, seven months."

"What happened to him?"

"Died."

"While you were living there?"

"Nope."

"After you moved, eh? How long after?"

"Week or two."

"Sick long?"

"No."

"Heart trouble, I suppose?"

"No. He was younger than me."

Della Street said soothingly, "I know just how he feels about it. He doesn't want to talk about it, do you, Mr. Lunk?"

"No."

She went on rapidly, "It's that way when someone near to you passes away. It's a shock. Your brother must have been smart, Mr. Lunk."

"What makes you say that?"

"Oh, just little things in the way you describe him. He seems to have been a man who wasn't taken in by anybody. That is, the Japanese houseboy didn't fool *him* any."

"I'll say he didn't!"

"It must have been rather hard to start doing the work by yourself after having had your brother help you in the garden."

"He didn't help me. He was there visiting. He hadn't been well for quite a while—not able to do any work."

"People of that sort sometimes live a lot longer than the husky, strong people who don't know what an ache or a pain is."

"That's right."

Della said, "Mr. Shore must have been a very fine man."

"Yes, ma'am. He sure was. He was certainly nice to me."

"Letting your brother stay in the house that way. I don't suppose they charged him board."

"Nope. They didn't," Lunk said. "And I'll never forget how Shore acted when my brother passed away. I'd been spending my money on doctors and things, and—well, Shore just called me in and told me how he understood the way I felt, and—know what he did?"

"No. What did he do?"

"Gave me three hundred and fifty dollars so I could ship him back East, and gave me time off from work so I could go along with him on the train. My mother was alive then, and it meant a lot to her having me bring Phil home that way and having the funeral right there."

"She's passed away since?" Della asked.

"Uh huh. Five years ago. Never had anything hit me quite as hard as the way Mr. Shore acted about that. I thanked him at the time. I wanted to thank him some more, but he was gone when I got back from burying Phil."

Mason nudged Della Street with his knee so that she wouldn't pounce on that opening and alarm the gardener. Then, after a moment or two, he asked casually, "That was right about the time he disappeared?"

"Just that time."

"Those Japs certainly are clever. The Orientals know a lot about drugs that we don't know."

Lunk leaned forward so he could look searchingly into the lawyer's face. "What made you say that?"

"Oh, I don't know," Mason said. "I was just thinking out loud. I sometimes get funny ideas."

"Well, what was funny about that idea?"

"It wasn't even an idea," Mason said. "I was just thinking."

Lunk said, significantly, "Well, *I've* been doing a lot of thinking too."

Mason waited a few seconds, then observed, casually, "If I had a Jap around and I didn't like him—I'd sure hate to be living in the house with him. . . . Have him fixing or serving food to me. I don't trust 'em."

"That's the same way I feel," Lunk said. "I'm going to tell you something, Mr.—what'd you say your name was?"

"Mason."

"Well, I'll tell you something, Mr. Mason. There was a while after I heard about Mr. Shore disappearing that I'd have bet dollars to doughnuts that the Jap had something to do with it. And then, later on, I began to wonder if maybe the Jap hadn't had something to do with the way Phil died. It could have been something, you know."

"Poison?" Mason asked.

"Well, I ain't saying anything. Personally, I ain't got any use for the sneaking, treacherous race, but I want to be fair. I've done him one injustice already."

"Oh, is that so?"

Lunk said, "Well, to tell you the truth, I sort of suspected him of having a hand in—well, I'll tell you. I thought for a while that maybe he wanted to get Mr. Shore out of the way, and he sort of practised first on my brother to see if he had the right dose and—you know, the way Mr. Shore disappeared and all that, and coming right on top of Phil's death. . . . I didn't think so much of it at the time, but I got to thinking more about it later on."

Mason again nudged Della with his elbow as he piloted the car round a corner toward the hospital. "Well, I don't see that that's doing the Jap any injustice."

"Nope," Lunk said positively. "He didn't do it. But up to a few hours ago, you couldn't have convinced me of that if you'd argued all night. Just goes to show how we get an idea into our heads and it sticks. To tell you the truth, the reason I didn't want to live on the place any more was on account of the way that Jap was hanging around. Phil was gettin' worse all the time. I got to feeling kind of sick myself and went to a doctor, and the doctor couldn't find nothing wrong with me, so I up and left."

"Did that cure you?" Mason asked.

"Perked right up," Lunk said, warming to his subject. "I got a place of my own, did all my own cooking, and carried my lunches with me. And I'll tell you something else, Mister, I didn't leave my lunches hanging around where anybody could open a box and sprinkle something on my sandwich, either. No, siree!"

"And you were cured immediately?"

"Within a week or two. But Phil was sick anyway. He didn't make it. He was all shot."

"What did Komo say when you moved out?"

"The damn Jap didn't say nothin'. He just looked at me, but I knew he knew what I was thinkin', and I didn't care."

"What made you change your mind? Why don't you think he poisoned Mr. Shore?"

"Nope," Lunk said, shaking his head positively. "He didn't poison the boss. I do think he poisoned Phil though, and I think he tried poisoning me; what's more, he poisoned that kitten, and if Matilda Shore got a dose of poison, you'll never convince me that Komo didn't do it. He ain't foolin' me none. You mark my words, he wanted to poison someone, but he wanted to see how the poison worked first. Ten years ago he used Phil to try things out on. Last night he used this here kitten. Thought for a while ten years ago he was practisin' up on Phil to have a go at the boss. Now I know it was me he was after."

"But if you thought your brother was poisoned, why didn't you go to the police, and . . ."

"Didn't have a thing to go on. When Phil died, I asked the doc about poison. He laughed at me. Said Phil had been living on borrowed time for five years."

Mason said, "Well, here's the hospital. You want to go in with me and see if the officers are still on duty?"

"I don't want to see no officers."

"Of course," Mason said. "But there's just a chance we can get through to see Mrs. Shore."

Della Street looked at him apprehensively. "I can run up, Chief," she said, "and see if they're on duty, and . . ."

"No," Mason said significantly. "I want to take Mr. Lunk up with me. You see," he explained to Lunk, "I was in to see her once this evening."

"Oh," the man said. "Didn't you say you were working for Gerald Shore?"

"Yes. He's a client of mine. I'm a lawyer."

Mason opened the car door. "Come on, Lunk. We'll run up. Della, you won't mind staying here?"

She shook her head, but there were little creases of worry down the centre of her forehead.

Mason took Lunk's arm, and the two climbed up the stone steps to the hospital.

As they walked down the long corridor past the receiving and admittance desk, Mason said, "Probably just as well to let me do the talking. But you listen carefully, and if I'm not doing all right, give me a nudge."

"All right," said Lunk.

Mason rang for the elevator, went up to the floor on which Matilda Shore's room was located. A nurse, working on some records at a desk, looked up from her work. Two men got up out of chairs at the far end of the corridor and came marching toward the visitors.

Mason had his hand on the door of Mrs. Shore's room when one of them said, truculently, "Hold it, buddy."

The other said, "That's Mason, the lawyer. He was here before. Lieutenant Tragg had a talk with him."

"What you want?" the man who seemed to be in charge asked.

"I want to talk with Mrs. Shore."

The other shook his head and grinned. "Nix on it. Nix on it," he said.

"This man with me wants to talk with her," Mason said.

"Well now, does he?" The officer grinned, surveying Lunk as though enjoying a huge joke. "So you *both* want to talk with her, eh?"

"That's right."

The man jerked his thumb down the corridor, and said, "Back down the elevator, boys. I'm sorry, but it's no go."

Mason, raising his voice, said, "Perhaps this man could do you some good if he could talk with Mrs. Shore. He's her gardener. I think Lieutenant Tragg would like to see him, too."

The officer nodded to his companion as his hand clapped down on Mason's shoulder. The other officer hooked his fingers in the back of Lunk's collar. "Come on now, boys. On your way, and don't act rough about it."

"I think we're really entitled to see her," Mason said.

"Got a pass?" the officer asked.

The nurse came efficiently forward on rubber heels. "There are other patients on this floor, and I'm responsible for them. I want no noise, no argument, and no disturbance."

One of the officers rang for the elevator. "There won't be any disturbance, Miss," he said. "These men are going *out*. That's all."

The elevator came to a stop. The door slid open. Propelled by insistent pressure from behind, Mason and Lunk entered the elevator.

"And don't try comin' back without a pass," the officer called as the elevator doors clanged shut.

Lunk started to say something as they walked down the corridor, after the elevator had left them at the street level, but Mason motioned him to silence. Nor did the lawyer speak until they were out on the sidewalk.

Della, sitting in the parked car, opened the door. "Things as you expected to find them?" she asked anxiously.

Mason was smiling. "Just exactly. Now then, we'll go some place where we can talk."

Lunk said doggedly, "I've got to reach Mrs. Shore. I don't want to talk to nobody else."

"I know," Mason said. "We'll see if we can't work out some plan of action."

"Listen," said Lunk, "I ain't got all night to work on this thing. It's hot. It's got to be handled right now. I've simply *got* to see her."

Mason turned the car into a broad street which, at this hour of the night, showed no traffic. Abruptly, he swung into the kerb, parked the car, switched off the headlights, and the ignition, turned to Lunk, and said sharply, "How do you *know* Franklin Shore is alive?"

Lunk started as though the other had jabbed him with a pin.

"Come on," Mason said. "Speak up."

"What makes you think I know any such thing?"

"Because you gave yourself away. Remember you said that up until a short time ago, all the talking in the world wouldn't have convinced you that Komo hadn't been mixed up in Franklin Shore's disappearance. You've held that belief for several years. You've held it so deeply and sincerely that it's become a fixed obsession with you. Now then, there's only one thing that could have changed your mind so suddenly. *You've seen or heard from Franklin Shore.*"

Lunk stiffened for a moment as though preparing to deny the statement; then settled back in the seat as the resistance oozed out of him.

"All right," he admitted, "I've seen him."

"Where is he?" Mason asked.

"He's at my place."

"He came there shortly before you took the street-car to go to see Mrs. Shore?"

"That's right."

"What did he want?"

"He wanted me to do something for him. I can't tell you what it was."

Mason said, "Wanted you to go to Mrs. Shore and find out if she'd take him back, or something of that sort."

Lunk hesitated a moment, then said, "I ain't goin' to tell you what he told me. I promised him I wouldn't ever tell that to any living man."

"How long was it after Franklin Shore came to your house that you went out to take the street-car?"

"Quite a little while."

"Why the delay?"

Lunk hesitated, then said, "There wasn't any delay."

Mason glanced at Della, then asked Lunk, "Had you gone to bed when Franklin Shore called on you?"

"Nope. I was listening to a news broadcast when he knocked at the door. I like to fall over dead when I seen who it was."

"You recognized him without any difficulty?"

"Yeah. Sure. He hadn't changed so much—not near as much as she has. Looks about like he did the day he left."

Mason glanced significantly at Della Street and said, "There's no reason why you should stay up any longer, Della. I'll take you down the street a few blocks to a taxi stand. You can take a taxi home."

She said, "You're not keeping me up. I wouldn't miss this for worlds. I . . ."

"You need *some* sleep, my dear," Mason interrupted solicitously. "Remember, you have to be at the office promptly at nine, and it will take you a *long* time to get home."

"Oh! I see—I guess so."

He switched on the ignition, drove rapidly to a nearby hotel where a taxi was parked at the kerb. Della Street jumped out with a quick "Good night. See you in the morning, Chief," and walked across to the taxicab.

Mason drove down the street for a couple of blocks, then parked the car again. "We'd better get this thing straight, Lunk," he said. "You say Franklin Shore *knocked* at your door?"

The gardener was sullen and suspicious. "*I've* got it all straight. Sure he knocked. The door-bell wasn't working."

Mason shook his head. "I'm not certain that you did right. It might make trouble for you with Mrs. Shore—trying to intercede on behalf of her husband."

"I know what I'm doin'," Lunk said.

"You owe Franklin Shore a debt of gratitude," Mason went on. "You want to do everything you can to help him, don't you?"

"Yes."

"And you know Mrs. Shore hates him, don't you?"

"No."

Mason said, "You must have talked with Franklin Shore for a couple of hours before you started out to see Mrs. Shore."

"Not that long."

"An hour, perhaps?"

"Perhaps."

"How did he seem mentally?" Mason asked abruptly.

"How do you mean?"

"Was his mind keen?"

"Oh, sure. He's smart as a steel trap—remembers things I've even forgotten. Asked about some poinsettia plants I'd put out just before he left. Damned if I hadn't clean forgotten about 'em until he asked. They didn't do so good and the old lady had 'em pulled up. We got some rose bushes in there now."

"Then he doesn't seem to have aged much?"

"No. He's older; but he's pretty much the same."

Mason said, "Why don't you tell me the truth, Lunk?"

"What are you getting at?"

Mason said, "Franklin B. Shore was a banker, a keen-minded business man. From all I can learn, he was clearheaded and quick-thinking. A man of that type wouldn't have come to you to ask you to intercede with Mrs. Shore on his behalf."

Lunk remained sullenly silent.

"It's a lot more likely," Mason went on, "that he'd have gone to your place knowing that you were under a debt of gratitude to him, looking for a place to spend the night where no one would be apt to look for him. You pretended you were going to give him a place to hide out, and then, after he'd gone to bed and to sleep, you sneaked quietly out in an attempt to go and tell Mrs. Shore where he was."

Lunk clamped his lips together in stolid, defiant silence.

"You may as well tell the truth," Mason said.

Lunk shook his head doggedly.

"The Homicide Squad wants to question Franklin Shore. They want to examine him about what happened after he communicated with a man named Henry Leech."

"What's that got to do with it?"

"Leech was murdered."

"When?"

"Some time early last night."

"Well?"

"Don't you see," Mason said, "if you conceal a witness, knowing he's a witness and wanted as such, you're guilty of a crime."

"How do I know he's a witness?"

"I'm telling you so. Now then, you'd better tell me everything that happened."

Lunk thought things over for a few minutes, then said, "Well, I guess I might's well. Franklin Shore came to my place. He was excited and scared. He said somebody was trying to kill him. That he had to have a place to hide. He told me about what he'd done for me in giving me a home for my brother and all that, and said it was up to me to help him out."

"And you asked him why he didn't go home?"

Lunk said, "I asked him some questions, but he wouldn't talk much. He acted like he was still the boss and I was just a hired man. He said he didn't want Mrs. Shore to know anything about his bein' here until after he'd found out what had been done with certain property. He said his wife was going to try to strip him of every penny and he didn't propose to stand for it."

"Then what?"

"So then I told him he could stay with me. It was just the way you doped it out. I got a spare bedroom in the back, and I put him to bed. After he got to sleep I sneaked out and went to tell Mrs. Shore."

"You hadn't gone to bed at all?"

"No."

"And you didn't go to bed?"

"Nope. Told him I had some letters to write."

"Franklin Shore didn't know you had sneaked out?"

"Nope. He was lyin' on his back with his mouth open, snoring, when I left."

"To betray the man who had once been so kind to you," Perry added.

Lunk's eyes shifted uneasily. "I wasn't going to tell her *where* Mr. Shore was—just that I'd heard from him."

"Did you know Henry Leech?" Mason asked suddenly.

"Yes, I knew him—a long time ago."

"What was he? What did he do?"

"He was a plumber—used to come to the house and do some work once in a while. Franklin Shore liked him. Mrs. Shore never did care much for him. He and my brother Phil used to get along pretty well, but I never cared too much for him. Thought he was full of hot air— always tellin' about how he was goin' to get rich in some mining deal. Told Phil a while before Phil died that Franklin Shore was goin' to finance him on a mining proposition—said he was goin' to be living on Easy Street in a couple of months. I've been wondering if maybe Franklin hadn't gone in partners with him, and when Franklin left he went out to work on that mine."

"Where was it?"

"In Nevada somewhere."

"Did Leech continue working after Franklin Shore disappeared?"

"No, he didn't. Mrs. Shore never liked him. Soon as she got in the saddle she canned him. He was puttin' in a lot of new plumbing up in the north end of the house, and every time he'd get a chance, he'd talk over this mining deal with Mr. Shore and with my brother. For some reason or other, Shore liked him, and would take time out to kid with him about his mine, an' when he was goin' to strike it rich."

Mason said, "When Franklin Shore showed up at your house, you asked him *some* questions about where he'd been, and whether he'd put any money in this mining deal. Now go ahead and tell me the truth."

Lunk blurted out, "The boss ran away with this woman. He went to Florida, but he had an interest in some mine out in Nevada. I don't know whether it was Leech's mine or not. They struck it kinda rich, and Shore's partner froze him out for a few thousand, when he could have made a lot more money if he'd held on."

"And that partner was Leech?" Mason asked.

Lunk faced Mason then with steady-eyed candour. "I'm goin' to tell you the truth, Mr. Mason. I don't know who that partner was. Shore wouldn't say. He dried up when I tried to pump him. It might have been Leech, and it might not."

"Didn't you ask him?"

"Well, I didn't come right out and ask him in so many words. When I was talkin' with him, I'd forgotten what Leech's name was. I did ask the boss what'd ever become of that plumber that was trying to interest him in a mining proposition, and the boss dried up like a clam."

"And you didn't press the inquiry?"

Lunk said, "I guess you don't know Franklin Shore very well, do you?"

"I don't know him at all."

"Well," Lunk said, "when Franklin Shore don't want to tell you a thing, he don't tell you. And that's all there is to it. I don't s'pose he's got any dough at all now, but you'd think he was still a high-and-mighty millionaire, the way he acts when you try to get any information out of him.

"Now, I can't stay away no longer. I've got him out there at the house and I've got to get back before he wakes up. If he wakes up and finds me gone, there's goin' to be hell to pay. Now you drive me back home and I'll find some way of gettin' in touch with Mrs. Shore. Ain't she got a telephone in that hospital?"

Mason said, "I was in the room for a few minutes. I saw that she had a telephone by the bed, but I don't think I'd try to telephone her except as a last resort. Even then, I wouldn't dare to tell her anything important over the telephone."

"Why?"

"Because Lieutenant Tragg will either have taken the telephone out, or have left instructions at the switchboard not to put through incoming calls."

"But she could ring up all right?" Lunk asked.

"She *might* be able to."

Lunk creased his forehead in thought. "I got a phone," he said, "and if we could think up some way of gettin' her to ring my number, I could give her the message."

Mason said, "I'll drive you home, and after we get there, we may be able to think up some way of getting her to put through a call. You might send her some flowers with your card on them and your telephone number on the card. The flowers would be delivered. The officers wouldn't stop them. When she saw your name and telephone number on the card, she'd know that you wanted her to call you on the phone. That might be a good way to work things."

Lunk said, "Now you're really talkin' sense. That'd work all right. The first thing she'd think of when she saw my card on the flowers would be what the hell I was sending her flowers for. But you understand they'd have to be bought flowers. If I sent her flowers out of the garden, it would be a natural thing to do. But bought flowers would tip her off right away that there was some reason for sending 'em."

Mason said, "I know a flower shop that's open all night. We can get an immediate delivery to the hospital. Have you got any money?"

"Only about a dollar and a half."

Mason said, "It should be a good big bouquet of expensive flowers. I'll drive up to the florist's with you, and then take you back home. I'll pay for the flowers."

"That's mighty white of you."

"Not at all. I'm glad to do it. Now there's one question I want to ask you, and I want you to think carefully before you answer it."

"What is it?"

"Henry Leech was interested in mines. Now, do you know whether he ever hired Gerald Shore as a lawyer to do anything in connection with his mining company?"

Lunk thought that question over for almost a minute, then said, "I can't tell you for sure, but I *think* he did. I'll let you in on something, Mr. Mason. I think Franklin Shore was double-crossed somehow—after he'd left."

"How do you mean?"

Lunk fidgeted uneasily, said, "Last time the boss was down in Florida he ran on a guy who looked just like him. They had their pictures taken together, an' this guy certainly was a ringer for the boss.

"Well, the boss kept kidding about it after he got back, said he was going to use this guy as a double when his wife had some of her social doings that he wanted to get out of. Mrs. Shore would get hopping mad every time he'd mention it.

"Now, I got an idea that the boss went down to Florida with this woman of his, and intended to educate this here double to go back and pretend *he* was Franklin Shore. This guy could live a swell life and send Franklin Shore money, and the boss could be happy with this woman he'd gone away with. Well, I think that after he'd sort of educated the guy, the bird got cold feet, or he may have died or somethin'.

"Get me? I think the boss was plannin' to have this other bird show up, claimin' it had been a loss of memory that was responsible for everything. People would have believed that, because the boss didn't take any money with him when he left. Well, somehow or other, it didn't pan out. Maybe he couldn't get this other guy educated right or something. That left the boss with his bridges burnt."

Mason held his eyes steadily on those of the gardener. "Might it not have been the other way around?"

"What do you mean? What you gettin' at?"

"This double might have got the idea and then made away with Franklin Shore, and returned to take his place."

"Nope. This man who came to my place is Franklin B. Shore. An' I knew from what he told me . . . say, wait a minute. I'm talkin' too damn much. You an' me will start gettin' along a hell of a lot better, Mr. Mason, if you quit askin' questions—beginnin' right now. Come on, let's go where we're goin' . . . or you can let me out right here an' I'll handle things myself."

Mason's laugh was good-natured. "Oh, come on, Lunk. I didn't mean to be nosy."

FIFTEEN

HOUSES IN THE neighbourhood were dark and silent as Mason stopped his car at 642½ South Belvedere. The chill which comes an hour or so before dawn was in the air.

He switched off the headlights and ignition and eased the automobile door shut after he and Lunk had alighted at the kerb.

"You live at the back?" Mason asked.

"Uh huh. That little house around at the back. You walk in along the drive. My place is built on to the garage."

"You have a car?" Mason asked.

Lunk said, grinning, "Well, it ain't a car like yours, but it gets me there all right."

"Keep it here in the garage?"

"Uh huh. I'd've taken it to go up to Shore's place to-night, only I was afraid that opening the garage door and starting the car would wake Franklin Shore up. So I sneaked out and took the street-car."

Mason nodded, started walking quietly up the drive.

"Look here," Lunk protested, "you ain't comin' in."

"Just far enough to make sure Franklin Shore is still there."

"You don't want to wake him up."

Mason said, "Certainly not. Those flowers will be delivered at almost any time now, and Mrs. Shore may ring you up. When she does, you'll have to talk with her in such a way that she'll know you have a message for her without telling her what it is."

"Why can't I tell her over the phone?"

"Because Franklin Shore will wake up when he hears the phone ring and listen to the conversation."

"Maybe he won't," Lunk said. "The phone is right by my bed. I can sort of muffle what I'm saying with a pillow."

"You might do that," Mason conceded, all the time walking toward the little bungalow on the back of the lot. "Or, you could just tell her that you'd seen me and that she could get in touch with me, and give her my number."

"Yes. That might work. What's your number?"

"I'll come in and write it out for you," Mason said.

"You can't make no noise," Lunk warned.

"I won't."

"Can't you write it down out here?"

"Not very well."

"Well, come on in. But don't make no noise."

Lunk tiptoed up the two stairs which led to the wooden porch, inserted a key in the lock, and noiselessly opened the door. He switched on a light which illuminated a small room cheaply furnished and bearing unmistakable evidences of masculine occupancy. It seemed even colder inside than it had been out in the air. The house was a flimsy structure, and the chill had penetrated through the walls. The air was impregnated with the smell of stale cigar smoke, and a cigar-butt, soggy and cold, was lying on an ash-tray.

Mason bent over to look at it. "His?" he asked.

"Yep. Expensive, too, I guess. Smelled good when he was smokin' it. Pipe and cigarettes are what I smoke."

Mason continued to lean over the little table on which the ash-tray reposed. Directly beside it was a card bearing the printed words "GEORGE ALBER," and, in a man's handwriting, "Called to see about the kitten. Rang the bell, got no answer. Guess everything's O.K. Knew Helen was worrying."

Lunk lit a gas-heater.

"Nice little place," Mason said in a low voice.

"Uh huh. Over here's my bedroom; other bedroom's at the back of that, with a bath between."

Mason said, "Better close the doors between the bedrooms so Franklin won't hear the phone ring."

"That's a good idea," Lunk said. "I think the door from the bathroom to the boss's room was left open. I closed the one from my room."

He tiptoed into the bedroom, and Mason followed along close behind.

The bedroom was a small, square room, furnished with a cheap bureau, a table, a straight-backed chair, and a single iron bed with a thin mattress and sagging wire springs.

In the light which filtered through from the living-room, Mason saw that the door to the bathroom was open, that the bed had not been made, and in the low spot in the centre of that bed, lying in the middle of a soiled and crumpled sheet, curled up in a furry ball, was a sleeping kitten.

The drawers of the bureau had been pulled out, the contents dumped on the floor. A clothes closet had been opened and garments pulled out and dropped into a careless pile near the closet door.

Lunk, standing half-way between the door and the bed, looked round in dazed surprise, and said, "Well, I'll be a son of a gun!"

Mason walked past him through the open door into the bathroom and looked into the adjoining bedroom.

It was empty.

This bedroom was even smaller than the other. A window in the far side of the bedroom, which looked out on the alley, was standing wide open. A night breeze blew somewhat grimy lace curtains in bellying folds. Covers had been turned back on the spring cot. Clean sheets were slightly rumpled. A pillow-case had a depression in it where a man's head would have rested.

Lunk came to stand beside Mason, looking with open-mouthed dismay at the bed and the window.

"He's skipped out," he said ruefully. "If I could've got to Matilda Shore while he was still here, she'd have . . ."

He stopped talking suddenly as though afraid he had said too much.

Mason made a cursory examination of the room. "These bathroom doors open when you left?" he inquired.

"I think this one was, but the one into my room wasn't. I was very careful to close it when I sneaked out."

Mason indicated a second door. "Where does this go?"

"Kitchen. And then from the kitchen you can get to the living-room."

"You have to go through one of the bedrooms to get to the bathroom?"

"That's right. This house is just a square box. The front room an' kitchen on one side, an' the two bedrooms on the other, with the bathroom in between the bedrooms."

Mason said, "I notice this door to the kitchen is open a crack—just an inch or two."

"Uh huh."

Mason said, "You can see the kitten walked through that door. There are the tracks of a kitten outlined in something white."

"That's right."

Mason bent over and touched his finger to the floor, rubbing it across one of the white tracks. "Feels something like flour. You can see where the kitten came through the door, walked over toward the bed. Yes, there are four tracks right together where it must have stood to jump up on the bed. Then it came down on the other side. You can see just a trace of the white powder here."

"That's right. But I don't think that powder is flour."

"Why not?"

"Because I keep my flour in a big tin, and I keep the lid on the tin. And I know the pantry door was closed."

"Let's take a look," Mason said, going into the kitchen.

Lunk opened the door of a little pantry, said, "Of course, I don't waste a lot of time keeping house. I cook my own grub and my cooking suits me all right. It might not suit some finicky housekeeper, but it suits me. Yep, there's the cover on the can all right. Of course, I spill a little occasionally when I'm gettin' it out for cooking. There's a little on the floor around the can, and it looks like the cat was chasing a mouse or somethin' an' jumped right into that pile of stuff. That's the most careless damn kitten I ever saw in my life. He ain't got sense enough to be afraid of anything. He'll run and butt his head up against a wall if he happens to be chasing something, or get on the back of a chair and fall down on his head. He's just awful careless. Either ain't got good sense, or don't know enough to be afraid."

Mason stood staring down at the flour. "If this pantry door was closed, how did the kitten get in here?"

Lunk thought that over. "Only one answer to that. Franklin was lookin' for somethin', an' he came snooping around in here, an' the cat followed him."

Mason said, "How about that stuff in the front bedroom where the drawers have been pulled out and the clothes dumped on the floor?"

Lunk said, somewhat ruefully, "I guess I slipped up. Shore must have got up right after I went out. When he found I was gone, he realized I'd gone out to tell Matilda Shore that he was here. Gosh, why did I let him catch me at that?"

"And then you think he searched the place?" Mason asked.

"He must have, what with him opening the pantry door and all that."

"What was he looking for?"

"I wouldn't know."

"You must have had *something* that Franklin Shore wanted."

Lunk thought for a moment or two, then said, "I'm not certain but what Shore was down on his luck. He may have been looking for money."

"Did you have any?"

Lunk hesitated, then said, "Yes, I had a little salted away."

"Where?"

Lunk was silent for eight or ten seconds, and Mason said, "Come on. Come on. *I'm* not going to hold you up."

"I kept it in the hip pocket of my best suit, hanging in the closet," Lunk said.

"Well, let's look and see if it's there now."

Lunk returned to the front room. The kitten opened its sleepy eyes, yawned, got up to its four feet, arched its back as high as it could possibly stretch, then reached out with its forepaws, elevated its hind legs, flexed its back in the other direction, and said, *"Miaow."*

Mason laughed. "I think your kitten's hungry. Have you got any milk in the house?"

Lunk said, "No fresh milk. I got some canned milk. Helen Kendal brought the kitten here so it wouldn't get no more poison." He walked across to the pile of clothes, picked them up, and started going through the pockets. An expression of dismay came over his face. "Cleaned out!" he muttered. "Damn him, he took every cent I had saved up."

"Tell me exactly how much it was," Mason said.

"Pretty close to three hundred dollars. He could get a long ways on that."

"You think he wants to get away?" Mason asked.

Once more, Lunk's mouth firmed into a position of sullen silence.

"Think he'll be back?" Mason asked.

"I don't know."

"Have you got any money at all?"

"Some in the bank. I ain't got no cash."

"Matilda Shore will be ringing up any minute now," Mason reminded him. "Are you going to tell her Franklin Shore was here and you let him get away?"

"Good gosh, no!"

"What *are* you going to tell her?"

"I don't know."

"What about the flowers? How are you going to explain sending her a bunch of hot-house roses with instructions to deliver them immediately—at about three o'clock in the morning?"

Lunk made a frowning effort at thought, then surrendered to say doggedly, "I don't know *what* I'm going to tell her—not now."

"Why tell her anything? Why not simply skip out?"

Lunk said, with feeling, "Gee, I'd like to do that, if I could get away with it."

"Well, why not? I could take you to an hotel, let you register under an assumed name, and then you could get in touch with Mrs. Shore whenever you wanted to, and make whatever explanations you wanted. In that way, you wouldn't have to tell anyone anything. You could keep in touch with me."

Lunk was nodding slowly. "I *could* stick some stuff in a bag," he said, "and maybe get a cheque cashed . . ."

Mason peeled off a couple of ten-dollar bills from a thick roll.

"You don't need to cash a cheque," he said. "I'll give you some money, and when you need more, you can telephone me. I've given you a number where you can always reach me."

Lunk suddenly gripped strong fingers around the lawyer's hand. "You're acting mighty square," he said, and, after a moment, added, "You stick by me in this, and I'll stick by you. And maybe later on, I'll tell you just what Franklin Shore *really* wanted. You let me think it over, and I'll give you a ring later on."

"Why can't you tell me now?"

The old sullen look came over Lunk's face. "Not now," he said. "I gotta be sure of somethin' first, but I *may* tell you later on—maybe about noon. Don't try to get it out of me now. I'm waiting for somethin' before I can tell you."

Mason studied his man. "Is that something," he asked, "the morning newspaper with the account of Leech's death?"

Lunk shook his head.

"Or the police report on Matilda Shore's poisoning?"

"Don't crowd me. I'm telling you straight," Lunk warned.

Mason laughed. "All right, come on, I'll put you in a nice, quiet hotel. Suppose you register as Thomas Trimmer? And I'll take the kitten along with me and see it's taken care of."

Lunk regarded the kitten somewhat wistfully. "You take good care of it."

"I will."

SIXTEEN

HELEN KENDAL SAT dry-eyed in the waiting-room at the hospital. It seemed she had been there for endless hours, so nervous that she couldn't sit still, so physically weary that she couldn't summon the energy to get up and pace the floor. A hundred times in the last hour she had looked at her wrist-watch. She knew now that it simply *couldn't* be much longer.

She heard the sound of quick, nervous steps in the corridor. Her tortured mind wondered if that might be someone coming to take her to the bedside of a dying man. Her heart choked up her throat with the thought that if it was only to tell her everything was all right, the messenger would be walking more slowly. These staccato footsteps could only indicate one thing, that they were coming for her, and the seconds were precious.

White-lipped, she came up out of the creaking rattan chair, started running toward the door of the reception room.

The steps turned into the door. A long, overcoated figure smiled reassuringly at her. "Hello, Miss Kendal. I guess you remember me."

Her eyes widened. "Why, Lieutenant Tragg! Tell me, have you heard . . . anything . . ."

Tragg shook his head. "They're operating on him. They had some delay getting donors for blood transfusions. They should be finished about now," Tragg said. "I've been talking on the telephone with the nurse."

"Oh, tell me, how's he standing it? How's he coming? Is it going to be . . ."

Tragg placed a hand on her quivering shoulder. "Take it easy," he said. "Take it easy. Things are going to be all right."

"They . . . they aren't sending for you because it's the last chance he'll have to tell . . ."

"Now listen," Tragg said, "take this thing like a soldier. You've been through so much to-night you're all unstrung. They're operating on him, and the last I heard was that he's taking it all right. I'm here right now to get just one thing."

"What?"

"That bullet—and a statement from him if he's able to talk."

"Not what they call a dying declaration?"

Tragg grinned. "You've been here all alone fighting your nerves, and you're jumpy."

She said, "I can take it! I want to know how he is—that's natural. And I'd be lying to you if I tried to tell you I wasn't frightened. But I'm not getting any heebie jeebies over it. I guess we used to think we were entitled to happiness as a matter of right. Now, people are dying all over the world and . . . well, I've got to learn how to take it—and so has everyone else."

Tragg's eyes were sympathetic. "You haven't been crying?"

"No—and don't you make me—either. Don't sympathize with me, and don't look at me like that. But, for heaven's sake, if you can really find out how he's getting on and what his chances are, go to it."

"You engaged?" Tragg asked abruptly.

Helen's eyes dropped and she flushed. "I—I—honestly don't know. He never—quite—asked me, but on the way over here in the taxi—— Well, I guess I let him see how much I cared. I didn't mean to, but I was so frightened that everything broke down. He was so game—and brave—I shouldn't have, of course."

"Shouldn't have *what*? You love him, don't you?"

Helen raised her head and looked at him defiantly. "Yes, I love him. And I told him so. I belong to him, and always shall, no matter what happens. I told him that, too, Lieutenant Tragg. And I told him I wanted to marry him *now*."

"What did he say to that?"

Helen turned away. "He didn't say anything," she replied dully. "He fainted."

Tragg controlled his twitching mouth. "Jerry lost a lot of blood, you know. I'm not surprised. Tell me, Miss Kendal, how long had you been home last night before Jerry arrived?"

"I don't know. Not very long."

"How did he happen to call—so late?"

She laughed nervously. "He said he tried to telephone me earlier, but of course I was out. He was passing and saw the house all lit up, so he just dropped in for a minute. We were talking, and then we heard this sound from Aunt Matilda's bedroom . . ."

"You said the noise sounded as though someone had knocked something over. The room was dark?"

"Yes."

"You're certain about that?"

"Yes. Unless whoever was in there had a torch. That may have been it, because the lovebirds started chirping."

"But there was no sign of a torch when you opened the door?"

"No."

"And the lights were on in the hall?"

"Yes. I never thought about *not* putting them on. I guess it would have been better if we'd kept the hall dark and turned on the lights in the bedroom."

"It would," Tragg said, "but that's all done now. No use bothering about it. What I'm getting at is that the lights *were* on in the hall and there were no lights on in your aunt's bedroom."

"That's right."

"And who opened the door? You or Jerry?"

"Jerry."

"And then what?"

"We knew, of course, someone was in there. Jerry was groping for the light switch and didn't know where it was, and I suddenly realized how terribly important it was to get the light on, so I ducked under his arm and reached for the light switch. It was then it happened."

"Two shots?"

"Yes."

"You never did get the lights on?"

"No."

"Was your hand near the light switch when the first shot was fired?"

"I think it was, but I can't be certain. That bullet whizzed right past my head, and smacked into the woodwork round the door. It threw splinters or plaster or something into my face, little stinging particles. I jumped back."

"And the next shot came how soon?"

"Almost at once."

"What happened after that?"

White-faced, she shook her head. "There's just a lot I can't remember. I heard that peculiar sound of the bullet—hitting Jerry."

Tragg said, "You're a brave kid. Don't think about Jerry. Just think of facts. Remember that's all we're interested in. That second shot came right after the first one, with hardly any interval in between, and it hit Jerry."

"Yes."

"Did he fall down immediately?"

"He seemed to spin right round as though something had hit him, you know, a blow."

"Then he fell?"

"I felt his knees buckle; then he was a dead weight against me. I tried to ease him to the floor, but he was too heavy. We both went down in a heap."

"What happened to the person who was in the room?"

"I don't know. All I can remember is seeing that awful pallor on Jerry's face. I put my hand down to his side, and it came away all bloody. He was unconscious. I thought he was dead. Naturally, I didn't think much about anything else. I talked to him—and told him things— and then his eyelids fluttered—after a while, then he smiled up at me and said, 'Let's see if I can get my legs under me, Babe.' "

Tragg frowned. "Has it occurred to you that the person who was standing in that room wasn't shooting at Jerry?"

"What do you mean?"

"I mean," Tragg said, "he was shooting at you. He shot at your head the first time, and almost hit it; then you jerked back, and in jerking back, you swung round so that your body was behind Jerry's; and when he took that second snap at you, he hit Jerry. Remember, the person who was there in the room could see *you* very plainly."

Her eyes were wide and startled. "I hadn't thought of that. I just thought that someone was in the room and didn't want to be discovered, and . . ."

"And you haven't any idea who that someone might have been?"

"No."

"Anyone who would find it to his advantage to have you out of the way?"

She shook her head.

"Not even if your aunt should die?"

"What makes you ask that?"

"Someone had made an attempt to poison your aunt earlier in the evening. He perhaps had reason to think he'd been successful, and that she was dying or dead. He might have come to the house to get you out of the way."

"No, I can't imagine anything like that."

"You can't think of anyone who would have stood to gain if . . ."

"No."

The efficient tread of rubber heels sounded just outside the door. The rustle of a stiffly starched uniform brought a nurse to the doorway, smiling. "He's down from the operating-room, Miss Kendal. You *are* Miss Kendal, aren't you?"

"Yes, oh, yes! Is he going to live? Is he conscious? Is he . . ."

"Of course he is, and you can go up if you want."

Tragg moved along at her side. The nurse looked at him inquiringly.

"Lieutenant Tragg. The police," he explained.

"Oh, yes."

"I came to get the bullet."

"You'll have to talk with Dr. Rosllyn. He'll be down from the operating-room very shortly."

Tragg said to Helen Kendal, "I hate to butt in on this, but I've got to ask him a question if the doctor thinks he can answer it."

"He's conscious," the nurse said. "They used a spinal anaesthetic."

Helen looked up at him pleadingly as they reached the elevator. "Aren't you more interested in that bullet, Lieutenant? That's awfully important. You know doctors are sometimes careless. He might throw it away or lose it—or something—unless you went right up."

Tragg burst out laughing. "All right, you win. Go in and see him alone. But don't get him tired, because I'm coming down in just a minute to talk to him."

The nurse frowned. "He's full of hypos, you understand, Lieutenant. He's groggy, and you can't rely too much on what he says."

"I know," Tragg said. "I only want to ask him a couple of simple questions. What floor is the operating-room?"

"Eleven. Mr. Templar is on the fourth. I'll show Miss Kendal the way."

He gave Helen an imperceptible nudge when the elevator stopped at the fourth floor. Then he turned to the nurse. "Couldn't you let Miss Kendal find Mr. Templar's room by herself, and take me up to the operating-room?"

"Why, yes. His room is 481—just down the corridor."

"She can find it."

Helen flashed him a grateful glance. "Thanks," she breathed, and sped down the corridor.

The elevator door slid shut, and the cage started on its upward journey.

"What are his chances?" Tragg asked.

The nurse shook her head. "I wouldn't know."

At the eleventh floor, she led the way to the operating-room. Dr. Rosllyn, stripped to the waist, was drying his arms on a towel.

"Lieutenant Tragg," the nurse announced.

"Oh, yes, Lieutenant. Got that slug for you. What the devil did I do with it? Miss Dewar, where's that bullet?"

"You put it in a tray, Doctor, and said you didn't want it touched."

"Damn it," Rosllyn said, "bet I put some bandages in on top of it. Here, wait a minute . . . Here, come this way."

He led the way into a room which opened off the operating room. The peculiar acrid smell of blood assailed Tragg's nostrils. A nurse pulled blood-soaked bits of cloth from an enamelled container, handed it, not to Tragg, but to the doctor. The doctor took a pair of forceps, reached in, and pulled out a red-stained chunk of metal. "Here you are, Lieutenant."

"Thanks. You'll have to swear that this is the bullet you took from the body of Jerry Templar, you know."

"Sure, this is the one."

Tragg turned the bullet over. "Make some identifying mark on the base here so you'll know it again."

The doctor took out his pocket-knife, scratched three parallel lines on the base of the bullet, then put crosses on each line. Tragg slipped the bullet in his vest pocket. "How are his chances?" he asked.

"Pretty good, so far. I'd have given him fifty-fifty before I started working on him. I'll give him nine out of ten now. Barring complications, he'll be all right. Strong, rugged type. That Army training does wonders for 'em, Lieutenant. That lad has the stamina of a billy-goat. Came through the operation in fine shape."

"All right for me to talk with him for just a minute?"

"I think so. He's full of dope, of course. Don't tire him, and don't ask him complicated questions. Simple things that he can hold his mind to. He'll start rambling if you let him keep on talking, but if you hold his mind to it and ask him simple questions, he'll give you the answers. Don't have any stenographer there, though. Some of his talk will be rambling and an isolated answer or two may be incorrect."

"All right," Tragg said. "Now, if there's any change, I want to know about it. And if it looks bad, I'll want to get a death-bed statement."

Dr. Rosllyn laughed. "I don't think you're going to have the chance. That boy *wants* to live. He's nuts over some girl or other, and, until I put him under with a whiff of gas, was rambling on how glad he was he got shot because that way he found out how much she loves him! Can you beat it? The only thing that's bothering him is that the bullet knocked him over and he couldn't get the man who did it. All right, Lieutenant, let me know when you want me to be a witness and identify that bullet."

Lieutenant Tragg made his way down to the fourth floor, tiptoed down the corridor to 481, gently pushed open the door.

A nurse was standing in the far corner of the room. Helen, self-conscious and embarrassed, was seated on a chair by the foot of the bed. "I'm so glad," she was saying as Tragg opened the door.

Jerry Templar frowned at the new interruption standing in the doorway.

Tragg smiled at him cheerfully. "Hello! You don't feel much like talking now, but I've got a couple of questions to ask you. Lieutenant Tragg of Homicide."

Templar closed his eyes, let the lids flutter open, looked at him for a moment as though having some difficulty getting his eyes in focus, then grinned back and said, "Shoot!"

"Not twice in the same night," the other protested. "Now you answer as briefly as you can, because you're not supposed to talk much."

Jerry nodded.

"Who fired the shots?"

"I don't know."

"Could you see anything at all?"

"Just a little motion—a blurred figure moving."

"Tall or short?"

"Couldn't say . . . a corner of the room moved, then came the shots."

"Could this person have been shooting at Helen instead of you?"

That thought galvanized Templar into hard-eyed attention. "How's that? Shooting at Helen?"

"Could that have been the case?"

"Don't know. Can't think that out. Yes—yes—might have. I never . . ."

"I'm sorry, but the patient mustn't be excited," came a droning voice from the nurse in the corner.

Tragg looked at Helen Kendal's proudly stiff figure, thought of the baffled, thwarted expression on Templar's face as he opened the door. He grinned at the nurse, and said, "Sister, I've been talking with the doctor, and I can tell you right now you're in the right church, but in the wrong pew. This shooting, mysterious as it is, has started to clear up some mighty important things that would get *all* cleared up once and for all if you'd just relax and go and get yourself a cup of coffee. I may not know a darn thing about medicine, but I know something of human nature, and if you'd get out of here for about five minutes and leave these two people alone, it would do your patient more good than anything in the world. He was telling the doctor all about it during the operation. Why not give him a chance to tell her about it now?"

The nurse glanced at Templar, then her garments rustled as she moved quietly round the foot of the bed toward the door.

Lieutenant Tragg said, "Well, I'll be seeing you."

"You only have a minute," the nurse warned Helen.

Tragg held the door open for her, caught the glint of Helen Kendal's eyes, and pushed the door shut behind him. "Give her as long as you can," he said to the nurse.

She walked with him down toward the elevator. "You certainly spoke *your* piece."

Tragg grinned. "I had to. Pride has busted up more romances than jealousy. Guy didn't want to say anything because he's in the Army. Girl shows how she feels when she's riding up to the hospital with him, and then becomes suddenly self-conscious, thinks she's been forward, and waits for him to make the next move. He's afraid perhaps she's changed her mind. Neither one of them want to say anything, and you standing there . . ."

"I stood back in the corner out of the way."

He grinned and said, "Well, I've started something, anyway."

Whistling a little tune, he pushed the button for the elevator, went down to the street floor, walked through the long lines of hushed corridors out into the cold, stinging tang of the night air.

He got into his police car, and drove rapidly to headquarters. An irritable Scotchman in the laboratory said, "I dinna suppose this could 'a' waited until nine o'clock."

"It couldn't," Tragg said. "You've got the bullet the autopsy surgeon gave you from the body of Henry Leech?"

"Yes."

Tragg handed him two bullets from his vest pocket. "The one with the three straight lines on it was recovered in an operation performed on Jerry Templar. The other one was dug out of some woodwork beside the door in which Templar and the girl were standing when Templar was shot. Now then, how long will it take you to tell me whether those three are from the same gun?"

"I don't know," the Scotchman said with singular pessimism. "It'll all depend. It may take a long while. It may take a short while."

"Make it take a short while," Tragg said. "I'm going down to my office. Give me a ring. And don't mix those bullets up. Perry Mason's on the other side of this case, and you know what he'll do to you on cross-examination."

"He'll na do a thing to me in cross-examination," the man at the laboratory bench said, adjusting the eyepieces on a comparison microscope. "He'll have no chance. I'll take microphotographs, and let the camera speak for me. A man's a fool to talk wi' his tongue when he can get a camera lens to do it for him."

Tragg smiled, then pausing in the doorway, announced, "I've declared open season on Mr. Perry Mason. I'm going to teach that boy not to cut corners."

"You'd better be buyin' yourself an alarm-clock," Angus MacIntosh grunted as he settled himself to his task. "Ye'll be gettin' up early in the morning, Mister Lieutenant."

Tragg paused in the act of closing the door to say, "I've already got one." Then he gently slipped the door shut and walked down to his office.

He made a little grimace, as the dead smell of stale smoke asailed his nostrils. He went to the windows, opened them, and shivered slightly as the dry cold of the before-dawn air stole into the room. He rubbed exploratory fingers across the angle of his jaw, feeling the stubble, and frowned as he noticed the oil which had been transferred from his skin to his fingertips. He felt sticky, dirty, and tired.

He crossed to the coat closet which contained a washstand, turned on hot water, washed his hands and face, and was drying himself with a towel when the telephone rang.

He walked over to pick up the receiver. "Yes?"

The voice of the Scotchman in the laboratory said, "I havena got 'em in the most advantageous positions yet so that I can make the best possible photograph, but I can tell you one thing. The three bullets came from the same gun. Noo then, how soon will ye be wantin' photographs?"

"Just as soon as I can get 'em."

The Scotchman groaned. "Ye was always an impatient lad," he observed, and hung up the receiver.

Tragg grinned his satisfaction.

Once more the telephone rang. The man on duty at the switchboard said hurriedly, "Here's an anonymous tip for you, Lieutenant. Won't talk with anyone else. Says he's going to hang up in exactly sixty seconds, and there's no use trying to trace the call."

"Got it so you can listen in?" Tragg asked.

"Yes."

"Okay, put him on."

A click came over the line as the operator plugged in a key and said, "Here's Lieutenant Tragg on the line."

"Hello," a peculiarly muffled voice said. The man at the other end of the line might well have been holding his fist cupped between his mouth and the transmitter. "Is this Lieutenant Tragg?"

"This is Tragg. Who is this talking?"

"Never mind. I'm just telling you something about Perry Mason, the lawyer, and the girl who drove him out to the Shore place a while after midnight."

"Go ahead," Tragg invited. "What d'you know about 'em?"

"They picked a man up. He's an important witness, one you want. They spirited him away where they've got him sewed up."

"Go on," Tragg said impatiently. "Who's the man, and where is he?"

"I don't know who he is, but I can tell you where he is."

"Where?"

The voice suddenly speeded up its tempo as though anxious to get the conversation terminated.

"Maple Leaf Hotel under the name Thomas Trimmer. Registered about a quarter past four this morning. He's in room 376."

Tragg said quickly, "Now, wait a minute. Let me get one thing straight. Are you absolutely certain that Perry Mason, the lawyer, is the one who put this man in the hotel? Is he at the back of that?"

"Back of it, hell," the voice said. "Mason was the one who came in with him, carrying a canvas-covered telescope-bag. The girl wasn't with him then."

The receiver abruptly slammed up at the other end of the line.

Lieutenant Tragg jiggled the hook. "Able to trace that call?" he asked.

"Call box, block from the hotel," the exchange operator said. "I got the call traced, and two radio cars rushing out there with instructions to pick up anyone they see within three blocks of the place for questioning. We'll know in fifteen minutes if they get any results."

There was the glint of a triumphant hunter in Tragg's eyes. "I'll wait fifteen minutes just on a chance."

It was twenty minutes before the report came in. Two radio cars had converged on the place. It was an all-night restaurant with a phone booth near the door. There was only one man on duty behind the counter, and he had been busy waiting on some customers. He had vaguely noticed a man enter the phone booth, but he couldn't describe him. The radio cars had picked up two men within a radius of four blocks of the place. It didn't seem probable that either man had put in the call, but the police had secured names and addresses from driving licences. Then the officers, stopping at the Maple Leaf Hotel, had found that a Thomas Trimmer had been checked in about four o'clock. He was a man in the late fifties with a slight stoop. He weighed a hundred and forty pounds, was about five feet six, wore somewhat shabby, but clean clothes, had high cheek-bones, and a grey drooping moustache. His only baggage had been an old-fashioned canvas telescope-case, fairly heavy. Trimmer had been brought in by a tall, well-dressed man.

A little pulse in Lieutenant Tragg's forehead began to pound as he listened to the report. "Keep the radio cars on the job," he ordered. "Sew the place up so that Trimmer doesn't get out. I'm on my way out there right now."

SEVENTEEN

MASON DROVE THE car slowly. The long hours of sleepless activity had lowered his resistance to the cold chill of the night air.

The kitten curled up on the seat beside him, snuggling closely for warmth. Occasionally, the lawyer, steadying the wheel with his left hand, placed his right hand down on the kitten's fur, leaving it there for a few seconds until Amber Eyes would start purring in drowsy contentment.

In the east, the stars were shrinking into invisibility. A faint illumination furnished a backdrop against which the roofs of the clustered apartment-houses showed in a serrated silhouette. He slowed the car as he neared the place where Della Street lived. The entire apartment-house was dark, save for that one vaguely lighted orange oblong which would be Della's window.

He parked his car, picked up the relaxed form of the purring kitten, and slipped it under his overcoat, holding it against the warmth of his body. He paused before the long list of tenants beside the mail-boxes, and pressed the bell of Della Street's apartment.

Almost instantly, the electric buzzer which released the catch on the street door brought her answering signal. He pushed through the door, and into the stuffy, warm air of the lobby. He crossed to the automatic elevator, pressed the button, and ascended to Della's floor. Amber Eyes, nestled under his coat, became apprehensive as he felt the upward motion, and squirmed about, digging sharp little claws into his clothes until an inquiring, startled head pushed its furry way out from the overcoat to stare curiously at the walls of the lift.

The elevator came to a stop. Mason opened the door, walked down the corridor and paused before Della Street's door to tap lightly with the tips of his fingers, giving their private code knock.

She opened the door. She was still wearing the clothes in which she had been attired when Mason had deposited her in front of the taxi stand at the hotel.

"Gosh, I'm glad to see you. Tell me, did I get your signals right?" she asked in a half whisper, as he eased his way through the door and entered the cosy warmth of her apartment.

"Darned if I know. What did you think I wanted?"

"For me to go out to Lunk's place."

"Right. What did you do with him?"

She said, "He wasn't there. Oh, you've got the kitten!"

He took off his hat, placed the kitten in her outstretched hands, and sat down without taking off his overcoat. He frowned thoughtfully at the carpet. "Got a drink?"

"Been keeping a pot of coffee hot for you. Spiked with brandy, it will fix you up in a jiffy——" She deposited the kitten on the davenport. "You sit there, Amber Eyes, and be a good kitten."

Mason said. "Wait a minute, Della. I want to talk with you about . . ."

"Not until you've had that coffee," she said, and vanished through the door into the kitchenette.

He sat motionless, elbows resting on his knees, staring fixedly at the pattern in the carpet.

Amber Eyes investigated the davenport, jumped down to the floor, allowed his nose to guide the way to the kitchenette, and stood at the door giving a high-pitched *"miaow."*

Della laughed and opened the door, saying, "And I suppose *you* want some warm milk."

Mason was still in the same position when she returned carrying a tray on which were two cups of steaming black coffee. The aroma of fine brandy mingled with that of the beverage to caress the nostrils.

He lifted a cup and saucer from the tray, and grinned at her.

"Here's to crime," he said.

She sat down on the davenport, balanced the saucer on her knee and said, "Sometimes that toast of yours scares me."

Mason sipped hot coffee, felt the brandy warming his blood into circulation. "What happened?" he asked.

"I wasn't certain you could keep Lunk occupied much longer. I told the cab driver to hurry."

"Give him the Belvedere address?" Mason asked.

"Not the address. I told him to stop at the corner of a cross street and wait. Then I walked back a block, turned the corner, checked the numbers until I came to the drive which led into Lunk's place. It's a little square house tacked on to the garage and . . ."

"I know," Mason interrupted. "I was inside the place. What did *you* do?"

"I saw the house was dark, so I barged up on the steps and rang the door-bell, big as life. No one answered. I kept leaning against the door-bell, and couldn't hear it ring, so I started to knock, and then I noticed that the front door wasn't quite closed. Believe me, Chief, I wished I'd been a mind reader right then and had known what you wanted me to do. But, after a while, I pushed the door open and went in."

"Turn on the lights?" he asked.

"Yes."

"What did you find?"

"There was no one in the house. The bed in the front bedroom hadn't been made. In the back bedroom . . ."

"Wait a minute. How did you get into the back bedroom? Through the kitchen or the connecting bathroom?"

"The connecting bathroom."

"Now be sure about this, Della. Were the doors between the two bedrooms open?"

"Yes, about half-way open—that is, the first door was about half open. The door from the bathroom to the back bedroom was *all* the way open. There was a window in the back bedroom that opened on an alley. That window was raised, and the wind was coming through there, gently blowing the curtains."

"How about the door from the bedroom into the kitchen?"

"It was open just an inch or two."

"Did you go through that?"

"No. I went into the kitchen by going back through the front bedroom and the living-room. But let me tell you about the front bedroom first. Drawers had been pulled out of the bureau and clothes from the closet were piled on the floor."

Mason said, "I know. Let's get back to the kitchen. Did you look in the pantry?"

"Yes."

"Was the pantry door open or closed?"

"Closed."

"Did you turn on a light in the pantry?"

"No. I opened the door, and enough light came in from the kitchen so I could see there was no one in the pantry. I wanted to make sure—I thought perhaps Franklin Shore had heard the bell ring and decided to hide, just in case it might be someone whom he didn't want to see."

"Did you notice any flour on the floor around the flour-bin in the pantry?"

"No—but I wouldn't have noticed it unless there'd been quite a bit of flour on the floor, because the light was behind me and I was only searching to make certain that someone wasn't hiding in there."

"Feel pretty shaky?"

"I'll say! Chills were chasing one another up and down my spine. If Franklin Shore *had* been standing in that pantry, he'd have scared the boots off me."

Mason finished the coffee, got up to put the cup and saucer over on the table. He slipped out of his overcoat, stretched his long arms, then lowered them to shove his hands deep down in his pockets. From the little kitchen the kitten *"miaowed"* a peremptory command to be readmitted to the room which contained human companionship. Della opened the door, and the kitten, its stomach bulging with warm milk, marched awkwardly into the room, made a little throaty noise of satisfaction, jumped up on the davenport, and settled down, curling its forepaws in under its chest. The alert interest slowly left its eyes, and, after a moment, they closed enough so that white membranes could be seen at the corners as it settled down to purring slumber.

Mason, still standing, jerked his head toward the kitten. "Where was Amber Eyes when you came in?"

"Curled up on the sheets right in the middle of the bed in the front bedroom."

"Near the centre of the bed?"

"Yes. The bed sags a little, and there was a low place right near the centre. The kitten was curled up, fast asleep."

He took his hands from his pockets, hooked his thumbs in the armholes of his waistcoat, and started pacing the floor.

"More coffee?" she asked.

He might not have heard her, but continued pacing the carpet, head pushed slightly forward, eyes lowered.

Abruptly, he turned. "Did you notice any tracks on the floor, such as might have been made if the kitten had walked through some white powder?"

Della Street frowned, said, "Let me think. I wasn't looking for anything smaller than a man, and I was scared stiff, but . . . I *think* there were some cat tracks across the kitchen. I carried away the general impression that it was a place in which a man had been living by himself, and that it needed a darn good cleaning. The sheets on the bed in the front bedroom were pretty soiled, and the pillow-case was filthy. The lace curtains needed cleaning. The dish-towels were in pretty bad shape. Oh, just a lot of little things like that. And I *think* there was something in the kitchen, some cat tracks or something spilled on the floor."

"But the pantry door was closed? You're certain of that?"

"Yes."

"How the devil could the kitten have got into flour in the pantry and left tracks across the floor—if the pantry door had been closed? It didn't go in when *you* opened the door?"

Della thought that over for a few seconds, then shook her head. "It's beyond me. The kitten never moved while I was there."

Mason thoughtfully regarded the sleeping kitten, abruptly picked up his overcoat, whipped it on, and reached for his hat.

She came to stand at his side as he reached for the doorknob.

"Please go to bed and get some sleep, Chief. You'll need it."

He looked down at her, and the granite lines of his face softened into a smile. "Get some yourself. *You'll* need it. When you were in the house, did you notice a visiting-card on the ash-tray with George Alber's name and some handwriting on it?"

"A card was there. I didn't notice the name on it. Why?"

"Oh, nothing. Forget it."

He circled her waist with his arm, drew her close to him.

She raised half-parted lips. His other arm circled her shoulder. For a moment, he held her close, then said, "Keep a stiff upper lip, Kid. I think we've pulled a boner."

Silently opening the door, he slipped out into the hall.

EIGHTEEN

DELLA STREET FOUGHT against the clamour of the alarm-clock. Her sleep-drugged struggle against the first spasm of ringing was successful. The bell ceased its clanging summons and she slipped off once more into deep slumber, only to be aroused by the irritating insistence of the second alarm.

She raised herself on one elbow, eyes still closed, groped for the shut-off. The clock eluded her, making it necessary for her to open her eyes.

The clock was not in its accustomed place by the bed, but over on the dresser where she had placed it as a precaution against shutting it off and going to sleep again.

Reluctantly, she threw back her covers, swung her legs out of bed, and started for it.

A faint *"miaow"* of protest came from the bed.

It took her a moment to account for that strange sound, then, switching off the alarm, she pulled up the covers which she had thrown back over Amber Eyes.

The kitten, curled in a warm little nest on top of the bed, purred its gratitude, got to its feet, arched its back, stretched, yawned, made two awkward zigzag cat jumps which brought it within reaching distance of her fingers.

The kitten accepted the ministrations of fingertips behind his ears, ventured in purring exploration over the slippery treachery of the rounded bedclothes, seeking to regain the warmth of Della's body.

She laughed and pushed him away. "Not now, Amber Eyes. The strident clang of the alarm calls me to industry."

She knew that she didn't have to get to the office on time, but there

were some matters in the mail which needed attention. A new typist
was working on an important brief, and Della knew she'd have to check
over that brief before letting Mason see it for final reading.

Warm needles of water from the shower, the scented lather of soap,
then, at the last, the sting of the cold water, tingled her into life. She
vigorously towelled her skin into glowing health, inspected stockings
for possible ladders, and was standing before the mirror in her under-
things, getting her face made up, when the buzzer on her inner door
exploded into noise.

For a while, she ignored it, then she opened the door a scant inch,
said, "Go away, I'm a working girl. I don't want to buy anything, I
can't subscribe to anything, and I'm late for the office now."

Lieutenant Tragg's voice said, "Well, I'll drive you down to the
office. That will save time."

Della tilted her head, placing her eyes close to the crack in the door
so that she could see Tragg's face.

"How'd you get past the street door?"

"It's a secret. You look sleepy."

"You look worse than that."

He grinned. "As far as I can tell, no one west of the Mississippi
got any sleep last night."

"I'm dressing."

"How long will it take you to finish?"

"Five or ten minutes."

"Breakfast?"

"Not here. I grab a cup of coffee at the drug-store on the corner."

"Bad for the health to eat that way," he said.

"Swell for the figure."

"I'll wait outside the door," he said.

"Is it that important?"

"It's that important."

Della closed the door. Her mirror showed her the reflection of a
scowling countenance. She moved over to the telephone, picked up the
receiver, started to dial Mason's unlisted number, then changed her
mind, dropped the receiver back into place, got into her dress, kicked
off her bedroom slippers, put on shoes, and then realized the problem
presented by the kitten.

She snatched the little fluff of fur up in her arms, said softly, "Now
listen, my love, that cop *eats* kittens, eats 'em alive. What's more, he'll
want your presence explained, and, frankly, you'd be harder to laugh
off than a man under the bed. It's the kitchen for you, and I'm praying
that lots of warm milk will keep you quiet."

Amber Eyes purred contentedly.

She stepped out into the little kitchenette, poured some top-milk from a bottle, warmed it until it felt just the right temperature, then fed the kitten.

"The doctor says you aren't to have anything solid," she told Amber Eyes, "and unless you want to give the show away you've got to be a good little kitten and keep your mouth shut. A good full stomach should help, so go ahead and fill up."

Purring its pleasure, the kitten lapped up the warm, creamy milk, and Della, slipping quietly out of the kitchen, gently closed the door so that Tragg wouldn't hear the click of the latch. She hastily threw the covers back into place on the bed, tucked the sheet in, fluffed the pillows, placed them in the clips at the foot of the bed, and pushed the bed back up against the wall, turning the revolving door so that it was concealed in the closet. She pushed the chairs back into position, working against time.

She put on her street coat, adjusted her hat more by instinct than any desire for facial adornment, opened the door and gave Lieutenant Tragg the benefit of her best smile. "All ready," she said. "Nice of you to offer to drive me to the office. I suppose, however, it's not entirely philanthropic."

"It isn't," Tragg said.

"A Greek, bearing gifts?"

"Exactly. Nice place you have there. Nice south-east exposure."

"Isn't it?" she said, tugging at the door-knob.

"You're all alone here?"

"Of course."

Tragg took a step forward so that his shoulder blocked the closing door. "Tell you what, Miss Street, we may as well talk in here for just a minute."

"I haven't time. I've got to be at the office."

"I think this is more important than being at the office," he said.

"Well, we could talk in your car, or . . ."

"It's hard to talk, driving a car," he said, moving into the apartment and walking apparently in a most casual manner over to the davenport.

Della sighed in exasperation, stood in the doorway, fully aware of the fact that his sharp, police-trained eyes were taking in every detail.

"I'm sorry, Lieutenant, but I simply *have* to get to work. I haven't time either to be interviewed or to argue about being interviewed . . . and I can't leave you here."

He apparently didn't hear her. "Certainly is a nice place. Well, if you insist, I'll come along, although I'd prefer to talk here."

He paused, apparently to adjust his tie in the mirror, but she realized that from the position in which he was standing he could see a reflection of the bathroom through the open door.

"Will you *please* come, Lieutenant?"

"Coming," he said. "Lord, I certainly look as though I'd been up all night. You won't mind driving with such a disreputable specimen?"

"Just so we get started," she said firmly.

"What's this door?" he asked, indicating the kitchen door.

"It's a door," she said angrily. "Surely, you've seen doors before, Lieutenant. They're composed of wood. They're hung on hinges, and they swing to and fro."

"Do they indeed!" he said, his eyes fastened on the door.

Della Street came angrily back into the apartment. "Now look here," she said sharply. "I don't know what you're after. You're not going to come in and snoop round my apartment any time you want to. If you want to search my place, go and get a warrant. If you have anything to say to me, say it on the way to the office. I'm starting now, and you're getting out!"

Tragg looked into the angry defiance of her eyes, and said with an ingratiating smile, "Surely, Miss Street, you don't object to my looking round your apartment."

"I most certainly do."

"Why? Are you hiding someone?"

"I give you my word of honour, there's no other human being in this apartment except myself. Now, does that satisfy you?"

He met the steady anger of her eyes and said, "Yes."

She let him start first for the door, followed along close behind, this time ready to slam the door shut and let the spring lock snap into position.

He was just stepping over the threshold, and her hand was on the door-knob when there came an ear-piercing scream of feline anguish, a scream which changed both its pitch and location with great speed.

"Oh, my heavens!" Della exclaimed, suddenly remembering that she habitually left the kitchen window open a few inches for ventilation.

There was no mistaking the sound. This was no mere cry of feline impatience, but a squall of agony.

That cry appealed to the maternal in her. She would no more have abandoned that kitten to its fate in order to save herself from a felony charge than she would have refused to rush to the aid of a child.

Tragg was right behind her as she raced through the apartment's living-room into the kitchenette. His head was at her shoulder as she flung open the kitchen window.

What had happened was only too apparent. The pulley which held the manila rope clothes-line was fastened directly beside the kitchen window. Amber Eyes, crawling to the sill and peering out, had been intrigued by the rope. He had hooked a paw round it and, in trying to withdraw that paw, his claws had caught and held. As his weight came against the clothes-line, it had started to slide through the well-oiled pulley. There was plenty of slack in that line and Amber Eyes had found himself sailing out through space at a dizzy height above the ground. His other paws had locked around the clothes-line, leaving him hanging head downward, squalling with pop-eyed terror, his tail switching to and fro, then fluffing out to huge proportions.

"You poor thing!" Della Street exclaimed and, reaching for the upper rope, started pulling Amber Eyes in. "Hang on now, kitty," she exhorted. "Don't let go."

The cat swayed to and fro, eyes shifting from Della Street in the safety of the window to the courtyard far below.

Tragg grinned. The grin became a chuckle, and, as she brought the kitten to within reaching distance and clutched it in her hand, the chuckle became a burst of laughter.

Not only did Amber Eyes have no intention of letting go, but terror had locked his claws into the rope so that Della had to disengage them as though they had been so many fishhooks. She held the trembling little body close to her, speaking reassuringly to it, quieting its fear.

"Go on and laugh," she blazed. "I suppose *you* think it's funny!"

"I do for a fact," Tragg admitted. "The cat makes a playful swipe at the rope, and the next thing he knows, he's flying through the air with the greatest of ease. It must have been a startling sensation for a kitten."

"Startling," Della said indignantly. "I'm glad you think it's funny."

"I didn't know you had a kitten," Tragg said.

"Indeed. I suppose the police department feels aggrieved that I should have adopted a kitten without consulting it. I suppose if I should tell you that my Aunt Rebecca had sprained her ankle ice skating, you'd call me on the carpet because I let her go out without permission from the police. If you'll just let me get to the office, I'll write you a letter 'Dear Lieutenant Tragg: I have a kitten. Does it meet with your approval?' "

Tragg said, "That is a very effective burst of indignation and sarcasm—but it doesn't tell me anything about the cat; and it isn't distracting my attention in the least."

"Oh, is that so!"

"How long have you had the cat?"

"Not very long."

"What do you mean by that?"

"It isn't a very old kitten."

"Have you had it ever since it was born?"

"No."

"About how long then?"

"Not so very long. Long enough to get to feel attached to it. You know how it is, after an animal has been with you a few weeks—or as far as that's concerned, even a few minutes, if you love animals, you get to feeling an attachment that . . ."

"Has the cat been with you a few weeks?" Tragg asked.

"No, I suppose not."

"Even a few days?"

"I fail to see where this concerns you in any way."

Tragg said, "Ordinarily, I would say you were quite right, Miss Street, but there are some circumstances which might alter the case."

"Such as what?" she asked impulsively, and then wished she had kept her mouth shut, realizing that she had given him just the opening he had been angling for.

"Oh," he said casually, "in case the kitten happened to be the one that belonged to Mrs. Matilda Shore, one that had been poisoned last night."

"Even so, what would that have to do with it?"

"The question of how that cat came into your possession," Tragg said, "might be interesting to the police. However, as you suggested, we can talk it over while we're riding to the office."

"Yes, I'm late now."

His smile was apologetic. "Perhaps," he said, "you are not referring to the same office that I am."

She turned to face him, fighting back a wobbly feeling in her knees.

"You know perfectly well to what office *I* am referring," she said, managing to keep firmness in her voice.

Lieutenant Tragg was not in the least impressed. He announced, "I am referring to the office of the district attorney. And you may as well bring the kitten along. Not only does it seem to be too careless to be left alone, but it may be a bit of very significant evidence."

NINETEEN

PERRY MASON SOAKED up slumber. The consciousness of broad daylight knifed its way through to his brain. He sat up in bed long enough to look at his watch, fling the pillows into a new position, and drop back with a sense of languid comfort. He started drifting comfortably down into the welcome warmth of nerve-healing oblivion. . . . The ringing of the buzzer on his door-bell irritated him into consciousness.

Mason decided to ignore the summons. He turned over, frowning in the determination of his concentration . . . damn the door-bell anyway . . . probably someone wanting to sell something. Why hadn't he shut it off? . . . The bell again . . . well, let them ring. He wouldn't pay any attention to it.

Again and again the bell rang. Mason found that his very determination to sleep was marshalling his faculties into wakefulness. He heard quick steps in the corridor, then knuckles banging imperatively on his door.

With an exclamation of irritation, he climbed out of bed, unlocked the door and jerked it open.

Paul Drake stood on the threshold, grinning at him. "How do you like it?" he asked.

"Damn it. I *don't* like it. Come in."

Drake followed the lawyer into the apartment, selected the most comfortable chair, twisted himself comfortably, and lit a cigarette. "Nice place you have here."

"Isn't it?" Mason said sarcastically.

"A little chilly. I'll close this window. The breeze is coming in through there. Sunlight's pouring in through the other one. It's eleven-thirty, Perry."

"What the devil do I care what time it is?"

Drake tried to blow a smoke ring, watched the blue clouds of smoke drift out into the shaft of sunlight, and said, "You're always getting me up about the middle of the night, when you and Della have been out making whoopee—and seem to think it's fun. Thought I'd interfere with your sleep just so you can see how it feels."

Mason, pulling the covers over his bare toes, grinned at the poetic justice of Drake's position, said, "It feels like hell," and reached for a cigarette.

"Thought you'd like a report of what's going on."

Mason tapped the end of the cigarette, carefully moistened the end with his tongue, lit a match, and said, "As soon as I finish with this cigarette, I'm going to throw you out and go back to sleep." He placed the match to the end of the cigarette.

"Lots of things have been happening," Drake said. "Those bullets all came from the same gun."

"That's nothing new."

"Tragg's turned the whole police force upside down. He's working on every angle of the case, squeezing out every last bit of information."

"I'm glad he is."

"The doctors give Jerry Templar nine chances out of ten to pull through. He stood the operation in fine shape."

"That's good."

"The kitten that was poisoned was taken down to the gardener's house for safe-keeping—chap by the name of Thomas Lunk."

"Uh huh."

"Lunk's disappeared. So has the kitten."

Mason said, "Listen, Paul. I can keep abreast of the current developments by reading the newspapers. I wanted you to get some angles everybody didn't know about, not trail along a few steps behind the police."

Drake went on as though he hadn't even heard Mason's remark, "Chap by the name of George Alber seems to stand ace-high with Her Majesty, Matilda Shore. Seems as though Matilda thinks Alber and Helen Kendal should get spliced. Alber thinks so too. Alber's going places. He's going to amount to something in the world. He's attractive and magnetic. Helen is throwing herself away on a man who isn't at all worthy of her. Aunt Matilda may leave her dough to Alber if Helen isn't a good girl."

Mason sucked in a prodigious yawn. "You are very annoying at times, Paul."

Drake looked at him with humourless eyes. "Do you find me that way?"

Mason knocked ashes off the end of his cigarette, snuggled back down under the covers.

"Matilda is out of the hospital and back at the house. Seems as though she's made a will in which she's tried to exert some pressure on Helen Kendal to make her marry young Alber. Alber apparently gets a very, very nice chunk of the Shore fortune one way or another. Either he gets it by marrying Helen, or, if Helen doesn't marry him, he is taken care of very handsomely. . . . Oh, yes, your friend Lieutenant Tragg is having the last few cheques that went through Franklin Shore's account carefully experted. A ten-thousand-dollar cheque to a man by the name of Rodney French seems to be the one he's particularly interested in. Rodney French is being looked for by the police. He seems to have taken a little vacation for himself, commencing yesterday evening. He neglected to tell anyone just where he was going."

Mason said, "Franklin Shore telephoned his book-keeper that he was putting that ten-thousand-dollar cheque through."

"That's right," Drake said, grinning, "he did."

"Well?" Mason asked.

"Tragg's working on a theory that perhaps Franklin *intended* to put that cheque through, but pulled his disappearing act before he'd made out the cheque. . . . That would make an interesting situation, wouldn't it, Perry? Put yourself in the position of a chap who is depending on a ten-thousand-dollar cheque from a chap whose name on the bottom of a cheque would have made it as good as a certificate of the United States Mint. Then the chap disappears and can't be found, and you've already committed yourself to the things you're going to do, on the assumption that cheque is going through."

"Anything else?" Mason asked.

"Oh, yes. Tragg's really working on that disappearance. It's a shame he wasn't in on it when it happened, but that was during the regime of our old friend, Sergeant Holcomb. Tragg's going over all the unidentified bodies that were found around that time—getting the records out for an airing. He's found one body. The description doesn't tally, however. He's also checking up on all the suicides around Florida in 1932, and he's checking up on some mining property Leech was interested in, also making a very close check on the finances of Gerald Shore as of January, 1932. A very, very resourceful chap, Tragg."

Mason said, "Phooey! Tragg's just a damned misanthrope."

"Of course, he covers a lot of territory," Drake went on. "Seems to think that kitten is rather an important factor in the entire situation."

"The kitten, eh?" Mason observed.

"Uh huh. Interesting chap, Tragg. When he goes after something, he really gets it."

"The kitten, for instance?" Mason asked, very casually.

"Oh, of course, the kitten. He has that kitten up at the district attorney's office."

Mason sat bolt upright in bed. "How's that?" he asked.

"Has the kitten up at the district attorney's office. Don't know just what he's doing with it, but . . ."

"Where did he get it?"

"I don't know. I pick up a lot of stuff from the newspaper boys, things that leak out through the police. He's asking questions of the chap who does the gardening out there, man by the name of Lunk. He . . ."

Mason became a moving mass of arms and legs, pinching out the cigarette, kicking the covers off, grabbing the telephone. The dial whirred through a number. Mason said, "Hello. . . . Hello. That you, Gertie? . . . Where's Della this morning?

"No word from her, eh? . . . Let me talk with Jackson. . . . Hello, Jackson. This is an emergency. Give it a right of way over everything in the office. Make out an application for a writ of *habeas corpus* for Della Street. Make it wide enough, big enough and broad enough to cover everything from rape to arson. She's being detained against her will. She's being examined concerning privileged communications, she's held without any charge being placed against her. She's abundantly able to furnish bail in any reasonable amount. Ask for a writ of *habeas corpus* and ask that she be admitted to bail pending the return and hearing on the writ. I'll sign and verify it. Get going on the thing!"

Mason slammed up the telephone, peeled off his pyjamas, splashed hurriedly into the shower, came out drying his body, jerking clean underwear out of a bureau drawer.

Drake sat curled up in the chair watching with a puzzled expression of growing concern while Mason hurried into his clothes.

"I have a six-volt electric razor in the glove department of my car," Drake said. "If you want to drive uptown with me, you could shave in the car."

Mason jerked open the door of a coat closet, struggled into his overcoat, grabbed his hat, pulled gloves out of his overcoat pocket, said, "Come on, Paul. What's holding us back?"

"Nothing," Drake said, uncoiling his double-jointed frame in a series of convolutions that would have done credit to a contortionist. "We're on our way. Your office or the D.A.'s?"

"My office first," Mason said. "When I talk with a D.A. I always like to be able to slap him in the face with a writ of *habeas corpus* in case he gets rough."

"This bird getting rough?" Drake asked.

"Uh huh. Where's that razor?"

TWENTY

HAMILTON BURGER, THE district attorney, was a man with a huge chest, a thick neck and heavy shoulders. There was about him a suggestion of the massive strength of a bear. He was given to making unpredictable moves with the swiftness of a man who concludes his deliberations before taking action. Once he started to act, he threw himself into that action with the concentrated force that eliminated any possibility of re-examining the situation. Lawyers who had come to know him well said that once Hamilton Burger started charging, it took a brick wall to stop him. As one attorney had expressed it, "Once Burger starts moving, he keeps moving until he's stopped, and it takes a hell of a lot to stop him."

Mason knew that a reception had been prepared for him as soon as he entered the outer office of the district attorney. No assistant or trial deputy was assigned to interview him; but with the clocklike precision of a carefully-thought-out bit of campaign strategy, he was whisked down the corridor and into the district attorney's office almost as soon as he had announced himself at the reception desk.

Hamilton Burger surveyed Mason with glittering, steady eyes. "Sit down," he said.

Mason took the chair across from Burger's desk.

"Do you want to talk to me or am I going to talk to you?" he asked.

"I'm talking to you," Burger said.

"Go ahead," Mason told him, "do your talking first. I'll say what I have to say when you've finished."

Hamilton Burger said, "You're unorthodox. Your methods are spectacular, dramatic, and bizarre."

"You might add one additional word."

For a moment, there was a flicker in the district attorney's eyes. "Effective?" he asked.

Mason nodded.

"That is the thing which bothers me," Burger said.

"I'm glad to hear you admit it."

"It doesn't bother me in the way that you think, however," Burger went on. "It simply means that if your spectacular, dramatic, swashbuckling methods *continue* to be effective, we'll have every attorney at the bar trying to cut corners, playing legal sleight of hand to outwit the police. And heaven knows, one of you in this county is *plenty*."

"If I beat the police to the correct solution of a crime, does that constitute outwitting the police?"

"That isn't what I meant," Burger objected. "It's not our policy to prosecute the innocent. And understand this, Mason, I'm talking, not only about what you do, but about how you do it."

"What's wrong with my means?"

"You don't try your cases in a court-room. You don't sit in your office and interview clients. You go tearing around the country, working by a catch-as-catch-can method of grabbing evidence, refusing to take the police into your confidence, and . . ."

"Wait a minute," Mason said. "Do the police take me into their confidence?"

Burger ignored the question. "There have been times when I've cooperated with you because I thought you were cooperating with me. But it's always been that same spectacular, flamboyant, pulling-the-rabbit-out-of-the-hat business with you."

Mason said, "Well, if the rabbit I'm looking for happens to be in a hat, why not pull him out?"

"Because you usually furnish the hat. You can't justify a legal hocus-pocus simply because you eventually squirm your way out. Now I'll quit talking generalities with you. I'll get down to specific instances."

"That would be fine."

"Specifically," Burger said, "last night you uncovered a valuable, vital witness in a murder case. If the police had had the testimony of that witness, they might have solved the case by this time. As it was, they were given no opportunity. You and your secretary whisked this witness out from under the noses of the police."

"You mean Lunk?"

"I mean Lunk."

"Go ahead."

"You took him to an hotel and secreted him. You did everything in your power to keep the police from finding him. The police have found him."

"What are they going to do with him?" Mason asked. "If he's so valuable, let him go ahead and solve the case."

"I'm afraid it isn't that simple," Burger said.

"Why not?"

"We've uncovered some evidence that up to now has been unnoticed in connection with Franklin Shore's disappearance."

"What?"

"Specifically, that ten-thousand-dollar cheque which was given to Rodney French may have been a forgery."

Mason settled back in his chair, crossed his long legs. "All right, let's discuss that."

"I'll be glad to hear your ideas on it," Burger said with stiff formality.

"In the first place," Mason replied easily, "Franklin Shore told his book-keeper he had put through such a cheque."

"I will correct you there," Burger interrupted, consulting his notes. "The testimony of the book-keeper as given ten years ago was to the effect that Franklin Shore said he *was putting* through such a cheque."

Mason waved the point aside. "All right, suppose he said he was putting through that cheque. That establishes its authenticity. But if the cheque *was* forged, the statute of limitations has run out. At present, that cheque business can have no legal significance."

Burger said, "That cheque could furnish a motive."

"For what?"

"For murder."

"Go ahead. I'm listening."

"If we had been able to get in touch with Lunk last night, it is quite possible we could have uncovered some very valuable additional evidence."

"Do you want to be more specific?"

"Yes. I think we could have found Franklin Shore."

"And I am accused of keeping you from getting in touch with Lunk?"

"Exactly."

Mason said, "I'll puncture that theory right now. The first thing I did with Lunk was to take him down to the hospital to see Matilda Shore. That was where he wanted to go. But—and get this point straight, Burger, because it's legally important—in place of trying to keep away from the police, I took him to the hospital knowing the police were guarding Matilda Shore. I told the police guards who Lunk was. I told them that he wanted to see Mrs. Shore, that he might have important evidence, and that Tragg might want to see him. What more can anyone ask?"

Burger nodded. "That's an outstanding example of your cleverness, Mason. As far as Lunk is concerned, that one very clever move virtually gives you immunity from any prosecution. You could make that stand up in front of a jury. And yet you know, and I know, that you deliberately staged that entire visit so that the guards *would* eject you and the man with you. You did it simply to give yourself a legal insurance policy."

Mason grinned. "I can't help it if you fill up your police force with morons. I took Lunk there, and told them who he was. They pushed him back in the elevator, told him to get out and stay out."

"I understand," Burger said patiently. "Now let me call your attention to something. Under our law, any person who wilfully prevents or dissuades a person who is, or who may become a witness, from attending upon any inquiry authorized by law is guilty of a misdemeanour."

Mason nodded.

"And, under another law, if any person gives or promises to give such a witness a bribe to keep him away, he's guilty of a felony."

"Go right ahead," Mason said. "I'm interested in your theory."

"Under the decisions," Burger said, "it isn't necessary that this attempt should be successful. Nor does the witness have to be actually kidnapped. It's been held in one of our sister states that it's a crime within the meaning of a similar law to get a witness intoxicated so that he couldn't testify."

Mason said, "Well, I didn't bribe anyone, and I didn't get anyone intoxicated. What's all the shooting about?"

Burger said, "Lunk adopts a sullen, defiant attitude toward the police, and won't tell us what he knows. However, he isn't too intelligent. Once you understand his peculiar psychology and take the time to work with him, it's possible to get a story out of him—a bit at a time."

"Well?"

"Lunk has told us enough so that we know that Franklin Shore was at his house, that your secretary went out and picked him up. Tragg had told you specifically that he wanted Franklin Shore as a witness to appear before the grand jury."

Mason said, "Go ahead and finish what you have to say, and then I'll tell you how I feel about it."

"You want the last word, eh?"

Mason nodded.

"Mason," said Burger, "I'm going to hit you where it hurts, and I'm going to hit you hard."

"By picking on my secretary, I suppose?"

Burger said, "You got her into this. I didn't. You kept Lunk tied up while she jumped in a cab and went to Lunk's residence, got Franklin Shore out of bed, told him that he had to get out, and made arrangements to conceal him."

"You can prove all this, I presume?"

"I can prove it by circumstantial evidence. You know very well, Mason, that you wanted to talk with Franklin Shore before the police did. You sent your secretary out there to pick up Franklin Shore and conceal him."

"Does she admit that?"

"No, she doesn't. She doesn't have to admit it. We've got the evidence to prove it."

"When you say prove, what do you mean?"

"I mean to the satisfaction of a jury."

"I don't believe it."

"It's circumstantial evidence," Burger said, "but we have it."

"You've got it like I've got the Hope diamond!" Mason said insultingly.

Hamilton Burger met his eyes unflinchingly. "I've sympathized with some of the things you've done in times past, Mason. I have been so intrigued by your rapid-fire methods and the results you have achieved that I haven't realized that as far as justice was concerned the viciousness of those methods more than offsets the benefits achieved. Now then, I'm going to pull your house of cards down."

"How?"

"I'm going to convict your secretary of spiriting off a material witness in a murder case. After that, I'm going to try you out as an accessory and I am going to convict you. Then I am going to have you disbarred on the strength of those convictions. Now, you probably have a writ of *habeas corpus* in your pocket that you've been preparing to slap down on my desk as your last word. Go ahead and slap it. I have no desire to be unduly harsh with Miss Street. I am proceeding against her because that's the only way I can get at you. I don't intend to confine Miss Street in jail. I am perfectly willing to let you have a writ of *habeas corpus*. I am perfectly willing to see that she is admitted to bail. I am, however, going to convict her of a crime. If she wants to apply for probation, that's all right. I won't stand in her way. Then I am going to convict you of a crime. I am not going to ask for a jail sentence. I am going to see that a fine is imposed, and then I am going to use that conviction to terminate your activities as a member of the Bar."

Burger pushed back his swivel chair and got to his feet. "Now then, that last word that you were talking about—that business of slapping the writ of *habeas corpus* on my desk, loses some of its dramatic punch, doesn't it, Mason?"

Mason also got to his feet, stared across the desk at the district attorney. "All right, I told you I was going to have the last word. Now I'll have it.

"Burger, the trouble with you is that you've hypnotized yourself by looking at Law entirely from the viewpoint of a district attorney. District attorneys have organized themselves and they've organized public sentiment. You have gradually lulled the public into a feeling of confidence that it can trust you to see that no innocent person is ever knowingly prosecuted."

Hamilton Burger said, "I am glad to hear you admit that, Mason."

"You shouldn't be. You should be sorry."

"Why?"

"Because the public has sat idly by and let the organized prosecutors amend the Law until the constitutional guarantees of the public were swept away. We're living in a period of changing times. It's quite possible that the definition of crime will be broadened to include things which we might at present list in the category of political crimes. When the ordinary citizen is dragged into court, he'll find that the cards have been stacked against him. Ostensibly, they were stacked against the professional criminal by organized public servants, but actually they've been stacked against Mr. and Mrs. Ordinary Citizen, because the whole legal procedure has been completely undermined.

"It's high time for citizens to wake up to the fact that it isn't a question of whether a man is guilty or innocent, but whether his guilt or innocence can be proved under a procedure which *leaves in the citizen the legal rights to which he is entitled under a constitutional government.*

"You object to spectacular, dramatic methods of defence. You overlook the fact that for the past twenty-five years you have beguiled the public into releasing its constitutional rights so that the only effective methods of defence which are left are the spectacular and the dramatic. Now then, Mr. District Attorney, you go ahead and arrest Della Street, and we'll thrash this thing out in a court-room."

Burger said, "That's right, Mason. We'll thrash it out in a court-room. And, if you ask me, your last word didn't amount to much."

Mason paused in the doorway, his face hard with anger. "I haven't had that last word yet," he said. "I'll have it in court."

And he slammed the door behind him.

TWENTY-ONE

JUDGE LANKERSHIM CAME to the bench amidst a swish of whispers from the crowded court-room, which subsided as a bailiff pounded a gavel.

"The People of the State of California versus Della Street," Judge Lankershim called.

Mason got to his feet. "The defendant is in court and on bail. Let the records show that she has surrendered for the purpose of trial."

"The record will so show," Judge Lankershim said. "She will remain on the same bail during the trial. I understand this action has been brought on for immediate trial pursuant to stipulation of counsel."

"That is right," Hamilton Burger said.

"I would like to hear from the prosecution as to the nature of the case."

Burger said, "Your Honour, I will make a brief preliminary statement. It is the contention of the prosecution that while the police officers were investigating a felony, to wit, an assault with a deadly weapon with intent to commit murder, committed by persons unknown upon one Jerry Templar, the defendant in this case wilfully spirited away a certain witness, one Franklin Shore, who had information which, if communicated to the police, would have materially aided the police in the solution of the crime. Specifically, it is charged that the defendant in this case, fully aware of the full significance of the facts which this witness knew, concealed him from the police and continues to so conceal him."

"And the defendant has pleaded not guilty?" Judge Lankershim asked.

"The defendant has pleaded not guilty, and asked for a trial by jury," Mason said. "And to prove our good faith in the matter, we will accept, without examination, the first twelve names which are called to the jury-box as jurymen to try this cause."

Judge Lankershim looked over his glasses at Perry Mason. "You are, however, insisting upon a trial by jury?"

"Exactly," Mason said. "Trial by jury is guaranteed by the constitution to the citizens of the State. We have lost too many of our constitutional guarantees by not insisting upon them. Upon behalf of this defendant, I insist upon a jury trial more as a gesture than otherwise. I would be perfectly willing to submit the matter to Your Honour's discretion otherwise."

"Do you wish to accept Mr. Mason's stipulation that the first twelve names called to the jury-box may constitute a jury, Mr. District Attorney?"

Hamilton Burger, who had personally embarked upon the trial of the case, relegating his assistants to subordinate positions at the far corners of the counsel table, got to his feet. "No, Your Honour, we will examine the jurors in the regular way."

Mason settled back in his chair. "I have no questions to ask of any juror," he announced with a smile. "I waive my challenges for cause. I waive my peremptory challenges. I am satisfied that any twelve American citizens who file into that jury-box will give the defendant the benefit of a square deal when the evidence is in—and that's all the defendant wants."

"The Court will observe," Burger said acidly, "that counsel is using the excuse of waiving his rights as a peg upon which to hang a dramatic statement intended to impress the jurors in advance with . . ."

"The Court understands the situation," Judge Lankershim interrupted promptly. "The jurors will pay no attention to the extraneous comments of either counsel. Let's get on with this case. Under the circumstances, Mr. Burger, it devolves upon you to examine the jurymen on their *voir dire*."

And examine them Burger did, with the painstaking, mathematical, searching questions which a man might have expected a prosecutor to use in a murder case, while Mason tilted back in his chair, an amused smile on his face, his bearing indicating that he was paying no attention either to questions or answers. And, somehow, the more Burger examined the jurymen, the more he made it appear that he was suspicious of their probity, of their impartiality, an attitude which contrasted unfavourably with that of counsel for the defence. Twice his associates tried to warn him of this, but Burger paid no attention to their warnings. He went doggedly ahead with his questions.

When he had finished, Judge Lankershim said, "Under the law, the

Court is called upon to examine the jurors for prejudice. It has never been the policy of this Court, however, to restrict the questions of counsel. Therefore, the Court has always permitted counsel to interrogate the jurors in the usual manner. But, under the circumstances of this case, the Court feels that it is incumbent upon it to see that no member of the jury is prejudiced for or against either side." Whereupon, the judge asked a few searching, but impartial questions, and said to Hamilton Burger, "The defendant has waived both challenges for cause and peremptory challenges. Do you have any challenges?"

Burger shook his head.

Mason turned to smile at the jury. Gradually it dawned on the courtroom that the ultimate effect of the entire procedure had been to accomplish what he had proposed in the first instance, namely, that the first twelve persons called should sit as jurors.

The jury smiled back at Mason.

Hamilton Burger made a brief statement to the jury, outlining simply what he expected to prove, followed that up by saying, "I will call as my first witness Helen Kendal."

Helen Kendal, obviously conscious of the eyes of the spectators in the crowded court-room, came forward and was sworn. She gave her name and address to the clerk, looked at Hamilton Burger expectantly for questions.

"You have occasion to remember the thirteenth of this month?"

"I do."

"I will call your attention to the evening of that day and ask if anything unusual happened."

"Yes, sir."

"What?"

"In the first place, my kitten was seized with spasms, and I rushed it to a veterinary, who said it was . . ."

Burger held up his hand. "Never mind what the veterinary said. That's hearsay. Just state what you know of your own knowledge."

"Yes, sir."

"Now, at about the time the kitten became ill, did anything else unusual happen?"

"Yes. I received a telephone call—from my uncle."

"What?"

"I received a telephone call."

"From whom?"

"From my uncle."

"You have two uncles?"

"Yes, sir. This call came from Uncle Franklin."

"And by the words Uncle Franklin, you refer to Franklin B. Shore?"

"Yes, sir."

"When had you last seen Franklin B. Shore?"

"Some ten years ago, shortly prior to his disappearance."

"Your uncle, Franklin Shore, had disappeared mysteriously some ten years earlier?"

"Yes, sir."

Hamilton Burger said to the Court, "I am asking leading questions on some of these points which are not disputed, but which I want to get before the jury."

"No objection," Mason said.

"What did your uncle say to you over the telephone?"

"Objected to," Mason said, "as hearsay. Incompetent, irrelevant, and immaterial."

"If the Court please," Burger announced, "I am not seeking to adduce any facts which will bind the defendant as to this conversation, but only to show the condition which existed there that night, and as to that only to the extent that it will be considered a part of the *res gestae*, explaining the moves of the various parties on that night."

"I will overrule the objection," Judge Lankershim said, "but will later limit the purposes for which the answer may be considered by the jury."

"What did your uncle say?"

"He asked me if I knew who was speaking. I told him that I didn't. He then told me his name and went on to prove his identity."

"That's a conclusion," Hamilton Burger said hastily. "That may go out. What did he say?"

"Well, he called my attention to certain things that only my uncle would have known about."

"What I am after particularly," Hamilton Burger said, "is what he told you to do."

"He told me to go to Mr. Perry Mason, the attorney, and then to go to the Castle Gate Hotel and ask for a Mr. Henry Leech, who, he said, would take us to him. He told me that I wasn't to take anyone else into my confidence; that, particularly, I wasn't to let my Aunt Matilda know anything about it."

"Your Aunt Matilda is the wife of Franklin Shore?"

"Yes."

"And later on that evening, in company with Mr. Mason, did you make any effort to get in touch with Mr. Leech?"

"Yes."

"What did you do?"

"We went to the Castle Gate Hotel. We were advised that Mr. Leech wasn't there. A note was delivered telling us where we could . . ."

"Just a moment," Hamilton Burger said. "I'll produce that note and ask you if this is the note."

"Yes."

Burger said, "I'll ask that it be received in evidence as People's Exhibit A, and I will then read it to the jury."

The document was duly stamped, and Burger read it to the jury.

"Now," he asked Helen Kendal, "what did you do with reference to that? In other words, what was your next step after you received that document?"

"We went to the place mentioned."

"There was a map with it?"

"Yes."

"I will show you this map and ask if this is the one."

"Yes, sir."

"I ask that this be received in evidence as People's Exhibit B."

"No objection," Mason said.

"So ordered," Judge Lankershim announced.

"And you went to the place indicated on that map?" Burger asked the witness.

"Yes."

"What did you find there?"

"It was up in the hills behind Hollywood. There was a reservoir. A car was parked near the reservoir. A man was sitting in the car, sort of slumped over the wheel. He was dead. He . . . he had been killed."

"That man was a stranger to you?"

"Yes."

"Who was with you at that time?"

"My uncle, Gerald Shore, Mr. Perry Mason and Miss Street."

"By Miss Street you mean Miss Della Street, the defendant in this action?"

"Yes, sir."

"And what happened next? What was done immediately after that?"

"We three remained near our car while Mr. Mason went to telephone the police."

"Then what happened?"

"The police came and asked questions and then my Uncle Gerald drove us home. After that, we went to a hospital to call on Aunt Matilda, and then Uncle Gerald drove me home again."

"By home, you mean to the Shore residence?"

"Yes, sir."

"Then what happened?"

"They dropped me at the residence. The others went to . . ."

"Never mind stating where they went, because you don't know—only what they told you. But the others left, did they?"

"Yes."

"Then what happened?"

"A friend came to call on me."

"What was his name?"

"Jerry Templar."

"He was a man with whom you had been quite friendly?"

"In a way, yes."

"And who was in the house at that time?"

"Komo, the servant, was sleeping in the basement. Mrs. Parker, a cook and housekeeper, was in her room over the garage. Mr. Templar and myself were in the living-room."

"What happened?"

"We heard a peculiar sound coming from my Aunt Matilda's bedroom, a sound as though something had been tipped over. Then we heard the chatter of her caged love-birds. Then, after a moment, we heard a peculiar noise which sounded like my aunt walking."

"Is there anything peculiar about her walk?"

"Yes, sir. She drags her right foot when she walks, and uses a cane. The thump of the cane, and the peculiar dragging noise of the right foot are very distinctive."

"And this walk sounded like your aunt's walk?"

"Yes, sir."

"Then what happened?"

"I knew that my aunt wasn't in the house. I told that to Jerry. He immediately walked down the corridor and opened the door of the bedroom. Jerry had always been so big and strong that I guess I considered him invincible. I never realized the danger in which I was placing him. I . . ."

"What happened?" Burger asked.

"Someone in the room shot twice. The first bullet just missed my head. The second one . . . hit Jerry."

"What did you do after that?"

"I don't know. I dragged Jerry away from the door, and then he recovered consciousness. He was unconscious for some little time. I don't know just how long. When he opened his eyes, I told him I must get an ambulance and a doctor. He said we could get a taxi-cab quicker, and I telephoned for a taxicab. We rushed him to the hospital, and an hour or two later on, Dr. Everett Rosllyn operated on him."

"You remained at the hospital?"

"Yes, sir, until after the operation, and until after—after I'd seen he was going to be all right."

"Cross-examine," Burger snapped.

Mason said, "You don't know how long Jerry Templar was unconscious?"

"No. It was all a nightmare to me."

"You don't know how long it was after the shot was fired before you got to the hospital?"

"No, sir. I can't tell you the time."

"And you don't know exactly how long it was after we left you at the house that last time before the shooting took place?"

"Well . . . it might have been . . . it might have been an hour. It might not have been more than half an hour. It was perhaps somewhere between half an hour and an hour."

"You can't fix it any closer than that?"

"No."

"You were about fourteen years of age when your uncle disappeared?"

"Yes, sir."

"Can you fix exactly the time when the kitten was first taken sick— that is, with reference to the time of that telephone conversation with your Uncle Franklin?"

"It was immediately after I hung up the telephone that I noticed the kitten was sick."

"Did *you* notice that?"

"My attention was first called to it by my aunt."

"By your aunt you mean Matilda Shore?"

"Yes, sir."

"What did you do with the kitten?"

"I took it to the veterinary."

Burger said, "Just a moment, Your Honour, one important question I forgot to ask. I would like to interrupt to get it in the record."

"No objection," Mason said affably.

"After dinner that night, did you go back to see the veterinary?"

"Yes, sir."

"And what was the condition of the kitten at that time?"

"The kitten seemed to be well, but weak."

"What did you do with him?"

"I took him with me. The veterinary suggested that . . ."

"Never mind what the veterinary suggested."

Mason said affably, "Oh, go ahead, let her tell it. I take it, Miss

Kendal, the veterinary suggested that if some person were trying to poison the kitten in the house, that it would be better to take it away from the house, and so you took it down and left it with Thomas Lunk, the gardener, did you not?"

"Yes, sir."

Mason said, "That's all." And Burger nodded.

Hamilton Burger called Lieutenant Tragg to the stand. Tragg testified in the close-clipped, efficient manner of the police officer who has been on the witness-stand on numerous occasions. He testified to receiving a telephone call, to going to the hills behind Hollywood, finding the body, identified the articles which were tied up in a handkerchief near the body, and testified as to the identity of the body.

Tragg then stated positively that he had advised Mr. Mason that night, while the lawyer was at the Shore residence, that he desired the presence of Franklin B. Shore as a witness to appear before the grand jury, and that he stated to Mason the importance to the police of finding and examining Franklin Shore.

He then went on to state his experiences at the Shore house later on that night when he had been summoned to investigate the shooting of Jerry Templar. He testified what he had found, calling particular attention to a writing-desk in which a lock had been forced open. He identified photographs showing the condition of the bedroom when he had arrived on the scene. Burger introduced these photographs in evidence.

On cross-examination, Mason adopted a manner of good-natured affability.

"Lieutenant, referring to this handkerchief, I call your attention to a laundry mark. Have you made any effort to trace that laundry mark?"

"Well, yes."

"And you found, did you not, that it was a mark given to Franklin Shore by a laundry in Miami, Florida, and that the laundry had been out of business for some six years?"

"That is right."

"You'll remember that when you first showed me the watch up in the hills behind Hollywood, I pointed out to you that, according to the indicator, the watch must have been wound at approximately four-thirty or five o'clock the day of the murder?"

"Yes."

"Now, have you examined the fountain-pen?"

"Yes."

"And what was the condition of that fountain-pen?"

Tragg said, "It was dry."

"According to your observations at the scene of the shooting of Jerry Templar, the assailant had entered through a ground-floor window on the north side of the house. Is that right?"

"Yes."

"And, in entering the room, had knocked over a night-stand or tabouret which was by the side of Mrs. Shore's bed?"

"Yes."

"Then had picked up a cane which apparently was in the room, and had imitated the steps of Mrs. Shore?"

"I think that's a fair deduction from the evidence. Of course, I don't know that of my own knowledge."

"But you did find a cane which was lying on the floor near the corner from which the shots had been fired?"

"Yes."

"By the way, Lieutenant, you stated, I believe, that you took Thomas Lunk into custody at a downtown hotel where he was registered under the name of Thomas Trimmer?"

"Yes."

"How did you happen to go to that hotel to make the arrest?"

Tragg smiled. "I am not going to divulge that."

"It's not proper cross-examination," Hamilton Burger objected. "The witness certainly is entitled to protect the source of his information."

Mason said, "I will withdraw that question and ask this in its place. Isn't it a fact, Lieutenant, that you went to that hotel because you received an anonymous telephone tip from some person who told you where Lunk was, the name under which he was registered, and the number of his room?"

"Same objection," Burger said.

Judge Lankershim deliberated the matter thoughtfully, then asked Mason, "What is the reason for asking this question, Mr. Mason?"

"It simply goes to show the entire *res gestae*," he said. "As a matter of fact, Your Honour, it may be quite material. Suppose, for instance, that *I* had been the one who had given Lieutenant Tragg that telephone tip?"

"You don't claim that you were?" Judge Lankershim asked.

"Not at present, Your Honour. But I think it's only fair to the defendant that the witness should answer that one question."

"I'll overrule the objection," Judge Lankershim said. "I doubt that it's entirely pertinent, but I am going to give the defence the benefit of the widest latitude in cross-examination. The question doesn't call upon the lieutenant to divulge in any way the source of his information. Answer the question."

Tragg picked his words cautiously. "I received an anonymous telephone communication, giving me approximately that information."

Mason smiled. "That's all."

"I call Matilda Shore as my next witness," Burger said.

Matilda Shore, who was sitting next to the aisle, raised herself from the seat by clinging to her cane with one hand, the back of the seat in front of her with the other, and walked to the witness chair, where the clerk administered the oath. While she was walking, the jurors, as well as the spectators, had an opportunity to listen to the peculiarly distinctive sound of her steps.

When she had given her name and address, Burger lost no time in getting to the point.

"You are the wife of Franklin B. Shore?"

"I am."

"And where is Mr. Shore now?"

"I don't know."

"When did you see him last?"

"Approximately ten years ago."

"Can you give us the exact date?"

"January 23, 1932."

"And what happened on that date?"

"He disappeared. Someone was talking with him in his study, someone who wanted money. The voices were raised for a while in angry altercation. Then they quieted down. I went to bed. I never saw my husband after that. He disappeared. I knew, however, that he wasn't dead. I knew that some day he would show up . . ."

"Never mind what you felt or surmised," Burger interrupted hastily. "I just want to establish certain things to prove a possible motivation for the entering of your house by a person who was interrupted before he could achieve the purpose for which he had come. For that purpose only, I'll ask you if there were some cheques which were cashed just before and after your husband's disappearance?"

"Yes."

"One of those cheques was for ten thousand dollars?"

"Yes, sir."

"To whom was it payable?"

"A man named Rodney French."

"There were several other cheques?"

"Yes, sir."

"Now, where were those cheques when you saw them last?"

"They were in my bedroom in a pigeonhole in a desk which was pushed back against the wall."

"That was a roll-top desk?"

"Yes, sir."

"An old one?"

"Yes, sir. It had been in my husband's study. It was his desk."

"You mean he had used it continuously up to the time of his disappearance as his desk?"

"Yes, sir."

"And you were using it on the thirteenth of this month?"

"That's right."

"And these cheques which I have mentioned were in there?"

"Yes, sir."

"How many of them?"

"There were about a dozen of them in an envelope, cheques which had been put through the account within the last few days prior to his disappearance, or cheques which had been written immediately before his disappearance and were cashed afterwards."

"Why were those cheques segregated in that manner?"

"Because I thought they might prove to be evidence. I put them in an envelope and kept them in this drawer."

"When did you leave your house on the night of the thirteenth?"

"I don't know exactly what time it was. I was getting ready for bed. It was probably about ten o'clock. I followed my usual custom of drinking a bottle of stout and shortly afterwards became violently ill. Remembering that the kitten had been poisoned, I took an emetic and went at once to the hospital."

"Where were the cheques which you have mentioned when you went to the hospital?"

"In that pigeonhole in the desk."

"How do you know?"

"I had been looking at them shortly before, and I hadn't left the bedroom except to go to the ice-box and get a bottle of stout and a glass."

"When did you next enter your bedroom?"

"The next morning about nine o'clock when I was discharged from the hospital."

"Did anyone accompany you?"

"Yes."

"Who?"

"Lieutenant Tragg."

"At his suggestion, did you search through your room to see if anything was missing?"

"Yes."

"Did you find anything missing?"

"No."

Burger produced the watch and fountain-pen which had been identified as having been found near Leech's body. Mrs. Shore stated positively they were the property of her husband, that he had had both these objects in his possession the night he had disappeared, and that she had never seen them again until the police had shown them to her.

"Cross-examine," Burger said.

"You couldn't find that *anything* was missing from your room when you searched it after your return from the hospital?"

"No."

Mason said, "That's all."

Swiftly Hamilton Burger laid the foundations for a complete case. He called the autopsy surgeon, called Dr. Rosllyn, identified the bullets which had been taken from the wound inflicted on Jerry Templar and from the body of Henry Leech. He then recalled Lieutenant Tragg to get the bullet which had embedded itself in the woodwork of the Shore home; following which he called the expert from the criminal laboratories who introduced photographs showing the distinctive scratches made by the rifling and by pits in the barrel of the gun, showing that these bullets had all been fired from the same gun.

Judge Lankershim glanced at the clock. "You will understand," he said to Burger, "that we are not trying the murder case at this time."

"Yes, Your Honour, but we are showing the circumstances which surrounded the commission of the alleged crime in this case. We are showing the significance of what had happened and the importance of having the police unimpeded in their efforts to solve these crimes."

Judge Lankershim nodded, glanced curiously at Mason, who seemed to be taking but very little interest in the entire procedure.

"I will now call Thomas Lunk," Burger announced with something of a flourish.

Lunk came shuffling forward. He seemed reluctant to testify, and Burger had to draw his story from him a bit at a time, frequently using leading questions, occasionally cross-examining his own witness, a procedure which Judge Lankershim allowed because of the apparent hostility of the witness.

Pieced together, Lunk's story made a convincing and dramatic climax to the case the district attorney had been building up. He told of how he had gone home from work that night, of how Helen Kendal had brought the kitten to his house where it was left for safe keeping, told of how he had listened to the radio, read a magazine, and while he was in the midst of reading this magazine, had heard steps on the porch, knocking at the door. He had opened the door, and then drawn back in surprise as he recognized the features of his former employer.

He mentioned but briefly that they had "talked for a while" and then he had given Shore the bed in his spare bedroom. He had waited until he felt certain that his visitor was asleep, then had quietly slipped out of the front door, taken a late street-car, got off at a point nearest the Shore residence, and started hurriedly for the house; that the defendant had intercepted him, asked him if he wanted to see Mrs. Shore, and, on being assured that he did, had taken him in an automobile, stating that she would take him to Mrs. Shore; that thereafter she had, as he reluctantly admitted, "stalled around" until Perry Mason had appeared on the scene, whereupon they had gone to a hospital, and Mason had told him Mrs. Shore was virtually in the custody of the police; that thereafter Mason had taken him to the Maple Leaf Hotel, had secured a room for him under the name of Thomas Trimmer; that he had gone to his room. After he had started to undress, there had been a knock at the door. Police radio officers had taken him into custody. He had no idea how they had found out where he was.

"What was the condition of Mr. Shore so far as his clothing was concerned when you left the house?"

"He was in bed, if that's what you mean."

"And undressed?"

"Yes."

"And you felt that he was asleep?"

"Never mind what the witness felt," Mason said. "What did he see? What did he hear?"

"Very well," Burger conceded with poor grace, "I will reframe the question. Was there anything in his appearance which you saw or heard which indicated whether he was asleep or awake?"

"Well, he was snoring," Lunk reluctantly admitted.

"And you, at that time, were fully dressed? You hadn't been to bed?"

"No, sir."

"And you left the house?"

"Yes, sir."

"Did you try to leave quietly?"

"Well, yes, I did."

"And you walked to the car line?"

"Yes, sir."

"How far?"

"A block."

"How long did you have to wait for a car?"

"There was a car coming when I got to the corner. I hopped aboard."

"How long were you on this street-car?"

"Not over ten minutes."

"And how long from the time you left the street-car until the defendant in this case accosted you and picked you up?"

"Oh, not very long."

"How long?"

"I don't know."

"Was it a minute, two minutes, five minutes, or twenty minutes?"

"Oh, a minute," Lunk said.

Hamilton Burger said, "I submit, Your Honour, that it's unreasonable to suppose that this man who was sleeping peacefully in his bed roused, investigated to find that Mr. Lunk had left, dressed himself, and left the house within that short space of time. I think it is a reasonable inference for the jury to draw that Mr. Shore was in that bed in that house at the very time Miss Street picked up this witness."

"That's an argument counsel can make to the jury," Mason said. "He has no right to make it now. If he wants to argue the case now, I'll say that . . ."

Judge Lankershim stopped him. "The jury will pay no attention to the arguments of counsel at the present time," he admonished the jury. "They are directed exclusively to the Court. Proceed with your examination of the witness, Mr. Burger."

"After the defendant in this case picked you up and took you in her automobile, Mr. Perry Mason joined you, did he not?"

"Yes."

"And thereafter Mr. Mason took you to this hotel?"

"Yes."

"Now was Miss Street, the defendant, with you all of that time?"

"No."

"When did she leave you?"

"I don't know."

"Do you know about what time it was?"

"No."

"Where did she leave you?"

"I don't remember."

"It was in front of an hotel, was it not?"

"I wouldn't want to say."

"But it was at some point where she took a taxi-cab, was it not?"

"I think there was a taxi-cab there."

"And afterwards Mr. Mason remained with you for some time, getting some flowers, sending them to Mrs. Shore in the hospital, going out to your house to inspect it, and then driving you to this hotel?"

The witness hesitated for several seconds, then gave a sullen, monosyllabic answer. "Yes."

Burger said, "You may cross-examine, Mr. Mason," and there was a smirk of triumph in his voice as he said it.

Mason looked at the witness. "Mr. Lunk, I want you to answer my questions frankly. Do you understand?"

"Yes."

"After Miss Street left us, we went to your house, did we not?"

"Yes."

"We arrived there about four or four-thirty in the morning?"

"I guess so, yes."

"It was cold?"

"Yes, sir."

"There was no fire going in the house?"

"No, sir."

"You lit a gas heater after we arrived?"

"That's right."

"When you first left the house, you had left the door between the *front* bedroom and the bathroom closed?"

"Yes."

"And when we arrived there, that door was open."

"Yes."

"And the contents of the dresser drawers had been dumped out and clothes taken from the closet?"

"That's right."

"Was anything missing?"

"Yes. Some money had been taken from where I'd been keeping it hid—in a pocket of my best suit."

"That suit had been left hanging in the closet?"

"Yes, sir."

"How much was missing?"

"Objected to," Burger said, "as incompetent, irrelevant, and immaterial. It's not proper cross-examination. It has nothing whatever to do with the facts of this case."

"Overruled," the Judge said. "The defendant is entitled to show the condition of the premises and anything which would reasonably make it appear that the departure of Franklin Shore might have been prior to the time the prosecution claims that departure took place."

"About three hundred dollars was missing," Lunk said.

"The door to the pantry was closed?"

"Yes, sir."

"Now, when you had been cooking, you had taken flour from a bin in the pantry?"

"Yes, sir."

"And some of that flour had been spilled on the floor round the bin?"

"Yes, sir."

"When we arrived, there was a kitten in the house?"

"That's right."

"This was a kitten which had previously been left with you by Helen Kendal?"

"Yes."

"And, I believe, I called your attention to the fact that the kitten had evidently run through this sprinkling of flour which surrounded the bin, and then had run across the kitchen, through the door of the kitchen, and into the back bedroom?"

"That's right."

"There were tracks showing that this had happened?"

"Yes. It ain't far from the pantry to the door of the back bedroom, only three or four feet, I guess."

"And not more than four or five feet from the bedroom door to the back bed?"

"Yes."

"And by the side of that bed I called your attention to a place where the tracks showed the kitten's paws had been bunched together as though it had jumped up on the bed?"

"Yes."

"The kitten was curled up in a little ball in the centre of the bed in the *front* room when we got there? Is that right?"

"That's right."

"But you remember distinctly that the pantry door was closed?"

"Yes."

"On a table in the sitting-room was an ash-tray, and a visiting-card bearing the name George Alber, some writing on this card, and the ash-tray held the stub of a cold cigar?"

"Yes. The cigar was left by Franklin Shore. I found the card stuck in the door when I went out."

"When you went *out*?"

"Yes."

"You didn't hear any knocking at the door or ringing of the doorbell while you were there?"

"No. That's why the card bothered me. Alber must have tried to ring the bell, and it didn't work. Sometimes it gets out of order."

The district attorney said to Mason, "May I withdraw this witness temporarily to put on two other witnesses who are anxious to get away? Then this witness can return to the box."

Mason bowed grave assent. "No objection."

Burger called in rapid succession the taxi-driver who told of taking Della Street to the neighbourhood, of the length of time she was absent from his cab, and of then driving her to her apartment. Tragg, recalled to the stand, testified as to finding the kitten in Della Street's apartment, and Helen Kendal, recalled, identified the kitten as the one which had been poisoned and which she had left with Thomas Lunk on the evening of the thirteenth.

Mason apparently paid not the slightest attention to any of these other witnesses. He did not bother with interposing any objections, nor did he use his right of cross-examination.

Then Lunk was recalled for further cross-examination.

Mason studied the witness for several seconds until the silence focused the attention of everyone in the court-room upon the importance of what he was about to say.

"When was the last time you remember opening that flour-bin in the pantry?"

"The morning of the thirteenth. I made some pancakes for breakfast."

"And, since I called your attention to the rather large amount of flour which was sprinkled around the base of the bin, you haven't taken the lid off the flour container?"

"No, sir. I haven't had any chance. The police took me from the hotel and have held me ever since."

"As a material witness," Hamilton Burger hastened to explain.

Lunk turned to him with some show of temper and said, "I don't care *why* you did it, but you sure did it!"

Judge Lankershim said, "The witness will confine himself to answering questions."

Mason looked up at Judge Lankershim. "If Your Honour will take recess for half an hour, I don't think it will be necessary to ask any more questions."

"Just what is the object of such a continuance?"

Mason was smiling now. "I couldn't help observing, Your Honour, that the moment I began this last phase of the cross-examination, Lieutenant Tragg rather hurriedly left the court-room. I think that thirty minutes will give him ample opportunity to get out to the house, search the flour-bin, and return."

"It is your contention that the cover was removed from that flour-bin sometime during the evening of the thirteenth, or the morning of the fourteenth by some person other than the witness Thomas Lunk?" Judge Lankershim asked.

Mason's smile broadened. "I think, Your Honour, Lieutenant Tragg will make a very interesting discovery. Your Honour appreciates my position. I am only interested in establishing the innocence of this defendant. Therefore, I don't care to make any statement as to what may be discovered, nor as to its evidentiary value."

Judge Lankershim said, "Very well, the Court will take a thirty-minute recess."

As the people shuffled out of the court-room to congregate in the passages, George Alber came pushing forward, a somewhat sheepish grin on his face.

"Sorry if that card mixed things up any," he said. "As it happens, I was driving by Lunk's place after the theatre. Thought I'd stop and see if a light was on. One was, so I went up and pushed the bell. No one answered, so I left the card—thought Helen might appreciate my thinking of the kitten—and I *was* a bit worried. To tell you the truth, it never occurred to me the bell might be out of order."

"A light was on?" Mason asked.

"Yes. I could see a light through the blinds. I just didn't knock, because I thought the bell was ringing."

"What time was this?"

"Oh, right around midnight."

Mason pursed his lips, said, "You might casually mention it to the district attorney."

"I have. He says he knows the bell was out of order, so it's unimportant."

Mason said, "I guess it is, then."

TWENTY-TWO

WHEN COURT RECONVENED, Hamilton Burger showed very plainly that he was labouring under great excitement. "If the Court please," he said, "a very startling situation has developed in this case. I ask permission to withdraw the witness Lunk from the box and recall Lieutenant Tragg."

"No objection," Mason said.

"Very well," Judge Lankershim ruled. "Lieutenant Tragg will once more go into the box. You have already been sworn, Lieutenant."

Tragg nodded and walked to the witness-box.

Burger asked, "Have you recently made a trip to the residence of the witness Lunk?"

"Yes, sir."

"That was within the last thirty minutes?"

"Yes, sir."

"What did you do?"

"I went into the pantry and took the lid off the bin of flour."

"Then what did you do?"

"I reached down inside the flour."

"What did you find?"

Tragg couldn't keep his voice from being nervously rapid. "I found a .38 calibre, double-action Smith & Wesson revolver."

"You may tell us what you did with reference to that revolver."

"I rushed it to the criminal laboratory to see if finger-prints could be developed. I took the number and, while I have traced that number to *my* satisfaction, I haven't as yet secured the necessary witnesses to appear and testify. I think I can have a witness here by to-morrow morning."

"Cross-examine," Burger said.

Mason said urbanely, "But you have satisfied yourself, Lieutenant, as to what the sales record will show?"

"I have. We have recently compiled statistics so that the sales of any guns within the county, over a period of fifteen years, can be instantly determined—that is, so far as the police are concerned. Of course, those records aren't anything we can take to court as evidence. We will have to get the original record from the dealer who made the sale."

Mason said, "I understand, Lieutenant. But those records do give you, for police use, the information which is contained on the dealers' registers of fire-arm sales?"

"Yes, sir."

Mason said, "I will waive all objections as to whether this is or is not the *best* evidence, and ask you if the police records don't show that this revolver was purchased by Franklin B. Shore some time prior to January, 1932?"

Tragg's eyes showed that Mason's question caught him by surprise, but he answered after a moment, "Yes, sir. That gun, according to our records, was purchased by Franklin B. Shore in October of 1931."

"And what do you deduce from all this, Lieutenant?" Mason asked.

Judge Lankershim frowned at Mason. "That question, Mr. Mason, calls for something which could hardly be binding upon the defendant, nor, of course, would it be permissible, if asked by the prosecution."

"I understand," Mason said, "but I take it there is no objection from the prosecution."

"None whatever," Burger said, with a triumphant leer at the jury. "I would like nothing better than to have Lieutenant Tragg answer that question."

Judge Lankershim still hesitated, then said, "There is only one theory upon which this would be admissible as cross-examination, and that would be to show the bias of the witness. In view of the fact that the question *may* be permissible upon that ground, since there is no objection on the part of the prosecution, I will permit it to be answered. The Court cannot, of course, tell what counsel for the defence has in mind. But the Court does feel that, so far as the proceedings against this defendant are concerned, the constitutional guarantees must be observed. Therefore, the Court will limit the consideration which the jury may give to the answer, as relating to and showing a possible bias on the part of the witness. Under those circumstances, the witness may answer the question."

Tragg said, "There is no question in my mind but what Franklin B.

Shore got up after Thomas Lunk left the house, went to the pantry and concealed this gun in the bin of flour; that this kitten followed him into the pantry, jumped in the flour, and that Mr. Shore pushed the kitten out, and the kitten thereupon ran into the bedroom and jumped in the bed which Mr. Shore had just vacated. I may state further that this simply goes to indicate how vitally important a witness Franklin Shore is and was, and emphasizes the gravity of any attempt which might have been made to spirit him away."

Mason smiled. "It also indicates that Franklin Shore was, very shortly after the shooting of Jerry Templar, in possession of the revolver with which the shooting was perpetrated, and of the same revolver which, in all probability, fired the fatal bullet into the body of Henry Leech, does it not?"

Burger said, "I'm going to object to that question, Your Honour, upon the ground that it is argumentative, and not proper cross-examination."

Judge Lankershim said, "It is highly irregular. It is far afield from the ordinary course of examination. It indicates what happens when a police witness is permitted to give his opinion and deductions under the guise of evidence. However, by failing to object to that other question, the prosecution has opened the door to this entire line of cross-examination. Only, however, for the purpose of showing the bias of the witness. If this witness is once permitted to give his deductions as to what the facts indicate, counsel for the defence should be permitted to point out to the witness a possible fallacy in his reasoning. I think I see the point counsel is driving at, and I think I appreciate what his next question will be—a question which might very seriously affect the case of the prosecution. By permitting the door to be opened at all, the district attorney has given counsel an opportunity to open it all the way. I am going to let the witness answer this question as well as the question which I feel certain will follow."

Tragg said cautiously, "I don't know that it's the same gun with which the crimes were committed. It is a gun of the same calibre and the same description. There were three discharged shells in the cylinder of that gun, and the remaining three cylinders were loaded with shells and bullets of the same general character as those recovered from the body of Henry Leech, from the woodwork at the Shore house, and from Jerry Templar at the time he was operated on."

Mason looked at Hamilton Burger and winked. He turned to the jury and smiled triumphantly. "And now, Lieutenant," he said to the witness, "I will ask you if it isn't equally fair to assume, if this weapon *should* prove to be the murderer's weapon, that Franklin Shore, having concealed that weapon in the residence of Thomas Lunk, *would then have been most anxious to make his escape?*"

"Objected to," Hamilton Burger shouted, "upon the ground that this is taking the witness far afield into the realm of conjecture. That is a matter which counsel can argue to the jury. It is not a question to be asked of this witness."

Judge Lankershim said, "It is precisely the question which I *thought* counsel would ask next. The objection is overruled. The witness will answer it—but remember, the answer is admissible only to show possible bias."

Tragg said, "I don't know. It is, of course, a possibility."

Judge Lankershim turned to the jury. "The jurors will understand that these last few questions have been permitted only for the purpose of showing the attitude of the witness. In other words, the possible bias of the witness, meaning by that any prejudice which he might entertain against the defendant. The questions and answers can have no evidentiary value except for that single purpose. You will consider them only for that purpose."

Mason settled back in his chair and said to Lieutenant Tragg, "Now when you found that gun in the flour, Lieutenant, you were somewhat excited, were you not?"

"Not exactly."

"You were in a hurry to get back to court and hand that gun to the police laboratory?"

"Yes."

"In so much of a hurry," Mason said, "that I take it you didn't search the bin of flour to see what else it might have contained."

The expression of sudden consternation upon Tragg's face foreshadowed his answer. "I . . . I didn't make any further search of the bin. But I did bring that bin along with me and give it to the police laboratory to search for fingerprints."

Mason glanced at Judge Lankershim and said, "I submit, Your Honour, that the case having gone this far, the witness should be permitted to . . ."

There was a commotion in the back of the court-room. The dour Scotchman who presided over the criminal laboratory of the police came pushing his way through the spectators who had gathered round the door.

Mason said, "However, Your Honour, I think that Angus MacIntosh is about to supply that information. We are perfectly willing to let Lieutenant Tragg step down and Mr. MacIntosh, who has already been sworn as a witness, take the stand."

Hamilton Burger said, cautiously, "I don't know what counsel is getting at. If the Court will pardon me a moment, I would like to talk with Mr. MacIntosh."

Burger arose hastily and stepped over to the rail which separated the counsel table from the spectators. He engaged in a whispered conference with Angus MacIntosh, then looked at Perry Mason with a puzzled frown, following which he said abruptly to Judge Lankershim, "If the Court please, we would like to have a recess until to-morrow morning."

"Any objection?" Judge Lankershim asked Perry Mason.

"Yes, Your Honour. If the district attorney won't put Angus MacIntosh on the stand, I want to call him as a witness for the defence."

Hamilton Burger said testily, "The prosecution has not yet concluded its evidence. The defence will have ample opportunity to call its own witnesses when the prosecution rests."

Judge Lankershim said acidly, "The request for a continuance is denied. Proceed with your cross-examination of Lieutenant Tragg, Mr. Mason."

Mason said, "I have no further questions, Your Honour. Nor have I any further questions of the witness Lunk whose cross-examination was interrupted to permit Lieutenant Tragg to be once more placed on the witness-stand."

Hamilton Burger said quickly, "Under those circumstances, I have some more questions to ask the witness Lunk on redirect examination."

Judge Lankershim's voice showed his impatience. "Very well. You may stand down, Lieutenant, and the witness Lunk will again go into the box. But, kindly don't waste time, Mr. District Attorney."

When Lunk had once more resumed his position in the witness-box, Hamilton Burger said, "Mr. Lunk, did you at any time after the morning of the thirteenth open that bin of flour in your pantry?"

"Objected to as already asked and answered," Mason said.

"It *has* been asked and answered, but under the circumstances, I will permit it to be asked again," Judge Lankershim said. "The witness will answer the question."

Lunk said, "No. After I made the pancakes on the morning of the thirteenth, I didn't take the lid off the flour-bin again."

"Did you use that flour-bin for any other purpose than storing flour—in other words, did you keep or did you put anything other than flour in that bin at any time?"

"No, sir."

Burger hesitated, then said, "That is all."

"No questions," Mason said.

Judge Lankershim looked at the clock, then at the district attorney. "Call your next witness."

Hamilton Burger said, with somewhat poor grace, "Angus MacIntosh will take the stand. Mr. MacIntosh has already been sworn and has testified to his position in the police laboratories."

MacIntosh returned to the witness-stand.

"You were given a bin of flour a few minutes ago by Lieutenant Tragg?" Hamilton Burger asked.

"Yes, sir."

"What did you do with that bin of flour?"

"I wanted to photograph the bin and develop latent fingerprints on it, so I dumped out the flour."

"What did you find?" Burger asked.

"I found currency in bills of fifty and one hundred dollars, making a total of $23,555."

There was a stir of excitement in the jury-box.

"Where are those bills now?"

"In the police laboratory."

"Cross-examine," Hamilton Burger snapped.

"No questions," Mason retorted promptly, and then smiling at the judge, said, "And now, Your Honour, the defence has no objection whatever to consenting to the continuance which the prosecution has requested."

"The prosecution doesn't want it now," Burger said shortly. "The prosecution rests."

"The defence rests," Mason said promptly. "It is four-thirty. I will stipulate that, so far as the defence is concerned, arguments on each side may be limited to ten minutes."

"I'm not prepared to argue the case at this time, or in that short time," Hamilton Burger said. "The recent startling developments have been such that I would like more time to correlate the various matters which have been discovered."

"Then why," Judge Lankershim asked, "did you object to an adjournment when the defence suggested it?"

Burger said nothing.

"Apparently," Judge Lankershim went on, "you wanted to see what the evidence of the defence would be. Counsel consented to a continuance, and you rejected it."

"But, Your Honour," Hamilton Burger protested, "I felt that I was in a position to go ahead with the case so far as the cross-examination of the defendant's witnesses were concerned, but that I was not prepared to argue the case."

Judge Lankershim shook his head. "Court will adjourn at five o'clock. You may proceed with your argument. The Court will limit the argument to twenty minutes to each side."

Hamilton Burger accepted the ruling of the Court, marched up to a position in front of the jurors and said, "In view of the limitation which has been placed on the argument, and the unexpected developments in this case, I am not prepared to make an extensive opening argument. I will conserve my time so as to make a longer closing argument. I will state, however, that the circumstantial evidence shows conclusively that the defendant in this case and her employer, Perry Mason, were engaged in activities which included spiriting away material witnesses. What was done with the witness Lunk is virtually uncontradicted. The defendant is not on trial for that, but her willingness to spirit away a witness is shown by the manner in which she and her employer got the witness Lunk away from the police and endeavoured to keep him in concealment.

"We are asking for a conviction of the defendant upon the evidence as it now stands. Regardless of what Franklin Shore may have done, I don't think any person on this jury doubts that Della Street's purpose in going to the residence of Thomas Lunk in the small hours of the morning of the fourteenth was to spirit Franklin Shore away. The Court will instruct you that it is not necessary that the attempt be successful in order to constitute a crime under sections 136 and 136½ of our Penal Code. The spiriting away of a witness, *with the intent of preventing him from testifying at a proper legal proceeding or an investigation, constitutes a crime.*

"That, ladies and gentlemen, is the contention of the prosecution. If the defendant wishes to adopt the position that Franklin Shore had already left the premises before Della Street's arrival, it is incumbent upon the defence to assume the burden of proving that fact.

"I will not consume any more time now, but will reserve such time as I have left for my closing argument."

Burger, glancing triumphantly at the clock, and realizing that he had jockeyed Perry Mason into the position of completing his opening argument prior to the evening adjournment, leaving the prosecution in the advantageous position of being able to sleep over the developments, before making its closing argument, marched back to his chair and sat down.

Mason slowly got to his feet, walked deliberately over to the jury-box and smiled at the puzzled jurors.

He opened quietly. "The prosecution can't shift the burden of proof to the defendant until it has first proven the defendant guilty beyond all reasonable doubt.

"I submit to you, ladies and gentlemen, that Franklin Shore was not present at Lunk's residence when Della Street arrived there. The reason I have introduced no testimony is that the evidence of the prosecution proves my point conclusively.

"I will not comment on the evidence of the flour. I will comment only on the actions of the kitten. Someone opened the flour-bin. Some object was placed in that bin, perhaps the gun, perhaps the currency, perhaps both. The kitten, a playful, careless, fearless animal, attracted by the motion of the hands over the bin of flour, jumped into the flour-bin and was promptly tossed out. The kitten thereupon ran through the partially opened door, into the back bedroom and jumped upon the bed.

"It must be perfectly obvious that the bed was then vacant, equally obvious that the kitten forthwith jumped down on the other side of the bed and went directly through the bathroom to jump on the bed in the front bedroom.

"Ladies and gentlemen, I will ask the prosecution, since this is a case of circumstantial evidence, to explain one thing to you—and preparatory to that, let me remind you that inasmuch as this is a case of circumstantial evidence, the law is that you must acquit the defendant unless the evidence not only indicates beyond all reasonable doubt the guilt of the defendant, but cannot be explained upon any *reasonable* hypothesis other than that of her guilt. Therefore, ladies and gentlemen, *why* did the kitten, after getting in the flour and after jumping on the bed of Franklin B. Shore, leave that bed to go into the front bedroom and curl up on the bed in there?

"Having relied upon circumstantial evidence, it is up to the district attorney to explain every bit of it. Therefore, in the morning, let the district attorney answer that interesting question as to the conduct of the kitten. And some of you, who are quite probably familiar with cats, their psychology, their habits, will doubtless have an answer of your own.

"And that, ladies and gentlemen, concludes my argument."

Several of the jurors looked puzzled, but two of the feminine members were nodding and smiling as though they had already grasped the point which was causing Hamilton Burger to scowl blackly.

Judge Lankershim himself seemed also to have some knowledge of kittens, for there was a smile playing about the corners of his lips, and a twinkle in his eyes as he admonished the jurors not to form any opinion as to the merits of the case, not to discuss it among themselves, or permit it to be discussed in their presence, and adjourned court until the next day at ten o'clock, remarking that the defendant was on bail and would be released upon that same bail until the next morning at ten o'clock.

TWENTY-THREE

AS SOON AS the court had adjourned and the Judge had left the bench, Hamilton Burger came pushing his way across to Mason.

"Mason, what the devil does this mean?"

Mason smiled affably. "I'm sure I couldn't say, Burger. All *I'm* doing is defending Miss Street against a criminal charge. I don't think the jury will convict her, do you?"

Burger said, "To hell with that. We all have a duty to perform—apprehending a murderer. Did Franklin Shore do it?"

"I'm sure I couldn't tell you."

Lunk came through the rail which separated the counsel tables from the spectators. "I want to talk with the district attorney."

"What is it?" Burger asked, turning to him.

Lunk said, "Franklin Shore may have put that gun in the flour, but I don't think he did. And I know darn well he didn't put the money in there."

"How do you know that?" Mason asked.

"Because Shore was trying to get me to give him some money."

"You didn't do it?"

"No."

"Why?" Mason asked.

"Because I wanted him to stay where he was until I'd had a chance to talk with Mrs. Shore."

"And why was he so anxious to get money and get away?" Mason asked. "Come on, Lunk. You told me that you might let me know what it was Shore really told you. Now, you've done a lot of covering up. Suppose you come clean now."

"I reckon I had better," Lunk said. "Shore came to the house. He was nervous. He said that he'd had some trouble with a man and had shot him. He said he had to get away quick, that he'd had to shoot to keep the other guy from shooting him, but he was afraid the police might think it was murder. He said Matilda wouldn't like anything better than to get him in a spot. I told him I thought he'd better talk with her anyway before he left, and he didn't want to, so I told him that he could hide at my place, but that as soon as I could get in touch with Mrs. Shore the next morning, I'd try and get an advance on my salary and give him a stake so he could get out. After I told him that, he went to bed to sleep. That's when I went out to see Mrs. Shore. I wanted to tell her I'd seen her husband. I wanted to see whether she wanted to stake him or whether she didn't."

"If she hadn't," Mason asked, "would you have surrendered Shore to the police?"

"I don't know, Mr. Mason. Shore had used me pretty square. Understand, I didn't intend to tell Mrs. Shore that he was staying at my house. I was going to tell her that I'd seen him. I was trying to give them both a square deal."

Mason said, "Go ahead, Lunk, tell the district attorney the whole truth. You've got to do it now. Tell him what Shore told you about where he'd been."

"He didn't . . . we didn't talk much."

"At least as long as it took him to smoke a cigar," Mason said. "Tell Mr. Burger what he said."

Lunk hesitated, then blurted, "Well, he ran away with that woman."

"Where and why?" Mason asked.

"It was like I told you," Lunk said. "When Franklin Shore was down in Florida people began to mistake him for another man. Shore looked this man up. They might have been twins. So they had a joke and had their pictures taken, and Shore started joshing his wife that he was going to tell this man all about the people he knew and have the guy be at the bridge parties as his stooge.

"Then Shore fell in love with this younger woman, so he got the idea that he maybe could disappear, take this dame with him, and go to Florida, and start training this other guy to be his double, telling him all about his business affairs and the people he was dealing with.

"Then after six months, when this man had everything all down pat, he would show up and claim he was Shore. He'd say his mind had suddenly gone blank, and even after his memory got back he was still shaky.

"Well, Shore did it. Things went fine. Inside of six months his double was all ready, so Shore sent a post card to his niece from Miami.

He figured police would come and find his double, apparently still in sort of a daze, but claiming to be Shore. And his memory would come back a little at a time. Of course, he'd be too sick to be very active in business, but he'd draw plenty of dough from his investments and he'd send the real Shore a cut out of it, and Franklin Shore would take the other guy's name, and marry this dame and it would be okay. Then the night Franklin Shore sent the card, this guy was killed in an auto accident. Well, there was Shore with his bridges all burned up, holding the sack."

"How about Leech?" Mason asked.

"Leech had got the boss keen on his mine. So the boss had given Leech some dough in cash to put in the mine, saying it wasn't from him, but from a guy in Florida—and Leech, thinking the Florida guy was a sucker, froze him out when he struck it rich. . . . Of course, the boss was the real Florida guy. He'd just given Leech a phoney name.

"Lately Shore got to needing money. He went to Leech. Leech was to have given him the dough, but he was stony broke by this time. . . . So Shore had to come back. The dame left him a couple of years ago and he was flat broke. And that's everything I know about it. That's the whole story the way the boss gave it to me there in the shack."

Hamilton Burger said, "The thing's incredible! That's the damnedest story I ever heard."

Lunk said in the flat, emotionless voice of a man who isn't trying to convince anyone, "It sounded all right to me. Maybe hearing it from the boss's own lips made it seem more convincin', but that's the story he told me."

Mason said to the district attorney, "Suppose it's all true—up to the point where the auto accident took place, Burger. Then suppose it was Shore who was killed. This double had been training to take Shore's place. He knew intimate things that Shore had told him, and he'd written them down and memorized them. A fortune was waiting for him if he could impersonate Franklin Shore and make it stick."

"Then why didn't he show up sooner?" Burger asked.

"One possible explanation is that Mrs. Shore knew about this double her husband had dug up," Mason replied. "Remember, Shore had started it as a joke, and his wife knew all about it. But if she should die, then the double could show up as the missing husband and claim the whole estate."

Burger gave a low whistle—then said, "Damn," explosively. "And *that* would explain the poison."

Mason lit a cigarette. Lunk said, "This wasn't no double that came to my place. It was the boss."

"How do you know?" Mason asked.

"Because he told me some things only the boss knew."

Mason smiled at Hamilton Burger.

Lunk frowned, then said suddenly, "Well, no matter *who* this was, he was broke. Why should he steal the few hundred I kept hid in my clothes and then leave a fortune in my flour-bin?"

Burger looked at Mason for an answer.

"No comment," Mason said, smiling.

"Do *you* think the man who called on Lunk was the double, or Shore himself?" Burger asked Mason.

"I don't know, Burger. I didn't see him. After all, you know you've said you'd prefer I minded my own business and let the police solve their murders. Suppose *you* wrestle with that problem?"

"Damn it, it *could* have been either one!" Burger exclaimed.

Mason seemed completely disinterested. "Well, I think my clients are in the clear, both Della Street and Gerald Shore."

Hamilton Burger's voice showed exasperation. "This is the *damnedest* case!"

Mason stretched and yawned. "I don't find it so," he said. "However, *I'm* not interested in anything except getting Miss Street acquitted."

"What the devil is that business about cat psychology you're talking about, and what does *it* have to do with the case?" Burger asked.

Mason said, "I'm afraid if I told you, Burger, you'd accuse me of trying to outwit the police. I've been thinking over what you said to me there in your office. I think there's a great deal to be said in favour of your position. You think an attorney has no business going out trying to solve murders, that he should confine himself to handling his own law practice, and I'm forced to agree with you. I'm representing Gerald Shore, and I'm representing Della Street. I have no interest in solving murders as such."

"But you want to get Gerald Shore entirely out in the clear, don't you?"

"Yes."

"There's no better way to do it than by showing us who committed the murders."

"No," Mason said, "that isn't the Law. It's what you were objecting to about my methods, Burger. You see, it's up to you to prove that my clients committed some crime. As long as I confine myself to representing those clients, I'm practising law in a staid, conventional manner. The minute I go out and try to 'outwit the police,' as you called it, I'm guilty of that unconventional conduct which has proved so irritating to you. In fact, Mr. District Attorney, I've decided to let you solve your own mysteries—and that's the last word I was telling you I was going to have. Come on, Della. Let's leave Lieutenant Tragg and the district attorney to work out their little picture puzzle. After all, it's no skin off *our* noses."

Burger said, "Look here, Mason, you can't do that! I'm satisfied you know a lot more about this case than we do."

"No, I don't," Mason said. "You have every essential fact that I have."

"Well, perhaps you've applied the knowledge we all have to better advantage."

Mason bowed. "Thank you, Mr. Attorney."

"All right, you owe it to us to tell us what conclusion you've reached."

"I'll tell you what I'll do, Burger. I'll put you on an equal footing with myself. There's one thing I know that you don't. Lunk told me that he was satisfied Komo, the houseboy, had been experimenting with poison, that he'd first started experimenting about ten years ago, that shortly before Franklin Shore's disappearance, Lunk's brother died, and Lunk has always been under the impression the houseboy poisoned him."

"Is that right?" Burger asked Lunk.

Lunk said, "That's right. I don't think that damn Jap had anything against my brother in particular, but I think he was experimenting with poison—just the way he started experimenting on the kitten."

Lieutenant Tragg, who had just come up to join the group, said, "There were four bottles of stout in the ice-box. Every one of them had been loaded with strychnine. Do you think the houseboy did that?"

"I know damn well he did it," Lunk said vehemently.

"How do you know?"

"Well, just from putting two and two together, the same as you know anything."

Burger said to Tragg, "There's some new and startling evidence here, Lieutenant. I want to talk with you."

Mason smiled and said, "What Lunk means, Lieutenant, is that he feels very positively Komo is the poisoner. You'll remember, Lieutenant, that you told me you thought the evidence would show the bullets had all been fired from the same gun, and that would mean that one person had been guilty of both crimes. Now, follow that reasoning out. Matilda Shore has a perfect alibi. She was in the hospital when the second crime was committed. Gerald Shore has an alibi. You probably know what it is, but I'm not going to stick my neck out by telling you

that because I don't want to be a witness. And you can eliminate Helen
Kendal and Jerry Templar. You can eliminate darn near everyone under
that theory except three or four people. There you are, Lieutenant. Pay
your money and take your choice. But if I were you, I really *would*
investigate the death of Lunk's brother, and see if it isn't possible that
the death was due to poison rather than natural causes.

"And now if you gentlemen will excuse me, I have a dinner date
with the defendant."

TWENTY-FOUR

THE DANCE ORCHESTRA was perfect. The lights were dim and on the floor only a few couples were dancing so that they were neither crowded nor conspicuous.

Without either having spoken for a long time, Perry Mason and Della Street were drifting through the strains of an Island song. As the orchestra swung into the chorus, Della Street began to sing the words very softly. Suddenly she stopped with an involuntary choke.

"S'matter? Swallow a fly?" he demanded. "Go on, do some more. I like it."

She shook her head.

"Something wrong?" he asked more seriously.

"No. I guess not. I've eaten, I've drunken, I've been merry, so I guess I'm all set for to-morrow."

The music stopped at that moment. Mason, with his arm still around her waist, swung her away so that he could look at her. His eyes were puzzled for an instant. Then they cleared. "I didn't get you. I see—to-morrow you die. Have you been worrying about that damn silly case?"

She laughed nervously. "Well—I suppose every nice girl has to go through this sort of thing sooner or later."

"But you haven't committed any crime."

"I wish you'd remember to tell Hamilton Burger when you see him. It seems ridiculous not to clear up this little misunderstanding, when all you have to do is say, 'Listen, Ham, old fellow, this little girl is . . .' Oh, hell's bells, let's sit down."

Perry followed her to their table.

"I thought *you* were worried," she went on, "when you brought the kitten out to me and found that Franklin Shore wasn't there."

"I was," Mason admitted. "If I'd used my head, though, I needn't have been."

"I don't get it," she said, lighting a cigarette.

"You should—if you know kittens."

"You mean the kitten jumping in the flour?"

"No, not that . . . What is it?" he asked, noticing that she was staring over his shoulder.

"Paul Drake."

"How did he find us here?" Mason asked, frowning.

Drake was close enough to hear his remark. He pulled out a chair and sat down.

"As you well know, I can find anybody, any time, any place. Here's my card. Aren't you going to order me a drink?"

"Cops and private dicks shouldn't drink when they're on duty."

"Paul Drake, the fellow I work for, is broad-minded. He's a swell guy. He's a prince. You ought to meet him."

Mason summoned a waiter. "Three Scotch and sodas."

"Five Scotches," Drake corrected. "But only three of 'em in my glass. I never could stand strong highballs."

The waiter hesitated, then deftly withdrew.

"You know, Perry, I didn't just drop in here to buy you and Della Scotch and sodas. There's something worrying me."

"Have *you* been arrested, too?" Della cried.

He ignored her comment to look steadily at the lawyer. "Perry," he said, "you weren't by any chance planning some especially dramatic blow-off for to-morrow, were you—using your friend, Tom Lunk?"

"Perhaps. Why?"

"You're not going to do it now," Drake said.

"Why not?"

"Lunk's dead, found at a road intersection a couple of blocks from his house, a hit-and-run car. A witness saw it happen and chased the car for half a dozen blocks, but couldn't even get close enough to see the licence number. The car swung round the corner just after Lunk got off the street-car he rides home on."

Mason drummed on the tablecloth with his fingers. "Burger was a damn fool to release him," he said.

"Apparently, he thought Lunk had told 'em everything he knew and there was no reason for holding him any longer."

Mason frowned.

"What were you intending to spring on Lunk?" Della asked.

"Quite a few things. Has it ever seemed curious to you, Della, that after I had taken all the precautions to get Lunk registered in an hotel under the name of Thomas Trimmer, the police should have picked him up so easily?"

"Someone must have followed you," Drake said.

Mason shook his head. "Don't kid yourself, Paul. When I don't want to be followed, no one follows me."

"Then who tipped them off? It couldn't have been the hotel clerk."

"No," Mason said. "And you can follow that process of elimination right on through. There's only one person who could have done it."

"Who?"

"Lunk."

Drake looked incredulous. "You mean that he telephoned the police himself?"

"Yes."

"But that was a goofy, crazy thing to do. Why would he do anything like that?"

Mason said, "That fact gives you the key to the whole business."

"But why?" Della Street asked.

Mason said, "There's only one reason I can think of."

"What's that?"

"He wanted to be arrested," he said dryly.

"You mean that he felt he was in danger?"

Mason shrugged his shoulders.

The waiter brought the drinks. Drake raised his glass to Della. "Here's to jail," he grinned. "Well, Perry, what do you do now?"

Mason said, "Nothing, absolutely nothing. Hamilton Burger is going to have to crack this nut by himself. That jury will never convict Della— not as long as there are two women on it who know something about cats."

Della Street put her glass down firmly. "If you don't explain what you mean by that, I will be convicted of a crime, and it will be murder."

"No prosecutor in this state would charge you with murder for killing Perry Mason," Drake pointed out. "You'd get a reward! But what *did* the kitten do that's so significant?"

Mason grinned. "It was a cold night," he said. "The kitten jumped into the flour when someone was hiding the gun in the bin. Naturally, it got thrown out, probably with a cuff on the ear. Now, that kitten had had a lot of kind treatment and didn't like the rough stuff. It ran out of the kitchen and into the back bedroom, and jumped up on the bed. It didn't stay there, though. It jumped off that bed and went to the other bed."

"Why?" Drake asked.

Della Street gave a sudden, quick gasp. "Oh," she cried, "*I* know why! Anyone would, if he stopped to think about it."

Drake shook his head and got up.

"Where are you going, Paul?" Della demanded.

"I'm going out to buy a cat so I can study him and learn about some of the important facts of life."

"You would, at that, you know," Mason told him seriously.

"Good night," Drake muttered lugubriously.

With Paul Drake gone, Mason turned to Della. "You know, Della, this has been more of a strain on you than I realized. As soon as the jury brings in its verdict to-morrow, what do you say we take a run out to the desert—around Palm Springs or Indio. We'll do some horseback riding, lie in the sun——"

"Perry, I may be convicted to-morrow."

Mason grinned. "You forget those two women on the jury who know cats."

"Aren't you going to explain any more to the jury?"

"Not a bit."

"Why?"

"Because if I did, I'd be explaining to Hamilton Burger. I'm going to let him fry in his own grease."

"What will Lieutenant Tragg do?"

"Eventually," Mason said, "Tragg will solve the case."

"But won't it take the jury a long while to get the whole idea through its head?"

Mason said, "Now that's something that would be a sporting bet. I'll bet you five dollars that jury will be out for at least three hours. It'll come in with a verdict of not guilty, but it'll be a dazed sort of jury, with two triumphant women smiling at you, and the men scowling. Then we'll start out for the desert, and Hamilton Burger will start talking with the jurors, trying to find out what it was about the kitten that broke the case. Then he'll try to get in touch with me, and we'll be out in the desert somewhere. Let's forget it and dance."

TWENTY-FIVE

THE BIG CAR purred smoothly out through the velvety darkness. As only in the desert, the stars, stretching in a vast, arching sweep, were no less brilliant over the clear horizon than they were directly overhead.

Mason said abruptly, "Let's pull off to the side of the road and soak it up, Della. It's an incomprehensible spectacle—makes you forget this strange human biped who commits murder."

They came to a wide place in the road. Mason drew off, switched off his ignition, cut off the headlights, settled down into the cushions.

"I love the desert," Mason said after a little while.

Della Street snuggled close. "We supposed to be working on this trip?" she asked.

"Uh huh. I've brought that brief along with me. We won't go back to the office until we've finished it."

She said, "Well, I owe you five dollars. It took that jury three hours and ten minutes to the dot. Chief, *I* know about the kitten, but what else happened?"

Mason said, "The kitten jumped up on the bed which was supposed to have been occupied by Franklin Shore; then it jumped down and went into the other bedroom and curled up in the middle of the bed which was supposed *not* to have been occupied by Tom Lunk. The kitten proves Lunk was a liar. The bed in the back bedroom hadn't been slept in, and was cold. The bed in the front bedroom had been occupied and was warm.

"I don't know whether you've ever thought about it, Della, but if a man has some hiding-place which he thinks is safe, he naturally hides everything there. For some time Lunk had been putting the money he collected for playing his part in the game into the flour-bin—a typical hiding-place for a crusty old bachelor. Then when he had to hide the gun quickly, he naturally hid it in the same place."

"Why did he have to hide the gun?"

"Because, dope, after he got to bed, Mrs. Shore telephoned him from the hospital and told him to rush out to the house, crawl in through the window, and get the gun out of the desk. She suddenly realized that the police were going to search the place. It's a wonder they hadn't found it when they made the first search, but at that time Tragg was concentrating on the medicine cabinet and looking for poison."

"I wish you'd tell me the whole story."

Mason said, "Somebody poisoned the kitten. It was an inside job. The kitten hadn't been out of the house. Komo *might* have done it, but he had no motive. The reason suggested by Lunk that he was trying out the poison was cockeyed because the kitten had been given such a large dose.

"You can figure out what happened. Mrs. Shore had a telephone call in the afternoon. After that call, she decided the time had come to commit the murder she'd planned so long and so carefully. She was tired of paying blackmail. She had to get Helen out of the house for some length of time, so Helen wouldn't know she was away from home. She knew that if she could poison the cat, Helen would dash madly to a veterinary hospital. Gerald came in unexpectedly, but he went along with Helen, of course. Then she sent Komo out to get some stout. With the coast clear, she took Franklin Shore's old gun, got into the car, and went up to the reservoir above Hollywood where Leech was waiting by appointment to collect another instalment of blackmail. She paid the last instalment with a .38 calibre bullet, came back, put the gun in the desk. She realized that suspicion *might* attach itself to her, so she poisoned the stout in the ice-box, pretended she had symptoms of poisoning, and was rushed to a hospital. That helped direct suspicion even more toward Franklin Shore. It didn't occur to her until after Tragg showed up that the police would make a thorough search of the house. She realized then that they'd find the gun. Police had her sewed up in the hospital, so she rushed through a telephone call to Lunk, and told him to go out and get the gun.

"Lunk was her accomplice. She'd groomed and trained him carefully in the details of what he had to do. All she had to do that afternoon was ring him up after she heard from Leech and tell him to go ahead."

Della objected, "But I thought Franklin Shore hadn't told Matilda or anyone about Helen's getting tight on the punch or rescuing the—"

Mason laughed. "Lunk, pretending to be Franklin Shore on the telephone, told Helen he hadn't said anything to Matilda."

Della said, "Well, I'll be——So Lunk came up to the house to get the gun—and shot to keep from being caught doing it."

"Yes. He crawled through the window, upset a night-stand, and thinking fast—no fool, Lunk—tried to cover up by making sounds as though Mrs. Shore were walking across the room. He hobbled over to the desk, got the gun, and was just getting over toward the window when Jerry Templar opened the door and started to switch on the light. He fired a couple of shots, dropped to the ground, and then beat it back to his shack, probably in his car.

"He was lying about not having gone to bed. He had been in bed when Matilda telephoned. When he went back to the shack, he hid the gun in the flour. Then he turned down the bed in the back bedroom, lay in it long enough to wrinkle the sheets, planted the cigar-butt, then dumped the things out of the bureau drawer, and out of the closet. He took a street-car to go back to the Shore house, hoping the police would pick him up and question him. Reluctantly he'd tell the story Matilda had cooked up about Franklin Shore turning up at his shack. The police would high tail it over there, and find all the planted evidence that Shore *had* been there but had flown the coop after robbing Lunk. Of course, Lunk never expected they'd search the flour-bin. That was his own particular secret hiding-place . . . and they wouldn't have searched it either if it hadn't been for me."

"How do you *know* all this?" she asked.

"The kitten's actions show conclusively that the bed in the front room was warm. The one in the back room wasn't. That is the key clue to the whole business. Lunk got up out of bed. The bed was warm. The kitten climbed into that bed. Lunk came back to hide the gun and the kitten got in the flour, was chased out, went to the bed in the back bedroom, jumped up on it, found it was cold, remembered the warm bed in the front room where it had previously been lying, and went back there to crawl up and go to sleep. Lunk went out with his carefully prepared story for the police, expecting to run into them at the Shore residence. You picked him up instead. He wasn't particularly anxious to tell his story to us because he wanted to tell it to the police; yet he had to *pretend* that he didn't want to have anything to do with the police. He was afraid I wouldn't pass it on to the police fast enough, so the minute he was free to do so, he gave an anonymous tip to Lieutenant Tragg over the telephone which resulted in his being picked up.

"Matilda had it planned out to kill a lot of birds with that one .38 slug by making it appear that her husband was still alive and had done the job. Incidentally, his being alive—and of course the police would never be able to find him—would keep Gerald Shore and Helen from proving the estate, keep Helen from becoming financially independent, and save forty thousand dollars in legacies."

"But why did she have Lunk telephone *Helen?*"

"Don't you see? That's the significant part of the whole business. Helen was the only one who really couldn't have recognized Franklin Shore's voice. She was only fourteen when he left. There's a great difference between fourteen and twenty-four. Lunk could deceive her, where his voice probably would not have deceived Gerald."

"What about Franklin's personal belongings in the car beside Leech?"

"Matilda got out some of her husband's old things and wrapped them up in one of his handkerchiefs and took them out with her. The laundry mark was a giveaway. Franklin Shore *wouldn't have carried the same handkerchief for ten years.* The fact that the watch was wound up at about four-thirty shows that that was when Matilda got things ready to go out on her little hunting trip. People don't wind watches at four in the afternoon. It's so plain it stands out like a sore thumb.

"You know, Della, she might have got away with it if it hadn't been for Amber Eyes. It was shrewdly worked out. She did one stupid thing, though."

"What?"

"That note, supposedly from Leech, directing us out to the reservoir that she mailed on the way back from the murder. She wrote it as a Jap would, trying to pull Komo in as a red herring to confuse the trail. That wasn't very smart."

"But why was Leech blackmailing her?"

"He found out the truth."

"What truth?"

"Remember the body that was found at about the time Franklin Shore disappeared—the unidentified body?"

"You mean that was Franklin Shore? Why, Chief, that's impossible. That . . ."

"No, it wasn't Franklin Shore. It was Phil Lunk."

"Phil Lunk?" Della gasped.

"You see, Matilda Shore didn't love her husband. What's more he was about to ruin the man she did love. If Matilda could get Franklin out of the way, she would inherit his fortune and be in a position to indulge her lust for power; she could save Stephen Alber financially, and, later on, marry him. Our friend Lunk was her man Friday from the beginning. His brother was dying. They knew that his death was only a matter of days—perhaps hours. Matilda laid her plans with that in mind. When he died, the doctor who had been in attendance came in response to Tom Lunk's call, and quite properly filled out a death certificate. But the body the undertaker picked up was that of Franklin Shore who had previously been given a dose of quick-acting poison. His body was waiting—probably outside in Lunk's car, all ready for a quick switch. After disposing of his brother's body, Lunk whisked Shore's body off to the East to bury in place of his brother, and later lied about the time he'd left, saying it was *before* Shore's disappearance."

"But he had a mother in the East. Wouldn't she have known it wasn't the brother Phil?"

Mason grinned. "You're still believing everything Lunk told you! I'll bet you that five bucks I won from you to-day that when Tragg investigates, he'll find Lunk never had lived in the place to which the body was taken for burial. Now here's another clue. George Alber went to Lunk's shack about midnight. Lights were on, but there was no sound from the inside. Lunk says he was listening to the radio before Franklin Shore came. If that had been true, Alber would have heard either voices or the radio."

"But how about that post card from Florida?"

"That post card is really as much of a giveaway as what the kitten did," Mason said.

"How?"

"Don't you see? Because it was written in the winter of 1931, not the spring of 1932."

"How can you tell?"

"He said he was enjoying the mild climate," Mason said. "Florida has a good summer climate; but people don't talk about enjoying a *mild* climate except in winter. Then he says, 'believe it or not,' he's enjoying the swimming. He certainly wouldn't have said that if he'd been writing from Florida in the summer, because then there wouldn't have been any *'believe it or not'* about enjoying the swimming."

"But the card was postmarked in June of 1932."

"Sure, it was," Mason said. "But there was no date on the card, only on the postmark. People seldom date picture post cards. Don't you see? There's only one explanation. It was a card he'd written Helen when he and Matilda Shore had been visiting there the winter before. He'd probably slipped it in the pocket of one of his suits and had forgotten to mail it. Matilda found it when she was cleaning out his closet soon after his disappearance. It gave her a chance to ring in an artistic touch to the whole case. So six months after the 'disappearance' Helen gets a card mailed from Florida. I don't know how Matilda got it mailed, but it could have been done in any number of ways. Too, that gave her a chance to concoct this story of the mysterious double, which would confuse the police even more when she wanted to arrange for a 'reappearance' and make it seem that Franklin Shore had really killed Leech." Mason sucked in a prodigious yawn. "I'm getting sleepy."

Della Street said, "I think you're the most baffling and most exasperating individual I've ever known."

"What's wrong now?"

She said, "All these clues are so plain once you explain them. That's what makes it so particularly exasperating. They're so *very, very* plain. The answer is obvious, once you really look at them properly arranged. But somehow I can't ever arrange them and interpret them."

Mason said, "But it's all there. The kitten jumping on to the warm bed, the handkerchief with a laundry mark ten years old, the watch that was wound at four o'clock in the afternoon—a time when no person would normally wind a watch. The post card sent in summer, but obviously written in winter . . ."

"And you're not going to help Hamilton Burger figure this out?"

"Not a bit of it. Let him fry."

"Are you going to let her get away with this, and . . ."

"She won't get away with it," Mason said. "Tragg will eventually figure it out. He probably has the kitten angle straight already. He'll go digging up the body of Phil Lunk, and find it's really that of Franklin Shore. He'll begin to wonder who could have driven the car that struck down Tom Lunk, and will reason it out that it must have been the person who had killed Leech, trying to silence the lips of a man who might talk too much. And you have to hand it to Lunk. He played that most deadly efficient of all parts—that of a witness who is smart, but pretends to be stupid. His lying about Franklin Shore's visit was a masterpiece. But that, of course, is one of the things an investigator has to remember. A murderer will naturally lie, and a person who is clever enough to work out an ingenious murder plan will be clever enough to work out an ingenious lie. Matilda had, of course, helped him. They'd worked that all out in detail. But if it hadn't been for that kitten, they'd have fooled us—for a while, anyway.

"And believe me, darling, the next time I get in on a case, Hamilton Burger and Tragg won't tell me the proper place for me is in my office waiting for clues to turn up. They're going to be in a hot, hot spot for some time now, and when they finally do get it solved, they'll realize I had the answers all along."

Della Street confessed, "Well, I'll tell you one thing. You had *me* scared."

"Afraid you were going to get convicted?"

"I . . . I didn't know. It seemed so darn hopeless when I saw all that circumstantial evidence piling up."

Mason took one hand from the steering-wheel to slip round her shoulders. "My dear, you should always have confidence in your lawyer," he told her gravely.

THE CASE OF THE
FIERY FINGERS

THE CASE OF THE FIERY FINGERS

Poker-faced Nellie Conway, who nurses bedridden Elizabeth Bain, brings trouble when she calls on Perry Mason with a glass phial containing four pills which she suspects are poison. Her employer, Nathan Bain, she says, had promised her money to give them to his wife. Perry Mason has them analysed and finds they consist of good old-fashioned aspirin! But when Bain accuses Nellie of theft and provides proof by ultra-violet light, the case which began like a hoax becomes suddenly sinister, and Perry is in it up to the neck.

Foreword

In all the earth there is probably no mental occupation quite as fascinating as that of finding clues and then accounting for them, which is all that detective work really is and about all that astronomy really is.

A detective, for instance, finds the head of an unburnt match broken off and lying by itself on the floor at the scene of a murder. Is it a clue or is it just one more bit of trivia?

Perhaps he will deduce that the murderer was given to the habit of snapping matches into flame with his thumbnail, that this particular match was slightly defective and therefore the head broke off in place of snapping into flame.

Then when the murderer is apprehended the detective will find out that the man simply wanted a small stick with which he could push a key out of the lock in a door, and had broken the head off a match and used the matchstick to fulfil his purpose.

And so it goes. Whenever a man feels that he has an explanation to account for some physical clue he is only too likely to find that his conclusions, while brilliant and logical, are completely incorrect.

But if these clues happen to have been discovered by an officer of the Massachusetts State Police there isn't much possibility of a brilliant but erroneous deduction.

Because such clues are sent to the laboratory of Doctor Joseph T. Walker, scientist, toxicologist and general all-around technical detective, who has an uncanny ability to separate mental wheat from imaginative chaff, the answers given are the right ones.

Let a discarded coat be picked up along one of the Massachusetts highways by a casual pedestrian who happens to notice what seems to be a bloodstain, and watch what happens.

Doctor Walker's piercing eyes make an examination which is different from the ordinary examination because he knows of a dozen things to look for, things that never would occur to the ordinary man.

That little hole, for instance, may seem to be of minor significance until by photographing it in infra-red light he brings out powder stains proving that it is a bullet hole. By using soft X-rays he will find bits of metallic fragments in the garment, and by a spectro-analysis of those fragments will name the manufacturer of the bullet in question.

Or perhaps that peculiar imprint which is visible only under a certain angle of transverse lighting will, when properly photographed, assume the form of a perfect circle indicating that the wearer of the coat may have been struck by a hit-and-run driver. The headlight of the offending automobile left its circular imprint in the garment, whereupon a microscopic examination is quite likely to bring out little slivers of glass, some of which may be distinctive enough to furnish an important clue.

A further microscopic examination of the threads of the garment may disclose a flake-like substance no bigger than the head of a pin, which Doctor Walker will turn on edge, and examine under a powerful microscope. He will then announce that this is a small chip or flake of paint peeled off from an automobile driven by the hit-and-run culprit. The automobile, he will announce, was first painted a robin's-egg blue when it came from the factory, it was next painted a conservative black, then covered with a neutral tan and is now a vivid red.

I have watched Doctor Walker at work in his laboratory. I have peered over his shoulder while he has discovered things that the average man would never even look for, and then has translated those things into clues which, properly evaluated, have on countless occasions led to the apprehension and conviction of a criminal.

I first became acquainted with Doctor Walker at one of Captain Frances G. Lee's seminars on homicide investigation at the Harvard Medical School. I have since had occasion to drop into his laboratory several times. Every time I do so, I find him engaged in some fascinating crime problem where his common sense, his uncanny keenness of mind and his marvellous technical training bring forth logical but unexpected conclusions, just as a magician reaches into an unpromising silk hat and brings forth a very live, very convincing, and very substantial rabbit.

Of course, the rabbit was there all the time, and from the viewpoint of the magician the silk hat was the logical place to look for it.

I know of many cases where Doctor Walker's mind, following physical clues as a bloodhound follows scent, has brought murderers to justice, and I know of some cases where the same mental qualities have been used to prevent innocent men from being unjustly convicted.

Quietly, modestly, unobtrusively, Doctor Walker goes to his work day after day, dedicating his life to the cause of practical justice.

Society needs more men like Doctor Joseph T. Walker. The time and money, spent in the highly technical training such men must have to become thoroughly competent, represents a profitable investment on the part of organised society.

But there is more than mere technical training that makes Joe Walker the man that he is. He has an unswerving loyalty to his ideals, a quiet courage, an inherent faith.

And so I dedicate this book to a competent scientist, a true friend, and a man whose pattern of life is a source of inspiration to those who are familiar with it,

DOCTOR JOSEPH T. WALKER.

Erle Stanley Gardner

ONE

PERRY MASON HAD just returned to the office after a long day in court. Della Street, his secretary, pushed a stack of half a dozen letters on his desk and said, "These are ready for you to sign, and before you go home there's one client in the office whom you should see. I told her I thought you'd see her if she'd wait."

"How long's she been waiting?" Mason asked, picking up the desk pen and starting to skim through the letters which Della Street had typed out for his signature.

"Over an hour."

"What's her name?"

"Nellie Conway."

Mason signed the first letter, Della Street efficiently blotted the signature, picked the letter up, folded it and slipped it in the envelope.

"What does she want?" Mason asked.

"She won't tell me, but she says it's an urgent matter."

Mason frowned, signed the second letter, and said, "It's late, Della. I've been in court all day and . . ."

"This girl's in trouble," Della Street said with quiet insistence.

Mason signed the next letter. "What does she look like?"

"Thirty-two or thirty-three, slender, dark hair, grey eyes, and the most perfect poker face you have ever seen."

"No expression?"

"Wooden."

"How do you know she's in trouble?"

"Just the way she acts. There's a peculiar tension about her and yet her face doesn't show it."

"Any signs of nervousness?"

"Nothing outward. She drops into a chair, sits in one position without moving her hands or her feet, her face is absolutely expressionless, her eyes move a little bit, but that's all. She doesn't read, she just sits there."

"But not relaxed?" Mason asked.

"Just like a cat sitting at a gopher hole waiting for the gopher to come out. Not a move that you can see, but you have the feeling of inner tension—waiting."

"You interest me," Mason said.

"I thought I would," Della Street said demurely.

Mason abruptly signed the rest of the letters in the pile of mail without even bothering to glance at them.

"All right, Della, let's get her in. I'll have a look at her."

Della Street took the mail, nodded, stepped out into the outer office and returned shortly with the client.

"Nellie Conway, Mr. Mason," she said crisply.

Mason motioned the woman to a seat in the soft, comfortable chair which he had installed in the office so that by lulling clients into complete physical relaxation he might relieve their emotional tension and so loosen their tongues.

Nellie Conway disregarded the motion and took one of the less comfortable wooden chairs, moving with a gliding silence as though she had trained herself to make no unnecessary sound.

"Good afternoon, Mr. Mason. Thank you for seeing me. I've heard a lot about you. I was hoping you'd get in earlier. I'm going to have to hurry because I have to be on duty at six o'clock."

"You work nights?"

"I'm a nurse."

"A trained nurse?"

"A practical nurse. I work on cases where the people can't afford hospitalisation or trained nurses. We work longer hours and, of course, we do things a trained nurse won't do, and we get less money."

Mason nodded.

Nellie Conway turned to fasten steady grey eyes on Della Street.

Mason said, "Miss Street is my confidential secretary. She will sit through the interview and make notes, if you don't mind. She has to know as much about my business as I do in order to keep things co-ordinated here in the office. Now, what did you want to see me about?"

Nellie Conway folded gloved hands, turned her triangular face towards Perry Mason and, without the faintest flicker of expression in voice or eyes, said, "Mr. Mason, how does one go about preventing a murder from being committed?"

Mason frowned. "I wouldn't know."

"I'm serious."

Mason regarded her with searching eyes, then said, "All right. This is out of my line. I specialise in defending people who are accused of crime and I try to see that my clients at least get an even break, but if you *really* want to know how to go about preventing a murder I would say there are four ways."

"What are they?"

Mason held up his hand and checked off the four ways on his fingers. "One," he said, "you remove the victim, or the potential victim, from the danger zone."

She nodded.

"Two," Mason said, "you remove the murderer, or the potential murderer from the place where he can have any contact with the victim."

Again she nodded.

"Three," Mason said, "you remove all weapons of murder, which is pretty difficult to do."

"So far they've all been difficult," she said. "What's the fourth?"

"The fourth," Mason said, "is the easy one and the practical one."

"What is it?"

"You go to the police."

"I've been to the police."

"And what happened?"

"They laughed at me."

"Then why come to me?"

"I don't think you'll laugh."

Mason said, "I won't laugh, but I don't like abstractions. My time's valuable. Apparently you're in a hurry. I'm in a hurry. I don't like this business of having a client say, 'A wants to murder B.' Let's get down to brass tacks."

"How much are you going to charge me?"

Mason said, "That depends on how soon you quit beating about the bush."

"I'm a working woman. I don't make a great deal of money."

Mason said, "Therefore it's to your interest to have the charge as low as possible."

"That's right."

"So," Mason said, "you'd better tell me what this is all about, and talk fast."

"*Then* how much will you charge me?"

Mason regarded the wooden face across the desk. He glanced amusedly at Della Street. His eyes turned back to his client and softened into a smile. "One dollar," he said, "for advice, if you've told your story within the next four minutes."

There was not the faintest sign of surprise in her face. She repeated merely, "One dollar?"

"That's right."

"Isn't that unusually low?"

Mason winked at Della Street. "What's your standard of comparison?"

She opened her purse, her gloved hands took out a coin purse. She opened it, selected a folded dollar note, smoothed it out and put it on the desk.

Mason didn't touch it. His eyes kept regarding her with puzzled curiosity.

She closed the coin purse, put it back in her bag, snapped the bag shut, put the bag on her lap, folded her gloved hands on the bag and said, "I think Mr. Bain wants to murder his wife. I'd like to prevent it."

"Who's Mr. Bain?"

"Nathan Bain. He's in the produce business. You may know him."

"I don't. Who's his wife?"

"Elizabeth Bain."

"How do you know all this?"

"By using my powers of observation."

"You're living in the house?"

"Yes."

"Waiting on someone?"

"Yes. Mrs. Bain. Elizabeth Bain."

"What's the matter with her?"

"She was hurt in an automobile accident."

"Bad?"

"I'm afraid worse than she realises. There's been an injury to the spine."

"Can she walk?"

"No, and she isn't ever going to walk again."

"Go ahead," Mason said.

"That's all."

Mason's face showed annoyance. "No, that isn't all," he said. "You think that he wants to murder her. You aren't a mind reader, are you?"

"Sometimes," was the unexpected answer, delivered in a calm voice.

"And you're getting this from reading his mind?"

"Well, not exactly."

"There are other things?"

"Yes."

"What are they?"

She said, "Nathan Bain wants to marry someone else."

"How old is he?"

"Thirty-eight."

"How old's his wife?"

"Thirty-two."

"How old's the girl he wants to marry?"

"About twenty-five."

"Does she want to marry him?"

"I don't know."

"Who is she?"

"Some woman who has an apartment in the city. I don't know exactly where."

"What's her name?"

"Her first name's Charlotte. I don't know the last name."

Mason said irritably, "I'm having to draw it out of you like pulling teeth. How do you know he wants to get married?"

"Because he's in love with this woman."

"How do you know?"

"They correspond. He met her at a convention. He loves her."

"All right," Mason said, "so what? Lots of healthy men thirty-eight years of age have restless eyes and a roving disposition. It's a dangerous age. They come back home if you leave them alone. Sometimes they don't. There are lots of divorces, but there aren't many murders."

Nellie Conway opened her purse. "Mr. Bain offered me five hundred dollars if I would give his wife some medicine."

Mason cocked a quizzical and somewhat sceptical eyebrow. "You're certain of what you're saying, Miss Conway?"

"Absolutely certain. I have the medicine here."

"Why did he say he wanted you to give it to his wife?"

"He didn't say. He just said that he thought that this medicine would be good for her. He doesn't like his wife's doctor."

"Why not?"

"The doctor was an old friend of Elizabeth's."

"You mean Bain is jealous?"

"I think so."

"Look," Mason said irritably, "all of this doesn't make sense. If Bain wants his wife out of the way he'd much rather have her divorce him and marry the doctor than to try and get rid of her by giving her poison. If he wanted to—let's take a look at this 'medicine'."

Without a word she handed him a small glass tube which contained four tablets about the size of a standard five-grain aspirin tablet.

"Were you to give these to her all at once?"

"Yes, at bedtime—when she was being quieted for the night."

"Did he pay you the money?"

"He said he'd pay me the money when I'd given her the medicine."

"How was he going to know if you gave it to her?"

"I don't know. I guess he trusts me. I wouldn't lie."

"Not to him?"

"Not to anyone. I don't believe in lying. It weakens your character."

"Why didn't *he* give her this medicine?"

"He can't go in the room with her."

"Why not?"

"The doctor has said he couldn't."

"You mean a doctor tells a husband he can't go in the room where . . . ?"

"Elizabeth hates the sight of him. She gets upset, almost hysterical every time she sees his face. We're forbidden even to mention his name."

"Why does she feel that way?"

"I think she really knows she'll never walk again. Mr. Bain was driving the car when the accident happened. She thinks it was avoidable."

"You mean that he deliberately tried to . . . ?"

"Don't put words in my mouth, Mr. Mason. I said she thinks the accident was avoidable."

Mason's facial expression was a combination of exasperation and curiosity.

"I gather you don't like Mr. Bain?"

"He's a very strong, fascinating man. I do like him, very much."

"Does he like you?"

"I'm afraid not."

"So," Mason said, "he comes to you and offers to pay you five hundred dollars to give his wife poison, thereby putting himself entirely in your power, leaving a witness who could testify in case anything did happen to his wife. . . . It doesn't make sense. . . . How do you know it's poison?"

"I just *feel* that it is."

"You don't know what the medicine is?"

"No."

"Did he tell you what it was?"

"No, just that it was medicine."

"Why did he tell you he wanted you to give it to his wife?"

"He said he thought it would make her feel better towards him."

"This whole thing is screwy," Mason said.

She said nothing.

"And you went to the police?"

"Yes."

"To whom did you go?"

"I went to the police station and told them I wanted to see about a murder, and they sent me to a room that had a sign on the door saying 'Homicide.' "

"And what did you do?" Mason asked curiously.

"I told someone my story and he laughed at me."

"Do you remember his name?"

"His name was Holcomb, he was a sergeant."

"Did you show him this bottle?"

"No."

"Why not?"

"I never got that far."

"What happened?"

"I told him, just as I've told you, that I thought Mr. Bain wanted to murder his wife, and I tried to tell Sergeant Holcomb why, but he laughed at me. He was in a big hurry. He had to go some place and he said . . . well, he said an unkind thing."

"What did he say?"

"He said I was neurotic, but I'm not."

"When did Mr. Bain give you this medicine?"

"Yesterday."

"Did you tell him you'd give it to his wife?"

"I made him think that I might."

"And you've been carrying that little bottle around in your purse ever since?"

"Yes."

"Taking it out from time to time when you wanted to get at something that was underneath?"

"I suppose so."

"In other words," Mason said, "there aren't any of his finger-prints left on that bottle by this time?"

"I don't suppose so."

Mason took the bottle, removed the cork, looked down at the contents, then spread out a sheet of paper and dumped all four of the tablets on the table. As far as the eye could determine, they were all identical. Mason picked out one of the tablets, returned the other three to the little tube.

He said, "Della, get me two plain envelopes, please."

Della Street opened the drawer of her secretarial desk, took out two envelopes and gave them to Mason.

Mason took the tablet he had taken from the tube, put it in an envelope, sealed the envelope, wrote his name across the flap, then took the tube containing the three tablets, placed it in the second envelope, sealed the flap, wrote his name across that flap and said to Nellie Conway, "Write your name across the flap so that part of the name is below the sealed flap and part of it is on the flap, just as I've done."

She took the pen and wrote the name as he had instructed.

"What's Bain's address?" Mason asked.

"Nineteen-twenty-five Monte Carlo Drive."

"You go on duty at six o'clock?"

"That's right."

"How late do you work?"

"Until eight in the morning."

"Then what happens?"

"A day nurse comes on."

"You have the longer shift?"

"Because the night nurse doesn't have so much to do."

"Why does she need a night nurse? Doesn't she sleep at night? In other words, couldn't the nurse be within call——"

"Mrs. Bain is a little difficult to manage at times."

"Why?"

"Well, her mind is upset. She's been worrying a lot, and . . . well, the fact she won't let her husband in the room . . . the doctor wants a nurse with her all the time. Expense doesn't mean anything to them."

"Who has the money?"

"She does."

"Bain is in the produce business?"

"He makes a living," she said, "but Mrs. Bain has the money. It's her separate property. She inherited it. She had it when she was married. That's why he married her."

"Does Mrs. Bain know about this other woman?" Mason asked.

"Of course. That's where I first got my information."

"From Mrs. Bain?"

"Yes."

"How long ago was this accident?"

"Somewhere around a month. She was at the hospital for ten days, then she came home."

"You've been working there ever since?"

"Yes."

"Who else is working there?"

"The day nurse."

"She's been on about as long as you have?"

"Yes."

"Who else?"

"A housekeeper."

"What's her name?"

"Imogene Ricker."

"How long's she been working there?"

"Oh, she's been working there a long time. She's very devoted to Mr. Bain."

"Does Mrs. Bain like her?"

"Oh, yes."

"And she goes into Mrs. Bain's room?"

"Certainly. Sometimes she takes spells for us nurses."

"How old is she?"

"Oh, I don't know. I'd say somewhere in the late thirties. One of those peculiar, shadowy women who seems to be everywhere and nowhere. You never know where she's going to turn up. She gives me the creeps, Mr. Mason. You've seen these cartoons of the haunted house with that thin woman sitting there with the dark eyes and the inscrutable expression? Well, she's just like that."

"The point I'm getting at," Mason said impatiently, "is whether Mr. Bain trusts her."

"Oh, I think Mr. Bain trusts her implicitly. She's been working for him for years. She worked for his first wife, and after his first wife died, well, then she kept right on as Mr. Bain's housekeeper——"

"How long ago did his first wife die?"

"I don't know exactly. He's been married to Elizabeth Bain a little over two years, I think, or right around two years, and I guess he was a widower for three years. Well, that would make his . . . I don't know, somewhere around five or six years. Why?"

Mason said, "Has it ever impressed you as being exceedingly improbable, young lady, that with a housekeeper in the house whom Mr. Bain had known for at least three years, and perhaps considerably longer, he'd pick on you, a total stranger, and out of a clear sky offer you five hundred dollars to poison his wife?"

"Yes," she said. "It's occurred to me as being unusual."

"Unusual," Mason said, "is a very, very mild designation. He gets along with the housckeeper all right?"

"Why, of course. They very seldom speak. She's quite taciturn."

"Any romantic attachment?"

"Heavens, no. She's angular, with deep-set, dark eyes——"

"So there's no reason for Mrs. Bain to be jealous of her?"

"Don't be silly, Mr. Mason. That housekeeper has no more sex than . . . than an angleworm."

"So the housekeeper could go into the room at any time and give Mrs. Bain medicine?"

"Why, certainly. I told you she helps out with the nursing when we want to get a few minutes off."

"Then *why* should Mr. Bain pick on you?"

"I don't know, Mr. Mason. I'm only telling you facts."

Mason shook his head. "It's all screwy. I'll get in touch with Sergeant Holcomb at Homicide and get his reaction. You keep the envelope with the medicine in it. I want to keep this one pill. I may get in touch with you later on. There's a telephone out there?"

"Yes."

"Is it all right to call you there?"

"Oh, yes."

"What's the number?"

"West 6-9841."

"Well," Mason said, "my advice to you is to keep those pills for evidence, not to commit yourself in talking with Mr. Bain, and let me talk with Sergeant Holcomb. If he wants to investigate, he can."

"He doesn't. He thinks I'm crazy."

"Your story has certain elements of improbability," Mason said dryly.

"Could I call you later on tonight?" she asked.

"Not very well."

"I have a feeling something may happen, Mr. Mason, when I go back there. Mr. Bain is going to ask me if I gave his wife the medicine and . . . well, if I tell him I didn't, he's going to get angry and suspicious."

"Then tell him you did."

"He'll know that I didn't."

"Why?"

"Because his wife is still alive."

Mason said, "I don't get this thing. It's a completely cockeyed story, it doesn't make sense any way you look at it. Yet somehow you seem to be completely convinced."

"Of course I am convinced, Mr. Mason."

Mason said, "I tell you what I'll do. I'll give you the number of the Drake Detective Agency."

"What's that?"

"They have offices on this floor," Mason said. "They do most of my detective work. I'll arrange to keep in touch with the Drake Detective Agency, and if anything of importance should develop, you can call there. They'll know where to reach me."

"Thank you, Mr. Mason."

Della Street wrote the number of the Drake Detective Agency on a card, arose from her secretarial desk and moved over to hand the card to Nellie Conway.

"Are they open at night?"

"Yes, they're open twenty-four hours a day," Della Street said.

"And you'll speak to them about me, so that I——?"

"I'll speak to them about you," Mason said, and glanced at his wrist watch.

"Thank you very much, Mr. Mason."

She arose from her chair, stopped and regarded the dollar note on the desk. "Do I get a receipt?"

Suddenly Mason's eyes narrowed. "I wouldn't try to charge you twice."

"I'd like a receipt. I'm very methodical in my bookkeeping."

Mason nodded to Della Street. "Make it for consultation, Della."

Della Street slipped a printed billhead into her typewriter, moved swift fingers over the keyboard, then handed the typewritten statement to Mason. Mason signed it, handed it across to Nellie Conway and said, "Here you are, Miss Conway, or is it Mrs. Conway?"

"Miss."

"All right. Here's your receipt. Now we have your dollar and you have the receipt and you will perhaps hear from me again."

"Thank you, Mr. Mason. Good-night to both of you."

She turned and walked with that strange gliding motion back across the office.

"You can go out this way," Della Street said, arising swiftly and escorting her out of the exit door that opened into the corridor.

When the door had clicked shut Della Street raised her eyebrows in a silent question at Perry Mason.

The lawyer was sitting at the desk, his face granite hard, his eyes level-lidded with thought.

"Well?" Della Street asked.

Mason said, "What a set-up! What a plan!"

"How do you mean?"

Mason said, "It was all right. I was just riding along, half-asleep at the switch, until she asked for the receipt. That did it."

"I'm afraid I don't get it. I . . . Whatever possessed you to only charge her a dollar, Chief?"

Mason laughed. "I knew she was sitting there expecting me to say ten dollars or twenty-five dollars, and then going to try to argue me into taking half of whatever figure I set, so I thought I'd trick some expression into her face by surprising her to death. I wish now I'd said a hundred dollars and got her out of here."

"Why?"

"Because I don't want to have anything to do with her," Mason said. "We're in a mess."

"I don't get it."

"Look," Mason said, "suppose something does happen to Mrs. Bain. See how the little minx has fixed things? Consider the position she's put us in. She's been to Homicide Squad. She's consulted me. She has my receipted bill to prove it. We all think she's a little screwy. We pass her off as one of these psychopathic screwballs and . . . Get me police headquarters. Let's see if we can get Sergeant Holcomb on the phone."

"You know he hates the ground you walk on, Chief."

"I don't feel too overly cordial toward him," Mason said, "but I want to try and verify that story, and I want to get myself on record as having tried to get Holcomb to do something. We'll steal a page from Nellie Conway's book and pass the buck."

"I get you," Della said, smiling. She moved over to the telephone, looked at her watch and said, "It's five-thirty. He's probably gone home."

"We'll try him anyway, and if he isn't there we'll talk to somebody in charge. Perhaps it would be better to get Lieutenant Tragg. Lieutenant Tragg has sense."

"Tragg likes you. He'd be more apt to listen. . . ."

"I don't care about whether anyone listens," Mason said, "I want to get my skirts clean. I don't like the smell of this. I don't like any part of it, and the more I think of it the less I like it."

Della Street tried for the outer switchboard and said, "I guess Gertie's gone home, Chief."

"Get him on my private line," Mason said.

Della dialled a number, then said, "I want Homicide Squad, please . . . Homicide Squad? This is Mr. Mason's office. Mr. Mason would like to talk with Lieutenant Tragg if he's there, or with Sergeant Holcomb if he . . . Will you put him on, please? . . . Yes, Mr. Mason is right here . . . Yes, I'll put him on the line."

She handed the telephone to Mason, saying, "Sergeant Holcomb."

Mason put the phone to his ear. "Hello . . . Hello . . . Holcomb?"

Holcomb's voice was uncordial. "Hello, Mason, what is it this time? Got a corpse?"

"I don't know," Mason said. "Did a woman see you some time today? A Nellie Conway?"

"That nut!" Holcomb said.

"What did she want?"

"Hell, I don't know. She's nuts. She's talking about someone who wants to murder someone, and I asked her how she knew, and she said it was just an intuition or something of that sort, and I told her she was barking up the wrong tree, that she didn't have any evidence."

"What makes you think she didn't have any evidence?"

"She didn't, did she?"

"I don't think you heard her whole story."

"Hell, Mason, I haven't time to sit here all day and listen to a lot of psychos . . . Good Lord, I can show you a thousand screwball letters we get down here in the course of a month that——"

Mason said, "This woman is peculiar. That doesn't mean she——"

"The hell it doesn't!" Holcomb said. "She's crazy!"

"Well," Mason said, "she's been in here and tried to tell me her story. I thought I'd pass it on to you."

"Thanks," Holcomb said. "You've listened to her, you've telephoned me, you've passed the buck. Okay, so what?"

Mason said, "I just thought I'd tell you it's a situation I don't like."

Holcomb said, "There's lots of things we don't like. How do you feel about the income tax?"

"I love it," Mason said.

"Go to hell," Sergeant Holcomb told him.

"Now wait a minute," Mason cautioned. "This woman tells a peculiar story in a peculiar way. She says the husband of the woman she's nursing——"

"I know," Holcomb interrupted, "is in love with some other gal and wants his wife out of the way. So you ask her how she knows, and she says she's intuitive."

"And the husband wanted her to give his wife some medicine and——"

"Oh, nuts!" Holcomb interrupted. "I'll tell you what I think. I think this gal is trying to get the husband in bad because she wants to discredit him."

"That could be."

"I'll bet it is. Why should the husband give *her* medicine to give his wife?"

"She thinks it's poison."

"I see, so the husband calls in a nurse who doesn't like him and

makes her a witness who can crucify him . . . Now I'll tell you something else. I know something about the background of that case. This
guy she's working for is okay. The wife is hysterical, neurotic, and this
little tramp of a nurse is . . ."

"Yes?" Mason prompted as Holcomb hesitated.

"Well, I don't think I should tell you *all* I know. She's been to you
as a client?"

"Yes."

Holcomb laughed. "Well, Mason, I hope she makes you a profitable
client—lots of business," and Holcomb roared with laughter.

"Well," Mason said, "I've reported to you."

"That's right. You've passed the buck. Go to hell and good-bye!"

Sergeant Holcomb, still laughing, banged up the phone.

Mason's face darkened as he dropped the telephone back into its
cradle. "Damn Holcomb," he said. "He's getting smart. Now he accuses
me of trying to pass the buck."

"Well, what were you doing?" Della Street asked, a mischievous
twinkle in her eye.

Mason grinned. "Passing the buck. Why else would I call the guy?"

TWO

PAUL DRAKE, HEAD of the Drake Detective Agency, moved with a shambling gait which to the casual observer seemed slow and tedious, but actually there was a double-jointed suppleness about the man that enabled him to perform a prodigious amount of work and cover a great deal of ground without seeming ever to be in a hurry.

Perry Mason at times likened him to a juggler who would drop a plate and then, when it was hardly more than three inches from the floor, reach down and catch it before it crashed, with a motion so perfectly timed that it seemed to be almost leisurely.

Drake jack-knifed himself into the overstuffed chair, swung his knees up over the arm, clasped his hands behind his head and eyed Mason with a bored indifference that was completely deceptive.

"What's the pitch, Perry?"

"I'm up against just about the goofiest problem I've ever encountered in my whole career."

"What is it?"

"A woman came in with a proposition that sounded entirely screwy. She wanted to know how much my advice was going to cost her and, just for the hell of it, I told her a dollar."

"What happened?"

"She paid the dollar."

"It's better to charge a dollar and get it in cash than to make a charge of a hundred dollars and get beat out of it." Drake said, grinning. "What's the trouble with her case?"

"I wish I'd never seen her."

"Why don't you give her her dollar back and tell her you can't do anything for her?"

"That's just the point, Paul. That's what I *think* she wants me to do."

"Well, what do you care what *she* wants? Just so you wash your hands and get out of it."

"There are some things you can't wash your hands of," Mason said. "It isn't that easy."

"Why not?"

"She comes to me with a completely cockeyed story about a wife being in danger, about a husband who's trying to get her to poison the wife——"

"That's easy," Drake said. "Advise her to go to the police."

"She's been to the police, Paul."

"What did the police do?"

"Laughed at her and kicked her out."

"That should make a precedent for you. What's the complete story?"

Mason told him.

When he had finished Drake said, "What do you want me to do, Perry?"

Mason handed Paul Drake the envelope containing the pill he had taken from the bottle Nellie Conway had shown him. "Let's find out what it is, Paul. It *might* be cyanide of potassium. Then I'd ring up my friend, Sergeant Holcomb, and have him jumping around like a cat on a piece of fly-paper."

Drake grinned.

"The point is," Mason went on, "we have only one tablet. If we use it up in an analysis——"

Drake said, "It's a cinch, Perry. I have a friend who has access to a crime laboratory where they have one of these new X-ray defractors that uses X-rays and gets a graph from the molecular defraction of a substance. I don't know how it works. All I know is, it does the work. You can take an unknown powder and get a pretty good idea of what's in it in a very short time, and it only takes a microscopic amount of powder to do the job."

"Okay," Mason said. "I want to be sure and keep this tablet so there won't be any possibility of substitution or loss. I've had it in an envelope, sealed, and with my name on it. Now I'll give it to you. You put it in an envelope, seal it and put your name on it, keep it in your possession and——"

"And be prepared to swear that that's the tablet I got from you just as you can swear that's the tablet you got from Nellie Conway?"

"That's right. How much is it going to cost to have this thing given a quick test?" Mason asked.

Drake said, smiling, "Well, this man is broad-minded. He always takes into consideration the ability of a client to pay. I'll suggest to him that he wouldn't want to charge more than twenty-five per cent of the fee you're getting for the entire case, and that'll probably sound all right to him, and I guess two bits won't be too much for you to pay, eh, Perry?"

Mason made as if to throw a book at the detective and Drake dodged.

"Go on," Mason told him. "Get the hell out of here and go to work. How long will it take to tell what's in the pill?"

"I may be able to get it done in an hour."

"Tell you what we'll do, Paul. Della and I will go out and put on the nosebags, then we'll come back and look in on you and then I'll drive Della home."

"The way he talks," Della Street said, "you'd think a girl never had a date."

"I beg your pardon," Mason said. "What do you have on for this evening, Della?"

"Well," she said demurely, "now that you bring it up that way, I haven't anything that I can't cancel in favour of a nice thick steak done medium rare, a stuffed, baked Idaho potato with lots of butter, some toasted French bread, a bottle of Tipo Chianti and——"

"Stop it!" Drake said. "You're driving me nuts. I'm going to have to get by with a hamburger sandwich which I'll hold in one hand while I drink a cup of coffee with the other."

"Don't let it worry you, Paul," Mason said, grinning. "That's just what she wants. What she gets may be different. I'll take her to a Chinese place and get her a bowl of white rice. Come on, Della, let's eat."

Mason switched out the lights in the office and held the door open for Della. "Another day," he said.

Della Street held up the dollar note which Nellie Conway had given the lawyer, and said to Paul Drake, "And another dollar!"

THREE

AN HOUR AND a half later, Mason and Della Street, leaving the elevator, sauntered into Paul Drake's office, exchanged greetings with a girl at the night switchboard and then walked into Drake's private office.

"I haven't anything yet," Drake said. "I'm expecting something any moment."

"How much of the tablet did you use, Paul?"

"Not much. This guy had a smart idea. He had a hairlike drill and bored a little hole right in the centre so he could get a cross-section right straight through. He had some other stuff he had to find out about on a rush order so that's what's causing the delay. He . . ."

The telephone rang. Drake reached for the receiver and said, "This will probably be it."

Drake said, "Hello . . . Yes, this is Paul Drake . . . All right, go ahead."

Drake flashed Mason a warning glance, then said, "Well now, just a minute. Just hold the phone. I'll see if I have his number where he can be reached."

Drake pushed his hand against the mouthpiece and said, "This is your girl friend. She's all excited. She wants you right away. She says it's very, very important."

"Oh-oh!" Mason said. "This is it!"

"What do I do? Tell her . . . ?"

"No," Mason said. "Tell her I just came in, that you'll try to find me."

Drake said into the telephone, "Well, I don't know where he is right at the moment. I have a number where I can reach him later on. If you could . . . Oh, wait a minute, there's somebody in the other office now.

I think I hear Mason's voice . . . Oh, Mason! . . . Was that Mason who just came in? Well, tell him I want him . . . Yes, tell him there's a phone call for him."

Drake waited a couple of seconds, then said, "He just this moment came in. Just hold the line. I'll get him on the phone for you."

Drake nodded to Mason, who took the telephone from the detective and said, "Hello."

Nellie Conway's voice, sharp with excitement, reached his ears. "Oh, Mr. Mason, something terrible, absolutely terrible has happened! I must see you right away."

"Where?" Mason asked. "At my office?"

"No, no. I can't leave here. I'm not free to come. Please, can't you come out here right away? It's 1925 Monte Carlo Drive. I . . . oh . . . !"

With that sharp exclamation and with no word of good-bye, she dropped the receiver into place at the other end of the line, severing the connection.

Mason grinned at Paul Drake and said, "Well, I guess I was right, Paul."

"What?"

"It's a frame-up of some sort."

"So what do you do?" Drake asked.

"It isn't what I do," Mason said, "it's what we do. Come on, Della, you're going to drive out with us. We may call you in, in case we want to have someone make a statement."

"Don't you want me to wait for the call to find out what's in that tablet?" Drake asked.

"The tablet," Mason said, "will either be cyanide or arsenic. And in all probability Mrs. Bain has just died. Come on, Paul, we're going out and discover a corpse."

"And then what?"

"Then," Mason said, "I'll try to get myself extricated from a very nasty predicament. Nellie Conway will be proclaiming to all and sundry that she told me the whole story while Mrs. Bain was still alive. People will think I'm a hell of a lawyer."

"I don't get it," Drake said. "I simply can't see where all this is going to leave your client. It makes her look like . . . just what *is* her position, Perry?"

Mason said, "All this little byplay leaves Nellie Conway in a position where she can accuse the husband of having administered the poison while she had her back turned, since she had refused to help him. Don't you see, the girl's given herself a perfect alibi. She's gone to the police and tried to get them to prevent a murder that was about to be committed; she's come to me and tried to get me to try to prevent a murder that was about to be committed, and then the murder is committed. My poker-faced client has given herself a beautiful alibi, or at least she thinks she has."

"Perhaps she has at that," Drake said.

"By making a goat out of me," Mason said grimly. "Come on, let's go."

FOUR

DELLA STREET WHIPPED Mason's car around corners, swerved in and out of traffic, making fast time, seldom putting on the brake to slow down, seldom pushing down hard on the throttle, managing despite traffic to maintain a steady, even speed.

Paul Drake, in the back seat, shook his head lugubriously. "Sometimes I'd rather you'd drive, Perry."

"You kicking again, Paul?" Della Street asked over her shoulder.

"Not kicking, just commenting," Drake said.

Mason said, "Paul just isn't accustomed to good driving, Della. He even kicks when *I* drive."

"Can you imagine *that?*" Della Street exclaimed.

"Just like a taxicab in Paris," Mason said. "At first I used to think they went like hell. They don't. They just hit one speed and stay there. The French driver knows that if he puts his foot on the brake it's going to cut down on his gasoline mileage, and the same holds true if he puts his foot on the throttle, so he just goes about thirty miles an hour steady, no matter what's in front of him."

"And you think I'm doing the same thing?" Della Street asked.

"Heaven forbid!" Drake interposed. "You're hitting fifty and not giving a damn about anything."

Della Street slowed. "Well, I get you there in less time, so you don't suffer so long, Paul. Monte Carlo Drive should be along here somewhere. It's within the next . . ."

"Here it is," Mason said.

Della Street swung the car to the right, still going fast enough so that the tyres screamed as she whipped around the corner.

Paul Drake made an exaggerated gesture of putting his hands over his eyes.

Della Street slid up to the big two-and-a-half-storey white house, with its lawn, hedge and wide verandas giving it the appearance of a country estate despite the fact that it was within thirty minutes of the centre of town.

"Do you want me to come in with you and bring a book?" she asked.

Mason said, "No, Drake will be with me. We'll declare ourselves. How is it they say it, Paul?"

"In no uncertain terms," Drake said.

"That's the stuff," Mason told him. "You wait here, Della. Keep the motor running. We may want to go places in a hurry."

"Regular cops and robbers," Della Street said, smiling. "Don't let anybody sell you boys a bill of goods."

"We'll try not to," Mason promised, and, with Paul Drake trailing behind him, hurried up the cement walk, ran up the steps to the porch and pressed the bell button by the side of the door.

The porch light clicked on almost as soon as the chimes sounded, and the door swung open.

A short man, who seemed to be bursting from the seams, said, "Well, it certainly didn't take you long to get here."

Mason said cautiously, "We didn't violate any speed laws. What seems to be the trouble?"

"Step right this way, please," the man said.

He turned and led the way across a reception hall into a big living-room.

Mason studied the man's back. The coat was well-tailored but tight. The man's heels pounded the floor with the quick, energetic steps of impatience. Like many short, heavy men he seemed buzzing around in a continual atmosphere of hectic futility, trying to pound time into oblivion by sheer nervous hurry.

"Right in here," he called over his shoulder. "Right this way, please."

He didn't even look back as he pushed his way through curtains and into a sumptuous living-room where everything seemed to have been carefully and systematically planned, a room which radiated the touch of an interior decorator. Each chair was in its proper place so that it balanced the mass and colour design of the room. The curtains had been pulled across the windows, but it was quite evident that the view was on the east, where the huge picture window was in the centre of the room with easy chairs and ottomans on each side.

Nellie Conway was standing near one corner, her eyes widened slightly. Aside from that her face held no trace of expression.

A tall, slender man, whose face had deep lines and who might have been fighting ulcers, was standing behind one of the overstuffed chairs, his forearms resting across the back of the chair, a cigarette dangling from the corner of his mouth. He seemed to be detached from the life in the room, wrapped only in the gloom of selfish dejection.

A woman of uncertain age, tall, gaunt, grim-faced, stood well back in the room. The room seemed to fit her exactly. It could have been her methodical, mathematical mind that had arranged the furniture with such careful precision and kept it so arranged.

She looked at Mason and for a moment her dark, inscrutable eyes locked with his, then she moved silently over to where Nellie Conway was sitting, placed a reassuring hand on her shoulder. "I think it's going to come out all right, dear," she said. "Don't be frightened." She gave Nellie a little pat, then turned and walked from the room.

"Mr. Mason," Nellie Conway said.

"Eh? How's that?" the fat man asked.

"This is Mr. Bain, my employer," she said.

"Eh? What's that? Who the hell is this?" Bain asked.

Nellie Conway went on talking to Mason without paying the slightest attention to Nathan Bain.

"Mr. Bain is my employer," she explained. "He has just had the temerity to accuse me of theft. This gentleman on the right is a private detective who seems to have been working on my case for some little time without doing me the courtesy of letting me know anything about it, and the police, I believe, are on their way."

"How's this?" Bain asked, whirling to Perry Mason. "Aren't you the police?"

The man Nellie Conway had described as a private detective said, dispiritedly, without moving the cigarette from its position, "Perry Mason, the famous criminal lawyer. That's Paul Drake with him, head of the Drake Detective Agency. Does most of Mason's work. Hello, Drake."

Drake said, "I don't think I place you."

"Jim Hallock."

"Oh yes. I place you now," Drake said without cordiality.

"What seems to be the trouble?" Mason asked.

"What the devil are you doing here?" Bain demanded. "I called the police."

"Thought I'd drop in and see what the trouble was."

"Well, where do you fit into the picture?"

Mason said, "Miss Conway asked me to call."

"Nellie?"

"That's right."

"You mean Nellie Conway asked you to call here?"

"That's right."

"For heaven's sake, why?"

"Because," Nellie Conway said, "I'm tired of being pushed around. You're trying to frame a crime on me and I don't propose to be framed. Mr. Mason is my attorney."

"Well, I'll be damned!" Bain said, and sat down abruptly in one of the occasional chairs, looking at Mason with gimlet eyes that had been pushed back into his head by the layers of fat that had grown around them.

Jim Hallock shifted his position enough to remove the cigarette and shake ashes from it casually on the expensive carpet. "She must have phoned Mason when she said she wanted to run upstairs and see how her patient was getting along," he explained to Bain.

"Mason! Perry Mason, employed by a cheap crook like this!" Bain said. "I can't believe it. It's preposterous."

"It's nothing to me," Hallock said to Bain. "You're the one who's doing it, but I think I'd qualify that 'cheap crook' business. We haven't proved anything yet and . . ."

"The hell we haven't proved anything yet. We've caught the thief. We've caught her red-handed."

Hallock shrugged his shoulders and said, "That's what I *thought.*"

"Well, it's so, isn't it?"

Hallock said nothing, merely stood there, leaning over the back of the big, overstuffed reading chair, as though smiling inwardly at some joke which appealed to him very much indeed. "I guess you've never seen Mason in court," he said.

"I don't get this," Bain said.

"I think," Mason told him, "that if someone will explain, we may clarify the situation."

"Are you representing Nellie Conway?" Bain demanded.

"Not yet," Mason told him.

"Why, yes, you are too, Mr. Mason. I paid you a retainer. I have your receipt."

"That was in another matter," Mason said dryly. "What seems to be the trouble here?"

Hallock said to Bain, "You don't need to talk if you don't want to. The police are coming here. They'll take charge."

Bain sputtered angrily, "I'll tell the whole story if I want to. All of a sudden, I seem to be the one that's on the defensive. *I* haven't anything to hide. My wife is sick, Mr. Mason. Nellie is the night nurse. She's not a trained nurse, just a practical nurse. Lately we've been losing jewellery and some cash. Personally, I suspected Nellie right from the first. But before I did anything I consulted Mr. Hallock, employed him as a detective. I wanted to get proof. I was only too well aware that any false accusation on my part might expose me to a suit for damages. A certain type of individual goes around looking for openings like that."

"I think that's unfair," Nellie Conway said.

Bain paid no attention, but went on, "Hallock had some very practical suggestions. We removed most of the really valuable pieces from my wife's jewel box and substituted imitations. Then we dusted the jewel box with a fluorescent powder so that if anyone touched that box some of the fluorescent powder would adhere to the fingers. Then we took pains to take the jewel box out of my wife's desk and leave it on top of the desk as though we'd overlooked putting it back. We made a complete inventory of the contents of the jewel box, Mr. Mason. All of the jewels were imitations but it was such an expensive jewel case no one would ever have thought the jewels were other than genuine.

"This afternoon Hallock and I again made an inventory of the contents of the jewel box. Nothing was missing. Tonight, when the day nurse went off duty, we once more checked the contents of the jewel box. Everything was in its place.

"About half an hour ago, when Nellie came down here to fix some hot malted milk for my wife, she was gone quite a long time. We purposely gave her an opportunity to be alone and undisturbed. Then we entered the room after she'd taken the hot malted milk upstairs, and inventoried the contents of the box. A diamond pendant was missing, so we called Nellie down here, turned off the lights and switched on some ultra-violet light. The results were all that anyone could have asked.

"I don't know how that stuff got on my fingers," Nellie said.

"Was there fluorescent powder on your fingers?" Mason asked.

Bain said, "See for yourself," and, with the self-importance of a showman who is putting on a good act, he marched over to the light switch and jabbed it with his thumb. Instantly the room was plunged in darkness. Then he pushed another switch. There was a buzzing noise and after a second the room was filled with ultra-violet light.

"Show the gentleman your hands, Nellie," Bain said with sarcasm.

Nellie Conway held up her hands. The finger-tips were flaming with iridescent light that had a peculiar bluish-green tinge and was exceedingly brilliant.

"There you are," Bain said. "Try and laugh *that* off."

He switched the ultra-violet light off and the room lights back on.

Nellie Conway turned pleadingly to Perry Mason. "Can't you see," she said, "this is all a—a part of that thing I was telling you about."

Nathan Bain said, "Let's get this straight, please. You're here representing Nellie. Is that right, Mr. Mason?"

"She asked me to come."

"And this gentleman with you is . . . ?"

"Mason's detective," Jim Hallock interposed. "I warned you, Bain."

"I see no reason why either of you gentlemen have any right to intrude upon these premises," Bain said. "I'm going to ask you to leave."

Mason said, "I'm a little dubious about whether Miss Conway is a client, Bain, but I'm not particularly impressed with *your* attitude."

"You don't have to be impressed with my attitude. This woman is a thief and . . ."

"Just a minute," Jim Hallock interrupted. "Let's not jump at conclusions, Mr. Bain, if you don't mind. There has been a series of jewel thefts. We're asking the police to investigate. There's certain evidence that Miss Conway will be called on to explain."

"That's it," Bain interposed hastily. "I'm not convicting her before she's tried. I've simply set a trap for her and she's . . . she's got that stuff all over her fingers."

Hallock smiled sceptically. "That's better, but it's too late to do any good."

Bain turned to Nellie Conway. "I don't see what you think you have to gain, Nellie. After all, I could bring myself to be lenient with you if you would make restitution, and . . ."

He broke off as the door-bell rang, and, saying to Hallock, "Keep an eye on them, Jim," he ran to the door, his short legs working like pistons. A moment later he called, "Well, here are the police. Now we'll see who's running this show."

The police needed no introductions. Bain, having made a brief explanation in the reception corridor, ushered the two uniformed radio officers into the room, and they immediately made their presence felt.

"Okay," one of the men said. "We'll dispense with the attorney and his stooge and see what this girl has to say for herself."

Mason said to Nellie Conway, "If that's the way they want it, don't say a word. That fluorescent powder is nice stuff but it doesn't actually *prove* anything. It's used in cases of petty crimes to trap a person and fill him with dismay at the idea of being caught with the evidence clinging to his fingers. A person usually becomes tearfully repentant under such circumstances and confesses."

"Shut up," one of the officers said to Mason. "Bain wants you to go home. It's his house."

"If it's an attempt to frame an innocent person it won't stand up in front of a jury," Mason went on, still talking to Nellie Conway. "Now mind what I'm telling you, the case won't stand up and . . ."

"That's enough," the officer said, moving belligerently forward.

Mason turned his eyes to the officer. "I'm advising a client," he said.

"I want them out," Mr. Bain said. "They have no business being here."

"You heard what the man said. Out!"

Mason said, "Right at the moment I'm trying to advise my client."

"Well, you can advise her some place else."

"And," Mason said, turning back to Nellie Conway, "don't let them kid you into believing that this is any serious crime. The most they can charge you with is petty larceny."

"What do you mean, petty larceny?" Bain sputtered. "Why, my wife's diamond pendant was worth five thousand dollars. It's . . ."

"Sure," Mason said, "but you outsmarted yourself. You put cheap imitations in the jewel box. It's the imitation that's missing. How much is that worth?"

"Why . . . I . . . How do you know it isn't the real pendant?"

"Don't get in an argument with him," one of the officers said. "Come on, Mason, on your way. You can advise your client after she's booked at police headquarters."

"Can you keep quiet?" Mason askcd Nellie Conway.

"If you tell me to."

The officers grabbed Mason and Paul Drake, pushed them out of the door.

"Don't say a word," Mason cautioned over his shoulder.

"Come on, buddy. Make it snappy," the officer said.

"Not even about . . . about that other matter?" Nellie Conway called after him.

"Don't talk, period," Mason shouted back as the officer propelled him out of the front door.

"Well?" Della Street asked, as Drake and Mason approached the car. "It looked as though you went out on your ear."

"That made me mad," Mason said. "Just for that I am going to represent Nellie Conway, and Bain will wish he had never ordered those cops to give us the bum's rush."

"What happened?" Della asked. "Who was murdered? The wife?"

"No murder," Mason said, "just a case of petty theft, and some smart private detective has been using fluorescent powder. I think I'm going to have to teach that pair a lesson."

"Specifically what are we going to do?" Della Street asked.

"Specifically," Mason said, "we're going to follow that police car. When they take Nellie Conway to jail we're going to bail her out."

"And then what?"

"And then," Mason said, "Paul Drake is going to telephone his chemist friend. We're going to find out just what particular brand of poison Nathan Bain was trying to get Nellie to administer to his sick wife. From that point on there's going to be hell to pay."

"You mean you'll call the police?"

Mason smiled and said, "No. I'll represent Nellie Conway in a petty larceny case just for the pleasure it will give me to cross-examine Mr. Nathan Bain."

"Will they bring her right out?" Della Street asked.

"If she follows my advice and refuses to talk, they're pretty sure to bring her right out. If they can get her talking, or trying to explain things, the situation may be a little different."

Paul Drake said, "We don't really need to follow that police car, Perry. We could just go on to headquarters and wait for them there."

"And have her taken to some outlying precinct where we wouldn't know where she was," Mason said. "I've had 'em do that before."

"In murder cases," Paul Drake said.

"They may do it in *this* case."

"Nuts. You've never monkeyed with this small stuff, Perry. They may not even charge her."

"Big oaks grow from tiny acorns," Mason said cryptically.

"Meaning what?" Drake asked.

"Meaning Nellie planted something," Mason told him. "I can feel it sprouting."

They were silent for a few minutes.

"We can't follow that police car without getting into trouble," Drake pointed out. "They'll use their siren and——"

"We'll make a stab at it," Mason told him. "Somehow I don't think they'll burn up the road. They may try to get nice and friendly with Nellie on the way to jail so that she'll talk. If she——"

"Here they come now," Della Street interrupted.

"Move over," Mason told her. "Let me get behind that wheel, Della. This may be the kind of driving that Paul *really* likes."

"Have a heart, Perry," Drake pleaded.

The officers escorted Nellie Conway down to the radio car. One of the officers walked over to where Mason's car was parked and said, "No need for you to stick around, Mason. Bain is going to follow us in his car and sign a complaint. He doesn't want to talk with you and we don't want you to talk with him. Get smart and go home."

"I am smart," Mason said.

"All right. On your way then."

Mason looked around at the kerb and said, "I don't see it."

"Don't see what?"

"The fire-plug."

"What fire-plug?"

"The way you were ordering me away I thought that I must have parked in front of a fire-plug. However, I don't see it and there seems to be no parking limit in this——"

"Okay, wise guy. See where it gets you," the officer said, and walked back to his car.

A few moments later a car came rolling out of the driveway and blinked its lights. The officers started their car and drove down the street. Bain's car fell in behind and Mason tagged on behind Bain.

Forty minutes later Nellie Conway was out on a two-thousand-dollar bail bond furnished by Perry Mason.

Then the lawyer walked upstairs and into the office of Homicide to encounter Sergeant Holcomb.

"I think you overlooked a bet on that Conway woman," Mason said.

"You usually do feel that way." Sergeant Holcomb seemed to be chortling inwardly.

"I'm warning you that you'd better look into it."

"I've already looked into it," Holcomb said, grinning. "In fact, I happen to know all about it. Bain and I have met, and when he began to suspect Nellie Conway of stealing cash and jewellery, he phoned me for advice.

"I'm the one who told him to get Jim Hallock and use fluorescent powder, and catch her red-handed—and that's just what he did.

"She evidently got wise. Bain had her under suspicion and she decided she'd plant an alibi by accusing him of trying to murder his wife. In that way he wouldn't dare to prosecute her.

"And you, the smart lawyer, walked right into the trap!"

Holcomb threw back his head and laughed. "For a man who's supposed to have been around, you do the damnedest things. You fell for that little tramp's story. Ha-ha-ha!"

Mason said, "Don't be too sure. The shoe may be on the *other* foot.

When Bain knew she wasn't going to give the poison to his wife, *he* decided to discredit *her*."

"Oh, nuts," Sergeant Holcomb said. "When Nellie knew he was getting on to her, she went and cooked up this story and got some tablets she claimed Bain was trying to get her to administer to his wife. I'd personally be willing to bet even money they're just props to back up her story, and that she grabbed 'em out of the first bottle she found in the bathroom. Nine chances out of ten they're aspirin tablets. That's what they looked like to me.

"Hell, Mason, figure it out. Would Bain be so dumb, even if he wanted his wife to have pills, to give them to a woman he was about to arrest for theft, and put himself in *her* power?"

And Holcomb once more threw back his head and roared with laughter. At length he calmed enough to say, "Don't let that little minx hypnotise you with a yarn that will arouse your sympathies, Mason. If you're going to be her lawyer, get your fee in advance, and in cash."

"Thank you so much," Mason said, and walked out.

Holcomb's booming laughter followed him down the hallway.

Mason rejoined Della Street and drove back to Drake's office.

Paul Drake, who had gone back by taxicab, was waiting for them. He handed Mason a graph some eighteen inches long, consisting of a long period of wavy lines running up into high peaks, down into troughs.

"What's that?" Mason asked.

"That's the way these X-ray defractors do their analysis. Here's the note from the chemist. He says:

" 'Dear Paul:
    " 'The graph is very distinctive. There's no question on earth but what the tablet you gave me consists of acetylsalicylic acid. I'm returning the tablet herewith, with a little hole drilled in the centre.' "

"Acetylsalicylic acid!" Della Street exclaimed. "What's that?"

"That," Mason said, "is exactly what Sergeant Holcomb said was in it."

"Well, what *is* it?" Della Street asked impatiently.

"Acetylsalicylic acid," Drake said, "is the chemical name for the active ingredient in good old-fashioned aspirin."

"Come on," Mason said. "Let's go home. We're all washed up—I can't withdraw from that Conway case now. I'll have to defend her. One thing, Paul, slap a subpœna on that housekeeper as a witness for the defence. That'll give Bain something to worry about. This has been the sort of day I *don't* like."

"Better take this pill along with you, Perry," Drake observed, grinning. "It's swell for headaches!"

FIVE

HARRY SAYBROOK, THE deputy District Attorney, seemed definitely annoyed that an ordinary petty larceny case had been turned into a jury trial, and his annoyance manifested itself in everything that he said and did.

Perry Mason, on the other hand, was urbane, fair, logical, and smilingly frank to the jury.

Judge Peabody from time to time cocked a quizzical eyebrow in Mason's direction as the noted criminal lawyer sat calmly complacent while James Hallock, private detective, testified that he had been employed by Mr. Nathan Bain, that he had understood generally a whole series of small thefts had been taking place at Nathan Bain's house, and that as a result the witness had secured a neutral coloured powder which would fluoresce to a vivid blue-green colour when exposed to ultraviolet light. He had placed this powder all over a jewel box in which certain articles of jewellery were being kept.

The witness further testified that he had been in the house when the defendant, who was employed as a practical nurse, had come to work on the evening of the tenth. He had, he explained, been introduced to the defendant as a business acquaintance who was selling Mr. Bain some mining property.

The witness further testified that in company with Mr. Bain he had previously made an inventory of articles contained in the jewel case. The articles, so far as he had seen, were pieces of jewellery. He had made no attempt to ascertain their value. Later on he had been given to understand that they were pieces of costume jewellery. However, at the time of his first examination the witness had contented himself with making a rough pencilled sketch of each article of jewellery and general description of the article.

At the time the defendant had come to work on the evening of the tenth he had examined the jewel case and had found every article which he had inventoried to be intact. Two hours later, at the request of Mr. Bain, he had made another inventory of the jewel box and had found that one of the articles, a diamond and pearl pendant, was missing. That thereupon, at the suggestion of Mr. Bain, they called the defendant into the living-room; that at a pre-arranged signal the ordinary incandescent bulbs had been switched off and the room had been flooded with powerful ultra-violet light; that under the influence of this light the fingers of the defendant showed as a fiery bluish-green.

Harry Saybrook turned to the jury and nodded, as much as to say, "So you see, it's as simple as that."

When Saybrook had assured himself that the jurors had fully realised the damning nature of Hallock's testimony, he turned to Perry Mason with something of a challenge and said, "You may cross-examine, Mr. Mason."

On the witness stand, Jim Hallock braced himself for the abusive cross-examination which attorneys for accused persons usually heaped upon the head of a private detective.

"Why," Mason said, apparently with some surprise, "I have no questions," and then, turning to the jury, added with the utmost candour, "I think this man is telling the truth."

"What?" Saybrook exclaimed in surprise.

"I think he's telling the simple truth," Mason said. "What's so surprising about that, Counsellor?"

"Nothing, nothing," Saybrook blurted. "I'll call my next witness, Nathan Bain."

Nathan Bain marched to the witness stand and under Saybrook's questions told his story. His wife was sick. It had been necessary to employ a day nurse and a night nurse. The case did not require trained nurses working in eight-hour shifts since there was a housekeeper to lend a hand on occasion, so Bain had hired two practical nurses, a day nurse and a night nurse. The defendant had been the night nurse.

Shortly after the nurses had started work certain things began to disappear around the house, small sums of cash, liquor, items of jewellery. Bain made a point of stating that he couldn't be certain that it was more than a coincidence, so far as the defendant was concerned. But he decided to set a trap. He had taken his wife's jewel case from the desk where it was usually kept, and had purchased articles of costume jewellery which had then been placed in the jewel box. The witness had then consulted James Hallock, the witness who had just testified. At Hallock's suggestion a fluorescent powder had been placed upon the box. The box had then been left on the writing desk as though someone had inadvertently neglected to return it to the interior of the desk.

Then Bain went on to describe the events of the evening of the tenth with particular detail.

Perry Mason yawned.

"Do you wish to cross-examine *this* witness?" Saybrook asked.

Mason hesitated just long enough so that Bain, feeling he was to escape without question, started to arise from the witness chair, then Mason said, "Just a moment, Mr. Bain, I do have one or two questions I want to ask you."

"Yes, sir," Mr. Bain said.

"When was this fluorescent powder placed upon the jewel case, Mr. Bain?"

"On the tenth."

"At what time?"

"About nine o'clock in the morning."

"The day nurse then was already on the job?"

"Yes, sir."

"Who placed the powder on the box?"

"Mr. Hallock did."

"And you stood by and watched him?"

"I did. Yes, sir."

"And previously you had placed these articles of costume jewellery in the jewel case?"

"Yes, sir."

"What type of jewel case was that, Mr. Bain?"

"It was a casket made in the form of an ancient trunk, covered with leather and studded with silver nails, with leather handles on each side."

"About what were the dimensions?"

"It was rather a large jewel case. I would say about fifteen inches by ten inches by ten inches."

"It was the property of your wife?"

"Yes, I'd given it to her for Christmas a year ago."

"And prior to the time the fluorescent powder was dusted on this jewel case, you had taken an inventory of the contents in company with Mr. Hallock?"

"Yes, sir. We did that together."

"Then the costume jewellery, or the imitation jewellery, was replaced in the casket, and then the casket was dusted with powder. Is that right?"

"That's right. Yes, sir."

"Now, did you have occasion to investigate that jewel box or casket during the day in order to see if the day nurse had taken something?"

"I did. Yes, sir."

"How many times?"

"Twice."

"When?"

"About two o'clock in the afternoon and then at six o'clock, shortly before the day nurse went off duty."

"And then you investigated it again in the evening?"

"Yes, sir."

"How many times?"

"Twice."

"When?"

"Immediately after the defendant came on duty so that we knew nothing was missing at that time, and then again about two hours later— which was when we found that one of the articles of jewellery was missing."

"Who made the examination?"

"Mr. Hallock and I."

"Who opened the jewel case, Mr. Bain?"

"I did."

"Do you mean that you left this jewel case lying around in plain sight with no lock?"

"No, sir, it was locked."

"And it was kept locked?"

"Yes, sir."

"Then how could anything have been missing?"

"The thief either had a duplicate key, which was not an impossibility, or the lock was picked, which would not have been difficult."

"I see. Mr. Hallock didn't have a key to the jewel case?"

"No, sir."

"You had a key?"

"Yes, sir."

"And your wife had a key?"

"Yes, sir."

"You weren't using your wife's key then?"

"No, sir."

"How did you happen to have a key to your wife's jewel box?"

"It was simply a matter of precaution, Mr. Mason."

"I'm afraid I don't understand."

"Women are always losing things," Bain said, rather self-righteously, "so as a matter of precaution against having my wife lose the key to her jewel box, I only gave her one key when I gave her the box. I retained one key in a safe place."

"Oh, I see," Mason said, with a swift glance at the five women who were on the jury. "You felt that that reserve key would be safe in your possession and would guard against your wife's negligence?"

"Yes, sir."

"That your wife would naturally be inclined to lose her key?"

"Well, I thought she might."

"As you expressed it, I believe, you have rather a contempt for the ability of women to keep things?"

"Just a moment, Your Honour," Saybrook shouted and jumped to his feet. "The witness didn't say that at all."

"I certainly understood him to say that," Mason said. "Perhaps not in those words, Counsellor, but——"

"If you're going to cross-examine the witness use his own words," Saybrook said.

Mason smiled and shook his head. "I know of no rule of law that requires me to do that, Mr. Saybrook. I simply ask the witness questions on cross-examination. The witness can correct me if I'm wrong. I certainly understood his testimony to be that he was rather contemptuous of the ability of women to be trusted with responsibilities, and I think the jury will bear me out in that."

And Mason flashed a quick glance at the jury.

"The witness didn't say any such thing," Saybrook said.

"Well, now," Mason said magnanimously, "I'm going to be the first to apologise if I misunderstood him. It's only a few pages back in the record, Counsellor, and I'm going to ask the court reporter to read back exactly what the witness said."

Saybrook, suddenly realising that Mason's tactics had been in the nature of a bait which had caused him to make an issue of what otherwise might have been passed over, and was now serving to emphasise it to the jury, said, "Oh well, there's no use wasting all that time. I'll withdraw the objection. The jurors will remember what the witness said and I know they're not going to let *you* put words in the witness's mouth or——"

"Not at all, not at all," Mason said. "I'm now interested in knowing exactly what the witness did say and I'm going to apologise to him if I've misunderstood what he said."

"Well, I didn't *mean* that," Bain interposed uncomfortably.

"You didn't mean what?" Mason asked.

"That women weren't to be trusted with things."

"I thought that was what you said."

"I didn't say anything of the sort."

"Well, now," Mason said, "let's have the record read by the court reporter."

Judge Peabody said, "All right, gentlemen, if you'll just keep quiet now so the court reporter can search back in his notes, he'll find the testimony in question."

There was a tense silence in the court-room. Saybrook found outlet for his nervous energy by running his hand through his thick black hair. He didn't like the turn that events were taking.

Bain sat self-righteously erect on the witness stand, waiting to be vindicated.

Mason settled back easily in his chair, waiting with the respectfully attentive attitude of the man who feels that the information which is about to be forthcoming is of the greatest importance.

The court reporter said, "Here it is. I'll read the question and answer:

'*Mr. Mason:* How did you happen to have a key to your wife's jewel box?

ANSWER: It was simply a matter of precaution, Mr. Mason.

QUESTION: I'm afraid I don't understand.

ANSWER: Women are always losing things, so as a matter of precaution against having my wife lose the key to her jewel box, I only gave her one key when I gave her the box. I retained one key in a safe place.

QUESTION: Oh, I see. You felt that that reserve key would be safe in your possession and would guard against your wife's negligence?

ANSWER: Yes, sir.

QUESTION: That your wife would naturally be inclined to lose her key?

ANSWER: Well, I thought she might.

QUESTION: As you expressed it, I believe, you have rather a contempt for the ability of women to keep things?' "

Bain squirmed uncomfortably on the witness stand as the court reporter finished reading.

"I thought that's what you said," Mason observed. "It was, wasn't it?"

"Well, it wasn't what I meant," Bain snapped.

"Oh, then you said something you didn't mean?"

"Yes, sir."

"Under oath?"

"Well, it was a slip of the tongue."

"What do you mean by a slip of the tongue, Mr. Bain? Did you say something that wasn't true?"

"Well, I said something that . . . I said it without thinking."

"Without thinking of what?"

"Well, I was only trying to say that my wife has a habit of losing things and . . ."

"And you did generalise by stating that that was a trait that women had generally?"

"Oh, Your Honour," Saybrook said, making his voice weary with exasperation. "Surely this is a minor matter. Good Lord, we've been over it time and time and time again. The question is already asked and answered in the record *ad nauseam*."

"I don't think so," Mason said. "I think that it's rather important to find out what attitude this witness may have, not only toward women generally, because my client is a woman, but also I'm particularly interested in finding out what's in the back of his mind when he states on cross-examination that he made statements he didn't mean. I'd like to find out how many *other* things in his testimony may have been incorrect."

"Nothing in his testimony is incorrect," Saybrook shouted.

"You mean then the witness really does feel that women are not to be trusted with responsibility?" Mason asked.

A few of the scattered spectators in the court-room laughed. Judge Peabody smiled and said, "Well, Mr. Mason, I think you've made your point."

"But I certainly desire to cross-examine this witness as to just what he means by what he says, Your Honour."

"Go ahead," Judge Peabody said.

"Is that the only thing in your testimony that is incorrect?" Mason asked.

"That isn't incorrect."

"Oh, you meant every word you said then?"

"Yes, I meant it," Bain shouted.

"I thought you did," Mason said, smiling. "Now let's be frank, Mr. Bain. After you realised that your statement might offend some of the women on the jury you tried to change it, but actually you meant it. Isn't that a fact?"

"Your Honour, I object," Saybrook shouted. "That's not proper cross-examination, and——"

"It goes to show the biased attitude of the witness," Mason said, "and is a reflection on his credibility."

"The objection is overruled. The witness may answer," Judge Peabody said.

"Isn't that it?" Mason asked.

"All right, if that's the way you want it, have it that way," Bain snapped angrily.

"Come, come," Mason said, soothingly. "It's not the way *I* want it, Mr. Bain. I'm simply trying to find out something about your mental processes. Isn't it a fact that you made this statement rather heedlessly without considering its possible effect and . . . ?"

"All right, I did. So what?"

"Nothing, nothing," Mason said, "I'm simply trying to get your frame of mind, your attitude. You meant what you said and you said what you meant, but when you realised the remark might have been impolite you tried to pass it off as a slip of the tongue. Is that right?"

"That's right."

"So it really wasn't a slip of the tongue, it was the truth. Is *that* right?"

"That's right."

"So you were stating an untruth when you said it was a slip of the tongue?"

"Call it a slip of the mind," Bain snapped.

"Thank you," Mason said, "now let's get back to the facts in the case."

"It's about time," Saybrook commented, his tone showing extreme weariness.

Mason smiled at him. "I'm sorry if I've bored you, Counsellor."

"That will do," Judge Peabody announced. "There will be no interchange between counsel. Confine your remarks to the court and your questions to the witness, Mr. Mason."

"Very well, Your Honour," Mason said cheerfully. "Now you want the jury to understand, Mr. Bain, that you yourself opened this jewel casket to look in it shortly after the defendant came on duty that night."

"I did. Yes, sir."

"You had your key?"

"Yes, sir."

"By the way, did you tell your wife that you had an extra key?"

"No, sir. I did not."

"Indeed," Mason said. "Why not?"

"Objected to as incompetent, irrelevant, and immaterial, and not proper cross-examination," Saybrook said.

"The objection is sustained," Judge Peabody ruled.

"But," Mason said, "you *did* have a key to your wife's jewel casket and you carefully kept that information from her. Isn't that right?"

"That isn't right," Saybrook shouted. "Your Honour, Counsel is deliberately distorting the testimony of this witness. He never said any such thing."

"I'm asking him now," Mason said. "He can answer that question yes or no."

"The objection is overruled," Judge Peabody said. "I'll permit an answer to that one question. I think we've gone over the matter several times but nevertheless I will permit the witness to answer this one question."

Bain hesitated.

"Yes or no?" Mason asked. "Is it a fact or isn't it?"

"Well, I didn't carefully keep the information from her."

"You kept it from her?" Mason suggested.

"Yes, I did," Bain snapped.

"You want the jury to understand that you kept it from her carelessly and negligently, that you simply overlooked mentioning it to her?"

"Well, I . . . I just wanted to have the extra key, then I'd surprise her in case she lost her key and couldn't find it. I . . ."

"But she never did lose her key, did she, Mr. Bain?"

"Not that I know of, no."

"And you feel that you would have known of it if she had lost it?"

"I suppose so."

"Then," Mason said, smiling, "you have to admit that your comments as to your wife's inefficiency in such matters were not well-founded."

"Objection," Saybrook shouted. "That's——"

"Sustained," Judge Peabody said. "I think we've gone into this matter far enough, Mr. Mason."

"Very well, Your Honour," Mason said. "I have just a couple more questions."

Mason shifted his position in the swivel chair at the counsel table and, catching the eye of one of the women members of the jury, let his face soften into a half smile.

The woman promptly smiled back.

Mason said, "Now, let's see, Mr. Bain. You opened that jewel case and I understand that when you did Mr. Hallock was there with you?"

"Yes, sir."

"And you pointed out that something was missing?"

"Yes, sir."

"And Mr. Hallock compared the contents of the jewel box with his list?"

"Yes, sir."

"Now, how was Mr. Hallock able to do that without touching the jewel box?"

"I never said he did it without touching the jewel box," Bain said. "Don't put words in my mouth!"

"Oh, then he *did* touch the jewel box?"

"I suppose so. He naturally would have. I didn't say he did, and I didn't say he didn't."

"But your best recollection now is that he did?"

"He may have."

"Do you know whether he did or not?"

"I assume that he did."

"So," Mason said, "after the fluorescent powder had been placed on the jewel box you touched the jewel box and *Mr. Hallock* touched the jewel box."

"Yes."

"So presumably at that time you and Mr. Hallock both had fluorescent powder on your fingers."

"I assume so. Yes."

"There were three people in the downstairs part of that house. All three of you had fluorescent powder on your finger-tips. You, Mr. Hallock and the defendant. Is that right?"

"Hallock and I had a right to have the fluorescent powder on our finger-tips. The defendant didn't."

"What do you mean, you had a right to?"

"We had a right to go to the jewel box."

"Certainly," Mason said, "but if you are going to rely on the assumption that the fluorescent powder on a person's finger-tips meant that a piece of imitation jewellery had been stolen, you could say that since Mr. Hallock had the fluorescent powder on his finger-tips that he had taken the piece of jewellery."

"Certainly not."

"Why not?"

"Because he wouldn't have."

"How do you know he wouldn't?"

"He was there for the purpose of preventing the theft."

"Oh, come, come," Mason said. "Not for the purpose of preventing the theft. You put the imitation jewellery in there because you felt some was going to be stolen. You left the jewel casket in a place where it was plainly obvious. In other words, you were baiting a trap. You *wanted* some of the jewellery to be stolen, didn't you?"

"Well, I thought we could catch the thief that way."

"Exactly," Mason said. "So, for all you know, Hallock may have gone to the jewel box and taken out that piece of jewellery."

"He didn't have a key to it."

"Neither did the defendant, did she?"

"I suppose she must have."

"Simply because you assume that she took the article of jewellery?"

"Well, she must have got into it in some way."

"And you had a key?" Mason said.

"I've told you I did a dozen times."

"And you might have gone to the jewel box and taken out that article of jewellery."

"I didn't."

"I'm not suggesting that you did," Mason said. "I am simply saying that you might have done so. You had the opportunity."

"Yes."

"And," Mason said, "you didn't put the fluorescent powder on the inside of that jewel box? You put it on the outside?"

"That's right."

"So that if the defendant had simply moved the jewel case for the purpose of getting at something that was behind it, or if she had inadvertently touched it, she would have had this powder on her fingers."

"Well, she had it on her fingers."

"I understand," Mason said, "but she could have got that on her fingers simply by touching the outside of the jewel case in an attempt to reach for something back of the jewel case—perhaps to pick up a magazine or——"

"There weren't any magazines around it."

"Just where was it, by the way?" Mason asked.

"Out on top of the writing desk."

"Was that where your wife usually left it?"

"No."

"Where did she usually leave it?"

"It was usually kept inside the writing desk."

"And the desk was kept locked?"

"I believe my wife kept it locked. Yes, sir."

"And did you have a key to that desk?"

The witness hesitated.

"Yes or no?" Mason snapped.

"Yes."

"Did you give that desk to your wife for Christmas?"

"No, sir."

"That desk was bought some time ago as part of the household furniture?"

"That's right."

"Your wife had a key to it?"

"Yes."

"And you had a duplicate key?"

"Yes."

"Did your wife know you had that duplicate key?"

"I don't know."

"You had retained a duplicate key to the desk without telling your wife that you had it?"

"I never said I didn't tell my wife."

"You said that you didn't know whether she knew that you had a key."

"Well, I can't remember whether I told her or not."

"I see," Mason said, smiling. "You made it a point to keep a key to your wife's writing desk, and then when you wanted to, shall we say, find some method of discharging the defendant in disgrace, you took the jewel case out of the desk and placed it on top of the desk in an inviting position?"

"Well, I wanted to get the thing cleared up one way or another."

"That jewel case was rather unusual in appearance, wasn't it?"

"Yes, sir."

"A woman would naturally want to look at it?"

"Well . . . Nellie Conway wouldn't have any business doing it."

"A woman who was living in the house, who was there, seeing this rather beautiful jewel case on top of a desk might not have had occasion to look at it?"

"Well, she wouldn't have had occasion to *touch* it."

"But if she had touched it, just to have felt the leather," Mason said, "she would have got this fluorescent powder on her fingers?"

"Yes."

"Now, when the defendant was arrested, you went to headquarters to sign a complaint?"

"Yes."

"So the defendant was taken from the house, and you went from the house. Did that leave your wife there all alone?"

"No, sir. I called the housekeeper, Mrs. Ricker, and asked her to sit with my wife until I could get back and get a relief nurse."

"Did you explain to Mrs. Ricker the reason it was necessary to call her?"

"Yes."

"Tell her you had had Miss Conway arrested?"

"Words to that effect."

"And she was willing to take on this extra work?"

"She certainly was. She was glad we'd caught the thief. She told me she'd been wondering all day why that jewel case had been left out of the desk. She said she'd tried to put it back in the desk twice, but the desk had been locked."

"Oh, *she'd* tried to put it back?"

"So she said."

"Then *she* must have picked it up after the fluorescent powder had been put on it?"

"Objected to," Saybrook snapped, "argumentative, calling for a conclusion of the witness, not proper cross-examination."

"Sustained," the judge said.

Mason smiled at Bain. "But you didn't examine the housekeeper's hands under ultra-violet light?"

"No."

"In the name of reason," Mason said, "why didn't you put that fluorescent powder on the inside of the jewel case so that——?"

"I don't know," Bain blurted. "That was all Hallock's idea. He handled that part of it."

"But you assisted him, didn't you?"

"I watched him."

"You were there and saw him do it?"

"Yes."

"And you were his employer? If you had told him that you wanted the fluorescent powder on the inside he would necessarily have had to follow your instructions."

"I don't know."

"But you were paying him?"

"Yes."

"By the day?"

"Well, I offered him a bonus."

"Oh," Mason said, "you offered him a bonus. What was the bonus for, Mr. Bain?"

"Well, I agreed to pay him so much a day and then if he cleared the job up satisfactorily I'd pay him a bonus."

"You'd pay him a bonus. How interesting. How much of a bonus?"

"A hundred dollars."

"So," Mason said, smiling, "if a piece of relatively inexpensive costume jewellery was missing from that jewel case and there was evidence that would link the defendant with that missing bit of jewellery, Mr. Hallock was to get a hundred dollars. Is that right?"

"I don't like the way you express it," Bain said.

"Well, express it in your own way."

"It was a bonus for completing the job."

"The job was to have been completed when Miss Conway was arrested?"

"When we caught the thief, whoever it was."

"How many people in that house?"

"My wife, Mrs. Ricker, Mr. Hallock, Nellie Conway and I."

"You didn't examine Mrs. Ricker's hands, notwithstanding you knew she'd handled the jewel box?"

"No. She's been with us for years."

"And everyone else in that house, except your wife, *did* have fluorescent powder on the fingers?"

"Well . . . yes."

"Yet you picked Miss Conway as the thief?"

"Yes. It had to be her or nobody."

"It had to be her?"

"Yes."

"So your bonus to Mr. Hallock was to get this one person arrested and convicted?"

"To get the thief."

"Have you paid the reward yet?"

"No."

"Why not?"

"The defendant hasn't been convicted. It was to be paid when the job was finished."

"I see, then you *do* have a doubt in your own mind as to whether this jury should or would convict the defendant?"

"Objection, argumentative."

"Sustained."

Mason smiled and said, "I have no further questions, Mr. Bain. Thank you."

Saybrook said angrily, "You didn't tell Hallock that he was to get a hundred dollars in case he got evidence that would convict this defendant, did you? You simply told him that if he could find out who was taking the jewellery you'd give him a hundred dollars."

"Just a moment, Your Honour," Mason said, "that question is viciously leading and suggestive. Counsel is putting words right in the mouth of the witness."

"Well, this is on redirect examination," Saybrook said, "and I'm simply trying to shorten an examination that has been already too prolonged."

"Come, come," Mason said, "let's not assume that just a few minutes spent inquiring into the issues is going to be——"

"Well, the court's time is valuable and Mr. Bain's time is valuable, even if yours isn't," Saybrook said.

"And think of the defendant," Mason said reproachfully. "If your attempt to save Mr. Bain just two or three minutes of his valuable time is going to obscure the issues, the defendant might be incarcerated in jail for a period of months. She'd have her good name blackened, she——"

"You don't need to go into that," Saybrook said, "that's simply to influence the jury."

"Well," Mason told him, smilingly, "your attempt to justify yourself for putting words into Mr. Bain's mouth was for the purpose of influencing the court."

Judge Peabody smiled. "The vice of a leading question, of course, consists in having asked it. The witness now pretty generally knows what Counsel has in mind. Go ahead, however, Mr. Saybrook, and ask a question so that it is a little less leading."

"Oh, I don't think there's any need of going into all this in any greater detail," Saybrook said.

"You have any further questions?" Judge Peabody inquired.

"That's all."

"Any further evidence?"

"That's the People's case, Your Honour."

Mason smiled at Judge Peabody and said, "We'd like to move at this time that the court instruct the jury to bring in a verdict of not guilty."

"The motion is denied."

"If I may have a ten minute recess, Your Honour," Mason said, "I would like to talk with the one person whom I have subpoenaed as a defence witness. Mrs. Imogene Ricker."

"Very well," Judge Peabody ruled.

In the back of the court-room the housekeeper stood up, gaunt, grim, and defiant. "I refuse to talk to Mr. Mason," she said.

"This woman has been subpoenaed as a defence witness, Your Honour," Mason explained. "She has heretofore refused to make any statement to me."

"I don't have to talk to him," Imogene Ricker said. "I came to court and that's all I have to do. I obeyed the subpoena. That doesn't mean I have to talk to him."

"Very well, then," Mason said, smiling, "just come forward, hold up your right hand to be sworn, and get on the witness stand."

"Do I have to do that?" she asked Judge Peabody.

"If you have been subpoenaed you have to do that," the Judge said.

She strode past Mason, held up her hand to be sworn, turned and flung herself down in the witness chair. "All right," she said grimly, "go ahead."

"You're a housekeeper in Mr. Bain's employ?" Mason asked.

"I am!" she snapped.

"How long have you been working for him?"

"Six years."

"On the evening of the tenth did you examine your hands by ultra-violet light to see if they were fluorescent?"

"That's none of your business."

Mason smiled. "If your fingers *hadn't* been fluorescent you would have answered the question, wouldn't you?"

"I don't have to tell you that either."

Mason grinned at the sympathetic jury. "Thank you. That's all, Mrs. Ricker. I just wanted the jurors to see how violently partisan you were."

"Oh, Your Honour," Saybrook said, "that——"

"The witness is excused," Judge Peabody ruled wearily. "The jury will pay no attention to comments of Counsel. Who's your next witness, Mr. Mason?"

"I don't have anyone," Mason said. "I think perhaps the jury have a pretty good concept of the case, Your Honour. An attractive jewel case was deliberately put in a position of prominence where anyone would be inclined to pick it up. We insist that——"

"There's been a ruling on the motion for a directed verdict," Judge Peabody said. "Go ahead and put on your defence."

"I'm certainly not going to put on any defence in the present state of this case," Mason said. "It's not incumbent on the defendant to prove herself innocent. It's up to the prosecution to prove her guilty. All they've proven so far is that this defendant, who was in a room where she was required to be under the terms of her employment, touched the outside of an attractive and unusual piece of bric-à-brac. The defendant will rest right now and we'll submit the case without argument to the jury."

"You have already made an argument," Saybrook said.

"Tut-tut," Mason told him. "I was merely explaining to the court why I intended to rest the defendant's case. Do you wish to submit it without argument?"

"I think I should argue it," Saybrook said.

Mason smiled at him. "Well, as far as I'm concerned I think this jury understands the issue very clearly. I'm satisfied that they're intelligent citizens and I see no reason for wasting their time. You were very concerned about the value of time a few minutes ago. I'll submit the case without argument. Go ahead and argue if you want to."

Saybrook thought the matter over, then said sulkily, "Very well, I'll submit it without argument."

Mason made a little bow to the Judge.

Judge Peabody said, "You ladies and gentlemen of the jury have heard the evidence. It is now the duty of the court to instruct you as to certain matters of law."

Judge Peabody read a stock list of instructions, emphasising the fact that it was incumbent upon the prosecution to prove a defendant guilty beyond all reasonable doubt, and that it was not incumbent upon the defendant to prove himself or herself innocent; that the jurors were the exclusive judges of the fact, although they should take the law as given to them in the instructions of the court.

The jury retired and returned in ten minutes with a verdict of not guilty.

Mason and Nellie Conway walked over to shake hands with the jurors.

The woman juror who had smiled at Mason said, exasperatedly, "That man Bain! You certainly gave him just what he had coming to him. The idea of his keeping a key to his wife's writing desk. Just a snoop, that's what he is! Poor woman, her lying there sick in bed and having a man like that around the place."

"I *thought* you were a pretty good judge of character," Mason said. "I felt as soon as I looked in your eyes that I didn't need to argue the case."

"Well, I certainly told them what I thought of *that* man," she said. "The only trouble was I didn't have a chance to tell them *all* that I thought, because everyone else felt the same way about it I did."

She turned to Nellie Conway. "You poor dear, having to work for a man like that, and now he's gone ahead and had you arrested and sworn to a complaint against you on the ground of theft and blasted your reputation. I certainly think that you should do something about it. I think you should sue him for damages."

"Thank you very much for the suggestion," Mason said. "I was going to advise her something of the sort myself, but I think the fact that the suggestion has come from one of the members of the jury will be something to remember."

"Well, you can certainly quote me. You have my name and address," the woman said, and again gave Mason a cordial smile and another handshake.

SIX

BACK IN MASON'S office, as Mason and Della Street were getting ready to close the office, the telephone rang. Della Street, taking the call, cupped her hand over the mouthpiece and said to Mason, "Do you want to talk with Nellie?"

"I definitely want to talk with her," Mason said. "Long enough to explain to her that she's no longer a client."

Mason took the telephone and Nellie Conway said in a calm level voice that was as expressionless as her face, "Mr. Mason, I want to thank you for what you did today."

"That's all right," Mason said.

"I suppose," she ventured somewhat diffidently, "I owe you some more money, Mr. Mason? The one dollar I paid you didn't cover all this extra work, did it?"

Mason said, "Well, of course, if I handled jury cases at a dollar a throw, it would be difficult for me to pay my office rent, my secretarial salaries and my taxicabs back and forth to the Hall of Justice."

"Oh, Mr. Mason, you're being sarcastic now, aren't you?"

"I was just pointing out a few economic facts."

"Can you tell me just how much I owe you? Would another ten or fifteen dollars be all right?"

Mason said, "How much money do you have, Nellie?"

"Does that need to enter into it?"

"It might have something to do with it."

"I'd rather not discuss that, Mr. Mason. I'd rather you'd just tell me how much your charges are."

Mason became serious. "You called me up to ask me that?"

"Yes."

Mason was curious now. "You didn't say anything about any additional compensation after the case was over, Nellie. You just shook hands with me and thanked me. Why have you become so concerned about it now?"

"Well, I . . . I was just thinking that perhaps . . ."

"Look here," Mason asked, "has Bain been in touch with you?"

She hesitated, then said, "Yes."

"And Bain is offering you some sort of a settlement?"

"Well . . . Mr. Bain and I are talking."

"You mean you're talking with Bain at the present moment? You mean he's with you?"

"I'm with him."

"Where?"

"At Mr. Bain's house."

"At the Bain house!" Mason repeated incredulously.

"Yes."

"What in the world are you doing there?"

"Why, getting my things, of course. When the officers took me away they didn't give me any opportunity to pack up my personal things."

"Let's get this straight," Mason said. "Were you *living* there at the Bain house?"

"Why, yes, of course. The day nurse and I shared an apartment over the garage."

"Well, I'll be damned!"

"Why, what's wrong with that, Mr. Mason? Mr. Bain has lots of room here, and——"

"But you didn't tell me that."

"Well, you didn't ask me."

"Who's taking care of the patient now?" Mason asked.

"Why, the same nurse."

"I mean as a night nurse. Who's taking your place?"

"They had a temporary nurse for a few days, but she left very abruptly. The housekeeper has been helping out, and, just as a favour, I'll stay on the rest of the night. Mrs. Ricker will take a spell with me while I'm packing."

"You've seen Mrs. Bain and talked with her?"

"Why, of course. Elizabeth Bain and I are real friendly. She'd like to have me stay right on at my old job. But I don't think I'll stay . . . I had to tell her all about my arrest, of course, and about the way you questioned—well, the witnesses."

"By that I take it you mean the way I tore into her husband on cross-examination?"

"Yes."

"How did she react to that?"

"She thought it was wonderful. She said she wanted to see you. She . . . well, I . . ."

"You mean you can't talk freely?" Mason asked as she hesitated and broke off.

"Oh, yes. That's right. Yes, indeed. Mr. Bain is right here."

"And you're negotiating some sort of a settlement with him?"

"I hope to."

"Then you'll go back to work for him?"

"I think not. Quite a few of Mrs. Bain's relatives are due here some time after midnight. They're flying in from Honolulu. She'll have lots of company. She . . . well, I'll tell you some other time. I wanted to ask you now . . . that is, Mr. Bain wanted to know . . . if you'd set a price on your services so——"

Mason said, "If Nathan Bain is going to pay the fee, you owe me five hundred dollars, and that cleans us up. Do you understand?"

"Well, I should think it would," she said, rather tartly.

"If Bain doesn't pay the fee, we're quits," Mason said. "The one dollar charge is all I'm making."

"Oh."

"You understand that?"

"Yes."

"And," Mason told her, "that winds us up, and let's have one thing understood, Nellie."

"What, Mr. Mason?"

"I'm not representing you in connection with any settlement you make with Bain. If you make a settlement with him that's up to you. I think perhaps you should have some lawyer represent you."

"Then I'd have to pay him, wouldn't I?"

"Most lawyers like to be paid," Mason told her. "They have to support themselves, you know."

"Well," she said indignantly, "I don't see why I should take money and pay it over to a lawyer. Mr. Bain is willing to be reasonable, and as he's pointed out he couldn't be any more reasonable if a lawyer were there to take fifty per cent out of what I am going to collect."

"Did he say that?"

"Yes. He pointed out that it would be coming right out of my pocket."

"All right," Mason said, "use your own judgment."

"I am," she said, "and please, Mr. Mason, so there won't be any misunderstanding, you're not representing me in the settlement. I'm just trying to find out how much I owe you for your lawyer's fees, but I'm not going to pay five hundred dollars."

"*You're not,*" Mason said. "Bain is."

"But I'm not going to let him pay that much. I think it's too much, Mr. Mason."

"How much do *you* think it should be?"

"Well, I would say not more than fifty dollars. You only did half a day's work."

Mason said, "I told you that if you were paying me you only owed me a dollar. If Bain was paying me, the bill would be five hundred dollars."

"Well, then, I'll get Mr. Bain to pay me and . . . well, I'll think it over, Mr. Mason. I'll . . . I'll do what's right."

"I'm satisfied you will," Mason said. "And now let's get this straight, Nellie. You and I are finished, the slate is wiped clean. I'm not your lawyer any——"

"I'll say you're not. At any such prices as those! Five hundred dollars for just a little over half a day's work . . . Why, I never heard of such a thing!"

And she slammed the receiver in Mason's ear.

The lawyer rubbed his ear, turned to Della Street. "That," he announced, "is gratitude. I have always said, Della, that the time to fix the amount of a fee is when the client is most anxious to secure the services. Miss Nellie Conway now feels ten or fifteen dollars would be ample compensation, and fifty would be munificent.

"Come on, Della, let's close up the joint and go home."

SEVEN

WHEN MASON ENTERED his office a few minutes after ten the next morning, Della Street said, "Congratulations, Chief!"

"A birthday or something?" Mason asked.

"You've missed her by five minutes. Therefore congratulations are in order."

"Missed who?"

"Your dollar client."

"Good Lord, don't tell me *she's* been on my trail."

"Called four times after nine-thirty. I told her I expected you'd be in at ten. She said she'd call at exactly ten o'clock and that was the latest call she could possibly make."

"What's it all about, Della?"

"Apparently she feels she may need a lawyer."

"For what?"

"She didn't deem it fit to confide in me."

"What did you tell her, Della?"

"In a nice way I told her she was poison, smallpox, and had B.O., bad breath, and, in short, that she stank. I told her you were far to busy to be able to handle anything else for her. I suggested that she get in touch with some other lawyer who wouldn't be quite so busy and would be more accessible."

"Then what?"

"She said no, she didn't have confidence in anyone else. She had to talk with you."

"Did she call again at ten?"

"Right on the dot. You could have set your watch by it. Just as the second hand on the electric clock got to fifty-nine seconds past nine-fifty-nine the telephone rang and it was Nellie. I told her you weren't here and she said that was a shame because then she couldn't explain things, and she did want to explain things."

"She'll probably call again," Mason said.

"I gathered that she wouldn't."

Mason grinned. "We've probably lost a chance to make another dollar! What else is new? Anything?"

"There's a woman waiting to see you. A Miss Braxton."

"What does she want?"

"Now there," Della Street said, "you have me. She won't tell me what she wants or what it's about."

"Tell her I won't see her then," Mason said. "Hang it, I waste more time talking with people who want some routine legal chore I wouldn't touch with a ten-foot pole—probably wants me to draw a contract or make a deed or——"

"You should see her," Della Street said archly.

"Huh?"

Della Street made motions with her hands as though outlining a feminine figure.

"Like that?" Mason asked.

"Wolf bait," Della Street said. "I mean she's *really* something."

"Now," Mason told her, grinning, "you *do* have me interested. Keep on."

"And," Della Street went on, "I think she's mad about something. She says that what she wants to see you about is a personal matter and too confidential to mention to anyone. She's been waiting ever since nine-fifteen."

Mason said, "I love beautiful women who are mad, Della. How old?"

"Twenty-three, on a guess."

"And neat?"

"Face, figure, clothes, eyes, complexion, even just a trace of the perfume that makes men go nuts. You should see Gertie out at the reception desk. She can't keep her eyes on the switchboard."

"That does it," Mason said. "We're going to see Miss Braxton, but if she doesn't measure up to your build-up I shall resort to stern disciplinary measures."

"Wait until you see her," Della Street said. "You want to take a look at the mail first or——?"

"No, not the mail—the female. Let's go."

"Prepare yourself," Della Street said. "Take a deep breath. Here she comes."

And Della Street went out to the outer office to escort Miss Braxton into Mason's private office.

Mason saw the young woman enter the office with a swinging confident stride, saw her hesitate, bow coolly, then walk over to stand perfectly calm and collected by Mason's desk.

"This is Mr. Mason," Della Street said. "Miss Braxton, Mr. Mason."

"How do you do?" Mason said. "Won't you sit down?"

"Thank you."

She crossed over to the big, overstuffed client's chair, settled herself, crossed her knees, smoothed her dress, and said to Mason, "Will you kindly tell me *just* what is happening to my sister?"

"Now, just a moment," Mason said, noticing the cold steely anger in her eyes. "I'm not certain that I know your sister and I certainly don't——"

"My sister is Elizabeth Bain. Nathan Bain, her husband, is trying to poison her. Just what has been done about it?"

"Wait a minute," Mason said. "You're getting several carts in front of one horse."

Miss Braxton said, "I don't think I was ever so mad in my life, Mr. Mason. You'll pardon me if I seem to be a little worked up."

"Go right ahead," Mason told her, "only don't take it out on me."

"I didn't come to you for that purpose, Mr. Mason. I'm not mad at you."

"Just why did you come to me?"

"I want to retain you as a lawyer. I think you're the only one who can handle this situation."

"What situation?"

"What situation?" she exclaimed angrily. "Good heavens, Mr. Mason, do you have the temerity to sit there and ask that question in good faith? Good Lord, my sister has been living in a hell on earth and no one seems to have taken sufficient interest to do anything about it!"

"Are *you* sure you have your facts right?" Mason asked.

"Mr. Mason, let's put it this way. My sister married very much beneath her. The man she married is a cold-blooded, scheming, nasty toad. Do I make myself clear?"

"I gather," Mason said, "that you're endeavouring to convey to my mind that you don't like the man."

"That," she said, "is a close approximation of the truth. I hate the ground he walks on."

"So I gathered."

She went on, angrily, "He married my sister entirely for her money. We warned her about it and—well, that's where we made our mistake."

"Who's 'we'?" Mason asked.

"The family. I'm her half-sister. There's a half-brother and—well, we should have kept our noses out of it. But we didn't, and as a result, there was a certain element of stiffness which crept into the family relations. We'd always been very close prior to that time, just as real brother and sisters, and now—well, thank heaven, now it's different. Now we're all back together again."

"Just what was it you wanted me to do?" Mason asked. "I have already been retained in connection with one matter involving the Bain household."

She threw back her head and laughed.

Mason raised his eyebrows.

"You'll pardon me," she said, "but I heard Nathan's description of what happened to him on the witness stand. I don't think I ever heard anything that amused me quite as much in all my life. The pompous, vain-glorious, self-centred, egotistical toad! And you ripped him up the back and down the front, Mr. Mason. You really did a job on him. Oh, how much I would have given to have been there!"

"You learned about all this from him?"

"From him and from Nellie Conway, the nurse."

"You talked with her?"

"Oh, yes."

Mason said, "I was rather surprised that she went back out to the house."

"I think Nathan was the one who was responsible for that. Nathan was simply frightened stiff, Mr. Mason, and I'll say one thing for Nellie Conway, she certainly knew how to keep pouring it on."

"Just what do you mean?"

"The way she put the hooks into Nathan was really something."

"Let's see if we can get this straight," Mason said. "First, I'd like to find out just what you want me to do and——"

"Why, I thought I'd made myself clear on that. It's not so much what I want you to do as to what my sister wants you to do."

"Elizabeth Bain?"

"Yes."

"What does she want?"

"She wants you to represent her."

"In doing what?"

"In doing lots of things."

"Go ahead."

"Well, in the first place, Elizabeth has now seen Nathan in his true colours. The man tried to kill her. He's been deliberately trying to kill her for some time. Heaven knows what that girl has put up with and heaven knows how many times she's been at the brink of the grave. All of those sicknesses she had, the food poisonings, the things she thought at the time were just stomach upsets, were probably all part of this scheme on Nathan's part to get rid of her."

Mason's eyes narrowed. "This has been going on for some time?"

"She's been living a perfect hell, Mr. Mason, and the poor girl doesn't know even now that her spinal cord is permanently injured. She thinks that after she has gone through a period of recuperation from the accident, someone is going to be able to operate on her, remove the pressure from the spinal cord and she'll walk again."

"And she won't?"

Miss Braxton shook her head. Tears came in her eyes. "She never will."

"What do you know about the accident?" Mason asked.

Her eyes glittered. "I know all about it. Nathan says that the brakes gave way on his automobile. He tried his best to stop it. When he found he couldn't he yelled to Elizabeth to jump. A fat chance she had of jumping! Nathan had very carefully engineered the thing so that he was on the inside of the road and Elizabeth was in the seat that looked right out over a yawning chasm. When Nathan yelled to jump he already had his door open. He just jumped out of the car and turned it loose.

"Elizabeth had sufficient presence of mind to reach over and grab the wheel. Then she tried to keep the thing on the road. When she saw that wasn't going to work, and the car was accelerating into terrific speed, she tried to run the car into the bank."

"The brakes really *were* out of order?"

"There wasn't a brake on the car," Miss Braxton said. "But that could have been arranged easily enough. All Nathan had to do was to fix it with a string running up through the floorboard so he could cut through one of the hoses on the hydraulic brakes and put the whole system out of order. And he picked a place to do it where the car would have naturally been expected to plunge over a perpendicular precipice. Fortunately Elizabeth's efforts to keep it on the road managed to get her past the most dangerous place so that when it left the road the car only rolled down the steep slope for a couple of hundred feet. Even so, it was a wonder she wasn't killed."

"Did anyone examine the car to see whether it had been tampered with?" Mason asked.

"What do *you* think?"

"I'm asking you."

She said, "Poor Elizabeth had her spinal cord crushed. She'd received a concussion and was unconscious. They got her to a hospital, and dear old Nathan went right back with a breakdown crew to see what could be done with the car. They managed to get it on a winch and hoist it back up to the highway; then they towed it away—and turned it over to Nathan. And during all the time they were fooling around out there with the winch, Nathan had every opportunity on earth to remove any evidence——"

"In other words, the police weren't called in?"

"The highway patrol made a routine inspection, but that was all. I don't think anyone actually went down to where the car was except Nathan and the garage men who hooked the cable on to the car and winched it back up to the road."

"Go on," Mason said.

She said, "You don't need to be so conservative, Mr. Mason. Nellie Conway told me her whole story this morning. I was never so completely flabbergasted in all my life. To think that such conditions could exist. Well, it certainly is time we got here. That's all I can say!"

"Have you talked with Nathan Bain about it?"

"No, I haven't said a word to him. I heard about you from Nellie Conway and I decided you were the attorney my sister wants. She wants to draw up a will that will completely disinherit him and she wants to file a suit for divorce. She hates the ground he walks on; she wants him out of the house."

"Has Nathan Bain been advised about this?"

"No, Mr. Mason. We want you to tell him."

"Me?"

"That's right. I want you to come out and talk with my sister. She'll tell you what to do, and then I want you to go out and see Mr. Bain, tell him he's done and tell him to pack up his things and get out of the house."

"Who owns the house?" Mason asked.

"My sister. She owns everything."

"Nathan's business is not profitable?"

"I think it's *quite* profitable," she said acidly, "but you'd never find it out from anything he tells you, and you wouldn't find it out from any books he keeps."

"What do you mean by that?"

"He does business on a cash basis wherever possible. He puts the cash in his pocket and no one knows how much it is or how much he makes. He doesn't believe in paying income tax and he doesn't believe in confiding in anyone. He's one of the most secretive men I know."

"Don't you think," Mason asked, "that it would be a better plan for your sister to call him in and tell him that as far as she's concerned she's all finished, that she wants him to leave, that she intends to file a suit for divorce, and——?"

"No, Mr. Mason. I don't think that would be the way to handle it. Elizabeth simply detests the sight of him. She gets almost hysterical every time she thinks of him. Remember that she's not well and she's been taking lots of sedatives which have had an effect on her nervous system. She wants to feel that he is entirely out of her life once and for all, and she doesn't ever want to see him again."

"All right," Mason said, "if that's the way she wants it."

"You'll do it?"

"I see no reason why not."

Miss Braxton opened her purse. "I told Elizabeth I'd come to you and put it right up to you, that if you'd do what she wanted and tell Nathan Bain where he got off, that she could be free of her worries. Elizabeth told me to give you this as a retainer."

She handed Mason a cheque, dated that day, drawn on the Farmer's and Mechanic's National for an amount of five hundred dollars, payable to "Perry Mason, attorney for Elizabeth Bain," and signed in a somewhat wobbly handwriting *"Elizabeth Bain."*

"This is a retainer?" Mason asked.

"That's right."

"And just what is it Mrs. Bain wants me to do?"

"You've started out very nicely showing her husband up. Just keep on doing it. Kick him out of the house and see that things are fixed so he can't ever get a penny of her property."

Mason said, "Your half-sister may make you her agent to deliver the cheque. I'll have to have those instructions from her own lips."

"Of course."

"When I'm alone with her, so I'll know there hasn't been any . . ."

"Undue influence, Mr. Mason?"

"If you want to put it that way, yes."

"Come on out and talk with her."

"I will."

"In the meantime, Mr. Mason," she said, "I want your opinion about this document—that is, Elizabeth does."

Miss Braxton opened her purse and took out a sheet of paper on which the date was written in the same wobbling handwriting that was on the cheque, and then the words:

I, Elizabeth Bain, knowing that my husband has tried to kill me on several occasions, having lost all confidence in him, and all affection for him, make

this my last will and testament, leaving everything I own share and share alike
to my beloved half-sister, Victoria Braxton, and my beloved half-brother, James
Braxton, with the understanding that they will take my property

Mason regarded the piece of paper somewhat quizzically, and said, "Just what is it you want to know about this?"

"Is it good?"

Mason said cautiously, "That depends."

"Well, good heavens, you're a lawyer, aren't you?"

"Yes."

"And you can't say that it's good or that it isn't good?"

Mason smiled and shook his head.

"Why not?"

"Suppose," Mason countered, "you tell me something of the circumstances under which this will was made."

"Well, I don't know as it's so terribly important, Mr. Mason. You'll notice that it's dated today. Elizabeth slept very soundly last night. One of the few good nights she's had. I think it was because she knew we were coming.

"Now, Mr. Mason, when she wakened about five o'clock this morning, she told me to come and see you, and give you that retainer. She instructed me to have you make a will which would fix it so Nathan Bain couldn't profit by her death. And then she . . . well, I don't know, I suppose perhaps . . . well, in a way she's been reading a lot and . . ."

"What are you getting at?" Mason asked.

"Well, of course, in pictures on the screen and in detective stories and all that, a person who is intending to disinherit someone . . . well, the interval that the lawyer is preparing the new will, you know, is always the most dangerous time. So Elizabeth talked that over with me, and decided that if she'd write it out, in her own handwriting, showing just what she wanted done with her property, that it would be good. Now is that right?"

"That's right," Mason said, "up to a certain point."

"What do you mean by that?"

"In this State, and, mind you, I'm talking now *only* about this State, a will is good if it is made, dated and signed in the handwriting of the testator. It takes those three things, the date, the will and the signature, all in the handwriting of the testator."

Miss Braxton nodded.

"Now," Mason went on, "you'll note that, in the ordinary sense of the word, your sister didn't sign this will."

"But she wrote her name, Elizabeth Bain, in her own handwriting."

"She wrote her name," Mason said, "in describing herself. In other words, there's a question whether the words 'Elizabeth Bain' as they appear in the will were intended as a signature or whether they were intended to be merely descriptive."

"Well, does it make any difference where the name appears on the will?"

"As a matter of law, it does not," Mason said, "provided the courts can establish clearly that the testator intended the writing of the name to be as a signature."

"Well, that's what Elizabeth intended."

Mason smiled and shook his head. "There have been several very interesting cases where the point has been raised. I can't give you the citations offhand, but there are cases where wills such as this have been offered for probate, and the question has always been whether the use of the testator's name was descriptive or whether it was intended as a signature. Now you'll notice one very peculiar thing about this writing."

"What?"

"There is," Mason said, "no final punctuation at the end of it."

"What do you mean by that?"

"After the word 'property,' " Mason said, "there is no full stop."

"Well, for heaven's sake! Do you mean to say that a little dot one-tenth the size of a pinhead on a piece of paper would——?"

"I mean to say so very definitely," Mason interrupted. "There's a case somewhere . . . wait a minute, perhaps I can put my hand on it."

He walked over to a shelf filled with books, pulled down a book, ran through the pages, then settled himself for a few minutes' intensive study.

Miss Braxton interrupted him to say, "Well, after all, it isn't that important, Mr. Mason. This is just sort of a . . . well, a stopgap. Elizabeth did it to ease her mind. She thought that if Nathan knew he had already been disinherited it would dissuade him from perhaps trying any last minute final attempt in desperation."

"You mean that he wouldn't try to kill her?"

"That's right."

Mason returned to the book, then said, "From a legal standpoint it's a most interesting question."

"Well, I've heard of a lot of technicalities," Miss Braxton said, "but if you're trying to tell me that a teeny, weeny dot on a piece of paper is going to make any difference as to the validity of a will, I'll say you lawyers are getting altogether too technical."

"The point is," Mason said, "that it goes to the intention of the testator. In other words, when your sister finished with this document, did she consider that it was a complete and final will, or did she start to make a will and was then interrupted by something and never did finish making the will?"

"Oh, I see what you're getting at now."

"For instance," Mason said, "if you're interested in the legal reasoning, here's the Estate of Kinney, reported in 104 Pacific (2d) at page 782, where it was held that the writing of the testator's name only in the beginning of the declaration is a sufficient signing to justify admitting a will to probate, even though there is no affirmative expression adopting the name so placed as the signature of the testator.

"Then in a recent case, Estate of Kaminski, reported in 115 Pacific (2d) at page 21, it was held that the name of the testator at the beginning of an alleged holographic will constitutes a sufficient signature where the instrument appears to be a *complete* testamentary expression of his desires.

"Now, in the Estate of Bauman, 300 Pacific, 62, it was held that in all cases of this sort the entire instrument must be examined to find out whether it was intended to be a complete will. The final expression, the abruptness in closing, and *even the final punctuation* are to be considered for the purpose of determining whether the writer intended to adopt the name as written in the opening clause as a signature or merely as words of description.

"Now you notice that your sister's will has some very peculiar closing words—'*with the understanding that they will take my property*' . . . The testator could very well have been intending to add 'subject to the following trust,' or 'to be used for the purpose of' . . ."

"But she didn't mean that at all," Miss Braxton interrupted. "She simply meant that the understanding was that by this will we were to take all of her property so that Nathan Bain wouldn't have any opportunity——"

"I understand that's your contention," Mason said, "but you hand me a sheet of paper, you ask me a legal question, and I'm giving you the best answer I can."

Miss Braxton smiled. "Well, I guess it won't make two bits' worth of difference, Mr. Mason, because you can draw up a formal will and have it executed with witnesses and everything. How soon can you get out there?"

"When would be convenient?"

"The sooner the better. All you need to do is to prepare a will made in conformity with this will and have it all ready for her to sign and——"

"That might not be advisable," Mason interrupted.

"Why not?"

"I haven't as yet talked with your sister."

"Well, I'm her agent. She sent me up here to tell you what to do, and gave me this cheque for your retainer."

Mason nodded and smiled, "Nathan Bain might contest the will. He might claim there was undue influence on your part."

"But good heavens, Mr. Mason, aren't we crossing a lot of bridges before we come to them? After all, a will wouldn't . . . well, there wouldn't be any occcasion for a will unless Elizabeth should die, and now that Jim and I are here she's not going to die; and if you can get Nathan Bain out of the house there won't be one chance in a million that——"

"A lawyer isn't paid to consider *probabilities*," Mason told her. "He's paid to consider *possibilities*."

"But that will mean a delay, won't it, Mr. Mason?"

Mason shook his head.

"Why not?"

"I'll take Della Street, my secretary, along with me. She'll take a portable typewriter, and just as soon as your sister tells me she wants the will prepared, my secretary will type it out, call in two witnesses who are completely disinterested, and——"

"What two witnesses?" Miss Braxton interrupted.

"Miss Street can sign as one witness and I'll sign as another."

"Oh, that'll be fine," she said, her face beaming. "That's the way to do it. How soon can you get out there, Mr. Mason?"

"Under the circumstances, I can get out there at . . . well, let me see, at two o'clock this afternoon?"

"Could you possibly make it at eleven-thirty this morning, Mr. Mason? That will give me time to get home and tell Elizabeth that you're coming out, and give her a chance to get straightened up a bit. After all, a woman wants to look her best, you know, and her hair's a mess! . . . They haven't been giving her the affectionate attention that a sister would give . . . you know, those little personal touches."

"Eleven-thirty will be all right," Mason said. "I'll be there——"

The telephone rang sharply. Della Street picked it up, said, "Hello . . . Who is it? . . . Vicki Braxton? . . . Just a moment, please."

She turned to Miss Braxton and said, "Someone wants to talk with you on this phone and says it's very important."

"And they asked for 'Vicki'?" Miss Braxton asked.

"Yes."

"Good heavens, I can't understand it. No one in the world knows that I am here, and I'm known as Vicki only to intimates and members of the family. Why, I . . . I can't understand it."

"Well, suppose you take the phone call," Della Street said, "and find out who it is. That is, if you want to."

From the receiver came a rasping chatter and Della Street said, "Just a moment." She placed the receiver to her ear and said, "What was that again? . . . Oh, yes, I'll tell her.

"It's your brother, Jim," she said.

Victoria Braxton walked over to the phone, said, "Hello, Jim. This is Vicki. What is it? . . . What? . . . No! . . . Oh, my God! . . . You're sure? . . . I'll be right over."

She slammed the phone back on the hook, turned around and said to Perry Mason, "My God, it's happened! Elizabeth is dying. They've been looking all over trying to find me. Jim, my brother, happened to remember . . . Let me out of here."

She started towards the door to the outer office, then saw the exit door opening into the corridor, swerved in her course, twisted the knob, jerked the door open, and dashed out.

Mason, looking at Della Street, ran his fingers through thick, wavy hair in a gesture of perplexity.

"This Bain case!" he said.

"I suppose you'd throw me out if I mentioned anything about the bane of your life!"

"I'd draw you and quarter you," he announced, as Della Street ducked defensively. "What happened to that holographic will?"

"She grabbed it, put it back in her purse, and took it with her."

Mason said, "There's just a chance, Della, that that document might assume the greatest importance."

"You mean, if Mrs. Bain is really dying?"

He nodded. "The peculiar wording of that last sentence in the holographic will, the absence of any closing punctuation——"

Della Street laughed cynically. "The next time you see that will, Chief, it will have a very complete period at the end of that sentence. Want to bet?"

Mason pursed his lips. "No, I don't think I do, Della. I guess you're right. In that event I'd be in a most peculiar position. I'd be bound to respect my client's confidences on the one hand, but, on the other hand, as an attorney at law, who is an officer of the court. . . . Get Paul Drake on the telephone. Tell him I want information about what's going on out there in the Bain household and I want it fast. Tell him I'm not particularly concerned how he gets it. . . . And Nellie Conway's last call was at ten o'clock?"

"Right on the second," she said.

"And she told you she couldn't call after that?"

"Yes."

"That," Mason said, "makes it *exceedingly* interesting. Also notice that Miss Braxton said no one knew she was here. That would mean her brother must know nothing about Elizabeth Bain's intentions to retain me, and nothing whatever about that rather mysterious holographic will."

Della nodded. "Shall we say the plot thickens, Chief?"

"Just like that gravy I tried to make on my last hunting trip, Della. It thickened in lumps. 'Thousand Island Gravy,' the boys called it."

EIGHT

AT 11.55 PAUL DRAKE telephoned.

"Hello, Perry. I'm out here at a service station about two blocks from the Bain house. Elizabeth Bain died about ten minutes ago according to information that was relayed to me by back door scuttlebutt."

"The cause?" Mason asked.

"Seems to be no doubt that it's arsenic poisoning. They felt she was too ill to be removed to a hospital. They've had a diagnosis of arsenic ever since nine-thirty this morning and have been treating her for it. Symptoms first appeared a little before nine."

"Any chance that it's suicide?" Mason asked.

Drake said, "The place is crawling with officers from the Homicide Squad. Your friend Sergeant Holcomb is pretty much in evidence."

Mason thought things over, then he said, "Paul, I have a job for you."

"What?"

"I not only want all the dope on everyone out there at Bain's place, but I want you to canvass the airports. I want to find out what planes left at ten-fifteen this morning. I want that done fast."

"Okay. I can check that pretty rapidly," Drake said. "You can check it yourself by calling the airports——"

Mason said, "That's only half of it, Paul. When you find what airplanes left, I want you to check descriptions of every woman on those planes. I'm particularly looking for a mousy, poker-faced woman, who will have signed her name on the passenger list with the initials. 'N.C.' That is, her first name will begin with an 'N,' her last name will begin with a 'C,' and I want information so fast that it isn't even going to be funny. How long will it take?"

"Perhaps an hour."

"Cut that in half," Mason said. "Make it fifteen minutes if you can. I'm going to be sitting right here at the telephone. Get going and call me."

Mason hung up the telephone and began pacing the floor.

"What is it?" Della Street asked.

Mason said, "Probably around nine this morning, perhaps a little before, Elizabeth Bain was taken violently ill. By nine-thirty they had diagnosed it as arsenic poisoning. About fifteen minutes ago she died."

"And?" Della Street asked.

"And," Mason said, "Nellie Conway was frantically trying to get me all morning, but she had a deadline of ten o'clock. She couldn't call me after that. That was the last minute she'd be able to talk with me."

"You mean she's on a plane somewhere?"

"She's on a plane," Mason said, "and let's hope she had sense enough to sign her name as Nellie Conway. In the event she didn't, her baggage is probably stamped 'N.C.' so she'll use a name that will fit with the initials on the baggage."

"And if Elizabeth Bain died from arsenic poisoning?" Della Street asked.

"Then," Mason said, "in view of the fact that I had certain tablets in my possession which Nellie Conway gave me with the story that Nathan had been bribing her to administer them to Elizabeth Bain, and in further view of the fact I gave those tablets back to Nellie——"

"But those were only aspirin tablets," Della Street said.

Mason sighed. "One of them was an aspirin tablet, Della. Whenever a lawyer begins to regard his work as routine and to think in terms of the average and the usual, he's riding for a fall. People don't pay a lawyer to think of what's probably going to happen. They expect him to think of and anticipate everything that could possibly happen.

"Look up Nathan Bain's telephone number. Ring the house. If Sergeant Holcomb's out there I want to talk with him."

Della Street said, "Nellie Conway left us a number, you know. Just a minute, I'll get it. . . ."

She ran through half a dozen cards, said, "Here it is. West 6-9841."

"All right," Mason said, "get Holcomb."

Della Street picked up the telephone, said, "Gertie, ring West 6-9841 and get Sergeant Holcomb on the line. It's important. Rush it."

Della Street held on to the phone for several seconds, then motioned to Mason and said, "He's coming on now, Chief."

Mason took the phone just as he heard a gruff voice saying, "Hello. This is Holcomb. Who is this?"

"Perry Mason."

"Oh, yes, Mason. How did you know I was out here?"

"I've been trying to reach you."

"All right, what is it?"

Mason said, "You will remember, Sergeant, that Nellie Conway, whom I spoke to you about a few days ago, had claimed that Nathan Bain had asked her to administer certain five-grain pills to his wife. I told you about that."

"Yeah, go on," Sergeant Holcomb said.

"And," Mason said, "in order to check her story I had one of those pills analysed. It contained aspirin. I thought you should know."

There was a long period of silence.

"You there?" Mason asked impatiently.

"I'm here," Sergeant Holcomb said.

"Well?" Mason asked.

"I don't remember the conversation that way," Sergeant Holcomb said, and hung up.

Mason jiggled the receiver twice, then dropped the telephone into place.

"Did he hang up?" Della Street asked.

Mason nodded, white-faced with anger.

"Go ahead, Chief," she said. "Let it go. I've heard all of the words before, and this is once I'd like to hear 'em again."

He shook his head.

"Why not?"

"Damn it, Della, I can't afford to get mad. I have to think."

"But, Chief, I was listening to that conversation. I know that you told him that——"

"Your testimony will be somewhat less than conclusive," Mason said dryly. "Moreover, you didn't hear what Holcomb said to me by way of reply."

"What does he *claim* he said?" she asked.

Mason made his lips into a sour grin. "He hasn't had time to think that up yet. What the hell do you think he hung up for?"

She said, "I wish you'd let go and cuss him. It's going to sound unladylike if I voice my thoughts on behalf of the firm."

Mason shook his head. "A good lawyer must always remember one thing. Never get mad unless someone pays him to do it."

"Can you imagine that damn cop deliberately lying?" Della Street asked, indignantly.

"I can imagine him doing anything," Mason said. "Lieutenant Tragg is tough but he's a square shooter. I should have insisted on getting in touch with Tragg; but the thing sounded like such a complete cock-and-bull story . . . I still don't get it. All I know is that I have a distinct feeling I'm in hot water and it's getting hotter."

He began pacing the floor. Della Street started to say something, then, changing her mind, stood watching him with worried eyes as he paced back and forth.

At 12.25 the telephone rang.

Della Street picked up the phone and Paul Drake said, "Hello, Della. I have the information Perry wanted about the airplane passenger."

Mason jerked himself up sharply. "That Drake?" he asked.

Della Street nodded.

"Tell him to give you the dope if he has any," Mason said.

"Shoot," Della said into the phone.

Drake said, "A ten-fifteen plane for New Orleans, Della. A woman who answered the description of the party Mason wanted gave her name as Nora Carson."

Della Street relayed the information to Perry Mason. Mason crossed the office in three swift strides, grabbed the telephone and said, "Paul, get in touch with whatever agency you correspond with in New Orleans. I want four men working in relays. I want Nora Carson picked up as soon as she leaves the plane. I want to have someone on her every minute of the time, and I don't care what it costs. I want to know where she goes, who she sees, what she does and when. Then wire to the Roosevelt Hotel and reserve a suite for two in *your* name. The registration will be Paul Drake and party.

"Della Street will get us tickets on the first available plane to New Orleans. Tell your men to report to us at the Roosevelt Hotel. Now jump in your car and get up here just as fast as you can because we're leaving on the first available plane and I don't know yet just what the schedules are——"

"There's one at one-fifteen," Paul Drake said, "but we can't make that. We——"

"Who the hell says we can't?" Mason asked. "Drive to the airport. I'll meet you there."

NINE

WITHIN TWO HOURS of the time Mason and Paul Drake had ensconced themselves in the Roosevelt Hotel in New Orleans, a representative of Paul Drake's affiliated detective agency was in the room making a report.

"We have the party located," he said. "She's taken an apartment in the old French Quarter. It was all ready for her. The lease was signed by a man from your city, a fellow by the name of Nathan Bain. Do you know him?"

Mason and Drake exchanged glances.

Mason said, "Go ahead."

"This apartment was leased about thirty days ago and Bain took out a six-months' lease on it."

"What sort of a place?" Mason asked.

"Well, you know how those apartments in the French Quarter are. They're old as the hills, but the place has a certain atmosphere that appeals to tourists and some of the local residents who want high ceilings and low rent. Some of the buildings have been fixed up pretty nice."

"When Bain negotiated for the lease did he say anything about who was going to occupy the apartment?"

"Simply took a lease on the apartment."

"How did he pay for the rent?" Mason asked. "By cheque?"

"No. There's something interesting. He paid by postal money order."

Mason nodded. "The girl is living there?"

"That's right. Living there under the name of Nora Carson, and she's dough-heavy."

"How heavy?" Mason asked.

"I don't know. She has quite a wad of bills in her purse, big bills. Right after she arrived she went to the Bourbon House for dinner and tried to change a hundred-dollar bill. It caused quite a little commotion. She said that was the smallest she had. The manager happened to get a glance at the inside of her purse and saw that it held quite a wad of currency. He thought she was lying and was trying to get rid of a big bill because it might be hot. That made him suspicious. He insisted that she dig up something smaller. She finally left the hundred-dollar bill as security, went out, and was back within twenty minutes with a bunch of small bills."

Mason digested that information. "Anything else?" he said.

"Yes. We've followed instructions and kept her spotted all the time."

"Does she have any idea she's being tailed?"

"Apparently not. She goes about her business just as though it was part of a regular routine. She doesn't seem to pay any attention to people on the sidewalk."

"All right. What's she doing down here?"

"Well, of course, she's only been here three or four hours, but——"

"What's she done to indicate the purpose of her visit in that time?"

"Nothing."

"How big a place is this French Quarter apartment house?" Mason asked.

"Not big. Two apartments to a floor, two floors. It's a narrow, three-storeyed place with a praline store on the ground floor, your party and one other woman have the apartments on the second floor, one bachelor and one vacant apartment on the third floor."

"Who has the other second-floor apartment?" Mason asked.

"A Miss Charlotte Moray. You know how these buildings are in the French Quarter—that is, I'm taking it for granted that you're familiar with it?" The question invited confidences.

"He's familiar with it," Drake said, shortly.

The New Orleans detective regarded Perry Mason thoughtfully. It was quite evident that he was interested in the identity of Drake's mysterious client, but his curiosity stopped short of actual questions.

"How long has this Moray woman been there?" Mason asked.

"About a week."

"Know where she comes from or anything about her?"

"Not a thing. We've only been on the job——"

"Yes, I know. Have you a description?"

The detective took a notebook from his pocket. "Around twenty-four or twenty-five, very dark, good figure, snapping black eyes, dark hair, a lot of personality and pep, wears good clothes and knows how to wear them. We haven't had time to find out much about her. We do know that she gets telegrams every day, sometimes two or three times a day. We don't know where they come from or anything about them, but we do know she gets them."

"Anything else?" Mason asked.

"That covers it to date. That Moray girl is a nice dish. Five feet four, a hundred and twenty pounds, curves in the right places, lots of fire, and evidently she keeps pretty much to herself. No boy friends, no particular interest in the scenery, seems to be fully familiar with New Orleans, knows where to shop, does some cooking in her apartment, eats out some of the time, very unapproachable, but gracious and smiling to the waitresses, just a woman keeping very much to herself."

"One more question," Mason said. "When did Charlotte Moray rent her apartment?"

"She sub-let it before she came here and was all ready to move in when she got off the plane."

"Sub-let it? From whom?"

"Why, this man Bain. I thought you understood. He leased the whole second floor, and——"

"Leased the whole second floor!" Mason exclaimed.

"Why, yes. You see, he——"

"Why the hell didn't you say so?"

"You didn't ask. I mean, you seemed to want information only on this Conway girl. Of course we've been working fast and . . . I'm sorry, sir. I thought you understood."

"The third floor—does Bain lease that too?"

"No, just the second floor, the two apartments there."

Mason turned to Paul Drake. "Pay them off, Paul, and call them off."

Drake raised his eyebrows.

"We're finished," Mason said. "Are these boys pretty good at forgetting things?"

"They should be," Drake said.

"We are," the New Orleans detective assured them, his eyes, however, filled with curiosity as he studied Mason.

"All right," Mason said, "we don't want any more coverage on the case. Lay the men off and be sure everyone is called off the job."

"As soon as we're paid off, we're off the job," the New Orleans detective said. "We're not anxious to work for nothing."

Drake pulled a notecase from his pocket, said, "This is a job where payments are made in cash. Come on in the other room and we'll get straightened up."

Five minutes later when Drake returned he said, "I didn't want to seem rude, Perry, but if I hadn't insisted on a private pay-off it would have been suspicious. He would have thought we were pretty closely associated. I wanted him to think you were just an ordinary client."

Mason nodded. "How soon will he have his men removed from the job, Paul?"

Drake said, "Give him fifteen minutes, Perry. I told him to go out and call the thing off. He said he was starting right away. We'll give him fifteen minutes."

Mason said, "That'll be fine."

"But what gets me," Drake told him, "is why you're so damn crazy to have this gal covered every minute of the day and night, and after the men have been working on her for four hours, you get in such a lather to have them called off the job. I don't get it."

"Because we have the information we want," Mason told him.

"Well, even so, why be in such a rush to get the men off the job?"

Mason lit a cigarette. "Nellie Conway is going to have a visitor, Paul. Later on, the police may be interested in Nellie Conway. They may find out these detectives were on the job and shake them down to find out what they know. If they don't know who this visitor is, they can't tell."

"You seem to be pretty sure of your facts," Drake said.

"I am."

"Then you probably know who this visitor is going to be—the one you don't want the police to find out about."

"I do."

"Who—Nathan Bain?"

"No."

"Who, then?"

"Perry Mason," the lawyer told him.

TEN

AFTER MIDNIGHT THE French Quarter of New Orleans takes on an individuality all its own.

Escorts who have gone to 'get the car' drive back down the narrow one-way streets, only to find that their party, instead of waiting on the sidewalk, is lingering over a last drink.

The driver sounds an indignant horn.

In the meantime, his car is blocking the choked one-way street. A car pulls up behind him and the driver sounds a couple of blasts just as a courteous reminder. The driver of the stalled car shows his good faith by blasting his horn in protest.

Two or three other cars fall in behind. Each car, from time to time, emits short, courteous reminders of sound, until, patience exhausted, they all start demanding the driver ahead to move on and clear the street.

At such times the exasperated roar of a dozen blasting horns shatters the night silence to ribbons.

Parties emerging from the noisy interiors of the nightclubs say goodbye to new-found acquaintances. There is an exchange of telephone numbers, and because ears and voices are not as yet oriented to the comparative stillness of the outer air, the information is usually given in a voice audible half a block away.

Then there are the exuberant souls who take advantage of the Quarter's custom of putting garbage cans out on the sidewalk for night collection. These revellers release their animal spirits by kicking the covers of garbage cans along the sidewalks.

Shortly before daylight, when other noises have quieted down, the garbage trucks rumble along, banging and clattering the collection of garbage into the big vans.

All in all, the person who craves quiet in the Quarter should not try to sleep before 6 a.m. Most of them don't.

Mason, threading his way through late revellers and denizens of the Quarter, walked twice around the block in order to make certain there were no shadows watching the entrance to the apartment house. Then he entered a narrow passageway which led to a patio, and climbed an ornamental flight of stairs, whose characteristic wrought-iron banisters led in a sweeping curve to the second floor. Here a hundred and fifty years of foundation settling in the damp soil had caused waving in-equalities in a typical floor, which, because of habit, the eye interpreted as being level, with disastrous results to the gait of a sober citizen, but seemingly without undue effect on the inebriated.

The door marked '1.A.' was by the head of the stairs. The door was slightly open. Mason could see the illuminated interior of the apartment.

There was a reclining chair by a table on which were newspapers and magazines; a reading lamp shed brilliance over the scene. In the shadowed area behind the reading lamp, heavy curtains had been par-tially pulled across french doors opening on a narrow balcony, which in turn stretched out over the sidewalk of the one-way street.

A door at the end of the corridor made a noise. Mason heard the sound of a cautious step, then a half-startled scream.

"How did *you* get here?" Nellie Conway demanded.

Mason said grimly, "Let's get a few things straightened out, Nellie."

They entered the apartment. Mason seated himself and indicated a chair for Nellie Conway.

"This isn't going to take long," he said.

She stood for a moment, dubiously, then fumbled with the catch of the purse which she had been carrying clutched under her arm.

"Honestly, Mr. Mason," she said, "you didn't *need* to do this. I intended to send you the money."

She sat down, opened the purse and took out two one-hundred-dollar notes, hesitated a moment, added another hundred-dollar note and pushed the three hundred dollars across the table to Mason.

Mason regarded the one-hundred-dollar notes thoughtfully. "Where did you get this?"

"That was part of the settlement."

"What settlement?"

"The one I made with Nathan Bain."

"All right," Mason said, still holding the money in his hand, "tell me about the settlement."

"Well, it was like I told you, Mr. Mason. Mr. Bain was worried and . . .

"Well, of course, when I came to get my things, Mr. Bain was a little embarrassed at first. I asked him about the relief nurse he had taking care of his wife, and it seemed she'd quit the job for some reason or other. The housekeeper was helping out. Mr. Bain said that he expected his wife's relatives to arrive shortly after midnight."

"Then what did you do?"

"I went in and talked with Elizabeth . . . Mrs. Bain, and helped the housekeeper. We managed to get her really quiet. She had the best sleep she'd had since the accident."

"Have any conversations with her?"

"Oh, yes. She asked me a lot of questions."

"What about?"

"About where I'd been and how much she hated to have me leave her, and how she'd missed me while I was gone, and asking me how it had happened that I was leaving."

"Did you tell her the truth—about being arrested and the trial?"

"Of course, why not?"

"I'm just asking," Mason said. "Go on. Did Nathan Bain come in there while you were there? Did he——?"

"Mr. Bain never enters his wife's room. It would have a very adverse effect on Elizabeth. The doctor knows that just as Mr. Bain knows it. It's lamentable, but it's one of the things that——"

"Never mind that," Mason said. "I just wanted to know if he went in."

"No, he didn't."

"And did you tell her about how he had tried to bribe you to give her medicine?"

"Oh, no."

"Why not?"

"That might have been bad for the patient. You shouldn't ever do or say anything to excite your patient."

Mason studied her thoughtfully. "All right. Now tell me about where you got this money."

"That was early in the evening, before I went in to see Mrs. Bain. When I first showed up, Mr. Bain asked me what I intended to do— you know, about the arrest and all that. That's when I telephoned you."

"Go ahead," Mason said.

"Well, I told him that as far as our relations were concerned, that is, Mr. Bain's and mine, they would have to be worked out by attorneys, that I didn't care to discuss that phase of the matter with him. I said I had come to get my things, and not to talk."

"And what did Bain do?"

478 THE PERRY MASON CASEBOOK

"Well, then Mr. Bain insisted we make some kind of a settlement. He wanted to have things worked out so we could . . . well, as he said, so we could act civilised about the thing."

"And you made a settlement with him?"

"Well, he explained to me that if an attorney represented me in making a settlement, the lawyer would charge me perhaps fifty per cent of what I received, at least thirty-three and a third per cent. He told me there was no reason why I couldn't have that money just as well as some lawyer. He said that he was willing to acknowledge the fact that he'd made a mistake. He said he'd been betrayed by that private detective who had posed as a smart guy, a sort of know-it-all."

"What kind of a settlement did you finally make?"

"I don't think that needs to enter into *our* discussions, Mr. Mason."

"What kind of a settlement did you finally make?"

"Well, he said he'd pay me what it would cost him to fight me in court, and in that way the lawyers wouldn't get it all. He said that if I got a lawyer to sue him he'd have to pay a lawyer to fight the case and I'd have to pay a lawyer to bring the case to court, and then they'd suggest a compromise, and he'd pay money to me, half of which would go into the pocket of the lawyer, and his lawyer would then charge——"

"What kind of a settlement did you make?"

"An adequate settlement."

"What kind of a settlement did you make?"

"I felt under the circumstances I had been fairly compensated."

"How much was it?"

She said, "Mr. Bain asked me not to discuss that matter with anyone and I don't feel free to do so, Mr. Mason. I . . . I had enough for your fee. I intended to send you a money order in the morning, the first thing. I really did."

"How much did he pay you?"

"I am sorry, Mr. Mason, I am not at liberty to discuss that. I've paid you your fee and I'd like for you to give me a receipt, please."

Mason said, "This money came from Nathan Bain?"

"Of course, where else would I get it?"

"I mean, did he give you a cheque and did you go to a bank and cash the cheque and then——?"

"No, no. He gave me the cash in currency."

"Did you sign anything?"

"I signed a complete release."

"Had it been drawn up by a lawyer?"

"I don't know."

"Was it typewritten?"

"Yes."

"On legal size stationery, or on letter size stationery?"

"On letter size stationery."

"Do you know whether he'd been to see an attorney?"

"I don't think so. I think he drew it up himself."

"You took the money?"

"Yes."

"How did you happen to come here?"

"I've always wanted to come to New Orleans and just relax and see the city. It has always fascinated me. It's a city with such a romantic background, and they say the restaurants here are——"

"How did you happen to come here?"

"Just an impulse, Mr. Mason."

"Did Mr. Bain suggest that you come here?"

"Mr. Bain? Good heavens, no!"

"How did you happen to get this apartment?"

She lowered her eyes for a moment, then said, "Really, Mr. Mason, I don't think I care to discuss any more of my private affairs. I'm certainly grateful to you but there are some things I can't go into. Please remember that you acted as my lawyer for just one matter. You're not my lawyer now. You defended me, and I've paid you. That winds up all matters between us. I don't want to seem rude, but——"

"Do you know anyone here in New Orleans?"

"Not a soul. No."

"There was no one you came here to see?"

"No."

Mason jerked his head towards the door. "Where were you when I came in?"

"I . . . I'd just dashed downstairs to mail a letter in the mail-box at the next corner."

"Who was the letter to?"

"To you. I wanted you to know where I was and to tell you I'd send you money for your fee."

Mason said, "You had some tablets in a little corked tube."

"You mean the ones we put in the envelope?"

"Yes. What did you do with those?"

She hesitated a moment, then said, "I tossed the whole thing in the trash."

"What do you mean by the whole thing?"

"The envelope, everything."

"You mean the envelope with our names written across the sealed flap?"

"Yes."

"You didn't open the envelope?"

"No."

"Why did you do that?"

"Because, well . . . I don't know. Perhaps I shouldn't have done it, Mr. Mason, but after I had made my settlement with Mr. Bain and he turned out to be . . . well, he was trying to do the square thing and I thought I'd let bygones be bygones."

"Did you tell him you were throwing the tablets away?"

"I'd rather not answer that."

Mason said, "Let's get a few cards face up on the table for a change. Did you tell him what you had done?"

"Yes. He saw me do it."

"Saw you throw the envelope in the trash?"

"Yes."

"What did you tell him?"

"I told him that I wasn't in a position to do what he'd wanted me to, that I'd told you about what had happened when . . . when I talked with you, and that if you'd wanted to, you could have confronted him with that envelope on cross-examination and put him in the position of having tried to see that drugs were given to his wife."

"What did he say?"

"He said that he had been anticipating such a move and that he was prepared for it."

"Did he say how he was prepared?"

"No."

"But he did say he had been anticipating it?"

"He said he thought I might try to pull something like that or that you might."

"And what did you tell him?"

"I told him that you hadn't needed to do anything like that, and that since he was trying to do the right thing by me, I'd try to do the right thing by him, and I took the envelope with that little bottle in it and tossed it into the waste basket back of the cook stove in the kitchen."

"Did you tell him you'd do that before he paid you money, or afterward?"

"I . . . I can't remember."

"Did you tell Nathan Bain you were going to New Orleans?"

"Certainly not. It was none of his business."

"You got off the plane and moved right into this apartment. You didn't go to a hotel first to get oriented, you just moved right in."

"Well, what's wrong with that?"

"Apartments aren't that easy to find in New Orleans."

"Well, what if they aren't? I found this one."

"You had this one before you ever came to New Orleans."

"Well, what if I did? I'm not accountable to you for my conduct."

"How is Mrs. Bain getting along?"

"Splendidly. Of course, she'll never walk again, but she's doing fine. She slept like a log, just the realisation that her relatives were there—and they're very nice people, those relatives of hers."

"You met them?"

"Of course. I was helping with the nursing as much as I could. After Mr. Bain made his settlement with me, I wanted to do what I could, you know."

"You didn't have any idea how long she might live when you last saw her?"

"Oh, she'll live for years."

Mason said, "Now we'll go back to where we started. How much of a settlement did you get out of Mr. Bain?"

"I'm not going to tell you that."

"You collected money from Mr. Bain for my attorney fee?"

"We talked, of course, about the expense I'd been to. That was why he was making a settlement."

"I told you over the telephone that if Mr. Bain was paying my fee, it was going to be five hundred dollars."

"Well, he wasn't paying your fee. I'm the one who's paying your fee."

"Nathan Bain was standing right there by the telephone when you talked with me?"

"Yes."

"And I told you it was going to cost him five hundred dollars for my fee?"

"Something to that effect."

Mason held out his hand.

She hesitated a long moment, then reluctantly opened her purse again, took out two one-hundred-dollar notes and literally threw them across the table.

Mason folded them, put them in his pocket and walked out.

As soon as he had left the apartment, she slammed the door, and Mason heard the sound of a bolt shooting into place.

Mason walked down the corridor, waited for a moment, then tapped gently on the door of Apartment 1.B.

The floor had sagged enough to leave a half-inch crack under the door. Mason could see a ribbon of light through the crack, could see a moving shadow as some person glided gently into position and stood listening intently.

Mason tapped once more with his finger-tips, a barely audible sound on the panels of the door.

The shadow on the other side of the door moved a few inches. The sound of the bolt being drawn back was almost inaudible. The door opened.

The very attractive woman who was standing on the threshold was clothed only in a filmy *négligé*. Light shining through it outlined her figure in sharp silhouette, the gossamer clothing forming a filmy aura about the well-shaped body.

"Oh!" she said, in an exclamation that was a mingling of surprise and dismay, and started to close the door.

Mason stepped forward.

She struggled with the door for a moment, then fell back.

"I'll scream," she warned.

"It won't get you anything."

"And this won't get *you* anything!" she retorted angrily.

Mason said, "Let's make this as painless as possible. I want to talk about the woman who was in here a few minutes ago, the one who has apartment 1.A."

"I don't know anything about her, except that I saw a young woman moving in there tonight, carrying a couple of suitcases. I haven't met her yet."

Mason said, "You'll have to do better than that. Let's talk about Nathan Bain. Does that name mean anything to you?"

"Certainly not."

"In case you don't know it already," Mason said, "Nathan Bain is going to be delayed quite a bit in coming to New Orleans. Now if you want to—"

She elevated a scornful chin. "Are you trying to intimate something?"

"Merely that Nathan Bain's plans are going to be changed materially."

"I don't know any Nathan Brame——"

"Bain," Mason corrected.

"All right, Bain or Brame, or whatever you want to call it. I don't know him and——"

"You've never met him?"

"Of course not. Now, if you don't get out I'm going to start screaming for the police."

She waited a few seconds, then started towards the window which opened on the patio.

"No telephone?" Mason asked.

"I don't need one. I'll show you how quickly the police——"

Mason waited until she was within inches of the window, then said, "Elizabeth Bain's death is going to cause Nathan Bain to——"

She whirled. "What are you saying?"

"I was telling you about Elizabeth Bain's death."

She straightened, turned and stood looking at him, as stiffly motionless as a statue. "*What* are you saying?"

"I'm trying to give you some information that may be of value."

She regained her self-possession. "Who is this Elizabeth Bain?"

"She's the wife of Nathan Bain, or rather she was."

"Would you mind telling me just who you are?"

"The name is Mason."

"And are you connected with the police in some way?"

"No. I'm an attorney."

"And just why do you come here to tell me this, Mr. Mason?"

"Because," he said, "I wanted to find out whether you already knew about Mrs. Bain's death."

"Mr. Mason, you certainly must have me confused with someone else."

She moved over to the big overstuffed chair, standing with one arm on its back, not bothering to hold the *négligé*. "How did it happen—this death of Mrs. Brame?"

"Calling it Brame the first time was a good act," Mason said. "The second time is corny. She was poisoned."

"Oh, good heavens!" she said, and her knees buckled her into the chair. "Did you say she was . . . was poisoned?"

"Yes."

"Was it . . . sleeping pills . . . suicide?"

"No."

"Oh!"

"However," Mason went on, turning back towards the door, "since you don't know the Bains, the thing can't be of any possible interest to you."

"Wait," she said sharply.

Mason paused.

"Who gave her . . . how did it happen?"

"What do you care? They're strangers to you—remember?"

"I . . . I meant . . . oh, all right, you win. What do you want?"

Mason said, "You look grown-up. I thought you might be able to act grown-up."

"What do you want?"

"Information."

"What information?"

"All you have."

"Suppose I don't give it?"

"That's your privilege."

"And you're a lawyer?"

"Yes."

She said, "Okay, sit down. I'll buy you a drink."

Mason sat down. She went to the sideboard, took out a bottle of Scotch, poured two stiff drinks, splashed in soda and said, "I hope you like Scotch and soda. It's all I have."

"That'll do fine," Mason said.

She brought the drink over to him and sat down in the chair, the *négligé* falling away to show glimpses of a figure that would have won a beauty contest anywhere.

"The sooner you begin," Mason said, "the sooner it will be over with."

"All right," she said. "I have nothing to hide. The big lug!"

Mason sipped his drink.

She said, "I met him at a convention six months ago. A producers' convention. He certainly has a good line and he's a good spender."

"Just what are you looking for?" Mason asked.

She said, "All right, I'll tell you that, too."

She took a couple of swallows from her drink, then met his eyes and said, "I was a green, trusting kid. I found out that men had a good line. I fell for it. It didn't buy me anything. Now I've started to get wise.

"I've worked, and worked hard, ever since I was seventeen years old. I see other women who don't have anything I haven't got, breezing around in expensvie automobiles with chauffeurs, all dolled up in furs and with some big sap footing the bills and thinking he's sugar when he's only gravy."

Mason grinned and said, "That's better."

"All right," she said, "I met Nathan Bain. I guess at one time he'd been God's gift to women. He can't realise that years and fat do things to a man. He started handing me a line, then when he saw he had to boost the ante he shelled out a little bit here and there."

"Money?" Mason asked.

"Gems, jewels—nice stuff."

Mason was thoughtful. "Did it come by messenger?"

"Don't be silly. He delivered in person," she said. "He'd take a nice little diamond something or other from his pocket, hold it on his hand for a while, then slip it around my neck. I'd go nuts with rapture."

"Nice work if you can get it," Mason said.

"Don't make any mistake about me, brother. I got it."

"Then what?"

"Then Nathan rented these apartments down here in New Orleans. I was to take a vacation down here. He'd have the adjoining apartment just for the sake of appearances. He wasn't supposed even to know me. Ostensibly he was down here on business, and he intended to have a business conference or two in his apartment so he could prove what he was here for if he had to."

"And then what?"

"Then," she said, "the damn fool let his wife get hold of my letters. She got them from his office."

"You wrote him passionate letters?" Mason asked.

"Sure. What did *I* have to lose? I took my pen in hand and drooled all over the paper. After all, I thought the guy had some sense."

"It bothered you when the wife got the letters?"

"Not a damn bit," she admitted. "It bothered him, and then all of a sudden, it bothered me. Up to then I hadn't realised how firmly he was hooked. He was hoping he could find a way to get a divorce with some sort of a property settlement from her, and marry me. Well, I decided to string along on that end of the game for a while."

"And then what?"

"Then," she said, "he got the letters back from his wife. I don't know how he got them but he got them and he sent this girl down to give them to me."

"You mean the one over in apartment 1.A.?"

"Yes. Nora Carson."

"What do you think of her?"

"All right in a negative sort of a way. She's kept herself under wraps until she doesn't know how to let herself go. She hasn't any voltage. She'd like to play the game my way but she doesn't know how it's done and she'll never find out. She doesn't have anything to show, and nothing to deliver. But she'd like to try. Since she delivered the letters, she's made an excuse to run in here three or four times. The way she looks me over you can see she's wondering what I've got she hasn't— and the pathetic part of it is, she'll never find out."

"She was sent here just to deliver those letters?"

"Yes. Nathan sent her down here to bring me my purple letters.

Wasn't that nice of him? My 'good name' is safe now. Think of it. I won't have to be a corespondent after all. I'll be—as though I give a damn—or do I?"

Mason said, "You're giving me a lot of information. Why?"

"Because I like your looks."

Mason smiled and shook his head.

"Yes, I do too. You look like a square shooter. You look like a man who knows his way around. You look like a man who will play square with me if I play square with you."

"And what do you want?"

She said, "I've put my cards face up on the table."

"All right, what do you want in return?"

She said, "If there's a murder, I don't want any part of it. Nathan Bain is a fellow you can have a lot of fun with and he does keep decorating the mahogany, but that isn't going to last. You know that as well as I do. Marriage to him would lead to a career in the kitchen. You have to get what you can out of him and then move on. He likes pastures while they're green and while they're on the other side of the fence. Give him the key to the gate and it would mean nothing."

"Go on," Mason said.

She said, "I have a right guy. He doesn't have quite as much as Nathan Bain, but there's just a chance that I might play it on the up-and-up with him. I've been thinking."

"And what do you want me to do?"

"Tell me what to do, so I can keep from being smeared in a murder case."

Mason said, "Start packing your things. Get out of this apartment within twenty minutes and get out of this city within thirty. You have your letters back. Burn them. The wind is going to blow. Go hunt yourself a cyclone cellar."

"I thought you were a good egg," she said. "Do you know, Mr. Mason, I sort of like this other guy. I might . . . hell, you don't suppose I'm falling for another line, do you?"

"I wouldn't know," Mason said, "but there's only one way to find out."

"You're right at that," she told him.

Mason finished his drink.

She followed him to the door, put her hand on his arm. "I'll remember you."

Mason said, "I'd get out quietly so that girl in the next apartment doesn't know that you're leaving."

The dark eyes showed sudden bitterness. "You aren't telling *me* anything," she said. "Listen, I've found out that a girl can't trust many men, and she can't trust *any* women."

"Good luck," Mason said, and walked down the narrow, winding stairs to the patio and the night noises of St. Peter Street.

ELEVEN

BACK IN THE Roosevelt Hotel, Mason found Paul Drake with his ear glued to a telephone, getting a long report.

When Drake had finished and hung up, Mason said, "Paul, I want to get copies of messages from the local files of the Western Union Telegraph Company."

Drake shook his head. "It's not only darned near impossible, Perry, but it's illegal."

Mason said, "Charlotte Moray, who has the apartment across from the one where Nellie Conway is living, has been receiving telegrams. I think they come from Nathan Bain."

Drake said, "I can help you out on the last one of those telegrams, Perry."

"How come?"

Drake said, "She may not even have received it as yet. Here it is." He picked up a sheet of paper on which he had scrawled pencilled handwriting, and read:

Unexpected and entirely unforeseen developments which may cause complications necessitate immediate conference. I am arriving on plane due nine-fifteen a.m. leaving on plane due to depart New Orleans one-thirty-five p.m. which will get me back here before my absence will have been noticed or commented on.

"And," Drake said, "the message is signed 'Your Falstaff.' "

"And it was sent by?"

"Nathan Bain."

"How did you get it, Paul?"

Drake said, "Nathan Bain was quote overcome with grief unquote. He enlisted the aid of a friendly physician who quote administered a sedative unquote, put Bain to bed in a private sanatorium and insisted that he remained undisturbed. A rather bad heart condition, you understand."

"Go ahead," Mason said.

"The police apparently fell for it and so did the newspaper reporters, although they grumbled a bit. My man smelled a rat. He found there was an alley exit through a garage. He watched it and sure enough Nathan Bain, showing no evidence whatever of having been given a hypodermic, came boiling out of the back, jumped into a closed car and was whisked away.

"My man followed as best he could, but I think he'd have lost the guy if Bain hadn't been so damn anxious to send this telegram. There was a branch of Western Union office about ten blocks down the street and Bain's car stopped there. Bain ran in and scribbled his message."

"How did your man get the copy?" Mason asked.

"That's a trick of the trade, Perry."

"Go on, come through," Mason told him. "If there's any way of getting Western Union messages that easy I want to know about it."

"It was dead easy, Perry."

"How much did it cost?"

"A dollar and ten cents."

"How come?"

"Bain grabbed a pencil and wrote this message down on a pad of telegraph blanks that was lying on the counter. My man boldly stepped up as soon as Bain had sent the message, took the same pad of telegraph blanks, tore off a couple of sheets and sent a telegram to his mother telling her he was too busy to write but that he wanted her to know he was thinking of her. The message cost him a dollar and ten cents. Naturally he didn't write it on the sheet of paper that had been immediately under the one on which Bain wrote his message. So it was only necessary for my man to take that sheet of paper, illuminate it with transverse lighting, photograph it and decipher the message which had been indented in the paper underneath by Bain's pencil. Bain writes with a heavy fist."

Mason grinned. "Good work, Paul."

Drake said, "Here's some stuff you won't like so well. The police searched the trash can back of Bain's kitchen stove. In there they found an envelope that had been sealed, and your name and the name of Nellie

Conway had been written across the flap. Then the envelope had been torn open and——"

"Was a phial in there?" Mason asked.

"Apparently not, but an outline on the envelope showed it had contained a little phial or bottle."

Mason thought that over. "Can the police tell just when the poison was administered, Paul? She must have taken some food——"

"It wasn't taken in food," Drake interposed.

"How was it taken?"

"It was taken in the form of three five-grain tablets washed down with a glass of water followed by coffee, and given by Mrs. Bain's sister, Victoria Braxton."

"Are you sure?"

"The police are," Drake said.

"How do they know?"

"Elizabeth Bain told them. Her half-sister gave her the tablets."

"What does Victoria Braxton have to say to that?" Mason asked.

"Apparently nothing," Drake said, "because the police can't find her."

"Oh-oh!"

"Your friend Sergeant Holcomb, seems to have taken charge of the affair. For some reason he had a sudden desire to search the Bain house from cellar to garret. He ordered everybody out just as soon as Elizabeth Bain died. He told them to go to hotels and report to the police where they were."

"So what happened?"

"So they did," Drake said, grinning. "Nathan Bain went to his club. He reported to the police that was there. James Braxton and his wife, Georgiana, went to a down-town hotel, registered and stayed there. Victoria Braxton went to another hotel, registered and notified the police she was there, and the police seem to be having some difficulty finding out exactly where she is. They want to question her. All they can learn so far is that she's completely broken up over her sister's death, is staying with friends somewhere and isn't in her room."

"What else do you know, Paul?"

Drake said, "Bain got a new night nurse after Nellie Conway was arrested. Evidently he made passes at her and she walked out in a huff.

"Mrs. Ricker, the housekeeper, had been on duty all day, but she said she'd try to see that the patient was comfortable. Then Nellie Conway walked in. Nathan Bain made a settlement of some sort with her, patched up his differences with her and put her to work.

"Mrs. Bain had a fine night. She went to sleep early and slept like a log, which was something she hadn't been doing. Sometime after midnight the plane bringing her half-brother, James Braxton, and her half-sister, Victoria Braxton, and Jim Braxton's wife, Georgiana, landed, and all three of them went directly to the house.

"Since Elizabeth Bain was sleeping, they decided they wouldn't disturb her at the moment, but would wait until she wakened.

"She wakened about three a.m. and asked if the folks had come. On being assured they had, she said she wanted to see them. She seemed a little sleepy and groggy, and a lot less nervous and hysterical than she had been. She greeted them warmly and went back to sleep.

"Now get this, Perry. Nellie Conway wasn't really working. She'd gone back to get her things. She made some sort of a settlement with Nathan Bain and she was just helping out because the housekeeper had been up all day. Nellie had said she'd help out until the folks came and then they could take over with the nursing."

Mason nodded.

"But," Drake went on, "the travellers had been flying from Honolulu and felt a little worn. They decided they'd get a little sleep, and Nellie Conway volunteered to stay on for a while longer.

"After about an hour's sleep, Victoria Braxton came in and told Nellie Conway she was completely rested now and Nellie could leave. The housekeeper had already gone to bed. I'm giving you all of this because I think it's important, Perry."

"Go ahead."

"Now, as nearly as we can tell, the doctor, a fellow by the name of Keener, had left three five-grain tablets to be given Mrs. Bain when she wakened at any time after six o'clock in the morning, but they weren't to be given to her before six. Those tablets had been left with Nellie Conway who was the nurse in charge."

"So what happened when Nellie Conway went off duty?"

"She put the tablets on a little saucer, put them on the table and told Victoria Braxton that she was to give them to Elizabeth Bain at any time after six o'clock, but not to wake her up to give them to her, to wait until she wakened naturally."

"Go on," Mason said.

"Mrs. Bain woke up around five o'clock, I believe, and was awake for a while, talking with her half-sister. Then she went back to sleep, wakened at right around seven o'clock.

"She still felt drowsy and completely relaxed. She didn't want any breakfast, but said she'd like coffee. She had a cup of coffee and took the three pills. Anyway, that's what she told the doctor. And get this, Perry, that coffee and the three pills are all that she took into her stomach from somewhere around eight-thirty the night before. So the arsenic *had* to be in the pills."

"Or in the coffee," Mason said.

"You can discount the coffee, because the coffee came out of an urn and several people drank it."

"Perhaps in the sugar?"

"She didn't take sugar or cream. She took the coffee black."

"Then what, Paul?"

"The day nurse came on duty at eight o'clock. She found Victoria Braxton on duty. Victoria said she wanted to take a bath, clean up and then she was going up-town for a while. The day nurse took over. Understand, this was a case where they only had two nurses. The night nurse worked from six to eight because she didn't have it quite so hard, and the day nurse worked from eight to six."

"Go on, Paul."

"The day nurse found Mrs. Bain sleeping, but she was twitching and moaning as though she might be in pain of some sort, but since she was sleeping soundly the nurse didn't disturb her.

"Mrs. Bain had been very restless, you know, and it was considered important for her to get sleep whenever possible, so, as it happened, the day nurse didn't do a darned thing about straightening up the room or anything. She just sat down and left everything the way it was so Mrs. Bain wouldn't be disturbed. That's important because it means that the evidence was left undisturbed."

"Go ahead, Paul. Then what?"

"Well, sometime shortly before nine, Mrs. Bain wakened and was immediately and violently ill, and she had such typical symptoms of arsenic poisoning that the day nurse, who seems to have been a really competent girl, and who had had training as a nurse, notified the doctor that she suspected arsenic poisoning. The doctor got on the job in a hurry, and by nine-thirty they had a definite diagnosis of arsenic—but in view of Mrs. Bain's weakened condition and the fact that she'd been sleeping so heavily and had absorbed so much of the arsenic before her stomach began to reject it, she couldn't pull through. She died sometime shortly after eleven-thirty.

"Victoria Braxton got home about a quarter to eleven. I think at that time Elizabeth Bain knew she was dying. Anyway, Miss Braxton told everyone to get out of the room, said she wanted to be alone for just two minutes with her sister, and since they were a little alarmed about Mrs. Bain's nervous condition, the doctor said that Victoria Braxton could see her for just five minutes. No one knows what they talked about."

"No question that it was arsenic poisoning?"

"Absolutely no question. They are making an autopsy and making an analysis of the vital organs, but the doctor saved some of the stomach contents."

"How about the time element?" Mason asked. "Is that all right?"

"That checks, Perry."

"Do the doctors say so?"

"The doctors aren't saying a damned thing, except to the District Attorney, but I've had my researchers making an investigation."

"What do you find?"

Once more Drake consulted his notes and said, "Well, take *Professor Glaister's Medical Jurisprudence and Toxicology*. He says that the symptoms usually appear within an hour. In one case, where the stomach was empty, the symptoms did not appear until after two hours. Then, of course, there have been cases where the symptoms didn't develop for seven to ten hours."

"And fifteen grains is a fatal dose?" Mason asked.

"Oh, sure. There has been a fatal case recorded where the amount of arsenic was only two grains, according to Professor Glaister."

"Gonzales, Vance and Helpern, in their book entitled *Legal Medicine and Toxicology*, state that three grains of arsenic absorbed into the system will kill a man of average weight. Of course, there have been cases where large doses have been taken without fatal results, but usually the poison was rejected by the stomach before it could get into the system."

The telephone rang sharply.

Drake answered, said, "Yes, hello . . . Yes, sure he is . . . Okay, I'll put him on."

He said, "Della Street calling you, Perry."

Mason glanced at his watch. "Gosh, there must be some major emergency to cause Della to call me at this hour."

He picked up the telephone, said, "Hello," and heard Della Street's voice, sharp with excitement, saying, "Chief, I don't want to mention names over the telephone, but do you remember the client who consulted you about the will?"

"The one that didn't have the dot at the end?"

"That's right."

"Yes, I remember her. What about her?"

"She's with me. People are looking for her, lots of people, and she doesn't want to see anyone until she's talked with you. Can she get in touch with you down there if she——?"

"Not very well," Mason said. "I'm coming back. Is there something she's trying to conceal?"

"She thinks someone is trying to frame something on her and——"

"All right," Mason said, "tell her not to say anything to anyone. Can you keep her out of circulation, Della?"

"I think so."

"All right. There's a plane leaving here at one-thirty-five in the afternoon. I'll be on it."

Drake's face showed surprise. "That's the plane that Bain——"

Mason nodded at Paul Drake, and said into the telephone. "I'll try and get that plane leaving here at one-thirty-five, Della."

"Okay."

"Don't let anything happen until I get there—you know what I mean."

"I'll try."

Mason said, "Okay, Della. I'll be seeing you."

Mason hung up the telephone, and as soon as he did so the bell started ringing rapidly and insistently.

Drake picked it up, said, "Hello," and then waited while the receiver rattled with a voice that was pouring words into it with a rapid insistence.

After a full two minutes, Drake said, "Thanks. I owe you one for that. We'll remember it."

He hung up.

"What gives?" Mason asked.

"That was the detective agency we hired to tail Nellie Conway," Drake said. "They were just giving me a tip. They have connections down here, you know."

"Go ahead."

"Seems the California police became interested in Nellie Conway. They found she'd taken the plane as Nora Carson. They phoned police here. They questioned the taxi drivers who cover the airport. The result is they spotted Nellie Conway in that apartment, and they got on the job just as you were leaving the joint.

"On general principles they tailed you here. Then they picked up Nellie. Where does that leave you?"

Mason looked at his watch. "Okay, Paul, I want that one-thirty-five plane. I don't want anyone to know that I'm taking it. Get a ticket in your name. Pay for the ticket, then go out to the airport, rent one of the parcel lockers, put the ticket in that locker, deposit twenty-five cents which will pay for twenty-four hours, close the locker, take the key out, and leave it with the girl at the news-stand. Tell her that when I show up and ask for the key to the locker, she's to give it to me without any question. Describe me if you have to."

"Will you know which locker?" Drake asked.

"Sure," Mason said, "the locker number is stamped on the key."

Drake asked, "Why don't you get a ticket in your own name? They may have tailed you here, Perry, but you're clean. You can tell——"

Mason shook his head. "I have five one-hundred-dollar bills in my pocket that may be hot as a stove lid. Here, Paul, put them in an envelope. Address and stamp the envelope and drop it down the mail chute.

"And I don't want to have any ticket for that plane in my pocket because I don't want anyone to know I'm on that plane when it gets in.

"I haven't time to explain, but this is one time I'm skating on thin ice——"

He broke off as knuckles sounded on the door. With a significant glance at Paul Drake, he tossed the folded five one-hundred-dollar notes far back under one of the twin beds, and opened the door.

Two men stood on the threshold.

"Either one of these the guy?" one of the men asked a plain-clothes man who was standing back in the corridor.

"This is the guy right here at the door."

The detective threw back his coat, showed a badge. "Come on, you're going places, mister," he said. "Somebody important wants to talk with you."

TWELVE

THE TAXICAB DROVE up to police headquarters. Mason was escorted into an office where the stale, close air gave forth that peculiar smell which clings to a room which is customarily occupied for twenty-four hours a day.

A desk sergeant said, "We don't like out-of-town guys who bust in here with a muscle racket. What's your name?"

"Suppose I should tell you it's John Doe?"

"Lots of 'em do. We'll book you that way if you want. Then when we throw you in the tank, we'll take all the stuff out of your pockets and maybe find a driving licence or something that will tell us who you are. But you'll still be booked as John Doe."

"What's the charge?"

"We haven't thought one up yet, but I think it's going to be vagrancy. You've been paying unchaperoned calls on single girls at two o'clock in the morning, and——"

"Is that a crime in this city?" Mason asked.

The desk sergeant grinned. "Could be, particularly if the California officers are interested. It'd be vagrancy. After we saw your driving licence, Mr. Doe, we'd know a lot more. Perhaps you'd like to co-operate a little better."

Mason took his wallet from his pocket, handed a card to the sergeant and said, "The name's Perry Mason. I'm a lawyer. I came here to interview a witness."

The desk sergeant whistled in surprise, took Mason's card, stepped out of the office, walked down the corridor and was back within two minutes.

"The Captain wants to see you," he said.

Officers escorted Mason down the corridor to a door that said 'Captain,' opened the door and pushed Mason in.

A big, middle-aged man with sagging pouches under his eyes, a close-clipped greying moustache, sat behind a desk. At a table beside the desk a shorthand stenographer was taking notes. At the other side of the room Nellie Conway sat on the edge of a plain wooden chair, her gloved hands folded in her lap, her face without expression, her eyes staring straight ahead.

She showed no sign of recognition as Mason was pushed into the room.

The police captain looked across at her. "Is this the man?" he said.

"Yes."

"This is Perry Mason, the lawyer, you're talking about?"

"Yes."

The police captain nodded to Mason. "Sit down."

Mason remained standing.

The captain said, coldly, "You're playing hard to get along with. That isn't going to get you anywhere, not in this town. You aren't in California now. Don't try throwing your weight around because in this place you haven't any weight to throw around. Do you want to sit down or do you want to stand up?"

"Thank you," Mason said, coldly. "I'll stand up."

"Want to make any statement?" the captain asked.

"No."

The captain turned to Nellie Conway. "All right," he said, "you said you did every single thing you did under the advice of counsel. You said the name of the lawyer was Perry Mason. Now this is Perry Mason. Go ahead and keep talking."

Mason said, "I'll advise you not to say a word, Nellie. You——"

"Shut up," the captain said.

"Are you going to keep right on being my lawyer?" Nellie Conway asked, eagerly.

"No."

"Then I'd better listen to these people," she said.

The captain grinned.

Mason took a cigarette case from his pocket, lit a cigarette.

"Keep talking," the captain said to Nellie Conway.

She said, "Nathan Bain gave me those pills. He offered to pay me five hundred dollars in cash if I would give the pills to his wife. I thought they were poison. I went to see a lawyer."

"What lawyer?" the captain asked.

"Perry Mason."

"That's the gentleman here?"

"Yes."

"What did he say?"

"There were four tablets," she said. "He took one of them out of the bottle and put it in an envelope and wrote his name on it. He put the other three tablets back in the bottle, corked the bottle, put it in an envelope, sealed the envelope and had me write my name across the flap of the envelope, and he wrote his name across the flap of the envelope, and he told me to save the envelope because he was going to find out what was in the tablets and was going to communicate with the police."

"Then what?" the captain asked.

"Then Nathan Bain had me arrested."

"Then what?"

"Then Mr. Mason got me acquitted and told me there wasn't anything in the tablets except aspirin. He intimated that I had been telling him a lie and trying to take him for a ride."

"Then what?"

"Then I went back to the Bain residence to get my things and Nathan Bain talked with me. He was very much concerned because he was afraid I was going to bring a suit against him for false arrest. He said there was no reason why we couldn't get along. He said we could act civilised about the thing. He said he wanted to make a settlement."

"What happened?"

"We talked for a while, and then he told me that he'd give me two thousand dollars and an airplane ticket to New Orleans and a key to an apartment where I could stay for two weeks and have a vacation. He told me all I had to do was to sign a release and give the three tablets to his wife.

"I thought those three tablets contained nothing but aspirin because that's what Mr. Mason had told me was in them, and I didn't see any reason why I shouldn't. I'd tried to do the best I could for myself under the circumstances. If a girl doesn't look out for herself, it's a cinch no one else is going to."

"So what did you do?"

"I signed a release Mr. Bain had drawn up. I got twenty one-hundred-dollar bills. I was helping that night with nursing his wife. I gave her the three pills about eight-thirty or nine o'clock."

"Did you tell Mr. Bain you had done so?"

"Yes."

"Did you have any trouble giving them to her?"

"Of course not. I was the nurse. I told her it was the medicine the doctor had left for her."

"What did she say?"

"She said she'd already had the medicine the doctor had left for her. I told her this was some other medicine, some special medicine that the doctor wanted her to have in addition to the regular medicine."

"Then what happened?"

"The medicine didn't hurt Mrs. Bain a bit. She took it and went right to sleep. I think it really must have been aspirin. It quieted her and she had a nice night. I left about seven o'clock in the morning, about an hour before the day nurse took over. I tried to see Mr. Mason to tell him what had happened, but I couldn't get him. He didn't come into his office before ten o'clock. That was the last minute I had to call him. My plane left at ten-fifteen and they called for passengers to get aboard at ten o'clock. I called him right on the dot of ten o'clock. His secretary said he hadn't come in."

"Did you leave word for him to call you?"

She hesitated. "No."

"Did you tell him where you were going?"

Again she hesitated.

"Come on," the captain said, "let's get this straight."

"No," she said, "I didn't tell him where I was going."

"When did you see him again?"

"About half-past two o'clock this morning."

"What did he do?"

"He came to my apartment."

"What did he want?"

"He wanted five hundred dollars."

"Did you pay him that?"

"Yes."

"Out of the money you received from Nathan Bain?"

"Yes."

"Did you tell him that's where you got the money?"

"Yes."

"And he took the five hundred dollars?"

"Yes."

"Did he give you a receipt for it?"

"No."

The captain turned to Perry Mason. "You've heard the statement that has been made in your presence, Mr. Mason. Do you wish to deny it?"

Mason said, "I don't like the way you run things down here. I don't intend to say a damn word."

The captain said, "Stick around and try to cut corners down here and you'll like the way we run things a hell of a lot less. The accusation has been made that you told this woman it was all right to give those three pills to Mrs. Nathan Bain. Do you deny that?"

Mason said, "I'm not making any statement. I will say, however, that she is entirely incorrect in that statement."

"I'm not either, Mr. Mason," Nellie Conway said with some spirit. "You told me that those tablets contained nothing but aspirin."

"The tablet that I took out of the bottle contained nothing but aspirin." Mason said.

"How do you know?" the captain asked.

"That's something I'll discuss at the proper time and in the proper place."

"All right, these statements have been made in your presence. You have an opportunity to deny them and make an explanation here and now if you want to."

"I have nothing to say."

The captain said to Mason, "That's all. You can go now. Don't try to cut corners here because we don't like smart guys. California may want you. Go back to your hotel and don't try to leave town until we tell you you can. You may be wanted as an accessory on a murder charge—five hundred dollars to give his wife three aspirin pills! You're a hell of a lawyer!"

Mason turned to Nellie Conway. "Nellie, what time did you give——?"

"I said you could go," the captain said.

He nodded to the two officers.

They each took one of Mason's arms, spun him around and propelled him out of the door.

The door slammed shut with an ominous bang.

THIRTEEN

THE TAXI THAT had taken Mason and the detectives from the hotel was parked in front of police headquarters.

Mason said in a weary voice, "Take me back to the Roosevelt Hotel."

"Yes, sir. Have a little trouble, sir?"

"Just lost a little sleep, that's all."

"Oh, well, you can always make that up."

"I suppose so," Mason told him, and settled back on the cushions.

At the Roosevelt Hotel, Mason paid the cab driver off, entered the hotel, walked to the desk, asked for the key to the suite, and, swinging the key carelessly, Mason entered the elevator and said, "Fifth floor."

Mason got off at the fifth floor and promptly walked back down the stairs as far as the mezzanine.

From the mezzanine he could look down and see the house detective who waited until the elevator had returned to the ground floor, then went over to the desk and put through a phone call. Mason, watching his opportunity, slipped down the stairs, went to the door at the other end of the block, and found a taxicab waiting.

"Drive straight down the street," he said. "I'll have to get the address I want."

"Going to be a nice day," the cab driver said. "You're up early."

"Uh-huh. What time do you quit work?"

"Me? I just went on about twenty minutes ago. I quit at four o'clock this afternoon."

Mason said, "That sounds like a nice shift."

"It is while I have it. I have to switch around."

"That doesn't sound so good."

"It isn't."

"Know the town pretty well?" Mason asked.

"Sure."

Mason said, "I've got a day in which I just don't have to do a damn thing. How much would it cost to get this cab by the hour?"

"Well, that depends on whether you want it for shopping and right around town, or——"

Mason took out a fifty-dollar note from his wallet, said, "I'll tell you what I'll do, driver. I'll just give you fifty dollars for the day. Is it a go?"

"What do you mean by all day?"

"Until you quit at four o'clock this afternoon."

"It's a go!"

Mason said, "Okay, shut off your radio because the damn thing makes me nervous. Tell your headquarters that you're going to be out of service all day."

"I'd have to telephone in and get permission, but I'm satisfied it can be done all right."

Mason said, "Okay. Tell them that you're going to go to Biloxi."

"I thought you said you wanted to look around the town."

"Hell, I don't know what I want to do," Mason said. "I used to know a girl in Biloxi."

"That's a long way to go for a girl," the cab driver said. "There are lots of good-looking women nearer than Biloxi."

"Are there?"

"So they tell me."

"Well," Mason said, "tell them you have a passenger to Biloxi. Ask them if fifty dollars is all right for a round trip."

"Okay. Wait and I'll telephone."

The cab driver went into an all-night restaurant, telephoned, came back and said, "I'm sorry. They say I'd have to get seventy-five for all day under circumstances like that. I think it's a stickup but——"

"What do we care?" Mason said. "Just so we have fun. Here's a hundred dollars. Now you're paid off for all day and we can go to Biloxi or not, just as we damn please. The extra twenty-five is for you."

"Say," the cab driver said, "you're a real sport."

"No, I'm not," Mason said. "I'm tired of a lot of routine and I want to settle down and enjoy life for a day without having a lot of telephones and a lot of radio. A little later on you can take me to a good place where we can get a nice breakfast and just sit around and enjoy life without being hurried."

The cab driver said, "I can find you a place all right. I hate to take all this money on a mileage basis to Biloxi and then let the company get rich just driving around town. If you're going to start to Biloxi we should get go——"

"I've changed my mind," Mason said. "I'll——"

"I can phone in and get a better rate for just being around the city."

"No, let the cab company get rich," Mason said. "I'll tell you what you do. Start your meter going and we'll run on the meter. Mileage and waiting time won't amount to as much as the price they gave you, and you can tell them afterwards that your passenger changed his mind."

"Okay, boss. Anything you say. I can sure use the money but I want to be on the up-and-up. You'd be surprised how strict they get with us and how closely they watch us. Lots of times they plant somebody to see if we'll cut a corner or——"

"There isn't any rule against cruising around with your meter running, is there?" Mason asked.

"Not a bit."

"Okay, let's go cruise."

They drove slowly around the city, the driver pointing out places of interest, then, after a while, as Mason started to doze, the driver asked, "How about that breakfast place now?"

"A good idea," Mason told him.

"Okay. I know a place that's run by a woman who's a friend of mine. She doesn't run a regular restaurant but she'd be glad to fix up any friend of mine. You'd get a lot better food than you'd get in any of the restaurants."

"That's what I want," Mason told him. "A chance to relax and feel that I don't have a darn thing to do."

"That's swell. This woman has a couple of daughters that are knockouts."

"I don't want to be knocked out this early in the morning."

The cab driver laughed. "Anyway, you'll like the food, and I mean there's some of the most marvellous Louisiana coffee you ever tasted, made with hot milk. Mister, you're going to have some cooking today that you'll remember as long as you live."

The cab driver drove toward the outskirts of town, stopped once to telephone ahead, then took Mason to a neat house where a negro admitted them to a spacious dining-room, with the morning sun just beginning to stream in through windows covered with lace curtains which, according to the cab driver, were "genuine heirlooms."

An hour and a half later, Mason, once more in the cab, suggested that they drive out to the airport. He said that he liked to watch planes come and go and it would be a good chance to see the town.

The driver felt that Mason might spend his time more profitably, but drove the lawyer out to the airport.

Mason sat in the cab.

The nine-fifteen plane was twenty minutes late.

Nathan Bain hurried from the plane towards a taxi. Two broad-shouldered men fell into step on each side. Bain's face showed startled surprise. The men piloted him across the street to a black sedan. They entered and drove away.

"Don't you want to get out and look around any?" the driver asked.

Mason stretched, yawned, said, "No, I'd like to find some place where we could walk and stroll around . . . Say, haven't you got a park here?"

"A park!" the cab driver exclaimed. "We've got several of the best parks in the world! Why, say, we've got parks here with live oaks that are bigger than any tree you ever saw in your life. We've got lawns and walks, and a zoo with all kinds of animals, lakes, canals——"

"That's for me," Mason said with enthusiasm. "Let's go down to a park some place where we can get out and lie on the grass and just bask in the sun, and then we can go out and look around the zoo and get some peanuts to feed to the animals, and after that . . . well, after that we'll do just as we damn please."

The cab driver said, "If I could only get a fare like you just about once every ten years, it would make up for all the grouchy old crabs that yell because I have to go around a block in order to get headed right on a one-way street. Come on, mister, you've called the turn. Say, do you like to fish? I know where we can get some fishing rods and get some of the best fishing . . ."

"Sounds good," Mason said. "Let's go."

Around eleven o'clock, Mason decided he was hungry. The cab driver found a quaint, isolated place, where Mason had an oyster cocktail, bouillabaisse, oysters Rockefeller, and a firm, white-meated fish that seemed to dissolve on the tongue. An olive-skinned girl with limpid, dark eyes, and exceedingly long lashes, served the meal, and from time to time glanced sidelong under her long lashes at Perry Mason, who was drowsily oblivious of everything except the food.

Shortly before one o'clock, Mason decided he would once more like to go down to the airport and see the planes come in.

This time he got out of the cab and said, "I'll walk around for a while."

"About how long?" the cab driver asked.

"Oh, I don't know," Mason said. "I just do things on impulse. Come on along, if you want."

Escorted by the cab driver, Mason moved slowly around the air terminal, then said, "I think I'll buy a newspaper."

He walked over to the news-stand while the cab driver was standing out of earshot, bought a newspaper and said, "I believe there's a key left here for me."

The girl looked at him curiously and said, "Yes, your friend said your bags would be in the locker."

She handed him a key.

Mason thanked her, gave her a two-dollar tip, walked back to the cab driver and said, "Go out and wait in the cab, will you? In case I don't show up within half an hour, shut your meter off, pocket the rest of the money and report back to duty."

Mason went to the locker and found that Paul Drake had packed his overnight travelling bag and left it in the locker, together with a letter in a plain envelope.

Mason opened the envelope and found the aeroplane ticket, together with a note which read:

Della knows you'll be on this plane. Things are moving too fast for me. I'm crawling into a hole and pulling the hole in after me. This is where I check out. I've had police in my hair at intervals all morning and have received intimations that if I don't get out of town I won't stay out of jail. I don't like the way these people play.

The note was unsigned.

Mason picked up the bag, strolled across to the registration desk for outgoing passengers.

"You'll have to hurry," the attendant told him. "They'll be calling the plane in a few minutes."

He weighed in Mason's bag, checked it, then the lawyer sauntered over to the gate, which opened almost the instant he arrived. He handed his boarding slip to an attendant, climbed aboard the plane, settled down, pulled a pillow out from the receptacle above his chair, and kept his eyes closed until after the plane had taxied down the field. As the plane took off, Mason straightened, looked out of the window and watched Lake Pontchartrain shimmering below. The plane made a half-circle and winged out so that New Orleans, with its buildings, its spacious parks, its busy waterfront, and the famous crescent in the Mississippi River became a panorama. Mason relaxed again and dozed fitfully until the plane landed in El Paso.

He noticed two people who boarded the plane, a man about thirty,

THE PERRY MASON CASEBOOK

who had an aura of dreamy-eyed futility about him, and a woman some
four or five years his junior, whose nervous alertness indicated that she
had taken on many of the responsibilities for her husband as a seeing-
eye dog takes over responsibilities for its master.

Mason looked out of the window at the airport. In the twilight he
saw that a cold, gusty wind was blowing, yawned, closed his eyes and
was dozing by the time the plane taxied down the runway. Half-asleep,
he felt the thrust as the powerful engines pushed the big plane into the
air, then wakened enough to watch the panorama flowing back beneath
him in the gathering dusk, the environs of El Paso, the Rio Grande
River, over on the other side the town of Ciudad Juarez.

Someone tapped his shoulder. Mason looked up.

It was the woman who had boarded the plane with the dreamy-eyed
individual.

"We'd like to talk with you," she said.

Mason regarded her thoughtfully, then smiled and shook his head.
"I'm not in the mood for conversation at the moment and . . ."

"Miss Street suggested that we get aboard the plane here."

"That," Mason said, "is different."

He walked back to the smoking compartment where the man was
sitting, waiting.

It was, Mason thought, quite typical that the man should send the
woman to make the contact.

"Did Miss Street give you any letter or anything?" Mason asked,
feeling his way cautiously.

"No. We talked with her over the telephone. Perhaps we'd better
introduce ourselves. I'm Mrs. James Braxton and this is James Braxton."

"You're the other members of the Bain family?"

"That's right. Jim is, or rather was, Elizabeth's half-brother, and
I'm his wife. Vicki Braxton is Jim's full sister."

The woman beamed at him.

"Well, now," Mason said, adjusting himself comfortably and taking
a cigarette case from his pocket, "that's very interesting. Would you
care to smoke?"

They accepted cigarettes and all three took lights from the same
match.

"I suppose you know what's happened?" the woman said.

"Just what has happened?" Mason asked.

She said, "That nurse, that Nellie Conway!"

"What about her?"

"She did give the poison after all. Nathan bribed her to do it."

Mason raised his eyebrows in silent interrogation, then smoked in silence.

The woman looked at him and said, "You're not saying a word, Mr. Mason."

"Your husband isn't saying a word," Mason said.

She laughed nervously. "He's a great listener. I'm the talkative one of the family. I go rambling on and on and on."

Mason nodded.

"We'd like to know what you think of it and what your ideas are concerning the case."

Mason said, "Lots of people would like to know that."

"I'm afraid I don't understand."

Mason said, "You tell me that you're Mr. and Mrs. Jim Braxton. I've never seen you before in my life. For all I know you could be newspaper reporters trying to get an exclusive interview."

"But, good heavens, Mr. Mason, your own secretary told us where we'd find you. We took a plane into El Paso and got in there just half an hour before this plane of yours pulled in. We've certainly been stewing and worrying and we wanted to see you at the earliest possible moment and warn you of what you're up against."

"Thanks."

"Mr. Mason, you must believe we're who we are. We . . . Jim, don't you have something, some means of identification?"

"Sure," Jim said, promptly rising to the occasion. "I have a driving license."

"Let's take a look at it," Mason said.

He studied the licence which the man handed him, then said, "Perhaps I can clear the matter up by asking a few questions. Where were you up until a few days ago?"

"Honolulu."

"Who was with you?"

"Just the three of us together. It was a family party. My sister, Vicki, and I have always been very close, and she gets along fine with Georgiana."

"Got any more means of identification on you?" Mason asked.

"Certainly. I have lodge cards, business cards, club memberships . . ."

"Let's see them," Mason said.

Mason went through the collection of cards which the man presented, said finally, "Okay. I guess that does it. Now suppose you tell me the thing Miss Street wanted you to tell me. She didn't have you fly down here just to ask me questions."

"Well," the woman said, laughing nervously, "I was just trying to get acquainted."

"We're acquainted now. What was it you told Miss Street that caused her to send you down here?"

"It sounds such a horrible thing to say," she said after a few moments, "when you blurt it right out this way."

"But, my dear," Jim Braxton interposed, "Mr. Mason is our lawyer. You have a right to tell him anything. You're supposed to tell him. Isn't that right, Mr. Mason?"

Mason said, "If you have any information which throws any light on the death of your sister-in-law, I suggest by all means that you tell me what it is."

She turned to her husband. "Jim, for the life of me I can't understand you. For the past year whenever I've mentioned that, you've told me I should keep my mouth shut, that I could get in serious trouble, and now you want me to tell the story to a man I've only known for a few minutes."

"But, dear, the situation is entirely different now. This would be . . . well, the law would protect you in this."

Mason glanced at his wrist watch. "We don't have too long to stall around, you know. There may be reporters coming aboard the plane at Tucson."

"Well," she said, "I may as well blurt it right out, Mr. Mason. Nathan Bain poisoned his first wife."

"She was supposed to have eaten something which disagreed with her," James Braxton said mildly.

"The symptoms were those of arsenic poisoning," Mrs. Braxton asserted.

"How do you know?" Mason asked.

"Because," she said, "I was suspicious of Nathan Bain from the moment he set foot in the house and started making eyes at Elizabeth."

"Go on," Mason said.

"Well, that's it, Mr. Mason. He's always said he didn't want to talk about it, but one time he told us all about it. It seems she had eaten something which disagreed with her, and the way he described the symptoms . . . well, I just started thinking, that's all."

"What about the symptoms?"

"All of the typical symptoms of arsensic poisoning. They are not very nice to describe, Mr. Mason, but I can assure you she had *all* of the typical symptoms."

"How do you know what the symptoms are?"

"I made it a point to read up about it."

"Why?"

"Because I was suspicious of Nathan Bain from the minute I clapped my eyes on him. I felt certain that he'd . . . I think he's a toad."

Mason said, "Let's get back to the death of his first wife. That *could* be one of the most important things in the case."

Jim Braxton said, "Your secretary thought so too. She wanted us to get in touch with you and tell you about it."

"Then tell me about it," Mason said. "And tell me how it happened that Nathan Bain got your sister to marry him. I gather that she was rather an attractive young woman."

"She was."

"Two and a half years ago Nathan Bain was a lot better looking than he is now," Jim Braxton interposed. "And he sure has a smooth line."

"But he was fat even then," his wife countered. "Don't you remember how he was complaining about his clothes being tight? He was always saying he was going to take off weight. First he'd say he was going to take off five pounds in the next six weeks. Then he said ten pounds in the next three months, then twenty pounds in the next six months.

"And all the time he kept putting it on. His clothes were always six months behind his figure. I always felt he was going to burst every time he leaned over. He just wouldn't watch his appetite. He ate everything. All the rich foods—used to boast about his stomach. He'd eat——"

"That isn't telling me about his first wife," Mason said impatiently, "and we haven't got all night."

"Well," she said, "his first wife died about three years before he married Elizabeth."

"Did he profit by her death?" Mason asked.

"I'll say he profited by her death! He picked up about fifty thousand dollars. He used that to gamble in the stock market and get himself established in the produce business. And then when he made some poor investments and found out that the financial shoe was pinching, he deliberately went out and set his cap for someone who had money.

"I tell you, Mr. Mason, that was all that he wanted of Elizabeth. He just wanted her money, that was all. I knew that the minute I clapped my eyes on that man. I could just look at him and tell.

"I've always been good at judging character that way. I can take a look at a person and tell what he's thinking about within the first ten minutes. And what's more, I never have to change my opinion of people. I come to a decision and I don't have to change it."

"She's good," Jim Braxton said.

Mrs. Braxton tried to look modest and failed.

"Go on," Mason said.

"Well, that's all there is to it, Mr. Mason. There's one thing I'll say about Nathan Bain. He's a marvellous talker. Give him a chance to get started and he can talk the birds right down out of the trees.

"And when he set his cap for Elizabeth he really made a good job of it. He was just the nicest, most considerate man you have ever seen. But as far as I was concerned, I could see the hypocrisy oozing out all over him. It was just like something filled with slime. He didn't fool me for a minute, and he knew it."

"You told Elizabeth how you felt?"

"I certainly did. I told her exactly how I felt about that man. I warned her against him and . . . well, she wouldn't listen to me."

"Then what?"

"Well, of course, that made the relationship a little strained because she was completely hypnotised. Nothing would do but she must run right to Nathan and tell him how I felt."

"Now, wait a minute, dear," Jim interposed. "You don't know that she went to Nathan and——"

"You mind your own business," Georgiana interrupted tartly. "I guess I know what she did and what she didn't do. I could tell the minute she spoke to Nathan. I could just see the change come over him. Before that time he'd been trying to hypnotise me as one of the members of the family, but the minute he knew I was on to him he drew into his shell and got on the defensive."

"Go ahead," Mason said. "Let's get down to something that we can use as evidence if we have to."

"Well, I'm just telling you, Mr. Mason, that after he married Elizabeth for a while he was the most attentive husband. Butter wouldn't melt in his mouth. He was always dancing attendance on her hand and foot. He did let himself go terribly when it came to putting on weight. He started to get real fat. He just ate and ate and ate——"

"Never mind that," Mason said. "Let's get back to first principles."

"Well, as I say, he was very nice for a while, always, however, trying to get Elizabeth to finance this and finance that, and then trying to get her to let him manage her property. But Elizabeth was too smart for that. She was a pretty shrewd business woman and she kept her own property so that she had it entirely in her own hands, and she intended to keep it that way.

"Well, you could just see Nathan change the minute he realised that he had tied himself up for life to a woman who wasn't going to let loose of her property, but was going to keep on handling it herself and regarding it as her own.

"I just knew something was going to happen. I told Jim a dozen times if I told him once. I said to him time after time, 'Jim,' I said, 'you watch that man, he's going to——' "

"We were talking about his first wife," Mason interrupted.

"Well, one day when he had been drinking and was unusually talkative, he was telling us about his early life, and then he mentioned his first wife, which was something he very seldom did."

"What was her name?"

"Marta."

"And what happened?"

"Well, they had been married about two years or a little better, and they went down into Mexico and she was supposed to have eaten some sea-food, and she became terribly, terribly ill. He described what a nightmare it was, driving her back across the border and getting to a point where they could get competent medical attention. By the time he got her home to her family doctor she was in very bad shape. The doctor said it was undoubtedly a case of food poisoning from eating tainted sea-food. Well, she died, and that's all there was to it."

"How do you know the symptoms were those of arsenic poisoning?"

"I'm telling you the man went into details, Mr. Mason. It was positively indecent, but he'd been drinking at the time and he told about all of the trouble he'd had driving this very sick woman through miles and miles of wild country. And it was then he mentioned the candy.

"With all Nathan Bain's craving for rich foods, there's one thing he can't touch, chocolate.

"Well, he told me about Marta having taken this box of chocolate creams along in the car, and the minute he said that, the very minute, mind you, I knew what had happened.

"I looked up the symptoms and, sure enough, there they all were. Marta was poisoned by arsenic in that box of candy which she opened and ate right after the sea-food luncheon."

"Where did she get the candy?" Mason asked.

"Heavens, how should I know? But you can bet one thing, he's the one who put the arsenic in it."

"He didn't go to a Mexican doctor?"

"No. Marta didn't want one and he didn't think it would be advisable. According to the way Nathan tells the story now, they both felt that she was suffering from food poisoning and that as soon as her system was cleaned out, she'd be all right. So they made a dash to get home.

"If you ask me, the reason he wanted to get her home was because he had a friendly doctor that he used to play golf with, and he knew the doctor would sign a death certificate without asking any embarrassing questions. The doctor accepted their diagnosis of sea-food poisoning, and when she died two days later, he very obligingly filled out the death certificate."

"Where were they living at the time?" Mason asked.

"San Diego."

"And what happened to Marta's body? Was she cremated or——"

"That's one thing," she said. "*He* wanted to have the body cremated, but her mother and father insisted that the girl be buried, so they had their way. She didn't leave any will or anything directing what should be done with her body, so she was buried."

"Where?"

"In San Diego, in the cemetery there."

"All right," Mason said, "that's fine. I'm glad you've told me that. *Now* we have something to work on."

"You see," Jim Braxton said to his wife, "I told you that was important."

Mason said, "Now I want you to get this and get it straight. I don't want either one of you to say a word about this to anyone until I tell you. Do you understand?"

They nodded.

Mason said, "This thing is terribly important. The facts in this case are all scrambled. Nellie Conway says that Nathan Bain wanted to pay her to give his wife medicine that would make her rest better and get her over being so nervous. She brought that medicine to me. I took one of the tablets and had it analysed. It was aspirin. . . . The thing simply doesn't make sense.

"Now then, Elizabeth Bain is dead. Nathan Bain is going to try to worm out from under. In order to do that he's going to try to involve everyone else. At the proper time I want to hit him with this thing so it will be a bombshell. . . . And I don't want any word of this to leak out in advance. Do you understand?"

"Anything you say," Braxton said.

"Well, that's it," Mason said, "and I want you to follow instructions on that to the letter. It may be a lot more important than you realise at the present time."

"Well, I guess *I* know when to keep *my* mouth shut," Mrs. Braxton said, "and as for Jim, he never talks, do you, Jim?"

"No, dear."

"And you'll follow Mr. Mason's instructions, won't you, Jim?"

"Yes, dear."

"You don't have anything to worry about," she said to Perry Mason."

Mason gave a wry grin. "That," he announced, "shows all you know about it."

FOURTEEN

IT WAS A calm, clear night. Stars were blazing down steadily, but paled into insignificance in the floodlights at the airport.

Mason joined the stream of passengers walking briskly to the exit.

Pursuant to his instructions, Jim and Georgiana Braxton had been among the first to leave the plane. Mason was at the tail end of the procession.

As the lawyer climbed up the ramp to the main floor level of the air terminal, he gave a swift searching glance, looking for Della Street.

She was not there.

Worried, Mason started crossing the big air terminal and suddenly caught sight of Lieutenant Tragg carrying a briefcase and pacing restlessly back and forth, his eye on the big clock.

Mason hurriedly walked towards the exit, carefully keeping his back turned to Lieutenant Tragg. He was just about to push his way through the heavy glass door when Tragg called his name, sharply, peremptorily.

Mason turned with every evidence of surprise.

Tragg was hurrying towards him.

"Hello, Tragg," Mason said, and waited, obviously impatient to be on his way.

Tragg, tall, intelligent, alert and a dangerous antagonist, gripped Mason's hand. "How are you, Counsellor?"

"Pretty good. How's everything?"

"I understand you were in New Orleans?"

Mason nodded.

Tragg laughed. "Police there reported that they told you not to leave New Orleans without permission."

"The New Orleans police," Mason said, "are abrupt, arbitrary, short-tempered and disrespectful."

Tragg laughed, then asked more seriously, "*Did* you have their permission to leave?"

"I'm not accustomed to asking *any* permission from *any* police officer before I do *anything*," Mason said.

Tragg grinned good-naturedly. "Well, let's hope nothing happens to change your habits."

"I don't think anything will."

"You always were an optimist."

"Are you here to meet me?" Mason asked.

Tragg said, "I have no official interest in you at the moment, Mason. My interest is in an airplane which is scheduled to leave for New Orleans sometime within the next twenty minutes. I'm one of those nervous travellers. I can't sit down and wait until someone calls the plane, but I have to pace the floor and look at the clock as though my eyes would push the minute hand around faster."

"Going to New Orleans to talk with Nellie Conway?" Mason asked.

"Officially," Tragg said, "I'm not supposed to make any statements, but off the record, Mason, there are some rather interesting developments in New Orleans."

"Of what sort?"

Tragg shook his head.

Mason said, "You don't need to be so damn secretive. I guess everyone knows Nathan Bain flew to New Orleans and was picked up by police as soon as he got off the plane."

Tragg tried to keep from showing surprise. "Is that so?"

Mason raised his eyebrows. "You didn't know I knew about that, eh?"

"You know lots of things, Mason. Sometimes you amaze me when I find out what you do know, and then again there are times when I'm afraid I never do find out what you know. So I have to try to keep you from finding out what I know."

"So," Mason said, "the fact that Nathan Bain was picked up by the police, that Nellie Conway was picked up by the police and was talking, and that you are impatiently pacing the terminal, waiting for a plane to take off for New Orleans is a pretty good indication that Nathan Bain has made some sort of a statement that is of the greatest importance, or that you expect him to by the time you get there."

Tragg said, "You really should get a turban and a crystal ball, Mason. Then you could go into the business of fortune-telling, mind-reading and predicting the future. It's a shame to have these talents wasted on an amateur."

"Has Bain confessed to the murder?" Mason asked.

"Why don't you look in your crystal ball?" Tragg asked.

"Not giving out any information, Lieutenant?"

Tragg shook his head.

Mason said, "I'm going to have trouble with your man, Holcomb, Tragg."

"You've had trouble with him before. It won't be anything new."

"I mean I'm going to have some real trouble with him. I'm going to put him on a spot."

"Are you?"

"You're damn right I am."

"What's he done now?"

"It's what he hasn't done. He's having a very convenient memory in connection with a conversation I had with him, in which I told him all about Nellie Conway."

Tragg was serious and thoughtful. "Sergeant Holcomb knows Nathan Bain. They've had quite a few talks together."

"So?"

"Just a matter of friendship, of course. Holcomb signed up for a class in public speaking that was open to police officers and deputy sheriffs—given under the auspices of one of the service clubs. Nathan Bain was one of the instructors at that class. He made quite an impression on Holcomb.

"Bain is a smooth, convincing talker. He has a good deal of personality when he's on his feet. Holcomb was very much impressed. He made it a point to compliment Bain, and they had quite a talk.

"A couple of months later Bain rang up Holcomb and told him that he was suspicious that a nurse named Nellie Conway, who was taking care of his wife, was stealing jewellery, and asked Holcomb what to do. Holcomb said it was out of his line and offered to refer it to the larceny detail, but after they'd talked for a while Holcomb suggested Bain get a private detective, and recommended James Hallock.

"Now does that answer your question?"

"It explains a lot of facts," Mason said. "It doesn't answer my question because I wasn't asking any question. I was making a statement."

"Well," Tragg said, "I thought you'd like to know the low-down on that. Naturally, when you approached Holcomb with a story about the medicine, Holcomb thought you were rigging up an elaborate defence for Nellie Conway, so you could use it later to trap Nathan Bain on cross-examination and get your client released."

A feminine voice on the public address system announced that passengers for Tragg's plane were being loaded at Gate 15, and Tragg, welcoming the interruption, grinned and said, "Good luck to you, Counsellor."

"Thanks, the same to you. Hope you bring back a confession from Nathan Bain and drop it on Holcomb's desk."

"Any message for the New Orleans police?" Tragg asked.

"Give them my love," Mason told him.

"They may want you back there."

Mason said, "If the New Orleans police want me back there, they can telegraph a fugitive warrant for my arrest, then they can try and find some law I've violated in the State of Louisiana so they can get me extradited. You might explain to them some of the legal facts of life, Lieutenant."

Tragg grinned, waved his hand and started walking briskly towards the gate.

Mason watched him out of sight, and was just turning, when he heard the patter of quick steps behind him, and Della Street came running up to him.

"Hello, Chief."

"Hello. Where have you been?"

She laughed. "You can imagine where I've been. When I saw Lieutenant Tragg waiting around here, I didn't know whether he was looking for you or for me, or just taking a plane. So I retired to the one place where Lieutenant Tragg and his minions would be unable to follow."

"And then?" Mason asked.

"Then," she said, "I kept watch on the situation, decided Tragg was taking a plane to New Orleans, and kept where I could watch him, hoping I would find an opportunity to tip you off, but he would have to be one of those big, restless he-men, and pace back and forth with one eye on the clock as befits a nervous traveller."

"Where's Victoria Braxton?"

"We're staying at an auto court."

"Registered all right?"

"Under our own names. That's the way you wanted it, isn't it?"

"That's fine. I'd hate to have it appear she was a fugitive from justice."

"She isn't."

"Anyone looking for her?"

"Newspaper people, but as nearly as I can find out, that's all. She's wanted for questioning at the district attorney's office at ten o'clock tomorrow morning."

"Have they notified her?" Mason asked.

"No, but it's in the press. They did notify her brother, Jim, and Georgiana. I see that they made connections with the plane all right. What did you think of them, Chief?"

"Okay," Mason said, "except that once that woman gets started she certainly talks a blue streak."

"She told you about . . . ?"

Mason nodded.

"What are you going to do with it? Do you want it released to the press so we can . . . ?"

"No," Mason said. "I want that information put in cold storage, to be used at the proper time, in the proper manner, and at the proper place. If Nathan Bain confesses to the murder of his wife, we'll pass the information on to Lieutenant Tragg—although Tragg will probably know all about it before we have a chance to tell him.

"On the other hand, if the police try to give Nathan Bain a coat of whitewash, we'll slap them in the face with it."

"*Why* should they try to give Nathan Bain a coat of whitewash?"

"Because," Mason said, "our dear friend, Sergeant Holcomb, has been taking lessons in public speaking from Nathan Bain. Isn't that just too ducky?"

"Quite a coincidence, isn't it?"

"It's a coincidence, if you want to look at it in one way."

"And if you want to look at it in another way, what is it?"

Mason said, "Suppose you were planning to commit a murder. Suppose you were a member of a service club that was asking for volunteers to coach a class in public speaking that was to be composed of top-flight detectives and peace officers. Suppose you were a smooth, forceful speaker and felt you could make a good impression on people. Wouldn't that be a nice way to make yourself a whole handful of friends who'd be in a position to do you some good, or, to look at it in another way, who'd be in a position to keep anyone from doing you harm?"

Della Street nodded.

"Well," Mason said, "apparently Sergeant Holcomb and Nathan Bain are just like that," and Mason held up two crossed fingers.

"And that may complicate the situation?" Della Street asked.

"That may raise hell with it. Where's the car, Della?"

"In the parking lot."

"Okay, I'll get my bag, you get the car, and I'll meet you in front. No newspaper reporters are expecting me back?"

She laughed. "Apparently not. They've been trying to get in touch with you, but they called the New Orleans police and were assured you wouldn't be leaving Louisiana until the police there had completed their investigations."

"Well, isn't that something!" Mason said.

"What did you do? Put up bail and then jump it?"

Mason said, "I walked out. Where did they get that idea that they could tell me not to leave town? The situation would have been different if a crime had been committed in Louisiana. They're trying to investigate a crime that was committed in California. To hell with them!"

"To hell with them is right," Della Street said, laughing. "Don't get so worked up about it, Chief. You're fifteen hundred miles from New Orleans now. You get your bag and I'll get the car."

She flashed him a quick smile and ran towards the parking place. Mason secured his bag from a porter and was standing by the kerb as she drove up. He tossed the bag in the back of the car, slid in the seat beside her and said, "Let's make sure we aren't wearing a tail, Della."

"Okay, you keep watch behind and I'll cut around some of the side streets."

Mason turned so he could watch the road behind him. "How's Vicki, Della?"

"She bothers me, Chief?"

"Why?"

"I don't know. There's something I can't put my finger on."

"Anything more about the will?"

Della Street said, "That will isn't the same now as when you saw it."

"No?"

"No."

"What's different about it?"

"At the end of the sentence," Della Street said, "there is now a very perfect piece of punctuation, a nice round dot made with ink."

"How nice."

"Chief, what could they do in a situation like that?"

"What could who do?"

"Would that be forgery?"

"Any mark that would be put on a document for the purpose of deceiving others and made after the document had been signed, would be an alteration of the document."

"Even a teeny-weeny dot no bigger than a fly speck?"

"Even a dot half that big, provided it was a significant part of the document and was intended to be such."

"Well, it's there now."

"Have you asked her about it?"

"She *said* her sister put it there."

There was an interval of silence.

Della Street said, "How are we coming, Chief?"

"No one seems to be taking any undue interest in our driving, Della."

"How about it? Do we hit the main boulevard?"

"Take one more swing, and then start travelling. I want to hear Vicki Braxton's story about the full stop at the end of the will."

FIFTEEN

VICTORIA BRAXTON, ATTIRED in a neatly tailored suit, looking very efficient and business-like, was waiting up for Perry Mason and Della Street in the well-furnished living-room of the de luxe auto court where Della Street had registered.

Mason lost no time with preliminaries.

"I don't know how much time we have," he said, "but it may be a lot shorter than we hope for, so let's hit the high spots."

"Can you tell me what happened in New Orleans?" she asked.

Mason shook his head. "It's too long to go into now."

She said, "I'd like to know. I'm very much interested in anything Nathan does."

"So are the police. We'll talk about that after a while if we have time. Right now I want to know certain things."

"What?"

"Exactly what happened in connection with Mrs. Bain's death."

"Mr. Mason, *I* gave her the poison."

"You're certain?"

"Yes."

"How did it happen?"

"Nellie Conway put those tablets on the saucer. She said to me, 'The first time Elizabeth wakes up after six o'clock in the morning she's to have this medicine. Don't give it to her before six but give it to her just as soon after six as she wakes up.' "

"There were three tablets?"

"Yes."

"Placed on a saucer by the side of the bed?"

"Yes."

"And then what happened?"

"Well, that's it, Mr. Mason. She wakened and I gave her the medicine. It must have been those tablets."

"To whom have you told this?"

"To Miss Street and to you."

"Did you tell it to the officers?"

"No, Mr. Mason, I didn't, because at the time—well, when the officers were out there making an investigation, we were all excited, and at the time it never occurred to me that by any extreme possibility could *I* have been the one who administered the poison."

"That's fine."

"What is?"

"That you didn't tell anyone. Don't tell anyone, don't mention it, don't say anything to the police, don't say anything to anyone."

"But, Mr. Mason, don't you understand, it's only through my testimony that they can really connect Nellie Conway with my sister's death, and Nellie Conway, of course, is the connecting link that leads to Nathan Bain."

"For the moment," Mason said, "we'll let the police worry about their connecting links."

"Mr. Mason, I don't think that's right. I think I should tell them. Those tablets Nellie left in that saucer were poison."

"Don't tell them."

"Will you please tell me why?"

"No," Mason said, "there isn't time. Now tell me about that will."

"What about it?"

"All about it. I don't think your brother or your sister-in-law know about it."

"Does that make any difference?"

"It might."

"Elizabeth didn't want Georgiana—that's Jim's wife—to know anything about it."

"Why not?"

"Because it would have made her even more extravagant, just the idea that she'd maybe some day come into some of Elizabeth's money."

"Is Georgiana that way?"

"Terribly—and she's always jumping at the wildest conclusions from the most trivial data. As it is now, she keeps poor Jim in debt all the time. Heaven knows how much they owe. If she knew about this will—I mean, if she had known about it—the way Elizabeth was injured and all—well, she'd have gone on another spending spree."

Mason digested that information thoughtfully. "Did you and Elizabeth discuss that?"

"Yes."

Mason said, "That may or may not explain something."

"What do you mean by that?"

Mason said, "There are some things about your story I don't like."

"What?"

"To begin with, when you came to my office you told me that your sister had sent you there, that you were to retain me and I was to draw a will."

"Well, what's wrong with that?"

"Then, when somebody telephoned and asked for 'Vicki,' you were surprised. You said only your intimates called you Vicki and no one knew you were there."

"Oh, you mean my brother and sister?"

"Yes."

"Well, they didn't know I was there. Only Elizabeth knew where I was, and I knew that Elizabeth wouldn't telephone me. But Jim knew I'd asked Nellie Conway where your office was—and he thought I *might* have gone up there to ask you something about her case or the settlement.

"They were, of course, trying frantically to get me. He tried half a dozen places and then he tried your office, just on a blind chance."

"All right, let's put cards on the table. Why didn't your brother and sister know you were there?"

"For the very reason I've been telling you, Mr. Mason. They weren't to know anything about the will. Elizabeth discussed it with me."

"When?"

"When she woke up about . . . oh, I guess it was about five o'clock in the morning."

"All right. Tell me what happened."

"Well, you understand, she woke up first sometime about three o'clock. We all went in there then and talked with her. It wasn't much of a talk. Just greetings and generalities. She kissed us and told us how glad she was to see us."

"Then what?"

"Then she went right back to sleep. We left Nellie Conway in charge and we all went into the other room to lie down for a while. I slept an hour or an hour and a half, and then I came back and told Nellie I was wide awake and could take over."

"Then what?"

"That was when she put the tablets on the saucer and told me to give them to Elizabeth whenever she woke up at any time after six a.m."

"Where had the tablets been before then?"

"In a little box in the pocket of her uniform—anyway, that's where she got them when I first saw them."

"Why didn't Nellie Conway leave them in the box and simply tell you that——?"

"Apparently she was afraid I'd forget them. She took the saucer out from under the glass that had the water in it, and put the tablets right there in plain sight by the side of the bed."

"How far from Elizabeth?"

"Why, right by the side of the bed. Not over . . . oh, a couple of feet perhaps."

"How far from you?"

"I was sitting right near there. They couldn't have been over three or four feet from me."

"How far from the door of the room?"

"The door of the room was right by the stand. It wasn't over . . . oh, eighteen inches or two feet from the door of the room."

"I just wanted to get it straight," Mason said. "Now, what happened after that?"

"Well, Elizabeth was sleeping. She wakened about five o'clock and that was when she started to talk with me. Then was when she made out the will."

"Then what?"

"I was thinking I'd give her the medicine—I guess it was about twenty minutes to six—but she went back to sleep again. She didn't wake up until around a quarter to seven, and then I gave her the medicine with some coffee."

"Tell me a little more about what happened when you were talking."

"She talked to me I guess for half an hour, Mr. Mason, telling me about what she'd been going through, about the fact that Nathan had been trying to kill her, that she had been talking with Nellie Conway about you, and that she wanted you to be her lawyer, that she wanted you to go out and tell Nathan Bain that he was all finished, that she intended to file a suit for divorce, and that she wanted to make a will disinheriting Nathan."

"Did she say anything about her grounds for divorce, about what proof she had?"

"She didn't go into details, but she told me she had documentary proof."

"*Documentary* proof?" Mason asked sharply.

"That's right."

"She was intending to get a divorce because he'd been trying to kill her, wasn't she?"

"I don't know—I presume so."

"And she had *documentary* proof?"

"That's what she said. I think it related to infidelity."

"Where did she keep it?"

"She didn't say."

"All right," Mason said, "go on. What happened?"

"Well, she told me that she wanted to have you come out and prepare a will for her to sign, and she asked me to go and see you. She asked for her cheque-book and told me it was in her purse in a bureau drawer. I brought it to her and she wrote out that cheque for you."

"Then what?"

"Then we had some discussion about the fact that she was really afraid of Nathan and she felt that before you could draw up a will and have her sign it, something might happen to her."

"That was rather melodramatic, wasn't it?" Mason asked.

"Not in the light of subsequent events," Miss Braxton said sharply.

"All right. Go ahead."

"Well, I told her I didn't think it was necessary. I told her I could go to see you and tell you what she wanted, and that you could probably be out there before noon with a will ready for her to sign. She said that she thought it would be better to execute a will first and have Nathan know that no matter what happened she wasn't going to let him have a cent of her money. She said she'd been thinking it over and had come to that conclusion, and that that was the thing to do."

"So what did she do?"

"She took a piece of paper and wrote out that will."

"Let me take another look at that will."

"But you've seen it, Mr. Mason."

"You have it with you?"

"Yes, of course."

With obvious reluctance she opened her purse and handed the will to the lawyer.

Mason looked at it carefully, then moved over to study it under the light.

"There's a full stop after the last word now," he said.

Victoria said nothing.

"When you came to my office," Mason said, "there was no stop at the end of the will. I pointed that out to you."

"I know you did."

"So then you took a fountain pen and added a stop," Mason said. "In order to try and gild the lily you've probably put your neck in a noose. They'll have a spectroscopic analysis made of the ink on that stop. If they have any idea that——"

"You're thinking that they'll show it was made with a different ink and a different fountain pen?" she asked. "Well, you don't need to worry about that, Mr. Mason. That stop was made with Elizabeth's fountain pen and it's the same pen that wrote the will."

"When did you do it?" Mason asked.

"I didn't do it."

"Who did?"

"Elizabeth."

"Do you," Mason asked, "know any more funny stories?"

She said, "I'm going to tell you the truth, Mr. Mason. I was very much disturbed about that stop not being at the end of the sentence. After you pointed it out to me, I realised that if anything happened— and then, of course, something did happen; I received word that Elizabeth had been poisoned. I dashed out there in a taxicab just as fast as I could get there, and I went right into the room. Elizabeth was very, very ill. She was suffering excruciating agony, but she was conscious. I told everyone to get out and leave me alone for a few minutes, and then I said, 'Elizabeth, Mr. Mason says you neglected to put a stop at the end of that will,' and I took the fountain pen and handed it to her."

"Did she reach for it?"

"Well, I . . . she was very sick at the time."

"Did she reach to take the fountain pen when you handed it to her?"

"I put it into her hand."

"And then what did you do?"

"I held the will close to her so she could make a dot at the proper place."

"Did she raise her head from the pillow?"

"No."

"How did she see where to make the dot then?"

"I guided her hand."

"I see," Mason said dryly.

"But she knew what was being done."

"I like the way you say that," Mason said. "In place of saying she knew what she *was doing*, you say that she knew what was *being done*."

"Well, she knew what she was doing, then."

Mason said, "You still aren't telling me the truth about that will."

"What do you mean?"

"I mean that the story you told isn't the right story."

"Why, Mr. Mason, how can you say that?"

"You're talking to a lawyer. Let's cut out the kid stuff and try the truth for a change."

"I don't know what you mean."

"That will wasn't finished when you brought it to my office, and you know it."

"Well, it certainly . . . it certainly is finished now."

"Why did Elizabeth Bain break off in the middle of making that will?"

Victoria Braxton hesitated. Her eyes moved around the room as though seeking some means of escape.

"Go ahead," Mason said remorselessly.

"If you *must* know," she blurted, "Elizabeth was writing the will when Georgiana opened the door and looked in the room to see what she could do—that is, to see if there was any way that she could help."

"That's better," Mason said. "What happened?"

"Elizabeth didn't want Georgiana to know she was making a will, so she whipped the piece of paper down under the bedclothes. Georgiana asked how everything was coming and if we were getting along all right, and I told her yes, to go back and go to sleep."

"Then what?"

"Then she went back into her room. Elizabeth waited a few moments, lying there with her eyes closed, and then suddenly I realised she'd gone to sleep. So I took the fountain pen from her fingers, but the will was under the bedclothes and I couldn't find it without waking her up. I decided I'd wait until I gave her the medicine and then get the will. I thought she'd entirely finished with it, because of something she said . . . she'd quit writing for a good minute or two before Georgiana opened the door."

"And when did you get the will?"

"Well, when I gave her the medicine, she took it with water but she wanted some coffee right after that, so I rang the bell and asked the housekeeper for some coffee. At about that time the day nurse came on and she said she'd give her the coffee. I only had time to fish the will out from under the bedclothes. Elizabeth saw what I was doing and smiled and nodded and said, 'It's all right, Vicki.' So I knew that she felt she'd finished it. Now that's the real honest-to-God truth, Mr. Mason."

"Why didn't you tell me that before?"

"Because I was afraid you might think that . . . well, that you might think the will really hadn't been finished."

"And no one else was in the room from the time Nellie Conway put those tablets on the saucer?"

"No."

Mason said, "We're going to drive you to the airport. I want you to take the first available plane for Honolulu. I want you to send a wire from the plane to the District Attorney that certain business matters in connection with your sister's affairs have made it necessary for you to rush to Honolulu, that you will keep in touch with him, and that he can count on your co-operation, but that there are business affairs of such a serious nature that your attorney advised you to make a personal trip to Honolulu at once."

"But what affairs?"

"Your sister owned property in Honolulu, didn't she?"

"Yes. Lots of it. We were staying at one of her cottages there. She has a whole string of them."

Mason said, "You don't need to tell anyone what the business affairs are."

"But, good heavens, what will I do when I get there?"

"You won't get there."

"What do you mean?"

"I mean you'll be called back."

"Then why go?"

Mason said, "Because it's a nice way to get you out of circulation. You're not running away, because you've sent the District Attorney a telegram under your own name. You're taking your travel transportation under your own name, and I'm taking the responsibility as your attorney for sending you there."

"That sounds like such a crazy thing to do," she said.

"That," Mason said, "far from being crazy, is the only sensible thing to do. Now, I'm warning you—do not discuss this case with anyone. Under no circumstances ever tell anyone you gave Elizabeth those tablets. Under no circumstances discuss the case with the police or the District Attorney unless I am there. Do you understand?"

"I still don't see——"

"Will you follow my instructions?"

"Yes."

"To the letter?"

"Yes."

Mason turned to Della Street and said, "Okay, Della. Take her to the airport."

SIXTEEN

EARLY THE NEXT afternoon, Paul Drake stopped in to see Perry Mason. Mason made no attempt to disguise his anxiety. "Paul, what's happening in New Orleans? Has Bain made a statement?"

"The police aren't releasing one single bit of information, Perry. . . . Well, I'll amend that statement. They have released one."

"What's that?"

"They have a warrant for you."

"What's the charge?"

"Vagrancy."

"Anything else?"

"You mean as a charge?"

"Yes."

"No. Isn't that enough?"

Mason grinned and said, "They can't extradite me on vagrancy. They know it. They made the charge just as a gesture."

"They're mad."

"Let them be mad. But you didn't come here just to tell me that."

"Lieutenant Tragg has uncovered something."

"What?"

"Something big."

"Evidence that Nathan Bain murdered his wife?"

"Apparently," Drake said, "evidence that he did not."

"I'd like to see *that* evidence."

Drake said, "I can tell you one thing, Perry. They have some secret evidence in this case, some evidence that they're keeping so closely guarded that no one knows what it is."

"What sort of evidence?"

"I can't find out."

"Does it point to Nathan Bain, does it point to the fact she committed suicide, or . . . ?"

"All I know is that it's some super secret evidence."

"Any chance you can find out?"

Drake said, "The grand jury is in session today. They're doing something in connection with this case. I have a man up there who has a pipeline into the grand jury. He may be able to give us the low-down.

"I also know that the District Attorney's office is furious because Victoria Braxton didn't show up for questioning."

"She's on a trip," Mason said. "She has business interests in Honolulu that she absolutely has to look after."

"So you told me," Drake said dryly.

"She is," Mason said, "as far as the business angle is concerned, acting on the advice of her counsel."

"Well, that makes it fine. Only the D.A. doesn't think so."

"He wouldn't. Anything else, Paul?"

"The police have been in consultation with Lieutenant Tragg in New Orleans. Something broke there this morning that they consider highly impor——"

The phone rang sharply. Della Street answered, then said, "It's for you, Paul."

Drake picked up the phone and said, "Hello . . . Yes . . . Okay, give it to me. . . . Who else knows about this? . . . Okay, thanks. Good-bye."

He hung up the telephone, turned to Mason and said, "There's your answer. The grand jury has just returned a secret indictment against Victoria Braxton, charging her with first-degree murder."

Mason whistled. "What's the evidence, Paul?"

"The evidence is secret."

"It won't be if they've put it before the grand jury."

"Don't worry, Perry, they didn't put anything before the grand jury that they aren't willing to shout from the housetops—that is, officially. They probably whispered something in the ear of the grand jury."

Mason said, "I had a hunch something like that might be in the wind."

He turned to Della Street. "Della, we'll send a wire to Victoria Braxton, on the plane en route to Honolulu, telling her to come home. I thought we'd have to do that, but I felt it would be a summons from the grand jury rather than an indictment."

"Telling her what's in the wind?" Della Street asked.

"No. We have to protect Paul Drake's pipeline. We don't dare to let it out that we know what the grand jury did—not yet."

"What do you want to tell her?" Della Street asked, holding her pencil over the notebook.

Mason thought a moment, then grinned wryly. "Take this wire," he said, "COME HOME AT ONCE ALL IS UNFORGIVEN."

SEVENTEEN

THE TRIAL OF the People of the State of California versus Victoria Braxton opened with all of that electric tension which underlies a championship prize fight between two men who have heretofore been undefeated.

Hamilton Burger, the big grizzly bear of a District Attorney, savagely triumphant in the assurance that at last he had a perfect case which contained no flaw, was making his preliminary moves with that quiet confidence which comes to a man who knows that he holds the winning cards.

Perry Mason, veteran court-room strategist, worked with cautious skill, taking advantage of each technicality which he felt could be of any possible benefit, feeling his way with caution, realising only too well that the prosecution had prepared a trap for him, and that at any moment the legal ground might fly out from under him.

Inside information was to the effect that the prosecution had carefully saved, as a surprise, evidence that would be completely devastating once it was introduced, and that Perry Mason, despite using every legal trick in the quiver to try and make the prosecution disclose its hand, had finally been forced to enter the court-room without any knowledge of his opponent's case other than the bare outline which had been utilised to support the indictment of the grand jury.

Betting among insiders was five to one against Mason's client.

Little time was wasted in selecting a jury. Mason had indicated that he wanted only a fair and impartial trial for his client, and Hamilton Burger had quite evidently been willing to accept any twelve individuals who would be guided by the evidence in the case.

Newspaper reporters waited eagerly for Hamilton Burger's opening statement to the jury outlining the case he expected to prove, but veteran lawyers knew that Burger would not even give a hint of the nature of his trump cards this early in the game.

After outlining the fact that he expected to prove Victoria Braxton had poisoned her sister by administering three five-grain tablets of arsenic, knowing that her sister had made a will leaving a full one-half of her property, valued at some half-million dollars, to the defendant, Burger went on to announce:

"I will further state to you, ladies and gentlemen of the jury, that in this case the prosecution has no desire to take any technical advantage of the defendant. The prosecution will produce evidence from various witnesses which will make you familiar with the chain of events which led up to the death of Elizabeth Bain.

"This evidence will not follow the usual legal pattern, but will be in the nature of unfolding a story. We will paint for you, ladies and gentlemen, a broad picture with swift, sure strokes of factual evidence. We want you to see the entire background. You will, perhaps, find the evidence in this case somewhat unusual as far as the ordinary cut-and-dried procedure is concerned, but if you will follow it closely you will be led to the inescapable conclusion that the defendant is guilty of first-degree murder, carefully and deliberately planned, executed in a most heartless manner, under such circumstances that it will be necessary for you to return a verdict of guilty of first-degree murder without recommendation, making mandatory the death penalty."

Hamilton Burger, with vast dignity, walked back to the counsel table, seated himself, and glanced significantly at the judge.

"Does the defence wish to make any opening statement at this time?" Judge Howison asked.

"Not at this time, Your Honour. We prefer to make our opening statement when we present our case," Mason said.

"Very well. Call your first witness, Mr. District Attorney."

Hamilton Burger settled back in the big counsel chair and turned the preliminary proceedings over to his two deputies, David Gresham, the assistant prosecutor, and Harry Saybrook, the deputy, who, having been ignominiously beaten by Mason in the trial of Nellie Conway, was thirsting for revenge, and so had managed to get himself assigned as an assistant in the present case.

In rapid order, witnesses were called to the stand, proving that Elizabeth Bain had died, that prior to her death she exhibited evidences of arsenic poisoning, that after her death an autopsy had shown sufficient quantities of arsenic in her vital organs to have made it certain that her death was produced solely by arsenic poison.

A certified copy of the probate record showed that a holographic will had been made in the handwriting of Elizabeth Bain, dated the day of her death, and leaving all of her property share and share alike to her half-brother, James Braxton, and her half-sister, Victoria Braxton, the defendant in the present case.

After these preliminaries were over, Hamilton Burger moved in to take personal charge of the case.

"Call Dr. Harvey Keener," he said.

Dr. Keener was a slim, professional-looking man with the air of a doctor, even to the well-trimmed Vandyke beard, the cold, analytical eyes, and the dark, plastic-rimmed spectacles.

Taking the witness stand, he speedily qualified himself as a practising physician and surgeon, who had been such on the seventeenth of September last.

"Now, early on the morning of September seventeenth," Hamilton Burger asked, "you were called on to treat one of your patients on an emergency call?"

"Yes, sir."

"At what time were you called, Doctor?"

"At approximately eight-forty-five. I can't give you the exact time, but it was somewhere between eight-forty-five and nine o'clock."

"And you immediately went to see that patient?"

"I did. Yes, sir."

"Who was that patient?"

"Elizabeth Bain."

"Now, Doctor, directing your attention specifically to the symptoms which you yourself found at the time you arrived and not those which may have been told to you by the nurse, will you tell us just what you found?"

"I found the typical symptoms of arsenic poisoning, manifested in a gastro-enteric disturbance, an intense thirst, painful cramps, typical vomitus, tenesmus, feeble irregular pulse, a face that was anxious and pinched, the skin cold and clammy. I may say that these are progressive symptoms, and I am referring to them as over a period of time, from approximately the time of my arrival until the time of death, which occurred around eleven-forty that morning."

"Was the patient conscious?"

"The patient was conscious until approximately eleven o'clock."

"Did you make any chemical tests to check your diagnosis?"

"I saved substances which were eliminated for more careful analysis, but a quick chemical check indicated the presence of arsenic in the vomitus, and the symptoms were so typical that I was virtually certain of my diagnosis within a few minutes of the time of my arrival."

"Now then, did you have any conversation with the patient in regard to the manner in which this poison might have been administered?"

"I did."

"Did she make any statement to you at that time as to who had administered the poison?"

"She did."

"Will you please state what she said as to the manner of administration of the poison, and by whom?"

"Just a moment, Your Honour," Mason said, "I object to this as incompetent, irrelevant and immaterial, and quite plainly hearsay."

"That is not hearsay," Hamilton Burger said. "The patient was even then dying of arsenic poisoning."

"The point is, Your Honour," Mason said, "did she *know* she was dying?"

"Yes," Judge Howison ruled. "I think that is a very essential prerequisite to a so-called death-bed declaration, Mr. District Attorney."

"Very well, if Counsel wishes to be technical, I will dispose of that feature of the case."

"Did the patient know she was dying, Doctor?"

"Objected to as leading and suggestive."

"The question is leading, Mr. Burger."

"Well, Your Honour," Burger said, with exasperation, "Dr. Keener is a trained professional man. He has heard the discussion and certainly understands the purpose of the question. However, if Counsel wishes to consume time with technicalities, I will go about it the long way. What was Mrs. Bain's mental condition at the time with reference to hope of ultimate recovery, Doctor?"

"Objected to on the ground that no proper foundation has been laid," Mason said.

"Surely," Judge Howison said, "you are not questioning Dr. Keener's qualifications now, Mr. Mason?"

"Not as a doctor, Your Honour, only as a mind reader," Mason said. "The test of a dying declaration, or a death-bed declaration as it is sometimes known, is whether the patient states as part of that declaration that the patient is dying and knows that death is impending, and with the solemnity of the seal of death placed upon the patient's lips, then proceeds to make a statement which can be used as evidence."

"Your Honour," Hamilton Burger said irritably, "I propose to show as part of my case that the defendant was left alone in this room with Elizabeth Bain, that medicine was placed on a saucer to be given to

Elizabeth Bain, that the defendant surreptitiously substituted for this medicine three five-grain tablets of arsenic, that when the decedent wakened at approximately six-forty-five, the defendant said to the decedent, 'Here is your medicine,' and gave her the three tablets or pills which had been substituted for the medicine which had previously been left by Dr. Keener."

"Go ahead and prove it then," Mason said, "but prove it by pertinent and relevant evidence."

"I think in order to show a death-bed declaration, you are going to have to show that the patient knew death was impending," Judge Howison said.

"That is exactly what I intend to do," Hamilton Burger said. "I have asked the doctor the question as to the patient's frame of mind."

"And that question," Mason said, "is to be answered not by the doctor's attempting to read the mind of the patient, but only by what the patient herself may have said."

"Very well," Hamilton Burger conceded. "Limit it to that point, Doctor, to what the patient said."

"She said she was dying."

Hamilton Burger smiled triumphantly at Mason.

"Can you give me her exact words?"

"I can," Dr. Keener said. "I made note of them at the time, thinking that they might be important. If I may be permitted to consult a memorandum which I made at the time, I will refresh my recollection."

The doctor's glib patter and his bearing on the witness stand indicated that he was no stranger to the court-room, and knew quite well how to take care of himself.

He produced a leather-backed notebook from his pocket.

"Just a moment," Mason said, "I'd like to consult the memorandum, that is, I'd like to look at it before the witness uses it to refresh his recollection."

"Help yourself," Hamilton Burger said sarcastically.

Mason walked up to the witness stand and examined the notebook.

"Before the doctor uses this to refresh his recollection," Mason said, "I would like to ask a few questions for the purpose of having it properly identified."

"Very well," Judge Howison ruled. "You may ask the questions."

"Doctor, this entry which appears here is in your own handwriting?"

"Yes, sir."

"It was made when, Doctor?"

"It was made at approximately the time the statement was made to me by the patient."

"And by the patient you mean Elizabeth Bain?"

"Yes, sir."

"It is written in pen and ink?"

"Yes, sir."

"What pen, what ink?"

"My own fountain pen filled with ink from a bottle which I keep in my office. I can assure you there is nothing sinister about the ink, Mr. Mason."

There was a ripple of merriment which Judge Howison frowned into silence.

"Quite so, Doctor," Mason said. "Now, at what time was this statement made?"

"It was made shortly before the patient lost consciousness."

"Shortly is a relative term, Doctor. Can you define it any better than that?"

"Well, I would say perhaps half an hour."

"The patient lost consciousness within an hour after this statement was made?"

"Yes, sir. There was a condition of coma."

Mason said, "Let me look at this notebook if you will, please, Doctor," and, without waiting for permission, he turned some of the pages.

"Just a moment," Hamilton Burger interposed. "I object to Counsel pawing through Dr. Keener's private documents."

"It's not a private document," Mason said. "It's a notebook which he is attempting to identify for the purpose of refreshing his recollection. I have the right to look at the adjoining pages of the notebook and to cross examine the doctor on it."

Before Burger could make any answer, Mason, holding the notebook, turned to Dr. Keener and said, "Is it your custom, Doctor, to make entries in this notebook methodically and in consecutive order, or do you simply open the book at random until you come to a vacant page and then make a note?"

"Certainly not. I keep the book in an orderly manner. I fill one page and then turn to the next page."

"I see," Mason said. "Now this entry which you have made here, and which you wish to use at the moment to refresh your recollection as to the words that Elizabeth Bain used in stating that she was dying, are the last words which appear in this notebook?"

"Yes, sir."

"That has been some little time ago, and I take it that you have treated quite a few patients since then?"

"I have. Yes, sir."

"Why then did you not make any further entries in this notebook after Elizabeth Bain made this statement to you?"

"Because I read the statement to the police when they appeared at the scene, and the police promptly took that book as evidence, and it has been in their possession ever since."

"Until when, Doctor?"

"Until this morning, when it was returned to me."

"By whom?"

"By the District Attorney."

"I see," Mason said smiling. "The idea was that the District Attorney was to ask you if you had jotted down the exact words of the decedent, and you would whip the notebook from your pocket——"

"I object," Hamilton Burger shouted. "That's not proper cross-examination."

"I think it goes to show the bias of the witness, Your Honour."

"I think it goes more to show the skill of the prosecutor," Judge Howison said, smiling. "I think you have made your point, Mr. Mason. I see no reason for permitting the question to be answered in its present form. The witness has already stated that the notebook was taken by the police and that it was returned to him this morning."

"And that is the reason there are no entries in the notebook subsequent to the entry by you of the statement made by Elizabeth Bain that she was dying and that she had been poisoned?"

"Yes, sir."

"*Now*, perhaps you will permit the witness to go ahead with his testimony," Hamilton Burger said sarcastically.

"Not now," Mason said, smiling. "I have a few more questions to ask concerning the identification of this written memorandum. This is in your own handwriting, Doctor?"

"Yes, sir."

"And was made within a few minutes of the time the statement was made?"

"Yes, sir."

"What do you mean by a few minutes?"

"I would say within four or five minutes at the most."

"You made notes of that statement because you considered it important?"

"I did."

"You knew that it would be important to get her exact words?"

"I did."

"In other words, you have been a witness in court before this, you knew the legal requirement of a death-bed statement, and you knew that in order to get a death-bed statement admitted, it would be necessary to show that the patient knew she was dying?"

"Yes, sir."

"And you made these notes because you were afraid to trust to your own memory?"

"I wouldn't say that. No, sir."

"Why *did* you make them then?"

"Because I knew some smart lawyer was going to ask me what her exact words were, and I decided I'd be able to tell him."

Again there was a ripple of merriment.

"I see," Mason said. "You knew that you were going to be questioned on this and you wanted to be in a position to cope with counsel on cross-examination?"

"If you want to put it that way, yes, sir."

"Now, then," Mason said, "without saying what her exact words were, did the patient make a statement to you as to who had administered the poison?"

"She did. Yes, sir."

"And yet you didn't consider that statement particularly important, Doctor?"

"Certainly I did. That was the most important part of the whole thing."

"Then why didn't you make a note of that in your notebook so that if some smart lawyer started to ask you for the exact words of the dying patient, you would be able to give them?"

"I did make such a notation," Dr. Keener said angrily. "If you will look back a page you will find the notation giving the exact words of the patient."

"And when was that notation made?"

"Within a few minutes of the time the patient made the statement."

"Within five minutes?"

"Within five minutes, yes. Probably less than that."

"Within four minutes?"

"I would say it was within one minute."

"And what about this statement that the patient made that she was dying? What's your best recollection as to when that was written in your notebook?"

"I would say that also was written within one minute."

"But," Mason said, smiling, "the statement from the patient as to who had administered the medicine to her is made on the page preceding her statement that she was dying."

"Naturally," Dr. Keener said sarcastically. "You have already questioned me about that. I told you I made my entries in this notebook in chronological order."

"Oh, then the statement as to who had administered the medicine was made *before* the patient said she knew she was dying?"

"I didn't say that."

"Well, I'm asking it."

"Frankly," Dr. Keener said, suddenly aware of the trap into which he had been led, "I can't remember the exact sequence of these statements."

"But you do know, do you not, Doctor, that you make your entries in this book in chronological order? You have said so very emphatically on at least two occasions."

"Well, yes."

"So that at the time the patient made the statement to you in regard to the administration of medicine, she had not made any statement to you to indicate that she knew she was dying?"

"I can't say that."

"You don't have to," Mason said. "Your notebook says it for you."

"Well, that's not exactly my recollection."

"But your recollection is hazy, isn't it, Doctor?"

"No, sir."

"You had reason to doubt it?"

"What do you mean by that?"

"You were afraid that you couldn't remember exactly what had happened and the exact sequence in which it happened, so you didn't trust your memory but made entries in this notebook so that no smart lawyer could trap you in cross-examination?"

Dr. Keener shifted his position uneasily.

"Oh, Your Honour," Hamilton Burger said, "I think this cross-examination is being unduly prolonged and I am sure——"

"I don't," Judge Howison ruled. "As the court understands the law it is plainly a prerequisite to a death-bed declaration that the person making it knows of impending death and makes a statement to that effect, so that the knowledge which is within the mind of the patient can be communicated to others."

"Well," Dr. Keener said, "I can't answer that question any better than I already have."

"Thank you," Mason said. "That's all."

"All right," Hamilton Burger said, "Counsel apparently is finished. Go ahead and state what Elizabeth Bain said, refreshing your recollection from the entry in your notebook, Doctor."

"I now object to the question," Mason said, "on the ground that it is incompetent, irrelevant and immaterial. It appears that the doctor is now testifying to a statement made by the patient at some considerable time interval *after* the statement made by the patient concerning the administration of the medicine, which the District Attorney is trying to get into evidence."

"The objection is sustained," Judge Howison said promptly.

Burger's face purpled. "Your Honour, I——"

"I think the situation is obvious as far as the testimony is concerned at the present time. If you wish to make a further examination of Dr. Keener for the purpose of showing the relative times at which these entries were made, those questions will be permitted, but in the present state of the evidence the objection must be sustained."

"Well, I will withdraw Dr. Keener from the stand temporarily and call another witness," Hamilton Burger said with poor grace. "I'll get at it in another way."

"Very well," Judge Howison said. "Call your next witness. That's all, Doctor. You may stand aside for the time being."

"Call Nellie Conway to the stand," Hamilton Burger said, with the manner of a man getting ready to play his high trumps.

Nellie Conway came forward to the witness stand, was sworn, and, after the usual preliminaries as to her name, address and occupation, was asked by Hamilton Burger, "You are acquainted with Nathan Bain, the surviving husband of Elizabeth Bain?"

"Yes, sir."

"And were employed by him as a nurse to nurse Elizabeth Bain?"

"Yes, sir."

"And on the evening of the sixteenth and the morning of the seventeenth of last September, you were so employed there as nurse?"

"Yes, sir."

"Now, did you at any time on the evening of the sixteenth or the morning of the seventeenth, give instructions to the defendant in this case as to medicine that was to be given to Elizabeth Bain?"

"I did. Yes, sir."

"And those instructions were communicated to the defendant?"

"Yes, sir."

"And the medicine was left where?"

"The medicine was left in a saucer on a bedside table within some two feet of Elizabeth Bain."

"What did the medicine consist of?"

"Three five-grain tablets."

"Who had given you that medicine?"

"Dr. Keener had left it with me to be given to Mrs. Bain."

"Where had this medicine been left?"

"It had been given me personally by Dr. Keener."

"When?"

"About seven o'clock on the evening of the sixteenth when Dr. Keener made his evening call."

"Who was present in the room when you had this conversation with the defendant?"

"Just Elizabeth Bain, who was sleeping, and Victoria Braxton."

"And what did you tell her?"

"I told her that if Mrs. Bain awakened after six o'clock in the morning she was to have this medicine, that it was not to be given to her before six."

"And that was medicine which you received directly from Dr. Keener?"

"Yes, sir."

"Cross-examine!" Hamilton Burger snapped.

Perry Mason's tone was casual and conversational. "You don't know what was in the medicine?"

"I know it was three tablets, that's all."

"It was part of your duties to give Mrs. Bain medicine which had been left by the physician?"

"Yes, sir."

"And you did do that?"

"Yes, sir."

"You were paid to do that?"

"Yes, sir. Although I wasn't paid for my services the night of the sixteenth and the seventeenth, that is, not specifically."

"Do you mean you weren't paid by anybody to give any medicine to Mrs. Bain on the night of the sixteenth and seventeenth?"

"I know what you're trying to get at," Hamilton Burger said, "and you don't need to go at it by indirection, Mr. Mason. The prosecution has no objection. The door is open, walk right in."

And Hamilton Burger smiled smugly.

Nellie Conway said, "I was paid some money by Nathan Bain on the night of the sixteenth. It was not a payment for services I was to render, it was payment for a settlement that had been made, but I did give Mrs. Bain some medicine that Mr. Bain wanted me to give her."

"Medicine?" Mason asked.

"Well, some pills or tablets."

"How many?"

"Three."

"What size?"

"Five-grain."

"And they had been given you by Mr. Bain to give to his wife?"

"Yes, sir. There had been four originally but I had given one of them to you, and the other three remained in my possession, and when Mr. Bain asked me to give them to his wife, I did."

"At what time?"

"Shortly after Dr. Keener had left, I gave Mrs. Bain those three pills or tablets."

"The ones that had been given you by Nathan Bain, her husband?"

"Yes, sir."

Hamilton Burger sat grinning delightedly.

"Where did you get these tablets that you gave Mrs. Bain?"

"From her husband."

"I mean immediately prior to administering them. Where were they?"

She said, as though she had carefully memorised the words, "I had taken those tablets to your office. I had told you about the conversation, and you had told me that the medicine was harmless, that it was nothing but aspirin. And you charged me a dollar for advice. You had returned three of those tablets to a small tube-like bottle which was just big enough to hold five-grain pills. That bottle had been sealed in an envelope with your name and my name written on it.

"So when Mr. Bain asked me once more to give those pills to his wife, I decided to do so since you had told me they contained only aspirin."

"Did I tell you that?" Mason asked.

"Yes, and you charged a fee for telling me so. I have the receipt."

"I told you that the pills you had contained only aspirin?"

"Well, you took one of the pills to be analysed and told me that it contained aspirin."

"One of the four," Mason said. "You don't know what was in the other three."

"No, only I supposed that if they had been anything harmful you wouldn't have given them back to me so I could give them to Mrs. Bain. I went to you for advice and paid you your fee."

Hamilton Burger chuckled audibly.

Mason said, "Then am I to understand that on the evening of the sixteenth you opened this envelope and took the three remaining tablets from the small bottle or phial, and gave them to Mrs. Bain?"

"I did. Yes, sir."

"With what effect?"

"No effect, except that she had a better and quieter night than she had had at any time."

"As far as you know," Mason said, "those pills might have contained arsenic or any other poison?"

"All I know is what Mr. Bain told me, that the pills were to give his wife a good sleep, and what you told me, that they were aspirin," she said, with the quick, pert manner of one who is giving a well-rehearsed answer to an anticipated question.

Hamilton Burger was grinning broadly.

"So," Mason said, "as far as you know of your own knowledge, you yourself may have given Elizabeth Bain three five-grain pills of arsenic on the evening of the sixteenth at some time shortly after seven o'clock in the evening?"

"I gave her the pills a little after eight o'clock."

"That's all," Mason said.

"No further questions," Hamilton Burger said. "Now we'll recall Dr. Keener to the stand if the Court please."

"Very well. Return to the stand, Doctor."

Dr. Keener returned to the witness stand.

"Doctor," Hamilton Burger said, "I want to ask you, in your opinion as a physician, if three five-grain arsenic tablets had been given to Elizabeth Bain at approximately eight o'clock on the evening of the sixteenth of September, when would the first symptoms of poison have manifested themselves?"

"In my opinion, and because of my knowledge of the patient's condition," Dr. Keener said, "I would have expected symptoms to have manifested themselves within a period of one to two hours after ingestion, a maximum period of two hours, certainly not later than that."

"Now then," Hamilton Burger went on, "you have heard the testimony of the last witness that you gave her three five-grain tablets to be administered to Elizabeth Bain in the morning."

"That's right. At any time when she wakened after six in the morning."

"What were the contents of those pills or tablets, Doctor?"

"They contained soda, acctylsalicylic acid and phenobarbital."

"There was no arsenic in them?"

"None whatever."

"Those pills or tablets had been compounded under your direction, Doctor?"

"In accordance with a prescription which I had given. There were certain very definite proportions. I may state that the problem at the time was that of administering proper sedatives which would, over a course of time, not upset the stomach, but would control a condition of extreme nervousness which had characterised the patient's reactions to her injuries and to surrounding circumstances."

"Now then," Hamilton Burger said triumphantly, "did you at any time after you gave those three tablets to the nurse, Nellie Conway, on the evening of the sixteenth, see those same three pills again?"

"I did. Yes, sir."

"When?"

"At about three p.m. on the afternoon of the seventeenth."

"Those same tablets?"

"Those same tablets. Yes, sir."

"Now then," Hamilton Burger said, smiling, "you may cross-examine, Mr. Mason."

"How do you know they were the same tablets?" Mason asked.

"Because I analysed them."

"You analysed them personally?"

"It was done under my supervision and in my presence."

"And what did you find?"

"I found they were the tablets I had prescribed. They contained identical proportions of soda, phenobarbital and acetylsalicylic acid."

"Where did you find those pills?" Mason asked.

"I found them in a waste-basket that was in the room for the purpose of collecting bandages which had been used, bits of waste cotton and other matter, which had been thrown away while the patient was being treated, things that were used in the treatment, in other words."

"What time were those pills or tablets found?"

"They were found——"

"Just a minute," Mason interrupted. "Before you answer that question, let me ask you one more. Did you find them yourself personally?"

"Yes, sir. That's right, I did. I suggested that a search be made of everything in the room. Frankly, I was looking for——"

"Never mind what you were looking for," Mason said. "Just answer the question, Doctor. You know better than to volunteer information. You've been a witness before. I am simply asking whether you personally found them."

"Yes, sir. I personally went through the contents of this waste-basket and I found one tablet, then I found two more."

"Then what did you do?"

"They were placed in a receptacle, called to the attention of the police, and certain tests were made."

"Can you describe the nature of those tests?"

"Just a moment, Your Honour, just a moment," Hamilton Burger objected. "That is not proper cross-examination. I have asked the witness on direct examination as to whether he ever saw those same pills or tablets again. Now I have no objection as to this witness testifying on cross-examination as to any tests that were made to determine the *identity* of the tablets, but as to any other matters, I object."

"But wouldn't the test be for the purpose of determining the identity of the pills?" Judge Howison asked.

"Not necessarily, Your Honour."

"Well, I feel that the objection is well-taken if the question is deemed to call for tests which were made for any other purpose and with which the witness is familiar. However, I don't see——"

"It will be explained in due time," Hamilton Burger said, "but I wish the privilege of putting on my own case in my own way, Your Honour."

"Very well, the witness will understand that the question is limited as to tests which were made for the purpose of identifying the tablets."

"Those tests were made by me, by a chemist of the police force, and a consulting chemist from one of the pharmaceutical houses, in the presence of two police officers. The tests disclosed unquestionably that these were the tablets I had prescribed. Those were the same three tablets that I had left to be given to Mrs. Bain after she wakened at six o'clock in the morning. There is no question but what a substitution had been made——"

"Just a moment, Doctor," Mason rebuked sharply. "You keep trying to go ahead and interject your surmises and arguments into the case. Please confine yourself to answering questions and stopping."

"Very well," Dr. Keener snapped. "There is no question but what they were the same tablets."

"In other words, they had an identical formula as the ones you had prescribed?"

"That's right."

"And, by the way, Doctor, do you use the term pills and tablets interchangeably?"

"Loosely speaking, the way we have been talking in lay terms, yes. I usually prefer to refer to a pill as something that is a ball of medication with a coating on the outside, whereas a tablet is more of a lozenge, a compressed, flat substance. However, in lay language I use the terms interchangeably."

"But technically what were these?"

"Technically these were tablets. It was a mixture that had been compounded and then compressed into small, lozenge-like tablets."

"How long had you been having trouble with a nervous condition on the part of the patient?"

"Ever since the accident—the injury."

"And you had used varying methods of sedation?"

"I used hypodermics for a while until the pain had subsided, and then, as I was dealing with a condition of nervousness that threatened to become chronic, I tried to get a treatment that would be a palliative yet without containing sufficient medication to be perhaps habit-forming."

"So this medication of soda, acetylsalicylic acid and phenobarbital was a part of a continuing treatment?"

"Yes, I had continued it for some time."

"How long?"

"About one week on this particular formula."

"And the patient responded?"

"As well as could be expected. I was, of course, finding it necessary to diminish dosage. After all, a patient cannot expect to depend indefinitely upon medication to control nervousness. The patient must cooperate, and there must be an adjustment to circumstances. Therefore, I was continually decreasing the dosage and, of course, the patient was, at the same time, developing a certain tolerance to the medication; therefore results were not entirely satisfactory from a layman's point of view, although as her physician I was keeping a careful watch on the situation and felt that progress was as good as could be expected."

"The point I am making," Mason said, "is that you didn't mix up these pills three at a time. The pills were mixed in quantities."

"Oh, I see what you're driving at," Dr. Keener said, with a somewhat nasty smile. "However, I will state that I was very careful never to leave more than three of these pills at any one time, so that these three must necessarily have been the ones that I left that evening on my departure. I had previously given the patient three similar pills or tablets, which I administered personally."

"Thank you for the benefit of your conclusions, Doctor," Mason said, "but all you know is that these three tablets had identical drug content with the ones you had prescribed. You don't know whether they were the three tablets you had left for her that night, or day before yesterday, or a week ago, do you?"

"I certainly do."

"How?"

"I know, because they were found in the trash basket, and the trash basket was emptied——"

"How do you know it was emptied?"

"The nurse reported it was emptied. Those were the orders that I had left."

"You didn't empty it yourself?"

"No."

"Then you're trying to testify from hearsay evidence, Doctor. You know better than that. I'm asking you of your own knowledge. As far as you're concerned, they might have been tablets that you had left for the patient to take the morning before or the morning before that, or the morning before that."

"Well, the patient would have told me if she hadn't been given the medicine, and the nurse would have reported——"

"I'm talking of your own knowledge, Doctor. Let's not engage in statements as to the probabilities of a given situation, but as to your own knowledge, is there any way you have of *knowing* that those tablets were the same tablets that you had left that morning, purely from the chemical content?"

"Not from the chemical content, no. However, there were other matters that——"

"I think I've pointed out, Doctor, that we're not going into those other matters at this time," Hamilton Burger interrupted sharply. "The questions that you are being asked concern entirely the chemical compounds of the pills or tablets, and the place and time at which they were found."

"Very well," Dr. Keener said.

"The point I am making," Mason said, "is that for perhaps the last four days you had been giving the patient identical medication?"

"For the last five days prior to her death, I had been giving her the same medication. Prior to that time the dosage had been somewhat stronger. I will further state that because I was afraid the patient might develop suicidal tendencies, I was very careful not to leave any surplus of pills or tablets so that the patient could accumulate a lethal dosage. Now does that answer your question, Mr. Mason?"

"That answers it very nicely," Mason said. "Thank you very much, Doctor."

Judge Howison glanced at Hamilton Burger. "It's four-thirty, Mr. Burger. Do you have some witness that you can put on who——?"

"I'm afraid not, Your Honour. The next witness is going to take some time, but I think we may as well get at it, because I expect his cross-examination will consume a very considerable period."

"Very well, go ahead."

"Call Nathan Bain."

Nathan Bain came forward and was sworn.

It was quite evident from the moment he took the witness stand that this was an entirely different Nathan Bain from the man whom Mason had made to appear at such disadvantage during the trial of Nellie Conway.

Nathan Bain had obviously been carefully prepared, thoroughly coached, and was enough of a public speaker to take full advantage of the situation.

Hamilton Burger stood up and faced the man with a manner which created the impression of a simple dignity and straightforward sincerity.

"Mr. Bain," he said, "you are the surviving husband of Elizabeth Bain, the decedent?"

"Yes, sir."

"And under the terms of the will, which has been filed for probate, you are not to inherit any part of her estate?"

"No, sir. Not one penny."

"You have heard the testimony of Nellie Conway that you gave her certain medication to be administered to your wife?"

"Yes, sir."

"Will you please tell me, and tell the jury, very frankly what the circumstances are in connection with that affair, Mr. Bain?"

Nathan Bain took a deep breath, turned and faced the jury.

"I had," he said, "placed myself in a most unfortunate and lamentable predicament, entirely through my own ill-advised stupidity. I regret that very greatly, but I wish to state the facts——"

"Go ahead and state them," Mason interrupted. "I object, Your Honour, to this man making an argument to the jury. Let him answer the question by stating the facts."

"Go right ahead and state the facts," Hamilton Burger said, with something of a smirk.

Nathan Bain's manner was that of a man who is baring his chest to his accusers. He said, in a voice that dripped with sorrow and humility, "For the past few months my relations with my wife had been anything but happy. I gave Nellie Conway four tablets and asked her to administer those tablets to my wife without the knowledge of her doctor or anyone else."

"What was the nature of those tablets?" Hamilton Burger asked.

"Those tablets," Nathan Bain said, "were four in number. Two of them were five-grain aspirin tablets, two of them were barbiturates."

Hamilton Burger, veteran jury lawyer and court-room strategist, managed to put into his tone just the right amount of feeling and sympathy, indicating that he disliked to subject Nathan Bain to this ordeal but that the interests of justice made it necessary.

"Please tell the jury the cause of the difference between you and your wife at the time of her death."

Once more Nathan Bain turned to look the jurors straight in the eyes, then lowered his own eyes, and in a voice of shamefaced humility said, "I had been untrue to my wife, unfaithful to my marriage vows, and she had learned of my infidelity."

"Was that the only cause?" Hamilton Burger asked.

"We had been drifting apart," Nathan Bain admitted, and then, raising his eyes to the jury in a burst of candour, he said, as though baring his very soul, "If it hadn't been for that I wouldn't have sought affection elsewhere, but . . ."

He broke off, made a little gesture of futility and once more lowered his eyes.

"You will understand that I dislike to go into this as much as you dislike to have me," Hamilton Burger said, "but I feel that it is necessary in order to give the jury a complete picture of the situation. *Why* did you want your wife to have this one dose, this heavy dose, of barbiturates?"

Nathan Bain kept his eyes on the floor. "My wife had intercepted certain letters, certain documentary proof of my infidelity. She was planning to bring a suit for divorce. I didn't want this to happen. I loved her. My other affair was simply one of those flings that a man will take heedlessly, thoughtlessly, when temptation offers, and without proper consideration of the horrible consequences which must inevitably develop. I didn't want my wife to get a divorce."

"*Why* did you arrange to give her the pills?"

"She wouldn't let me come in the room, yet the door was always unlocked. The nurses were not in there all the time. They came and went. When she was asleep the nurse would step out down to the kitchen to get some hot milk or coffee, or something of that sort. I wanted an opportunity to go into the room and search and find those letters."

"Couldn't you have done it without drugging her?"

"She was very nervous and very restless after the accident. The poor girl's spine was crushed and I suppose that that injury had a deep-seated effect upon her entire nervous system, but in addition to that there was, of course, the knowledge of her injuries, and I think towards the last she had the feeling that she might never be able to walk again. She slept very fitfully, wakening at the slightest noise. I knew that if she detected me in the room, trying to get those documents, it would be disastrous. Even my presence in the room irritated her, and Dr. Keener had warned me not to excite her. He had told me definitely to stay out of the room."

"How long had that situation been in existence?"

"From the day she returned home from the hospital."

"So what happened on the evening of the sixteenth?"

"On the evening of the sixteenth, this dosage of barbiturates, added to the phenobarbital that Dr. Keener had prescribed, put my wife in a deep, restful sleep. She was drugged to a point of insensibility. I waited until both the housekeeper, Imogene Ricker, and the nurse, Nellie Conway, were out of the room. They were down in the kitchen drinking coffee and talking. I felt certain they would be there for some minutes, because my wife was sleeping very soundly that night, and they knew that for some reason she was having a very deep, restful sleep. So I entered the room and after some five minutes' search found the documents and took them back into my possession."

Nathan Bain looked down at his shoes, took a deep breath and let it out in a sigh. His attitude was that of one who condemns himself most strongly, yet who, after all, recognises that he has been actuated only by human frailties which are a part of every man's make-up. It was a consummate job of acting.

It would have been possible to have heard a pin drop in the courtroom.

Hamilton Burger managed to give the impression of one who is respecting another's great sorrow. "What did you do with these documents after you recovered them, Mr. Bain?"

Bain said, "I arranged to return the letters to the woman who had written them so she could destroy them."

"And I believe you went to New Orleans immediately after your wife's death?"

Judge Howison looked down at Mason and said, "Of course, an objection is usually up to opposing counsel, but it seems to me that some of this matter is entirely collateral."

"I think not," Hamilton Burger said, with slow, ponderous dignity. "*I* want the jury to get the entire picture here. We want to put all our cards face up and on the table, those that are good and those that are bad. We want the jurors to see the interior of this man's house. We want them to see into his mind, into his soul——"

Mason interrupted dryly, "One of the reasons I hadn't been objecting, Your Honour, was that I knew Hamilton Burger had this touching speech all prepared and I didn't want to give him his cue."

There was a slight ripple of merriment. Judge Howison, himself, couldn't help but smile, and Burger frowned as he realised that this emotional release was undermining the effect he was trying to create.

He drew himself up and said with simple, austere dignity, "If Court and Counsel will bear with me, I think I can convince them of this man's sincerity, of his repentance and of his grief."

And without waiting, Burger turned to Nathan Bain and said, "Why did you go to New Orleans, Mr. Bain?"

"I went there," Bain said, "because the woman who had entered into my life was there, and I wanted to tell her personally that I never wanted to see her again, that the affair had been the result of an unthinking venture and had left me emotionally bankrupt."

Nathan Bain's words and manner carried conviction. A veteran speaker would have noticed that much of this was due to tricks of delivery, carefully studied, synthetic oratorical accessories, but the average listener heard only a bereaved husband being forced by the exigencies of the situation to make public confession of his wrongdoing, and trying his best to conceal a broken heart beneath a rigid exterior of Spartan self-control.

"Now then," Hamilton Burger went on, "you spoke of a settlement that had been made with Nellie Conway, and there has been some talk here of a settlement. Will you describe that and tell us what that actually was?"

"That," Nathan Bain said, "was an attempt on my part to adjust what had been a wrong."

"Tell us about it, please."

"I was instrumental in having Nellie Conway arrested for theft. I realise now that not only was my action impulsive, but that it was ill-advised. She was represented by Mr. Perry Mason, the attorney who is now representing Victoria Braxton, and Mr. Mason, I am afraid, caused me to cut rather a sorry spectacle in the court-room. That was because I hadn't fully thought over the various ramifications of the situation. I am afraid I was tempted to act hastily—much too hastily."

"Just what did you do, specifically?"

"I appealed to the police, and, on their advice, hired a private detective. Things had been missing from the house and I had reason, or thought I did, to suspect Nellie Conway. I took my wife's jewel casket from the desk where it was kept under lock and key, and left it out in plain sight. I filled it with synthetic costume jewellery and made an inventory of the articles. I dusted the outside of the casket with a fluorescent powder."

"Just describe that to us, if you will, Mr. Bain."

"Well, it was a powder which was furnished me by the private detective whom I employed. I understand it is quite generally used by private detectives for the purpose of catching sneak thieves, particularly in the case of locker burglaries and schoolroom sneak thieves."

"Can you describe this powder?"

"It is virtually . . . well, it's rather neutral in shade, and when you put it on an object such as this leather-covered jewel case which belonged to my wife, it is practically invisible. It has a quality which makes it adhere to the fingers. It is remarkable in its clinging qualities, yet there is no feeling of stickiness in connection with it."

"Now you have described that as a fluorescent powder?"

"Yes, sir. When ultra-violet light shines upon that powder it gives forth a very vivid light, that is, it fluoresces."

"I would, if possible, like to have you tell the jury something more about the case against Nellie Conway. In other words, I want to have it appear why you paid her such a sum of money."

"Because of the false arrest."

"You're now satisfied it was a false arrest?"

"After Mr. Mason got done with me," Nathan Bain said, with a wry smile, "I don't think there was anyone who had any doubt about it, myself included."

Some of the jurors smiled sympathetically.

"How much did you pay her, by the way?"

"Two thousand dollars for herself, and five hundred dollars for an attorney fee."

"Now just go ahead and describe the arrest a little more, if you will, please."

"Well, we dusted the fluorescent powder on this jewel case."

"And I take it the powder wasn't placed anywhere else?"

"No, sir. Only on the jewel case."

"And what happened?"

"Well, from time to time, the detective and I would look at the contents of the jewel case to keep an inventory. Nothing was missing until shortly after Nellie Conway came to work, then a diamond pendant was missing. By that I mean a synthetic diamond pendant, a bit of costume jewellery. We made an excuse to switch off the lights and switch on the ultra-violet light, and Nellie Conway's finger-tips blazed into brilliance. That was circumstantial evidence and we jumped at conclusions from it, and naturally jumped at the wrong conclusion, as Mr. Mason so ably pointed out."

"What happened in that case?"

"Nellie Conway was found not guilty in, I believe, record time."

"By a jury?"

"Yes, sir."

"Now then," Hamilton Burger said, "with reference to those three tablets which were found in the waste-basket, according to Dr. Keener's testimony, were you there when the basket was searched?"

"I was. Yes, sir."

"And what was done with those three tablets?"

"Well, they were examined and placed in a small box and . . . well, when it began to appear that in all human probability the substitution must have been made by the defendant in this case, I suggested to the police officers that when I had told the defendant something about the case against Nellie Conway and how it had been handled, the defendant had wanted to see the jewel case. So I opened the desk, got out the jewel case and let the defendant look at it."

"Did she handle it?"

"Yes. She took it in her hands."

"Did anyone else handle it?"

"No, sir. At about that time the defendant's brother, who was upstairs, called to her, and she returned the jewel case to me. I hurriedly placed it on top of the desk and followed her upstairs."

"Later on, you told the police about this?"

"Yes, sir. I told them that perhaps some of the fluorescent powder which still adhered to the jewel case might . . . well, I suggested to the police officers it might be well to look at those three tablets or pills under ultra-violet light."

"Did they do so in your presence?"

"Yes, sir."

"And what happened?"

"There was a very faint, but unmistakable fluorescence."

There was a startled gasp from the spectators in the court-room, then the buzz of whispering.

It was at that moment that Hamilton Burger, apparently suddenly aware of the time, of which he had previously been unconscious, glanced apprehensively at the clock on the court-room wall, and said, "Your Honour, I find that I have exceeded the time of adjournment by some ten minutes."

"So you have," Judge Howison said, his voice plainly indicating that he himself had been so interested in this dramatic phase of the testimony that he had not noticed the passing of time.

"I'm sorry," Hamilton Burger said simply.

Judge Howison said, "It appearing that the examination and cross-examination of this witness will occupy a very considerable period of time, and it now having passed the usual hour for the evening adjournment, the Court will take a recess until tomorrow morning at ten o'clock. During that time the members of the jury are admonished not to discuss the case among themselves or with others, nor permit it to be discussed in their presence. You jurors are not to form or express any opinion as to the guilt or innocence of the defendant until the case is finally submitted to you. The defendant is remanded to custody. The Court will adjourn until tomorrow morning at ten o'clock."

Judge Howison left the bench and there was instantly a great commotion of voices throughout the court-room.

Mason turned to Victoria Braxton. "Did you handle that jewel chest?" he asked.

"Yes. I was curious. I asked him about it. He took me downstairs and opened the desk. When we went back upstairs he left it on the top of the desk. But while I am the only one who handled it at the time, the others did later."

"What others?"

"Why, Jim and Georgiana."

"Did you see them handle it?"

"No, but they went downstairs, and Georgiana asked me when she came back up why Elizabeth's jewel case was out in plain sight—so if they saw it they must have handled it. Georgiana has an insatiable curiosity."

"And Nathan Bain handled it when he gave it to you, didn't he?"

"Why, yes. I hadn't thought of that."

"And who put it back in the desk? Did he?"

"The housekeeper, I think."

"It's the same old story," Mason said. "Everyone handled it, yet by building up to this climax just at adjournment, the District Attorney conveys the impression he's proven your guilt.

"That's always the way with these fluorescent powder cases. The thing is so dramatic, the fluorescent finger-tips seem so damning, that everyone loses his mental perspective.

"Now, couldn't Nathan Bain have opened the door of his wife's bedroom, picked up the tablets from the saucer and switched the poison tablets?"

"No . . . I don't think so, not while I was there."

"They were close to the door?"

"Yes. If he'd opened the door to look in he could have done it, but he didn't. But couldn't he have substituted them while Nellie Conway had them, carrying them around in that box?"

"Don't worry," Mason interrupted. "I'm going to cover that phase of the case on cross-examination. What I'm asking now is whether he could have made the substitution after Nellie Conway had put the tablets on the saucer and left them with you."

"No. That would have been impossible."

"And what time was it that you were handling the jewel case and got that powder on your fingers?"

"Shortly before three in the morning. We got to the airport at one-forty-five, and by the time we arrived at the house it must have been two-thirty."

"And at about three o'clock you went in to see Elizabeth?"

"Yes."

"The three of you?"

"Yes."

"Keep a stiff upper lip," Mason said, as the deputy sheriff touched her arm.

"Don't worry," she told him, and followed the officer to the prisoner's exit.

Jim Braxton and his wife, waiting for Mason immediately outside the bar which segregated the space reserved for attorneys and officers of the court from the rest of the court-room, grabbed the lawyer, one by each arm.

It was Georgiana who did the talking.

"That dirty hypocrite," she said. "He's sitting there so butter wouldn't melt in his mouth, and the worst of it is, he's getting away with it. That's what I told you about him, Mr. Mason, the . . . the toad, the big, fat toad! That's all he is, a toad!"

"Take it easy," Mason said. "It's not going to do any good running up a blood pressure over it."

"He's sitting there just trying to lie his way out of it. He's fixed it up with this Nellie Conway, and between them they're telling a great story for the jury, trying to make it appear that Vicki must have been the one who gave her that poisoned medicine. Mr. Mason, you've simply *got* to do something, you can't let him get away with this."

"I'm going to do the best I can," Mason said.

"We all know who murdered Elizabeth. It was Nathan Bain, and he and that Conway woman have cooked up a story that will look good in print and will lull the suspicions of the jurors. We know the real Nathan Bain, Mr. Mason, and he's not like this at all. He's just a shrewd, selfish, cunning individual—unbelievably cunning—but he does have the knack of standing up and talking to people in a way that makes it seem he's baring his very soul, that he's giving them an insight into his innermost thoughts. Actually the man's innermost thoughts are just as black and impenetrable as . . . as . . . as an ink-well full of ink."

Mason said, "I've torn him wide open once. I may be able to do it again, but this time he's been very carefully coached."

"Hmph!" she said. "The probabilities are he's the one who coached that District Attorney. Between them they're putting on a great show."

"Aren't they?" Mason said.

"Couldn't you have objected to a lot of that stuff?" Jim interposed timidly.

"Sure," Mason said, "but I want it in. The more of this stuff he's putting in, the more latitude it gives me in cross-examination. The more I try to keep out, the more the jurors suspect we're afraid to have them learn all the facts."

Georgiana said, "Don't depend too much on cross-examination. He's been prepared for that. Between him and that District Attorney they've rehearsed that act until they're black in the face. They're both birds of a stripe—I mean a feather. Just a couple of actors putting on a big razzle-dazzle. If you could only know Nathan the way he really is, and then see him the way he is on the witness stand, you'd appreciate some of the things I've been telling you."

"Well," Mason said, reassuringly, "perhaps we can find some way of letting the jury see him the way he really is."

EIGHTEEN

MASON, IN MIDNIGHT conference with Paul Drake and Della Street, paced the floor of his office.

"Damn Burger," Mason said. "He has some devastating bomb he's going to drop."

"That fluorescent powder? Could that have been it?" Paul Drake asked.

"No. That doesn't really prove as much as they're trying to make it appear. Anyone in the house could have touched the casket. Nathan Bain saw the defendant touching it, but . . . that damn housekeeper, Paul, what have you been able to find out about her?"

"Just what our reports have shown, Perry. She keeps pretty much to herself, and has no close friends. She apparently was devoted to Bain's first wife and she was devoted to Elizabeth. How she feels toward Nathan is a question."

"If she felt that Nathan Bain poisoned Elizabeth . . ."

"But she doesn't, Perry. She's positive Vicki Braxton did it. She says Vicki is a pretty smooth article, and she knows about other evidence in the case. She's positive Vicki wheedled Elizabeth into making a will, and then when Elizabeth became suspicious and refused to complete the will, Vicki poisoned her."

Mason thought that over, then said, "If she could be *made* to believe that Nathan poisoned Elizabeth, and then that he might have poisoned his first wife, Marta, don't you think she then might tell us something that could help?"

Drake said, "I don't know. I've had one of my cleverest woman operatives make her casual acquaintance, and get her talking as well as anyone can. Of course, we've asked no questions about Marta's death.

The housekeeper says the doctor gave Nellie those three pills. Nellie had them in a little box. She saw them on the kitchen table when she and Nellie had coffee together just before midnight, and knows they were the same pills. She says Hamilton Burger can prove they were, that it had to be Nellie or Vicki who made the switch. The police have positive proof. And, of course, she says Nellie had no motive."

Mason, pacing the floor, said, "How do we know she had no motive? That's only what the housekeeper says."

"We can't find any motive, Perry. Vicki, of course, had the big motive."

"Nellie had enough motive to give those three sleeping tablets, Paul."

"Sure—money."

"Well, why couldn't more money have been the motive for the poison tablets? Those extra three tablets after the confession stuff on the first three would be a masterly touch. Good Lord, Paul, we have every element of proof. Bain gave Nellie money to administer sleeping tablets. They both admit it. Then he gave her more money, and someone changed the doctor's three tablets to poison tablets. Nellie and Nathan Bain knew that if he gave her a lot of money it would be traced, so instead of being surreptitious about it, he did it right under our noses.

"He arrested Nellie on a charge where he had no real proof. Nellie had previously contacted me, so he knew I'd rush to her rescue. Then I get her acquitted, and Nathan pays her a lot of dough and puts her back in the room where she has the last three tablets Elizabeth ever took."

Drake said, "Gosh, Perry, when you look at it that way it sure seems dead open-and-shut."

"Sure it does, Paul. It's all this razzle-dazzle stuff that confuses the issues."

Drake said, "Just strip the issues down to bare fact like that, Perry, and you may be able to sell the jury on the idea—unless Burger comes up with something new. Even I never realised how damning the bare facts are. It's only when they're all dressed up in this hocus-pocus that they seem to become innocuous. Nellie and Bain could have staged that whole act, the fluorescent powder and everything.

"When you come right down to it, that fluorescent powder on the tablets and on Vicki Braxton's fingers is a terribly damning bit of circumstantial evidence—and yet it was deliberately planted by Bain. By using the case against Nellie as a red herring . . . dammit, Perry, I believe you're right!"

Mason, continuing to pace the floor, said, "The only thing that I have to be sure of is that Hamilton Burger gets the door wide open."

"What do you mean?"

"Opens the door so I can start cross-examining Nathan Bain about the death of his first wife, without having Burger be in a position to yell that it's incompetent, irrelevant and immaterial; and that because he didn't touch on anything dealing with her in his direct examination, I can't cross-examine on it."

"Of course," Drake said, "you haven't made a move toward getting the body exhumed."

"Why should I? I'm going to put that up to the prosecution. I'll dare them to do it."

"They'd never try to exhume that body in a thousand years. If it *should* turn out she'd died of arsenic poisoning, it would knock the case against Victoria Braxton sky-high. They know that."

"That's fine," Mason told him. "We'll leave the body in the grave but we'll certainly drag her ghost in front of that jury—if I can only find some way to make it relevant and material. Tell me all you've found out about her, Paul."

Drake said, "She came from a rather wealthy family. Her parents were opposed to the marriage. They're Eastern people. This girl, Marta, evidently had a lot of spirit. She fell for Nathan Bain like a ton of bricks. Between you and me, Perry, Nathan Bain, with that ability to impress people and that gift of gab, must have been quite some ladies' man before he started putting on all that weight."

"Apparently so. Go on, Paul. Tell me more about Marta."

"Well, Marta was independent and high-strung. She had some money of her own, quite a little money. It had come to her from an uncle and was in trust, to be delivered to her when she was twenty-five. Prior to that time she had the income from it."

"How much money?"

"Something over fifty thousand."

"Go ahead. What happened?"

"Well, either Nathan Bain convinced her that her parents were persecuting him, or she got the idea in some way. Anyhow, after the marriage there was a very distinct coolness—she tried to be the dutiful daughter all right, but she had thrown in her lot with Nathan Bain and she wanted her parents to understand it. The old folks thought it was simply the fling of a high-strung, impetuous girl, and that she'd get over it and would probably come back home."

"Tell me some more about the fifty thousand bucks."

"She was twenty-five on the seventeenth of June. She got the money in her own name. On the first of August of the same year she was dead. Nathan Bain got the money. He was a big shot for a while, and then horse racing and poor investments got him down, and he picked out another girl with money. This time a good wad of money. Elizabeth Bain had at least half a million, and it may run more than that. He thought he was going to get his hands on her money, and she had other ideas, so then Elizabeth Bain died. The trouble is that he made a couple of false passes first and she became suspicious, so she disinherited him with that will. Good Lord, when you summarise the naked facts they make Bain look like a fiend, but when you see him on that witness stand, clothed in grief, humility and repentance, and being so damned human about it all. . . . Hell, Perry, I'll bet there isn't a man on that jury but what's found himself in Bain's shoes at one time or another. I tell you Bain has won them over.

"Perry, I don't want to inquire into your business when it's none of my business, but does it seem to you that there's anything phony about that will?"

"What about it?"

"Well, it was made in the handwriting of the decedent on the morning of the date she died, but the wording sounds a little funny, as though she had been interrupted in the middle of the thing in some way. The housekeeper tells my operative she thinks Vicki was trying to high-pressure Elizabeth into making the will and that Elizabeth balked and refused to complete it and sign it."

Mason said, "That's something Nathan Bain's lawyers will have to prove in the Probate Court."

"I was wondering if you'd noticed the way the will seems to break off in the middle."

Mason's reply to that was complete silence.

"Well," Drake said, "that's the story, Perry. I *could* have people whisper a word or two into the ears of Marta's parents. . . ."

Mason shook his head. "Then it wouldn't come as any surprise to Hamilton Burger, and he'll keep the door closed so I can't use it on Bain's cross-examination. No, Paul, I'm going to go into court tomorrow and when Hamilton Burger gets the door opened so I can cross-examine Nathan Bain, I'm going to spring the point. Just as soon as I've done that, I want you to get Marta's parents on the phone, tell them what's happened, and get them to raise hell yelling for an exhumation and autopsy. Remember, Paul, do that the *minute* I spring the point. Have it so you can get to a phone at once."

"Leave it to me," Drake said. "If you play it right you may blast

Bain out of that humble, repentant sinner act. And if you can't do it, Perry, that jury's going against you."

"I know it," Mason said, grimly. "You're not telling me anything, Paul."

NINETEEN

AS COURT CONVENED the next day, Hamilton Burger's manner gave no doubt but what he was now moving in for the kill.

Once or twice he glanced sidelong at Perry Mason, a glance of sneering triumph.

"Your Honour," he said, "Nathan Bain was on the stand, and I'll ask him to resume his place on the witness stand if he will."

Nathan Bain, moving like an elephant walking on eggs, marched up to the witness stand, composed himself in the chair, and looked at Hamilton Burger with the expression of a repentant but loyal dog, quite evidently a man who had stripped himself to the bone in the interests of justice, and was willing, if necessary, to make even further sacrifices.

"Mr. Bain, directing your attention to events which took place immediately after your wife's death."

"Yes, sir."

"Did you assist the officers in making any search of the premises?"

"I did. Yes, sir."

"Now will you describe the premises, please, generally?"

"Well, the house is a two-and-a-half-storey house. There is a garage at the back, and a patio."

"Is there shrubbery in the patio?"

"Surrounding the patio, yes. Shrubbery and a hedge."

"Now in searching this patio did you find anything, or were you present when the officers found anything?"

"Yes, sir."

"What?"

"A bottle wrapped in paper."

"Were you present when the officers unwrapped that paper?"

"I was. Yes, sir."

"And what was in the paper?"

"A bottle containing a label from a Honolulu drugstore, with the word 'arsenic' printed on it."

Perry Mason heard a commotion back of him.

Victoria Braxton got to her feet, choked, started to say something.

The deputy sheriff, who had her in custody, rushed to her side, and then suddenly wild screams of hysterical laughter penetrated the court-room as Victoria Braxton, laughing, screaming and crying, had hysterics.

"Pardon me," Hamilton Burger said, with a bow at Perry Mason. "Your client seems to be emotionally upset. I think, Your Honour, we should have a recess until the defendant is able to proceed with the trial."

"Recess until eleven o'clock," Judge Howison said, banging his gavel on the desk. "Is there a physician in the court-room?"

"Dr. Keener is here."

"He'd better have a look at this defendant," Judge Howison said, and promptly retired to chambers.

Complete pandemonium broke loose in the court-room, spectators surging forward, deputy sheriffs in attendance grappling with Victoria Braxton, newspaper photographers battling for places to secure photographs from a point of vantage, the jurors, heedless of the admonition of the court, craning their necks to get a glimpse of what was going on.

It was almost forty-five minutes before a white, emotionally-shaken, trembling Victoria Braxton could even talk with Perry Mason in a witness room adjoining the judge's chambers.

"Well?" Mason asked, coldly.

She said, "Don't start blaming me or I'll blow my top again. I took a chance on disposing of that arsenic, and lost, that's all."

"Would you mind telling me what it's all about?"

She said, "It's simple. I bought that arsenic in Honolulu for a cat that had been making life hideous there in the bungalows. The bottle was in my baggage. When I got back to the house and learned that Elizabeth had died from arsenic poisoning, I suddenly remembered having it and thought perhaps the possession of it might be miscon-strued. I'd signed the poison register in Honolulu and ... well, I knew that the police were snooping around and I felt quite certain they'd manage to inspect my baggage, so I stepped to my upstairs bedroom window and threw it out into the shrubbery. Someone must have seen me, otherwise I can't imagine why they'd have searched the premises. Now that's the whole story."

Mason was silent.

"How bad is it?" she asked.

Mason said, "Short of some sort of a legal miracle, it's bad enough to get you a verdict of first-degree murder at the hands of the jury, probably with the death penalty."

"That's what I thought," she said.

Mason got up and started pacing the floor.

"What do we do?" she asked. "Or is there anything we *can* do?"

Mason said, "I could probably get a continuance for a couple of days on the ground that you're emotionally upset. If I did that, it would ruin whatever last faint, glimmering chance we have. If you're telling the truth and can get on the stand and tell it so you convince at least one of the jurors, we can get a hung jury. Our only hope now is to hurry this trial to a conclusion so fast that public opinion doesn't have a chance to crystallise into a feeling of complete hostility. Do you feel that you can go back to the court-room and go through with the thing?"

"I can go through with anything now, I guess. I'm shaking like an autumn leaf, but I'll take it on my chin now."

Mason said, "You *might* have told me this before, you know."

"If I had, you wouldn't have handled my case. I'm grown-up, Mr. Mason. I'm a big girl now. I took a gamble and I lost. Don't rub it in. I'm the one who will be executed, not you."

"Let's go back to court," Mason said, tersely.

"Will you," she asked, "make any explanation of my hysterics to the jury?"

"Sure."

"When?"

"When I can think up an explanation that won't raise more hell with your case," Mason said.

There was sudden hope in her eyes. "Do you think you can do that now—before the bad impression I made has had a chance to sink in?"

"No," Mason said, "we can't make any explanation until we can win at least one friend on that jury. Come on, we're going to have to face it." Turning, he walked back to a court-room which now regarded him with a concentrated stare of sullen hostility.

Judge Howison took the bench and called the court to order. Hamilton Burger, unduly solicitous, inquired of Mason. "Is your client able to proceed?"

"Quite!" Mason snapped at him.

"Very well," Hamilton Burger said. "But I can appreciate the shock she has sustained. The prosecution wishes to be just, but it wants to be humane. If this upset, white-faced, trembling defendant is in as bad shape as she seems, we——"

"She isn't," Mason interrupted. "Go on with the case and save your sympathies for your star witness."

"I can understand and so forgive your short temper," Burger said with a smirk. "Mr. Nathan Bain, will you resume your position on the stand? Now, Mr. Bain, I am going to ask you if you would know that bottle when you saw it again."

"Yes, sir. My initials are marked on the label as well as those of the officers who were participating in the search."

"Is this the bottle?"

Hamilton Burger handed him a box with a glass top, containing a small bottle.

"That is it."

"We ask that this be received in evidence, Your Honour," Hamilton Burger said.

Mason said shortly, "Objected to as incompetent, irrelevant and immaterial. No connection whatever has been shown between the bottle and the defendant, and the Court will notice that this bottle contains a white powder. The unmistakable evidence is that if Elizabeth Bain was poisoned she was poisoned with three five-grain tablets."

"Just a moment," Hamilton Burger said. "We can connect this up if the Court please, but it will be necessary to call two witnesses in order to do so. In view of Mr. Mason's objection, I will ask that Mr. Bain now step aside for just a moment and make way for two witnesses who will be able to dispose of the points raised in the objection."

"In that case," Judge Howison said, "I would suggest that you simply mark the exhibit for identification and then, after you are finished with this witness, you can put the others on."

That did not suit Burger's strategy and his face showed it. "Your Honour," he said, "one of these witnesses is from Honolulu. It is very important that he get back. If I could call him just briefly."

"What's he going to testify to?" Mason asked.

Hamilton Burger welcomed the opportunity to turn to Mason. "That witness," he said, "is a clerk in a drugstore on Hotel Street in Honolulu. He is going to identify the defendant as being the woman who entered his drugstore and asked for arsenic in order to poison a cat that had been terrorising the neighbourhood, killing kittens, carrying off birds, and making a general nuisance of himself. He is going to produce a poison register on which will appear the date and the signature of the defendant."

Mason said casually, "Why, there's no need to call *him!* We'll stipulate to all that."

"You'll stipulate to it?"

"Good heavens, yes," Mason said. "Of course we'll stipulate to it. It's the truth."

"Oh, I see," Burger said slyly. "In view of the defendant's hysterics——"

"That will do," Judge Howison said tartly. "Confine your remarks to the Court, Mr. District Attorney. In view of the stipulation of Counsel, the statement of proof just made by the District Attorney will be considered as part of the evidence in this case."

"And," Hamilton Burger went on, obviously taken aback, "he will identify the bottle and the label as being the bottle that was given to the defendant, and will produce samples of typewriting made on the typewriter of the drugstore, which we expect to prove by a handwriting expert will show that this label——"

"No question about it," Mason said. "We'll stipulate it. We admit it."

"And by that stipulation, that, too, will be considered in evidence," Judge Howison said. "In view of Mr. Mason's stipulation, that disposes of the defendant's objection that the bottle has not been connected with the defendant?"

"Quite right, Your Honour," Mason said, smiling urbanely. "I just wanted to make sure the proof was in. That was the sole object of my objection. Now then, I would like to ask at this time if there is any *other* proof connecting this bottle with the defendant? If there is, let's have it all at this time and then we'll stipulate the bottle can be received in evidence."

Hamilton Burger said, "There is other evidence."

"Let's have it."

"I would prefer to introduce it later."

"Then," Mason said, "I'll renew the objection to the fact that the bottle is incompetent, irrelevant and immaterial. There is no evidence connecting this particular bottle with the defendant."

"Oh, all right," Hamilton Burger said. "The wrapping paper contains a finger-print of the defendant in the same fluorescent powder that was dusted on that jewel box. It fluoresces under ultra-violet light and it can be seen and identified as a finger-print of the defendant."

"You are certain of that?" Mason asked.

"I'm certain of it, and I have a finger-print expert sitting right here in court who can swear to it."

"Then I'll stipulate it," Mason said, cheerfully.

Judge Howison frowned. "I am not certain that in a case of this gravity I want Counsel to make stipulations as to such an important piece of evidence. I think, Mr. District Attorney, I'm going to ask you to put that witness on the stand."

"Very well," the District Attorney said. "If the Court will permit Nathan Bain to step to one side, I'll call Sergeant Holcomb."

"Very well," the Court said, "for this limited purpose of identifying the bottle, we will call Sergeant Holcomb."

Nathan Bain left the stand. Sergeant Holcomb held up his right hand, was sworn, and took the witness stand.

Nor could he resist a glance of triumph at Perry Mason.

Hamilton Burger said, "I show you this bottle and ask if you have ever seen it before?"

"Yes, sir."

"Where?"

"It was found on the seventeenth day of September on the premises of Nathan Bain, in a hedge in the patio."

"I now hand you a piece of paper and ask you what that paper is?"

"That is the paper that surrounded the bottle, in which the bottle was wrapped."

"Did you make any test of that paper?"

"I did. Yes, sir."

"What did you find on it?"

"I found the finger-print of the middle finger of the right hand of the defendant. That finger-print, incidentally, bore faint traces of fluorescence. In other words, in ultra-violet light it showed the same unmistakable characteristics as the powder which had been placed on the jewel case in the living-room of Nathan Bain."

"Cross-examine," Hamilton Burger said.

"That paper was on the outside of the bottle?" Mason asked.

"Yes, sir."

"And the finger-print was on it?"

"Yes, sir."

"Any other prints?"

"No prints that were such as could be identified, but there were numerous smudges which were faintly fluorescent. In other words, they had been made with the fingers of a hand that had touched fluorescent powder, but they were mere smudges."

"And the fluorescence was quite faint?"

"Yes, sir."

"Now how did that compare with the fluorescence on the tablets which were found in the waste-basket?"

"That on the tablets was much stronger."

"There were no fluorescent prints, smudges or traces on the bottle, on the label on the bottle, or the inside of the paper in which the bottle had been wrapped, or in fact, on any single thing inside that paper?"

"Well, no."

"And if the defendant, with enough of that fluorescent powder on her fingers to have left smudges or prints on the paper covering the bottle, had opened the paper to get at the bottle, or had opened the bottle to get at the contents, there would have been such traces of fluorescence, would there not?"

"I am not prepared to say."

"Why? You're testifying as an expert."

"Well . . . I don't know when she got the arsenic out of the bottle. That may have been before . . . I don't know, Mr. Mason. I can't answer your question. There are too many uncertain factors involved."

"I thought you couldn't answer it," Mason said with exaggerated courtesy. "Thank you very much, Sergeant. That is all."

"Nathan Bain, will you return to the stand, please," Hamilton Burger said. "Now, Your Honour, I renew my offer that this bottle and the wrapping paper be received as People's exhibits."

"They will be so received. Now let's see, the three tablets have been identified as People's Exhibit A, the bottle will be People's Exhibit B, and the wrapping paper will be People's Exhibit C."

"Cross-examine the witness, Bain," Hamilton Burger said sharply.

Mason glanced anxiously at the clock. He had time for only a few questions before the noon adjournment. Any impression he was to make on the jury before adjournment must be done quickly.

"You were estranged from your wife, Mr. Bain?"

"Yes. Yes, sir. Unfortunately . . . and as I have been forced to admit, due entirely to my fault."

It was apparent that any further attempt on the part of Mason to persecute this repentant sinner could only result in further alienating the jury.

Mason said, "Did you see your wife in her last illness?"

"At the very end, yes, when she was hardly conscious."

"You have been married once before?"

"Yes."

"Your first wife died?"

"Yes, sir."

"You did not see your wife, Elizabeth Bain, during the first part of her illness?"

"No. Due to the matters I have mentioned, she did not wish me to be in the room with her."

"Were you interested in learning about her symptoms?"

"Certainly I was interested. I paced the floor of my bedroom in an agony of self-torture, Mr. Mason. I asked for bulletins from my wife's bedside. I asked the doctor to describe her symptoms. I wanted to make certain that everything that could possibly be done by medical science was being done."

"You knew that those symptoms as described to you were said to be those of arsenic poisoning?"

"Yes."

"You were familiar with those symptoms?"

"No."

"You were not?"

"No."

"You had never seen them before?"

"Why, certainly not, Mr. Mason."

Mason got to his feet. "I will ask you, Mr. Bain, if at the time of her final and fatal illness your first wife, Marta, didn't exhibit each and every symptom that was exhibited by your wife, Elizabeth Bain?"

"Oh, Your Honour," Hamilton Burger shouted, "this is certainly going too far. This is an attempt by innuendo. Why, this is an inhuman, illegal——"

"I don't think so," Judge Howison said, watching Nathan Bain's face shrewdly. "The prosecution threw all doors wide open with this witness. I think under the circumstances I am going to give the defence every latitude for cross-examination. The objection is overruled."

"Answer the question," Mason said.

"That was different," Nathan Bain told him, his manner suddenly stripped of all its poise. In his own way he was as badly shocked as Victoria Braxton had been, and he showed it.

"What was different about it?"

"It was a different cause. She died from food poisoning. The doctors said so. The death certificate shows——"

"Was there any autopsy?"

"No. I tell you there was a certificate of death."

"An autopsy was performed on your wife, Elizabeth, was it not?"

"Yes, sir."

"For the purpose of *proving* that she died of arsenic poisoning?"

"I believe the District Attorney ordered the autopsy."

"But no autopsy was performed on your wife, Marta?"

"No." Nathan Bain seemed to have sagged within his clothes.

"You stood to inherit some half a million dollars from your wife, Elizabeth?"

"Apparently not. She seems to have left a will that———"

"You are going to contest that will, are you not?"

"Now, Your Honour," Hamilton Burger interposed, "I wish to object to this on the ground that it is calling for something that is far afield———"

"It goes to show the state of mind of this witness," Mason said. "He has testified at great length in mealy-mouthed repentance. Let's find out how deep that repentance goes."

"I think your language is unduly vigorous, Mr. Mason," Judge Howison said, "but I'm going to permit the witness to answer the question."

"Answer the question," Mason said. "Are you going to contest the will?"

"Yes," Nathan Bain snapped. "That will is a complete phony. It is———"

"You expect to keep it from being probated, do you not?"

"I do."

"And thereby you will inherit some half-million dollars?"

"Possibly," Bain said, savagely angry.

"Now then," Mason said, "tell the jury how much you inherited after your first wife so unfortunately passed away with symptoms so similar to those exhibited by Elizabeth Bain during her last illness."

"Your Honour!" Hamilton Burger shouted. "This is an insinuation that is not warranted by the evidence. This is not proper cross-examination———"

"I think I will sustain that objection in the form in which the question is asked," Judge Howison ruled.

"Can you," Mason said, "point out to the jury any symptom that your wife, Marta, had that was not a symptom of your wife, Elizabeth Bain, in her last illness?"

Nathan Bain was uncomfortably silent.

"Can you?" Mason asked.

"I wasn't there to see the symptoms of Elizabeth's illness," Nathan Bain said at length.

"How much money did you inherit from your first wife, roughly speaking?"

"Objected to," Hamilton Burger said. "That is———"

"Overruled," Judge Howison snapped.

"Fifty thousand dollars."

"How long were you married to her before her death?"

"About two years."

"How long were you married to Elizabeth Bain before her death?"

"Two years, approximately."

Judge Howison glanced at the clock. "I dislike to interrupt Counsel's cross-examination," he said, "but this examination has already continued some few minutes past the usual hour for the Court's recess."

"I understand, Your Honour," Mason said.

"Court will adjourn until two o'clock this afternoon," Judge Howison said. "The defendant is remanded to custody and the jurors will remember the admonition of the Court."

Nathan Bain took advantage of that moment to dash down from the witness stand while the jurors were still leaving the jury box.

He shouted at Mason in a paroxysm of rage, "Why you . . . you . . . you dirty, despicable shyster! . . . I could kill you!"

Mason raised his voice. "No, no! Don't kill me, Mr. Bain! You wouldn't inherit a dime!"

A newspaper reporter roared with laughter.

Court attendants crowded forward to separate the two men, and the jury filed slowly and thoughtfully from the jury box.

TWENTY

PERRY MASON, DELLA Street and Paul Drake sat huddled in conference in the little restaurant across the street from the Hall of Justice. The proprietor, an old friend, had ensconced them in a private dining-room and brought in an extension telephone.

Mason, eating a baked ham sandwich and sipping a glass of milk, said, "Hang it, Paul, I still can't get a clear picture."

"Well, the jury have a clear picture," Drake said. "Of course, you did a masterful job with Nathan Bain. You may have won over some members of the jury if your client can get on the stand and tell a decent story. But you know she can't do it, Perry."

"Why not?"

"There's too much against her. Her finger-print on the wrapper, the fact that she hurled that bottle out of the window. She must have hurled it out of the window, and there must have been some witness who saw her. You can't believe that those men would have gone out and started searching the grounds just on the strength of a general investigation. Holcomb hasn't brains enough for that."

"No," Mason conceded. "Some witness saw her throw the bottle out of the window, or saw someone throw it out of the window, that's a cinch."

"Well, there you are," Drake said. "She gets on the stand and tries to tell a story, and then Hamilton Burger jumps up and starts to cross-examine her, and by the time he gets done with her she'll be the greatest poisoner since Lucrezia Borgia."

Mason nodded glumly.

Drake said, "I've been watching that court-room, Perry; I've been talking with people who have listened to the evidence, and while you certainly made a magnificent job of stripping the mask off Nathan Bain, nevertheless your client is in a mess. That fit of hysterics put a noose around her neck."

"I'll say it did," Mason said wearily. "This business of getting into court representing a woman and then finding she's been holding out on you is tough on the nerves."

"Well, what would you have done under similar circumstances?" Della Street asked. "She thought her secret was safe. She knew that if she told you it would prevent you or any other reputable lawyer from taking the case."

"I suppose so," Mason agreed glumly, "but I still don't get the picture. Did you notice Nathan Bain's face when I asked him about the death of his first wife?"

Drake said, "You surely flabbergasted him."

"Why?" Mason asked.

"He'd been drilled and rehearsed on how to take your cross-examination; but this was an unexpected blow in a particularly vulnerable place."

"You agree with me it hit him hard?" Mason asked.

"He damn near fainted," Paul said.

Mason frowned thoughtfully, then, after a minute or two, asked, "You phoned Marta's parents?"

"The minute you made the point."

"How did they take it, Paul?"

"They're catching a plane, demanding the body be exhumed and raising hell generally."

Mason grinned.

"As I see it," Drake warned, "if the body *is* exhumed and if she did die of arsenic poisoning, you may get a hung jury *if* the defendant can tell a convincing story. But if the body is exhumed and she didn't die of arsenic poisoning, Perry, you're a gone goose. You'll have made a martyr out of Nathan and a shyster out of yourself."

Mason nodded. "It's not a gamble I like, but it's a gamble I have to take. A lawyer has to throw all his chips out on the table when he gets in a situation like this."

"If your client could only explain that bottle of arsenic," Drake said.

"She can. She wanted it for a cat."

Drake shook his head. "The jury won't believe her, Perry. Just wait until you hear Burger's argument to the jury."

"Yes," Mason said sarcastically, "I can imagine Hamilton Burger saying, 'The murderess thought the wool had been pulled over the eyes of everyone, and then when this damning, this tell-tale piece of evidence, which her Counsel is now trying to minimise, was brought into Court, what did she do?—Ladies and gentlemen of the jury, I don't ask you to accept my valuation of this damning bit of evidence. I ask you only to accept the valuation which the defendant herself placed upon it.' . . . And so and so on, ad infinitum."

"You make it sound damn convincing," Drake said.

"So will Hamilton Burger," Mason told him. "Call your office, Paul. See if there's anything new."

Drake put through a call to his office and said, "I'm eating lunch. Anything new in the Bain case? . . . What? . . . Let me have that again. . . . Hold the phone."

He turned to Mason and said, "A peculiar development. We've been shadowing Nathan Bain, you know."

Mason nodded.

"Apparently Bain has no idea he's being tailed. Now I told you that Bain, like all these men who have exploited women by the exercise of irresistible charm, has a fatal weakness himself. As those fellows get older, they almost invariably fall for their own line. Some shrewd, selfish, scheming woman who is younger, is attractive, and on the make, gets them head-over-heels in love with them."

"Go ahead," Mason said. "What's the pitch, Paul?"

"Despite his attitude on the stand, Nathan Bain is absolutely nuts about Charlotte Moray. She's now back here in the Rapidex Apartments."

"Under what name?" Mason asked.

"Under her own name. She's been living there for months. Nathan Bain went to see her this morning just before he came to court."

Mason, pacing the floor, gave that matter thoughtful consideration.

"That should give you something to smear him with on further cross-examination," Drake said.

Again Mason nodded.

"Any instructions?" Drake asked.

Mason said suddenly, "Paul, I've got an idea."

"It's about time," Drake told him.

"Who will be in Nathan Bain's house this afternoon? Anyone?"

Drake said, "Let's see, Perry. I guess not. Bain and the housekeeper will both be in court and——"

Mason's interruption was sharp. "Paul, I want you to get a stakeout in some place near-by, where you can instal a recording machine. I want you to get into Bain's house and put a bug in the room that has the telephone."

Drake's face showed dismay. "Have a heart, Perry! You can't do that!"

Mason's face was hard as granite. "Paul, I'm gambling my reputation on this thing, and you're going to gamble right along with me. I want you to get a microphone in that room, a stake-out, and a complete recording device."

"Good Lord, Perry, he'll find the bug——"

"Put it where he won't find it."

"But he'll find it eventually, Perry. They'll be dusting or——"

"And by that time," Mason said, "they'll trace the wires and only find two loose, dangling ends."

Drake's face showed a glimmer of hope. "How long would we have to be on the job, Perry?"

Mason said, "Put two men on the house. I want to know when Bain comes in. I want to know who else comes in, and when they come in. Within an hour after Bain arrives he's going to get one telephone call. After that you can cut the wires, pick up your equipment and get out."

"It'll mean my licence if I get caught," Drake said.

"Then," Mason told him coldly, "don't get caught."

TWENTY-ONE

AT THE TWO o'clock session, Judge Howison addressed the crowded court-room.

"Somewhat against my better judgment," he said, "I have permitted the deputy sheriffs to admit spectators for whom there are no seats. These spectators will remain standing at the extreme edges of the court-room, along the walls, so as not to block the aisles. I wish to warn every spectator that his bearing must be compatible with the dignity of the Court. If there are untoward incidents I will clear the court-room.

"Mr. Nathan Bain was on the stand being cross-examined. You will resume the witness stand, Mr. Bain, and Mr. Mason will continue your cross-examination."

Nathan Bain had lost some of his assurance. Apparently the few questions Mason had asked him prior to the noon adjournment, and his loss of temper, had led him to realise that even the detailed coaching of Hamilton Burger was insufficient armour to protect him against Mason's thrusts.

Mason assumed a conversational tone of voice. "Mr. Bain," he said, "going back to your testimony concerning the use of this fluorescent powder. As I understand it, there had been persistent thefts from your house over a period of time?"

"Yes, sir."

"Coincident with the employment of Nellie Conway?"

"That's right, although I realise now that was merely a coincidence as far as time is concerned."

"Jewellery had been missing?"

"Yes, sir."

"And there had been no missing jewellery prior to the time Nellie Conway was employed?"

"No, sir."

"There had been no complaint from any member of the household as to things that were missing?"

"No, sir."

"Now, your wife kept her jewellery in a jewel case that was customarily locked in the desk in the living-room?"

"Yes, sir."

"And Nellie Conway, of course, was employed as a nurse to wait on your wife after the unfortunate accident which had damaged her spinal cord?"

"Yes, sir."

"And immediately after that accident, and at all times thereafter, your wife developed a feeling of bitterness toward you and would not permit you in the room?"

"My wife was nervous."

"Answer the question. *Did* your wife develop a bitterness of feeling toward you and would not allow you in the room?"

"Yes, sir."

"So you had no direct oral communication with your wife from the time of the accident until her death?"

"Unfortunately, that is right."

"Then you must have known prior to the accident that she had those incriminating papers secreted in her room."

"I did."

"How much prior to the accident?"

"I can't remember."

"Use your best recollection."

"Well, I . . ."

"Immediately before the accident, isn't that right?"

"Well, it may have been. She told me about those papers on . . . let me see, the . . . the memory of the accident has, of course, obliterated so many things . . . it was such a shock. . . ."

"As a matter of fact, she told you on the very day of the accident that she had the goods on you, that she had the evidence of your infidelity, and she was going to divorce you, didn't she?"

"I . . ."

Mason opened his brief-case and whipped out a letter which had been sent to Victoria Braxton.

"Yes or no, Mr. Bain?" he asked sharply, jerking the letter out of the envelope and whipping it open dramatically.

"Yes," Nathan Bain admitted, shamefacedly.

"Now then," Mason said, "you're positive that items of jewellery had been missing from the house over a period of time after Nellie Conway was employed?"

"Yes, but I have repeatedly told you, and I wish to tell you again, that while you are using Nellie Conway's employment as referring to a measure of time, that is *all* it refers to. I am satisfied that Miss Conway had nothing to do with the loss of the jewellery."

"But it was disappearing?"

"Yes, sir."

Mason got up and faced him dramatically, standing with his eyes boring into those of the witness, until every person in the court-room felt the tension, then he asked in slow, level tones, "How—did—you—know?"

"How did I know what?"

"That your wife's jewellery was missing?"

"Why, I know generally what she had and——"

"You weren't communicating with your wife?"

"No."

"Therefore your wife couldn't have told you?"

"No."

"The jewel case was kept in the desk?"

"Yes."

"Your wife couldn't walk?"

"No."

"How did *you* know the jewellery was missing?"

Bain shifted his position uneasily on the witness stand.

"How did you know?" Mason thundered.

"Well," Nathan Bain began, "I . . . I just happened to notice that . . ."

"This desk was your wife's private writing desk, wasn't it?"

"Yes."

"But you had retained a duplicate key to that desk without her knowledge?"

"I had a key."

"The jewel case was kept locked?"

"Yes."

"And you had retained a duplicate key to that jewel box without her knowledge?"

"I explained that all to you once before, Mr. Mason."

"I am not asking for an explanation, I am asking for an answer. Did you or did you not retain a key to that jewel case without your wife's knowledge or consent?"

"Well, in a way, yes."

"Yes or no."

"I object to the question on the ground that it has already been asked and answered," Hamilton Burger said.

"Objection overruled!" Judge Howison snapped.

"Yes or no?" Mason asked.

"Yes," Nathan Bain said.

"Therefore," Mason said, "the only way for you to have known that items of jewellery had been missing *after* your wife's injury was for you to have surreptitiously opened that desk, surreptitiously opened her jewel box, and made a surreptitious inventory of the contents of the jewel box without her knowledge or consent, and without her specific permission. Isn't that right?"

"I was just checking up."

"Now then," Mason said, "*what* items of jewellery were missing from your wife's jewel case?"

"A diamond pendant. That is, an imitation——"

"I'm not talking about the items of synthetic jewellery that you placed there, but the items of genuine jewellery."

"I couldn't say."

"You didn't have an inventory of the contents?"

"No, sir, not of my wife's jewellery. Not a specific inventory."

"Then why did you go to the jewel case to make an inspection?"

"Just to check up."

"But if you didn't know what was in there how could you tell if anything was missing?"

"Well, I . . . I was just looking."

"And you can't tell us of any single specific item that is missing, or that was missing?"

"No, sir."

Once more Mason fixed Bain with accusing eyes.

"This girl friend of yours—with whom you had your affair, did you give her presents of jewellery?"

"Sir, do you mean to insinuate——"

"Did you give her presents of jewellery? Answer the question."

Bain ran his hand across his forehead.

"Yes or no?" Mason thundered.

"Yes."

"Thank you," Mason said sarcastically. "Now, were those presents of jewellery given to her in the boxes in which they came, or did you take them from your pocket and put them on her?"

"I can't remember."

"Can you remember any store where you bought any one, any single one of the articles of jewellery you gave her?"

"I . . . I mostly bought them at auctions."

"Do you have any single bill of sale for any one of those articles you now claim you purchased at auctions?"

"No, sir. I destroyed them."

Mason said, "I have been advised that the parents of Marta Bain, your first wife, wish to make an application to have the body exhumed. Would you have any objection?"

"Your Honour, Your Honour!" Hamilton Burger shouted. "I object to that question. It's argumentative. It's not proper cross-examination. It's foreign to the issues in this case. It's incompetent, irrelevant and immaterial and . . ."

"I think I will sustain the objection on the ground that it is argumentative," Judge Howison ruled. "However, I am disposed to allow Counsel for the defence a wide margin of cross-examination, particularly in view of the peculiar nature of the direct examination and the large amount of territory explored by you on direct."

"Are you willing to have Marta Bain's body exhumed?" Mason asked.

"Same objection."

"Same ruling."

Mason said, "Your Honour, I now ask that this case be adjourned until proceedings can be had for the exhumation of the body of Marta Bain, deceased. I feel that it is vital to the issues in this case to determine whether or not she met her death from arsenic poisoning."

"Oh, Your Honour," Hamilton Burger said, his tone showing an exasperation that indicated there was after all a limit to human endurance. "This is just a very adroit red herring drawn across the trail which is getting too hot to suit Counsel.

"If he had been so concerned about the death of Marta Bain, he could have made application for an adjournment before the case was tried. Now that we have a jury empanelled——"

"Nevertheless," Judge Howison interrupted, "the Court is inclined to think there may be something to the motion. I'm not going to rule on it immediately. I will take time to consider the matter and rule on it tomorrow morning. In the meantime, are you gentlemen prepared to proceed with the trial?"

Perry Mason shook his head. "Your Honour, the question of whether this motion is granted will effect my entire strategy in the trial. I do not care to go ahead until there has been a definite ruling."

"Very well." Judge Howison said, "I am going to reserve ruling until tomorrow morning at ten o'clock, and in the meantime Court will stand adjourned. The defendant is remanded to the custody of the sheriff, and the jury will remember the admonition of the Court not to converse among themselves or with any other person about the case, or permit it to be discussed in their presence; nor shall the jury reach any opinion as to the guilt or innocence of the defendant until the evidence is all in and the case has been finally submitted to it for decision.

"Court adjourned until ten o'cock tomorrow morning. In the meantime, I'm going to ask Counsel to cite any authorities they may have bearing on the question of the pertinency of an adjournment pending proceedings for the exhumation.

"Court's adjourned."

TWENTY-TWO

PAUL DRAKE'S TINY cubbyhole of an office was the nerve centre of the operations.

Mason and Della Street sat huddled around Drake's battle-scarred desk. The detective, with four or five telephones in front of him, reported operations from time to time as there were new developments.

"That early adjournment damn near wrecked us," he said. "If Nathan Bain had gone straight home he might have caught us. I certainly don't like this, Perry. It's taking last-minute, desperate chan——"

"They're taken now," Mason interrupted. "There's no use worrying about them. Where the deuce do you suppose Nathan Bain is?"

"He left Hamilton Burger's office half an hour ago," Drake said. "My shadow hasn't had a chance to report on him yet."

"If he should go to the Rapidex Apartments we're sunk," Mason said.

"Why?"

"I'll tell you after a while."

Drake said, "You're playing a desperate game. It's too filled with risk for you to let me know what it is. You're afraid that I'll refuse to ride along."

"No, that isn't it. You'll work better if you don't have your mind occupied with other stuff. Dammit, Paul, why don't you get an office that's big enough to walk around in?"

"Can't afford it."

"One would never suspect it from the bills you send. Quit worrying, Paul. A lawyer and detective who won't take chances for a client aren't worth their salt. Planting a bug isn't such a heinous offence."

"It isn't that," Drake said, "it's the chances you take getting in so you can plant the bug."

"I know," Mason sympathised. "But we can't pick and choose, Paul. We have to get certain information. We can't get it the easy way, so we have to get it the hard way. How did your man get in? With a pass key?"

"Sure."

"No one knows anything about it? No one saw him?"

"I don't think so. A neighbour *might* have noticed, but my man was carrying a basket of groceries, just as though he were a delivery boy."

"Where's your stake-out?"

"In a garage that we rented. I'm not too happy about that."

"Why not?"

"We had to rent it in too much of a hurry. I think the woman who owns the place thinks we're planning to hide stolen cars. I have a hunch she may notify the police."

Mason looked at his watch. "Well, we should be out of there within another hour anyway."

A telephone rang. Drake picked up the receiver, answered the phone, then nodded and said, "That's a lot better. Keep me posted. I want to know the minute anything happens."

He hung up the telephone, and turned to Mason. "All right, Perry, your trap's set, whatever it is. Nathan Bain and the housekeeper arrived at the house five minutes ago. My man tailed them there. This was his first opportunity to get to a telephone and make a report."

"There's someone else on duty?"

"Sure, sure," Drake said. "Don't worry about that. That's all part of the routine. We have enough men on the job so we can let you know if anyone goes in or out, and keep you posted on developments."

Mason turned to Della Street. "Okay, Della, do your stuff."

Della Street pulled a piece of paper from her pocketbook, spread it out on the desk and said, "I want an outside line, Paul."

Drake threw a switch. "All right. That phone's connected. Dial your number."

Della Street's skilled fingers flew rapidly over the dial of the telephone.

"What's the number?" Drake asked, curiously.

"Nathan Bain," Mason said tersely.

Della Street sat with the receiver at her ear, waiting for an answer.

"Is it ringing?" Mason asked.

Della Street nodded.

Drake said in a low voice, "You do the damndest things, Perry. That letter that you pulled out of your brief-case and flashed in front of Nathan Bain, was that really a letter which Elizabeth wrote her sister, or was it——?"

"It was a recipe for a fruitcake," Mason said. "Dammit, Paul, you don't suppose they're not going to answer? Wouldn't your men——?"

He broke off as Della Street motioned for silence. Placing her mouth close to the telephone, she said in close, clipped, emotionless tones, "Mr. Nathan Bain? ... Very well, please call him at once upon a matter of the greatest urgency. ... Hello, is this Mr. Nathan Bain? Very well. This is the Receiving Hospital. A patient giving the name of Miss Charlotte Moray, residing at the Rapidex Apartments, has just arrived by ambulance and is being treated for arsenic poisoning. She claims this could only have come from eating chocolate creams which she received through the mail. She has asked us to notify you that she is being given emergency treatment, but suggests that if possible you come to see her at once."

Della Street waited a half-second, then in the same professional, efficient voice, "That is right. The name is Charlotte Moray. The address the Rapidex Apartments. Good-bye."

She hung up.

Drake looked at Mason with wide, incredulous eyes. "Of all the crazy, damn-fool things to do!"

Mason made an impatient gesture. "It's the only thing we *can* do, Paul. I have a theory. I have to find out whether it will hold water."

"But that isn't going to fool him," Drake said. "It will simply——"

Mason interrupted to say, "You keep your men on the job out there, recording any conversations that are heard over the microphone."

"But good heavens, Perry, you're not going to get anything that way."

"You can't tell," Mason told him.

They settled down for a period of anxious waiting.

After ten minutes, Mason said, "Hang it, Paul, I'll go crazy if I can't start moving around. How much longer do you suppose it will be before we get a report from your men in the stake-out?"

"Whenever they finish recording whatever there is to record. They're making regular routine reports every hour on the hour, but they'll report any developments that aren't routine."

"This won't be routine," Mason said. "It's like putting a camera out in the woods with a thread running to the flash-gun, coming back the next morning and seeing what's on the film. It may be a deer or it may be a skunk. You just have to wait until the film's developed to find out what tripped the shutter. That's the way it is with this stake-out."

"Perhaps it won't be the shutter that gets tripped," Drake said. "It may be a lawyer."

"It could be," Mason admitted.

"But, my gosh," Drake said, "the first thing he'll do will be to call Charlotte Moray."

"If he does, it will be interesting to know what he says to her."

Mason looked at his wrist watch and started drumming with the tips of his fingers on the desk.

Drake started to say something, then, after studying the expression on the lawyer's face, changed his mind and remained silent.

At the end of another five minutes Mason said anxiously, "How far would your men have to go to get to a telephone, Paul?"

"You mean the men who are watching the front of the Bain house?"

"No, no. The men who are on that stake-out."

"Not far, Perry. Just to a petrol station on the corner."

"How far in terms of minutes or seconds?"

"Two minutes at the outside."

Mason looked at his wrist watch again, then took a pencil from his pocket and nervously started sliding his finger-tips up and down the pencil, reversing it with each operation.

"Just what are you expecting, Perry?" Drake asked.

Mason shook his head, said, "With every minute now I am expecting less and less. We should have heard before this."

Another five minutes passed.

Mason lit a cigarette, settled back in the chair with a sigh and said, "Well, Paul, I guess we've lost our gamble."

"It would help," Drake said, "if I knew what it was we'd bet on, how much we'd bet, and just how much we stand to lose."

Mason said impatiently, "Nathan Bain *must* have been in touch with Charlotte Moray and must have known that phone call was a plant."

"He didn't go out there," Drake said. "He and the housekeeper were at the District Attorney's office in conference with Hamilton Burger. When they came out they went directly home."

"Didn't stop anywhere and telephone?" Mason asked.

"I don't think so," Drake said. "I think my man would have reported it if they had. I told him to give me a report on everything they did, and he made that report fifteen or twenty minutes ago."

Mason wearily got up from his chair. "Then for some reason they must have called Charlotte Moray from the D.A.'s office. Now we'll have to figure something else. Tell your men at the first opportunity to cut the wires leading to the bug and go home. Clean out their equipment so the police won't find anything if they start following the wires."

"We'll cut the wires close to the house," Drake said. "And we'll do it just as soon as it gets dark."

"When will you be in touch with your men?"

"Within another twenty minutes. They report on the hour, even if nothing happens."

"All right," Mason said, "I guess that's it. He's probably suspicious."

The telephone, shattering the silence, caused Della Street to jump nervously.

"This may be it," Drake said, grabbing the telephone. Mason stood poised and tense, waiting.

Drake said, "Hello . . . Yes, go ahead . . . What is it? . . . Well, do the best you can. Give me a line on it. You'll have to speak louder, I can't hear you. Get up closer to the telephone. . . ."

Suddenly Drake's face lightened. He looked up at Mason and nodded, said into the telephone, "Go ahead, keep feeding it into the line. Give me what you have."

Finally Drake said, "Hold the phone a minute. Wait there for instructions. Just hang on."

Drake pushed the palm of his hand over the mouthpiece of the telephone and said to Mason, "Bain and his housekeeper had a hell of a fight, standing right there by the telephone. Bain accused her of sending arsenic candy to Charlotte Moray. The housekeeper called him a liar and a bungler, pointed out how clumsy he'd been trying to kill his wife in that automobile accident . . . and then Bain evidently popped her one, and they started throwing mud back and forth. It came in perfectly."

"Does your man have all of it on the wax cylinders?" Mason asked.

"He's got it."

Mason grinned. "Tell him to sit out there for a while longer, then report again when it gets dark. Also let us know at once if anything new turns up."

Mason turned to Della Street, said, "Get Lieutenant Tragg at Homicide Squad, Della."

Della started dialling. Drake relayed Mason's instructions into the telephone.

A moment later Della Street nodded to Mason and the lawyer picked up the telephone, said, "Hello, Lieutenant. This is Perry Mason."

"What the hell do you want now?" Tragg asked.

"What makes you think I want anything, Tragg?"

"The tone of your voice. It's your polite act."

Mason laughed. "How grateful would you be if we gave you the solution of a couple of murders, all wrapped up with pink ribbon in a nice little package?"

"How grateful would I have to be?" Tragg asked cautiously.

Mason said, "A microphone would have to be police property."

"You mean that I'd planted it?"

"Yes."

"How certain are the solutions?"

"The cases are on ice."

"I guess it could be arranged," Tragg said, "but I wouldn't want to be a cat's paw. I'd want to be mighty certain I was playing a sure thing."

"You would be," Mason assured him. "Come on up to Paul Drake's office. By the time you get here we'll have everything ready."

"Okay, I'll ride along that far," Tragg told him. "This guy, Bain, doesn't look as good to me as he does to Holcomb and the DA. . . . But, even so, you're going to have to show me."

Mason said, "Come on and be shown." He hung up the telephone, said to Della Street, "All right. Get Nathan Bain on the telephone."

"Nathan Bain!" Drake exclaimed. "Are you crazy?"

Mason shook his head.

Della Street's fingers were already busy with the manipulation of the dial.

"Hello," she said. "Hello . . . Mr. Bain? Just a moment, hold the line, please."

She passed the receiver to Mason.

Mason picked up the telephone, said, "Good afternoon, Mr. Bain. This is Perry Mason calling."

Bain said, "I have nothing to say to you, Mr. Mason. The District Attorney has promised me he's going to put a stop to your persecution of me. I'll see you in court tomorrow."

"Perhaps you won't."

"You're damn right I will!" Bain said angrily. "And when I do———"

"Just a moment," Mason interrupted, "before you make any definite appointments, Bain, you'd better look around the room and find the microphone. Good-bye."

Mason hung up the telephone.

Drake came all the way up out of the chair in startled protest. "Good Lord, Perry, do you know what you're doing? Do you realise———?"

"I think I do," Mason said, grinning. "Flight, you know, is an evidence of guilt. I think that within about ten minutes your man who's watching the house will report that Nathan Bain has dashed out and driven away in a hurry. I want Lieutenant Tragg to have a strong enough case so Hamilton Burger won't start punching holes in it."

TWENTY-THREE

THE GARAGE HAD the dank, musty smell which seems to be spontaneously generated in buildings that are kept too long closed and where sunlight cannot penetrate.

It was cold and draughty. Paul Drake's men, bundled in overcoats, regulated the mechanism which turned the wax cylinders.

Lieutenant Tragg, flanked by Perry Mason and Della Street, leaned over the records, listening.

Paul Drake, nervously apprehensive, was standing slightly to one side, talking with one of his men.

The voices which were played back from the wax cylinder, amplified by a small loudspeaker, were sufficiently clear to be distinctly audible, although there was a slight distortion of the tones due to the amplification of the microphone.

At the end of some ten minutes, Tragg straightened as the voices on the end of the record ceased.

"Well, that's it," Mason said.

"How did you figure out what had happened, Mason?" Tragg asked.

"I was watching Bain's face when I accused him of having murdered his first wife. I saw that the thing hit him like a blow from a sledge-hammer. I thought at the moment it was because he was guilty, but later on I began to think about it and started putting two and two together.

"Of course, if his first wife had been poisoned by eating chocolate creams filled with arsenic, it stood to reason——"

"Wait a minute," Lieutenant Tragg said, "why didn't Nathan Bain get some of it if it was in the candy?"

"Because Bain doesn't eat chocolates. That's one thing he's allergic to. That narrows down the field. It had to be either Nathan Bain or the housekeeper.

"So then I started thinking. I wondered what would happen if the housekeeper had fallen in love with him, if she was one of those quiet, repressed, mousy women who would develop into a possessive——"

"Well, she was," Tragg said, "there's no question about it, now that I've listened to this conversation. They certainly are a pretty pair, and when they let go at each other hammer and tongs they told plenty."

"The housekeeper killed the first wife through jealousy. Then when she found she really was only one more woman as far as Nathan Bain was concerned, she still kept on in his employ just to be near him. Nathan Bain married money, and when he found he couldn't get hold of that money, he started trying to kill his wife. That guy sure has a way with women, and he sure played the field.

"It's interesting to hear the housekeeper on that record tell him what a clumsy, inefficient murderer he turned out to be, and how she had to step in and do the job, switching the arsenic tablets in place of the medicine the doctor had left when Nellie Conway, leaving the pill-box on the kitchen table, had moved over to the stove to warm up her coffee. That's when Bain popped her—a great pair they turned out to be."

Tragg suddenly turned to Drake. "What's the dope, Paul? What's happened over there? You have men watching the place."

Drake said, "Nathan Bain left in a hell of a hurry. He threw some stuff in a bag and was on his way. My man tried to tail him but there was absolutely no chance. Bain was hitting fifty miles an hour before he'd got to the end of the block."

"And the housekeeper hasn't shown?"

"No, she's still there."

Tragg smoked a thoughtful cigarette. "I guess it was pretty plain after all," he said. "Once you stop to figure it out, if the first wife was murdered and if Bain *didn't* do it, it almost *had* to be the housekeeper. It had to be someone who knew their intimate habits, who was in a position to slip poison into the candy, who knew that Nathan Bain was allergic to chocolate and wouldn't touch it. They're both of them a pretty kettle of fish. So Nathan Bain really did manipulate the accident that crushed his wife's spine, hoping he could kill her. What I don't see, Perry, is why he didn't get the housekeeper to give the sleeping medicine to his wife if they were that intimate."

"Don't you see," Mason pointed out, "that's the one thing that was the dead give away. He was afraid to let the housekeeper know what he was after, because the minute the housekeeper knew what he wanted *she* would have been the one to get those letters from Charlotte Moray.

Bain had really fallen for the Moray woman, and he was afraid of what that crazy, insane, jealous housekeeper would have done to Charlotte Moray."

"I'm not too certain but what we'd better do something ourselves," Tragg said, "before she gets any ideas. I think I'll go over and pick this Imogene Ricker up. I'll want those records delivered down at headquarters."

"You'll have them," Drake promised.

Tragg looked at Drake thoughtfully and said, "You took a lot of chances on this thing, Paul."

Drake's eyes shifted.

"He was acting under my orders," Mason said.

Tragg cocked a quizzical eyebrow. "Okay, Perry, you reached in your thumb and pulled out a plum. But one of these days the plum won't be there. You'll just get your thumb burnt and then it's going to be too damn bad."

"Oh, I don't know," Mason said. "I didn't take so many chances on this one. After all, it was almost a mathematical certainty, and the minute it became apparent that Nathan Bain was afraid to trust the housekeeper to get the purple letters written by Charlotte Moray——"

"Okay, you win," Tragg interrupted. "You don't have to explain when you've won. Winners never explain. Losers always do. I'm going over to pick up Imogene Ricker. You folks want to tag along behind?"

Mason nodded.

"I'll stay here," Drake said.

"You get those records down to headquarters," Tragg said, "and *be damn certain nothing happens to them.*"

"Are you telling me," Drake said with feeling.

Tragg got in his police car. "It's only around the block, Perry, but I want my car there because I'll be taking that Ricker woman to headquarters. Do you want to drive your bus?"

"I think so, Lieutenant. I'll park right behind your car. If she should want to make a statement you can borrow Della Street to take it down in shorthand."

"I'd have to want that statement pretty damn bad to borrow your secretary," Tragg said. "I'm going to keep the Perry Mason angle out of this just as much as possible. The D.A. won't like it."

"To hell with the D.A.," Mason told him. "If you get a confession, call in the newspaper reporters and let the D.A. read about it in the headlines tomorrow."

"Are you," Tragg asked, "telling me how to run my business?"

"Sure," Mason said, grinning.

"Well, it won't work quite that way," Tragg admitted. "I'd get the D.A. on the phone and explain to him what it was all about and tell him he'd better come up to headquarters in a rush, but before he got there, somehow or other the newspaper men would have had a tip. They'd be phoning in the story about the time the D.A. arrived. . . . You give me about two minutes head start," Tragg went on, suddenly becoming crisply business-like, "then you can drive up to the house and see what the score is. And you fellows keep those records tuned in on that live microphone so that you hear everything. If she wants to get it off her chest, I'll see that she does the talking in the room by the telephone. Okay, let's go."

Tragg drove away. Mason gave him a two-minute start, then he and Della Street followed.

The police car was in front of the house. There was no sign of Lieutenant Tragg.

One of Paul Drake's men, who was shadowing the house, sauntered over to Mason's car. "Tragg just went in a few minutes ago," he said.

"I know," Mason told him. "Who let him in? The housekeeper?"

"No. The front door was unlatched. When he didn't get an answer, he opened it and walked in."

"Oh-oh!" Mason said.

At that moment, the door opened. Lieutenant Tragg beckoned.

The lawyer ran up the steps to the porch.

Tragg said, "Get your car, pick up Drake's men and get the hell out of here, Perry. I've just telephoned headquarters to send out the squad car."

"You mean," Mason asked, "that she——?"

"Evidently he throttled her . . . he was crazy in love with that Moray woman. When he and Imogene got to hurling verbal brick-bats at each other, he started choking her. Perhaps he only intended to make her lose consciousness so he could get away. . . . Anyway, it's a mess now, and I've got to play it my way. Remember, that's been my microphone all along. Round up Paul Drake's men. Tell them to get the hell out of here, and fast."

"How about Bain?" Mason asked apprehensively. "That Charlotte Moray woman may be in danger. If he should start for there and——"

"You don't have to *keep* telling me how to run my business," Lieutenant Tragg said. "Within sixty seconds a radio car will be staked out in front of the Rapidex Apartments. If Bain shows up they'll collar him. Shake a leg, Mason, get those agency men cleaned out of here."

Mason nodded, turned, took Della Street's arm, and started running down the porch stairs.

"Well," Della Street said, as Tragg gently closed the front door, "perhaps after all it was better that way, Chief. That poor housekeeper must have been about half-crazy. Don't you think it was better?"

"A hell of a lot better," Mason said grimly. "I'll chase Paul Drake's men out of here and then you go call up the hotel and get a nice airy room with a good, big bath."

Della Street raised her eyebrows. "What cooks?"

"Tell them," Mason explained, "that it's for Victoria Braxton, and that she'll be in sometime late this evening."